KW-621-575

Legendary couturière, Alouette Doré, queen of the French fashion scene for most of the century, has always avoided giving interviews about her past. But now, in her nineties, she wants to set the record straight. And the only person she'll talk to is journalist Andrea Vincent – famous for her no-holds-barred investigations . . .

# Mademoiselle

Merle Jones

HEADLINE

Copyright © Merle Jones 1988

First published in 1988
by HEADLINE BOOK PUBLISHING PLC

First published in paperback in 1989
by HEADLINE BOOK PUBLISHING PLC

All rights reserved. No part of this publication may be reproduced, stored in a retrieval system, or transmitted, in any form or by any means without the prior written permission of the publisher, nor be otherwise circulated in any form of binding or cover other than that in which it is published and without a similar condition being imposed on the subsequent purchaser.

ISBN 0–7472–3124–9

Typeset in 10/11¼ pt English Times
by Colset Private Limited, Singapore

Printed and bound in Great Britain by
Collins, Glasgow

HEADLINE PUBLISHING PLC
Headline House
79 Great Titchfield Street
London W1P 7FN

To my mother, a born survivor.

# Prelude

## Doré
## Paris, June 1978

The camera closed in on the figure on the stretcher. She lay on her belly, face turned sideways. A dark bloodstain spread from her buttocks up across her back. The woman's mass of dark blonde hair was swept to the side to reveal an ashen face. She was unconscious.

'Yes, shrapnel wounds, but pretty deep and she's in shock. It's hard to give a prognosis in these conditions. . . .' The harassed paramedic was rushing wounded troops and civilians from a helicopter to a field dressing station while simultaneously trying to answer the TV reporter's questions. He obviously wished the reporter were anywhere but beside him.

The English language soundtrack faded and the French voice-over cut in. 'Andrea Vincent was lucky. That was the second time she was wounded while accompanying a unit into action. This time she was hospitalised for two months and for a while it looked as if she might be paralysed for life. But she made a full recovery and later returned to Vietnam until the Americans evacuated Saigon.'

The next piece of film showed a gaunt but obviously fit woman disembarking from a plane, presumably on her return to the Far East. It faded into another newsreel clip, this time of an international property speculator looking drawn and apprehensive as he arrived at an official enquiry into his activities on the British stock market. Again the voice-over cut in.

'Within a year of her return to Europe, the shadier

members of London's financial community probably wished that Vincent had remained in South-East Asia. She abandoned stills photography and took to TV journalism, first with a documentary on her Vietnam experiences, then moving into the field of investigative reporting. She showed a natural talent for unearthing stories on questionable financial dealings. Her film "Just When You Thought It Was Safe To Go Back In The Water . . ." on offshore funds was responsible for the collapse of James Hyett's international business empire.

'She won the Investigative Reporter of the Year award in 1976, then took a break to research and write a book on the Mafia's expansion into the world of legitimate commerce. She then returned to television with another award-winning series of films, this time covering alleged links between the world drugs trade and the intelligence services of the Eastern and Western blocs.'

A more up-to-date clip showed Andrea Vincent, looking years younger than she had during her last Vietnam appearance, clad in a superb evening gown and receiving her latest award from the Prince of Wales. The final footage showed her on location at Ascot during the shooting of a series about crime in the world of horse racing.

'Although she is half French and finished her education at the Sorbonne, Andrea Vincent has no plans to pursue her career here,' concluded the commentator. 'She pays infrequent visits to her mother, the writer Marie-Louise Chabrol, in Brittany, but otherwise is a confirmed Londoner.'

The French TV presenter turned to the next subject in his survey of women in European media. This one was a home grown tele-journalist who had followed the more traditional female path by concentrating on fashion and domestic subjects. The woman who had been watching the documentary in the huge opulent drawing-room of her apartment above the Rue Cambon, in the most fashionable arrondissement of Paris, had sat riveted by the old Vietnam newsreel clips which formed much of the Andrea

Vincent footage. Hearing a summary of the next subject's more homely achievements, she gave an impatient hiss and snapped the off button on the TV's remote control panel.

She turned imperiously to her male companion. 'Get her, Eugène. She's the only one I'll consider.'

'Mademoiselle, are you sure you wish to consider anyone at all? I know we have had this conversation before, but I still think you might regret this. Look what happened in the past. . . .'

'It's *because* of what's happened in the past that I want it this way. I've delayed too long for all the wrong reasons. Of course it has to be her! I got it wrong before because I chose the wrong people. All the time the answer was staring me in the face. Only my stupid pride prevented me from acknowledging it.'

Eugène St-Meurice knew it was pointless to argue. Alouette Doré had been getting her own way for more than seventy years and was unlikely to accept anything less now. The possible results of her folly were painful to contemplate. But there, he thought, it will be her pain, so why should I concern myself with it? My problem will be persuading this wretched TV personality to join us for a couple of months.

# Chapter One

## Andrea
## London, June 1978

The TV crew were bickering a shade too long about the best way to tackle their subject, to the despair of Mark Trent, the senior cameraman. He turned impatiently on the supposed leader of the gossiping technicians, convinced the afternoon light would fail before they had finished the shoot.

'Come on, Nev, for Christ's sake! A bridge is a bridge is a bridge, and it'll be an invisible bridge if you don't get your skates on. I'm not in the business of filming black cats down coal holes at midnight!'

Nev, the number two cameraman, stopped talking to the woman reporter and grinned at him. 'Not much point in getting a stunning shot of the stonework in the afternoon sun if we don't give the viewers any idea of how inaccessible the scene of the crime was, is there? Calm down and we'll be with you in a minute.'

The blonde he had just been talking to intervened. 'He's right, Nev. Unless we get going now we'll lose the light, and I'd rather wrap this up today if we can. I'm feeling about as inconspicuous as a pork chop at a bar mitzvah at the moment. The sooner we get away from here, the happier I'll be.'

'Whatever you say, love. You're the boss. Anyhow, I think it's sorted now.'

Andrea Vincent spoke her piece to the camera, describing the last hours of Paolo Umberto, an international financier, before his corpse was discovered by a cleaning woman on her way over the bridge just after dawn. To follow Andrea's introduction, the crew needed more footage showing general views of the area and close-up shots of the bridge's sub-structure. As she came off camera she noticed that two of them had turned to watch someone descending the steps from the Embankment to the foreshore, where the cameras had been set up.

No one spoke. They looked on silently, suspicion giving way to incredulity as the man started across the Thames mud towards them. Andrea was the wariest of all. She and the crew were all dressed to suit the location, in Barbours and rubber boots. The newcomer, by contrast, would have been thoroughly at his ease on that June morning in Bond Street. He was an incongruous sight here, or perhaps a sinister one . . .? Reaching them, he ignored the crew and spoke directly to Andrea.

'Mam'selle Vincent?' The French accent seemed almost affected. 'Mam'selle, forgive me for pursuing you 'ere, but I 'ave been unable to reach you at the office for over one week.'

Too right, mate. With the Mafia breathing down my neck, the fewer people who can get to me the better, she thought. Somehow, though, this exquisite did not strike her as a suitable candidate for the Brotherhood.

'What can I do for you, M'sieur – er – ?' She awaited an introduction which came reinforced with a card, engraved and expensive.

'St-Meurice. Eugène St-Meurice.' He paused as though expecting a round of applause. Andrea simply nodded and murmured a stock pleasantry. The name meant nothing to her.

'I wish to discuss a major assignment with you, Mam'selle. We can go somewhere and talk?'

A derisive sound escaped the lips of one of the cameramen. The others were silent but the mixture of grins and grimaces must have warned St-Meurice of her likely response. Fortunately his error was so immense as to deprive her of her power to blaspheme.

Instead, with a measure of scornful kindness, she said:

'I can only assume from that remark that you haven't the remotest idea what I'm working on. These boys are the best news team in the UK. That bridge up there served as a gallows for one of the biggest crooks in Europe a couple of weeks ago. The whole world is still arguing about whether he jumped or the Mafia pushed him, and *you're* asking me to go somewhere and talk about a major assignment?'

The visitor reddened but held his ground. 'There are other matters of importance beside squalid crimes, Mam'selle. I am offering you the story of a lifetime . . .'

This was too much! At this rate he would hold them up until tide and light were all to hell. 'Look,' she said angrily, 'you can see for yourself I can't possibly talk to you now. In fact, I'm amazed at your nerve, barging in like this when I'm already on the story of a lifetime! I'll promise you one thing – to call you at your hotel this evening – but only if you leave me in peace now. Okay?'

'Excellent, Mam'selle Vincent. I assure you I would not pester you if it were a trivial matter. I am at the Berkeley.' He bowed and walked away. Andrea grimaced at what the mud had done to his hand-lasted shoes.

An hour later the light really had gone. They managed to complete the last few background shots in time, then stood talking just north of the bridge while looking out for a cab for Andrea.

'So what d'you plan to do about the Empress Eugène?' said Nev. 'Surely you don't intend getting together with him after all Vic Halliwell's said to you about suspicious foreigners in expensive suits?'

'I hardly think he meant that sort of foreigner – or that sort of expensive suit, either. That one was Faubourg St-Honoré, not Via Veneto. I should think the only thing he's ever murdered is a dry Martini.'

'Look, Andy, take care, will you? Sure, he's probably okay. But he could be doing a mate a favour and taking you somewhere convenient to meet the big kids. Why not just forget you ever saw him and go back to your hotel for a pizza and a glass of plonk?'

'Nev, how could you? I'll never feel the same about pizza if I live to be ninety! Come to think of it, that doesn't seem too likely right now, does it?'

'Cheer up, love. You've been bloody marvellous about it so far. Don't start getting pessimistic now. You'll come through.'

'Any minute now you'll shout "Are we downhearted?" as the ship disappears beneath the waves!' Nevertheless Andrea was touched by his concern, and on her way back to the hotel decided to go along with his warning that contact with strangers was unwise at present.

They were on the last lap of what looked like becoming Andrea's most dangerous job to date. It had started routinely enough a month before, when she began work on a short documentary for Channel Five on the financial skulduggery leading up to a foreign banker's suicide in London. Her first couple of background interviews made her wonder whether it was suicide after all. The threatening phone calls which followed convinced her she was on the right track.

After that matters got worse very quickly. By the time she had finished her research, she had been forced to move out of her South Kensington mews house and into an hotel. The threatening calls continued and her boss at the TV company suggested giving her a temporary bodyguard. Andrea laughed at the idea. Leaving the studios that evening, she was about to cross the street when a car swerved towards her and attempted to crush her against the side of the building. Only her reflex leap from its path saved her. The car struck the wall a glancing blow, swung back on to the road and away before Andrea was fully aware of what had happened. After that she changed hotels twice a week and was driven to and from the studios by a different car hire company each day.

The production team teased her about her sudden unwanted celebrity but they were genuinely worried about her safety. On location they always made sure that two of them were close to her. No strangers were allowed to break into the closed group.

They had now completed the last day's filming. Tomorrow she would be back at Channel Five House editing for a few days. Then the Director of Public Prosecutions would get a copy of her Umberto dossier and the finished film. They were all carefully avoiding talking about what might happen after that. Theoretically the villains would be rounded up by Scotland Yard and Interpol, Andrea would go home again and everything would return to normal. They assured each other over-heartily that vendettas were not pursued outside Sicily. In the silence that inevitably followed, Andrea often wondered how long it would be before she learned to walk down a dark street again without looking back every ten paces. Of course Nev was right in warning her against going off with a stranger – and a foreigner at that.

But she was tired of eating alone in her hotel room. Books were losing their charm and she had no appetite for other people's documentaries on television. Eugène St-Meurice would be better than no company at all, and she had never seen a *mafioso* with so much money invested in such unobtrusive clothes. Little by little she convinced herself he was genuine. She telephoned him just after seven o'clock.

'Thank you for calling, Mam'selle. Would you care to join me here for dinner? The restaurant is superb, even – may I say it? – by French standards.'

'Uh-huh, not a chance. You're not the only one who appreciates the Berkeley's *risotto Milanese*! Meet me in half an hour at the Wan Kei in Rupert Court off Shaftesbury Avenue. They serve the best Chinese food in London.'

'Really, Mam'selle Vincent, do you have to be so secretive? I don't care for this creeping about to obscure places for a straightforward meeting. I like a civilised meal in civilised surroundings, not a hasty bowl of rice up a back street.'

'Please yourself. It's that or nothing. I may sound

paranoid but there are some Italian gentlemen who are deadly serious about finding me, if you get my drift. If you're that keen to do business with me, you'll do it on my terms, Monsieur St-Meurice.'

He was at the Wan Kei by eight p.m. As they ate their way through a succession of superb Cantonese dishes, he relaxed in spite of the laminate-topped tables and black chain store teapots. His subsequent proposal took Andrea completely by surprise.

'Fashion? Me? You have to be kidding! I may look quite smart, it's part of my job, but in my book clothes are strictly for enjoying and wearing, not forever! I find all that "darling, you're a great artist" crap, to a dress-maker, quite nauseating. What on earth made you think I'd be interested in doing a couturière's biography, even straight from the clothes horse's mouth?'

'Mam'selle, even you must accept that Eliane Doré is not just a couturière. She virtually invented the emancipated woman, and she did it through dress and lifestyle not political posturing. Surely you are aware that every top journalist and biographer in two continents has attempted to write the definitive life story?'

'Yeah, sure. A few years ago the gossip columns could find nothing else to talk about. But it seems to me that the heart of what they were saying was that La Doré didn't want to spill the beans. All they had to report was rows between those top writers and your top couturière, which invariably ended with much stamping of well-shod feet and much walking out of expensive doors. Why should you think she'd treat me any differently?'

'Because she has asked specifically for you, Mam'selle Vincent. No other journalist will do. She admires your work in your own field and thinks her trouble so far has arisen from allowing authors too close to the fashion business to take on the commission. They cannot bring to the task the objectivity which she feels necessary, and that inevitably leads to disputes. Mademoiselle is above all a perfectionist.'

'Well, bully for Mademoiselle! No, I'm sorry to have

brought you all this way for nothing, but I love what I'm doing now and have no desire to break into haute couture.'

He was beginning to look desperate. 'Please reconsider, Mam'selle Vincent. She is never prepared to take no for an answer.'

'Well, love, it's never too late to learn, even at a hundred and ten, or however old she is now. Christ, someone as old as that must have been turned down some time!'

St-Meurice had turned slightly pale at her tone, as though she were discussing the Virgin Mary with excessive familiarity. 'There is no need to speak of her in that manner. She is a great woman. Please, let me ask you again, at least consider it. My Paris numbers are on the card I gave you – home as well as office. Think about it when you finish your present job and, I implore you, don't dismiss it too lightly. I think you will find the story far more fascinating than you anticipate.'

She agreed to call him if she changed her mind, but assured him it was unlikely. They left the little restaurant together but Andrea belatedly remembered Nev's warning and watched St-Meurice depart by taxi before heading for her own hotel.

At first the notion of her working on a dress designer's biography struck her as amusing nonsense, but the meeting with St-Meurice led Andrea to consider Eliane Doré from an angle which had never occurred to her before. Yes, of course he had exaggerated her importance, but in a way he was right. Whatever the politicians said, it was clothing – or lack of it – and social attitudes that produced radical change. And Doré had certainly revolutionised fashion. Mmm, it was an intriguing thought. Had La Grande Mademoiselle, as Doré was nicknamed by the press, done more for women's liberation than the entire Pankhurst family? It might be interesting to find out. . . .

In the end, though, Andrea decided that fear for her own skin had temporarily overcome her news sense. Dismissing Eugène St-Meurice, Eliane Doré and haute couture in general, she jotted down a few notes on loose ends in the Umberto story which needed tying up tomorrow, and went to bed. But having entered her mind, Doré seemed determined not to depart. When Andrea went for coffee at the studio cafeteria next morning, she ran into a producer who had started her professional life as a fashion assistant on *Vogue*.

'Do you know off-hand whether we've ever done any specials on Alouette Doré?' Andrea asked, keeping her voice as casual as possible.

'Mmm, let's see. . . . Yes, there was a fifty-minute feature in that ten-part series we did on the great designers a few years back. I'm afraid it wasn't the best of the bunch by any means. She let them into her salon but wouldn't do an interview and clammed up completely about her early life. They should have known better than to try, because in all those years in the fashion business she's never once given a press or TV interview.

'As the whole point of the thing was "Meet the personality behind the big name" that ruined the programme before it got going. Still, it showed her gorgeous clothes, and they padded it out with a string of short interviews with the big names who'd known her in the Thirties. There's a hefty file on her, too, because at first the researchers were determined to do as good a job on her as they managed on Balenciaga and St Laurent. What's so interesting about her all of a sudden? If *you're* on her trail, does it mean she's been running heroin across frontiers sewn into beaded evening tops?'

'No, I just got curious about this secrecy thing she appears to have. From what you've just said, it's every bit as strong as I've heard.'

'Oh, no question about that. It seems to cover two main areas, her origins and her love life. Apparently she never tells the same story twice on the first and never tells any story at all on the second – just lets gossip exaggerate her glamour until she sounds like the greatest thing since Cleopatra. But the less enchanted have been heard to mutter: "So how come she's wound up alone in her old age?" It would be fascinating to find out, but I doubt whether anyone ever will, now.'

'I might just give it a whirl. Thanks for the information, Maggie.'

But Andrea's interest might have ended there had not her film editor gone down with a virulent stomach bug.

'If you can hang on for a couple of hours, we'll get Josh Egan for you,' Vic Halliwell told her. 'You always say you like working with him and he'll have finished his present job by mid-afternoon. I'd tell anyone else to go for a three-hour lunch, but seeing that it's you, you're going to have to hide here until he's free. There's a Women's Institute group doing the studio tour in a few minutes. You could always tag along – you might learn something!'

'Funny! If you weren't so important I'd tell you what I thought of that little idea! Don't worry about me. I'll keep myself amused somehow.'

Halliwell became serious. 'Just as long as you stay inside, Andy. I know it's a bore, but this is probably the most dangerous time of all for you.'

'And wouldn't it be a nuisance if I got knocked off before the damned story was finished?'

'Get out, you hard-bitten bitch – you know it's your safety we're worried about!'

She made a face at him and left. There was only one place to go – the studio reference library, and then a viewing room, with the file on Alouette Doré and a tape of the documentary special.

On closer consideration, Eliane 'Alouette' Doré's biography began to look like the all time plum writing assignment. Now in her ninety-fourth year, she still towered above the other style-setters of the twentieth century. Single-handed, it seemed, she had invented the modern woman back in the early 1920s. But it had not ended there. Having changed the shape, style and behaviour of the female sex, she had gone on to make herself fabulously rich.

Then, while the rest of her generation were settling into comfortable middle age, Doré had captured the heart of the richest man in England, the Duke of Conway. Their affair lasted years and it was said that she eventually chose a wife for him, rather than abdicate her title of queen of fashion to become a mere duchess.

Throughout the 1930s she had ruled fashionable Parisian society. If you were brilliant, eccentric or avant garde the chances were you went to her salons, for clothes or intellectual stimulation. To be merely rich was not enough. Only the attractive or talented rich were welcome *chez* Doré. Somehow this fashion immortal had managed to survive even the disgrace of collaboration with the Germans. She had closed her fashion house throughout the war but remained in Paris, living in the Ritz with a high-ranking Nazi.

When hostilities ceased she departed to exile in Switzerland, only to sweep back to the centre stage of world fashion when she re-opened in the mid 1950s. Since then she had been riding high as a true fashion immortal, incalculably rich, eternally chic. Right now it appeared that only death would defeat her, and her interest in an official biography hinted that she felt she might cheat even this final eclipse by immortalising her achievements in an Authorised Version.

What a life story! Rags to riches, ignorant waif to cultural lioness, little tart to Grande Mademoiselle. The eminent writers were queueing up to chronicle her story by the time she had reached her mid-seventies. But somehow the biographies remained stillborn. Mademoiselle sifted through the contenders with the eye of a connoisseur. One by one, some of the greatest names in modern European and American letters trooped in through the doors of her Rue Cambon apartment - and trooped out again. They all started off enthralled by her tales of acquaintance with the great, the brilliant, the notorious. After a couple of months of interviews, however, their relationships with Alouette altered. The more bedazzled discovered that she expected to exercise an absolute right of censorship over their work. The cynics began to notice that her accounts of a Breton girlhood altered unrecognisably from day to day. The only consistency in these memories lay in their strong resemblance to the trashy newspaper serials which she had read compulsively in those far off days. Over a period of ten years, author after author undertook her life story with the most radiant optimism, only to leave after a bitter quarrel not long afterwards. The most determined, a top French magazine editor, lasted a year. The most disillusioned, an American Pulitzer prizewinner, stormed out after only three weeks. As the years passed and the list of literary casualties lengthened, there were fewer contenders for the post of official biographer.

Doré had been nearly ninety when the Channel Five feature was made. As Maggie said, the designer had refused to participate directly and the most viewers were permitted to see was a shot of her sitting on the staircase which led from the salon up to her private apartment, watching the models parade in her latest creations as she had twice a year throughout her couture career. Painters, sculptors, a choreographer and several authors, as well as half European high society and a scattering of film stars, were interviewed to pad the documentary. It made fascinating viewing, even if it lacked Doré's personal involvement. The huge background information file which went with the tape was even better.

Andrea watched the video through twice, then sat for a long time in the empty viewing room, thinking about the legend the stuff of whose life she had just glimpsed. The temptation to take Eugène St-Meurice up on his offer was becoming almost irresistible. She had not changed her view on the essential silliness of a major industry which insisted on regarding itself as a branch of the fine arts, but this woman was in a class of her own. Andrea found herself gripped by the prospect of producing the definitive account of such a life; of painting an accurate portrait despite the sitter's determination to veil herself in mystery.

Suddenly she realised that the delay in getting hold of Josh Egan to edit her Umberto tapes must be over. She went to find him, and long hours in the cutting room pushed thoughts of Mademoiselle into the background for the rest of the day. But that evening she took the Doré tape back to the hotel and ran through it again. Several times she was on the point of telephoning Eugène St-Meurice and saying she had changed her mind. Several times she decided against it.

Over the years Andrea had built up a wide circle of acquaintances in the literary world. Joel Handford was a friend she had not seen for a long time. He was also the Pulitzer prizewinner who had stormed out on Mademoiselle. It was now well after midnight in London but still only part-way through the working day in Arizona, where Joel lived. Andrea telephoned him. He gave a whoop of pleasure at hearing from her after so long and asked about her current activities. The Mafia investigation intrigued him and he asked a lot of questions about it. Then she mentioned the Eliane Doré project and his manner changed abruptly.

'That senile old bitch should be put away for endangering the sanity of simple-minded authors! Keep away from her, kid. She makes poison ivy look like lilac!'

'Come on, Joel, you've cracked some of the toughest egos in the business in your time. Surely the brain that defeated the Teamsters' boss and President de Gaulle within one year wasn't beaten by a little old lady in a Paris suit?'

'You got it – game, set and match! I was so addled by the time she'd finished with me I went on a five-day drunk to recover my sanity. Believe me, Andy, that woman's contact with reality is fleeting – and I'm being kind! She's also selfish, devious, shifty, pathologically secretive . . . and above all there's something way back in her past that she can't live with, so she's deceiving herself as well as the rest of us with her pathetic fantasies.'

'But that sounds like the basis for the all time great biography. Why walk away from it?'

'Yeah, you'd be right if there were a snowball in hell's chance of her coming up with the truth eventually. Don't forget that she's outlived her whole generation. There's simply no one left alive who could tell you the real story if not Mademoiselle. But don't expect it from her. It's less a matter of won't than can't, I think, but she finds that impossible to live with so inevitably she blames the would-be biographer for ineptitude. She may be over the hill but she's still a shrewd old cow and when she starts pitching in like that she's pure poison. Leave her be, Andy. She'll be too much for you to handle and that's no reflection on your ability. Choose someone straightforward like Howard Hughes!'

She thanked him and said goodbye, enthusiasm quenched. Nobody was worth the sort of torment outlined by Joel. Just as well there was someone with first-hand experience who could warn me off, she thought.

But Andrea had bargained without the outcome of her present assignment. The next morning she made her normal check-in call to Vic Halliwell before starting out for the studio. The tone of thinly disguised panic in his normally phlegmatic voice swiftly alerted her that something was wrong.

'Andy, you're okay? Thank God! I was just beginning to wonder how bright it had been not to know your location.'

'Why, what happened? You sound as if the roof just collapsed!'

'It did, and until a couple of seconds ago I wasn't sure if you were under it.' Halliwell laughed humourlessly. 'At six a.m. this morning someone blew the front off your house.'

'They did what?' Andy's knees buckled with fright and she sank wearily down upon the bed of her hotel room. She had no need to ask who had done it.

'The Bomb Squad is still going through the rubble. Nev had just come in when we got the news. He panicked at the thought that you'd got so fed up with camping in hotels you might just have gone home to Kensington last night, after you'd finished editing the report. The only witness was a newspaper boy who saw a new blue Porsche just outside the archway into your mews. He was admiring it from across the street when your place blew and the car drove off. The police are assuming whoever was in it triggered the explosion by remote control. I don't know what we're going to do with you for the next couple of months.'

'What do the police suggest?'

'Well, they've offered round-the-clock protection, but you know as well as I do that you'll be unable to work for five minutes in those conditions. If we could only find a safe bolt-hole for you, my feeling is you should be sent on a longish sabbatical until this is sewn up. You can always write the book of the TV programme while you're off.'

'Vic, in your own little way you're a bit of a genius sometimes! That's just what I could do – only not the book you're thinking of.'

'You're talking nonsense. I know it's a shock to have your house blown away, but please try and make sense.'

'I have somewhere to go, Vic. Somewhere that will keep me out of the way for at least two months, maybe more, and where the Honoured Society would never dream of looking for me. There's also a chance that I'll come back with the basis of the glossy documentary series of the decade. How about "The Woman Who Created the Twentieth Century"?'

'Now I know you've lost your marbles!'

'Not this time, Vic. Just off to do a honey of a job. See you in three months!'

Eugène St-Meurice's delight at Andrea's change of heart quickly turned to exasperation when he learned he was to be cheated of the pleasure of personally delivering his trophy to his employer.

'Look, Eugène, I've said I'll do it. Isn't that enough to be going on with? How I get there is up to me. All I can tell you is that it will take at least a couple of days. If you arrange to be at your home number in Paris by Friday, I'll ring you there between, say, Friday noon and Saturday noon. And I promise I shan't be more than half an hour away from you.'

'But why can't you do it in a more straightforward manner? Surely you'd prefer to travel on Mademoiselle's private jet and be collected by her limousine at the airport? It will be a more comfortable journey than anything you are likely to arrange.'

'No doubt about it, but comfort isn't my top priority just now. Look, why not return to Paris, saying I've turned you down, and in a couple of days I get you out of a spot by ringing to say I've changed my mind about the commision. Will that help?'

'I suspect it will have to, Mam'selle Vincent.'

'Hey, Eugène, your ooh la-la accent has almost gone.'

'You are not the only one who can assume protective colouring at will. It often helps me to complete a sale. Now I have some advice for you. You have a reputation for paying attention to detail. I recommend that you live up to that for the next few weeks because unless you listen closely, remember and analyse, you will be no more successful with La Grande Mademoiselle than any of the others.'

'Why should you care?'

'One day I might tell you, but I doubt it. Let us say merely that I want to see a true record after she has gone, not a collection of melodramatic fairytales.'

'Since you've started to unwind, tell me something. Is she as hard to pin down as they all say she is?'

'Worse.'

'Why?'

'There are many things in Mademoiselle's life which she prefers to keep hidden.'

'Then why the obsession with a biography?'

'It is her chance of immortality, Mam'selle.'

'But what earthly point is there in preserving a lie for posterity?'

'You will have to ask her that, if you dare. I truly have

not the faintest idea. If my past were as I suspect hers to have been, I should take my secrets with me to the grave. And now, Mam'selle Vincent, I have told you enough to cost me my job if she ever hears of this conversation. I won't be so frank with you again. Shall we say this is a small token of my gratitude that you have decided to take on the assignment after all?'

'But you've told me nothing!'

'Perhaps; perhaps not.' He rose to leave the small café where they had arranged to meet. 'Now I must go back to the Berkeley and prepare to leave. Unless you prefer to reconsider coming with me?'

'No, thanks all the same, Eugène. See you in Paris in a couple of days.'

'*Au revoir, Mam'selle, et bonne chance!*'

Kastrup looked just like any other middle-sized international airport in north-western Europe. Its main advantage as far as Andrea Vincent was concerned was that few people travelled through it en route from London to Paris. If anybody had been waiting for her to do a bunk, they were unlikely to get further in pursuit of her than the Royal Hotel in Copenhagen. On her arrival in Denmark she boarded the SAS bus and sat watching the featureless landscape on the journey between the airport and the capital. Disembarking at the airline terminal in Vesterbrogade, she went to register in the Hilton-style SAS Royal next door. Her first act after locking herself into her room was to ring the hotel's hairdressing salon and make an appointment for half an hour hence. Then she carefully removed all her make-up.

The reflection which looked back at her from the bathroom mirror was that of a big, handsome woman in her mid-thirties. The hair was thick and honey-coloured and fell in a softly flattering style to her shoulders. Stripped of their make-up her storm-grey eyes looked slightly less significant, but she was still strikingly good-looking. Andrea would never be easily hidden. Nearly six feet tall and with big bones, she moved with an easy grace which came of fitness and self-confidence. Now the time had come for disguise, she was too intelligent to think a brown wig and a pair of sunglasses could transform her. What she needed was a change of appearance which would not make passport controllers delay her passage across frontiers, but would prevent instant recognition by someone who might be tailing her from a description rather than from personal knowledge.

Two hours later she had achieved the main element of the disguise. The glowing dark blonde hair lay on the salon floor and she sported an urchin-short flame-coloured hairstyle instead. Along with the hair she had apparently shed ten years. She flagged down a taxi, took it to Magasin du Nord on Kongens Nytorv and bought a completely new range of cosmetics. After that she went round the corner to a boutique and emerged in a designer version of a black leather biker's suit over a yellow 'Jesus Saves – With First National' teeshirt. She looked more like a twenty-five-year-old follower of street fashion than a thirty-five-year-old TV reporter.

Andrea had brought no luggage with her from England apart from a briefcase. At Magasin du Nord she had acquired a leather overnight bag together with a change of clothes and underwear – the former rather less striking than her leather gear. Now she checked in at the Hotel Angleterre. From her room she telephoned the SAS Royal Hotel, said she was checking out and gave her AmEx number to settle the account. Then she spent an enjoyable half hour experimenting with the new make-up before trying out Andrea Vincent Mark Two on the restaurant. Whatever its effectiveness as a disguise, the new look certainly seemed to pull the men, she thought, smugly ignoring several smouldering glances while tucking into her *gravad lax*. Gentlemen might prefer blondes, but would-be seducers obviously went for redheads.

She knew and loved Copenhagen from years back, but decided not to risk a stroll through the mile-long pedestrian precinct which connected Kongens Nytorv with the town hall square, and beyond with the irresistible Tivoli Gardens. It looked as if her scheme was working but she had planned it too carefully to risk chance discovery for the sake of a stroll up memory lane.

After enjoying her first untroubled night's sleep for more than a month, Andrea checked out of the Angleterre, travelled to the Central Station and boarded the Nord Express for Paris. Oh, Eugène, you're in for a shock when you see the new me, she thought. I'll bet anything La Grande Mademoiselle isn't into either phony red hair or leathers. I wonder if she wants me enough to put up with it?

In her dimly lit apartment, high above her Paris salon, Alouette Doré tried, not very hard, to curb her impatience. It was difficult to remember how long it had been since anyone had failed to satisfy her smallest whim. Now it seemed that someone was ready to thwart her in a matter of the gravest importance. She hissed almost inaudibly through clenched teeth, a lifelong mannerism when irritated, and reached for the telephone.

'Eugène? Are you certain she is coming? It's already after nine. She did say yes, not just perhaps?'

Her aide's voice was patient but weary. 'Yes, Mademoiselle. I have already explained many times, I would not have made such a mistake, knowing how important this matter is to you. She said between noon today and noon tomorrow. There are still fifteen hours left before she is even late. I cannot make a spell and conjure her out of the air for you.'

'No, but you might have had the intelligence to make sure she came back with you instead of going off alone like that. So stupid! Why would she want to travel on some dirty train or aeroplane when she could have come on the jet with you?'

'Mademoiselle, she has been working on a very delicate assignment. I think she has fears for her own safety. It would be of little use to you if anyone – er – followed her here.'

'Oh, stop being so melodramatic! What if someone did follow her? At worst we'd have some Eddie Constantine type in a raincoat standing down below staring up at the windows. It might even be amusing.'

'I do not think the people who follow Andrea Vincent will be content to stare up at windows, Mademoiselle. They are accustomed to be inside, not out in the cold, and if they are not invited in they have ways of making themselves at home anyway.'

'Nonsense – it's all some childish excuse for keeping me waiting and making herself seem more important than me. I expect she has heard I'm a prima donna and wants to lay claim to the role first. Well, she'll have to do much better than this!'

St-Meurice sighed, resigned to an evening of self-centred ranting. Doré had no real comprehension of other people's lives independent of her. Others existed only as secondary characters in the great drama which was Alouette Doré's life.

'You'd better come over here,' she ordered sharply. 'I shall order supper for two and if she arrives she'll just have to take pot luck. Come on, hurry. I'm beginning to feel hungry and you know it depresses me to eat alone!'

'But, Mademoiselle, have you forgotten? I would not presume to give anyone your personal number. She can contact only me. I cannot go out, I have to stay at home until she calls.'

Her sharp intake of breath told him Doré really had forgotten, but he knew she would never admit it. In moments she had thought up an excuse.

'Idiot, of course I remember! Seraphine is still downstairs. I'll send her over in a taxi and she can stay at your place for the call. I want to discuss this girl again before I meet her.'

'I think it unlikely that she will arrive at all tonight, Mademoiselle. Why not dine with one of your friends?

Monsieur le Comte d'Agde was telling me just this morning that it was too long since he had seen you, and asking whether you would be available this evening. You know he dines late and I'm sure if you telephoned. . . .'

'Eugène, even you must have more sense than to think I would invite myself to the home of Henri or anyone else at this ungodly notice. It would look as if I had been let down at the last minute. No, get over here as soon as Seraphine reaches you. Once we've done with this stubborn child, I want to talk over the collection anyway.'

'She is a mature woman, Mademoiselle. I think you will achieve nothing if you treat her like a gamine.'

'I know, I know. I've heard it all before! These days if you're over thirty you're already an old hag. Eugène, when I was over forty my real life was just beginning! I tell you this girl is still a child. Now let me go. I have to send Seraphine and order some dinner. Don't be long. I shall tell her to make the taxi wait for you when it brings her.'

She disconnected without saying goodbye. Eugène St-Meurice glanced across his drawing-room at the golden-haired young man with the silky eyelashes who sat waiting on the sofa, and cursed Alouette Doré with quiet savagery.

# Chapter Two
## Doré

*I was cold tonight, maybe that's why I thought of Papa. That and this crazy scheme I've dreamed up to use the English girl as my myth-maker. I can never think of Papa without thinking of snow. Hardly surprising considering the way it was coming down that day. Like something straight out of a novelette! Hmm, those idiot men of letters were always so pleased when they thought they'd caught me out telling them a pack of lies from the cheap romances of my childhood days. It never occurred to them that the truth could have been so close to fiction.*

*I can see him now, so handsome, so embarrassed and oh, so determined to be rid of me, urging me forward towards the Sister of Mercy at the orphanage. 'Go to the Little Sister, Elie. She'll look after you while I'm making our fortunes! Go along now.' 'No thank you, Papa, I'd rather come and help you make the fortune. Shall we go now? I don't like it here.' Oh, I was so sure he'd listen! Instead he turned to the Sister, raised his eyes in a melodramatic gesture which said, Kids! Where do they get their ideas?*

*Then he turned back to me, less jolly now. 'Don't be stubborn, Elie. What will the nuns think? You always say you want to help me. Well, the best way is to be good, learn your lessons and wait until I come to get you. I don't want to have to tell you again.' He kissed me hurriedly, already wanting to be gone. 'Au revoir, little one. Take care.'*

*'But Papa, really, I could look after you. I wouldn't be any trouble, I promise' – now I was getting desperate; he*

*was close to the courtyard gate and heading away from me – 'I can keep house and do some work, washing perhaps, or selling some of your goods . . .' The nun interrupted me, not unkindly but in a tone that would brook no defiance.*

*'Eliane, you are being silly. You are ten years old! How could you look after a grown man and earn money? Your papa cannot support himself and look after you. The sooner you let him start working, the quicker he will be able to come back and fetch you.' I caught Papa's eye as he gave the nun a look of pure gratitude. I hated her and for a moment I hated him, too. But there wasn't enough time for that. He was back at the gate again. I made one last desperate appeal.*

*'Papa, it's not fair, just because I'm a girl! Gaston and Paul aren't coming here, only me! Why should it just be me?'*

*He sighed as if I were slow and had missed something that was obvious to everyone else. 'Paul is twelve and Gaston is nearly fifteen. They really are old enough to work – at least to earn enough for me to send them to stay with Ninette, knowing they'll bring in enough for their keep. I cannot do that with you, lovey, and your sister is too poor herself to keep you.'*

*I knew there was no point in further argument. His face told me he wanted to be somewhere else. Even my distress was beginning to bore him. I think I learned then not to plead. You never achieve anything by it. People make up their own minds and if you're in their power, you're just lucky or unlucky. You can't affect their decision unless you have the power to escape. That's what it's all about, power.*

*The door closed and he was gone. I'm still sure I heard a woman say his name and laugh as she added something about freedom – but that could be a trick of my imagination, embroidering the way it might have been. One thing I know: if he ever made the fortune, someone else benefited from it because I never saw him again, rich or poor.*

*All these years that's been locked up inside my head. When Eugène told me he had* la vedette, *the English reporter from the television, I promised myself that it would be different with her, that this time I would tell the whole truth, no fancy embroidery. But will I be able to go through with it? I feel myself going red with shame just lying here alone thinking about it. If only those clowns knew that's why I sleep on my couch so much. It's not affectation – it's just that there I go on good journeys of the mind. Here in my bed they're all bad or sad or plain unthinkable. Well, can I tell this Andrea Vincent such a story? Will she care that my father abandoned me to a bunch of cold-hearted nuns when I was too young to stop him?*

*She might not, but I do. I'll probably lose my nerve when the moment comes, as always. None of them would understand, of course. They're all too stupid and totally lacking finesse. They'd all think I was ashamed of the orphanage. I couldn't care less if the whole world knew about the orphanage, but it wouldn't end there; they'd all work out that if I went to live there while my father was still alive and able-bodied, it was because he didn't want me. No one has ever been told that a man didn't want me, and I find it impossible to start now.*

*Eliane, Eliane, this is ridiculous! This girl makes fifteen who have come to write about you at your invitation. You promised yourself she would be the first who wouldn't need to leave empty-handed. After all, you owe her that at least. . . . You owe yourself something, too, and there's not much more time to pay your debt. Just think, you could sit back and stop feeling nervous that someone would drag out your disreputable brothers and embarrass you with them; or that some gutter journalist might prove publicly that those middle-class land-owning aunts were just figments of your imagination.*

*The fear preoccupies me so much now that I'll have no peace until I can really bury it. Here I am, tottering on the edge of eternity and not even sure whether Eugène will keep his mouth shut once I'm gone. Not that he knows it all by any means, but he knows more than anyone else now. All the others are dead.*

*I was so unjust to Magda until the very end; so jealous, so full of envy. And why? All those years after her heyday she was utterly eclipsed, while I carried on from strength to strength, age only increasing my fame. Magda never did me a bad turn and I'd certainly never have made it without her. Successful, yes, but the leader of the intellectual élite of Paris? Not without Magda! I'd still be reading those shop girl romances if it weren't for her. She could have told such a lot about me that I wanted covered up, and God knows in the last years she could have used the money they would have paid her. But she never gave the slightest sign she knew anything worth telling about me. She never even hinted at the reasons the rich bitch had for throwing around so much cash, proving herself the Queen of Culture by paying for the funerals of dead avant garde geniuses.*

*Yes, Magda was probably my best friend of all. And to think I told myself I was repaying her friendship by dressing her head to toe in Doré, free of charge. She knew as well as I that because I created the clothes, all I was really giving her was a few metres of jersey or* mousseline de soie. *Not a great deal for half a lifetime of help and support. About the only real service I was able to do her was to prepare her properly for her own funeral. So like Magda to die at the height of the preparations for the Spring Collection, but I sent her off properly just the same. She went to her rest looking more beautiful than when Bonnard painted her, all in white – even the flowers in white – like a snow maiden, apart from that soft pink lipstick and a pink silk sash. She looked more like a Slav princess on that last journey than at any time while she lived.*

*Who'll do it for me? Not Eugène, that's for sure. Even if he were willing, I've had to share my physical privacy with too many men to put up with it when I'm in my coffin. And anyway, it would make the damned pansy sick. Loulou? She'd leave me for the rubbish cart. Perhaps Andrea Vincent. . . . Careful, Eliane. You're taking too much for granted. See how she takes your story first. See how she reacts when you tell her . . . if you tell her.*

*Hell and damnation! This is getting almost as bad as the night before the '54 Re-opening Collection. I shan't sleep tonight and I want her to see me strong, not old and weak. I can't wipe away the wrinkles and the bent back, but I can give them a few shreds of glamour if I've had a chance to rest! It looks as if it will have to be a little pill. There, that should do it. Now I can lie here and plan my big entrance when this wonderful woman journalist arrives, and by the time I've set it all in order, I shall be drifting off. Whatever I do, I mustn't discuss Loulou with her yet. That would put her off straight away. I wish I could have taken a look at her before this all started. Eugène is observant enough, but he misses the things that a woman will instinctively pick up. I'd only need to have seen her once in the flesh and I'd know whether she was likely to love me or hate me on sight. She'll do one or the other, that's for sure. No half measures for that one, from what I hear.*

*I imagine she'll expect to have nothing in common with me. From what Eugène says she's due for a shock there! She obviously expects me to try and persuade her that fashion is a fine art, and that the designer should be taken as seriously as the painter or composer. I'll have fun changing her mind on that score. I've seen enough pictures of the girl to know that she dresses well. Clearly she has the proper attitude to clothes. It will be fun to teach her to appreciate the couturière's skills. If she hasn't stormed off by then I might let her watch me at work on the Autumn Collection. Yes, that could be interesting, if she's still here . . . if I've hardened my resolve enough to tell her . . . tell her everything. . . .*

But morning changed things, as mornings have a habit of doing. She had planned to receive Andrea Vincent in the Rue Cambon apartment. Although she no longer slept there, Doré always felt the place showed her off in her proper setting. But the Ritz was her personal haunt, the place where she had done her intimate living since the late 1930s. Over the years her suite there had become almost a facsimile of her earlier home above the salon, and these days it felt somehow safer than the couture house. She had dined at the Rue Cambon with Eugène, but close to midnight had told him to order the car to take her the little journey back to the Ritz, and then to drop him at his apartment.

Safe in her suite, she dismissed him. 'Bring *la vedette* here if she ever materialises,' she told him.

St-Meurice called her at noon. 'She is here, Mademoiselle. Shall I bring her now?'

Panic. Even in old age she despised the habit of faded beauties of sitting in shaded rooms. At night there was an excuse for drawn blinds and subtle lamplight. Over lunch it was pathetic. But she could not face a young woman at the height of her own beauty seeing her like this by the savage glare of summer daylight.

'It's not convenient now, Eugène. Keep her amused for now, then you can bring her over for dinner around nine. No earlier.'

Why here? Why not at the salon? For a moment she wavered, unsure whether to call him again and change the rendezvous. But no. This time instinct told her she should be on home ground. Home ground, that was a laugh! It suggested a comfortable house, with children and grandchildren growing older around you; dogs on the rug and horses in the stable; memories surrounding rooms full of furniture and pictures collected over decades of shared happiness. And here she was, exiled in a set of rented rooms, the furniture and memories consigned to locked warehouses, children and grandchildren unthought of. Well, perhaps not quite.

Doré breathed slow and deep to still the flutter of terror that rose within her. Slowly, take it slowly. You always manage well alone. You will manage this as well as anything else. This time you must not lose control. This time there will be only the truth – no nonsensical fantasies.

But they started of their own accord. Hours later, alone again after her first meeting with her would-be biographer, she cursed herself for a fool. Still, it had been only a small lapse. She would leave it for the moment and perhaps cover it again when they had achieved a closer relationship.

Liar! said a silent voice inside her. She stilled it. Her shock at the girl's air of youth was to blame, that was all. She had expected a mature woman, someone the age she had been when she first met Conway, not this *gamin manqué* with her childish haircut and complete lack of formality. At least they had got on well, and her own ill-judged remarks had been only passing references as they ranged over a multitude of things after dinner.

'No artist could have endured my family. I got all my spirit from my dear, unspeakable father who had gone to America. My aunts were thrifty, respectable members of the bourgeoisie. They lived on the rent of the farmland they owned. They were quite prosperous but mean; everything was used carefully until it wore out. I never went hungry but I never knew the joy of over-indulgence, either. Nothing was done simply for fun; everything had to have a purpose or it could not be justified.'

In fact she had often gone hungry. The finances of the orphanage at Josselin were precarious. In a bad year, when wealthy patrons were less charitable than usual, potato soup and black bread were the most regular dishes on the menu. Later, as a couturière, Eliane had always shied away from the stiff heavyweight wools which occasionally came into fashion. She hated them because she had been forced to wear them in their cheapest, ugliest form. Those indestructible serges had been her skirts and coats for eight interminable years. . . . 'I wore little dresses in soft black wool with fine linen smocks over them to keep them clean. In summer the dresses were black cotton. They had neat white lace collars which one removed for washing.'

Those were the clothes she would have liked to have worn. When she was sent out on errands, Eliane occasionally ran into a group of convent schoolgirls, walking demurely in pairs behind a nun. One day, seeing such a party approach, she shrank into a dark doorway, shamed by her shabby frock and hideous apron of sacking. On weekdays she even had to wear sabots. Her one pair of second-hand boots were for Sundays only. She stood in someone's hallway and yearned to feel the softness of that fine wool against her skin. She imagined the swish of the cotton petticoats they wore underneath. In her fantasy she danced, light-footed, in a little pair of soft kid boots.

'Out, out, you scruffy little bitch!' It was the concierge of the building in which she had taken refuge. 'Dodging your work, were you, sneaking off to idle away the morning? I know your sort. Just because you're a non-paying guest of the good Sisters up the road, you think you don't owe them anything. Well, my girl, I'm telling you now I'll not encourage you!'

He chased her from the building, into the path of the schoolgirls. The first pair shied away with ill-concealed distaste. 'Don't let her touch you, Cécile, you've no idea where she's been. Bet she's got lice! Look at that apron, and those hands – yeuch! Mama always says you know a peasant from their horrid sunburned hands!'

The nun who accompanied them admonished them to behave more discreetly, but it never crossed her mind to make them apologise to the girl they had so insulted. She turned to Eliane, kindly enough but distantly. 'Go along, little one. Clearly you have a task to complete. You will be late. Hurry now!'

Eliane bit back a furious retort. If she reacted as she wished, this old hag might report her to Reverend Mother at the orphanage and then she wouldn't be allowed out for weeks. She turned away, eyes averted, hands concealed beneath her rough apron. One day there would be time for revenge. . . .

'I said, how did you ever manage to persuade them to let you leave home, Mademoiselle?'

Doré came back to the present with a jolt. Why had she not told this woman what Josselin had really been like? Too late now, she must fill the silence somehow.

'Oh, I had to run away, naturally! Those aunts would have turned Mata Hari into a nice marriageable middle-class girl! Time enough to discuss all that when we really get started. At the moment I'm curious to know more about what you could have been doing to cause you so many problems this week.'

For an hour, she charmed Andrea, not with the obvious fawning of the inexpert flatterer but with the subtlety of a professional. After all, she had been doing it since she was eighteen.

## Extract From Andrea Vincent's Working Diary

*Sunday June 6, 1978*

Things begin to look promising! She's a tough old bird, as I expected, but beyond that, quite different from my expectations. For a start she's completely down to earth about the fashion business.

These notes are going to be dreadfully disjointed at first because I'm trying to take in such a welter of impressions. Once Mademoiselle is warmed up, I shall be taping most of the interviews for the book, but I prefer to try and straighten out my views every couple of days by jotting down a commentary on what's happening. When she's speaking, it all seems so vivid, but it fades so quickly that I'll need a written record when I start the serious work.

Best bit first: I was unjust to Doré in assuming she'd do the great artist act; quite the reverse. She started off by being very cold and haughty but Eugène had warned me about that. She's so tiny and frail that my first instinct was to protect her. Then I looked into those eyes and, oh brother, I started wanting to protect myself! They're marvellous eyes – they reminded me of the granite you see at the bottom of fast, clear streams in Wales; almost black, with the running water appearing to strike sparks from them. Imagine being looked at by sparking granite through ice cold water and you might begin to understand what I'm attempting to describe.

She greeted me in her sensational sitting-room in the Ritz. Many of the famous bits and pieces – notably her Coromandel screens – were transferred there twenty-odd years ago when she stopped living in her apartment over the salon. Now the whole suite is like a frame for a rare old painting. You forget that the basic furnishings are hotel standard stuff, albeit one of the grandest of grand hotels. Instead, all you see is Doré: in the decor; in the textiles; in the knick-knacks. Of course, even they are something special. You point out some particularly delightful ornament, only to be told it's a piece by Fabergé – 'One of the pieces he made for fun' she tells you – and that it was given to her by Diaghilev. The icon over there? 'Ah yes, Stravinsky gave me that to watch over me. So sentimental, these Russians, but irresistible, no?'

Well, I don't know about the Russians, but *she's* pretty irresistible, and I really expected to be immune to her. How wrong can you be? True, she started by being glacial and remote, raising the famously unplucked eyebrows ever so slightly at the sight of my carroty hair – just enough for me to notice but not enough for melodrama – every reaction understated, all in the best taste, of course.

Dinner was a little poem, but I *mean* little! I should have guessed that she'd have no interest in food. She pretends she has, but no one who eats like a bird can have! The truth is that she carries her sense of style through everything. So we get this magnificent display of Ritz porcelain, glass and silver, on which is presented gorgeous food. The only drawback is that you need a magnifying glass to see it! She must have ordered one dinner which was served to all three of us. Poor old Eugène took one look at my face and refused all but a crumb of everything – which left me with two crumbs. After she let us out of school at the end of the evening, he took me off to a bistro and filled me up with *confit d'oie* and *vin de Cahors*. I needed it by then, too.

Anyway, back to Mademoiselle. While we were attacking our teeny weeny crudités and our twenty grams of veal escalope, she started off at a brisk clip on a run-down of her view of Life, Art and What It All Means. I thought, ho, hum, here we go with the pseudery, and went on to automatic pilot, only to be snapped back to attention seconds later when she said: 'Costume designers work with a pencil; it is art. Couturiers with scissors and pins; it's a news item, no more.'

My jaw dropped, I was so surprised. And that was when she smiled at me for the first time, *really* smiled, not the polite lip-curls she'd thrown off earlier. I realised then what she was like seventy years ago, why she conquered the whole bitchy smart world. She ravished them.

Now she just tilted her head slightly and said, very quietly, 'Ah, so we have it! Now I understand. You were reluctant because you thought I took it all seriously. What nonsense! I should have been locked in the madhouse years ago if I had. I succeeded for two reasons. One, the lesser, was talent. The other was that I understood from the beginning that fashion does not exist unless it reaches the streets. The fashion that remains in the salons has no more significance than a costume ball.'

There was a fair bit more in the same vein. She overplayed it just a little; I think she has more vanity than this meeting would suggest, but that nevertheless she was telling me her idea of the truth.

She's a born strategist; I recall from the background file someone famous saying she reminded him of one of Napoleon's young generals, brilliant, ambitious, and in a hurry. That's still true. She starts in straight away with the '*tu-toi*'. I wonder how she'd ever get by in England, without such a perfect Gallic opportunity to wrong-foot people. How could an English speaker ever fully appreciate the ambiguity of being addressed in a manner reserved for babies and servants on one hand, and for your most intimate friends on the other? She's off winning the game while you're still wondering whether you're an infant, an inferior, or someone infinitely precious.

# Chapter Three

## Doré

## 1897–1899: In the Beginning

When she cried with cold or hunger as a child, Eliane's father comforted her by offering their family name as a talisman. 'Others have only a silver spoon in their mouths, my girl; you have a solid gold name. Doré means gilded. With Doré after your given name, you have a handsome start in life. Always remember that!'

When he said it, it was plausible. When he took her along with him around the fairs and markets where he scratched a living, everything sparkled. Women had a ready smile for him and a sweet for the little girl; cronies shared a baguette and a bottle of cider or wine. She had no need of warm stockings and nourishing stews when he was around.

As the years passed, though, the child spent more and more time with her mother. Lucette Doré was delicate, worn out early by chest trouble and too much child-bearing. There had been four children before Eliane and there were three after her. Doré did not bother to marry her until long after Eliane was born, but he gave his name to all the children. Lucette never fully recovered her feeble strength after the last, and tuberculosis killed her a week after Eliane's tenth birthday. Immediately after the funeral, Alain Doré abandoned Eliane to the nuns of Josselin.

For two years she did not know what happiness meant. The Sisters did not ill-treat her, but their concept of love did not include cuddles or laughter, and their idea of decorous behaviour made no allowances for childish exuberance. She received fleeting visits from relatives who were not much better off than her father. After six months, Eliane's younger sister Elise joined her. The girl had been sent to their elder married sister Ninette when Eliane went to Josselin, but Ninette's slender resources were unequal to the task of supporting Elise and soon the youngest Doré sister became a permanent guest of the nuns too.

Life improved minutely for Eliane when Elise joined her. Her greatest misery had lain in the loss of family identity. Now she felt a sense of responsibility for the younger child which gave her back a little of her self-esteem. But a far bigger change occurred when she reached the age of twelve.

The nuns did not like sending their older charges out of the orphanage. Once a girl was past puberty, the temptations of even a sleepy provincial place like Josselin were enough to turn her thoughts away from the convent. In the nuns' eyes, there were only two possible futures open to orphan girls: to take the veil or to find employment as shop girls or servants. No respectable Frenchman would be interested in marriage with the likes of them, for they had no dowries. With such grim prospects ahead of them, it was unsurprising that many girls simply slipped away if they were allowed out unaccompanied too often.

It was different for the younger ones. In Paris they, too, would have been at risk, for the metropolis was at the centre of a flourishing trade in child prostitutes. But here in the depths of rural Brittany, girls were generally quite safe until they grew into young women. So reasoned the nuns, and used their eleven- and twelve-year-old charges for outside errands in preference to the more nubile teenage orphans.

Perhaps their unworldliness prevented them from noticing that Eliane was already exceptional. She had a presence and a sparkle that seemed to triumph over the dowdiest cast-offs and the most meagre food. A small powerhouse of energy, she skipped and ran everywhere, drawing the attention of amused or curious townspeople as she went about the nuns' business.

Jean-Baptiste Longchamps certainly noticed her. He was an aristocratic widower, living in modest luxury in a handsome modern town house in Josselin. He had rented out the family château a few years earlier after his wife's death. He seldom saw his grown-up daughter and there seemed no point in throwing away money on maintaining a vast house which would only benefit her in the end. Longchamps had always found grown women somewhat intimidating. Throughout his life, it seemed, they had been issuing orders and he had been jumping to obey them. Occasionally he visited Tours or Paris and picked up a girl for the night, but it gave him little satisfaction. Even in their company he felt vaguely insecure.

Eliane came to him like a refreshing spring shower.

Among their other small enterprises, the nuns ran a laundry for the finest hand washing. They also produced delicate embroidery - handkerchieves, pillowcases and ladies' shifts and nightgowns - all finished in the most exquisite work. Monsieur Longchamps used both services. His bedlinen was supplied by the nuns, he placated his waspish daughter on her Saint's Day and at Christmas with gifts of fine lawn blouses and handkerchieves, and all his laundry went to the Sisters.

The first time he saw Eliane, she came to deliver a parcel of dress shirts which he had asked to have returned especially quickly for a series of dinner parties. Longchamps was strolling along the leafy avenue towards his house when he became conscious of a small figure leaping jubilantly ahead of him. It was Eliane, the parcel of shirts tucked beneath her arm, capering with the sheer joy of temporary freedom from the orphanage. Her pleasure was infectious and he slowed deliberately to stay behind her. He had already decided to follow her beyond his front gate when she turned through it.

By the time he reached her she had operated the ornate bell-pull and was bobbing about as she waited for a reply.

'You wait in vain, Mam'selle,' said Longchamps. 'The housekeeper is out and the master of the house is taking a walk.'

She gave him a smile that was pure enchantment. 'Then I shall wait here for him and enjoy his garden in the sunshine, M'sieur. It's far nicer than what's waiting for me anywhere else!'

Strange, he thought. Another child would have said 'waiting for me at home'. This one sounds as if she has no home. He surrendered to the temptation which had been forming since he first saw her skipping figure. 'Perhaps you would care for a glass of lemonade while you await him?'

She smiled again, face tilted sideways, peeping archly over the large parcel which she carried shield-like before her. 'Perhaps I would. Perhaps I would also wonder how M'sieur came to possess a key to the house.'

'Well done, Mam'selle! Yes, you're right. I'm the man you came to see. This is my laundry, is it not?' He gestured at the parcel with its familiar wrapping of smooth brown paper and brown and white twine. 'As you've unmasked me, would you care for that lemonade anyway?'

'Oh, yes please! I love being out and they'll not allow me to go anywhere else today.'

Longchamps let them both into the house. 'They? You speak as if you were in the keeping of prison warders.'

'But I am, M'sieur! My papa left me in the care of the Sisters while he went to make our fortunes, but I'm sure he didn't mean to let them treat me like an orphan! After all, I'm only half an orphan. Only Mama died.'

'Child, one cannot be half an orphan. When a parent dies, one is orphaned. It's as simple as that.'

'Not to me! One day Papa will come to get me and it will be a different tale then, see if it's not!'

The expression on her small face warned him not to pursue the subject. He smiled, shrugged, and took her through to the kitchen, where he fetched cold lemonade from the stillroom for her and a glass of Vouvray for himself.

He gestured to the larger garden at the rear of the house. 'Come, Mam'selle, we shall drink under the trees.'

Eliane stepped into wonderland. Here for the first time she found a place where nothing was ugly, where no one could pursue her and where she could talk unrestrainedly to an admiring audience of one, seated in a white iron chair beside a little round table. She fell instantly in love.

So did Jean-Baptiste Longchamps. As he sipped his wine and listened to his small guest's chatter, he watched her with a hunger which he grew increasingly determined to satisfy. The child was perfect! Her face was small and heart-shaped, the black brows and pink lips echoing each other's upward curves. Her cheekbones were high and round; her eyes a riveting dark grey, almost black, with little sparkling lights in their depths. Thick, glossy black hair sprang back from a fine high forehead, and was braided down her back into a thick pigtail.

Today Eliane was wearing the orphanage version of a summer dress: cheap black cotton with no white trimmings that would get dirty too quickly. The sacking apron had been discarded as too rough for her to be seen in at the smart end of town. She wore black cotton stockings and the only permitted dash of white, her petticoat, was a sober affair with one mean flounce and no embroidery. To Longchamps it could have been silk and lace, so captivated was he. She kicked her legs in amusement at a small joke and the white cotton flashed, it seemed to him, in myriad flounces. And how he longed to finger them. . . .

Too soon, the little vision was saying she must go. She asked the time, and when he told her clapped hand to mouth in mock horror. 'They will roast me on a spit, M'sieur! I have been gone two hours. What shall I say?'

He was not so besotted that he failed to notice the real fear in her bravura performance. 'I think perhaps a little note from me might help. Now, what is your name? With all this chatter we have not introduced ourselves.'

'I am Eliane Doré, and you must be the Monsieur Longchamps of the fancy shirts!'

'None other. Now, shall we tell a small diplomatic lie in order to smooth your path with the good Sisters.'

They went indoors and Longchamps quickly wrote a note to Reverend Mother on his expensive writing paper. In it he apologised for keeping her charge so long, but said his housekeeper had found her help most useful. The girl also seemed to enjoy it, so if Reverend Mother could spare the Doré child on Saturday afternoons for two or three hours, it would help his household and give her a chance of earning a few sous. He neglected to mention that his housekeeper, Madame du Plessis, took every Saturday afternoon off to visit her sister in St Malo.

Reverend Mother was a snob, the horse-faced daughter of a prosperous bourgeois family, who had preferred to be a Bride of Christ rather than to hitch herself to any of the money-mad suitors her father kept pushing at her. Her dowry to the church had ensured a smooth passage through its lower hierarchy and now she was in charge of a small convent tucked away in the provinces, the pinnacle of her idea of achievement. She regarded people in Jean-Baptiste Longchamps' social position as virtual demi-gods. They had breeding and background as well as money. Their manners were courtly and they were never at a loss for the correct phrase. She was far too naïve to observe his fear of women and thence to speculate on its possible consequences for an immature but pretty female child.

Longchamps' letter impressed her. She beamed at Eliane, previously far from her favourite charge. 'Well, child, for once you appear to have done the right thing. Can I trust you to go on doing so if I send you to Monsieur Longchamps and his housekeeper every Saturday? I might even let you keep some of the money he pays if you behave properly.'

A silent Eliane nodded and smiled her agreement. She wanted to yell her delight at the successful deception, but knew that would spoil everything. The nun assumed her mute response was due to excitement and dismissed her quite kindly.

All the way to Longchamps' house on her first return visit, Eliane almost hugged herself with excitement. Imagine – she had a friend at last, someone who would conspire with her to deceive the nuns so he and she could go off and have fun together! She could hardly wait.

It started better than Eliane could have hoped. A sumptuous lunch awaited her, set out on a little wheeled cart ready to be steered into the garden and placed on the round table in the rose arbour. Longchamps bowed her in, gestured at the meal, then stopped her as she began to head for the garden.

'A moment, if you please, Mam'selle. One does not attend grand opera en déshabille, eh? I thought you would wish to dress for the occasion.'

He indicated a stack of expensive-looking boxes on the hall table. 'Perhaps you would care to take them to the guest room and change.'

For the first time, Eliane managed to exercise the self-control which was to become her legendary sang-froid in later life. She smiled coolly, returned his bow, swept up the boxes and moved towards the staircase. Longchamps smiled, enjoying the girl's spirit. 'First left at the top of the stairs, Mam'selle. There is a bathroom next to the guest room.'

Once inside the bedroom, Eliane's self-control deserted her and she let out a little whoop of joy. She dropped the boxes on the bed with its carved mahogany frame then wandered around the room, looking at the expensive toilet set, the cheval glass, the handsome carpet and bedlinen. Some day she would live in such surroundings!

Then she remembered the packages. They contained a complete outfit, all in white, frothing with lace and embroidery. The petticoats, camisole and knickers were of silk, the snowy dress of lawn. There were gossamer-fine white silk stockings, lace garters with blue satin ribbons and a beautiful pair of white kid boots, slightly too large but easily wearable if she laced them tightly.

Eliane had scrubbed herself from top to toe before leaving the orphanage. After dressing, she paused in the bathroom only long enough to attend to her hair. Instinctively she undid her braid and brushed out her hair in a long black fountain, tying it back with the blue satin hair ribbon which had been in the box with the garters. She returned to the bedroom to pirouette in front of the cheval glass then, delighted with her new image, went down to join her benefactor.

Jean-Baptiste Longchamps gasped in admiration as the child descended the stairs, a picture of fake maturity. She's perfect, quite perfect, he thought. If I'm careful, what a summer this will be!

They ate luncheon in the garden, Eliane in her excitement merely picking at the foie gras mousse and the chicken mayonnaise. She loved the champagne, though, and drank a lot. By the time they had finished their meal, she was giggling and flirting like an adult. The fact that she was not one enabled Longchamps to flirt back. Flushed with wine and excitement, he relished every movement of her slender legs, which accentuated the froth of virginal petticoats above the little white boots.

Eventually, he said: 'Why not come over here and keep me company, my dear? I haven't had a beautiful girl on my lap for years.'

Giggling, Eliane accepted the invitation and flounced down on his knee, even dropping a butterfly kiss on his forehead. His excitement was almost unbearable as he put his arms round her and felt the small body squirming eagerly in his grasp. Almost of its own volition, his hand slid down on to her silk-clad leg.

'Do you like that? You have such pretty little legs, it's nice to touch them.'

'Oh, yes, M'sieur. I feel wonderful sitting here with your arms around me – safe from the whole world. You can cuddle me all you want!'

He did not look at her face until he was naked and ready to join her in the big bed.

She gazed back at him expressionlessly. 'Will it hurt?'

Her directness startled him. 'Uh – I – hope not. Don't worry, my dear. . . .' Then his excitement overcame his momentary discomfiture and he got into bed with her, pushing himself roughly on to her and entering her almost immediately.

It hurt less than it puzzled her. Eliane watched almost as a spectator as he panted and sweated over her, finally achieving orgasm with a choking cry which made her wonder if he were having a heart attack. Then he collapsed against her, and amazed her by starting to cry. She had never seen a man cry before.

'M'sieur Longchamps – I thought I was the one who was supposed to cry. What's wrong with you?'

That stopped his weeping. 'Yes – yes of course . . . are you all right, Eliane, did I hurt you much?' He was instantly solicitous.

'A bit, but not as much as my papa when he used to beat my backside with a strap after he'd drunk too much.'

Initially Longchamps was nonplussed by her matter-of-fact attitude. To cover his confusion, he began fussing about her well-being. 'There seems to be some blood . . . I know – let's give you a bath!'

Immediately Eliane was animated again. 'In the big tub with water from the taps? I've never done that!'

'Well, now's your chance, my dear. I have some marvellous scented oil which you might like. Come on, let's go and investigate.'

They ended up in his big bath together, the twelve-year-old charity orphan and the fifty-year-old aristocrat. Up to her neck in warm water, Eliane lost all interest in their sexual encounter and abandoned herself to the pleasures of her first bath in a proper bathroom. At first Longchamps shared her pure childish pleasure but then his re-awakened desire intervened. He lifted her from the bath, rubbed her dry in big white Turkish towels, then carried ber back to the bedroom. By now it was late afternoon and shadows were beginning to wipe the bars of sunlight from the bed cover. He laid her back on the sheets and climbed into the bed with her.

'Do you really like all that?' She was nothing if not direct. Longchamps was once more too excited by her small, erect pink nipples and lithe little body to hesitate long.

'Yes, yes – otherwise I wouldn't want to do it, would I? Come here, let me show you what I want you to do . . . Ah – oh, Jesus, that's marvellous. Just go on. I'll tell you when to stop . . . Yes, please, please go on. . . .'

He was insatiable until dusk, when he drifted off to sleep for half an hour. Eliane lay and stared at him, chin propped in the palm of her hand. If only they could just have been friends, but oh, no, he had to own her! Why did people always make claims? She brooded privately, on the edge of tears, until he awoke. He had done nothing terrible to her body; he was not generously endowed and after the first time he had not hurt her at all. But she belonged to herself and now she felt as if he had taken a bit of her. It was not a good feeling.

Then Eliane looked around her. This was a comfortable house, and if she were sensible she could come here every Saturday, put on gorgeous clothes, have a good lunch, spend the afternoon without having religion rammed down her throat, and take a bath in the wonderful big tub. Surely it was worth letting this harmless old man put his hand up her skirt and take her dress off in exchange?

She decided it was worth the indignity. Shortly afterwards he woke, gave her a lot more money than the few sous he had mentioned to Reverend Mother, helped her back into her orphanage clothing and insisted on plaiting her hair for her. That was a big mistake because he almost started on her again in his excitement, and now it really was late. Eventually, contenting himself with sliding his hand up her skirt for a few minutes, he bade her farewell.

* * *

The weeks that followed were a time of delirious pleasure for Jean-Baptiste Longchamps. The ultra-modern house, chosen to irritate his traditionalist daughter more than for any other reason, enchanted Eliane and drew her back irresistibly. Electric light; bathrooms with hot and cold running water; lavatories flushed clean by more running water; a refrigerator which thundered away to itself while keeping cream desserts chilled and producing ice chunks for her lemonade – to her it was Aladdin's cave brought to Brittany.

She was quick to learn and grasped instinctively that Longchamps needed to believe she shared his enjoyment of their sexual encounters. She did not, but they did not repel her sufficiently to prevent her from coming back. From that first day, her indifference continued to stem from the same cause: when she surrendered her body to him she felt as if she ceased to own herself and that he had literally become her possessor for a while. That thought galled her. Had she been able to forget it she might even have learned to take pleasure in his love play. Longchamps made every effort to stimulate passion in his child-mistress. After that first uncontrolled possession he took her gently and slowly, relishing the build-up of tension and prolonging his pleasure as long as possible.

It was easy enough to convince him that she was drawn with him along the path of ecstasy; after all, his own experience amounted to a frigid, disapproving wife and a succession of bored prostitutes. All Eliane had to do was to maintain the teasing flirtatious character she had created for him in the garden. As this was genuine when they were talking and eating there, she had little trouble in carrying over the pretence to the bedroom. Back in her curtained space at the orphanage dormitory, however, she often sobbed at the humiliation of that weekly surrender. But the bitterness she felt then was far less than that which her father's desertion had caused her.

Between such brief intervals of misery, Eliane relished the secret relationship, her weekly treats and luxuries, and above all the small cache of money which was building up behind a loosened brick she had discovered in an abandoned outhouse in the orphanage grounds. Her liaison with Longchamps progressed without a hitch throughout the summer until the country fair which marked the end of harvest. Then her first personal brush with one of the more barbaric orphanage practices almost resulted in disaster.

The nuns at the convent-orphanage of Josselin were not intentionally cruel to their charges. But they shared the contemporary peasant and bourgeois view which maintained that recipients paid by whatever means they could for the charity they received.

As the nuns' own lives of poverty, chastity and obedience taught them personal vanity was to be abhorred and conquered, they had no sympathy with those of their charges who wished to be physically attractive. The women's fashions of the period called for huge, padded coiffures, and few women had the volume of hair necessary to create the more elaborate styles. They relied on false pieces, made of animal hair for the less well off and human hair for ladies of fashion and fortune. The fairs that toured the countryside were a useful collection ground for the valuable tresses. Most had two or more barbers' stalls, often run by sheep-shearers, not for restyling hair but to cut off and buy it from poor country girls in need of ready cash. Some of their trade came from deserted wives or servant girls, impregnated then turned out penniless by their employers. Impoverished fathers lined up their daughters to be shorn as a contribution to the family budget. But orphanages were by far the greatest source of supply. Soon after each fair set up, the local nuns marched their charity charges down to the barbers' tents and masses of long hair were exchanged for much-needed funds.

Eliane had missed the barbers in previous years, the first time because she was a new arrival and her hair still harboured lice. The second year she had been ill, and by the time her racking cough was better the fair was long gone. This time, though, there was to be no escape. Always optimistic, she told herself they would take no more than a few inches form the bottom of her hair. There was plenty of it; when she brushed it out it reached almost to her knees. If they took even half a metre she could spare it if she had to. . . .

They took it all. She felt apprehensive when Giselle, the blonde girl from the next cubicle in her dormitory, was led into the tent and emerged sobbing, her head hidden beneath a scarf. Before Eliane had time to ask why she was so upset, it was her own turn. The barber, a taciturn, mustachioed Auvergnat, pressed her on to a hard kitchen chair and swathed her in a soiled rough cloth to catch the small trimmings.

Eliane waited for him to loosen her thick plait, but he wasted no time on such refinements. Taking a large pair of shears he made one decisive cut at the nape of her neck and stood back, clasping in his big fist all but a handful of her precious black hair. Momentarily, horror made her speechless. She sat silently on the hard chair, lips parted, staring at the huge plait which still dangled from his grasp. Finally the barber put it down and made some pretence of tidying up the jagged edges of hair which stuck out around the collar of her rough frock. As he worked he grinned at her, attempting to dispel her misery.

'Come on, duckling, you don't look so bad! If you'd just smile, you'd be every bit as pretty as before you lost your hair. It'll grow again in no time.'

She jumped up so abruptly that the chair overturned. Snatching the shears from his hand she brandished them under his nose. 'I should geld you with this, you old bastard! How can you do this for money to little kids like us who can't stop you? Swine!'

She hurled the shears across the tent but not the way a child does. Her stance was more that of a professional knife thrower and the terrified barber yelped with fear as he ducked to avoid the missile. The blades cartwheeled across the tent and slashed into the canvas walls. The barber was on his feet as they met their target. 'You murderous little bitch – that could have been my throat!'

'It should have been. It would have stopped you buying and selling pieces of children!'

But her triumphant anger was short-lived. He was on her in a moment, seizing her skinny wrists and twisting them behind her with savage satisfaction. 'I should be handing you over to the gendarmes, not the Sisters. Thank your lucky stars I'm such a good chap, otherwise you'd really be in for it!'

The nuns were shocked, embarrassed and angry, their feelings intensified by the impossibility of fully conveying the gravity of her act to their young charge. She was hurried back to the orphanage and packed off to the chapel with instructions to pray for forgiveness. She passed the time crouching there alone, biting her lip and silently swearing vengeance on nuns, barbers and anyone else who could conceivably have been involved. God was not in her thoughts.

Later, looking in a cracked mirror at her newly cropped reflection, she wept afresh with shame, partly at the destruction of one of her chief physical attractions, but mainly because this was further proof that she did not own her own body. Her own fury was as nothing against Jean-Baptiste Longchamps' reaction when she next saw him.

He gave a cry of horror as he opened the front door and saw her cropped head. 'Your lovely hair! What happened, child? Was it an accident?' The butchery was still only three days away and the humiliation was fresh in Eliane's mind. She flung herself against him, her only protector, and sobbed out an explanation of what had happened.

When she finished, he was white-faced and shaking with anger. 'This is an affront to all decency! They cannot subject a child to such treatment and get away with it, they cannot!'

'But they have, M'sieur Jean-Baptiste! Look at me if you doubt it. I can do nothing to stop them and I don't see that you can, either.'

'You don't, eh? Well, I'm not letting them get away with it. Let me think it over. I shall protest, I tell you!'

Later, embracing her, he wept for the loss of the luxuriant hair which had excited him so. But by now Eliane was wishing she had hidden her misery. Her intuition told her he was more aggrieved by the loss of a source of pleasure than by real concern for her feelings, and she feared that his outraged self-interest might get them both into trouble.

Sure enough, when she emerged from the bathroom later that afternoon, she found him writing a furious letter of protest to Reverend Mother. One glance at the text filled her with fear. One did not need to be a woman of the world to understand what motivated the note. Even an unsophisticated orphan – or a provincial Mother Superior – would read far more into his words than the objective interest of an occasional benefactor.

'If you send that, we're finished. They'll guess what we're up to and never let me come back, and I expect you'll be in awful trouble too for letting it happen.'

At first it was hard to dissuade him. Longchamps had been thwarted. Unable to turn his displeasure on Eliane, the real victim, he was determined to protest to someone. Eventually, grudgingly, he agreed that the tone of his letter was wildly inappropriate, coming from a man whose only interest in Eliane was allegedly as a casual helper to his housekeeper. But having admitted this, he was determined to place his childish mistress beyond the reach of the nuns and started working on a scheme to remove her from their care. Clearly it was impossible for him to adopt her. That would lead to all sorts of awkward questions and conceivably to a medical examination for Eliane. Then he pondered on the possibility of farming her out to her relatives. Two or three branches of the Doré family lived within reach of Josselin. All were too poor to maintain either Eliane or her sister Elise from their own income, but what if Longchamps were to provide them with the funds to do so? Perhaps that would work.

Eliane was filled with misgivings. She loathed the nuns

and longed to be with her family, but she was fairly sure they would take a more cynical view than the orphanage of her weekly visits to Longchamps. The day those visits stopped would see the end of his financial support. Then she would be back in the orphanage within weeks, without the relief of her escapist Saturdays.

Try as she might, Eliane was powerless to dissuade Longchamps from planning an adoption campaign. She knew him well enough now to recognise the wilful streak in him which would not tolerate resistance so she deferred further discussion. Nevertheless she was uneasy. From the week of her haircut, Eliane sensed that their affair was doomed.

The end came from an unexpected quarter. Reverend Mother had gone to visit an old priest in St Malo one week-end and was returning to Josselin by train on the Saturday evening. As she waited at the station she recognised one of her regular laundry and embroidery customers further down the platform. Wondering what the woman might be doing here on a Saturday, she went to speak to her.

'Madame du Plessis? I hope everything is well at the Avenue Rousseau? No sickness in your family?'

Longchamps' housekeeper was bewildered. 'Why no, Reverend Mother. What makes you think anything is wrong?'

'Well, it being Saturday, your busy day . . . seeing you up here I wondered . . . I thought the Doré girl had come to you as usual today. I hope she did not fail to pass on a message about her presence being unnecessary this week.'

'Doré girl? Who is she? Forgive me, Reverend Mother, but this conversation is making no sense at all to me. Why should I be interested in one of your charges – I take it that's who this girl is – and why should you think it at all unusual for me to be in St Malo today? I come here every Saturday to spend the afternoon with my sister. What makes you think Saturday is a busy day for me? Quite the reverse – I stop work at 11.30 on the dot and catch the noon train.'

As she finished speaking, the Josselin train pulled in at the platform. White-faced, the nun drew Madame du Plessis aside. 'I beg you, Madame, permit me to pay a supplement for us both to travel back in a first-class compartment. I believe we need to talk in private.'

Their journey sealed the fate of Jean-Baptiste Longchamps' middle- aged passion for Eliane Doré. On her arrival back at the convent, Reverend Mother's first act was to check that Eliane had returned from the Longchamps house. Minutely reassured by the news that the girl was peacefully eating supper in the orphans' refectory, she shut herself in her study to consider the appropriate course of action. It was the worst dilemma of her previously uneventful career.

Reverend Mother's worldly side told her that there could be little profit in publicly disgracing Josselin's most distinguished citizen. And to what purpose? No one would care a jot for the scrawny orphan who had been up to who knew what with that terrible man these two months and more. But what a tidal wave she might cause in this peaceful provincial millpond! There would be unanswerable questions about whether the nuns provided adequate supervision for their charges. The anti-clerical elements might take it further and imply that nubile virgins were deliberately supplied to salacious old men. . . . No, that was quite unthinkable! Hurriedly she thought over the other implications of revelation. It promised to create an appalling mess.

On the other hand, she was the product of a lifetime's orthodox Catholicism, more than half of it strengthened by the discipline of holy orders. Her religion meant a great deal to her, whatever her social ambitions and snobberies might do to distort it. She was profoundly conscious that somewhere along the line the convent had failed Eliane Doré. Of course the child bore a share of the blame – this business could not have occurred without her active cooperation – but she was still just a few months beyond her twelfth birthday. She was in their care precisely because the world recognised the inability of children to make their own moral judgements. Reverend Mother shuddered at the thought of what had been done to her.

Her spiritual conflict continued long into the night. Finally, in the chapel after dawn, she resolved she must be prepared to bear the full brunt of whatever blame descended on the convent.

Eliane put a stop to her anguish. Confronted after breakfast with Reverend Mother's discovery, she at first remained silent. The nun tried cajoling her. 'Come along, Eliane. You know you were wicked to collude with Monsieur Longchamps, but given your extreme youth and his great importance, I quite understand that you felt you had to. No one will punish you, but we must take action to see this does not happen again.'

Suddenly the girl found her voice. 'I did nothing more than go and talk with him, Reverend Mother. I think Monsieur Longchamps is a very lonely man.' Her eyes never left those of the Mother Superior and both of them were aware that the girl was lying.

'Nobody will believe that, Eliane. What about the letter, asking for you to help his housekeeper? Madame du Plessis had never heard of you before yesterday!'

'Perhaps Madame du Plessis is not interested in gossiping about what Monsieur Longchamps gets up to when she's away, Reverend Mother. He said something about her coming from the north coast and not knowing anyone down here.' All the time her eyes never left the nun's. A small flicker of hope lit the blackness of Reverend Mother's depression.

'Eliane, I repeat, no one will hurt you. Now please tell me exactly what has been happening between you and Monsieur Longchamps on Saturday afternoons for the past nine weeks.'

'When I went there to take the shirts that first time, he

gave me some lemonade in the garden and we talked for ages. He said I made him laugh a lot, and wouldn't it be fun if I came to visit every Saturday? I said I couldn't because I'd never get permission and he said it wouldn't hurt to pretend the housekeeper needed a bit of help. So then he wrote to you and you said yes.

'I'm afraid I didn't do any work, I just went on making him laugh. He used to have a wonderful meal waiting in the garden and lots of lemonade, and he'd tell me about all the marvellous parties they used to give in his château. Then he'd give me a few francs for the orphanage and a few sous for me –' a picture of the five hundred francs stowed in the outhouse popped into her mind – 'and I'd come back in time for supper. We both knew somehow his housekeeper wouldn't think it was right for me to be there like that when she was out, and neither would you, but there wasn't any harm in it really.'

Reverend Mother wanted to believe Eliane more than she had wanted anything since her appointment as Mother Superior, but she was aware of her duty. She could not let matters rest here.

'While you were with him, Eliane, did he, uh, put his hands on you anywhere, or, er, try to take any of your clothes off? You must tell me if he did. Remember, you'll not be punished. You have done nothing wrong beyond the initial deceit.'

The child reacted with appropriate horror. 'Never, Reverend Mother! I would have died rather than go back there if he'd ever done anything like that! He once took my hand to help me up when I tripped over, but that is all.'

'Where did you go in the house? Did you ever see the bedrooms?'

'Reverend Mother, I went there to sit in the garden, not to look at his furniture! I went through the front hall and out through the kitchen to the garden. Once we went through the drawing-room – that has glass doors which open on to the garden terrace – but otherwise I don't know what the inside of the place looks like.'

Reverend Mother's resolve was weakening by the minute. Deep inside she knew that Longchamps had been violating this child for weeks, but for her own reasons the girl chose to deny it. Her entire manner proclaimed that she was not merely prepared to go on denying it, but to back her denial with completely convincing evidence. If Monsieur Longchamps could deal with Madame du Plessis, it might yet be possible to avoid disaster and to end Eliane's exposure to moral corruption without further fuss. The girl was making the entire business much easier. But what if the housekeeper were not prepared to stay silent? And what if the authorities, alerted by reports from her, demanded that Eliane Doré be medically examined? Whatever Eliane said, Reverend Mother was sure she knew what such examination would confirm.

Well, she might as well know the worst now. 'Eliane, I want to believe you, but there is one obstacle which can be overcome only if you are telling the truth. Madame du Plessis can hardly be expected to do as we ask if we decide to take this matter no further. If she wishes to complain to the authorities about what has happened, they will question you at least as closely as I have this morning –' she raised her hand to silence Eliane's protest that she could handle such interrogation – 'and they will then seek to prove or disprove their suspicions by subjecting you to a thorough physical examination by a doctor.'

'What if they do? It's not as if Monsieur Longchamps has been beating me or anything.' Eliane's confidence was growing by the minute.

'I wish it were that simple, my child. It is very easy for a medical man, or even an experienced midwife, to discover whether a young girl has been – interfered with – by a man. If they examined you, could you be sure they would not make discoveries which substantiated Madame du Plessis' suspicions?'

But Eliane was ahead of her. Sniffling a touch theatrically, she made much of finding the scruffy handkerchief in her sleeve. 'Then they would learn things that displeased you, Reverend Mother, but it would be nothing to do with Monsieur Longchamps. I didn't know you meant that sort of thing. When I was still with Papa, a little time before my mother died, there was a rough boy working at one of the inns where my father sold things. When Papa was off drinking with his friends one day, the boy got me into the stables, saying he'd show me a new foal. Then he –' a well-timed pause, then – 'he pulled off my skirt and did things to me that hurt me a lot! There was some blood and he tore away the bit of skirt so Papa wouldn't see and told me to say it had caught on a nail. He just left me there after he'd finished messing about with me and said I'd get into trouble if I told anyone, ever. I stayed there and cried for a while and then I heard Papa shouting for me, so I went to him and said I'd fallen and torn my skirt and hurt myself, and that was that. He never asked any more about it and it stopped hurting by next day.'

The tale had come into her head from nowhere. In fact she had been so small in those days that even at ten she had looked little more than seven or eight, and all the men and boys around the inn yards had treated her as a protected mascot more than anything else. But her story accomplished all she could have wished with Reverend Mother. There were tears in the nun's eyes as she rose, came round the big desk and embraced Eliane.

'Oh, you poor child! And no one ever knew. How frightened you must have been!' Eliane obligingly sniffled a little more. 'We cannot subject you to another ordeal now, just because you were party to a harmless deceit. Of course, your visits to the Avenue Rousseau will have to stop immediately. I shall see Monsieur Longchamps myself and explain matters. As for you, just take a little time to recover from the whole thing and then we shall talk again. Pray to Our Lady for guidance. It always helps.'

More relieved than she would have thought possible an hour earlier, Reverend Mother dismissed Eliane then wrote a note to Jean-Baptiste Longchamps, requesting that he come to see her as soon as it was convenient.

Their discussion remained private. A few weeks later, Madame du Plessis retired to live with her sister in St Malo, where she opened a small hotel on the capital sum she had received from a grateful employer on her departure. At the end of the summer, Longchamps sold the house in the Avenue Rousseau and went to live in Italy.

# Chapter Four
## Andrea

Andrea had spent little time in Paris since her days in the Sorbonne immediately preceding 1968. The events of that year had turned her away from the capital for good, first to another continent and, on subsequent visits to France, to the provinces. Now she began to experience a Paris she had not known as a student.

Alouette Doré was obviously taken with her. The first evening's meeting was followed by another on the Sunday night. Doré still hung back from facing the younger woman in the full glare of summer daylight, but she was coming round to the idea. Andrea had been booked into the Ritz in order to be closer to her subject, but on Sunday morning Doré decided something more intimate was appropriate.

Eugène St-Meurice groaned as his telephone rang at 8 a.m. on Sunday. Of all his acquaintances, only Mademoiselle would call at such a barbaric time. What could have gone wrong so early today?

'Eugène – *La vedette*, I thoroughly approve. A bit more outré than I'd expected, but after all it doesn't do always to blend with the scenery! No, on balance I'm most impressed. And I've been thinking: as this whole affair is so – so intimate, it would be more appropriate to install her at the Rue Cambon than to coop her up in an ordinary guest room at the Ritz for a couple of months. Please arrange it.'

He was dumbfounded. 'But, Mademoiselle, the Rue Cambon . . . it's you, your symbol. I know you seldom sleep there now but it breathes Doré to the whole world, like . . . like. . . .'

'. . . Like a mausoleum. Go on, say it!'

'I was thinking more of a temple to your fame, Mademoiselle.' But he was improvising wildly. She was right. To St-Meurice the apartment was a fitting tomb for the Doré who had reigned supreme in the Paris of the 1930s. There was something vaguely blasphemous about the idea of another person, particularly a woman, living there.

'I shall contact Seraphine and instruct her to have the Oriental Room made up for Mam'selle Vincent.'

'No, no, no! The whole point of this is to expose her to my personality in my setting. Put her in my bedroom.'

'Impossible! That is . . . well, what if you did decide to stay overnight? You still do occasionally.'

'Eugène, you know as well as I do that I've never felt the same about that room since 1938. I always sleep on my magic sofa when I stay there.'

Magic sofa, the silly old fool! What a mass of meaningless superstition she is, thought St-Meurice. Then he subdued his irritation. It always brought out the worst in him when Mademoiselle found a new pet and he felt particularly waspish about this one. If Doré's razor-sharp intuition got wind of his resentment she'd be merciless. Best keep it under firm control.

'I'll arrange to meet Seraphine there in an hour or so, Mademoiselle, and see that everything is in order. Then what? Do you propose to tell Mam'selle Vincent yourself?'

'No, I shan't have time to see her before this evening, about the same time as last night. If she's free, give her some lunch and take her over there this afternoon. She'll be able to take stock and settle in before we meet for dinner. Bring her at 8.30.' The usual unannounced disconnection followed.

Andrea had a secret weakness for grand hotels. Growing up in England in the 1950s, she had been exposed to a succession of indifferent middle-range establishments during school holidays in the country and on visits to London. As a student she had done the usual round of pensions and youth hostels. Her French mother had introduced her to grand luxe when she checked Andrea into the Plaza Athenée in the wake of the 1968 student troubles to talk over Andrea's decision to go to Vietnam. Marie-Louise Chabrol was far too sensible to think she could dissuade her daughter from the venture but she was willing to offer a little bribery on the off-chance. It did not work, but the hotel's thick carpets, marble bathrooms and superb food had made a lasting impression on the girl. From then on she veered wildly between sleeping in ditches, haystacks and other people's apartments while working, and at the best hotels in the capital cities of five continents between times.

That Sunday morning she awoke to the incomparable surroundings of the Paris Ritz. Primrose-coloured sunlight spilled through the tall windows and freshened the soft greys and whites of the painted woodwork. Vast acreages of Savonnerie carpet separated the gilded ebony furniture which gave the room its main decorative theme. Somewhere, she knew, an impeccably-clad waiter was on the way to her room, bearing her a tray of fresh croissants, Normandy butter, her favourite *myrtille* jam and piping hot coffee. Savouring every second, she wiggled her toes against the silky-smooth linen sheets. There were days when she wondered what it would be like to live like this always. . . .

Eugène St-Meurice telephoned just after she had finished breakfast. 'Hi, Eugène – don't you ever get any time off for good behaviour? Your job must be like painting the Forth Bridge!'

'Please? I do not understand you. What bridge, Mam'selle Vincent?'

'Forget it, it would take too long to explain. But, Eugène, isn't it about time you started calling me Andy, or Andrea at least? Your boss started right in with the "*tu-toi*" as soon as we shook hands. It seems a bit daft for you to be so formal when all around are dropping their manners!'

'Well, you had not given me permission. . . .'

'You didn't give me permission either, I just did it. We reckless young things have a habit of behaving badly. Come on, don't be so starchy!'

'Very well – Andy. Andrea seems even more staid than Mam'selle Vincent.'

'Thanks! Now, what did you want to say?'

'La Grande Mademoiselle has asked me to look after you today, unless you wish to be left to your own devices, of course. She has lined up something of a surprise which I shall show you this afternoon. In the meantime, I am at your disposal. Perhaps you would care to join me and a couple of friends for lunch?'

'That's kind of you, Eugène, and don't think I've missed the treatment Mademoiselle's been doling out to you. It doesn't really matter whether you like me or not, does it? You have to smile and be polite whatever you feel like doing. I'll try to behave reasonably, but feel free to slap my wrist if I become too unbearable!'

He warmed to her in spite of himself. 'Thank you, Andy. She does not make it easy, it is true. Now, do you want us to meet immediately or in time for lunch?'

'Oh, later is fine. Try to salvage something of your morning, at least. I don't know whether you're aware of it, but I lived in Paris for three years in my early twenties and I'm sure the city hasn't changed too much. I'll enjoy getting my bearings again.'

'Thank you again. We can meet at the Relais Plaza at 1 p.m. Oh – it's new since your day. It's at the Plaza Athenée and *le tout Paris* meets there for lunch.'

'My God, you're not one for obscure little Latin Quarter bistros, are you?'

'One can see too much of those at the wrong age, Mam'selle – er, forgive me – Andy. Just one last thing. Knowing La Grande Mademoiselle, she will want the reason for your visit to Paris to remain secret. She has not actually forbidden me to introduce you to other people but I suspect that is only because it has not crossed her mind that I might do so. When my friends ask about the purpose of your visit, I should be obliged if you could tell them you are undertaking general research on Paris fashion for a new book. They will respect your desire for confidentiality then because they are in the couture business too and it is vital to them. Leaked secrets can be murderously expensive. Now, until lunch-time, au revoir.'

'Take care, Eugène. 'Bye.'

Andy was not over-keen on meeting too many people, for obvious reasons, so was unconcerned about whatever restrictions Doré might decide to impose on her social life. But there was one person she had to tell of her arrival. She booked a call to Paimpont, in the Île et Vilaine region of Brittany.

'Good morning, Marie-Louise Chabrol here. Who is calling?'

Andy never heard that voice without experiencing a small thrill. It was the closest sound would ever come to a mixture of woodsmoke and wild honey. Andrea could instantly picture her mother, bundled up in a snowy towelling bathrobe, her storm-grey eyes still sleepy.

'Marie-Louise? It's Andy. I'm back in God's country again. How are you?'

'Andy, darling, how marvellous to hear you! It's been months. . . . I hope you intend coming to see me before you go back to London.'

'I'll try. I'm in Paris – staying for a couple of months, probably. I'd rather not discuss the job on the phone. Tell you all about it if I have a chance to come and see you, okay?'

'Sounds intriguing – I can hardly wait. I shall be at Barenton all summer, so as long as you give me twenty-four hours' warning there should be no problems. When you do come, I'll probably have a shopping list of goodies for you to bring. I'm just finishing a book, and when I stick "The End" on the bottom of the last page I've promised myself a blow-out on the most expensive goodies Fauchon can supply!'

'Now I'm the one who can hardly wait! I'll bring enough for both of us. But don't expect me too soon, Ma. It may be a couple of months yet – certainly not before August.'

'All right, darling, but for goodness' sake try not to get involved in anything dangerous. When you came back from Vietnam I thought I could say goodbye to worrying about your safety, but you seem to have been in more scrapes since you got home than you ever went through out there. Your letter the other week made my hair stand on end.'

'Yeah, but they don't shoot as straight as the Viet Cong in this part of the world.'

'Don't tempt Providence!'

'Right. Take care of yourself, Marie-Louise. I can't leave a 'phone number right now – obvious reasons – but I'll get back to you as soon as I can.' Andrea said goodbye and hung up.

She managed to squeeze another cup of coffee out of the pot while she thought about how she would spend the next couple of hours. A summer Sunday in Paris was not the best time to see the capital: its international fame ensured that too many tourists from all over the world were out competing with the Parisians, who would be taking advantage of the Sunday half price or free museum admission to see as many sights as possible. The morning was a lot better than the afternoon, but unless she got going quickly she knew that none of the famous places of interest would be approachable.

Andrea took a quick shower, applied make-up and put on the light-weight jacket and skirt she had bought the previous morning before calling St-Meurice to announce her arrival. She had decided on a destination before she was out of the shower. It was too many years since she had seen the Lady and the Unicorn. Time for a reunion, and the Musée de Cluny was unlikely to be too crowded before noon.

The Hôtel de Cluny is one of the only three great medieval

mansions which survive in modern Paris. It was built in the fourteenth century by the Abbot of Cluny in Burgundy, over the ruins of a vast Gallo-Roman public bath-house. After the Revolution it fell on hard times but was bought by the State in the mid-nineteenth century for use as a museum. Today it houses an unrivalled collection of medieval decorative objects and the house itself is a treasure, boasting flamboyant balustrades, mullioned windows and elaborately-carved gargoyles. Dormer windows crowd the roof line and the whole edifice completes its fairytale image with a pentagonal tower containing a wide spiral staircase.

The star exhibits of the collection, the six tapestries of the Lady and the Unicorn, were the object of Andrea's visit. Her mother had introduced her to the hangings when she was very young. They had captivated her so completely that she had demanded bedtime stories about the figures for months afterwards. When she went back to Paris at the age of twenty to attend the Sorbonne, the Musée de Cluny was close at hand and she seldom let a month go by without slipping in to see the Lady and the magical beasts and plants which accompanied her.

The morning was bright and sunny, so the first arrivals were lingering in the mansion's gardens rather than going indoors to see the collections. Andrea preferred to make her tour the other way round. She hurried to the first-floor rotunda where the tapestries were displayed.

As always, the sight of them made her gasp in wonder at their freshness. Almost five centuries after their manufacture, their colours sang in tune with the bright day. Lost to everything else, Andrea stood absorbing their beauty.

'They sweep away everything else with a rush of springtime, don't they?' The French was fluent but the speaker's accent was from somewhere further south. She turned slowly, reluctant to glance away from the Lady but wishing to acknowledge another's admiration for the tapestries' beauty.

The man who had spoken was worth attention. In spite

of her considerable height, she had to look up at him. What she saw might have been part of a work of art itself – but from Quattrocento Florence, not medieval Paris, she decided. His skin was the smooth clear olive seldom seen outside Renaissance portraits. The eyes were heavy-lidded and slanted upward at the outer edges. Their velvety dark brown was disturbingly flecked with light hazel. All the surfaces of his face were so smooth and shapely they might have been chiselled and finished to perfection by a sculptor. With such looks, Providence need not have given him a beautiful body, but she had done so. He was lean and muscular. Made for Florentine dress, Andrea thought inconsequentially. Imagine those legs in skin-tight silks and soft leather boots. . . . The image was so beguiling she had to shake her head to clear it.

'Forgive me, Mam'selle, I thought you were French. You did not understand me?' It was the most reasonable explanation for her dreamy reaction.

'No, no! I understand you perfectly. Sorry, I was a bit dazzled by the tapestries. As you said, they sweep everything else away. They've been doing that for me ever since I was about six years old.'

'Ah, so they are old friends! They are quite new to me, but I plan to get to know them well. Textiles are my job and I've been told I can learn a lot from these. Now I begin to see what my friends meant.'

'Really? What sort of textiles?'

'Fashion – specifically women's knitwear. I'm a sort of wandering fashion gypsy. I'm from Spain, work for one of the big Italian ready-to-wear houses, and now they've lent me to a couture house here and I'm hoping to be head-hunted for the big time. Of course, I've seen reproductions of these beauties before, but nothing quite prepares you for the reality, does it? God, imagine those colours and the flower motif in soft, loose jerseys! They'd look wonderful, particularly on someone like you – although somehow I see you with blonde hair rather than red.'

Andrea felt herself blush for the first time in years.

Surprised by her girlish response, she hurriedly turned to face the tapestries. He stood next to her. 'Tell me more about them. You seem to be quite an expert.'

So she took him from tapestry to tapestry, happy to explain the intricacies of the allegories of the senses depicted in them. He can't get this sort of detail from his Michelin Green Guide, she thought with satisfaction. Eventually they had completed their circuit of the rotunda.

'Where now, lovely lady?'

Reluctantly she shook her head. 'I have an unbreakable house rule when I come here: either I look at the tapestries and then go, or I stay away from them and look at one of the other galleries. I never mix the two, I'd get cultural overkill otherwise. In any case, I really should start heading somewhere else, although I'm not exactly in a rush.'

'Then perhaps I might come with you, at least part of the way?'

She hesitated. Nev seemed a world away but his half-forgotten warning about foreign strangers drifted back. Irritated by her own timidity, she dismissed it. For God's sake, the man was a Spaniard!

'I don't see why not.'

They strolled along the Boulevard St-Michel, Andrea looking around her wonderingly. 'Good God, it really is all gone. There are no ghosts.'

'Ghosts? I don't understand.'

'Oh, ancient history now. I was here in 1968, when all the smartest students were wearing paving stones and the gendarmes had the cutest capes loaded with lead shot.'

'Were you on the wrong side?'

'There was no wrong side, nor any right one, just the absurdity of half-baked youth against the extremism of reactionary middle age. It was the greatest waste of human anger and guts since World War One. The Boul' Mich' stopped being one of my favourite streets and turned into somewhere I was determined not to be seen dead in. If I was going out young, I wanted my blood to flow some place where it would matter!'

'Which was?'

'Oh, a long way from Paris, but almost as much ancient history as my student days now.' Caution abruptly put a brake on her impulse to confide in this attractive stranger whose name she still did not know. Not that it mattered. She doubted she'd be seeing him again.

Soon they reached the junction of the Boulevard St-Michel and the Rue St-Severin. Andrea seized the opportunity to talk about a less personal subject. 'If you like churches, let's go down here for a few minutes. It has a glorious fifteenth-century stained glass window showing the Tree of Jesse which you might like to see for inspiration too – and there's a nice macabre story about the place.'

In the small garden within the St-Severin charnel house precincts, she told him the gruesome tale. It seemed that an archer, condemned to execution in the fifteenth century, was offered his freedom if he agreed to undergo an experimental gallstone operation – he was a sufferer – and survived.

'They carved him here,' she said, 'and believe it or not, he came through it. I've often wondered how strong he must have been to survive their notions of sterile operating conditions, let alone the pain.'

Still wincing at the thought, they cut back through the church and Andrea remembered something else. This church had been modernised by the original Grande Mademoiselle – a cousin of Louis XIV. Looking around, she decided that the earlier holder of the title lacked the panache of Alouette Doré. There was something ponderous about the seventeenth-century refurbishment. She was tempted to share the reflection with her new friend, but refrained. It might betray her assignment, and Eugène had made a point of asking her to keep it secret.

They returned to the street and within minutes had arrived at the St-Michel Métro station. 'Where to now?' he asked.

'Well, I don't know about you but I have a lunch engagement, and I'm hopping on a train.'

'Oh, please don't let's part like this! I can't hang around outside the Musée de Cluny in the hope that you might decide to go and visit your tapestries again. At least let me introduce myself and persuade you to give me your telephone number.'

He looked so forlorn - and handsome - that she was swayed. 'Okay. My name's Andy Vincent. What's yours?'

'Ortiz - Esteban Ortiz, from San Sebastian.'

'I don't see you in modern Spain, you're definitely a Quattrocento type. Hullo, Renaissance Man!'

'Hullo, Twentieth-Century Woman. You couldn't be from any time but the present!'

As they spoke they had been moving towards the ticket office. Now Esteban put a hand on her arm and said: 'At least let me escort you to your date. Unless you'd rather not be seen with a man, that is.'

She bridled. 'Nobody owns me! Anyway, this is just a meeting with a group of new acquaintances, otherwise I'd invite you along. Yes, of course you can take me there. It's at the Relais Plaza in about twenty minutes.'

They left the Métro at Franklin D. Roosevelt and he was still with her when she arrived at the Relais Plaza. At the entrance she turned to him. 'What now? I can hardly take you in as a lunch guest when I'm one myself.'

As she spoke she caught sight of Eugène, sitting with two other men and a woman. He waved, came over, and immediately solved her dilemma in surprising fashion. 'Steb, you're a mind-reader! I was going to introduce this young woman to you once she'd settled in, and you turn up with her the day after she arrives!'

Andrea, speechless, looked from one to the other.

'Andy, forgive me,' Eugène apologised. 'Paris really is much smaller than London, you know. You've obviously been away long enough to forget. Couture is an even smaller world. Steb's working with Castellane, I met him a couple of weeks ago, and Castellane is sitting just over there, waiting to meet our bright young authoress. Where did you two meet?'

He guided them across to the table, made the appropriate introductions and insisted that Esteban Ortiz join them for lunch. Pierre Castellane claimed all the credit for their chance meeting at the Musée de Cluny.

'I told Steb about the tapestries – to me the glory of the collections. Don't you agree that they would make the basis for a wonderful knitwear collection if they were handled sympathetically, Andy?'

She relaxed, her last shreds of wariness about the strange coincidence dissolving. 'Why, yes, but I admit it had never crossed my mind until Steb mentioned it today. Then I swallowed it so completely that I took him to see the Jesse Tree window in St-Séverin with a similar treatment in mind.'

'Ah, La Grande Mademoiselle's church.' This was from Eugène, and too quietly for anyone but Andrea to hear. She turned to him, amused that he too knew of the association, and nodded. Around them the conversation flowed, Esteban Ortiz joining in as if he were long established in Parisian couture circles.

Eugène's lunch guests were Castellane, a Paris couturier who had started his rapid climb to the top in Milan about the same time as St Laurent left Dior in Paris; his wife Bibi, a French countess whose title pre-dated the reign of the Sun King; and Egon Klarsfeld, probably the only male designer whose name Mademoiselle would hear without a contemptuous sneer.

After St-Meurice's telephone call inviting her to lunch, Andrea had worried momentarily about being noticed by the wrong people. She had come to Paris to avoid danger and if too many people met her there, eventually word might leak out. But she shook off the thought by reminding herself that only the criminals directly involved were aware of her recently completed investigation of the Umberto death. Anyone else meeting her here would think only of her earlier work. The lunch party strengthened this feeling. St-Meurice's guests were fascinated by her Vietnam experiences and, after that, interested in her reactions to Paris after so long away from it. They showed all the happy chauvinism of residents of the City of Light, and were ready to talk for hours about its charms.

Andrea did a lot of listening as well as talking. These were some of the star talents in the world of couture today. They knew their business inside out and were refreshingly honest about it. When she mentioned her previous prejudice about designers thinking they were great artists, Castellane waved a hand dismissively.

'Ah, the ivory tower dwellers! Every industry has a few of that sort. I have a theory that even in aero engineering or shipbuilding you get a few who stand back and dream dreams of some day seeing their blueprints hanging in art galleries. We have them too and because they tend to be at the more expensive, exotic end of the business, the fashion press is always giving them editorial space to air their pretensions. But look at those of us who concentrate on dressing rich, elegant women who want to look wonderful but not eccentric. We say very little about art apart from coyly confessing to having six Picassos on the walls of our apartments!'

Steb Ortiz did not agree entirely. 'I know that one or two designers seem precious,' he said, 'but if there is no fine art involvement in fashion, how do you explain your advice to me to go and look at a room full of medieval works of art as inspiration for a knitwear collection?'

'Because, Steb, you misunderstood them. The Lady and the Unicorn series may look like fine art now because we have put them in a museum. But they were commissioned as superior wallpaper, remember. If anyone were capable of designing and producing them today, they would be manufactured for sale in interior design shops, not art galleries. Don't make the mistake of thinking that by classing couture as trade, instead of art, we belittle it. The best tradesmen are as talented in their line as the best artists. It's simply a matter of snobbery.'

And so the conversation continued, interspersed with happily greedy comments on the food. 'We dine again with Mademoiselle tonight,' murmured Eugène to Andrea. 'Eat as much as you can while you have the chance.'

All of them were sufficiently egotistical to want to dominate the converstaion, so Andrea had plenty of opportunity to study Esteban Ortiz. He was a few years younger than her, a fact she noted with no more than passing interest. He was a good linguist, even handsomer on closer acquaintance than at first glance, and, if Castellane's and Eugène's reaction were an accurate indicator, very talented. Above all, he was the sexiest-looking man she had seen for months. It might be pleasant to indulge in a little fling with him if she could fit it in with everything else. Ortiz appeared to have something similar in mind and kept trying to nudge her into a more personal conversation than their surroundings permitted.

Eventually, Pierre and Bibi departed. Andy was mildly amused when Eugène St-Meurice said it was time for him to take her to their next appointment: Steb had obviously been on the point of inviting her off somewhere else and did not react well to being intercepted. Egon Klarsfeld was talking to some acquaintances at another table and Eugène moved across to say their goodbyes. Ortiz, looking decidedly sulky, pounced on Andrea.

'Getting you alone is worse than cornering Greta Garbo. At least say I can call you, and give me your number.'

She was reluctant to be pinned down. 'It might be easier if you give me yours and I'll get in touch. I don't really know at the moment where I'll be from day to day.'

'Some men might regard that as a put-down.'

'Well, some men had better stop being so goddamned touchy!'

He reacted as if she had bitten him but Andrea was into her stride by then. 'I'm used to having grown-ups as friends, not kids. If it's okay for you to call me and arrange another meeting, why shouldn't the same hold true for me? I'm not trying to escape gracefully. I really am busy and you'd have the devil's own job tracking me down. Now, do you want to give me the number or not?'

Ortiz smiled, apparently with difficulty. 'Okay, okay, I apologise. What's got into you?'

'Nothing. It's just I've never thought it's a woman's place to sit at home, waiting for her dream man to call. Let's start again. Give me your number and I'll ring you some time in the next couple of days, if you still want me to.'

'Very well, Andy.' He scribbled a number and an address on a plain card which he had taken from his wallet. 'It's a friend's apartment. He lent it to me while he's abroad for a few weeks. Try to call me soon; I'd like to get to know you properly.'

He made much of the last sentence, gazing intensely at her as he spoke. Just as well he looks so good, she thought. Apart from that he really isn't my type.

The awkward silence which followed was broken by Eugène's return. 'If you're ready, Andy, I really do have a lot to discuss with you. Esteban, Egon is staying on with the people over there. He says that if you'd like to join them they'd be delighted. . . .'

Ortiz took his leave and went to sit with the group which had absorbed Klarsfeld. St-Meurice and Andy went to get a cab.

'You've come a long way in one morning,' he said approvingly. 'I suspect Esteban will be a far more entertaining companion than me!'

## Extract From Andrea Vincent's Working Diary

*Monday June 7, 1978*

Things are moving so fast it's hard to keep up with them. When Mademoiselle decides to unwind, she really goes to town. After an interesting but complicated lunch date with St-Meurice and friends, Eugène shepherded me off alone. I was half-expecting a sneak preview of the salon, so when he took me to Rue Cambon by taxi I wasn't too surprised. That came when we got out of the lift, not in the first floor salon as I'd expected but in Mademoiselle's private domain upstairs. And then he announced that she's lending me the place for the duration of my stay!

It's a bit like being given Buckingham Palace while the Queen is away on a trip. I love it, she's right to think it gives me more of a feel of her life, but it *is* weird. It's so strongly imbued with her personality that I keep expecting her to come in through the bedroom door. For some reason, Eugène is furious about it, although he's trying very hard to conceal his feelings. It seems an odd reaction. How can I possibly be a threat to him? He's worked for Mademoiselle since his early twenties and he must be in his fifties by now, although he's very well-preserved. He is the obvious choice to take over the House of Doré when La Grande Mademoiselle finally lets go. She treats him rough sometimes, but it's just as clear that she depends on his judgement and trusts him more than anyone else. So what can he possibly fear from me? Perhaps there's something really juicy to come up in the biographical material, but I don't see what.

After a lot of brooding, I'm begining to think he idolises her to such an extent that he sees my live-in presence at the Rue Cambon as sacrilege. But the odd thing is that he understands her faults and frailties completely, not the usual accompaniment to hero-worship.

Being here in Doré's apartment is worth a bit of aggro with Eugène, though. When I said she brought all her precious things to the Ritz on her removal, I didn't have the remotest idea of how many precious things she possessed. Now I think of it, I remember someone writing that she had bought thirty or forty of those wonderful Coromandel screens over the years, so even allowing for the collection at the Ritz and in the country, there are plenty left for Rue Cambon. The drawing-room is a treasure house of French and Italian traditional, Far Eastern exotic, Art Deco perfect and Post-War eclectic. If that sounds like a mess, it's anything but. It all blends into a brilliant melange of luxury, culture and comfort. In fact, it's the interior design version of what she's always achieved with clothes.

There are two equally elaborate guest bedrooms, but her own room – temporarily mine – is almost spartan in comparison. Just a big comfortable bed with plain sheets and covers, a few unobtrusive pieces of furniture, plenty of good books and gentle lighting. The adjoining bathroom, on the other hand, is like an operating theatre. Killer lights, designed to show up every physical fault – presumably with the aim of making them easily correctable – and cabinets full of every expensive toiletry one can imagine. No wonder she went on looking so good for so long. She treated her physical appearance like a military campaign!

I moved in from the Ritz late yesterday afternoon before going back there to join her and Eugène for dinner. He was right when he told me to eat as much as possible at lunchtime because we had a dinner which was only marginally bigger than Saturday's. She then spent a couple of hours completing the high speed preview of her career and told me what she has in store for the next week or two.

Eugène is to be banished back to his job – and presumably, his private life – from today. Unbelievably at her age, Mademoiselle is working till all hours finishing off the collection for the August showing. It never crossed my mind that she was still so active in the business, but she is. She has suggested that I sit in on the fitting sessions which will fill her working day from now until the big show. Eugène tells me – a bit brusquely – that they are an unforgettable experience.

She often re-works the entire collection on the model, apparently, cutting away seams, re-draping material, withdrawing some designs altogether. The senior fitters and tailors are there with her and either Eugène or Seraphine Junot, a brilliant organiser, is present at all times. She intends to slot in our initial interviews for the book around this little lot, coming back up to the apartment when she's had enough of the collection. The new régime starts this afternoon. She doesn't want to tie me up for all the fittings, just as many as I like. Between times, I assume I can alternate between getting my notes in order and conducting whatever degree of private life is possible.

I was beginning to wonder whether I'd be let off the leash at all while I was here, but Mademoiselle apparently realises that this might lead to a claustrophobic atmosphere which could spill over into the finished book. Or is it that she's afraid I'll unearth too many unwelcome truths if she keeps me too close for too long?

# Chapter Five

## Doré
## Up and Away

The years stretched ahead of her, sterile, empty and constricted. There seemed no prospect of improvement. Even Cinderella lived in a world where there were men, Eliane reflected, and Providence had already taught her that they were the only escape route from poverty for orphan girls.

After Reverend Mother put an abrupt end to her affair with Jean-Baptiste Longchamps, someone always seemed to be watching Eliane. At first she thought it was her imagination, but then she noticed that she was no longer used for outside errands as the other younger girls were. Initially she took it philosophically. One way and another she had got off lightly, she knew. For weeks she had expected more than such confinement and the constant exhortations to prayer, but that seemed to be the extent of the nuns' reaction.

Then she began to realise that they had no intention of relaxing their surveillance of her. Shortly after her thirteenth birthday, the Mother Superior sent for her. It was the first time they had been alone together since the confrontation after the nun's unfortunate encounter with Madame du Plessis. Momentarily, Eliane was worried that there had been further revelations about what had gone on at the Avenue Rousseau. She was wrong, but the real reason was infinitely worse.

'Eliane, you are approaching womanhood and we have to consider what is to happen to you.' Reverend Mother's tone was decisive. 'During the recent – uh – difficulties, you told me something which I promise no one else shall ever know. Nevertheless, I have thought a lot about it and it has occurred to me that such an experience, so young, might have made you dread the prospect of being out in the world, unprotected by money or family. I think, therefore, it might help you considerably if you were able to contemplate a secure and tranquil future.'

Eliane was mystified. What was the old chatterbox trying to say? Clarification chilled her.

'You have behaved well since last summer. If you continue like this, we are willing to offer you a novitiate when you reach the age of sixteen.'

She sat back, smiling smugly as though she had given the girl a substantial present. Indeed, in her view she had offered the greatest gift in her power. Fortunately the effect on Eliane was so electrifying that she was unable to reply. Reverend Mother misunderstood.

'Don't try to make up your mind now, my dear. It's the most important undertaking you will ever make and is not to be approached lightly.'

Nevertheless there was no doubt in her mind that the girl would accept. Anything else was unthinkable. Such an honour for a little nobody with no dowry to offer the church; nothing, in short, beyond her own frail self? It was better than any other offer she might receive. Eliane was sent away to think and pray for guidance.

Always the prayers for guidance, she snarled to herself. Always they send me for guidance to the very place I want guidance to avoid! She put aside the need to deal with the question; for the moment it was enough to know that if they killed her she would never accept their gift. If she was going to do any praying, it would be for an excuse to hold off Reverend Mother as long as possible. Even at thirteen, Eliane was a natural strategist who knew that the nun would react like a jilted suitor if her offer of marriage to Christ was rejected.

She was also naturally superstitious and when the perfect excuse materialised she glanced heavenward, momentarily suspecting for the first time that there might after all be a God.

Salvation came in the shapely form of her Aunt Geneviève, though 'Aunt' was a misleading appellation, for Geneviève Doré was the child of Eliane's grandfather's old age, a beautiful afterthought fathered on his mistress less than two years before Eliane herself was born. Grandfather Doré had now died and his estate could not support all the surviving children so Geneviève became another uninvited guest of the orphanage.

'Christ, if this goes on Mother Church will be supporting more Doré girls than the Doré family!' said Eliane as she embraced her kinswoman. The two had always been close and Geneviève was the one member of the family who had come to see her regularly.

Geneviève looked around glumly. 'Any bright ideas about how we get out of this dump?' she asked.

'I don't know about that, but at least you've given me an excuse to get out from under the veil!'

Eliane went to see the Mother Superior as soon as possible and acted out a touching scene of family love and humility. 'I must ask you to be patient with me, Reverend Mother. I know you have offered me a wonderful opportunity and I'm honoured. But Geneviève must be having a terrible time – it's not so long since I went through it that I've forgotten. Elise and I are really all she has left for the moment and I can't tell her that I plan to desert her and become a nun. Perhaps you would be kind enough to give me another chance when I'm older?'

Reverend Mother was forced to accept her small charge's excuses. In fact, they seemed to be inspired by the best motives. But she had an uneasy feeling that the Doré girl was deceiving her; she was at a loss to understand why. She tried to be civilised about the matter, with only limited success. 'Very well, Eliane. I can see that you are in a difficult position. But you must bear in mind that the offer might not be made again.'

Thank God for that, if for nothing else, thought Eliane.

At least she had been able to offer an excuse which gave no cause for overt resentment. With anything like luck she would not be bothered again.

She was right. With Geneviève's companionship she blossomed and matured very fast. The fifteen-year-old had learned a lot about the world first-hand before her father's death had snatched her out of it temporarily. After contemplating their plight for a while, Geneviève came up with a plan of action.

'You're too young for us to run away and stand on our own feet,' she said. 'If you were big and well-developed, it would be different, but you're as flat as a boy and you still look about ten years old.'

Eliane was indignant. 'Some people think that's quite exciting.'

'Yes, and they chew up little girls like you and spit them out before breakfast! We've got to face up to staying here until you're a bit bigger and older-looking, and while we're here we might as well learn something. Some day we might really have to earn our living if we can't be rich or famous.'

'What about Elise? If you think I'm young, look at her. She could pass for seven or eight.'

'Oh, we can't wait for her. It would be far better if we could get ourselves set up and send enough money for her to join us. Now what can we do here that would help us to earn some sort of living outside?'

'Hmmm . . . d'you fancy being a laundress?'

'Don't be stupid! I could have done better as a farm servant if I'd wanted to do that sort of thing!'

'Well, it's the sort of work they do here, that's why I suggested it.'

'But they embroider and sew, too. That's much more interesting and less tiring than bashing away at a copper full of wet sheets all day.'

'You're as crazy as Papa's sister Antoinette! Embroidery's so badly paid that you have to be a nun living in a convent to do it, because nobody else can earn enough to live on! How could that help us?'

'Start thinking, kid. You don't only learn to embroider when you sew. If we want to get away, we need to look right. You've cried to me often enough when I visited about how awful it was to be dressed in cheap rough clothes while the paying pupils wore good dresses. Well, think how impossible it would be for us to be anything much wearing these shabby things. If we learn to sew properly, at least we'll be able to make nice things so that when we run off, we won't look as if we came from the orphanage.'

A moment's reflection satisfied Eliane that Geneviève was right. It also set her speculating about how much worsted, lace and linen her hidden five hundred francs would buy them. From that day on, the two girls were better able to cope with the constraints of orphanage life. They had a goal and all their energy was devoted to achieving it. Eliane concentrated on learning about making up the big lengths of linen into fine sheets; how to cut lawn and eventually silk to make up the blouses and shifts the nuns produced. Geneviève showed a talent for embroidery and was occupied in producing the delicate trimmings for handkerchieves and underwear.

After her initial irritation with Eliane's postponement of a decision about her novitiate, Reverend Mother was mollified by her charge's new-found industriousness. 'If she goes on like this, she might be really useful to us if ever she does decide she wants to join the Order,' she told the priest when he came visiting one day that summer.

A year later, such a hope would have been unthinkable, because by then Eliane and Geneviève had absconded together to try their luck in Paris.

They had planned their escape in great detail. A portion of Eliane's five hundred francs was spent on material for an outfit for each of them. After that, they had enough to travel to Paris and to stay in a cheap rooming house for a few days. The clothes were made up in odd moments. It took them far longer than they had imagined because of the need for secrecy, and their original intended departure date soon after Eliane's fourteenth birthday had to be postponed by almost six months because of the hold-up.

'Unless we can go looking the part, we might as well not go at all,' said Geneviève. 'We certainly shan't get another chance if we mess this one up.'

Eliane had only the vaguest idea of what they would do in Paris. What notions she did harbour involved the stage. Geneviève was surprised at this thought.

'What do you plan to do?' she asked. 'I know you can manage a few cartwheels, but somehow I think they expect a bit more than that at the Moulin Rouge.'

'You say yourself that I've got a nice voice, and the nuns always make a fuss about it. I might make it as a singer.'

'You're nuts, girl. If we were bourgeoises, you'd be asked to warble along while your husband or brother played the piano, and all the relatives would applaud after you'd finished and say you should go on the stage. That doesn't mean you really *should* go on the stage! I've a feeling that you're tough enough to make it, but you don't have enough talent, my love. Face up to it now, not when they break your heart in a few months' time!'

'Oh, it won't break my heart! I haven't got this big love affair with the footlights and all that rubbish. I just couldn't think of anything else we could do to earn money in Paris. No one's going to pay us to be apprentice midinettes, are they?'

'Not unless things have changed a lot since Mother had a go, and I don't think they have. But there's always one way.'

'If you've found one you're brighter than me.'

'No, Eliane, just a couple of years older. What about earning a living the way you spent all those Saturdays with the old boy at Josselin?'

Eliane was scornful. 'It took me a couple of months to get five hundred francs! We'd need a lot more than that, starting from nothing!'

'And what about the lovely clothes and meals and things? He got you cheap and he knew it. Those little tasters were all things he could only lend you because you had to come back to the orphanage at the end of the afternoon. If you didn't have to do that, your admirers would have to give you the things for keeps, wouldn't they? And that would mean they'd be paying for all your meals and nice clothes. You didn't much mind what he did to you, did you?'

'Mmm, not really, I suppose, but it used to make me cry a bit when I got back.' Then she brightened: 'Still, it beats the novitiate any day! Tell you what – if I can't make something from singing, I'll give it a try!'

'I think that just means you'll give it a try.' At that point they arrived at the railway station.

They had been talking as they walked along the road which led from the orphanage into town. The girls were confident they would escape detection because the nuns would be in Chapel at this hour. By the time their absence was noticed they would be aboard the evening train for Paris. Their new clothes also acted as protection. They certainly bore no resemblance to convent dwellers in their grown-up dresses and jackets. Although proud of the overall effect, it never occurred to either of them that the standard they had achieved was remarkable. After all, they had no basis of comparison beyond the excellence of the nuns' basic technique, acquired over lifetimes of dedication to little else but God and needlework.

At the station, Geneviève watched as Eliane counted out the money for their fare. 'What are you doing? We don't need returns – that's far too much!'

Eliane swept past her to the ticket office. 'My days at the bottom are finished. We're going first class.' And she parted with a quarter of their remaining funds to do it.

Paris was a disaster. The first set-back occurred when Eliane went to explore the possibilities of employment as a singer. The café-concert was still popular in the capital and there were plenty of places at which to apply. In the third, she thought she had struck lucky. The proprietor looked her over and liked what he saw.

'I wouldn't take on anyone as a regular artiste unless I had a personal recommendation from someone,' he said, 'but you're a nice-looking girl and I'll give you a try as a *poseuse* if you want to take your chances.'

Eliane's feet hardly touched the ground as she raced home to tell Geneviève. Her aunt could hardly believe it. 'What did you do, hypnotise him into thinking you were a professional singer?'

'Oh, I'm the lowest form of life around there, but at least he's giving me a chance. I'm not a featured singer or anything.'

'So what are you doing?'

'I'm something called a *poseuse*. He didn't spell out what I'll be doing but he said I'll get a chance to sing.'

Geneviève tried not to laugh. She was considerably more worldly than Eliane and knew immediately that the girl was a non-starter in her new role.

Cafés-concerts had become too much of a craze in Paris and there were a couple in every other street. The rougher ones brought in a lower type of customer who bought the minimum number of the cheapest drinks and stayed on for the entertainment. Proprietors, desperate for a paying clientèle to cover the cost of the artistes, had hit on the idea of *poseuses*. These were young female hopefuls who received no formal wages but who sat looking attractive in a half-circle behind the featured players. During the intervals they took turns at their chosen dramatic monologues or songs, passing a collecting plate afterwards to cover their expenses and make a little ready cash. For a while it had up-graded the image of the establishments which used these girls, as much by adding to the customers' expenditure as anything else. There were worse ways of getting a start as an entertainer, but there was one qualification for being a *poseuse* of which Eliane was obviously ignorant. Geneviève reflected to herself that it was better thus. It would prevent Eliane from ever knowing whether she was gifted enough to succeed on the stage, which her aunt sincerely doubted.

'I'm afraid you won't find out whether you were destined to be a music hall immortal, unless you've been concealing something in our luggage and not telling me about it.'

'Why? What are you on about?'

'I'm surprised he didn't tell you. He must have assumed you already knew. A *poseuse* has to wear evening dress. It's a condition of being allowed to sit up on the stage and then to perform.'

'Oh. Well that's it, then, isn't it?'

Eliane slumped on a chair for a moment, deflated by the news. Then, to Geneviève's astonishment, she jumped up and started rummaging in their meagre baggage. Picking up a pile of assorted garments, she retreated behind the scrappy screen which concealed the bidet.

'Eliane, why have you suddenly gone coy on me? I've seen you naked often enough to forgive you a little immodesty now.'

'Nothing to do with it. I just want to give this a little bit of drama, that's all.'

As time passed, Geneviève's attention began to wander. 'I don't know about drama, love, you'll be shaking me awake if it takes much longer.'

'Be patient. How - about - this?' She stepped from behind the screen, transformed. In spite of herself, Geneviève let out a gasp of admiration.

'I don't know how you did it, Eliane, but in a minute you're going to do the same for me!'

'Oh, no I'm not! This isn't hard to do but I'm wearing nearly everything we both possess, apart from our day clothes.'

'Just how *did* you do it?'

'I'm not quite sure, but I suddenly saw it in my head and it all came together.'

Eliane had taken a pile of the white petticoats they had made in considerable quantity and put them one on top of another to form a foaming pile of skirts. She had topped them with the elegant hand-embroidereed blouse Geneviève had created for herself and decorated ornately with lace, embroidery and scarlet satin ribbon. The outfit had been transformed from extravagant underwear to unorthodox evening dress by the addition of the one precious thing in their joint possession: an Indian silk shawl, in a magnificent range of gold, bronze and red tones. Although almost two metres square, it was of such fine material that it threaded through a wedding ring with little difficulty. Alain Doré had won it at one of his fairground sales pitches in a game of chance, and had presented it to the young Geneviève in a generous gesture typical of the feckless poor. She and Eliane (who had been hurt that her father hadn't thought first of her) had shared it since her arrival at the orphanage. Now Eliane had somehow flattened and folded it into a sash and knotted it so that it concealed the drawstring waistline of the petticoats and married them to the blouse, transforming them into a proper skirt.

'I don't know about the voice, Eliane, but the clothes will kill 'em!'

Unfortunately, the voice did not. On the first three evenings, they took a little money, enough to pay for their room, with Geneviève in her day clothes passing around the collecting plate to save Eliane's delicate outfit from the dirty floor and wine-stained tables. But by the fourth morning the whites were looking bedraggled and they had not made enough to have them laundered. Lacking the resources to wash the garments in their mean room, they admitted defeat. There was to be no fourth appearance.

With the same spirit that had led to their purchase of first-class tickets from Josselin, Eliane insisted they go out for a square meal in the bistro at the corner of their street. 'If I'm going to start lying down for old men, I want to do it with a good meal inside me,' she said.

'It's not that bad. Just think of something else and it's over quite quickly,' Geneviève told her. 'If it hadn't been for the odd bit of money from old men, I'd have joined you at the orphanage a lot faster than I did. Just keep it in your mind that it mustn't be for long, otherwise you'll never be any good for anything else. It's only to set us up for better things, understand?'

Eliane nodded, wide-eyed and silent, then took a hefty gulp of white wine and tackled her dinner. The following morning she felt as if she never wanted to eat again.

As Eliane had never done this sort of thing before, Geneviève suggested that she should use their room in the hotel. 'I've talked to the concierge and as long as I see him all right tomorrow, he'll give you no trouble. I'd rather you didn't have to work the street or go back to their places with them for a while,' she told Eliane.

Even so, it was rough going. For the first time, Eliane fully appreciated Jean-Baptiste Longchamps. He might have been self-centred, but at least he was gentle and cultivated. Only one of the five men she picked up that night was either. The others treated her as if she were a bottle of wine or a pack of cigarettes, consumed her, paid, and were gone. One of them was drunk, two stank, one said virtually nothing. The fifth satisfied himself and then launched into a monologue aimed at reforming her. On balance she detested him most, although he was cleaner and more polite than the others. He was the last of them. When he had gone she slumped on the bed, too tired and depressed even to cry.

Geneviève arrived an hour later, dispirited and haggard. They both washed themselves thoroughly then climbed into bed and slept until nearly noon. When they woke, dressed and went down to the bistro, Eliane recovered rapidly with the aid of quantities of coffee.

Geneviève watched her narrowly. 'Well? Can you stand it?'

'I'll probably get used to it. So far it's not quite as bad as the orphanage.'

Unexpectedly, Geneviève burst into tears. 'I don't think I can. I did it around the villages after Papa died but that was different. Here it's – it's as if the bastards are out shopping, and they sort of thumb through you to choose what they want. And for some reason they seem so much dirtier than in Brittany! I'm scared, Eliane, scared we'll catch one of those awful diseases, or have a baby, or – or even maybe get murdered.

'The last one gave me the creeps. He took me back to an awful little room and went on and on for ages. Then he wrapped a red silk scarf round my neck and started on me again, and as he got more excited, he – he tightened the scarf until I could hardly breathe. Suddenly he just sort of ran out of steam. If he hadn't, I think I'd be dead now . . . and that was just our first night. What if it goes on being like this?'

She had regained control of herself when she started talking, but now she was crying again. Eliane was perplexed. She had regarded Geneviève as the leader. Now she was surviving and the older girl was a wreck. Not that Eliane blamed her, given her experience last night, but it was obvious that Geneviève was not going to be the rock on which their Parisian future could be built.

'So what d'you want to do now?' she asked. 'I don't think you're up to another night like last night for a while, but we haven't really got enough to live on more than today and tomorrow once we've given the concierge his cut, and there doesn't seem to be anything else we can do. I don't know whether I could handle enough men to keep us going on my own.'

That set Geneviève crying again. 'Oh, what a stupid little bitch I was! You weren't happy in that stinking orphanage, but at least you were safe, then along I came with my idiotic ideas and talked you into running off. Now we've nowhere to go and I've failed you, but you're still ready to try and keep us both. I do love you, Eliane!'

Eliane was close to crying herself now. She had received so little real affection in her short life that she recognised the real thing when it was offered. 'Come on, we'll manage. I've an idea. . . .'

It wasn't a great idea, but it was the best she could do, given Geneviève's state. They packed their few possessions, paid the concierge his bribe and left the hotel. They had enough money to buy two tickets back to Brittany. That evening they arrived on Geneviève's mother's doorstep. She was taken aback and stood indecisively at the door, hedging until she realised they did not plan to stay permanently. After that she was positively relieved, took them in, gave them a glass of milk apiece, and agreed to help them.

It was a simple enough plan. Eliane had reasoned that the best they could achieve was a return to the orphanage. After an exploit like theirs they ran the risk of ending up at a state correctional institution, a place which made the convent seem like a haven. That was the last thing Eliane wanted. She got Geneviève's mother to play along with their tale that her daughter had been so lonely and homesick she had needed the reassurance of seeing Madame Doré again. Reluctant to travel the country roads alone, she had persuaded Eliane to go along as her chaperone. Now, having been home and being satisfied that all was as well as could be, the girl was prepared to return to Josselin. Their prolonged absence was explained by the fact that the nuns would assume they had no money and that they had been forced to walk to Madame Doré's village, sleeping rough and begging lifts from farm carts. To give the plan authenticity, it was necessary to leave the travel bag with their smart new clothes at the Doré house. Eliane had little hope of seeing them again. Luckily they had put their Sunday orphanage dresses in with their other things, otherwise they would have been forced to give themselves away by wearing the new clothes back. Now they were able to don the drab black frocks as though they had worn nothing else.

Next morning Madame Doré sent a neighbour's son to tell the priest the agreed story and he arranged for the girls to return to Josselin. The nuns were understanding, if cold, and the exploit put an end to any suggestion that Eliane should be asked again whether she wished to enter the novitiate. She resigned herself to the grey drudgery of convent life, concentrated on her sewing and tried not to dwell on how remote adulthood and freedom seemed. Her brief sojourn in the outside world had taught her two things: she must be free and she must have money. Perhaps they were not two things, but different aspects of the same principle.

# Chapter Six

## Andrea and Doré

This time they met without Eugène, and ate lunch in the Ritz restaurant. Andrea was entranced. Where the couturière had feared the younger woman would see wrinkles and decay, she saw only gallantry and pride. Her admiration communicated itself, unspoken, and worked a small miracle. Doré recognised it as the respect of one top professional for another, devoid of sycophancy or self-interest, and for the first time she began to tell a little of the truth about herself.

She could not quite bring herself to discuss her origins, but she was prepared to talk a little about her lovers. 'Strange,' she said with a laugh, 'I was determined not to go places on my back, but when I try to describe it now, it sounds rather as if I did it on my lovers' backs – the same thing, really, I suppose.'

Afraid to break the reminiscent mood, Andrea remained silent.

'Bonnie Charles wasn't the first, of course, but he was the most important – the most important ever. I should have married him, and maybe I would have if I'd been given the chance. Apart from him, the centre of my life was Conway – but he came along much later. The really strange thing is that the one who made it all possible, who set my life on this course, meant far less to me than either of them – come to that, I meant far less to him than his horses and his horsy friends. But if ever I should have thanked God for anything, I should have thanked Him for throwing me at Christian de Selincourt. Without him I might have lived and died a provincial shop girl.'

'What did he do, sweep you off to the world of fashion?' Andy's friendly tone robbed the question of any hint of malice.

'I don't think it ever happens that easily outside the cheap romances I used to read in the newspapers. No, but he certainly set the stage for my star performance! He was an officer with one of the cavalry regiments garrisoned at Saumur – terribly smart, like the Blues and Royals in England. I was a shop assistant with ideas about going on the stage in those days. No need to look surprised, my dear, I've not been hiding a great talent all these years. I was pretty awful, but I looked good and my voice was passable so I could always fill in on some concert bill during the Season. I'd never have made a living at it, but it got me out of my cold little apartment over the shop and introduced me to lots of handsome admirers among the younger officers.

'They were all right for a few drinks and a few laughs, but not much more. None of them would have dared to fall head over heels in love with me; they all came from terribly respectable families who would insist on good marriages when the time came. Imagine how impossible it would have been for them to take a glorified servant home – and one who was a penniless orphan into the bargain! I didn't fit into one world or the other. I certainly wasn't part of the haut monde, and the demi-monde would have fallen over itself laughing if I'd claimed membership.'

She puffed herself up, looking oddly girlish behind the wrinkles. 'You had to be big and baroque and trimmed with feathers to be let into that world, plump enough to subside under a man like a feather mattress. I was still the size of a little girl, with no bosom, no backside, no nothing, just a long neck, lots of hair and a naughty smile. "Sorry, Mademoiselle, you don't have the entrance fee!"

'But Christian didn't fit into the Society mould. His parents had been killed in some freak storm out in Indo-China and he'd grown up under the care of a guardian, a remote elderly relative. The old boy was dead too by the time Christi came of age and there was no one else he gave a damn about. So when he got his money – and there was a lot of it – he was able to please himself. There was no disapproving Mama at home to say he was only allowed to see nice girls; no tolerant Papa to take him off to naughty bordellos but bring him back into the sheep pen for mating. He could please himself and he did just that. In those days he planned to spend his whole life chasing what he liked the most – no, not women, they came second – horses!'

She broke off. Andrea was becoming a little uneasy and the anxiety communicated itself. 'What's wrong? Not boring you, am I?'

'Quite the reverse.' Andy was embarrassed by her own unpreparedness, but she had not expected La Grande Mademoiselle to unwind so fast. 'I – I was going to put a lot of what you told me on tape so we could edit it later. It's so fascinating I don't want to get any of it wrong when I start putting it together, that's all. But we got started so suddenly I haven't brought along a machine yet.'

Doré was unconcerned. 'No problem. I was just rambling, anyway. We'll go over it again when we're at the apartment sometime. I'm telling you all out of order anyway; it'll keep for re-telling.'

She was still perfectly at ease but the nostalgic mood had evaporated. Suddenly she was all today. Andy silently cursed herself for spoiling a promising opportunity. Mademoiselle started talking fashion.

'We'll go to the Rue Cambon afterwards and you can take a look at how a collection gets on the road, or at least how mine does. Some of the poseurs who call themselves couturiers these days just stick their heads round the atelier door once a week to see if the designs are coming along nicely. You don't have to be an expert in the couture to know which ones, either. Their finished styles scream shoddy thinking.'

'I was amazed to hear that you actually work on the collections yourself,' said Andrea.

'Why? Surely you can see that all my designs come from one mind. There's not a committee outfit among them.'

'Yes, I appreciate that, but I've read time and time again that you can't even sew.'

The little black head bobbed and Doré shouted with laughter. 'So you believe some of the propaganda, too, do you? A little fib I told centuries ago when I was leading some idiot débutante up the garden path about having an aristocratic background. Convent-educated, apprenticed in a mercer's shop and couldn't sew? I wouldn't have lasted five minutes! I don't like sewing, never have, but if I had to I could sit down now and construct every garment you're wearing, right down to the underwear. Don't listen to fairy stories without applying a little healthy cynicism, my girl. Your background should give you a natural talent for it . . .'

'My background, what's that got to do with anything?'

Doré became inexplicably waggish, smiling like some theatrical fairy godmother with a big secret.

'Perhaps a lot more than you think. Wait and see. Different stories for different times. Now please pay attention. We were talking about my next collection. I start by making notes, developing ideas from the previous season and the number of outfits I shall want to show. Then I order the bolts of cloth and start cutting on the model: no drawings, no toiles at that stage. I like to see how the real fabric hangs. The fitters go crazy! They can't bear to see so much top quality cloth going to waste. Sometimes, on a really complicated design, I get through a whole bolt before it's right. It never seems to occur to them that at our prices I can afford to do it that way. I can guarantee there'll be a fight some time around this stage before a collection, with one of the cutters bringing in his design in percaline when he should have been using silk. I say fight but that's not quite true. I am an autocrat. I don't fight, I give orders, so in this case it means the poor man has to go off and do it all again in silk. I am respected but not loved.'

The last words had a forlorn note. 'I'm sure you're wrong!' Andy's response sprang from instinct, not flattery. 'The proof of your genius is all around them – there must be love mixed in with the respect.'

The designer gave one of her marvellous smiles. 'I wish I could believe it. As I'm mellow after a good lunch, I'll confide in you. Somewhere along the line I got it wrong. I thought if I coddled and coaxed and loved my business above everything else, I had more chance of happiness than if I lived any other way. It's a hell of a time to find out I was wrong, isn't it?' Her voice was thick with tears but she continued to smile.

'Sometimes I lie on my magic couch late at night and I wonder where I went wrong. Should I have done things differently, or have I just lived too long? In a way I hope it's the latter – I do hate making mistakes, but old age is something I have no control over.'

During this short speech she had mastered her emotions and a glimmer of mischief was coming back. 'Of course, the day after I drop dead, the showroom, the apartment, the Madeleine or wherever else they see me off, will be crammed with friends who swear they were with me every moment right up to the end. There are a handful of them around right now. They're solicitous, interested, friendly, but they manage to slot me in when their other social commitments permit it. I'm the wrong sort for slotting in!'

'Perhaps that's the real reason for your solitude.'

Doré stopped in her tracks at this heresy. 'And what do you mean by that? Some of the most famous names of two generations were falling over themselves to court my company once. They never expected me to sit in a quiet corner and lionise them – they always made a fuss of *me*. Why should the nonentities who pass as celebrities today think they're better than Diaghilev or Picasso or Stravinsky?'

'Maybe they don't. Maybe you have a tendency to make them aware that you think they're nonentities compared with Diaghilev or Picasso or Stravinsky. Even if it's true, people have their pride.'

This is it, Andrea thought. I've blown it before I even begin. She's going to send me packing before we get to the coffee.

Instead, Mademoiselle looked at her speculatively for a moment, then said: 'You're certainly no nonentity and you seem to like my company.'

Andy heaved a silent sigh of relief. 'Quite. You're terrific company but you also make me feel as if *I'm* terrific company. Look, this is crazy! Even I'm not arrogant enough to presume to correct the social mannerisms of a woman of your maturity.'

Doré burst out laughing. 'Improve the manners of a decrepit old bag, you mean! Oh, please stay around for a long, long time. You brush away the years, Andrea. By the way, you don't call me anything. Why not?'

'Hmm, don't know really. Mademoiselle seems too impersonal; for some reason I get the feeling you dislike Alouette, although it's what most of your circle call you; and you just aren't an Eliane. So what's left?'

'How do you think of me – or is that a dangerous question?'

'No, not at all. There's only one name in my head for you: Doré. That says it all. I just thought you might regard it as impolite if I addressed you directly like that.'

There was, once more, a hint of tears in the couturière's voice. 'I would regard it as a great compliment, my dear. Doré is the only name I've ever valued' – then the mischief glimmered again – 'although I do have a weakness for La Grande Mademoiselle. The trouble is, that one can really only be used behind my back!'

She glanced at her watch. 'My God, we'd better go round to Rue Cambon, or the wage slaves will be moaning about wanting to go home before we even get started!' She rose and led the way out, walking as firm and straight as a twenty-year-old.

It was almost four o'clock by the time they reached the Rue Cambon. Andrea noticed a few resigned expressions as they moved through the main showroom. Mademoiselle went off to find Seraphine and Andy took the opportunity of a quiet word with Eugène, who had been talking to the senior fitters.

'They didn't seem exactly overjoyed to see her,' she said quietly. 'I'd have thought that this close to a collection, she'd set the place alight with her arrival.'

Eugène, like the more junior workers, was irritable. 'She would have done if she'd arrived at 11 a.m. Most of the people you see here have been in and hard at work since eight this morning, a few since seven. They're supposed to finish at five and go home to live their own lives. Mademoiselle is a little too fond of sailing in here any time after four and starting a full day's work. She expects the staff to stay with her, so now the poor devils will be off trying to sort out a rota so that at least some of them get a free evening.'

'But she's an old woman, Eugène. Surely they don't expect her to put in a nine to five day at her age, or on the other hand to finish for the day bang on time so close to the collection?'

'Not every night, no. But they don't expect this to happen every night, either, and at this time of year it usually does.' He sighed. 'I'd better find Seraphine. I know she has a dinner engagement tonight and I don't want her to miss it. I'll stay and she can disappear before Mademoiselle realises she's still around. Bet I'm already too late, though.'

It's not just Doré's lateness that's bugging him, thought Andy. He's still unhappy about me – he's giving it off in waves. What the hell can I do about it? I'll never handle this thing if I can't get him batting for me. The idea slid to the back of her mind as a junior brought her a cup of coffee and took her to sit somewhere where she would not be in the way. In spite of the tension, Andy was intensely curious about what the evening session held in store.

She was not disappointed. Once the work force had resigned themselves to another late night and had sorted out a list of people to stay on, the atmosphere lightened. Clearly they were fascinated by Mademoiselle's approach, although some of them had been through almost 50 collections with her since she reopened in 1954.

The first all-pervasive impression was that nobody said no to Doré. Whatever she ordered, asked, suggested, received the same response: Yes, Mademoiselle. Of course, Mademoiselle. Immediately, Mademoiselle. At this stage, at least, there was no discussion. Andy wondered whether discussion took place anywhere along the line. Within ten minutes she realised that Eugène St-Meurice must have one huge headache: there could never be any question of grooming another designer as Mademoiselle's heir apparent. When Doré died, so did her house, unless St-Meurice had a secret contender lined up and was keeping the knowledge to himself.

For half an hour, Doré busied herself with different groups of people. Then, around five, she gave St-Meurice some sort of private signal and her working session began. Between then and nine p.m. she worked on two suits. In each case it was the same: the model walked in and stood on the mirrored podium where the clients would get their first view of the finished outfit. Then Mademoiselle called her down into the brightly lit salon and the girl stood immobile while the couturière slashed at a seam here, re-pinned a hem there. The first time she ripped away a sleeve head, Andrea turned away nervously, convinced the garment would be damaged beyond repair. But Doré still knew what she was doing. The razor-sharp shears she carried on a ribbon about her neck slashed through the sewing thread, Doré reached for pins and re-positioned the sleeve with almost demonic thrusts. After more than two hours she stood back, satisfied. Andrea was at a loss to see any difference between the garment now and before it was altered.

With the second suit it was a shorter job: a minor alteration to a skirt length which also involved adjustment of the front seams. Again, Doré removed the original stitching herself, marked with pins what she wanted re-done, then handed over model and garment to the fitter who was responsible for it. She sighed and picked up the glass of water which was always close at hand.

'Enough for me. I'm finished. I'm seeing someone at the Ritz at 9.30. Time for everyone to go home!'

The silence, absolute until now beyond the occasional brief discussions between Doré and a tailor or fitter, was punctured by a dozen relieved voices, all betraying their earlier fears that they would be required until after midnight. Eugène St-Meurice slid across to Andy as she headed for the staircase to the apartment upstairs.

'Will you be all right this evening? I did not expect her to cast you adrift so suddenly and I had made a few plans of my own, but . . .'

Andrea cut him off with a laughing protest. 'I'm a big girl, Eugène, or hadn't you noticed? I'm quite capable of amusing myself, though I'm grateful for your kindness. Tell me, though, how do I get in and out?'

He smiled. 'Well, for obvious reasons, we can't give you a latchkey. Come down to Reception for a moment and I'll show you where the main bell is outside. You just ring it and the security man lets you in. You'll need to do the same thing before you go out, too. Pick up the telephone and dial the code in the front of the blotter folder on Mademoiselle's desk with all the internal salon numbers.'

After he had gone, Andy collapsed on to the sofa upstairs and sipped gratefully at a very big drink. All the adrenalin that been been flowing unchecked in the salon had left her feeling drained. But she revived fast and by the time she had finished her Martini, she wanted a change of scene. Right now, there was too much Doré all around her and, temporarily at least, the atmosphere was becoming oppressive. Her mood lightened. Perhaps Steb Ortiz would be free.

Andy telephoned the number he had written down for

her. She was childishly pleased when she heard his husky voice at the other end of the line.

'Esteban? Andrea Vincent. Are you too busy to renew our acquaintance?'

'Andy! No, wonderful! I'm not doing anything that can't wait. As a matter of fact I was knitting.'

'Now I *know* we're approaching the fall of Civilisation As We Know It.'

'I'm not churning out sweaters for the boutique round the corner, you idiot! You know how I make my living – as it happens, I'm working through the prototype of a design inspired by your famous tapestries.'

'Sorry, but it was irresistible. May I take a look?'

Now it was his turn to laugh. 'I'll bet this is the first time a man has ever lured you to his apartment to see his knitting!'

'I can't wait. I'll be there in half an hour. Is there anywhere I can pick up some junk food on the way? I haven't eaten yet.'

'Yes, but I shall be insulted if you do. I dine late, I'm an excellent cook and you're invited.'

'Done. As my contribution I'll bring a bottle of something bubbly.'

She hung up and went to rifle the fridge in the tiny service kitchen which Doré appeared to use solely to keep champagne on ice. Taking a bottle of Bollinger, she left to find a taxi.

Steb Ortiz obviously had rich friends. His borrowed apartment was in the centre of the ultra-chic Marais quarter, between the Rue de Rivoli and the Place des Vosges, Paris's oldest square. When she saw Ortiz's knitting, Andy felt slightly guilty about her frivolous reaction over the phone. A large industrial knitting machine was set up near the drawing-room window, with a part-worked design on it. Stretched on a frame for finishing was a completed sweater. Another version of the machine design lay on the sofa, also partially worked but this time by hand.

'You do take it seriously, don't you? Sorry I was so flip. You must get as sick of knitting wisecracks as I used to about jokey advice to take care I had film in my camera.'

'Yes, but of course people never expect knitwear designers to knit. They think we draw pretty pictures, then go find a little old lady down a back street to do the real work. Well, some people might, but I like to get hold of the yarn and make sure my ideas work before I go on to that stage.'

He dismissed his work momentarily. 'Come on, let's eat. We can talk about this lot later if you're interested.'

'Mmm, fine with me. Something smells marvellous and I'm a dreadful glutton. What is it?'

'It's called *saupiquet des amognes*: slices of fried Morvan ham in a savoury sour sauce made from wine vinegar, shallots, cream, and about a litre of pure veal stock concentrated down to a few spoonfuls. There are just potatoes Anna and a tomato salad to go with it, I'm afraid.'

'Don't apologise. It certainly puts the hamburger I'd planned to shame!' She produced the champagne. 'The taxi driver delivered me here *con brio*, so I hope this doesn't explode when opened. At least it's good and cold still.'

They chattered companionably through the delicious meal, no hint of his momentary irritation at their first meeting re-surfacing now. By the time they had drunk coffee together, cocooned in the huge sofa, they were on very friendly terms. Steb slipped his arm round Andy's shoulders and she turned to face him. They exchanged a long, exploratory kiss and he moved closer, the pressure of his lips and tongue increasing as her taste and scent stirred him. 'This promises to be a much nicer evening than I was expecting, Renaissance Man.'

'I hope you still think so in the morning, Twentieth-Century Woman.'

# Chapter Seven

## Doré
## 1906: A New Beginning

Like all children, Eliane was convinced that the condition of the moment would last forever. But even within the orphanage, time passed. Her little sister Elise began to develop an individual personality and as this revolved around worship of Eliane, the older girl found it comforting. Even more flattering was the realisation that since their abortive trip to Paris, the worldly Geneviève held her in similar esteem.

The morning after their return to Josselin, she embraced Eliane and said: 'You saved us. I'll never forget it, never. Whatever happens when we're older, remember you can come to me. If I have a chance of doing anything now, I owe it to you.'

'Come on, Geneviève, you're not in a play! I only used a bit of good sense.'

'Sure, if you'd been grown up. But you were a little kid, far too young to be away from home, let alone shoved into something like that. You could have lost your head the way I did, then we'd both have wound up in the reformatory. Instead of that you behaved marvellously.'

'I can't have been so good only to have got us back to this pig-pen!'

'Ssh – you don't know what you're saying! Mama once took me to see a cousin of ours in the reformatory at Rennes. I think it was supposed to be an awful lesson. It was. If you think this is bad, you should've seen that!'

'Well, I'm glad you're so keen on it. We're going to be prisoners here for long enough.'

But that was true only for Eliane. Both Geneviève and Elise achieved freedom of a kind before she escaped the convent. Geneviève's departure was inevitable when she had passed her seventeenth birthday. The orphanage rule was that the nuns' responsibility for their charges ended as each girl reached her eighteenth birthday. In order to avoid embarrassment, they began trying to place a girl as soon as she was seventeen and she left when they obtained a situation for her.

There was no problem with Geneviève. She was a beautiful girl and a talented needlewoman. Within a few weeks the Mother Superior had obtained an apprenticeship for her in a fine linen shop at Saumur. Geneviève's looks would have been a handicap in many establishments, where a wife might have feared that her husband's attention would wander to the comely new assistant. But Chez Ninon was owned by a widow. Geneviève's striking appearance was a positive bonus as many of her customers were cavalry officers from the town's garrison, shopping for trinkets for their latest mistress. A good-looking salesgirl would improve business enormously.

Accommodation was arranged in the guest wing of a girls' seminary. Geneviève thought that arrangement unlikely to last long. She parted from a tearful Eliane with promises to prepare the way for them to be together in Saumur in a couple of years. Eliane clung more closely to Elise after Geneviève had gone, but even her companionship proved short-lived.

Elise was fond of small children and had spent much of her time at the orphanage helping the nuns to look after the six- and seven-year-olds. One afternoon soon after she reached the age of fourteen, the Mother Superior sent for her.

The nun who came to find her in the babies' classroom said: 'Reverend Mother won't need you for about half an hour. Go to the dormitory and change into your best dress and boots. Are you clean? If not, make sure you scrub yourself thoroughly before you come down. There's someone important who will want to see you.'

Bewildered, Elise did as she was told. When she reported to the Mother Superior's office, she found the nun talking to a pleasant-faced couple. Their expensive clothes made it obvious that they had not come to leave a child at the orphanage.

Reverend Mother was unusually friendly. 'Ah, come in, child. Here she is, Madame Lepine. This is Elise Doré. Elise, Monsieur and Madame Lepine are here to choose a clean, well-behaved young girl to look after their children. Please, Monsieur and Madame, talk to Elise for a while. I shall arrange for some tea.' Radiating tact and discretion, she left the room.

Elise suddenly felt like a trapped animal. She had settled in only recently, her short life having been even more beset by disruptions than Eliane's. She did not remember her mother at all, her father only vaguely. Her big sister Ninette was a little more substantial, but the last days of their time together, with money getting shorter and Ninette's cough getting worse, made that a grim memory. Then there was the convent. She minded it far less than Eliane or Geneviève. To her it was the greatest security she had ever experienced. Now someone was going to drag her away again when she had imagined the next three or four years stretching ahead, dull but safe.

Perhaps Madame Lepine understood a little of what was going through her mind. She smiled, more the smile of a mother than of a potential employer. 'Don't worry, Elise. We shan't force you if you prefer to stay here, but let me explain why we have come.'

They had four children, and the nanny they employed found it difficult to look after them all properly. She loved the children but she had been Madame Lepine's nurse when Madame was a child, and was due to retire long before the children had grown up. She had suggested that if the Lepines found a young girl who was fond of children, she could train her as the next nanny, so that by the time the girl was about eighteen, she would be ready to take over.

'Mademoiselle Charlotte is a Breton and she wouldn't hear of us taking a local girl from around Vichy where we live,' explained Madame Lepine. 'The convent here has an excellent reputation, so we came to ask Reverend Mother's advice. She says that you love children and are very good with them. How would you like to come and live with us to look after our son and daughters?'

Elise faced a dilemma. She trusted the couple instinctively and the proposal sounded like heaven after the cold formality of the orphanage. But what about Eliane? No, it was out of the question! She could not leave her sister all alone so soon after Geneviève's departure.

'Madame, I . . . I would like to come, but I . . . that is, my sister . . .' The strain was too much and she started to cry. Madame Lepine, instantly all concern, was on her feet, embracing and comforting her.

'I told you, my dear, no one would force you. But what's this about a sister? Reverend Mother mentioned there were two of you here but I thought your sister was older. Surely she wouldn't mind your going to a good place?'

'But I'm all she has, Madame! How can I go off like that? When would you want me?'

'We were planning to take you back with us tomorrow. Look, why don't we wait until Reverend Mother comes back and then ask her to get your sister in and see what she thinks about it?'

Elise smiled doubtfully. Reverend Mother returned and the problem was explained. She flashed a poisonous look at Elise as she rang her bell to summon the nun who carried her messages. 'Please fetch Eliane Doré, too, Sister Thérèse. She will be in the sewing room at this time of day, I imagine.'

In her short life Eliane had had plenty of practice at maintaining an impassive exterior. This confrontation required all her self-control. One look at the Lepines told her they could give Elise a better time than the orphanage. If they didn't take her, what would happen to the kid when she herself went to work in a year or two? Even after that, how long would it be before she was in a position to look after Elise? One thing was certain: no one else ever would.

'I don't have to go if I don't want to, Eliane, Madame Lepine told me that. What shall I do?'

'Go with them, my love. I can't do anything to help either of us yet, can I?'

She would have liked to behave as the young heroines of her favourite serials and throw off a line like 'Who needs a snivelling little baby like you around anyway?' to make sure that her kid sister took advantage of her great opportunity without worrying about leaving her in the lurch. But Eliane knew the certainty of her love was the one constant thing in Elise's life at present. Such a remark would only make her unhappy in order to bolster Eliane's momentary feeling of heroism.

'Reverend Mother, may I speak to Elise alone for a minute?' The nun nodded, radiating suspicion. The two girls went into the outer office.

'Listen, Elise, you're only fourteen. If I'm lucky, I'll get out of here as soon as I'm seventeen, like Geneviève did. Even if I'm not, I'll be out a few months later. You'd have to stay here on your own for another two years after that, and who knows what sort of work you'd be offered at the end of it? They look like decent enough people. Go with them, but don't lose touch with me whatever you do. As soon as I can, I'll get you back. Just promise me one thing: don't get too attached to them. I don't know what I'd do if I sorted something out for us and then you didn't want to leave them.' Angrily, she blinked back tears. Elise was crying openly.

'How can I go? You'll be all on your own and you hate it much more than I do.'

Eliane turned fierce. 'Get back in there and tell them you'll be ready to go with them in the morning! I told you, there's nothing better around the corner. Only don't forget me. Promise?'

'Promise.' Elise sniffed and gave her a radiant smile.

Like the child she was, her thoughts had immediately jumped ahead to the adventure in store for her. 'Isn't she a beautiful lady? That great big hat and all that lace!'

Eliane stifled more tears and grinned back at her. 'Go on, clever girl! That old bag Reverend Mother must have given you one hell of a report to get them wanting you without taking a look at anyone else.'

Next day she watched as the carriage took the Lepines and Elise away to the station. There goes my family, she thought. In her effort not to cry she bit the insides of her cheeks until they bled. It was going to be a long, cold two years.

The time passed somehow. Eliane did not escape at seventeen. There was no vacancy at the girls' seminary in Saumur and the only jobs available had no accommodation with them. Eliane flatly refused to go to work as a farm servant and until she was eighteen the nuns were powerless to force her.

Geneviève had moved out of the girls' seminary long ago. She had visited Eliane at Christmas in each of the two years since her departure and, when they went out in Josselin for the afternoon during the second visit, made it clear that the linen shop was not her main source of income.

'I'd never manage to have my own apartment if I were just a shop apprentice,' said Geneviève, 'but I could hardly have stayed at the seminary or in respectable lodgings and done what I am doing now.' Her giggle made it clear that she felt no guilt about her second occupation.

Eliane remembered their awful Parisian experiences. 'Do you mind it very much?'

Geneviève laughed again. 'Good God, no! That awful business in Paris is best forgotten. Saumur is quite different. Of course, I can't give up the shop job. That's what makes me respectable. If I didn't do that, apparently the gendarmes would be around within five minutes to see how I made my living, then it would be official registration, regular medical examinations, the lot. No, darling, if we can get you a decent job there when you're old enough to leave, we'll be all set. Don't let the sisters push you off into domestic service or anything like that. Of course, we shall have to find rich men to support us eventually because once you're too well-known you lose your attraction for the officers and it's all downhill unless you sort out something else. But I'm working on that.'

'It certainly doesn't seem to have hurt you so far. You look marvellous.'

'I feel it, too, just having decent clothes and not having to be polite to the Sisters. I shall never be polite to another nun as long as I live!'

She opened her bag and took out a little square box. 'This isn't very grand, Eliane, but I saved up for it and it's nicer than anything else you have. It should fit because our hands are the same size and I tried it. Happy Christmas, my love, and let's hope we both spend the next one together in Saumur.'

Inside the box was a topaz ring, inexpensive but very pretty. Choking with gratitude, Eliane put it on. 'I shall always wear it, Geneviève, even when I'm rich and famous.'

'Well, darling, hurry and outgrow that awful place and we can start trying to be.'

It was against the orphanage rules for Eliane to accompany Geneviève to the station. The older girl had to see her back to the convent and then depart. 'God knows why,' said Geneviève. 'You'd think they'd be glad to get rid of one more unwelcome guest.'

'You know as well as I do that it's not worry about us doing a bunk, it's in case we do something else and dump the result back on the convent doorstep a few months later.'

'Don't tempt Providence!'

After her departure, Eliane resigned herself to the usual desolate Christmas. Elise, who had settled in Vichy like a member of the Lepine family, wrote loving letters but was too far away to visit. Don't feel sorry for yourself, Eliane told herself. It has to end some time, then you'll show the bastards! She was unsure of just what she would show them, but knew that when she did, it would be spectacular.

Eventually Eliane's eighteenth birthday was only weeks away and the Mother Superior had already summoned her three times to urge her to accept farm service. At their third meeting, her patience almost snapped.

'You have made your distaste for the farmyard quite clear on several occasions, and I'm aware you have talents as a needlewoman which would be wasted at such work. But we also offered you an opportunity to develop your skills as a novice here and I recall you were equally dismissive about that. Only girls with families can pick and choose what they do, Eliane. We have been more than generous to you already and it cannot go on much longer. Now the job at Lesneven is better than either of the others. The farm is prosperous - almost a small château - and you could well eventually learn the skills necessary to become a housekeeper. I cannot turn you out on the street when you are eighteen so unless something else comes along in the next fortnight, you will go to the Souézecs at Lesneven in a month's time.'

She looked down and began consulting her appointments book. Eliane was dismissed. It was close to the mid-day meal time and she had no intention of returning to the workrooms for the twenty minutes or so that remained. Desolate, she wandered into the convent's extensive grounds. For once even her inventiveness was at an end. It would not be difficult to run away, but where, to what? She could hardly turn up on Geneviève's doorstep without any contribution to get herself started, or even the respectable cover of a job. Her secret bank in the outhouse had been exhausted by their trip to Paris and she had never found a way of replenishing it. But a farm? If she descended to that she would never escape. Shopkeepers did not take on inexperienced peasant girls as assistants. She would end up like her mother, coughing out her life in her early thirties from poverty and too many children . . .

The prospect was so horrific that she lost track of time and of where she was going. She wandered across the lawn beneath the Mother Superior's study window. Suddenly a sharp voice disturbed her reverie. 'Doré – Eliane Doré! Yes, girl, I mean you. Stop day-dreaming and come up here immediately. Someone has been looking for you for ten minutes!'

Reverend Mother was leaning through her open casement window, clearly irritated at the undignified position forced on her by the girl's elusiveness. Eliane was so surprised to be wanted twice in one morning that she turned and hurried back to the building, misery forgotten in a flood of anxiety about Elise or Geneviève. Something must have happened to one of them, otherwise she would not have been sent for so dramatically!

But it was nothing to do with either her sister or her young aunt. Salvation had arrived in the shape of a mercer from Saumur. By the time Eliane got back to the office, Reverend Mother was more serene.

'Ah, there you are at last! What a good thing that Monsieur and Madame Chaillot went into town to eat before meeting you. They would never have been interested in you had they known you just disappear when you feel like it. It seems there is a chance that you will get your own way after all, Eliane. The Chaillots have a job for a young woman and are able to offer accommodation along with it.'

It seemed too good to be true, and to an extent it was. The accommodation – her own apartment over the mercer's shop in the centre of Saumur – turned out to be an unheated garret. Little wonder that Chaillot was willing to pay for what he described as an apprentice, and to offer free lodgings. Normal practice for proper apprentices was for their families to pay the shopkeeper to train their daughters. But this was no proper apprenticeship. The Chaillots wanted a fully experienced shop assistant, preferably with additional skills as a seamstress to satisfy the constant requests of customers for a dressmaking service. For once Eliane benefited from the very system she had feared would swallow her. The only other candidates for the job were two farm servant girls. Apparently they were neat and attractive, but Chaillot dismissed them as country bumpkins. Besides their obscure origins, they were unable to provide references to attest to their honesty. Eliane's reference from the orphanage would be impeccable on this count. If Eliane was interested, said Madame Chaillot, she could start next week. The Mother Superior asked the visitors to wait in her private parlour while she advised her charge.

'This might seem like a golden opportunity, Eliane, but I have no high hopes of the standard of accommodation they are offering. It seems obvious that if it were desirable, they would have experienced applicants from Saumur, instead of having to take an inexperienced beginner. The pay is low, it is true, but the apartment cannot be very good either, so don't expect too much. Are you sure you would prefer to try this than the Lesneven situation?'

'Yes, Reverend Mother. It's a proper job in a town. I shan't be anyone's slave and I'll obviously have the chance to make up my money by doing some dressmaking for the customers.'

Mother Superior sighed. She could not deny that the Doré child was prepared to work hard for her freedom. Such a shame she was doomed by her background to obscurity. She was a pretty and clever girl, and with a little money behind her she could have gone a long way. Still, such things only happened in silly romantic stories. In real life the Eliane Dorés lived and died in poverty. It was useless to question the justice of such a state of affairs, it was the will of God.

There was no one at the convent who meant anything to Eliane. Apart from Geneviève and Elise, she had made no friends there. To her the other charity girls were nonentities, and the paying pupils her natural enemies.

The nuns had failed utterly either to understand or to inspire her. They had succeeded only in teaching her to sew. When she finally departed from the orphanage early in March, she did so with a light heart and no regrets. The journey was timed to enable her to travel to the town of Saumur on a Saturday morning, and settle into her new home before starting work on the Monday. As the small postern gate in the convent wall closed behind her, Eliane involuntarily gave a little skip, as she used to on her way to the Avenue Rousseau. Whatever lay ahead could hardly be worse than the convent-orphanage of Josselin.

Monsieur Chaillot was not in when Eliane arrived at the shop late that afternoon. Madame, neatly attired in black with a white lace collar, presided behind the counter. Business was slack that day, so she was able to introduce Eliane to the intricacies of her new job with few interruptions. To her pleasure, the girl gathered she was to be virtually alone there.

'The shop does not merit my full-time attention,' explained Madame, 'but it would not really be worthwhile to put in an experienced manageress in her mid-twenties; not enough takings. As the apartment upstairs was empty, we thought it would suit someone like you and make it worth our while taking someone on. You're a pretty girl and if you can improve business from the garrison, good luck to you – I'll see you benefit by it too. I'll also pay you if you're interested in dressmaking in your spare time for any of my customers from our other shops. Just remember one thing and we'll all get on well together: we're not trying to cheat you and we don't expect you to cheat us. If you do, it'll show up sooner or later and after that your job prospects will be the streets or the farms.'

She gave Eliane a wintry smile. 'I hope the nuns gave you a set of bed linen as a parting gift. We don't supply any in the apartment, although there's furniture, blankets and pots and pans. I've put out food for the week-end in your kitchen but after Monday you'll have to supply your own. Any questions?'

Eliane shook her head. It was no harder than anything else she had lived through; better than much of it. At least here she was free to come and go once the shop was shut. Ignorant of the nuns' one generous gesture to girls who left to set up on their own, she had made a set of sheets and pillowcases for herself from material she had managed to save from the ends of rolls. Already a skilled cutter, Eliane had worked out economical ways of making yardage allowed for a pillowcase stretch to a child's bedsheet and a child's bedsheet length to one for a small adult bed. She regarded such economies as legitimate perks of her unpaid job in the convent sewing rooms. As a result she had one good quality set of fine cotton sheets, and one coarser but still serviceable set as a parting gift from the nuns.

By six o'clock Madame Chaillot had locked up and left the building to Eliane. The girl surveyed her new home with scant affection. The Chaillots had exaggerated in calling it an apartment. The first floor, directly over the shop, would have offered spacious accommodation. As this was where the couple had started their married life, presumably it had once been their quarters. But now it was the main storage space for the shop below. Boxes of ribbons, thread and all sorts of dressmakers' sundries were crammed from floor to ceiling into the two rooms and spilled out on to the landing. The staircase, fairly spacious up to this point, became much steeper above the first floor landing as it dog-legged to reach the attic floor. This was Eliane's domain: one large room with a small kitchen adjoining it. For water she had to take a large canister or a bucket down to the ground floor. There was no indoor lavatory, just an earth closet at the end of the yard behind the shop. Eliane shrugged. A farm would have been at least this bad.

The apartment was not improved by its furnishings. The large brass bed was substantial enough and the blankets, although much mended, were scrupulously clean. A built-in cupboard and a chest of drawers provided storage for her minute wardrobe. There were two cheap armchairs, one a rocker which creaked hideously, a small table with two hard chairs beside it, and a gimcrack wash-stand with a chipped enamel jug and basin on top and an equally worn chamberpot on the shelf beneath. A scrap screen concealing the bidet completed the fittings. In the kitchen were a table, a small paraffin cooking stove, a food cupboard and a porcelain sink with a waste pipe but no water supply.

The only heating was provided by a small, ugly cast iron wood-burning stove which sulked when the wind turned northerly. At least Madame Chaillot had taken the trouble to light it and bring in a supply of wood for Eliane's arrival. Each room was lit by a dormer window. A pane in the living-room was cracked and even on this mild evening a vicious draught came through. Eliane determined to buy another screen as soon as she could. The paper-thin curtains were unlikely to keep out the cold.

In their way, the Chaillots were not unkind. A *pot au feu* had been left for her in a covered container, with enough for two meals. All she had to do was re-heat it. There was even a litre of rough red wine. Eliane made her supper, drank some wine then went out for a stroll, exulting in her new freedom to roam without retribution. When she returned to her mean apartment, she could almost believe she was entering a mansion. Snuggling down for the night between fresh sheets, she was full of happy anticipation. Tomorrow she would see Geneviève, and after that her whole life would really begin afresh!

'Forget your *pot au feu*, darling. I've been looking forward to this reunion and it's time you saw a little Saumur society!'

It was hardly beau monde, but it was enough to be going on with. Geneviève took Eliane to a lively bar-restaurant in Saumur where the young officers liked to drink, gossip and flirt. Geneviève was obviously popular and her pretty sister ('Don't you dare tell them I'm your aunt!' Geneviève threatened) was a welcome addition to the group. Eliane would have plunged into the intoxicating social whirlpool without further thought but Geneviève had other ideas.

One of the young men who was particularly proud of his English public school education had flung himself down on one knee beside Geneviève and, gesturing at Eliane, began singing in fractured English: 'Tell me, pretty maiden, are there any more at home like you?' Eliane was in heaven and ready to follow the youth, or any of his companions, to the ends of the earth. Laughing, Geneviève helped him to his feet and shooed him back to an adjoining table.

Amid the resulting ribaldry she turned to Eliane and said quietly: 'You come home with me this afternoon – alone. We need a little talk. Now, enjoy yourself but remember, no assignations this week!'

Eliane was about to ask why on earth she had been brought here if not to meet eligible men, but the gaiety all around them drowned her protests. When they left the restaurant it was after four o'clock. Accompanied by a train of male admirers, they strolled beside the river, Eliane feeling cosmopolitan and glamorous. She was disappointed but impressed at Geneviève's efficiency in dismissing their escorts at the junction of the embankment and the road leading to her part of town. Laughing and waving, they melted away back towards the town centre. Geneviève guided Eliane down the quiet side streets.

'How did you manage that? I thought they'd spirit us off by force if necessary, but you say au revoir and they go like lambs. Why?'

'They understand the conventions, my love, and the sooner you do too, the better. Come on – I've got some nice wine back at the flat. By the time you have to go back to your hovel you'll be aglow with it. Much safer than love for the moment.'

In her small, comfortable sitting-room, Geneviève poured them a drink and explained the ground rules of her new life to Eliane.

'There's a very thin line between merry young pieces like us and street girls, and we're the only ones who'll preserve it. If you cross over to the wrong side, that's it forever. You'll find the boys understand that as well as we do and they'll help us to keep our place. But once we slip, they'll grind us down as easily as if they'd never known us.'

'But you made it pretty obvious that we could get quite a bit of money on the side by going to bed with them! How can we do that if . . . if . . .'

Geneviève laughed. 'Always ready to run before you walk, silly girl! You can either do it blatantly as a common street girl or by working permanently in a house, or you can do it the way I do and still have pretty high hopes of improving yourself later. It's always done tactfully, with grace. We flirt and have admirers in the restaurants. A group of them can buy lunch or dinner for both of us or one of us, but that's all quite respectable and we go home unaccompanied afterwards. If it's an engagement *à deux* it should be in a quieter, more discreet restaurant and there should be no horseplay like that nonsense today. That's just a bit of real fun and it's also an advertisement that we're pretty and available. If they're interested enough, they come round to the places where we work and they buy something, ask our advice on their purchases and make arrangements for a more romantic meeting.

'Remember, we have to keep our jobs to have a respectable means of meeting them and to stop the gendarmes registering us as full-time tarts. We are not prostitutes, and we never want to be known as anything worse than jolly girls who like a good time.'

The down to earth Eliane snorted contemptuously. 'What does the world think we do alone with them – play bezique?'

'It doesn't matter what the world thinks, as long as we give it an excuse for not airing such thoughts in public. I'm interested in reality, and reality is often very dishonest. You can have principles when we get rich. For now, let's concentrate on getting you a bit of security. You're a gorgeous new face in town. For the next couple of weeks you're going to be very busy at your job, learning the ropes and getting used to living at a different pace from the orphanage. For heaven's sake make sure you give a good impression to the Chaillots from the start. They're giving you a roof, remember, such as it is.

'We'll show you off again next week-end, and the following week I suspect you'll start getting a few gentlemen callers at the shop. That will please the Chaillots – it's always good for business to have a popular young shopgirl in your store. Don't accept more than one or two invitations during the first week, and set the dates a week or so ahead of that. Learn the ropes with them – they'll want to show you off before doing the usual – and don't worry about that. None of these boys is any trouble. Once you've been seen in the right places and the right company, you'll have a nice stream of similar arrangements and your own little crowd of admirers. After that we'll see how things develop.'

'What about my room? It's really crummy. I can't imagine entertaining a better class of lover in there.'

'No, I've been thinking about that. It'll be all right with the young officers. They're all still struck by *la vie bohème* and they'll see it as part of the romance. But as soon as you get an older admirer, fix something with him well ahead and talk to me. I'll make myself scarce and you can bring him here. After he's thirty a man goes off cracked windows and enamel washbowls.'

'What if you have someone coming as well?'

'Mmm. I've been working on something I haven't had a chance to tell you about yet. If I'm not careful I'll wear out my welcome in Saumur. It's nearly time for me to change the way I operate. No, don't panic, I'm not going to buzz off the minute you arrive. It's just that I've been at this game for nearly two years now. I'm as popular as ever – more so if anything – but there's a funny snobbery even in selling yourself. They'll be expecting me to move up the ladder, just like them and their military ranks.

'The permanent faces around Saumur, the ones who really matter, will expect me to have made my mark by now. I should be moving on either to one permanent protector or to three or four regulars. But for that I can't operate from the apartment. I need to have a chaperone and work through a house of assignation. I'm just getting to know a woman who'll be perfect. Once I've set that up, I'll live here very respectably, but I shan't need to worry about a shop job any more and I shan't be entertaining any men here - well, only occasionally if it's for fun. Once I'm set up, you can use this place for your little adventures as often as you like.'

Geneviève's advice proved invaluable to Eliane. She steered the younger girl away from danger and into a succession of profitable and on the whole amusing liaisons. The shop job was no problem, although Eliane would have hated it had she been wholly dependent on it. She had a natural head for money and could count change, discuss stock and recommend new items almost simultaneously. For the first week Madame Chaillot watched her like a hawk. When they closed on the Saturday evening, she turned to Eliane with a surprisingly genuine smile.

'Here's your first pay packet, my dear. I confess I didn't expect a lot when we took you on, but if you go on like this you'll never be out of work. There's more than you were expecting in that envelope. It's self-interest, not generosity. You're too good to lose and if someone else gets their eye on you they'll offer you more than we did at first. I don't want to see you working for Dupont or Chevalier, so I've matched what they'd be likely to give you. Just remember you didn't have to ask, eh?'

It was the start of a euphoric couple of months. The pay was still not wonderful, but Eliane was able to buy her screen and start building up a decent wardrobe. And she followed Geneviève's strategy for acquiring admirers with considerable success.

All went well until the autumn. Then the unthinkable

happened. Three successive mornings of nausea and weakness convinced Eliane she was pregnant. Panic-stricken, she met Geneviève for their regular Sunday lunch date at the Rivoli bar-restaurant. For once she was deaf and blind to her young military admirers. 'How soon can we decently leave, Geneviève? There's something I have to tell you.'

She had no need to say any more. Geneviève had been through enough close calls herself to recognise the symptoms of unwanted motherhood in Eliane. They had a couple of drinks to preserve some pretence of normality, then left, pleading a family visit. Back in the Rue Franchot apartment, Geneviève brewed coffee and heard her fears confirmed.

'What am I to do? I can't look after a kid and work in the shop, even if the Chaillots would consider keeping me. In any case, imagine trying to raise a baby in that hole! I did just what you said, never missed. Can I really be pregnant?'

'Darling, I told you it wasn't absolutely certain and warned you not to go all the way at your most dangerous time. Did you?'

'No, I . . . oh, Christ, I must have! It must have been that Henriot boy with the gorgeous dark eyes. Too much champagne and singing and a perfect June night. What a silly little fool I am!'

'Yes, dear. Well, now we know you have a weakness for champagne and dark eyes, let's concentrate on doing something about it! If you can face it, I know a midwife who'll help you get rid of it, but she made a mess of one girl I know. I'd hate that to happen to you.'

'So would I! Look, what if I went through with it? I'm strong and small. It wouldn't show. If only we could do something about the kid once it was born . . .'

Geneviève's eyes were sombre. 'We could, but remember how you grew up. Would you let any kid of yours go through that?'

'Not a chance! No, I mean would there be some way of

getting it decently placed? If there were, perhaps I could manage.'

'I don't see why not. God knows with the skeletons in our family closet, no one's going to call you names for adding another little bastard to the list. Mama is a good enough soul, if a bit poor. With enough money to care for the baby, she'd do it like a shot. It wouldn't need to be forever. As soon as we were on a firmer footing we could make other arrangements.'

'We? I can't ask you to take on any responsibility in this. You've enough on your hands getting yourself up the ladder.' Geneviève had managed to realise her plan of working through a house of assignation and was now entertaining select clients through the offices of a good-looking widow with a house nearby.

'I told you a long time ago that if you ever needed me, I'd be there. Listen, I've been thinking. If you go on as long as you can at Chaillot's, wearing a good corset to hide the bulge, when you get near your time you can come here. We'll get you into the hospital to have the baby, then back here to stay for a couple of weeks while we get ready for Mama to take it. After that we'll provide the cash between us to look after the brat, and if the Chaillots have kept your job open you go back to it.'

'What if they dismiss me?'

'You don't give them a chance, girl. When you think you can't go on any more, say you have to go back to the country to nurse Ninette. Someone will have to do it soon, anyhow. Tell Madame Chaillot you'll be gone at least three months, but if she wants you afterwards you'll be glad to return. If she says she can't hold the job, ask for a reference for when you start again. She can hardly refuse and once you've got a written testimonial you'll have no trouble getting another job in Saumur. The Chaillots have a reputation for shrewdness. If they recommend you, you're bound to be good.'

Geneviève managed to answer every objection Eliane could produce. She relaxed for the first time in days and started looking beyond the blackness of the next few months. She was still young and still determined to make good. Why should a little thing like a baby stop her?

Deep in the winter she wondered why she had ever felt so optimistic. Geneviève helped her along and Eliane was right about her own physical strength, but her room was primitive and the need to save meant she could no longer spice up the drabness of her days with expensive treats. For a while she had continued her discreet little affairs, but all too soon Geneviève warned her to desist in case one of her lovers noticed her changing shape and spread the word that she was pregnant.

She continued as a part-time artiste until she was more than seven months pregnant. Even then her condition was not obvious, but Eliane was getting tired more easily now and she wanted to reserve all her flagging energy for the shop. It was vital that Madame Chaillot continued to regard her as a skilful and conscientious worker.

It was not difficult to give up the theatre. After the novelty of her first few appearances, she became just another little girl with stars in her eyes. Eliane learned quickly that she did not possess the spark which drew the attention of an audience to a potential star, however small her part. She quit in mid-January and managed to hold out in the shop until the end of February. Her tight corset and small frame enabled her to keep her secret, but it was getting harder. Finally, with what Geneviève was contributing, she decided she had enough to survive until after the birth and went to announce her departure to Madame Chaillot.

Her employer, down for her weekly visit from the large shop in the smarter part of Saumur, listened impassively. When Eliane had finished the tale of her sick sister, she said: 'If you are not going out immediately after you close tonight, I will come and see you for a few minutes. Is that convenient?'

'Of course, Madame. I hope there is nothing wrong.'

'Nothing to worry about. I simply want to talk to you.'

Later, she arrived on Eliane's threshold with a small bottle of very good cognac and two glasses. The girl offered her a seat and Madame poured them each a drink.

'To your new baby, my dear. I hope you are able to return after its birth.'

Eliane let out an involuntary gasp. 'Oh, you know! I thought I was keeping it well hidden.'

'My dear child, you are. If you were not, believe me, you would no longer be employed here. My husband has no idea about your condition. I don't think it would bother him personally but he wouldn't let you stay while you were expecting, in case one of our lady customers noticed. I admire your guts in handling it as you have – and I'm interested in the child.'

'You're what? Whatever for?'

'I have a daughter, Mademoiselle Doré, married to a linen draper in Rennes. She is twenty-five and can never have children. The unhappiness is forcing her and her husband apart and I think that only a baby will help them. But I'm not happy about them taking a foundling. I want to know where my grandchild comes from.'

Hope leapt wildly within Eliane but she had to surmount all the obstacles first. 'You hardly know where this one is coming from!'

'Oh, but there you are wrong, girl! I know everything that goes on in this town. You come from good sturdy peasant stock. You're strong, healthy and very clever. And the boys you go around with are hardly scum, are they? You have to be well-heeled to be a cavalry officer in Saumur garrison.'

Blushing, Eliane agreed.

'Well then, if I can't have a grandchild who's my own flesh and blood, yours is good enough for me. Complete your arrangements as you planned, but when you are ready to part with the baby, I'll take charge of it. Of course, I'll pay you all the time you're away and the apartment will be yours again when you're ready to come back.

The story about your sick sister will do as an explanation for your boyfriends and the people in the neighbourhood. One more thing: does the father know? No, I guessed as much. Good. We can keep it between ourselves.'

So, miraculously, it was arranged. Two weeks after Eliane gave birth in a charity hospital at Rennes, Adèle and Edouard St-Meurice came to claim their adopted son. It was ten years before Eliane saw him again.

# Chapter Eight

## Doré

## 1907–1911: Knight On a White Charger

Pregnancy and motherhood wrought changes in Eliane. They were not physical, her boyish shape returned within a couple of weeks of the birth, but the whole episode gave her a sense of invulnerability. Madame Chaillot's intervention seemed ordained by Providence, and however hard Geneviève tried, she was unable to convince Eliane that she was just another little girl who had got lucky, instead of a favourite of Fortune.

'I know you think I'm crazy, but I feel it here –' Eliane rubbed her midriff. At least she doesn't think it's in her heart, reflected Geneviève – 'I'm just like one of those girls Decourcelle writes about in the newspaper serials. You know, they have all sorts of terrible adventures but in the end they're recognised for their true worth and the hero carries them off to a life of luxury.'

'You're not just optimistic, you need to be certified if you believe that!' Geneviève was aghast. Her little Eliane, tough as old shoe leather, confessing to a liking for those sugary bits of nonsense in the papers, and believing the same thing could happen to her? She must be joking.

It seemed she was not. 'You wait and see, Doubting Thomas. I shall go about my business quietly, not expecting anything, and one day, pouf! The man of my dreams will sweep all this away!'

'But you've always said there *is* no man of your dreams!' Geneviève was getting exasperated now.

'Well, I meant for messing about with me, you know . . . I like having them around, I just think it's a bit of a waste of time when they start taking my clothes off and fiddling around. I don't think heroes do that sort of thing, do they?'

'Eliane, you have better cause than most to know that *all* men do that sort of thing. Why do you think the hero carried off the heroine in the first place, to play hopscotch?'

Now Eliane was getting exasperated, too. 'If you're going to be so cynical there's no point in carrying on with this conversation. You just wait and see. I shall try not to say I told you so.'

Geneviève dissolved the tension by bursting out laughing. 'Okay, kid, you win. If it makes you happy, you believe that. I only hope a little of it comes true. God knows you deserve it a bit easier now.'

A gentle spring unfolded into the most perfect summer either girl could remember. The wonderful garden country of the Loire bloomed fatly and they blossomed in its warmth. It was just what Eliane needed after the cold and worry of the previous winter. Freed from the need to provide for the baby, she was even reasonably comfortable financially, particularly when she resumed her casual liaisons with the cavalry officers.

Once Geneviève was satisfied she did not miss her son or harbour any daydreams about reclaiming him, she started trying to assure a less hazardous future for Eliane. Geneviève's own existence was developing along the lines she had hoped. A casual introduction to Gabrielle Printemps set her on course. Madame Printemps was a respectable widow with good connections and a solid town house on the island suburb of Saumur, the Faubourg des Ponts. The etiquette of coquetry said that to attract an affluent male protector of the right type, a girl had to have plusher surroundings than Geneviève's modest apartment. Although her easy virtue was an essential element of her way of life, she must outwardly appear respectable and comfortably off. If she aspired to become a kept woman, Geneviève must become inaccessible to casual admirers.

Hence the respectable female chaperone. Hence the assignations at this chaperone's house.

To the participants in this odd set of social conventions, there was nothing contradictory about the fact that having met his lady at such a house, the suitor would then take her to a bedroom, undress and make love to her with as much abandon as if she were a shopgirl and he a young cavalry officer. All those involved would have been horrified had anyone suggested that Madame Printemps was actually a procuress. At worst, she saw herself as a well-connected widow whose reduced circumstances turned her to match-making in search of a little extra income. It was irrelevant to all of them that this match-making was never intended to end in the marriage bed.

Now Geneviève was interested in drawing Eliane into a similar arrangement. The conventions of this odd world said that Madame Printemps could not decently chaperone both of them – presumably that would make her look too much like the procuress she really was. No, they would need to find a similar lady for Eliane, but she was not at all sure that such an arrangement appealed to her.

'What do you have against it?' Geneviève asked, exasperated. 'I can't see any other way for you to get out of the rut. In a year or so you'll have been here as long as I was before you arrived, and you won't be able to go on as the toast of the cavalry school much longer than that.'

'I don't intend to, and I'm not running down the understanding you have with Madame Printemps. That works fine for you, but it wouldn't for me.'

'Don't say Longchamps put you off older men? You never mentioned it before.'

'No, it's not that, it's men in general. I know I spend all my spare time with them now, being the life and soul of the party, but that's different. In a way what happens in bed doesn't seem to matter. They like me because I make them laugh and I'm pretty. I have to tell you I'm no Cleopatra when they get me on my own.'

'Who says you have to be? With most of them, looking

as pretty as you do, all you need to do is lie down and be available. If you're a bit slow to respond it's still an improvement on their wives; they've been known to fight the men off!'

'You won't understand, will you, Geneviève? I'm trying to tell you something important. What you're doing works all right for you, and sooner or later you'll be lucky and find one man to keep you in high style. God knows, you're lovely enough. But if that happened to me, I'd feel I'd been sold into slavery. I can't ever put myself so much in a man's hands. I'd feel trapped like I did all those years in the convent.'

A great sadness swept over Geneviève, not for herself but for Eliane. 'Oh, little girl, you still have to grow up. What else does either of us have to offer except our looks and our quick little brains? The trouble is that the quick little brains aren't trained for anything but pleasing lovers and working in shops. The shops will never make us rich but the lovers might. I know it's hardly a perfect world, but it's the only chance we've got. Unless you do something like this, you'll end up a tart or a dirt-poor middle-aged shop assistant. I know which I'd prefer.'

'I don't pretend I've got an answer, I just know I can't face finding my own Madame Printemps yet. You said yourself I've got a year or so more, so give me time to find my feet. I'll think of something.'

It was the summer she discovered the races. Saumur, with its reputation as an equestrian centre, attracted all the rich horsy young men who wanted to acquire the cachet of a cavalry regiment background and to indulge their love of horses. Naturally there was a racetrack, and naturally her young admirers invited her to join them there.

Eliane loved it. Her first sight of the graceful thoroughbreds with their gaily liveried jockeys convinced her she must learn to ride. In the meantime it was enough to watch and thrill to the competition. Geneviève no longer accompanied her on such adventures. They met decorously now at the older girl's apartment, although they remained as close as ever. When they met in public, Geneviève was invariably accompanied by Madame Printemps. Eliane's honour guard of cadets and officers would bow respectfully, acknowledging the altered status of their erstwhile companion, Geneviève and Eliane would exchange a secret wink, and both parties would go about their separate business. Somehow, though, it always left Eliane feeling slightly depressed.

Emerging from such an encounter at the racetrack one Sunday, she allowed herself to be drawn over to where a group of jockeys and enthusiasts were discussing the horses – not regarded as an acceptable pastime for a lady.

'Come on, Eliane, you must meet Christi – you'll love him. At least, I'm pretty sure he'll love you! Never mind the jockeys, we'll never separate him from them. Come on!'

Moments later she was shaking hands with a stocky young man, casually dressed in expensive civilian clothes. She was surprised.

'Oh – uh – Monsieur de Selincourt, why did I think you were a cavalryman? Your friends gave me the impression you were a member of the regiment.'

'I was, until about three days ago. Then I gave it all up for love – no Mademoiselle, don't run away,' he added, laughing. 'Love of horses, not of a lady!'

'But surely the cavalry's the best place to be if you love horses?'

'Other people's, yes. Your own, no. I said I'd serve my time, and I did. But my horses are my life and it's time I got back to them. So this week I kissed the cavalry goodbye and here I am, ready to be a sportsman again. Have you any objection to being seen in the company of a mere civilian?'

She gave him her most bewitching smile. 'On the contrary, M'sieur. I'd value your expert opinion. I was just wondering how I'd have to go about learning to ride. Perhaps you could advise me.' Bowing, he smiled his assent and offered his arm. She took it and swept away from her posse of military escorts, oblivious to their semi-serious cries of protest.

Within moments she got a demonstration of his commitment to horses. He had two competing in that week's race meeting; one outsider running that afternoon, the other favourite in tomorrow's big race. De Selincourt was to ride the favourite himself. One of his team of jockeys was taking the outsider today. She went with him to inspect the horse before it lined up to start. The big silver grey mare was plunging and jibbing, the jockey virtually unable to control her. De Selincourt quietened the beast and ordered the rider to dismount. They exchanged a few heated words and he ordered the little man back to the changing rooms.

The trainer, perplexed, hurried over. 'What're you doing, Christi? We haven't time for any messing around this close to the start.'

De Selincourt was seething with rage. 'Might as well not run her as put that snivelling little bastard up! I know Shantung will never be a Derby winner but she's all right when she knows who's boss. That ninny always lets the brute take over.'

'He's the only ninny we've got, Christi. What else have you in mind? Scratch our entry?'

''Course not. I'll take her.'

'You? Come off it, you barely make the weight! Shantung was doubtful with Pierre's featherweight on her back. With you up she'll come in miles behind.'

'We'll soon see about that! I haven't brought my whip. Give me your cane.' He snatched the fine silver-topped cane carried by the dandified trainer and snapped it before the horrified man could protest. 'Too long to use as it was,' he growled. Without further ado he took off his jacket, handed it to Eliane, said 'Back in a few minutes,' and strode off towards the changing rooms.

He returned soon, more dashing than ever in his colours, kingfisher and black shirt with a black cap.

'Why did you make me hold your jacket if you were going to change anyway?' asked Eliane.

'You might have got bored and gone away if I'd left you empty-handed. Now you have to stay and watch the race. Georges will look after you, otherwise I shan't replace his broken cane!'

De Selincourt relieved her of the jacket and passed it over to the trainer. Then he mounted Shantung and left them together as he headed for the start line, calling over his shoulder, 'See you at the winning post!'

She turned to Georges. 'Well, M'sieur, you seem to have an unwanted guest for the race. I'm sorry if you have other things to do.'

He gave her a broad smile. 'Nothing as pleasant as keeping you company, Mam'selle. If you get to know Christi any better you'll find this is typical behaviour. I'd had that cane all of three weeks! Come on, I'll find us a good place to watch the race.'

While they waited for the start, Georges Varenne explained why de Selincourt was so touchy about putting up a good show in today's race. 'One of his factories is just a few miles away and the workers got to hear this would be Christi's first civilian race meeting. Of course, they all decided to come along and support him today – he's very popular with them. But they didn't know his big race was tomorrow and most of them bet on his horse for today. They'll all be back at work tomorrow anyway. When Christi saw that little clown mishandling Shantung just now he had visions of all the lads losing their shirts and he got a bit short-tempered. That's why he's riding.'

Eliane was starry-eyed. 'Just like a Decourcelle hero!'

'Yeah, only Decourcelle never tells you how in real life the hero usually comes in last when he weighs four kilos more than the horse should be carrying!'

But nothing could shake Eliane's enchantment. The story had already made her half in love with de Selincourt. What followed completed the infatuation.

There was a sizeable entry and for some time de Selincourt's blue and black silk was swamped in the sea of colour as the tightly bunched riders began to pull ahead of him. He stayed well back and Eliane began to lose faith in her fairytale hero. Then, suddenly, it was as if he had been stung into action. His muscular legs thrust vigorously and his arms flailed demonically, the rhythmic beats of Varenne's broken cane slapping the grey's flank in perfect time with her hoofbeats on the turf. As the mare flashed past the stand the crowd could hear the impact of stick against flesh. They went wild as huge strides took the horse past rival after rival, and then in a final burst of effort she made it first past the post.

Eliane was shrieking encouragement like any of Christian's factory hands. Her enthusiasm was so wild that Varenne had forgotten his own excitement and was watching her, grinning with frank admiration. She blushed and resumed a more lady-like posture. 'I suspect Christi has won more than the race,' he murmured.

As they walked down to the winners' enclosure she was triumphant. 'See? I told you it would be just like a Decourcelle story, and it was.'

'Well, don't expect a Decourcelle meeting down in the enclosure. It won't be like that at all.'

De Selincourt certainly did not look like a triumphant jockey. He still appeared to be in an explosive temper, thrusting the leading rein into Varenne's hand and turning abruptly away. Almost as an afterthought, he said: 'I'm going back to Paris. Pierre can ride the favourite tomorrow. No skill involved there; the horse will do all the work.' Then he was off, as gloomy as if he had trailed the field instead of snatching victory.

Surprise and indignation swept away any reticence that Eliane might otherwise have felt. She dashed after him, instinctively using the diminutive she had heard his cavalry friends calling him. 'Christi – Christi, wait! What on earth's wrong?'

He strode on and she was forced to run to overtake him. Finally, breathlessly tagging along beside him, she repeated her question. He stopped and turned to face her, still furious. 'It's just a waste, that's all, a bloody stupid waste, and unfair to pressurise an ordinary animal to be something special. I shoved that horse further than she should decently be pushed so I wouldn't look an arsehole in front of my factory hands. What a rotten reason to behave like a brute!'

Eliane wanted to burst out laughing and bit back the impulse to say: 'Is that all?' Egocentric that she was, she had thought that at the very least someone had told him she was a tramp and he was brushing her off. Instead it seemed he was angry only with himself. She humoured him.

'Come on, it can't be that bad. Tell me about it.'

The outburst had already calmed him considerably. He made a fist and half-heartedly punched at the air, embarrassed at his own display of feeling. 'Oh, I get like this at times. My temper gets the better of me and I'm damned if I'll let anything beat me if there's something I feel I have to live up to. But when I do it at the price of making a poor dumb animal suffer, I hate myself.'

'But surely the horse is all right? She seemed okay in the enclosure when you handed her over to Georges.'

'No permanent damage; she's probably almost forgotten already that she was pushed too hard. But Shantung isn't in the class of some of the nags she beat today. It was my will that won, not her talent, and that meant she had to suffer unnecessarily. No horse should be made to win a race on anything other than its own capabilities.'

'It sounds as if you think more of horses than you do of people.'

'No doubt at all about that, my dear. They're a bloody sight nicer for one thing. They don't tell lies, drop heavy hints or fail to keep appointments. And above all, they don't expect anything of you.'

'Hey, can you introduce me to a few? My life's been missing friends like that until now!'

His black mood melted and he rewarded her with a smile. 'Mam'selle Doré – Eliane – has anyone ever told you what a bewitching little face you have? You could charm a Calvinist preacher out of a sulk! What are you doing after the races?'

'Well, I'm not going to Paris, that's for sure! Too far for a working girl who has to report for duty on Monday.'

'Paris? Who said anything about Paris?'

'You did, just now, to poor old Georges. Bit his head off and threw your reins at him.'

'Oh, yes, so I did. Well, a chap could change his mind with the prospect of a little civilised company. How about dinner?'

'Delighted. But I'll have to find my escorts again in a minute, otherwise it'll be a walk back to town for me.'

'My dear young lady, permit me to put a miracle of the twentieth century at your service! We'll go back in my motor car.'

Eliane made no attempt to hide her wonder. 'You have an automobile? Oh, how wonderful! Can we go and try it out now?'

He glanced down at his sweat-stained silks, shrugged and laughed. 'Why not? If I'm going to catch pneumonia I already have it, and if you don't mind being seen publicly with a sweaty jockey, I'd love to take you for a drive. Come on, she's over by the paddocks.'

A chauffeur in elegant coffee-coloured livery stood guard beside the car. Race-goers eyed it, some critically but all of them clearly impressed. A motor car was still uncommon enough in the provinces to attract plenty of attention. De Selincourt told the chauffeur to take a little time off, arranged to meet him later near the jockeys' changing rooms, and handed Eliane into the front passenger seat of the vehicle.

'Are you sure you don't mind travelling with the hood down? Your smart clothes will get covered in dust.'

'Let them! This might be my only chance this summer to go for a ride like this and I'm not letting a few dust stains stop me!'

He drove away from the race course and the car popped and snorted around the country lanes. Eventually they stopped in a quiet backwater beside the River Loire. Eliane got out and strolled along the bank while de Selincourt fussed with the motor for a few minutes. When he joined her, she failed to notice him immediately and went on humming a popular song that had been flitting through her head all day.

'I knew it!' he said. 'You're not a girl at all, you're a little songbird. Hang on while I find a cage to put you in.'

She was only half joking as she said, 'No cages – that's the one thing that'll make this little bird fly away fast!'

'Okay, but from now on you're Alouette, my skylark. Eliane's much too ordinary a name for you.'

She did not try to hide her delight at the endearing nickname. It made her hope that perhaps she had made a permanent impression on Christian de Selincourt.

She saw Christian every evening that week. Each time she asked when he was leaving Saumur, he put the date farther ahead. 'I've no pressing business anywhere this week – I prefer to stay here and lead you astray.'

'Well, I admire your persistence, considering your progress so far!'

While receiving his attentions with grace and pleasure, Eliane had kept their encounters romantic but chaste. She was unsure why or even how she had managed this, because when she liked a young man enough to go out with him she invariably took him back to her apartment and her bed. She told herself that her delay must have something to do with the unavailability of Geneviève's apartment until Friday. De Selincourt was not an admirer she would care to introduce to the rooms above the mercer's shop. But at heart she sensed that he was special, and was reluctant to spoil the delicacy of their flirtation.

As he was staying with highly respectable friends of his dead guardian, the possibility of his taking her home did not arise, so the main initiative remained with Eliane. While making sure that she understood the strength of his interest in her, de Selincourt made it clear that, at least for the moment, any further advance in their relationship was strictly in her gift.

The mercer's shop in the Rue Gilbert closed a little earlier on Thursdays than the rest of the week. When she had locked up, Eliane hurried around to meet Geneviève at her apartment, to tell her of her latest conquest and arrange to use the apartment for the next few nights.

Geneviève was impressed by the girl's news. 'Hold on to him, darling. He's your best catch so far. I've heard about young Master Christi in Madame Printemps's salon. He does terrible things to my gentlemen's tempers! They think that someone as rich and eligible as de Selincourt should be proposing to their daughters, not galloping about on expensive horses in between propositioning the likes of Eliane Doré.'

'Then he's not pulling my leg about being rich?'

'Eliane, where did you learn to be so cynical? Of course he isn't pulling your leg. How do you think he comes by his automobile and horses and servants – hires them for the day to impress you, perhaps? He's one of the richest young men in the Western Loire, unmarried and determined to remain so. He has an eye for the girls only second to his craze for horses. He must be really nuts about you if he's kept his hands off you since Sunday. I'd start to consider a graceful surrender if I were you. He could be your passport from behind the counter.'

The same thought had occurred long ago to Eliane, but she had not dared to believe in his wealth until Geneviève confirmed it. Loth though she was to admit it, there was something else about Christian de Selincourt that all her previous admirers had lacked. He was the first ever to have excited her. She was puzzled and intrigued by the headiness of her emotions. She who was always so hard-headed, always ready to give the most ardent man only what he could buy, and then to wait with scarcely-concealed impatience for him to be done – here she was fluttering at the thought of de Selincourt's strong horseman's hand on her arm, of his breath warm against her cheek. Why? What was so special about him?

Realisation came in a flash as she watched him exercising one of his horses at the cavalry school later that evening. He was the first man of talent and ability she had known. The others had been bourgeois nonentities. Christi shared the financial security of the haute bourgeoisie but his talent as a horseman was all his own. And his unaffected manners sprang from a depth of human understanding unusual in a man of such privileged background. His straightforwardness was a mixed blessing, although Eliane adored it. He thought nothing of using the language of the stable yard in the drawing-room and Eliane's immunity to his verbal coarseness was one of her many attractions for him. He had known ladies and demi-mondaines who had fled from his uncouth tongue and he had despised them for it. He treated his grooms, his men and women friends alike, and those who expected him to behave more conventionally were quickly shaken off.

De Selincourt also had an enlightened attitude to sex. He made no bones about finding Eliane desirable but he was quite prepared to wait until she was ready for a more intimate encounter. The obverse of his casual toughness was an intuitive understanding of mutual physical attraction and he knew that the girl was his given a little time and the illusion that the initiative was hers alone. He did not have to wait much longer.

On Friday evening he took her out to supper, as he had every night that week. But tonight her heightened mood seemed to have communicated itself to him. Instead of one of the bright, noisy establishments in the centre of Saumur, he had arranged for them to eat at a lovely old inn on the banks of the Loire a few miles out of town. Even his beloved motor was banished for the evening as unsuitable for a romantic encounter. When he called at Geneviève's apartment for Eliane, he did so with an immaculately turned-out carriage and pair. Eliane was starry-eyed as he handed her into it.

'And now, Mademoiselle Alouette, we shall find a forest grove appropriate to your beauty,' he announced grandly, 'and I shall ply you with the finest corn to plump up your feathers!'

She giggled deliciously. 'I can't wait – quick, drive out of this boring town before the magic forest disappears!'

As they drove she looked at him intently, trying to analyse what it was about him that appealed to her so much. De Selincourt was sturdy and well-knit, of no more than average height but radiating strength and self-confidence. He was square-jawed, with a high forehead. His hair and eyes were an everyday shade of brown and he wore the sort of moustache which was virtually standard to all young men of his age at the time. At first glance there was nothing particularly remarkable about him. She decided that most of his charm lay in the way he moved. He radiated controlled energy. All his movements were accomplished economically and he always appeared to have reserves of untapped strength. His sudden outbursts of temper did not detract from this appeal; they simply reinforced the feeling of energy building up behind the relaxed façade. He was the only person Eliane had ever met who appeared to have a store of vitality to equal her own.

They dined on a terrace hung with vines overlooking the river. As the waiter left them to their first bottle of champagne, de Selincourt played the stage seducer.

'And now, to tempt the innocent little bird to forget her nest, some exquisite oysters from the Breton beds, to excite you beyond measure!'

Eliane had eaten oysters as a child, but never in the appropriate surroundings. She had been introduced to the rare delicacy at a stall run by one of her mother's relatives down on the Quiberon sea front. The old oyster-man had shucked the shells off some Belons with expert twists of his short-bladed knife. She remembered the bloodiness of his gnarled hands and how he had told her that even the most skilled openers constantly cut themselves on the fiercely closed shells. Even in that bleak wintry setting the taste had been divine. Now, with the appropriate background, it was nearly magical. She ate a dozen and would have accepted more had not de Selincourt warned her of the large meal to come.

'Never eat too much of the best, little one. Why suppose there's not something even better to come, and limit one's expectations?'

De Selincourt had chosen an elaborate seduction supper but had the experience to order it in tiny quantities. The result was a gastronomic symphony in which each course led Eliane on to the next in childlike delight. Jellied consommé was another wonder. 'It looks like a big puddle of amber!' she cried, clapping her hands in pleasure. Then there were crayfish cooked in champagne, and a spring chicken sautéd with fresh herbs. After a few leaves of lightly-dressed green salad, they finished with *fraises* Marguerite, tiny wild strawberries on a bed of pomegranate ice.

'Pomegranates to melt your resistance,' Christi told her, then chuckled. 'It's no use, little Alouette, you make me want to smile each time I look at you. Can you pretend I said those lines in the best seducer's manner?'

'Only if you twirl your moustache – it doesn't count otherwise. Anyway, you rogue, what d'you mean by saying I make you smile? Is my poor monkey face so frightful?'

'Not like that, idiot! I just feel as though you're my best friend and every time I try to say something stupid or pretentious it's as if you're looking right through me and I want to laugh with you.' Abruptly he became serious. 'It still doesn't stop me from wanting to make love to you, Eliane. Don't you like me that way?'

She steered him back towards light-heartedness. 'Which way would that be? Do I gather that your intentions are anything but honourable, M'sieur? What would my governess say?'

That set him laughing again. 'Listen, I've been fighting the temptation to say this, but the hell with it! I've never gone much on caution so why spoil the habits of a lifetime now? I have to leave Saumur on Sunday evening. Why not come with me? I'd like to have you around all the time, Alouette.'

Why did she hesitate? Here was the golden opportunity. Without even trying very hard she had been offered a chance to leap-frog the complex diplomacy of a house of assignation straight into the home of a rich, vigorous, amusing young lover. What more could any penniless shop girl ask? And yet she hesitated.

'Give me a little time, Christi. No –' she raised her hand to hush his immediate protest – 'I'm not turning you down. I'd be very happy if you came back to the apartment with me tonight, but I must think carefully before following you from Saumur. A girl who makes you laugh for a few days is one thing. A girl you have to support and see every day is quite another. What would happen to me if you tired of me?'

He was exasperated. 'I'm mad about you and already you're asking what will happen when I lose interest! I'm no villain, Alouette. Trust me.'

'I've never dared trust anyone, don't you understand? There's never been anyone to trust except myself. I daren't, Christi, I just daren't. But that doesn't mean we can't enjoy the champagne and . . . and other things. Cheer up, I'm not running away.'

They clip-clopped back to Saumur in the warm summer darkness and strolled through silent streets to Geneviève's cosy flat after leaving the rig at the local livery stable. During the journey their easy companionship had been re-established and now it felt natural for him to go into the apartment with her. She fetched cognac and glasses from the cupboard and went to set the coffee brewing. De Selincourt had waited long enough for an extra half-hour or so not to matter. She slipped off to the bedroom to undress. Eventually she called him in. One lamp shed soft golden light across the big bed and she stood wrapped in a long robe of crisp embroidered cotton cutwork, looking wonderful.

He reached out to her. 'I've been wanting to do this since

the first time I saw you without a hat on.' He took the combs and clips from her hair and it cascaded about her like an ebony waterfall, reaching below her hips. The nuns had never managed to get her anywhere near the fair-ground barbers' tents after that first time. Her marvellous tresses were thick and heavy and needed no artificial padding to form the fashionable piled-up hair style. As a result, when the pins were dislodged, it really did tumble free as the romances described, instead of hanging lank and spiky.

De Selincourt picked up a long strand and caressed his face with it. 'It smells like a hayfield, all fresh-cut grass,' he said.

She smiled and nuzzled gently against him. 'As long as it doesn't look like one.'

He picked her up and carried her over to the bed, laying her down gently then reaching over to unbutton the white robe. Eliane's skin had a naturally dark cast and showed up smooth and golden against the whiteness of the garment and the surrounding bedlinen. 'My little brown Arab,' he said softly. 'Christ, Alouette, you're beautiful!'

He knelt over her for a moment, studying her small, softly rounded breasts and flat belly. He took a lock of her own hair and stroked her body with it. She wriggled convulsively and giggled. 'Ouch! That tickled! Don't be so unromantic!'

'I've never felt more romantic in my life. Just stay still, don't move an inch. I'll be with you in a moment.' Hastily he took off his clothes. She watched him, for the first time looking at a prospective lover with anticipation instead of contempt. He turned back to her in time to catch an expression of concentration on her face. 'What are you thinking about, my love?'

'I just couldn't get over what a tiny little bum you've got.'

'Wretch! Here's something that's not so tiny!' He bounded on to the brass bed and pressed her hand against his penis. It was swollen and stiff, eager for her, and she responded immediately, sighing with excitement as his hard hands slid over her.

Eliane relaxed on to her back, expecting his full weight to fall on her, but he raised her to a half-sitting position. 'No, I want to see you all the time, my beauty. Up on your knees, come on . . .' He positioned her so that she was kneeling astride him. 'That's better! Now gently, gently, just - sit - uhh - oh, that's wonderful!'

She had never experienced anything quite like it before. The stance pressed her forward, stimulating her to intense enjoyment, but the position of physical dominance also added to Eliane's pleasure. For once she had no sense of being exploited or possessed. She felt more like a feather-light jockey, riding a big powerful steed. The image was so compelling that it heightened her excitement until she was carried away on a huge wave of physical sensation.

De Selincourt was gazing up at her through half-closed eyes, caressing her cloak of black hair with one hand and the golden flesh of her clenched thigh with the other. A moment after her own passion exploded in a tidal wave of sensations, his climax came and he reared up convulsively beneath her before relaxing, sweating and trembling.

Very gently, he reached up and lifted her so that once more she lay beside him. 'I never knew a little bird who could do that before, but I'm glad I've found one now! Will you sing like that again when I ask?'

'Just try me! I might even have second thoughts about that trip.'

But it took him longer than three days to make her commit herself so irrevocably. In the end he departed alone that week-end, but he returned with increasing frequency. Eliane tried to pick up the threads of her previous existence but somehow the young officers seemed mere boys next to Christi, and the love-making which previously had been little more than a tiresome chore became actively distasteful to her now that she had a standard of real sensual pleasure against which to judge it.

Early in September Christian de Selincourt marched

briskly into the shop one Monday morning. Barely waiting for the solitary woman customer to depart, he said: 'Right, my skylark, you have until the end of this week to say your farewells to Madame Chaillot and anyone else you care to name, then I'm kidnapping you. No arguments this time. I miss you. You're coming to live at Gaillard and I don't want any arguments.'

That was before she knew about Ottilie Deslys.

The day Eliane left Saumur was bleak and autumnal. Down on the *quais* it was beautiful, but her spartan rooms reflected none of this. On her last day she stood at the threshold, trying to focus on something which would produce affectionate memories of the life she was leaving. There was nothing. The cracked pane in the dormer window overlooking the street still made a faint whistling sound as the harsh north-east wind infiltrated the gap. The enamel washbowl which stood with its matching jug on the rickety table still showed an ugly chipped spot. Now that she had sent her pretty screen and curtains to Geneviève's apartment, there was only one attractive item in the room – a lace-trimmed white linen runner on the dresser. Momentarily she was tempted to take it. She reached out for the piece of white cloth, then stopped, contemptuous of her own pettiness. She was hardly poor enough to strip this hovel of its only pleasant feature. Eliane picked up her cardboard suitcase, turned her back on the sordid flat and started down the stairs towards her new life.

When she saw Gaillard, her superstitious nature insisted it was her reward for not stealing the linen runner. The estate was glamorous beyond her wildest imaginings. Deer roamed in the endless acres of parkland; an avenue of grotesquely gnarled Spanish chestnuts guided visitors up to the fairytale house which was the home of her Prince Charming. Here all the linen was crisp and sparkling. Beds were heaped with fat feathery quilts. Fresh flowers appeared miraculously in painted vases on the window sills. All the newspapers were laid out in the library. Coffee and croissants appeared each morning. Plates of wafer thin sandwiches were left out for her at night. Food and drink were constantly at hand, no matter how late or how early the hour.

Above all, Eliane gazed wonderingly at the autumn landscape. In the Saumur backstreets it had been bleak and cold. Here in Gaillard the trees were bronze and gold and flame red. The sky was steely blue and sunshine glowed on the forest ponds.

'Why is it so much brighter here?' she asked Christian.

'It's the shine of freshly-minted money, my love. New francs can put a sparkle on the dullest day!'

She nodded silently, impressed by the eternal truth he had expressed to her in one throwaway remark. It was to be the central axis of her new philosophy of life.

But even the Garden of Eden had a serpent. Gaillard had Ottilie Deslys. She was a magnificent sight, virtually a collector's piece from another age. She was one of the *grandes horizontales*, courtesans who also made careers on the Paris stage, either in light opera or in the theatre. Fabulously rich, thanks to affairs with some of France's wealthiest aristocrats, she boasted one of Europe's finest collections of diamonds and pearls. Christian de Selincourt had enjoyed a long-standing sexual relationship with her which varied in its intensity according to any other current involvements of either party. He had told Eliane that Ottilie spent quite a lot of time at Gaillard, but hearing of their mellow relationship, Eliane had convinced herself that the older woman was no more than a platonic friend. One look made it clear that she would never be that.

At thirty-two, Ottilie was at the height of her beauty and had enough real talent to have carved herself a career on the musical stage which did not rest on her success in the bedroom. She was tall – almost five feet ten – and heroically built, with the monumental breasts of her calling and thighs apparently made to subdue spirited stallions, equine or human. Her glossy caramel-coloured hair complemented peachy skin and shining chestnut eyes. She looked like a deliciously edible human dessert.

She was not amused when de Selincourt introduced her to Eliane. Momentarily the warm brown eyes were hard as pebbles, then she forced an apparently friendly smile. 'Alouette, eh! How appropriate.' She broke into song, her rich voice tugging suggestively at the words:

*'Alouette, gentille alouette;*
*Alouette, je te plumerai!'*

Little lark, pretty little lark, little lark, I'll pluck you clean!

'And he will, too, you wait. He eats little girls like you for after supper snacks and spits out the bones by breakfast time. You have to be big and strong and independent to survive with Christi, not a skinny little nobody with nothing but a sexy backside.'

De Selincourt had moved over to watch a horse in the paddock and had caught only Ottilie's snatch of song. He turned back to the two women with a tolerant smile. 'Don't tease the kid, Ottie. It's all new to her and you're a bit overpowering to people who don't know you!' Then he turned back to the horses.

'That's nothing to the way I can be when you know me better, unless you're a man.' Ottilie spoke in an undertone, with a friendly smile pasted on her face. De Selincourt assumed she was being kind and took no further notice. Satisfied he was out of earshot, Ottilie continued: 'Listen, kid, if I were you I'd push off back where you came from. There's only crumbs for you here. Christi's all heart, he collects waifs and strays, but if you have ideas about being the châtelaine around here, forget them. The position's taken.' She wheeled away and stalked regally back to the house, treating Christian to a glowing smile on the way.

De Selincourt strolled back to Eliane, who stood numb and shaking. 'See, I told you she gets on with everyone.

We'll all rub along together without any trouble just so long as you understand that one woman at a time has never been enough for me, and I'm unlikely to change now. Ottie's a great sport.'

'Yes . . . I can see that. Perhaps you shouldn't have brought me here, Christi. It might not work out.'

'Silly girl, of course it will! She knows she's not threatened. I'm very fond of you and I want to look after you for as long as you enjoy being here. But when she's around – which isn't all that often – Ottie's the grande dame. She heads the table and greets the guests. If that makes you upset we'll just have to spirit you somewhere else while she's holding court. God knows, this place is big enough! Come on, forget about all that now. Take a look at some really lovely horseflesh.'

Experience had taught Eliane not to cry when girls of more delicate sensibility might have done. Forcing a smile she followed Christian, making herself appear interested in what he said and captivated by the beasts he showed her so proudly. She was beginning to realise that Ottilie's remarks might have been the unvarnished truth, not, as she had first assumed, the malice of a woman threatened with displacement. If she was to survive with Christian, she must give the impression that she was happy with her role here. He was not at all the considerate romantic she had believed him to be.

The stables were a useful distraction from her misery. Eliane's pretence of interest in them worked on de Selincourt and after a while she found herself being carried along by it too. Christian was a mine of information about horses. His animals were magnificent and as Eliane was introduced to horse after horse as if they were people, she caught his enthusiasm like a disease. Soon she had forgotten Ottilie Deslys's existence – or at any rate had pushed it to the back of her mind. She wanted to ride these lovely animals, to learn how to take care of them and to have them welcome her as companions. Suddenly she realised that de Selincourt had stopped talking and was watching her with an odd smile on his face. As she returned his look with a level stare, he laughed outright.

'Well, I'll be damned! You've caught the bug already, haven't you, little skylark? One whiff of horse dung and you were as enslaved by the brutes as I am!'

She nodded. 'Please teach me to ride soon, Christi – please! I can't wait!'

'You can't start just like that, dear girl. Neat tailored skirts and button boots are hardly riding gear. We'll have to get you a proper habit.'

'But that could take ages! Surely all I need is the freedom to swing up into the saddle?'

'Well, not quite, Alouette. If you want to grow up to be a grande dame you have to dress *à l'anglaise* – bowler or top hat, veil, tailored jacket, shirt and cravat, breeches covered decorously by a special wrapover skirt. And of course you have to ride side saddle. I think we have a couple of those but we'll have to buy the clothing.'

'But surely I don't have to dress like that with no one to see me?'

'What makes you think no one'll see you?'

'What would they think I am, your niece from the country? Ottilie's hardly likely to welcome me as a companion on morning gallops. Someone might even think I was *her* niece from the country! So I shall be all alone with nobody to be shocked by my clothes.'

He roared with laughter. 'I think maybe the little songbird has a snarl after all! Well, Mam'selle, what d'you suggest?'

'Look at those grooms over there, Christi. They're about my build, even if they are boys. They must have spare breeches and sweaters and shirts. Why can't I dress like that?'

'Simple – they don't ride side saddle. I couldn't teach you without collapsing every time I looked at you sitting up there sideways in a pair of breeches.'

'Who said anything about a side saddle? I refuse to believe anyone can enjoy riding around on one of these great mountains of muscle when they're only half on. If the idea is to preserve my precious virginity intact, it's a bit late now, isn't it?'

He laughed again. 'You are an impossible child! It's nothing to do with virginity! It's just considered more decorous for ladies to cover their legs, and side saddle is the only position anyone's discovered which permits them to do so.'

'I keep telling you, Christi, no one is going to see me! I might as well make it clear now that as long as Ottilie Deslys is around, I shan't be moving far from the estate. Even if I find we get to be great pals, I don't believe in being seen poaching in someone else's park. So if I'm going to ride around here, it'll be in private. I'll wear boy's clothes and ride astride like the stable lads. Tell you what, though – if it makes you any happier – when you've taught me to ride astride, afterwards we can stick a side saddle on the horse, I'll pin a blanket around me over the breeches and you can show me the way ladies do it, to prepare me for my public début. Will that suit you?'

'Okay, okay, you win.' He shook his head, grinning at her belligerent little face. 'You'll probably try it once, hate it and never mount again anyhow, so none of this will matter.'

He could not have been more wrong. Eliane was a natural horsewoman, with an excellent sense of balance, a light touch and an empathy with the animals which enabled her to learn the basics of horsemanship in next to no time. Few things amused her more than swinging herself on to a horse without saddle or bridle and galloping it around the paddock – a trick that quickly earned her the nickname of the Little Red Indian with the stable lads.

She needed the diversions of riding, her inevitable popularity in the stables, and Christian's surprised admiration of her developing skill. Ottilie Deslys gave her a rough time when she was staying at the château. After a devastatingly humiliating incident designed by the actress to show the little shopgirl who was the real mistress, Eliane accepted at least temporary defeat and kept out of her way as much as possible.

At first she was convinced she had the upper hand over Ottilie without even trying. The illusion did not last long. De Selincourt was moodier than his superficial bonhomie suggested. When he became Eliane's lover, he was in a sentimental frame of mind and treated her as he seldom had any other mistress. Now she discovered that her sensitive dream man shared all too many qualities with the crass young officers of Saumur.

On her first evening, de Selincourt made much of her, showing her off to a couple of his racing cronies, and seeming not to notice when Ottilie made a sweeping departure quite early on. But she was to make a devastating re-entry later.

Eventually Christian climbed the stairs to his bedroom with Eliane plus a bottle of champagne. The great chamber could have been a stage set for seduction, with subtle pink lights and a crackling log fire, satin sheets on the big gilded bed and a general air of boyish sexual fantasy accomplished.

De Selincourt swept Eliane into his arms and laid her down on the bed, then knelt over her to unfasten the small mother of pearl buttons of her dress. He gave a moan of pleasure when he had finished, as if he had just unwrapped a particularly pleasing purchase. 'Come on, little one, help me out of my things, too,' he said. As he spoke he propelled her hand towards his flies, pressing her fingers hard against himself, crushing them between his hand and his already impressive erection.

She was a little clumsy, startled by these minimal preliminaries compared with the finesse he had shown in courting her at Saumur. He writhed against her for a few moments then made an impatient sound, got up and undressed himself. 'All right, now, are you ready?' He turned back and joined her again.

'Christi, you're not usually like this. What's wrong?'

'Nobody's always the same. I'm just ready for it

tonight, that's all. Come on, you're not usually this standoffish!'

He lunged at her, and for the first time ever, she felt panic-stricken at the thought of sex. It had never meant much to her but now, for the first time, she realised she was completely in a man's power. It scared her. Fortunately for her Christi mistook her wriggling for excitement and she managed to subdue the worst of her panic without his noticing that anything was amiss. His strong male body straddled her and his mouth clamped down on hers. His tongue pressed against her teeth, forcing them apart and then filling her mouth. At that point he sensed something of her resistance, and sat back for a moment. Tonight he was definitely different from the Christi she thought she knew. Instead of putting him off, her fear seemed to excite him more. He forced her arms above her head, bent over her and began licking, caressing and biting her breasts and belly. Eliane was getting really scared now and her resistance was beginning to irritate him.

That was when the bedroom door opened to reveal Ottilie. She was changed almost beyond recognition and Eliane did not know whether to hate her even more or welcome her as a saviour. The purpose of her visit was fairly obvious even to a recently retired shopgirl.

Ottilie's chestnut hair hung loose and lustrous down her back. She was clad in the most salacious imaginable parody of a man's riding kit. Thigh-high leather boots like those of a British cavalryman, but made of the finest kid, were worn over white doeskin breeches. Over them was a black satin shirt, open to the waist, baring her big firm breasts. She carried a riding whip.

Striding forward across the big room, she stood looking down at them with an ambiguous half smile. 'Well, Christi, don't say you still haven't licked that stable lad into line! Really, I can't leave anything to you!'

She climbed into the bed, momentarily ignoring de Selincourt and addressing herself directly to Eliane.

'Come on, little Skylark, nothing here to make you flutter! I'm just a girl like you, see?'

With almost hypnotic slowness she lifted one of Eliane's trembling hands and drew the fingers gently inside her satin shirt, moving them rhythmically over her body. 'See? No demons or big bad weapons there. Now, let's give you a little champagne to relax you and you'll feel much friendlier . . .'

She made sure Eliane drank a lot more, then went to work on her again, soothing, stroking, caressing, always moving slowly and reassuringly. When Eliane felt really relaxed, Ottilie's experienced hands and mouth moved over the girl as if she were a sensitive musical instrument. Soon Eliane was quivering with excitement. The actress was covering her body with small, butterfly-light kisses. Eliane opened her eyes momentarily and found herself gazing straight at de Selincourt, who was watching her with mounting excitement.

'Okay, Ottie, that's enough – I want her now!' Before Eliane was fully aware of the change, he was on her again. This time her fear was gone and she sailed away on a wave of pleasure created by Ottilie and consummated by Christian.

Later, she simply wanted to disappear. She could never quite remember afterwards whether she had passed out due to champagne and excitement, or merely drifted off to sleep. She did remember waking several times in the embrace of one or the other of them. Ottilie's skintight riding breeches had been made with an opening along the crotch seam and she made love to them both without removing them or the boots. Eliane did not want to be excited by the woman; she still hated her – more than ever, if anything – but tonight she was literally irresistible and revealed to Eliane sensations she had never experienced with a man. Finally she surfaced to find Ottilie riding de Selincourt around the room piggyback, uninhibitedly slapping his bare buttocks with the riding whip. That was when Eliane slid out of the bed and ran from the room, not pausing until she had locked herself into her own bedroom off the adjoining landing.

Next morning she was downstairs early, sitting out on the terrace in the unseasonably warm autumn sunshine and dunking a croissant in a big bowl of *café au lait*. De Selincourt joined her there. There was no sign of Ottilie. He gave Eliane a light kiss on the top of her head then sat down with his own coffee. He radiated well-being and grinned broadly at her.

'Well, how's Alouette this fine morning? Feeling as good as you look?'

Unable to bottle up her misery and shame, she flung out: 'So that was why you brought me here – as a doll for that old bag!' Then she snapped her mouth shut. Where could she go if Christian turned her out?

But he showed no sign of anger, merely roared with laughter. 'You didn't seem to mind much last night, kid! No, it's not why I brought you here. But I didn't bring you as Ottie's replacement, either. Your trouble is that you don't understand that a man can be changeable, have different needs at different times. Ottie knows that instinctively and works on it. What's more, she enjoys it. That's why she'll always have a string of admirers. Now let's have no more sulks and tantrums. In any case, you're usually a bit slow to get going when we're alone. There was precious little of that last night, was there? You couldn't get enough of it, from her or me. You're quite safe here but not at the top of the heap. One day it might happen, but certainly not yet. Either get used to that or think about moving on, because Ottilie's not going anywhere until she feels like it!'

Still smiling, but clearly meaning every word he said, de Selincourt tossed back his coffee, stood up and turned away towards the stables. 'Don't take life so seriously, Alouette. It's never worth it!'

It is when you're poor and have nowhere to go, she thought bitterly, watching his retreating figure.

* * *

De Selincourt enjoyed entertaining, and apart from his horsy friends knew a lot of people from the world of Paris show business. His estate, in the fashionable horsemen's paradise of the Compiègne Forest, was easily accessible from the capital, so there were frequent visits from his and Ottilie's theatrical friends. When such parties were held at Gaillard, there were suppers and dances where she was as much hostess as if she were Christian's wife. Christi would have had no objection to Eliane's attending them, and Ottilie would have revelled in the girl's semi-public humiliation, but Eliane would not have dreamed of showing herself. The night of the first such party she locked herself in her room and wept bitterly until dawn. Then she went for a ride and did some serious thinking. Tears had never achieved anything for her in the past and she had no illusions that they might do so now. Strategy was better. She set to working one out.

Just as when she and Geneviève had been in trouble in Paris, she concluded that any constructive action, however feeble, was better than lying down and feeling humiliated. If she was excluded from the ballroom by her own pride, she would make use of the servants' hall.

Her first appearance there, the evening of de Selincourt's second house party after her arrival, caused a subdued riot among the servants. But she behaved as though joining them were the most natural thing in the world, asked their permission to share their table and said she would like to learn more about riding from the horsemaster and his lads. From that moment on she had the undying devotion of everyone below stairs. Ottilie Deslys had always been popular with them, for she tipped generously and they enjoyed being able to boast that they knew a famous singer-actress. But Ottilie had never shared their supper and their talk; had never remembered their day-to-day problems and asked about them. Eliane was their new heroine. Mademoiselle Alouette was the rising star of Gaillard.

The next objective was to ease Ottilie from her throne.

If there could be only one queen at Gaillard, Eliane had reserved the role of crown princess for herself and now she set about hastening the succession. Ottilie was seldom around for the smaller race meetings and the informal polo games in the Compiègne area. For her, racing meant dressing herself up in lace and jewels and parading to be admired on the lawns at St Cloud or Longchamp on a Sunday afternoon.

Eliane began to go with de Selincourt to the smaller meetings, but from the beginning she stood out from the other kept women in the most disconcerting way. She dressed simply, almost mannishly. No sweeping lace trains and goffered blouses for her; she had no wish to be taken for a cocotte. For the same reason she kept right away from the fashionable enclosures, staying down close to the paddocks, taking refuge behind her field glasses. She got to know jockeys and trainers, and she got to know de Selincourt's sporting friends.

At first, Christian failed to notice her clothes. Then the good-natured teasing of his friends drew his attention to Eliane's unique appearance. At that point he started giving her a dress allowance. It began after a small mid-week meeting in Compiègne. Eliane had made her usual appearance, in a brown gaberdine skirt with a plain cream shirt-waist blouse, and an untrimmed camel hair coat with topstitched seams, hanging loose to mid-calf length. It resembled the coats worn on cold days by English schoolboys who were too old for the fitted shapes of childhood and too young to aspire to an adult's topcoat. Eliane's outfit was completed by an austere straw boater, soft brown leather gloves and a pair of highly-polished black leather boots. The clothes were admirably suited to the chilly day and to her practice of striding about the course, binoculars slung round her neck, eternally active to disguise the fact that she would not set foot inside the enclosure reserved for the smart set. After the race meeting, when their few mid-week guests had dispersed to change for dinner, Christian held her back.

'Alouette – I've been a bit slow on the uptake, and I'm sorry. Didn't mean to embarrass you . . .'

'About what?'

'Well, you know, clothes. It must be damned awkward for you to dress on the few francs pocket money I hand out. Can't expect you to look like a fashion plate on that. Take this –' he handed her a bulky envelope – 'I'll let you have half what's in there every three months from now on, and you spend it on clothes. If you have any doubts about what to get, order a few fashion magazines from Paris. That should get you started.'

She accepted the envelope without comment, only gasping in surprise when she opened it in the privacy of her room and discovered what a substantial sum it contained. Her first reaction had been irritation that he should imagine her choice of dress was dictated by poverty. True, she could not afford the quality she would otherwise have chosen, but otherwise the style she wore was a perfect reflection of the way she wished to look. But Eliane learned quickly. She had suppressed her indignation and had taken the money. Let Christi find out for himself how she would dress if she could afford it – he'd notice soon enough.

She took a trip to Paris on the strength of de Selincourt's recommendation that she study current fashion. Ottilie had just ensconced herself for three weeks at Gaillard, so Eliane assumed she would scarcely be missed. The city thrilled and intimidated her at the same time. This was no place to be if you were poor and helpless – but if you were rich and independent, what a spectacle! She stayed at de Selincourt's small town apartment, but every morning she would stroll to the Place Vendôme and enjoy her breakfast at a pavement café while she watched the rich guests coming and going from the Ritz. That was the life!

Then she found somewhere that impressed her even more, though she would have died rather than admit it – Galeries Lafayette.

By the 1900s, shopping in Paris had descended from the

heights of exclusivity to scoop up the mass profits lining the pockets of a newly-prosperous middle class. Before the days of the department stores, shopfronts had been tiny and forbidding with minimal window displays. Such items as appeared never bore price tags, so the shy or uninformed seldom dared enter in case the goods on offer were beyond their means. The department stores changed all that. They were constructed as cathedrals of the flesh, with wordly temptation displayed as proudly as the sacraments in a Christian cathedral. Silks, furniture, scents and novelties appeared on dazzling display against an opulent background of white and gold paint and red velvet upholstery.

Galeries Lafayette was literally the collection of galleries implicit in its name. Three tiers soared above a broad ground floor general sales area, the whole emporium topped by fancy cast iron vaulting and a glass dome. Garlands of artificial flowers and fairy lights were slung across the huge open spaces between the opalescent globe lampshades and electroliers which kept the place brightly lit even on the gloomiest day. Uniformed attendants stood at the foot of the central staircase, worthy of a château, which divided around an enormous mezzanine plant stand, its two branches then climbing to serve the galleries on either side. As an alternative for the less energetic shopper, there were passenger lifts lined in pink velvet. Potted palms were arranged everywhere, giving the impression that the shoppers were pursuing their errands within a vast, glamorous conservatory. Between all this grandeur were displayed gloves, feathers and personal ornaments. The more prosaic items were stored in drawers built into mahogany counters and chests.

Galeries Lafayette displayed the smartest clothing it was possible to buy ready-made – although women of substance still preferred custom made clothing from personal dressmakers, unless they could afford to patronise a couture establishment. But, impressed though she was, Eliane had not come for the store's fashionable tea gowns and afternoon frocks. After browsing through the dress showrooms, she moved on to the boys' department.

She approached a salesman who looked young enough to be easily fooled and smiled with assumed self-confidence. 'M'sieur, please help me solve a silly problem which I got into by being too kind-hearted.'

He flushed. She was very pretty. 'If I can, Mam'selle.'

'My younger brother refuses to have his riding kit from the local shop in Compiègne. Because I'm in Paris with Aunt Ottilie –' she enjoyed that bit – 'he insists I should come to you for the clothes. I know he should be here himself to try them on, but I've written down his measurements. D'you think you could . . .?'

'Oblige, Mam'selle? Of course. It will be a pleasure.'

He busied himself among his stock, then returned, a little puzzled. 'I – er – don't wish to embarrass you with any indelicacy, Mam'selle, but it seems . . . that is . . . well, er, his waist seems very small for his, er, other, lower, measurements. Could there be any mistake?'

Alouette lowered her eyelashes modestly and murmured, 'He's had a most unpleasant illness, M'sieur. They had to remove two of the lower ribs to save him. Of course, his waist is abnormally small as a result. It's a cause of considerable distress to him.' She raised her perfect eyes to meet his and smiled piteously. 'I suspect that's really why he was so eager for me to get the things . . . he hates having to explain.'

Now the young man was completely flustered, and enslaved by this divine nymph who would so embarrass herself to save her sickly brother's blushes.

'Say no more, Mam'selle. How very thoughtful of you! Of course, we'll kit him out. Our alteration hands will make any adjustments if stock size cannot accommodate his needs.'

'I regret I cannot stay long enough in Paris for the work to be done. But if you told me which way was best . . . I'm good with a needle but I don't know whether to go for the proper waist size and enlarge – you know – or the other way round and make the waist smaller.'

'It will be my pleasure to arrange for the alteration hand to advise you, at no extra charge.' And Eliane got a free lesson in fitting breeches, learning that it was vitally important to get the right cut in crotch and seat, while the waist could always stand considerable manipulation. The alteration hand took a motherly interest in this eager young customer. 'The main thing with riding breeches is to see no creases show on the inside of the leg when the rider is seated. You should check that out by seeing the garment on the wearer, and get him sitting in the right position before you finish the alterations. If you go for the right leg and hip size from the start, and ignore the waist until later, you don't need to be such an expert to make a good job of the alteration.'

Eliane rewarded the young salesman's courtesy by purchasing half a dozen pairs of breeches. His commission would be substantial. The alteration hand seemed happy enough to have been consulted for once as though she were the fountain of all knowledge instead of a menial. Having dealt with the breeches, Eliane repeated the tale of her sickly brother and bought jackets, shirts and a coat, instructing the store to deliver everything to her at the château. Then she went into the dress fabric department.

Here, she was less self-assured. Her instinct might let her down when it came to competing with the cocottes or the great ladies on their own territory. She knew her slender form looked silly and impoverished under the whalebone and satin that flattered them so much, but the originality which allowed her to see herself looking elegant in boys' clothes abandoned her at the threshold of the ballroom. Then she remembered her gallant gesture of defiance on an earlier trip to Paris. Underwear and shawls had combined as something wonderful then . . . why not work along those lines now? Her thinking turned her away from the dress fabrics and into the haberdashery department, where they also sold lining fabrics and the lightweight silks from which ladies' underwear was made. She bought vast quantities of silk foulard, crêpe-de-chine and mousseline de soie – all materials more closely associated with the boudoir than the salon. Then she selected varying widths of lace and ribbons, always in delicate neutrals or apricots, browns and black. She returned to the dress fabric department and bought lengths of dull but rich basics – a fine cream wool and some tobacco-coloured silk foulard. Finally, as a sort of insurance policy, she bought, ready-made, the most simple and youthful-looking dinner gown she could find. She looked so absurdly young in it that the saleswoman kept asking where her mother was, and whether she had permission to be out choosing her own gowns.

On her way out of the store, Eliane was fascinated by a glimpse of plaster model display heads. They appeared to be showing off the sort of hats she saw at race meetings and in town, but shorn of their elaborate fruit, feather and flower decoration. She turned back for a closer look and discovered she had been looking at the blank hat forms in the specialist haberdashery department normally frequented only by professional milliners or women too poor to buy made-up hats. The appearance of these uncluttered shapes as frames for her mop of black hair made her ecstatic. This was what she'd always wanted!

Only one salesman was on duty and he was dealing with another customer. By the time he got to her, Eliane had piled up four hat forms to take with her, had replaced another seven on their bases, and was trying on the last three in quick succession.

'Was Mademoiselle waiting for assistance, or merely for her mother?' The middle-aged man found it impossible to keep the patronising tone out of his voice. Eliane quelled him with one look. 'Unless you object, I'm planning to buy that lot. Any problems with that?'

The man reddened. 'I – er – beg your pardon, Mam'selle. You seemed so young to be making hats . . .' His explanation petered out. She did not bother to be more than barely civil to him.

'My family believe in child labour. Wrap that lot up, if you can bear to handle my money. I'll take them with me.' Already she was itching to experiment with the hat forms. She had no intention of waiting until she returned to Gaillard. She would practise here in Paris.

Half an hour later, having made another diversion into the trimmings department, Eliane left Galeries Lafayette and took a cab back to the apartment. For the next two days she hardly went out, spending every waking moment playing about with the hat forms. She ruined two of them, but they were so cheap it hardly mattered. The rest were highly successful. None of them was trimmed with anything more than a simple wisp of tulle and a single artificial flower, or a two-coloured strip of grosgrain ribbon, drawn into a flat bow at the side. At the end of the week, Eliane found she could pack the six hats she had finally made up into two hatboxes. They were such simple creations that there was nothing to crush, and they fitted easily inside each other.

It did not take Christian long to notice the difference in her dress, but to her delight he was not ashamed of her unconventional approach. When it looked cheap, he had felt humiliated. Now that Eliane had the money to manufacture her style from expensive materials, he revelled in it.

So did his sporty friends. They were a much younger set than the Parisian playboys who hung around Ottilie Deslys. Most of them were still in their mid-twenties and even the older members of the group were fitter, more active types than Ottilie's crowd. They had liked Eliane from the start. She was quite different from any other women they knew. For a start she knew as much about horses as most of them and talked about the beasts without sentimentality, in the raw language of the stable yard. She read all the racing papers. She had no desire to chatter about the latest operettas or café singers in Paris because she seldom went there. And now she drew the eyes of everyone around her as she appeared in public in the strange hats and frocks which she created for herself. After a while they began wondering loudly, in de Selincourt's presence, why they were never invited to house parties at Gaillard hosted by Eliane. Eventually Christian got the message. He tried out one party, during a week-end when Ottilie was staying in Paris to rehearse a new music hall routine.

It was a roaring success. Instinctively, it seemed, Eliane had known they were really a collection of overgrown boys, so she gave them three days of adolescent fun which no one else had offered them since they were twelve years old. They all went riding, of course, but there was also a mounted paper chase and wildly juvenile amateur dramatics masterminded by Eliane, where they all had a chance to dress up and act the fool. Prevented from bringing their 'official' mistresses because the cocottes tended to be friends of Ottilie, the men with such long-term attachments arrived instead with younger, more informal girl friends, far more like Eliane in temperament than the gold-digging cocottes of the older generation.

Those who had no firmer involvements came along with casual girl friends, too – two actresses and an aspiring singer – but girls who were pursuing straight stage careers, not using the theatre as a shop window for glorified prostitution.

The freshness and spontaneity of the whole occasion made de Selincourt conscious that his regular receptions with Ottilie were growing staid and he began to think about changing them to be more like Eliane's party. He tried it – once. Ottilie did not find scavenger hunts amusing. And as for the idea of everyone sitting around the breakfast table reading the papers in their dressing gowns . . . She reacted as though she were de Selincourt's wife rather than his mistress, although it was the thought of how she would look without corset or make-up rather than the promptings of convention which influenced her. Reluctantly, Christian put aside the idea for the moment, but now and then, when Ottilie was otherwise engaged, he set up another informal party run by Eliane.

Her new fashion look really set her apart from everyone else. She made up the lengths of wool and silk foulard into plain overdresses, with ankle-length skirts and collarless necklines open to the waist. The straight, tubular sleeves stopped between elbow and wrist. Beneath each gown went an underdress - of ivory lawn with tobacco velvet ribbon insertion beneath the brown silk; of bronze mousseline de soie trimmed with cream lace beneath the cream wool. Pintucked rows of self-coloured lace edged the neckline, cuffs and hem, all of which extended three to six inches below the gowns. The clothes looked sad and restrained over corsets, but as Eliane had no surplus flesh to subdue, she discarded hers when she wore the new styles. The result was a picture of fluid elegance. When she greeted de Selincourt's friends at the château, when she rode with them in the forest, when she appeared at Compiègne racetrack, it was impossible to miss her. She was the best-dressed woman present, and she looked unlike anyone else.

The hats completed the unorthodox new look. Elaborate trimmings would have killed the dresses. Two shapes - a vast cartwheel of felt and another of straw - she wore without any trim. She put each on a plaster head base, then boiled a couple of kettles and steamed the brims. While they were damp and limp, she swiftly re-shaped them, leaving them to dry off and shrink into the new lines she had devised. Her favourite of the other forms, a small, highly-varnished black straw boater shape, she trimmed with a broad grosgrain ribbon. There was another boater in natural straw, which she permitted the flamboyance of ribbon in two colours. Two small felt billycock shapes acquired pheasant feathers and a pert little piece of spotted tulle veiling. And there it ended.

The new models looked as though they had cost a fortune. Eliane reflected silently on the true price and hugged herself with smug pleasure. She was guided by nothing apart from the sense that superfluities looked grotesque in dress. The bigger the frame, the easier it was to get away with them. But for anyone with a slender, small-boned physique they were death. Self-preoccupation turned Eliane into a first class innovator.

Now that Eliane could sense things shifting her way, she was in no hurry. Every week that passed gave her more confidence. She watched the way other women walked, talked and ate. She improved her riding skills. Much as she sneered at riding side saddle, she mastered it and eventually appeared at the polo ground in Compiègne, in immaculate riding clothes *à l'anglaise* and riding as though born in the saddle. She had the good sense not to attempt tailoring the riding habit herself, but went to the best equestrian tailor in Compiègne. The cost of the riding habit was more than the bill for her entire self-created wardrobe, and it was worth every penny.

Two years slipped away as she polished herself and learned about her new world. At the end of that time she still looked little more than seventeen. By now Ottilie Deslys's hostility was becoming noticeable even to the easy-going de Selincourt. He was also beginning to realise that he preferred the company of Eliane to that of his longer-established mistress. The younger girl would never amount to a physical lover in Ottilie's class, but then sex was easy to come by when one wanted it. The kid had a way of making you feel you were in bed with her when you were having a dinner table conversation, or riding in the woods . . . in short she was growing up to be irresistible.

In the end it was Christi's best friend, the Englishman Bonnie Charles, who overturned the old order and started Eliane's life on its most momentous phase.

# Chapter Nine

## Andrea and Esteban

For a week or so, Andy saw relatively little of Doré. The couturière was immersed in work on the new collection, and after Andy had spent a fascinated afternoon watching a repetition of her first evening at the salon, she decided to limit her presence there. It was interesting but wearing to watch the strain intensify on the faces of the skilled craftsmen and women as weeks of work disappeared in moments beneath Mademoiselle's razor sharp scissors. I'll come back when it's closer to completion, Andy told herself as an excuse. Then she turned with some relief to the pleasures of Parisian shopping, and of getting better acquainted with Esteban Ortiz.

Their relationship blossomed in spite of Andy's initial misgivings. She had grown up with a mother who had not so much encouraged her to compete with men as to reject any possibility of discrimination on the grounds of gender. With such a background, together with good looks, a first-rate education and a sharp intellect, Andy never had any doubts about her abilities. Years of working in the world's war zones had added a veneer of toughness and now she had no time for the sort of man who wanted a submissive feminine playmate at his side. A few brushes with such characters had made her touchy on this subject and Steb Ortiz came into the firing line as a result. Things reached flashpoint on their second date when they took a taxi back to his apartment from a fashionable restaurant. The cab driver was a surly misogynist and behaved so churlishly towards Andy when she started to pay him that Ortiz leapt to her defence. To his indignation, Andy promptly turned on him.

'You keep out of this! I always fight my own battles and this crabby son of a bitch isn't giving me any trouble at all.'

Before Steb could pursue the matter, she switched her attention back to the unfortunate cabby. 'And as for you, dog-breath, I suggest you sell this bone-shaker and look for a job shovelling camel-shit. Your temperament should suit you for it.' She counted out the considerable fare in small coins, leaned inside the taxi window and dropped them on the vehicle's floor. 'Don't bother to count it. There's no tip.'

As she turned to stalk away from the kerb, the driver recovered his wits and snarled at Steb: 'What are you, a galloping masochist or something? Sooner you give her a good thrashing, the better we'll all be!' Before Steb had time to retort, he crashed the gears and screeched off into the Paris traffic.

Andy was already in the lobby of the apartment building, pressing the lift button. Ortiz stormed past her and started up the stairs. 'What are you doing? Who needs to walk up eighty stairs after the sort of meal we've had?'

He called without looking back, 'I either walk or strangle you. Which do you prefer?'

Andy was waiting when he arrived, and scowled as he took out his keys. 'Shall I leave now or are you going to be more civilised about this?'

'I suggest we discuss that inside. I wasn't planning to take the taxi driver's advice, if that reassures you, but I'm tempted.'

Then he opened the front door and stood aside to usher her in. By the time they entered the drawing-room, Andy was simmering. Silently, he poured her a drink and made one for himself. She could contain herself no longer.

'Look, Steb, you can't expect me to get all sweet and shy when a bastard like that has a go at me. I've seen off tougher guys than him in every continent, and I'm not about to be bested by a cheap cab driver!'

He did not answer immediately. Instead he continued to

stare at her gloomily and took a sip of his drink. His silence was beginning to make her nervous and she looked away, preparing to launch into another tirade. Finally he said: 'I assume that this sort of tantrum makes you feel better when you've got too wound up. The only other excuse I can think of is that your mental development was arrested at a very early stage.'

'Come on, you saw the way he behaved. What would you have done?'

'If you'd kept your mouth shut for another ten seconds, you might have found out. I certainly wouldn't have come across with a bad impersonation of Scarlett O'Hara!'

'That's it, isn't it? It's okay for men to be aggressive, but the girls have to keep to their place. How bloody cosy!'

'Nothing so infantile. You, dear girl, have one of the quickest tempers I've ever seen. Now I have a couple of male friends who are a bit touchy, too. If I were out with them, I'd have a damned good try at getting in ahead of them to deal with trouble. I happen not to like getting into brawls on the pavement. In this case, I had even better reason for barging in. However much of a slob that driver was, I doubt very much whether he'd have hit a woman. But you'd wound him up so tight he was ready to smack someone and *I* was the likely candidate. He was a big boy and I can live without a black eye, thanks.

'Given the level of your reasoning just now, I don't expect you to grasp this immediately. Call me when you have. I'll be in the kitchen.'

He strode past her and quietly shut the door. Andy stood staring after him, as speechless as she had left the taxi driver. Her tantrum lasted all of thirty seconds, then her underlying good sense started to surface and she realised what an ass she had made of herself. She glanced round the room. A glass cylinder on the low table was full of white and yellow moon daisies. She scooped them out, shook the water from the stems, then knocked on the kitchen door. By the time Ortiz opened it, she was down on one knee, flourishing the bouquet at him.

'I was a total fool, you're quite right. Would you care to accept this small token of my remorse? It would have been platinum cufflinks, but Gucci were closed and anyway you only seem to wear sweaters.'

His frown dissolved and he pulled her to her feet with a little shake. 'Yes, you are a fool – one day you're the one who'll get punched – but you also know how to apologise. That's something I can never get the hang of.'

'Admit it, I'm also gorgeous and you can't wait to get my clothes off.'

'That too, but if you'd gone on like that much longer I'd have decided it wasn't worth the pain.'

She became serious again momentarily. 'I really am sorry, Steb. I'm beginning to realise I got you wrong and I feel a bit sheepish about it. I'll try to behave better, but it would help if you'd remember how crabby I get when people start bossing me around.'

'No guarantees. Sometimes it's quite a strain keeping my temper with you, and at times it's downright impossible.'

'Like tonight, for instance?'

'Like tonight. Only if there's ever a next time, I might just forget how much I fancy you, turn you over in the street and slap your backside until you scream for mercy.'

She was becoming indignant again. 'If you ever tried that . . .'

'Andy – you're doing it again less than ten minutes after you apologised for the first tantrum. Shut up!'

'Make me!'

As they talked, he had moved back into the drawing room, heading for the drinks cupboard to refill their glasses. Now he stopped, turned back towards her and stood inches away from her. She was a tall woman and they were practically the same height. For a long moment they met each other's eyes, both throwing out a silent challenge. Then he burst out laughing. 'This is utterly crazy! You strut around telling me how you have no intention of being put down, and your entire lifestyle is a string of non-stop challenges to any man to oppress you. The hell with it – why should I make you? It's what you half want me to do, isn't it?'

The tension was gone. She smiled too. 'Game, set and match to the Spaniard in the corner,' she said. 'Come on, let's have another drink and be nice to each other.'

It was a decisive incident. They saw each other most evenings over the following two weeks and went through several stormy sessions, but the squabbles were little more than two temperamental people letting off steam. Both had a sense of humour and both were beginning to acknowledge that they had an instinctive rapport.

They were both fond of food and Esteban was a better cook than Andy. As a result their dates tended to be long dinners at good restaurants, or dinner, conversation and lovemaking at Ortiz's apartment. One evening they were in the kitchen, Andy sitting on a high stool as she watched him slice vegetables with the expertise of a professional chef.

'I should remember that no male chauvinist would be as good a cook as you, and so proud of it,' she told him. 'But you really did give off macho waves that first day, you know, and it set the scene for how I saw you from then on.'

'Let's get one thing straight. I come across like that in self-defence, almost without thinking about it. I realise now that this is your first writing job inside the rag trade, but when we met I assumed you were a fashion journalist. If you knew the business, you'd know that practically all the male designers are gay. Castellane is one of the few exceptions, and I'm another. He's in the fortunate position of being able to present his wife to everyone, so he doesn't give off the wrong signals. Anyhow, he's not exactly everyone's dream lover! I, on the other hand, appear to hold as much appeal for boys as girls. I don't mind – it's quite flattering – but I'm boringly heterosexual. It's much less embarrassing for them as well as me if I make my tastes clear from the start. All that macho bit is no more than sexual tact.'

'But you must be a bit of a male supremo – what about all that conservative Latin blood?'

He laughed. 'You really can be absurd at times! You must have got your stereotypes from the turn of the century. Next thing I know you'll be insisting that all Spaniards fight bulls in their spare time and march in the Penitents' Procession in Holy Week. My mother could have taught you more about liberated relationships than all your globetrotting has done.'

'I suppose she managed to keep house for a family of fourteen, do beautiful embroidery and complete a college degree without losing her femininity!'

'Bitch! Actually, she's a professional cellist. Perhaps you've heard of Maria Ricardo?'

'Oh-oh, something tells me I've made a fool of myself again.'

'You could say that. It's not just intellectual Frenchwomen who keep their maiden names on marriage, you know. My father taught music at a high school and took pupils at home. He was a brilliant teacher but he'd never have made a solo artist. It never caused them any problems; they were very happy together. She went off on tour a couple of times a year and he stayed home to keep an eye on us. During our summer vacation we all went on tour together with Mama. Neither of them could cook an egg or wash a shirt. I learned to cook in self-defence against a succession of pleasant middle-aged housekeepers who thought paella was the highest form of culinary art.'

'And I'm going to have to learn to be more tolerant and open-minded, aren't I? Seems I've turned into a bit of a brat during my travels.'

He nodded, smiling. 'What were your parents like, by the way? I know I get at you about your attitude, but you certainly aren't the orthodox image of the man-hating, unmade-up feminist.'

'For "parents" read "parent". My father died when I was too young for his influence to count. My mother is a very special lady. Perhaps I'll take you to meet her one day. My father was English, and after he died, she brought me up all on her own in a foreign country, with very few friends. She did a grand job. All the over-the-top bits are my own work, I'm afraid.'

'So she was no great theoretical women's libber?'

'Oh yes, she was, but more as part of being politically active in general. She saw it was all part of the class struggle. Yeah, I know, boring, but not with Marie-Louise. She'd joined the Communist Party when she was very young – during the war when she was a student at the Sorbonne. But at heart she was really a raving anarchist, and by the 1950s she'd got thoroughly disillusioned with the whole Red Dawn bit. Not that I knew that. As a kid, I still thought she was a good Party member. She had recordings of all those lovely gut-wrenching Communist songs – *Bandiera Rossa* and stuff like that – and I learned to sing them along with "Baa baa black sheep". I didn't realise she'd got fed up with the whole thing until I made my one and only political gesture in Paris in the 1968 riots.

'Like just about every student I knew, I was out on the streets jemmying up paving stones and shouting dirty names at the CRS. But after a while I started wondering what my lot were thinking of setting up in place of the old order. None of my mates seemed to have a clear idea. I was feeling more and more sheepish about it but I didn't quite have the nerve to clear out. It smacked of betrayal, somehow.

'Marie-Louise was living in France again by then. She came looking for me when the troubles got going and tried to convince me it would all come to nothing. You can imagine how that went down with someone like me at the age of twenty-three! This was my mother and I had to rebel, although anyone you'd less want to rebel against than Marie-Louise I can't imagine. In the end, she said, "Okay, you win. But I'll be around to pick up the pieces if you get tired of it all." '

'And was she?'

'With a vengeance. The next day there was a particularly bloody set-to. One big brute of a CRS type had kicked a girl unconscious next to me and the boys got him. I expected them to thrash him but – God, I'll never forget it – they managed to get his shield and crash hat away from him and they started literally tearing him to pieces. I stood and watched for a couple of minutes and then I knew they were as bad as the other side. All I wanted was to get away, but I was sure I was going to be sick all over the place and I seemed to be trapped. At that moment a voice beside me said: "Come on, love, we're going home." I turned round and there was Marie-Louise. She looks pretty good even now but in those days she could have passed for my sister. She was wearing an old pair of Levis and a pea jacket, and carrying an aerosol can of paint.

'I said, "Ma, we'll never get out of here, it's bloody murder!" She just smiled and reminded me: "I worked these streets for the Resistance, remember?" We were away in seconds. We were almost clear of the whole mess when we turned a corner into a bunch of real death or glory fanatics who were determined not to let anyone chicken out. Marie-Louise took it all in her stride. She pointed back at the worst of the action. "Fight's up there – and it's a good one. We've just come back to write a love letter to the pigs!"

'Then she took out her little aerosol and started writing on the wall. "See you later, boys, we'll be back soon." They left us in peace fortunately. I was just about ready to collapse. She said, "Come on, kid, I'm taking you home. But before we go, memorise that slogan and never forget it. You'll be a lot happier in future if you refuse to take politics any more seriously than that." I looked up at the wall, and she'd sprayed, in bright red, with those thugs twenty yards away: "*Je suis Marxiste – tendence Groucho!*" I think we've seen eye to eye ever since.'

'She sounds like quite a woman.'

'She is.'

They dined together as tranquilly as an old married couple. Soon after eleven, Esteban said, 'Tonight I'm going to throw you out, much as I hate to do it. Come on, we'll find you a cab down in the square. I'm trying out a new design project of my own, and I should have been working on it this evening instead of enjoying myself with you. Now I really have to get on with it. It'll probably keep me up all night and I don't want any beautiful distractions.'

'Anything interesting?'

'I'll show you when I've finished, if it works out. You had a lot to do with my starting off on it. I'll be out of circulation tomorrow and the day after, because I have to do some extra work for the knitwear people and put in a lot of time on this other thing. Okay?'

'Of course. I've been neglecting my own work. It'll give me a chance to catch up. We can get together at the end of the week.'

'Right. I take it I still have to wait till you contact me.'

'You should know better than to ask! But bear with me, I could just change my mind soon.'

Andy still felt more drawn towards the Paris shops than her work, but realising that she must start formally interviewing Doré soon, she bought a good portable tape recorder and a stock of blank cassettes. She had no intention of being caught again unable to record the flow of reminiscences. Then she treated herself to a lot of expensive ready-made clothes and costume jewellery in the designer boutiques around the Rue Cambon, Place Vendôme and Faubourg St-Honoré. At this stage she stopped telling herself it was part of her research. She had begun by pretending to compare Doré boutique merchandise with that of other houses, but soon simply gave herself up to enjoying luxury shopping.

She was in the enviable position of genuinely needing to buy clothes and accessories, having arrived with almost nothing, and of possessing the money necessary to buy at least some of the expensive high fashion which surrounded her. The years as a top photographer and reporter had not been undertaken simply for glory. Her income was as high as her reputation and she had been too busy over recent months to spend much of it. Now she did a lot of catching up.

Halfway through the week, she ran into Eugène St-Meurice as they both left the Rue Cambon salon.

'Why Andy, you're becoming a stranger! I hope you don't feel neglected, but you've seen for yourself how things are.' He raised his eyes significantly towards the upper floor and she nodded.

'It's almost one o'clock. Let me give you lunch. I'd like to talk to you about your progress so far. Are you busy?'

'No, Eugène – thanks a lot. I'd like that.' Andy was surprised to notice that for once he seemed not to feel threatened by her. The invitation had an air of true spontaneity, not of a relayed edict from Mademoiselle. She smiled at him. 'Don't tell me – the Ritz. I know how you feel about bistros!'

'For once you're wrong. We won't go to a workmen's dive, but I can assure you that the Ritz is the last place I want to patronise today!'

'My God, they must be quivering with anxiety! What have they done?'

He laughed. 'Nothing, nothing! But guess who'll be there today at her usual table, and guess who would find it impossible to resist the temptation of dragging you back to the salon at four o'clock to watch her massacre of the fitters?'

'Oh, no – I couldn't take that today. Lead on somewhere else.'

'You see? You're becoming a seasoned foot soldier at last.'

Immediately her bantering mood dissolved and she shivered slightly. He was all concern. 'What's wrong, Andy? Do you feel ill?'

'N-no, just a silly touch of superstition. It's simply that the – er – gentlemen I was trying to avoid when I took up this assignment call their men "foot soldiers". I seem to have got away lightly but I still shiver when their terminology crops up by accident.'

'Are you really still afraid of them? Surely they'll have lost interest now you seem to have packed up and moved on?'

'I'm afraid it's not that simple. This is the second time I've done a probe piece about them. I don't think they're likely to dismiss me this time round. I'm just hoping to stay ahead long enough for one of their feuds to put someone else on top of the hitlist. Once that happens they'll be too interested in internal warfare to bother with the likes of me. Sorry, Eugène, I'm being neurotic. Come on, let's go and get a damned good lunch and forget them and La Grande Mademoiselle for a couple of hours!'

He managed to make her laugh by saying very quietly, 'We might be able to dismiss the Mafia, but Mademoiselle – never!'

Eugène was a natural host who knew instinctively what would please his guests. Today it had to be somewhere special to smooth away Andrea's worries as much as possible. 'It's the last time this summer that you'll get a chance to sample the best duck in Paris, so let's go and make sure they can fit us in,' he told her. 'Next week they close until September.'

A short while later they were at Pharamond, a Michelin-starred restaurant in the Rue Grande-Truanderie, where St-Meurice ordered Barbary duckling with green peppercorn sauce. He devoted all his attention to the menu and wine list until he had given their order. Andy watched him with some amusement.

'Eugène, I confess that after a bad beginning I'm getting fond of you. You know what you want, you know where to get it, and your taste is impeccable. When you *can't* get what you want, you don't make a fuss. Either you give up and forget about it, or – and I suspect this is what you usually do – you go off and work out some other way of getting it.'

'All this from watching me order lunch? Surely you're reading a little too much into it?'

'Oh, no, Eugène – that's only a little bit of it. I mean

the total you. I feel as if we have far more in common than I ever expected. Isn't that strange?'

'Less so than you might think. We actually have a great deal in common.'

'Now you're beginning to sound positively cryptic! What are you leading up to?'

'Hmm – later, perhaps. It requires considerable preparation and I don't know yet if I'm equal to it, let alone whether you are. In the meantime, let's drink some good wine and talk about what you've been doing while Mademoiselle is off slaying cutters.'

'Oh, I've been spending as if money were going out of style, buying up half the ready-to-wear fashion in Paris. One day I'll learn how to pass a boutique without going inside!'

'Andy, are you telling me that you've been paying the full price? You really *are* crazy!'

'Why, what had you in mind? Daylight robbery?'

'Did it not occur to you to ask me? I'd have got you everything at a fraction of the retail price. I have a contact in every fashion house in Paris.'

She flushed, embarrassed. 'I – er – that is, I've known from the start that Mademoiselle insisted on you getting hold of me to do the biography, you made no secret of it. But I got the impression that it wasn't simply a case of feeling neutral and tolerating me because boss lady wanted it – I felt you actively resented me for some reason, and that I was a king-sized pain in the arse to you. So naturally, when it came to something unofficial like this, the last thing I wanted to do was to impose on you.'

'Forgive me, Andy. I fear I was somewhat hostile, but it was Mademoiselle's fault, not yours. In fact, I should have been happy to arrange a little cut-price shopping for you, and I insist that you get the maximum discount in the Doré boutique at least. It will probably be unnecessary, though. I suspect you will enrage La Grande Mademoiselle if you dare to try paying for anything there.'

'Oh? That's the last thing I expected.' She brightened.

'Do you dare let me loose in there after telling me that?'

'After my apparent churlishness early in our acquaintance, I should deserve it.' He hesitated, then appeared to make a decision. 'I am not working later today and would like to talk to you about something which concerns us both, and your work with Mademoiselle. Have you time to come back to my apartment for an hour or so after lunch?'

Seeing his solemn expression, Andy stifled her impulse to make a flippant remark about dishonourable intentions. Instead she merely said: 'I don't mind talking here if you'd rather. Where better than over the remains of a wonderful meal?'

He glanced about, looking positively conspiratorial. 'No, too public. I want to discuss something with you in total privacy. As I told you a week or two ago, Paris is a very small city.'

Now she was completely hooked. The food at Pharamond was sensational but she was hard pressed not to gallop through her meal and drag St-Meurice away to hear what he had to tell her. But he refused to be drawn into serious discussion, determinedly comparing the Barbary duck with other breeds, other recipes, other sauces. Similar attention was given to the wine, the vegetables and the cheese. They did not linger over their cognac; by now Andy was far too intrigued by what he was going to tell her. St-Meurice himself was nervous about it and now he, too, seemed anxious to make the disclosure as soon as possible.

'Shall we go to your place, then?' Andy pressed him. 'Mademoiselle is hardly likely to give us any peace back at Rue Cambon and anywhere public would be as inappropriate as this restaurant.'

'Yes, I'd like that,' said St-Meurice. 'You'll find it interesting, too, I hope. The atmosphere is quite different from your present home.'

The apartment was in the First Arrondissement – 'It would be folly to live too far from the Ritz when one considers Mademoiselle's nocturnal need for company' – but otherwise anything less like Doré's elegant baroque surroundings would have been difficult to imagine. Eugène St-Meurice's large, airy apartment seemed effortlessly to combine a welcoming atmosphere with hard-edged avant garde chic.

'Wow! How d'you keep it clean?' Andy conjured the flip remark to minimise her wonder at the black and white interior whose occasional splashes of primary colour were reminiscent of Mondrian.

'Simple, my dear. No children, no wife, no permanent lover, no pets – who would clutter it? Only Mademoiselle makes my life untidy, and Mademoiselle is not welcome here.'

Impulsively, Andy put her arm around him and gave him an affectionate hug. He stiffened momentarily and then relaxed, smiling.

'Thank you,' he said quietly. 'You understand.' It was not a question.

He opened a bottle of chilled Sancerre and served it in tall, moisture-beaded goblets, with a wry smile. 'Damn Ernest Hemingway! I've always loved this stuff but nowadays everyone over the age of forty thinks people drink it because he made it glamorous. In fact, I just enjoy the flavour of blackcurrant leaves and no other wine seems to have it.'

They sipped appreciatively for a while. St-Meurice fiddled with cigarettes and lighter, prowled about and generally delayed. In the end Andy decided to force the issue. 'Okay, Eugène, let's have it. Is La Grande Mademoiselle telling me a pack of lies as an alternative to her life story?'

'I suspect not a *pack* of lies, but I do think she may be editing the truth yet again. How confident are you that she is being completely honest?'

'Who is ever completely honest? I think she's telling more of the truth than she ever has. A couple of times I've caught her hesitating over some point in a story, and I've had a gut feeling in every case but one that she was frank with me.'

'I think she means to be honest with you, and apart from the odd lapse she's making a good beginning. But when you get into the detailed revelations, I don't know if she will have the strength . . . If that happens, you should at least have some pointers to enable you to distinguish between fantasy and reality. What I tell you may not cover quite everything but it will, I think, make sense of the worst inconsistencies. I shan't attempt to fill in the detail of Mademoiselle's life. She has started that and I want most of it to retain its freshness. I'll tell you only about the areas where you might be misled.

'Before she ever started out as a couturière, Alouette Doré earned her living as a shopgirl in Saumur. As many girls of her class did in garrison towns in those days, she padded her income by casual affairs with the young officers: nothing as vulgar as formal prostitution, you understand, but probably providing herself with almost as much again as she received in her weekly pay packet. Has she hinted at any of this? If not, it might be quite an embarrassment trying to make her confess it rather than whatever the day's fantasy might be.'

'Oh, yes, she's told me that. In fact it's almost as far as we've got. She started trying to tell me some fancy fibs about going on the stage, then she burst out laughing, said "What the hell? Who am I kidding? I was a part-time tart" and told me about herself and her Aunt Geneviève.'

'Well, in the course of those transactions she got a little careless and conceived a child.'

'She certainly hasn't mentioned that, and we've moved on from her Saumur days now. I wonder why not.'

'Doré likes to be stronger than her enemies and there is one area where she feels vulnerable: in the eyes of the world she was never a wife or a mother. She imagines they point at her and whisper that she is a barren vine. It infuriates her to have to defend herself by saying she merely chose not to have children. Imagine how much more galling it is that she has been a mother twice but feels she can never admit it.'

'Why not? These days millionairesses and the proverbial woman in the street are all announcing they've had a child without choosing to marry the father. I realise that at Doré's age one's perspective on things is different, but given the way attitudes have changed, why should she care now?'

'Because to a certain extent, the children are incidental. They are no use as a weapon unless she can boast about marriage as well. It's not a matter of respectability but of being able to get her man and keep him, you see. Over the years, enemies have undoubtedly taunted her about this. God knows, the lack of husband and children must have been her only visible weaknesses in the days of her glory. Think how frustrating she must have found it not to admit to having two children. But the inhibition was so strong in the past, I think she will baulk even now and cut it out of her story. This is at the heart of my anxiety and the reason why I had to speak to you.

'It's odd to say someone as deprived as Alouette Doré in those days was fortunate, but in a sense she was. Geneviève helped to protect her, and her employer was a better friend than she might have expected. The employer wanted a baby for adoption by her childless daughter and son-in-law. Years later, the boy's adoptive mother was in a bad way financially – she was widowed by then – and she wrote to Doré asking for help. Mademoiselle was in a sentimental mood. Apparently she told her friend Bonnie Charles that the boy was her nephew – unless he was a simpleton that illusion would have been dispelled the moment he saw Edouard's resemblance to Alouette – and he insisted they should send for the child.' Here St-Meurice paused for a moment to pour more wine.

'That particular lie might not have washed with Bonnie Charles but the rest of the world accepted it,' said Andy. 'I assume that's the lad who's referred to as her nephew in a couple of the potboilers that have already been published about her?'

Eugène nodded. 'Perhaps at least partly due to the fact that he's been dead for years and was never a very interesting figure while he lived. Being taken up by her didn't help him much. He was a small town boy, eleven years old, shy, gangling, conscious that he did not fit into this fashionable world where he had suddenly been dropped. Before, his Mama had idolised him. He was still made much of by Doré, but in the manner that smart people pet a new dog or canary. He was the craze of the moment, nothing more. And naturally Mademoiselle soon tired of him.

'After a few months, she was preoccupied with the business. She had tried to turn the little boy into an amusing companion, but he was shy and withdrawn. When he was brought to the exotic luncheon parties she gave for Bonnie's international friends, little Edouard asked why he had to have rich sauces with his beef, or said he didn't like crayfish. He said that Maman always cooked her lamb plainly with haricot beans and that sugar pancakes were all he liked for dessert. One way and another, he was dull.'

'So Doré sent him back to his mother?' Andy hazarded.

Eugène almost spat the next sentence: 'Did she, hell! No son of hers was going to grow up a country bumpkin, even if he did bore her to stupefaction, so she packed him off to an English boarding school!'

'Oh, no! Not a little French boy with that sort of background. It must have been sheer hell.'

'I gather that it was. As a concession to his Catholicism, she did move him from Harrow to Beaumont, but that was the most she would do. And he was forced to endure six months at an Anglican prep school before she relented on the religious side. They called him Froggy, of course. Boys of that age are seldom original. He never forgave Mademoiselle.'

'What happened to him? Did he go back to his adoptive mother as soon as he was old enough?'

'That sort of thing only happens in storybooks. No, she

died of cancer before he finished at Beaumont. She saw him for the holidays each summer, but that was all. And until he grew old enough to make her feel middle-aged, Mademoiselle would insist on Edouard's paying court to her for regular periods. She finally lost interest in him when he left school in the mid-1920s, as she lost interest in everything else for a while. After that he was off the hook for the rest of his life.'

'Mmm, lucky lad. How did he manage that?'

'He died – obscurely. Another unexplained casualty of the war, unconnected with Mademoiselle by then. He's not an important personality but his existence is important, because of the way Mademoiselle over-reacts about herself and motherhood.'

'What about the other child? You mentioned two.'

'Ah, now that one is different – and potentially a far bigger story for you. That is the important matter I wanted to speak to you about. Mademoiselle had a child with the Duke of Conway.'

'She *what*? Christ, Eugène, if that's true I'll be able to write my own cheque for a British newspaper serialisation. Everyone says the only reason she never married him was that she couldn't give him a child. Now you're saying she did. So why did they split?'

'Correction: she'd have married him if there had been a *son*. It was a daughter.'

'I see. But in any case, the child would have been illegitimate, so even a son couldn't have inherited the title.'

He stared at her expressionlessly for a moment, then said: 'You still have a great deal to learn about Alouette Doré, and if most of it comes from her own lips perhaps you will understand her better in the end. I suspect that for her own reasons she'll be more forthcoming with you about the second child than about the first, but I still felt I must warn you of potential inaccuracies in case it wrecked your book. The other areas where she has been difficult with others are her wartime behaviour and her precise relationships with certain men.'

'And?'

'Well, what do you think? Of course she had sexual affairs with them! The age in which fornication and adultery were officially frowned on was also the age in which they were obligatory if you lived the way she did, in her kind of society. As for the wartime experience: there is a very shocking story buried there. On that, all I can do is to urge you to press her. I myself do not know precisely what happened. Just don't let her side-track you with tales of the Nazis sticking to their end of the Ritz and her sticking to hers. Their end was the whole hotel.'

But Andy was less interested in the wartime story than in Eugène's first revelation. 'To go back to her affair with the Duke. How on earth could such a public figure have a child without the world knowing? There must have been gossip.'

'I should not dream of spoiling Mademoiselle's pleasure in telling you all about that. However, I'd banish any doubts you might harbour about her being able to conceal the pregnancy. Secretly producing a child while working full time as a shop girl in Saumur was within her capacity at nineteen. I am sure that a similar trick was simplicity itself when she was thirty-eight and as rich as Croesus.'

He stopped talking. Silence lapped the room, deep enough to drown in, and Andy wondered how much more St-Meurice knew but chose not to tell. Questions crowded in but she knew she must save them for Doré.

With a conscious effort, she glanced at her watch. It was almost six o'clock. 'Eugène, thanks for being so candid. I confess I didn't realise you were so concerned to make sure I succeeded at this job. I promise not to do or say anything foolish to Mademoiselle, and I shan't let on that you've said anything unless you give me the go-ahead.'

Eugène smiled. 'I suspect her antennae are still sensitive enough to tell her you know something and I am the source. If she suggests as much, you have my permission to admit I have divulged a little – uh – family history! I merely ask that you use great discretion and do not volunteer any of the information I have given you unless she first raises the matter.'

'Of course, you have my word. Now take care of yourself, and I'll see you soon.' She leaned forward and kissed him on both cheeks. He touched her arm lightly and escorted her to the door.

After she'd gone, he went to pour himself another drink. Even in solitude, his expression was unreadable. Eugène St-Meurice had accustomed himself to concealing his inner world, even from the bathroom mirror.

Andy was walking back in the general direction of Rue Cambon, wondering how best to use the information she had just been given. On the face of it, although Eugène's revelations were fascinating, she could see no way of persuading Doré to fill in the gaps without running the risk of alienating the couturière altogether.

It was comforting to think that even without the crucial secret of Doré's motherhood, the official biography would still be worth writing, but there had to be some tactful method of making her spill the beans . . . Then Andy would have a scoop worth many additional thousands. But what was in it for Eugène if she got the story straight? Why should he care whether or not she knew all the dirt about Mademoiselle? From the start, he'd made it clear that he regarded the entire biography project as ill-conceived. Perhaps his revelation of this afternoon was not prompted by altruism so much as by a jealous desire to muddy the waters between Mademoiselle and Andy. Eugène mightn't be an ally at all. . . .

Andy was still deeply absorbed by her train of thought when she stopped under the colonnade at the corner of the Rue d'Alger and the Rue de Rivoli. Cars were rushing westward along the major road and a dribble of vehicles filtered from the Rue d'Alger to join them. As she looked along the side street there was a break in the traffic and Andy started to cross.

Immediately an anonymous saloon slid away from the kerb and accelerated at a rate far beyond the modest power suggested by its bodywork. She quickened her pace slightly to stay out of its way and realised with dawning horror that it was changing course to stay with her. Suddenly the opposite pavement seemed miles away and the memory of a similar vehicle in a dark street outside Channel Five House came flooding back.

Instinct had saved her then and it saved her now. Instead of trying to race the murderous car to the opposite side, she doubled back, relying on the break in traffic having continued. She made it to the other side and shot on at right angles, out into the Rue de Rivoli, again without looking. This time a clear crossing was more than she could have hoped for. Horns blared and brakes shrieked as the hurtling traffic vainly attempted to slow its headlong progress and avoid hitting her. She was almost on the far side when a Deux Chevaux van gave up the unequal struggle with its elderly brakes and helped her on her way, catching her a glancing blow on her thigh which lifted her into the air en route to the far pavement.

Andy did not even stop to find out where it hurt. She was still mobile and took full advantage of the fact. Immediately ahead was the Tuileries, the elegant central Paris park. She dodged through and peeled off to the left, not stopping until she was well away from the gate. Only then did she collapse gratefully on to a bench and try to assess how badly she had been injured.

To her surprise, it didn't seem at all serious. The vigorous throbbing of her thigh and buttocks was more like the burn felt after intense exertion than the anguish of a broken bone or torn muscle. She would be bruised and sore tomorrow, no doubt, but it was a miracle she was still alive. . . . The thought brought her up with a jolt. How long was she going to stay that way? The change of scene and the apparent success of her escape route through Copenhagen had made her careless. They'd almost got her with the same method they had tried in London. What would they try next time? Now there would clearly be a next time, and a time after that until they finally got her.

Andy shook her head angrily, inwardly debating her wisest course of action. No – she wasn't giving up now! Even if they had tracked her down, she was less vulnerable here in Paris than she would have been in London. The Rue Cambon apartment was only a little less secure than Fort Knox. Apart from that she spent little time outside the select circle of Doré, St-Meurice and a couple of his big designer friends. She might need to be careful about seeing Steb Ortiz so often. As long she still insisted on visiting him, she was alone and unguarded when she travelled to and from his apartment. Andy tucked that thought away. No point in rearranging her social calendar before she was even sure she could get back to Rue Cambon in one piece.

She stood up, gingerly testing her damaged leg. Minor injury or not, she was not sure how long it would carry her. She'd have to find out. There was only one sensible escape route: straight across the gardens, through the arch under the elevated terrace and down on to the Quai des Tuileries beside the Seine. She set off, forcing herself to walk normally. By the time she reached the Quai she was having real trouble moving without limping perceptibly. It was no use; she couldn't drag along obscurely forever. Better draw attention to herself now, risk being spotted and get out of the way before she seized up altogether. She stepped forward and signalled madly for a cab. She was lucky and got one quickly. As she tucked herself into the back seat and slammed the door, she saw two men come tearing down the steps from the Tuileries' Waterside Terrace and start down on to the Quai.

'Rue Cambon, please, driver.' She spent the rest of the journey parrying his teasing remarks about shopping cheaply by window gazing after Maison Doré was closed for the night.

Back at the couture house she dismissed the security man's solicitude about her obvious difficulty in walking, managed to dodge the salon floor where another of Doré's late sessions was proceeding, and finally collapsed into a hot bath up in the apartment. For the first time in over an hour she felt safe.

## Extract From Andrea Vincent's Working Diary

*Monday June 21, 1978*

So here they are, the Honoured Society, mixed up with my work with Doré. I really must have been naïve to think I could dodge them here for ever, but somehow this is such a different world that I managed to fool myself. After due consideration I think all I can do is go on as if they didn't exist, and trust to Mademoiselle's personal security system to cut down the risks.

The whole Doré story is getting far too interesting to drop now, even if my continued presence here begins to look like a matter of life and death. If they're that eager, they're going to get me somewhere eventually so it might as well be here. My leg is aching as if I'd been kicked by a horse and turning blue-black, but apart from that I'm okay. And when I dragged myself out of a bath back at Rue Cambon, Doré rang me from the Ritz to fix a whole string of appointments throughout next week. She wants to record a big slab of reminiscences before she goes to work on finishing the collection. I can hardly wait!

There's quite a bonus at the end, too. She plans to go to the races for the first time since the 1930s – says it'll sharpen her powers of recall. It's the Prix de Paris at Longchamp next Sunday and she's planning to make up a party. What an end to a key week! She's even making noises about kitting me out in one of her outfits – *prêt à porter*, not couture, of course, there wouldn't be time for the latter – and I confess my first head to toe Doré is a tempting prospect. It almost makes up for sinister men attempting to mow me down in their souped-up cars.

# Chapter Ten

## Doré

## 1911–1922: Birth and Death of a Dream

*Damn it to hell, I can't be suffering a guilty conscience this far along the line! I've never known what it was like to feel guilty. Well . . . maybe just a little, once or twice, but nothing like this. The girl's getting to me, so here I am unable to sleep again instead of drifting off contentedly as I thought I'd be able to once we got started. All right, Mademoiselle, if you can't sleep then you can give a little thought to how well it's gone so far.*

*For a start, how much have you told her that you can be so pleased with? Now there you know the answer. Oh, the relief of letting someone else know the truth about the orphanage, and the awful non-existent aunts, and Papa leaving me, not going off to make the family fortunes. I've come a long way with* la vedette *in a very short time. I've never told any of that to anybody. But I still couldn't face telling her about the first baby, could I? Skipped over that one good and proper with a little dismissive remark about trying to make it as a singer for longer than I really did. Funny, when I lost my nerve about telling her that, it seemed reasonable enough. A girl like Andy wouldn't really give a damn about me dropping a bastard all those years ago, and yet when I looked at her, suddenly she was all the upper class girls of my own girlhood, all ready to mock and condemn, so I lost my nerve.*

*I wonder how it will work out when we get up to date and I'm talking about the more recent past. Mmm, so many problems there that if any of them get solved, this little bit of deceit will seem like nothing. How am I going to handle Otto? Or the re-opening with Eugène working for me? Oh shit, I'd better take one of my little pills, otherwise the thought of all that will keep me awake until the Spring Collection.*

*Apart from the baby, though, there's nothing amiss with what I've already told her. I can almost see myself telling her about Conway. Oh, Conway, it's so strange! I thought you'd be the one who would be close to me now, but you're as remote as a star. I thought that this girl, this visible thread from you and me to the future, would bring you back to my side, but it's not you that I dream of, it's Bonnie. I keep pretending it's just because I'm getting to his part of my story, but I don't really believe that. I, the great atheist, the godless superstitious Breton peasant, believe he's there looking out for me, waiting for me, my one real love, the one I should have been with forever if only both of us had been content with a little less. . . .*

He stood on the turf in the sparkling sunshine, grinning up at her on her big bay horse. Bonnie Charles radiated good health, success, good breeding and self-confidence. His hair was as black as Eliane's, thick and shiny, and his eyes had a granite-and-water look which was also reminiscent of her. Strangers who saw them together often wondered momentarily whether they were brother and sister. Beyond their similar colouring, though, the physical resemblance ended. He was a big, muscular man, over six feet tall, with the sort of whip-hard horseman's body which tended to lean strength rather than bulk. His legs were long and well-muscled and showed to great advantage in immaculate English-cut riding clothes and boots. Charles's face had a pagan look. His cheekbones were high and broad and his eyes slanted upward slightly at the outer corners. One look from them had been known to make respectable matrons believe he had made an indecent proposal when really he had said nothing.

'Urchin! Only you would turn out in a perfect lady's rig

with your hair caught up in that absurd little horsetail behind. Why d'you do it?'

She returned his grin. 'I don't like people to get too comfortable in my company. Any girl can stick her hair in a chignon and cram on a bowler over it. I happen to find it more comfortable like this.'

'And it happens to distinguish you in yet another way from all the other well turned-out little women down here whom the men admire and instantly forget. I bet no one forgets Alouette Doré in a hurry!'

'Exactly. I have no intention that they should.'

'But you ought to be remembered for more than a hank of hair and a daring manner. What else d'you plan they should remember you for?'

'I haven't worked that one out yet – but I will, just you wait!'

He laughed outright. 'You've heard of Oscar Wilde, of course.'

'No. Is he one of Christi's theatrical friends?'

Charles stopped laughing instantly. He knew intuitively that one day Eliane would find out who Wilde was, and if she thought he had mocked her ignorance she would never forgive him. 'Not quite. A bit before our Christi's time. He was a fashionable English writer who was disgraced because he liked the boys a little too much. Anyway, he wrote a story called *The Sphinx Without a Secret*. I recommend you read it some time. It holds a valuable lesson for you.'

'Come on, Bonnie, you know my reading is the racing press and the latest serial! How will I ever get to read something some literary snob wrote years ago? You'll have to tell me the story or I shall never know what you're on about!'

'Very well, but you're a frightful little philistine whose only charm is that she's honest enough to admit it. The sooner we do something about educating you, the better. The story is about a beautiful married woman who goes off alone in her carriage every afternoon and returns a couple of hours later without any explanation. Her husband is convinced she must be having an affair so he has her followed. Sure enough, she goes to a house of assignation, enters alone and emerges after staying most of the afternoon. He jumps to the obvious conclusion that she is meeting her lover there and their marriage ends in her disgrace. The truth is that she has been going to the house and sitting there in respectable solitude each day because she thinks her prosaic life makes her boring and that she needs to add an exotic touch of mystery to the proceedings. In doing so, she loses everything.'

'And why do you think such a story might apply to me?'

'You seem to be doing things for no better reason than to make people notice you. I was merely hinting that you should think it through more thoroughly, and make sure there's something behind the intriguing details. Otherwise, if anyone discovers it's only a façade, you'll be dropped and never taken seriously when you do something worthwhile.'

He fell silent, half expecting a resentful outburst, but she appeared to be considering what he had said. Eventually she replied: 'Mmm, I suppose you have a point. Now what shall I think up to convince them it's more than just a load of old horsehair?' She grinned at him wickedly and touched her spurs to the horse's flanks. Charles jumped aside, only just in time, as the big animal leaped away.

'Hey, idiot, that doesn't mean manslaughter's a good idea!' But he was laughing as he watched the pint-sized figure dash away in perfect control of her mount.

Bonnie Charles was Christian de Selincourt's best friend. Their love of horses and pretty women gave them much in common, but Charles was an infinitely more complex personality than de Selincourt. Culturally, Christi had never progressed much beyond the sporting press, the stud book and the odd salacious novel. He enjoyed the theatre but the most avid fan could hardly have described contemporary

French drama as the pinnacle of art. Charles had read widely and in many languages and his Paris apartment included a sizeable library. He enjoyed opera and his visits to the ballet were not undertaken merely in order to shower flowers and indecent proposals on the girls of the corps de ballet.

When Eliane first went to live at Gaillard, he was out of France on a long business trip. She did not meet him until she had been with Christian for more than a year and even then it was some time before he became a regular visitor at the château. He fascinated her from the moment she met him. She never claimed love at first sight: she was astute enough even then to know he attracted her simply because he was unlike any other man she had known. Charles was as different from Christi and his other friends as de Selincourt himself had been from the callow young officers of Saumur.

The trouble was that on first acquaintance, de Selincourt had seemed to be what he was not. Occasionally, untypically, he reflected a degree of sensitivity and understanding which was really lacking from his nature. He was not devoid of such qualities but they surfaced more readily with his men friends than with his mistresses. When he was treating Eliane as a friend, he could be as considerate and tender as any woman would wish; but when he became conscious of her as a lover, the sensitivity vanished and he could be a tyrant. He was determinded to escape matrimony and fended it off by going to extraordinary lengths to show his mistress of the moment that he saw her as nothing special. In Eliane's case such churlishness was doubly apparent because he never subjected Ottilie to the same treatment. After all, it was quite clear that she was not interested in marrying him or any other man. She had all the fame, admiration and lovers she could want; and, more important, she was as rich as de Selincourt in her own right. Eliane was still naïve and she did not understand the reasoning behind his behaviour. She was too insecure to realise that his continued interest in her after nearly four years was sufficient indication of his feelings. She needed a more open demonstration – and there was no question of that from Christi.

Bonnie Charles was different. He adored women on many different levels: he had a huge sexual appetite and satisfied it unashamedly with a constantly changing stream of young and middle-aged women; he was curious about their lifestyle – at the time totally different from the lives their men led; he was particularly fascinated by women of intelligence, because he believed that female sensibilities were more highly developed than men's, and that therefore if a woman had a good brain too she was potentially a man's superior. In spite of such unorthodox views, he was equally at home in the company of men, a brilliant all-round horseman with special talent as a polo player; a strong swimmer; a good tennis player. He delighted in the amateur dramatics which were a constant feature of the social life at Gaillard, his talent as a raconteur was legendary, and he invariably arrived for visits bearing hampers crammed with the freshest delicacies from the best shops in London or Paris.

All this added up to a picture of the man she had thought she saw in Christian de Selincourt a few years before. Charles offered two additional attributes which made him particularly attractive to Eliane: he was a self-made business success, having increased a hundredfold by his own efforts a very modest inheritance, and he could not endure Ottilie Deslys.

At first it was this antipathy rather than his other qualities which drew her to him. She was outside Compiègne railway station one Monday morning, exercising one of the more unmanageable horses from de Selincourt's stables. In her hands it behaved like a gentle old hack. Eliane was chatting with the station master, in private life a keen member of the racing fraternity, when Charles strode out of the booking hall, looking positively ferocious. She had been introduced to the dashing Englishman a couple of months before when he returned from abroad, but since then he had been along to a couple of Ottilie's week-ends when Eliane deliberately kept out of the way. His air of irritation was so obvious that she could not resist speaking to him.

'Why so out of spirits so early in the morning, Monsieur Charles?' she called out to him.

He stopped and turned towards her, apparently undecided whether he could bear the strain of conversation. When he saw who had called out to him, he relaxed visibly. 'Bonnie, please, Alouette – as long as I may use your first name, of course!'

She smiled her agreement. 'Come on, you don't escape so easily. Why are you so cross? Gaillard doesn't usually have such an effect on Christi's guests.'

His handsome face darkened again. 'It does for me when Deslys is part of the bargain! I've just been seeing her on to her train for Paris - so vital that she gets to her public to avoid disappointing them! I hope for their sakes she's a bit livelier by tonight than she's been for the past three days.'

'Good gracious, Bonnie, are you saying that our prima donna has failed to ensnare you?'

'You could put it that way, I suppose. Why on earth doesn't Christi get rid of her? She's like last week's newspapers.'

Eliane was beginning to enjoy herself for the first time in several days. 'But I thought her grace and beauty were every man's ideal.'

'If you enjoy constant doses of hot chocolate with heavy cream and a plate of sweet cakes, perhaps, but I like lean game and astringent wines.' His eyes abruptly focused on Eliane, taking in the slender frame and boyish clothing approvingly. 'That woman thinks the main function of men is to buy diamonds and open carriage doors. In return she believes they expect fawning coquetry or mindless tantrums.'

'Is she wrong?'

'No girl should try that line dressed as you are. The outfit gives too much away.'

'Like what?'

'Like the fact that you have a mind of your own; that you have no intention of conforming with the *horizontales'* ideas of acceptable attire; in short, that you'd probably loathe her as much as I do even without your additional grounds.'

'Oh, surely you exaggerate. Gaillard is a big place. There's room for everyone.'

'Balderdash. There'd never be room for more than one female in any establishment of mine if you were that female. I imagine you find the arrangement wildly unsatisfactory. Only a harum scarum like Christi would ever think it could work – but he shows élan in even trying it!'

'Remember it required my consent.'

'Give me leave to doubt that. I'd lay bets that you came here thinking you'd be sharing our hero with no one but his horses. Once you were installed, it must have been too late to change your mind. My God, your pride must have taken a bashing!'

She found it impossible to dissemble with this apparently omniscient man. 'If I had my way she'd be under that damned train, not on it.'

'Then she goes with similar wishes from us both.'

Eliane rewarded him with a dazzling smile. 'Perhaps we should plan an alternative future for her.'

'Allow me – it will be my pleasure. I'll make it my present to you on your next birthday.'

'So soon? That gives you only a few weeks. And there must be a price tag. Nothing I want so much can be free.'

'Oh, there'll be a price all right, but I shan't rush you and I think you might enjoy paying it when the time comes!' His long, significant look left her in no doubt what the price would be. Eliane realised that the prospect filled her with unalloyed excitement.

As they talked, she had turned her horse and begun walking it back along the station approach. Now she reined in. 'This is silly. I can't drag you all the way back to Gaillard on foot. How did you get here?'

'What? Oh, carriage, of course. I wouldn't come in the car and Deslys wouldn't hear of me riding beside the rig, so I strung my hunter behind, then got Jules to drive us down and take the carriage back afterwards. Nimrod is tethered in the station yard. Come on, let's get him.'

As they rode back along the lanes with their winter backdrop of frosty fields and crisp bare branches, Charles explained his errand. 'It's as if the woman senses that I'm the one man in Gaillard who can't stand her and focuses on me in the hope of winning me over. All she succeeds in doing is to make me more hostile. We're like oil and vinegar. She started that overgrown little girl wheedling for me to escort her, and I could only have avoided it by being churlish.'

'For her it might have been worth it.'

He laughed. 'But not for my Christi. I love the man, in spite of his nonsense. No silly vain actress is worth the loss of his friendship. But that's enough of Ottilie. I've talked about her more in the past ten minutes than ever before and I've no intention of prolonging the experience! I'll see you get your birthday present, though.'

The rest of the journey was uneventful and they parted at the gates of Gaillard. Bonnie wanted to ride a little longer. Eliane had promised to return the stallion by mid-morning and it was already 10.30. She watched him depart with some regret. He was an attractive companion and she welcomed the opportunity to insult Ottilie without fear of repercussions.

She never knew how much Bonnie Charles had to do with Ottilie's permanent eclipse, but from that day on the actress's reign at Gaillard drew swiftly to its close. For three successive week-ends, de Selincourt asked Eliane to organise impromptu house parties and the great château was full of laughter, disorderly mixed breakfasts and childish amateur theatricals. Bonnie Charles attended the middle week-end and then disappeared, pleading urgent business in England. He did not come again until the day before her birthday when he arrived bearing her gift, an exquisite bronze statuette of a racehorse.

Eliane gave a cry of pleasure as the soft paper fell away from the beautiful object. 'Oh, Bonnie, thank you. It's the loveliest thing I've ever owned!'

He feigned coolness. 'Just a small memento. You've had your main present, of course.'

She looked up sharply. Gaby Soustelle, the actress girl friend of one of the other guests, was watching, round-eyed and impressed. 'You've given her something else? But the bronze alone must have cost a tidy sum!'

Charles's lazy smile was pure poison as he looked significantly at Eliane. 'Oh, her main present was worth a lot more than the horse, Gaby, a lot more.' Doré hugged the horse statue and said nothing, merely returning his smile.

Ottilie never returned to Gaillard, although her parting from de Selincourt seemed amicable enough and they met occasionally in Paris. After a while there was talk of her having embarked on a passionate affair with a much younger man – an Englishman. Eliane was not sure how Bonnie Charles had managed to dislodge her, but she was convinced it must be his doing.

Now her world should have been perfect. There was no longer any need for her to remain in the shadows; de Selincourt was proud of her and enjoyed showing her off. The château was always full of his – and increasingly Eliane's – sporting friends. The older theatrical crowd no longer attended, but younger faces from the theatre and music hall worlds constantly came and went. The atmosphere was light and cheerful. In a sense it gave Eliane an opportunity to catch up on all the things she had missed in her drab orphanage days. Their activities were wildly childish – charades, pantomimes, paper chases, games of hide and seek. Gaby Soustelle devised the dramas and Doré invariably found herself assembling collections of costumes, sometimes fantastic, sometimes prosaic.

She played the odd practical joke, turning up soon after dawn one day convincingly disguised as a drunken old flower seller who had got on an empty train in Paris the previous night for a sleep, only to waken at Compiègne. All the guests were temporarily taken in and chaos ensued as they tried to palm her off on one another while she whined and sniffled about losing her flowers and having no money to get home. Eventually Bonnie unmasked her and they all descended for an early breakfast over the racing papers, which she had picked up off the early train before playing her trick.

As time passed, Eliane became a fixture in the Compiègne area, intriguing, uniquely dressed, unapproachable to anyone not part of the charmed inner circle around Christian de Selincourt. It was a better life than the little *gommeuse* of Saumur could ever have imagined – but it was not what Eliane wanted. She knew when she began waking early that something was badly wrong. In her days at the shop, the hardest thing of all had been to get up in the morning. She would waken before dawn in winter thanks only to the big double-belled alarm clock supplied by Madame Chaillot, and wriggle deeper beneath the blankets in a vain attempt to shut out the cold morning. Finally she would fling herself from her warm nest for just long enough to light the stove and put on a pan of water to heat. Then it was back to bed to contemplate a future in which she could rise when she wanted and take her time over a leisurely breakfast.

At Gaillard, not even the servants had to start their day in such conditions. Now Eliane was free to lie as late as she wished, and at first she was inclined to lounge between the smooth expensive sheets until quite late, unless she had planned a morning gallop. But as time passed she became restive and edgy, waking with a jump at dawn, lying on her back beside the sleeping Christian, staring at the ceiling and wondering what was missing from her life. The early gallops became twice weekly, then daily affairs. One morning she was so early that she was at Compiègne station even before the Paris train arrived with the newspapers. It was over these, sitting on the terrace outside the drawing room on another, brilliantly sunny morning, that she got a first inkling of what was wrong.

Gaby Soustelle and Natalie Defarges were with her. Gaby had arrived that weekend bubbling with excitement at having landed her first leading role in a top comedy production on the Paris stage.

Natalie, the only regular visitor at Gaillard whose looks put Eliane in the shade, sighed. 'What a lucky girl you are, Gaby, to have another talent apart from pleasing men. You'll still be going strong when we're starving in some provincial boarding house.'

Eliane felt as if someone had switched off the sun. She muttered an excuse about feeling unwell – even in extremis she did not want Gaby to think she grudged the actress her triumph – and hurried away indoors. Once inside she raced upstairs and locked herself into a bathroom, where she sat down on the wooden lavatory seat and pressed her burning face against the cool tiled wall beside her. She sat thus for an interminable period, her mind full of boiling, unquiet images which refused to settle into any specific pattern. Then the shock waves finally began to subside and she almost wished the turmoil would return for suddenly she was faced with the true cause of all her disturbed early mornings, and she hated what confronted her.

All this comfort, all this security, were an illusion, because for Eliane and the girls like her – universally known in France as *irrégulières* to distinguish them from virtuous women – there was no such thing. The comfort lasted as long as the beauty, maybe not even that long. After all, if she was honest, Ottilie Deslys was still physically lovely, but that hadn't prevented Christi from dismissing her like a sacked servant when he tired of her. Ottilie, like Gaby, was the fortunate possessor of a talent which made her independent of men when she needed to be. Eliane had been capable of such independence, even on a limited, impoverished level, when she worked for the Chaillots. At least then the roof over her head and the food in her belly were provided by her own skill. Here the bread might be richer and the rooms infinitely more glamorous, but they were available only on loan and could be snatched from her the moment she became a nuisance.

Panic swept over her again. There must be something, something she could do! But what? She certainly had no talent for the stage. The only other thing she could do was serve in a shop. But she could hardly open a shop under Christi's nose – he'd be livid! Why, the very idea. . . .

She snapped her head away from the tiled wall and stood up. For the past two weeks, Gaby Soustelle had been flitting around Paris wearing a series of hats Eliane had made for her after Gaby admired the styles she had been making and wearing herself for almost a year. As on that first occasion, she still bought the basic materials from Galeries Lafayette on her rare visits to Paris.

By the time Eliane had finished with them, they didn't look remotely like Galeries Lafayette hat forms. Nor did they look at all like the towering mountains of ornaments which women habitually wore on their heads at the time. She had become expert at the skills she discovered in those halting first attempts with the steaming kettles and assorted trimmings. Nowadays, her creations seldom failed. They were simple, distinctive and very stylish. The previous night, Gaby had laughingly said she was sure it was the jaunty little black straw hat she wore to her audition which had first attracted the theatrical impresario's attention.

The more Eliane thought about the idea, the more she liked it. Okay, so it wasn't great strategy. Neither was the tactical retreat from Paris to Josselin in her orphange days, but it had saved her and Geneviève from the reformatory. This latest idea might just save her from an impoverished old age in a provincial boarding house, as visualised by Natalie. That was enough to be going on with.

She had more sense than to broach the matter directly with de Selincourt. He would have to be approached tactfully, if at all. Better try building up a little custom first . . .

It was much easier than she had begun to imagine. Gaby had a nature as superstitious as Eliane's own, and was more than ready to go on wearing Doré hats for fear that, if she stopped, her new-found theatrical luck would run out. The part she had landed was in a modern comedy and the heroine was a lady of fashion. A Paris couturier was designing the costumes and Gaby required minimal persuasion to suggest that the hats should come from Mademoiselle Alouette Doré, whom she boosted as a cross between Worth and Madame Du Barry.

Thanks to that one contact, Doré hats were seen on the head of the girl who turned everyone's heads in Paris that season as the star of the daring new comedy *Lilith*. The programme notes credited Eliane for her hats and soon both Gaby and the theatre management were referring fashionable women to her.

The theatrical commission had paid only a nominal fee – far less than the monthly pocket money she received from Christian – but the commercial business it brought her was a different matter. Eliane set herself up in a pretty English-style summerhouse in a remote spot at Gaillard. De Selincourt was taking the whole matter lightly because he still saw it as an innocent diversion. He had no idea of how hard she was working because he spent so much time in the stables. He had no idea, either, of the size of the cheques which were beginning to arrive in the mail for his little *irrégulière*, because she paid them into her new bank account without mentioning them. Each time she saw the amount she had on deposit, Eliane grew more excited, but a full realisation of her success did not really take root until the weekend when Gaby arrived, breathless with the news that a recent order had been placed on behalf of Ottilie Deslys under the name of one of her women friends.

'Can you imagine how much she must have wanted to get her hands on a Doré hat to go that far?' Gaby was bubbling with all the satisfaction that Eliane was trying to suppress. 'You really should be in Paris, Alouette – tucked away up here you don't get any true idea of how your hats are sweeping through the fashionable set.'

'Don't be crazy! If they were that popular I'd have been

killed by overwork by now. It's true that I've been thinking of getting a couple of girls to help me, but I haven't turned out anything like enough to be that well known.'

'For a kid from the streets, you can be really naïve at times. Ever heard of imitation being the sincerest form of flattery? There are Doré copies on half the heads along the Rue de Rivoli. It's time you were making more money from it, my dear, and the only way you'll do that is by opening in Paris.'

They were sipping pre-dinner drinks in the ground floor salon at Gaillard. De Selincourt was at the far end of the room, regaling two male friends fresh from Paris with a snippet of horsy gossip from Compiègne. Gaby's remark made Eliane glance sharply in his direction and the actress caught the look. At that moment Christian's story ended and the air was filled with a roar of masculine laughter. One of his friends slapped him on the back and they started on another story. Gaby shook her head sympathetically and smiled at Eliane.

'One day it will have to be him or the hats – or whatever else you're up to by then. Surely you realise that, my dear?'

'No – why should I? If I do a little business, what concern is it of Christi's? I never noticed him objecting to that fat old cow Deslys going off to earn her living.'

'You're being naïve again, Alouette. For Christi – for all these men – the stage is different. It's the sort of thing we little tarts do as another string to our bows. It doesn't matter if we're straight artists with real talent – they still say that stage success is just an extension of what we do in their bedrooms, take off our clothes and tickle their fancies. As long as they can think like that, we're no threat. But what you propose is business, trade, a man's world. He'll tell you it's undignified but that's not really it. It's fear that you'll be as good at making money as a man, or even better. Try not to be too hard on Christi. He's no worse than the rest and a damned sight better than some. At least he encourages you to ride like a man, and in private at least to be funny and clever. That's a lot more than many lovers would let you get away with.'

'What do you think I should do about it? I can confide in you, Gaby. I'm doing this because of what Natalie said a few months ago about you succeeding while we gradually faded away. I don't intend to fade away, but at the moment I can't manage without Christi – I'm not even sure I want to. So how do I manage going on with my hats and not letting on to him?'

'Mmm, well for a start you begin looking for a likelier lad to replace him. You may never need to move on to someone else but it's always a good idea to have a remount in case your hunter goes lame.'

They giggled at the idea, but Gaby was making a serious point and now she pursued it. 'Eliane, I'm very fond of you. I'm – I'm almost afraid to go on with this in case you take it the wrong way. I'd hate it if we weren't friends any more. But I think it's something you need to know. Promise not to be cross if I tell?'

'Of course not – not unless you're about to do an Ottilie on me and start bitching with the excuse that it'll do me good in the end!'

'No such thing. This is serious. Look, you and I are both street kids, right? Me from the back streets of Paris, you from some Breton bog. Both common as dirt but pretty and clever. How d'you think *They* see us?'

Eliane had no need to ask who *They* were. They were the class of society which treated the likes of her and Gaby as barely tolerated guests, somewhere between paid companions and entertainers. At their best they were the Christian de Selincourts. At worst they were the patronising women who gossiped about them in the enclosure at race meetings. Eliane considered the question.

'Mmm – mildly amusing but strictly temporary. That's what bothers me.'

'Yes, but go a bit deeper. Don't you ever wonder what they see when they look at us – what they want to see? Forget the dowagers for a minute. Think about Christian and his friends. Think of us and the girls like us and what we have in common.'

'We're young and pretty, of course. What else? Well, we've been around a bit, enough to know which knives and forks to use. We dress well, if strangely in my case, and we talk nicely.'

'Stop there for a minute. How did you learn?'

'It's about the only thing I have to thank the nuns for, apart from a cheap set of bedlinen. They hammered out our awful peasant accents. Every time one of us came out with that high Breton "antz" sound, they'd make us feel so ridiculous we were soon talking like Jesuits. I hated it then, but I'm damned glad of it now!'

'Exactly. With me it was the old wreck of a has-been tragic actor who picked me out of a back alley when I was fourteen and got me a job in the chorus. Think of the other *irrégulières*. They all talk like us. Have you ever wondered how come these lovely, so unsnobbish boys we all hang around with never happened to take up with girls who had accents straight off the Marseille waterfront or the Auvergne farms? We're welcome here as long as we sound and look like ladies.'

'That's interesting, Gaby. I'd never thought about it before, but I must have realised it deep down or I wouldn't have been so busy ever since I moved in here learning to ride side-saddle, and what to do with my orange peel, and how to hold up the back of my skirt. But I don't quite see why you're bringing it up now.'

'Because I'm trying to make you see us as the men do, make you see what we have to be in order to keep them. We all have perfect manners, as good as any Society woman, and who's to know if we learned ours as domestic servants or from an acting coach? We also behave like whores in private and like ladies in public. Now that's what I was trying to get around to. If we want to stay in this world, we have to behave publicly like ladies.'

'Of course. So what? I've spent most of the last few years skulking around in nondescript clothes in my efforts not to be vulgar and flashy. Nobody knows better than me about that.'

'Then why can't you see that it will have to be Christi or the hats – or rather, Christi and every man like him or the hats? Ladies do not work. Above all, ladies do not go into business. Christi may be madly bohemian and have rejected convention, but he's still got all the insecurities of the nouveau riche. You might stand more of a chance if you were with Leon or Etienne – they're both from the old nobility who really don't give a damn. But although he's so rich, Christi's just two generations on from his bourgeois shopkeeper ancestors. He wants the world to see he knows a lady when he sees one, even if she's his mistress. He won't put up with the world thinking he approves of his mistress being a shopkeeper.'

Eliane was staring at her, numb with the awful truth of what Gaby was saying. Her friend sighed and put an arm around her.

'Please don't be cross with me! It sounds so heartless of me to pour cold water on things, and really I'm not. I just think you must understand that you're not likely to be able to have the business and Christi – or any of his set, for that matter.'

Eliane took the point. She knew instinctively that Gaby was telling the truth. It was unlikely that she could have it all – but she intended to try. Over the next few weeks she gave a lot of thought to possible ways of discussing her hat venture with de Selincourt, and to a prospective alternative protector to whom she could go if he became impossible. In the end she decided she had to tell him a little about it.

She broke it to him airily, trying to lessen the impact of her announcement by reducing it to a morsel of gossip, to be mentioned then forgotten. 'Oh, Christi, I'm about to become an employer!'

He smiled at her, ready to humour and maybe sidetrack some request for a lady's maid. 'Really? And why do you need employees?'

'Well, you know I did those hats for Gaby's début? They made quite a stir and . . . and I got a lot of orders from ladies in Paris who wanted to emulate her chic. Anyway, it's so time-consuming now that I need a couple of girls to help. You know I've been using the English summerhouse?'

His face was darkening with disapproval. 'Yes – I thought it was some bit of nonsense for our week-end charades, though. I didn't realise you were going back into trade.'

She flushed, angry at the implied contempt, but forced herself to remain sweetly persuasive. 'I know it's hardly appropriate to be doing that sort of thing around the château. That's why I – I'd thought of opening a little shop in Compiègne.'

There! It was out. Before he had time to break in she went on, pouring out enthusiastic imaginings of a bandbox-smart little establishment which would reflect nothing but credit on him. It was no use, he was furious. She prattled on for a few moments but he slapped the table and shouted to silence her.

'Enough! I will not be talked down in my own house – and I'll not become a tradesman for your amusement either. It's out of the question. If you're bored, come out riding more. You haven't been on a horse for over a fortnight.'

So he had at least noticed her absence. Perhaps she was sufficiently firmly established with him to risk a little defiance. She'd soon find out. . . .

'I'm not asking you to become a tradesman, Christi.' The tone was all sweet submissiveness. The message was the exact opposite. 'I have enough cash to put a deposit on shop premises and to cover the girls' wages for the first few months. If I haven't succeeded by then, I shall give up. But if my orders so far are anything to go by, that's unlikely. I'm not asking you to finance me; I just don't want to do anything to annoy you.'

Momentarily, surprise displaced his irritation. 'You've made enough already to set yourself up?'

'Only in Compiègne. I couldn't possibly manage it in Paris.' She paused significantly, hoping against hope that he would offer his support. She was disappointed, but at least news of her initial success stemmed his opposition to the Compiègne venture.

'Hmm . . . seems a lot of nonsense to me. Plenty of girls in your position would thank their lucky stars they didn't have to work from morning till night, not go out looking for some way of keeping their fingers busy. Hat shop, indeed! Who wants to be a shopkeeper when there's racing and polo and parties to be had?' But he did not tell her she could not go ahead.

Eliane knew that she had won more of an armed truce than a victory. She was by no means indispensable though Christi was delighted at her popularity with his friends. Lately, too, Gaby had told her that smart Paris was talking about this beautiful mysterious Alouette who had succeeded in holding on to one of Society's most eligible bachelors for more than four years, who dressed with unique individuality, who rode as though born in the saddle, and was in general totally captivating. De Selincourt could not have failed to hear the talk, or to have been teased flatteringly by his men friends, and this could only add to her allure for him. Nevertheless the first intensity of his sexual passion had faded long ago.

Although Eliane told herself she could take or leave sex, generally speaking she preferred to leave it, even with de Selincourt. That she continued to entertain and fascinate him in spite of this was a great tribute to her other social talents, but she was too intelligent to think it would last indefinitely. One day he would be captivated by another, lustier, younger girl and Eliane's sun would set.

She intended to have moved on in triumph before that happened. But where should she look? Two or three members of de Selincourt's inner circle had made it clear their interest in her could amount to far more than friendship but essentially they were alternative versions of Christi himself. In any case, she had recognised the truth in what

Gaby Soustelle had told her. The men were entranced now. If they knew she was going into the hat business, it might be a different matter. There were lots of Alouettes hanging around the provincial towns, longing to live in idleness with rich young men. There was a strictly limited supply of rich young men. If she was failing to get on with Christian because of her private drive for security, it would be no different with them. It was not as if she could hope to snare them forever by her wonderful prowess as a lover. She dismissed the problem for the moment and set about opening her shop in Compiègne.

By anyone else's standards, it would have been a triumph. Suddenly there was a rush of female guests at the châteaux in the area and fashionable women would always go for a stroll in Compiègne during their stay. It became a requirement of one's country weekend that one peeped in at Christi de Selincourt's funny little milliner, who just happened to make such ravishing hats that one found one-self staying to try them on, then placing a big order. Such reasonable prices, and she wore such unusual clothes her-self it was a shame that one couldn't buy clothes there, too! Still, perhaps that would come later. One never knew.

Within six months Eliane felt she was a one-woman annexe to the Faubourg St-Honoré. Her work force of two had expanded to four. Then she received a letter from her sister in Vichy which further strengthened her determination to open in Paris.

Elise was now twenty-two and had become the Lepines' nanny when she completed her training under the former nurse some years before. They treated her almost as a daughter and it never occurred to her to consider working for anyone else. But there was a complication which had not been mentioned when the Lepines took Elise from the orphanage.

Madame Lepine had a younger brother. Their parents had died soon after her marriage and she had taken responsibility for giving a home to Paul, who had been at a military academy when the young Elise had joined them.

Paul returned to their estate near Vichy for holidays and eventually for more frequent breaks. He fell in love with Elise and she with him. He had acquired a veneer of sophistication during his military training, or Elise would have become pregnant a lot sooner than she did. As it was, their affair lasted for more than four years.

She did not even tell Eliane, who thought her younger sister confided everything. So it was something of a shock to Eliane when she received a letter from Madame Lepine, followed almost immediately by a tear-stained, incoherent note from Elise.

*Les Moustiers*
*August 3, 1911*

*Dear Mademoiselle Doré*
*It is my painful duty to tell you that we are unable to keep Elise with us any longer. As she has been with us so long, and as we have grown so fond of her, I felt I must write to you in an attempt to arrange a safe place for her to go. I must tell you now that I am expressing such concern only because we were so close and because I feel my family bears part of the blame for what happened to her.*

*A month ago, your sister was taken ill with serious abdominal cramps and it soon became clear that she was suffering a miscarriage. As we had no idea that she was pregnant, it came as a considerable shock. I am sure you will have gathered from your own correspondence with Elise that we have always tried to ensure that her welfare and her morals were safeguarded. At first we were at a loss to understand how such a terrible thing could have happened. Close questioning of the other servants produced no information, then, to my unspeakable shame, my brother Paul came to me and confessed that the child would have been his; also that their relationship had been going on for years. He expressed a wish to marry Elise, but of course this is out of the question. Even if I felt such a match had any chance of success, it would be doomed now by the fact that the servants and, inevitably, other local people have some notion of what has happened. Marriage now would only result in lifelong misery for them both, as respectable society would not receive them.*

*We have kept Elise with us until she was fully restored to health and we shall not put pressure on her to move until satisfactory arrangements have been made for her elsewhere. At present I do not quite know what I am able to do about giving her a reference. Elise might in any case not wish to take such a post again. We shall pay her wages for the rest of the year. Paul has no money of his own until his twenty-fifth birthday, but in the meantime I have arranged to pay her a small annuity which should maintain her in modest circumstances should she be unable to find suitable work. When Paul has his own money he might care to make alternative provision.*

*While there is no great hurry for Elise to move, she is obviously distressed at present and has no one in whom she can confide, so if you are able to arrange for her to come to you, at least temporarily, it will perhaps help.*

*I cannot begin to express my regret that such a terrible thing could have happened when Elise was under my supervision. My one hope is that she is still young enough to put the whole business behind her and make a new life for herself.*
*Yours sincerely*
*Marguerite Lepine*

*Dearest Eliane*
*Please, oh please, don't be cross about what I've done. Madame is writing to you and you'll probably know all about it by the time you get this, but please don't turn your back on me! I love Paul so much and we really tried not to have a baby, it just happened. I wasn't even sure I was pregnant but I'd missed and I was getting a bit fatter. I kept trying to lace myself in so people*

*wouldn't suspect. Then it started hurting terribly and I fainted and when I woke up Madame was there crying. I was in bed and it still hurt really badly and she said I'd lost it and whose fault was it?*

*I couldn't say it was Paul so I pretended to faint again and they asked all the others so everyone knows now and I can't stand looking at any of them. Then Paul told her and they sort of shut me away. I'm not locked up or anything but they gave me a cottage in the park away from the nursery wing and now there's somebody else come to look after the children and my Paul has been sent away. I love him so much but we mustn't get married because Madame says everyone would know and make me miserable as well as him.*

*Please let me come to you if you can. I think I may be able to afford a cheap boarding house if it's difficult with your living arrangements. Please, oh please, come and get me. I'm so lonely and miserable.*

*Your loving Elise*

Furious, Eliane balled up Madame Lepine's letter, muttering a stream of abuse. To think that even a decent, kind woman like her, who had been virtually the mother Elise had lacked, could be such a slave to convention that she would do this to the kid. Marriage out of the question, was it? If the little swine was decent enough to suggest it himself, he might even have had the guts to make a go of it, but this cow was stopping it with her hoity toity attitudes and concern that the right thing should be done. Sorry, was she? So she should have been! Elise was a child, completely ignorant of that sort of thing when she went to the Lepines, yet their attitude now was that they were only 'partly' to blame. Eliane knew where she'd stick the blame. And she knew precisely what she had to do now.

She found de Selincourt, as usual, at the stables. She showed him the two letters and he let out a grunt of anger. 'The bitch – she could at least have let her precious brother do the right thing if he was willing. I know what you're about to say and you don't have to ask. I've just bought a pair of cottages in Compiègne to house visiting jockeys and trainers. Elise can have one for as long as she likes and I'll confine my visitors to the other for the moment. If she needs to stay a long time or feels cut off down there, we can always find her room up at the house, but right now I suspect she'll be happier away from where rich young men with a roving eye can get at her.'

'Christi, at times you're the best friend a girl ever had!'

He grinned, then put on a pretend glower. 'Only at times? Who's your full-time best friend then?' She slapped his shoulder playfully, then turned and hurried away to plan her trip to collect Elise.

Elise's presence made a huge difference to Eliane's life, more than she would have believed possible. It gave her a sense of family stability for the first time ever, perhaps because she sensed she was moving towards becoming the family breadwinner. Elise was very like Eliane in some respects and totally different in others. The privation and repression that had given Eliane her fighting spirit and sense of adventure had made Elise timid, gentle and grateful for whatever attention or affection she might receive. After their first evening together, Eliane was fired by the impulse to protect and cherish the younger girl, an impulse which lasted until Elise's death. Her sister repaid her with a doglike devotion which would brook no criticism of Eliane from anyone.

She fitted in quietly at Christian's cottage in the village, occasionally joining the week-end parties at Gaillard but always remaining a shy figure in the background. She proved invaluable in the shop and soon Eliane was wondering how she had managed without her. Elise's lack of training as a needlewoman at the convent had been more than made good during her years as a nursemaid. The senior nanny was a fine plain seamstress who believed that such skills should be second nature to nursemaids; Madame Lepine was a cutwork embroideress of near genius who enjoyed passing on her expertise, so now Eliane had acquired a good worker. But it was on the administrative side that Elise soon began to show exceptional ability. Her winning manner and unfailing sweet courtesy charmed the fashionable women who came to the shop in a way which Eliane's acerbic wit could never do. Somehow, too, Elise had an infallible eye for the type of style which went with the looks and clothes of the clients. Such thoughts never occurred to Eliane. She created hats because she liked the feel and look of the materials and form shapes. The preferences and style of the clients had no influence on her creativity and it was useless for them to ask her for suggestions for designs they might specially commission to go with a particular outfit.

Elise grasped all this within days and unobtrusively steered her sister away from clients who might want such a service, taking over the orders herself. The scale of their business quickly began to reflect her tactful policy. Instead of standing by while Eliane treated a valuable potential client to the sort of dismissive responses normally doled out by bad-tempered Parisian concierges, Elise fussed over them, praised their choice of dress or suit, then said she would discuss with Mademoiselle exactly the type of hat such an outfit needed and come round to see them at home if they wished. This was seldom necessary. They were so frequently charmed by the little milliner, so frequently intrigued by the non-business activities of the little milliner's big sister, that they invariably returned to inspect the headgear Eliane had devised after Elise's diplomatic suggestion of something to complement a rose tulle theatre gown or a grey worsted afternoon frock. Eliane knew she was being manipulated, but that it was for her own benefit. The customers simply revelled in the welter of attention they received – and loved the hats.

Elise's initial few weeks at Compiègne lengthened into months. Business was excellent, but Eliane was increasingly conscious that the scope of Compiègne was limited. She was beginning to get a taste for independence but remained acutely conscious that her hard-won success could be swept away overnight if the women who came to peep at her found a new source of amusement. For permanence she needed Paris. She also wanted to give Elise a broader stage. After the girl's first heartbroken outpourings about her lost lover, she had said no more. But Eliane wanted her to meet someone else, someone who would expunge Paul Gallimard from her mind. A hat shop in Compiègne was hardly the place where such a man was likely to appear. Then Elise came up with a suggestion which made such a move even more attractive.

A woman had been buying hats in the Compiègne shop and had asked Elise to set aside for her a delightful confection of straw and ribbon which had formed Eliane's window display that week.

'I love it so much I'm tempted simply to buy it now,' she said, 'but I've been finding lately that Mademoiselle Doré's designs are so unusual it's sometimes impossible to get clothes which have the right feel to match the hats. I want to see what's available in Paris to go with this one. Sometimes I specially commission a hat from you to match a particular dress, but the other way round I find I can't do a lot of her styles justice.'

Elise reported the conversation later. 'I've been wondering for ages why you don't do clothes as well, Eliane. If you have the eye for such gorgeous hats, you're sure to be able to whip up frocks to go with them.'

Eliane was flattered but dismissive. 'What it is to have a heroworshipping little sister! I'm a complete fraud, idiot. All I do is what they could do if they wanted: go to Galeries Lafayette, buy a stack of plain hat forms and get a good range of assorted trimmings, then I play until I like the result. There's no great talent involved in that, is there? The miracle is that anyone wants to buy the things when they could make their own for a few sous. Turn me loose with a bale of cloth and a pair of scissors and I'd make a fool of myself in no time flat.'

'And what about the things you designed and made for

yourself and Geneviève years back? A lot of that came close to tailor's standards. What about all the things you have now which no other woman has in her wardrobe? They must have come from somewhere.'

Eliane laughed again. 'Three-quarters of them are pinched from Christi's and his men friends' closets. Men's clothes are very comfortable and some of them can look quite good on women if they're not built like those great big cocottes.'

'Yes, but who else ever thought of it? Anyway, that's not really true about you borrowing things from Christian and his friends. You may pinch the odd coat or sweater from them, but you get the breeches and jackets from shops. Then there's those lovely plain afternoon frocks with the fancy underdresses that you wear when other women are lacing themselves up fit to bust. And what about that marvellous frock you designed for Gaby Soustelle to have made up in Paris?'

Eliane was finally beginning to take her seriously. The kid had a point after all. It might be just as easy to trick these silly rich women into believing she knew how to design clothes as it had been with the hats. Gaby's dress had certainly been a success.

She had come down to Gaillard a month before a big Paris showbusiness party when she was to be fêted as the girl who made *Lilith* the theatrical hit of the year. She was going crazy trying to find a dress which would make her stand out from all the other beauties who would be vying to eclipse her. She had a good dressmaker in Paris but the woman was just that – a dressmaker. She took styles from the fashion papers and re-created them faithfully, but that would leave Gaby competing in a well-made frock against couture gowns. Sometimes it helped to be a grande cocotte when you were starting out on the stage – it was the only way a poor girl could finance a couture wardrobe.

'Oh, Alouette, what shall I do? I don't want to go to my own party looking like a smart off-duty shop girl, but I can't afford couture yet!' The two girls were sitting together, poring over a fashion magazine. Eliane came across a delightful drawing of an Empire-style tea gown, the waist high under the bosom, skirt falling long and uncluttered from it to the floor. Suddenly she had an idea.

'You know, I look different when I hang around the racetrack because I take the simplest clothes and touch them up a little. Suppose we got your dressmaker to make a basic shape like that – nice and simple – and touch it up so it didn't look like anything any of the others were wearing?'

'It's a lovely idea, Alouette, but she really isn't anything more than a good craftswoman. She wouldn't know what the touching up involved.'

'Suppose I did the trimmings and she copied them. She'd only have to imagine them in the magazine to get the same effect as she does with a straightforward copy.'

Gaby was beginning to believe in Eliane's idea. 'D'you really think it might work?'

'No doubt of that – as long as I keep telling myself it's a hat, not a frock! Go on, clear off and give me some quiet time to think – and be prepared to dash off for some materials for me to work with.'

Eliane forgot all about dinner that evening. She went through Gaby's wardrobe – her own was calculated to inspire no one apart from transvestite stable lads – then went to inspect the closet where Ottilie Deslys had abandoned a few gowns for which she had no further use. There was no question of adapting the style, for they were some seasons out of date, but Eliane wanted to get the feel of good fabrics and try to understand what would fall best in the style she and Gaby had seen in the magazine. Finally she opted for a soft, middle-weight silk velvet. The quality of this fabric in Ottilie's cast-offs was gorgeous, but the pastel colours would have been quite wrong for Gaby's dark, elfin looks. Provisionally she decided on either a rich shade of garnet or midnight blue. The final choice would depend on what she and Gaby saw in the shops.

Next she sat down, fingering the material and looking at

the style, and started asking herself the sort of questions she normally went through in creating a special hat. What were the qualities of the base? How must they be enhanced to maximise the appeal of the wearer? What did the wearer want the resulting style to say about her? What she came up with was so apparently simple that Gaby secretly wondered how she would wriggle out of taking her friend's advice. What Alouette was suggesting would consign her, unseen, to the darkest corner. No one would even notice her. . . .

But now that Eliane's interest was kindled, little Gaby no longer had the choice of withdrawal. The gown project had become something Eliane wanted to see through to completion. The full weight of her small, assertive frame was thrown into convincing Gaby that it would work. 'If it doesn't, you'll still have time to get a more spectacular outfit and I promise I shall pay for this gown if you do. Is it agreed?'

Dubious, Gaby consented. On the Monday morning Eliane bustled her aboard the Paris train, bound for the drapers' shops to seek the right materials for her new creation.

The gown was marvellous. At first glance it had the simplicity of a fairy's robe in a guileless children's book illustration. That was where its impact lay. Against the cocottes' lace and satin acreages it screamed silently for attention. Eliane chose garnet-coloured velvet, glorious and expensive, the colour of a glowing ruby when it caught the light; darkening to the tone of a mature Burgundy when in shadow. She had raised the low neckline of the fashion illustration.

'A high neck for evening?' said Gaby doubtfully. 'Everyone else will be bared to the navel!'

'That's why they'll notice you,' said Eliane.

The sleeves in the fashion illustration were short and puffed high at the shoulder. Eliane kept the puffs, but instead of ending the sleeve there she continued it as a long tight tube to the wrist, concealing everything and hinting at undisclosed beauty beneath. Then came her *coup de grâce*.

Against Gaby's black hair, dark eyes and ivory skin, a mass of unrelieved dark red would have been too sombre. Eliane cut a stylised petal shape from a piece of the stiff paper which dressmakers used to make master patterns. Later, in the dressmaker's atelier, she explained: 'These shapes must be cut out double, in the finest cream muslin, and stitched inside the neck band of the gown so that they flow out to form a collar which looks like the petals of a daisy. Watch – I'll show you with handkerchiefs.'

She unpacked six plain handkerchiefs which she had bought for the purpose, shook them out, tucked one corner of each inside the neckline of her own frock and let the rest of the fabric hang loose over the dark cloth of the dress. 'Now I know it looks a bit untidy like this, but with the self-backed muslin it will be enchanting, just you wait and see.'

The dressmaker could see it already – Eliane could tell from the new respect with which the woman was treating her. But poor Gaby was still dubious and after they had left the woman with her instructions, Eliane had to take her off for a stiff drink to calm her anxiety. 'Come on, it's not that bad! I promise I shan't be offended if you dislike the finished article. I must confess I like the idea so much myself I'd be tempted to have it altered to fit me. If you decide you prefer to go garnished *à la cocotte,* have no fears about my temper. I'll be sweetness itself.'

But when the gown was completed, Gaby needed no further reassurance. When she tried it on, she was convinced she looked more alluring than ever before. The party was a personal and professional triumph. Every man in the room was riveted by her beauty and one of Europe's leading impresarios promised her the lead in his new production of *La Dame aux Camélias*, subject to a cursory audition.

The incident might have given her ideas about expanding her business, but the renewal of her acquaintance with

Bonnie Charles at Gaillard stopped that. When Eliane got off the train at Compiègne after another fabric-buying trip to Paris, he was waiting as though it was something he did every week. 'I brought a carriage,' he said. 'Thought about horses, but even you'd have problems riding up to the house on horseback in your town clothes – although I'm quite sure you'd have a try.'

She was disproportionately pleased to see him, considering that to her he was supposed to be just another occasional visitor, however close his friendship to Christi. But watching him sidelong as he drove the rig back to Gaillard, she knew this dismissal of him was pure pretence on her part. His uniquely attractive face had imprinted itself permanently somewhere in the back of her mind a long time ago and she would never dislodge it. Eliane did not even begin to speculate about where their relationship would go from here. In a sense this was unnecessary, for intuition told her they would go together. It was hardly surprising, therefore, that all thoughts of expanding the business should temporarily dissolve. But inevitably her personal drive towards independence re-asserted itself. When it did, Bonnie proved himself an unexpected ally.

Every autumn, Christian moved his training establishment south to the vicinity of Pau in the Pyrenean foothills, where he rented a large house and stabling until March drew him north again. Eliane found it boring because they had far fewer glamorous visitors from Paris down there and this year she had planned to use the shop as an excuse to remain in Compiègne, paying only flying visits to Pau. But when it became clear that Charles was going along for at least a month, she hastily changed her mind and joined them.

Her conversation with Elise about expanding into dress production took place shortly before the move. Elise's encouragement revived the Paris plan. Later, in Pau, Bonnie's sympathetic interest in her strengthened her resolve to tackle Christi one evening as they sat around together after dinner.

Bonnie knew that Eliane had a wholly realistic idea of

her own standing with de Selincourt. Clowning with her at the stables one day, he had lifted her from the saddle in parody of a grand romantic gesture.

'Personal transport from heaven to earth for the Queen of this domain!' he told her.

Eliane had sniffed self-deprecatingly. 'Provisional Queen, you mean! Watch me get guillotined the minute Christi spots an heiress apparent!'

'You're crazy! Haven't I cleared Deslys out of the place for you? You've no competitors now, Alouette.'

'If you only knew! It's not that Christi's actually looking out for another girl, it's just that he doesn't like the way I behave and if I don't knuckle under he might go off me.'

Intrigued, Bonnie had probed the matter with de Selincourt. 'She really is an exquisite creature, isn't she? You must be tempted to make a permanent financial settlement on her and tie her to you for good.'

'Come on, Bonnie boy, you're slipping. Even the loveliest flower fades at the end of summer. I want to be free to pick a fresh bloom when that happens.'

'In that case, old boy, I might be interested in carrying away this particular beauty.'

'Oh, no you don't! I'm glad you approve my taste, but just remember she has dinner here every night.'

That had closed the subject – until the evening in the salon at Pau. Eliane was looking particularly lovely in a creamy lace blouse and multi-layered chiffon skirt. Her marvellous black hair was piled in a great shining coil, accentuating the length and slenderness of her neck. Watching her throughout dinner, Charles had become almost intoxicated by her beauty and was swept by a sense of recklessness. He felt ready for anything.

Abruptly, Eliane appeared to make a decision, although she attempted to conceal the importance to herself of what she now said. 'Christi, I've had a splendid idea. I'm bored with the shop in Compiègne and –' here she took a deep breath as though plunging into cold water – 'you were telling Etienne Kroll only last week that you'd like to sink some money in some new sort of investment. . . .'

'Well?'

'Well, why don't I sell the shop in Compiègne, and put that and the money you're planning to invest into a hat shop in Paris. You could be my backer.' She finished in a rush and sat, lips parted, awaiting his reaction.

De Selincourt eyed her expressionlessly for a moment, then said: 'And that's it? Well, my dear, the answer is no.'

His tone had sharpened perceptibly as he finished speaking. Eliane looked so deflated that Charles felt obliged to intervene. 'It's a very intelligent suggestion, Christi.'

'For someone else. I'm not a banker.'

The earlier sense of recklessness pushed Bonnie onward. Instinctively he lapsed into English, a language Eliane neither spoke nor understood. 'Have a heart, Christi, and think about it at least. If you don't do this little favour for her, I . . .' He dried up but there was no need to continue. De Selincourt understood what Bonnie was getting at before he did himself.

Also in English, he snapped, 'Please don't let me stand in your way.' Without a pause he switched back to French and called to the butler: 'Marquand, two bottles of Bollinger. It seems Mademoiselle is leaving us. We must wish her bon voyage!'

Eliane laughed nervously, her eyes darting back and forth between the two men. She might not have known the literal meaning of Charles's few English sentences, but she had fully grasped their implication. These two stags were locking antlers over her. It was so long since she had entered the Forest of Compiègne that she was unsure now whether she would survive outside it. Then she looked at Charles and knew that with him she could survive anything. His glance hardly wavered from de Selincourt's face, but she caught it for long enough to be reassured. He would keep her safe until she could stand alone.

After a significant silence, de Selincourt broke the

impasse with a laugh. 'This is crazy! Who knows how we'll all feel in the morning? Come along, children, drink your drinks and let's talk of less serious matters, like my new polo pony!'

The evening reverted to the pattern of a normal relaxed after-dinner session. At bedtime de Selincourt put a proprietorial arm around Eliane and escorted her upstairs. That night he made love to her with greater vigour and passion than he had shown for some time. Amazing how a little rivalry kindles a man's interest, Eliane reflected as he embraced her.

Eventually Christian drifted off to sleep, but Eliane remained restless. It was a calm night with a full moon and eventually she got up, bundled on a Turkish towelling robe and a pair of sandals, then went quietly out and downstairs. She walked across the big lawn, silver and magical in the moonlight, part of a new world. Suddenly a slight movement where there should be none at this hour startled her from her reverie. It was Bonnie Charles.

She smiled at him. 'Worrying already about there being no going back? I shan't hold you to anything, you know!'

He shook his head. 'I wish you would, but I . . . I'm frightfully fond of Christi. I have to give him at least one chance to win you back. I've some horse business around the area tomorrow but then I shan't come back here as I'd intended. I'll get *le Sleeping* back to Paris at ten o'clock. Then you and he can work things out and I'll return in due course to learn whether the prize is to be mine.'

'But it is, Bonnie - you know it is!' She was suddenly scared that if he left alone now she might never see him again.

He raised a hand to her lips to silence her protests. 'It's only a little separation and we shall still be business partners, whatever you decide to do about - about the rest. Nevertheless I mustn't crowd Christi so I'll be off tomorrow until he has had a chance to settle everything. After all, he was damned decent tonight once he saw he was beaten.'

Privately Eliane wondered at male ideas of decency. She did not find it particularly noble of de Selincourt to have dragged her off upstairs for a quick bout of lovemaking after supposedly having surrendered her to Charles. Such thoughts did not appear to have crossed Bonnie's mind, or if they had he found de Selincourt's behaviour acceptable.

Whatever Bonnie said about returning for her, she had too many memories of human perfidy from her father on to be reassured by such words now. She swayed close to him, hoping that if she forced a physical consummation of their friendship, he would forget such hare-brained chivalry. But he anticipated her and held her firmly at arm's length.

'No, little bird - without trickery or not at all. You're talented and beautiful enough not to need to play games.'

He kissed her lightly on the forehead, turned and melted away into the moon-stained shrubbery. Eliane stood alone for a long time staring at the blank space where he had been. Okay, so she was talented. Now was the time to put her talent to work - and not to design a hat.

There was only one Paris-bound express each day which stopped at Pau; it arrived around 9.30 at night and left at 10.00. If Bonnie Charles was going to be on it, Eliane decided, so was she. De Selincourt had already arranged to spend the day looking at polo ponies at a nearby stud, and Charles was currently their only house guest. Eliane had the place to herself so she could plan her departure like a military campaign.

A cool look through her cupboards and drawers confirmed her feeling that she was risking little. Four years with de Selincourt had left her with nothing permanent beyond a good seat on a horse and a well-developed sense of personal style. The cupboards held pretty but inexpensive clothes and the trinket boxes contained no important jewellery. Good! All the better for making a sensational exit.

It was Monday and the household servants had been given the day off. Cold food had been laid out under covers for her and Christian. She ate a substantial meal at seven, knowing he was unlikely to return before nine. Then she bathed and dressed in a calculatedly simple shirt and skirt, almost masculine in cut but softened by a big bow at the neck.

The horsemaster kept a supply of chalk in the stables to mark up instructions on a slate notice board for his staff. Eliane had taken some that morning after finishing her last ride. Now, in de Selincourt's bedroom, she used it to scrawl a farewell message on the tabletop beside his bed. *'Christi – please understand. I love Bonnie and I've gone with him to Paris. Forgive me. Eliane.'*

Then she picked up a small handbag, consigned the room to memory with one sweeping glance, and went down to the stables. There she had already arranged to have a rig harnessed and ready. She told the lad to come and collect it at the station yard about 10 p.m. She drove off down the avenue to the wrought iron double gates and the illusion of freedom. And that was the end of her four years with Christian de Selincourt.

By the time she reached Pau station, Eliane had re-arranged the events of the past twenty-four hours into a satisfactory interlude from a Decourcelle romance. De Selincourt's curt dismissal was a symptom of well-hidden hurt. Charles's temporary self-effacement was the height of chivalry. Her own little plot was the madcap impulse of a lovestruck girl – already she was rejecting the idea of herself as a twenty-five-year-old – and now she could look forward to a classic love scene aboard a racing express train. Even if it all came to nothing, it was exciting.

She guided the horse into the station yard, tethered it and found it a bag of oats. Then she left instructions with the station master to keep an eye on the equipage until the lad turned up, and went off to wait in the darkness at the far end of the platform. The station master watched her, puzzled. Why hang around there when there was a cosy waiting room just by the booking hall?

He got his answer at ten minutes to ten. Bonnie Charles strode through the booking hall on to the platform, swaggering in an English-cut overcoat and carrying a large leather travel bag. He was in the act of swinging himself up the steps into the sleeping car when a familiar voice stopped him.

'Bonnie – Bonnie, wait! I can't let you go without me!' The sleeping car attendant saw a knowing grin flit across the dark man's face before he turned back towards the girl who was calling him.

'Why, Alouette. What are you doing here? No, I needn't ask that, need I?'

Tears were streaming down her cheeks. She ran towards him and practically leapt into his arms. He prised her loose and handed her up into the car, following her aboard. His sleeping compartment was four doors along the corridor. As they reached it he bent impulsively over her, lifted her and carried her in. By the time the train drew away from Pau they were already making love, Eliane with unparalleled, frenzied excitement. For once she was acting out the climax of one of her novels in real life, and nothing could stop her. The notion carried her over the edge of mere excitement and into an ecstasy which she had never known before.

The train was already far north of Pau when Bonnie raised himself on one elbow and gently swept a lock of hair out of Eliane's eyes. She gazed at him dreamily, for once convinced that she was in the arms of the world's greatest lover.

'Look at you, little urchin, all hair and eyes! You look about ten years old.'

'Hmm, you a dirty old man or something? I thought you were falling for me because I was a smooth woman of the world.'

'Oh, my Alouette, you're much, much more than that. You're a free wild thing and you don't try to hide it. I'll bet no one else has ever known the one thing that frightens you.'

'I wouldn't be too sure that you do, either!'

'I know you as well as I know myself. All that scares you is being possessed. If you thought someone owned you, you'd simply shrivel and die, wouldn't you?'

'How can you tell? I've never –'

'You've never told anyone. Neither have I. I know because I feel just the same, always have, and from the moment I met you I recognised it in you, too. Don't worry. Whatever my other shortcomings – and I have plenty – I'll never try to be your master.'

She wrapped her arms around his neck, drawing him tightly down against her slender body. Bonnie kissed her, long and searching. Excitement stirred sleepily in her again, then built quickly, pushing aside her gratitude and romantic admiration. She disentangled his hand from her hair and pressed it against her breast.

Charles cupped it lovingly, stroking its small roundness. He kissed her face and neck, then his lips moved down over her throat to her nipple. He sucked gently until it hardened between his fingers. He continued to move downward over her flesh, softly kissing her belly and thighs. Soon he rolled sideways into the narrow berth. 'Come on, then. Now you love me.'

He was already hard with desire for her and her mouth moved hesitantly to imprison him. He gave a deep moan of excitement as her lips closed softly around him and began to press him. As his excitement increased he hardened and grew until it was difficult for her to continue, but now she too was so stirred that she was oblivious to it. She drew her hands down his muscular belly, entwining them in the thick mat of curly black pubic hair, making him moan and writhe in an exquisite anguish. When he was sure it could only continue for seconds, she slipped out of the berth and drew him to the edge.

Holding herself steady against the train's forward rush by grasping the overhead rail, she lowered herself on to him and took in his full rigidity with one sweeping downward thrust of her slight body. Then she simply held on while the train hurtled them forward, her smile of reckless enjoyment somehow enhancing his passion. He exploded into her and dragged her down from her perch as he did so, searching for her hot moist mouth again, subduing her body beneath his own as she raged to her peak of ecstasy. As she achieved fulfilment she let out one cry, then collapsed back against the pillows. For Eliane there could never again be love-making like this.

This time Paris was all any girl could wish for. Finally Eliane had come home to the city of her dreams, a city which had seemed mere fantasy when she solicited there at the age of fifteen or made occasional unremarkable shopping trips from Compiègne.

Christian de Selincourt had never shown enthusiasm for taking Eliane to the theatre or the smart restaurants of Paris, and she had always been too proud to ask. Bonnie Charles was different. He recognised the rare quality of her beauty and it pleased him to show her off. It added considerably to her satisfaction to know that he *was* just showing her off and not silently proclaiming that he owned her. Somehow that mattered more than anything else.

They lived at the Ritz, establishing a lifelong habit for Eliane. 'Who wants to live modestly when the best is available in the Place Vendôme?' said Bonnie when she questioned his extravagance. Embarking on her liaison with Charles, Eliane had not given a thought to the social side of the capital. Her two aims had been to capture a new lover and to move her business to Paris. Maxim's and the Opera could not have been further from her mind. Now she found herself sleeping at the world's grandest hotel, dining at the most famous restaurants and preparing to open an expensive hat shop in the Avenue Gabriel. Bonnie had clearly meant what he said about freedom. He discussed the amount of finance she needed, agreed a sum then took her off to the bank the day after they arrived in Paris and deposited the required amount in her account. She was aghast.

'You – you're not going to keep an eye on what I'm doing with it? You're not bothered about giving it to me all at once in case I run off somewhere?'

'Just pay in the money, Alouette, then we'll go for lunch and discuss it in more convivial surroundings.'

Le Grand Vefour was the original eating place, the establishment which had introduced the term 'restaurant' into civilised vocabulary. It continued to live up to its name by attracting the survivors of the *belle époque* and their heirs – both the French nobility and coming men like Bonnie Charles. Eliane revelled at her arrival within the charmed circle. Charles noticed her excitement and understood her well enough to refrain from comment. Instead he steered her through the daunting menu, then returned to the matter of their joint business venture.

Eliane resumed her expostulation about the sum he had deposited. He held up his hand to still her chatter. 'Alouette: if I were going into a new venture with a male acquaintance, I would no more dream of suggesting he take my investment in monthly dribbles than I would wish to know the colour of his underwear. It would be quite unbusinesslike. You are the one who wishes to break away from the ways of the cocotte. Don't you see, if you take the money any other way than this, you're condemning yourself to be treated as a kept woman.'

She reddened but quickly countered his accusation. 'If that's true, you have to back it up with all the provisions of a proper business deal – legal agreement, share of profits, all the rest of it. You haven't even suggested that, so it's hardly a normal business set-up, is it?'

He laughed in her face. 'My God, darling, you have a wonderfully outmoded view of modern business! I don't do four deals a year on that basis – although I lose count of the number of transactions I *do* complete. I move fast and I move to improve my lot dramatically. One doesn't often make the sort of profits I go for with neatly-notarised documentation. Most of my business agreements are written in my brain. I have a very good memory.

Now – what did you have in mind, that we'd be spending every evening together at the fireside where you could ask me for a little more cash occasionally to keep the hat shop going? I thought you didn't believe in people owning people and all the conventions that went with that.'

'I – I don't. I just didn't think anyone, even a lover, would be as generous as this. I'll repay your investment, Bonnie, and I'll do it at the proper rates of interest, you wait and see. This really *is* a business deal!'

'Well, we'll discuss that when the time comes, shall we? I'd like it if you came to me for advice in running the whole thing – not in the designs, of course, you're on your own there – but when it comes to strategy and tactics, I think I could be quite useful to you.'

It was an understatement. He made her. While she was still getting ready to open, Elise forwarded from Compiègne a letter from Geneviève, who had been living near Saumur for some years as a nobleman's mistress. Things were going badly and she wrote to suggest that Eliane might pay her an extended visit.

She showed Bonnie the letter. 'What should I do? She's the only other person I love as much as Elise, and I trust her judgment and experience more than my own. I can't stop everything now but I can't let her down, either.'

Charles read the letter carefully. 'Get her here with you. This chap is obviously leading her a merry dance at the moment and she can't hurt herself with him by disappearing for a while. From your point of view it would be wonderful. I'm sure she shares the Doré looks and dash, and if she's as remarkable as you say, you'll be an unbeatable team. Get Elise here as well and you'll sell out a week after you open, simply because you'll intrigue Society.'

He was right, just as he proved to be right on many other aspects of the business. Geneviève jumped at the chance to let absence make her lover's heart grow fonder, and she proved invaluable in the business. Elise left a manageress at Compiègne and joined them. Bonnie had moved swiftly to make sure there was no permanent rupture between himself and Christian de Selincourt. Soon their – and Alouette's – mutual friends were calling on the new lovers at the Ritz. When Eliane opened her bandbox-smart shop on the Avenue Gabriel, and did so with two glamorous look-alikes sharing her premises, the gallants swarmed there to flirt and gossip.

At first it did wonders for business. Society women and cocottes alike could not resist going to look at these dashing young women who always had a stream of male admirers in the one place a man could never be tempted to visit, a hat shop. But after a while they grew exasperated by the inevitable interruptions in service as their attractive milliners broke off to flirt or arrange that evening's social programme. Eliane had no business skills to back her flair with hats and clothes, and no understanding of what drove the customers away. She revelled in the attention of the handsome young men and was first puzzled, then anxious, when the flood of well-heeled female customers slowed to a trickle.

Bonnie saw the danger signals and counselled her to banish the young men until after closing time. Once again, he was right. The women soon flocked back. They were still intrigued by the milliners they christened the Three Musketeers, but without the inconvenience previously caused by the girls' suitors the customers stayed and spent more.

Eliane was furious with herself for being so short-sighted. 'Why on earth didn't I see for myself that all those lovely lads around the place would be quite the wrong thing for those women? Leave me unsupervised for a minute and I'll sink without trace!'

Bonnie had no time for such posturing. 'Come on, Alouette, you're no helpless little country girl! No one would expect you to leap into business with all the skills at your fingertips. Good God, people like Madame Vionnet came up through every department at Worth before they went out alone. You've never even worked in an atelier.

It's a miracle you've come so far, so fast, but it'll be a few years yet before you overtake them.'

'Me in the same league as Madame Vionnet? Oh, darling, you must be blinded by love if you believe that. She's a proper couturière. All I ask is to be a successful milliner.'

'That's this year. I have a feeling that by next year you'll be wanting to fly a little higher.'

Before opening in Paris, Eliane had discussed with Charles the range of products she would sell. It was on his advice that she restricted herself to hats at first. 'Stick to what you know while you're learning about what you don't know,' he said. 'When the hats are a success, that's the time to start on the frocks and blouses.'

Is the man never wrong? she asked herself shortly after they opened. No doubt about it, if she had tried to design and produce dresses on top of launching a business, she would have closed within a couple of weeks. Merely coming to grips with stocking and running a shop in a busy, high fashion location was more than a full-time job. But the dresses had become a minor obsession. Elise's instinct had been right and the amount of interest created in the customers by the clothes Eliane made for herself was enough to convince her, too. It was just a matter of time.

It took them a year to establish the hat shop as a truly profitable enterprise. In that time Eliane learned that she had to make her profit between the beginning of September and the end of June. Once July began, sales shrank to a trickle and after the Bastille Day holiday they dried up altogether. 'I suppose we just close down,' she said gloomily, 'but it's such a shame we miss so much summer trade when they all take off to the sea.'

'Why not take off to the sea with them?' It was Bonnie, as usual presenting her with a winning idea, apparently effortlessly.

'But where? I wouldn't know how to start.'

'Deauville, where else? In any case, I spend a lot of my time there in July and August and this way I'd be able to spend it with my favourite milliner without keeping her from her work.'

'But it's much too late to do anything for next summer. We're already well past Christmas.'

'Why on earth d'you say that? You opened in the Avenue Gabriel about two months after we arrived in Paris. If you aim to get going in Deauville in June you have at least five months left.'

'No, no – there was one crucial difference with the Paris opening. I didn't have to design a hat collection before I got going. Anything I had was new to the customers last year. This time I can't repeat myself, so if it's to work I have to produce a range of town hats and another line suitable for resort wear to launch in the new shop. Still. . . .'

That first summer by the sea was a revelation to Eliane. Shop girls did not make trips to the seaside; nor did orphans. De Selincourt was uninterested in beach or casino so they had stayed at Gaillard in July and August. At first, Eliane had no intention of quitting Paris that summer of 1912, but when business came to a standstill in mid-July she admitted defeat and joined Bonnie at Deauville. She found it hard to believe what she saw on her first morning stroll to the beach. The men were elegant and relaxed in white duck trousers, striped blazers or lightweight shantung jackets. They exuded holiday spirit. The women, by contrast, looked just the same as they did at Longchamp or Auteuil: corseted, coiffured, painted and ornamented in spite of sunshine and sea. Eliane was wearing one of her casual Compiègne summer ensembles, a simple cotton shirt and lightweight skirt. She attracted scandalised looks from the women of fashion.

'What on earth are they all staring at?' she asked Bonnie.

He was amused. 'I don't think that, before today, they thought a woman *had* arms in the daytime. Haven't you noticed? They cover them with yards of silk, lace and leather gloves until dinner time and then they expose every thing as a startling display case for their jewellery. They've never seen anything quite like you and I have a feeling that this is only the beginning.'

'You're so right! I was feeling a bit dowdy but now I can see I've got it right and they're wrong. Correction – not wrong but imprisoned by the way their men want them to be.'

He looked at her with new respect. 'What put that idea into your head?'

'I'd have thought it was pretty obvious. If I were a man I wouldn't want women getting notions of independence and self-reliance. It's bad enough having all those other men to compete against, after all. They've been quite clever about it, really. They've convinced the women that they *want* to look the way they do. And as long as women are locked up inside all that whalebone and tulle, men can forget them as a possible threat. They can never be more than spectators.'

'Well done, Alouette, I never realised you were so incisive.'

She snorted contemptuously. 'Don't patronise me, or I shall forget how much I adore you! It's damned obvious, no great observation. Well, if those silly cocottes want to go on living locked up in ivory towers, they're welcome to. This is the twentieth century and I plan to dress for it.'

'D'you think the men dress more sensibly, then?'

'Of course they do. Softer shirts, fewer clothes, loosely cut jackets, lightweight trousers. . . .'

'Hmmm, and daft little straw hats and unnecessary walking sticks which give them the appearance of a resting concert party when they sit down on the beach.'

'It's still a damned sight better than what the women wear.'

'Alouette, dearest, you're looking at the wrong men. The men you're thinking of dress perfectly for the city, because that's their working environment. Here they're no more than visitors and that's what they look like. If you want to see really practical seaside clothing, look at what's worn by the men who live and work here all year. It's their clothes which would free women, just as the stable boys' rig freed you at Gaillard.'

He laughed as she turned away from him and strode off along the Esplanade. She glanced back, pretending anger, and said: 'Girls in matelot sweaters, perhaps? Very droll! I'll offer them for sale next season at the Avenue Gabriel!' She stalked ahead as he merely continued to laugh. Heads turned as her odd appearance was noticed and commented on.

Bonnie did not see her again until dinner time, when she was more conventionally dressed for dining and gambling. He bowed and gave her a quizzical smile. 'We're not going to start a dress revolution in that gown, although we might attract some new admirers.'

She failed to rise to the bait. 'I'll leave them their evening gowns for the present. It's their day clothes that interest me. Wait till you see what I've found.'

She refused to be drawn further on the matter, throwing herself into an evening's pleasure which the grandest of *horizontales* would have found acceptable. A splendidly opulent dinner was followed by a profitable session at the casino and ended with passionate love-making in Bonnie's room.

Next morning she dashed off to her own room before he was out of bed and returned with a bulky garment. She shook it out for his inspection. 'There! My answer to the problem of what to wear over my little shirts and skirts! If it's good enough for the fishermen, it's good enough for a woman of fashion by the sea. Thanks for the advice.'

Although still sleepy, he was interested in what she had found and pressed her for an explanation. 'After we parted I started thinking over what you'd said and realised that perhaps a matelot's sweater wouldn't be such a hare-brained idea after all. Of course, it would look disastrous worn over a corset, but then we're doing away with those, aren't we? Anyhow, I put that thought aside for a while because I wanted something I could put on and off in public, so it would be no good dragging it over my head and wrecking my hair. Here's the answer – an ordinary jacket but made in knitted fabric instead of woven cloth. Thanks for the idea, genius, you'll be challenging Monsieur Worth at this rate!'

The jacket she held out for his inspection had obviously started life as a fisherman's pull-on sweater. Eliane had slit it down the front, faced the raw edges in woven fabric to keep them firm, then overlapped them to provide space for buttons and buttonholes. The result was hardly tailored, but it was immensely attractive.

'I shall wear it to the beach today,' she said. 'How long d'you think it will be before women are asking me where I got it?'

'About ten minutes. And after that, perhaps English-style sailors' trousers? That would be quite a look!'

She was fascinated by his practical and original ideas. She knew that women's clothes were wrong for the new world that was coming, but could not always quite envisage the most suitable alternatives. He knew immediately when to look away from bourgeois to artisan dress; when to tailor clothes, in the male fashion, for female wear. Every day Eliane wandered about mentally noting the way women looked and acted on holiday. How different their lifestyle could be if they were dressed differently. It was an education as important as her entire stay at Gaillard, because it introduced her to her best potential market if she were ever to become a couturière.

As they boarded a train to return to Paris early in September, Bonnie said: 'Will you miss it when you're hard at work back in the Avenue Gabriel?'

'Miss what? This lot? They'll all be back there with us, won't they, strolling in the Champs Elysées? As for this place, it'll virtually cease to exist after we've all gone, only to wake up again next summer. No, I'm looking forward to being back at work. I took a holiday because I couldn't sell any hats, remember.'

Later, she wondered why it had not occurred to her then

to plan a shop in Deauville. Instead, she flung herself into producing a collection of autumn and winter hats that seemed to float straight out of the shop on to the heads of the most fashionable women in Paris.

The next time the idea of designing clothes for sale cropped up was when she and Charles discussed it after Christmas. By now Eliane realised she needed a base like Deauville if she was ever to progress further. A smart hat shop was all well and good but she was not going to be the most interesting new face in the capital indefinitely. Once her novelty value had gone, and the sensation of the simplicity she had introduced had died down, they would start to see for themselves that she had given them magic with a cheap Galeries Lafayette hat form and some grosgrain ribbon. Then they would drop her and go elsewhere. She needed to diversify. If she got it wrong in Paris, she was finished for good. A few mistakes in Deauville would pass unnoticed in the general off-duty feeling of the place, and she could try again and again until practice made her perfect.

Bonnie was delighted at her decision. 'You're at your best when you push yourself, my girl. With Geneviève and Elise to back you, you'll manage it with no trouble.'

'But will we all need to be there?'

'The Three Musketeers tag is a good selling point. Pity to lose it. Anyway, you need lessons in diversification. You create the clothes. Elise manages the shop – she's a better business manager than you'll ever be and you know it – and the willowy, glorious Geneviève models the garments. Not in the shop, though, out on the Esplanade. Create a new wardrobe for her and send her out in it each morning. No woman in her right mind would pass up a chance to look like Geneviève!'

'Mmm – I'm beginning to feel jealous!'

'No need, my love. She's beautiful, you're unique – and I prize uniqueness above everything. Come here and put me to the test!'

She slid into his arms. The unreasoning, smothering

fear which had started to blight the tail-end of her relationship with Christi de Selincourt was absent with Bonnie. Each time she sank into the warmth of his love-making it was with a feeling of security, not unfounded terror. Now his strong, sensitive horseman's hands began to caress her neck and shoulders, his fingers pausing momentarily to press lightly on the pulse which was thudding heavily in her throat as her passion mounted. He laughed gently against her hair as he began to undress her.

'With you it's like holding a timid little bird,' he said, 'always having to be careful in case it panics and flies away, or even dies of fright. But when you calm down and open up your plumage you're so beautiful it's worth all my patience.'

The stroking went on, slow, rhythmic, gradually extending from her small breasts over her flat belly and thighs. As he caressed her, he discarded her clothing. 'You're going to have to leave that corset on,' he growled, his voice thickening with excitement, 'it's too complicated to take off gracefully and I like this far too much to stop.' Incoherent with pleasure, she simply raised her hands to stroke his dark, passionate face, murmuring half-formed words of endearment and stretching, cat-like, to allow his exploring hands to caress her more fully.

Bonnie slid down her body, touching, pleasing, exciting her. He drew back momentarily and regarded her with enjoyment, his pleasure heightened by the effect of the tight white corset with its blue ribbon trimmings which contrasted erotically with her gold-tinged flesh. He bent and buried his face in the silky dark crop of hair between her thighs, his tongue pressing and searching, raising her to a state of near frenzy which she had never achieved by more orthodox love-making. Aroused to distraction, she pressed his head hard against her belly, relishing the slight rasp of his chin against the silky flesh of her inner thighs. Still gently, but exerting considerable strength to disengage her, Charles pulled away. 'Wait a little, my Alouette – I know it's heavenly but I want to come there with you!'

He slid on top of her, entering her with a huge rigidity which shocked her after the electric delicacy of his foreplay. But the effect was momentary. As always with Bonnie, soon she was riding forward inexorably into a fantasy kingdom of soft brilliant colours and sensations where there was no passage of time and no pain. It ended with a blooming shower of complete release and she surfaced lazily through the afterglow of the miracle he had just given her.

That night was the last time Eliane wore a corset. Bonnie teased her, saying she had abandoned her whalebone and lace because it slowed down their love-making, but they both knew that her new clothes would work only if women's real shapes showed underneath. A hint of stiffness turned them into hideous caricatures of men's work wear.

Together Eliane, Geneviève and Elise settled down to a few months of frenzied planning and production. They managed to maintain the Compiègne hat shop, produce a gorgeous summer hat collection for the Avenue Gabriel and to find and fit out a shop in Deauville. By July 1913 they were all shattered, but there, in one of Deauville's most fashionable streets, was an elegant shop front with *Eliane Doré* emblazoned in white lettering on its black sun awning. No description was offered, or apparently needed, of what was for sale there. She had arrived.

Inside were informal seaside versions of Eliane's celebrated hats: the basic theme was natural-coloured straw, with styles ranging from feminine versions of the fashionable young man's straw boater to the extravagance of the wide turned-back brims and straight-sided, flat-tipped crowns traditionally worn by the seamen of Brittany. The trimmings were stark – plain black grosgrain, or at most a little cluster of silk spring flowers in pastel colours. Feathers, veils, stuffed birds and what Eliane called greengrocery were absolutely outlawed. The hats were marvellously fresh but would have remained unsold had she not provided clothes to be worn with them. No one could have carried off the simplicity of the headgear with the acres of organza, voile and lace which had hitherto made up smart women's resort wardrobes.

The clothes hit holidaymaking Society with the impact of a shower of cold water: shocking at first, then refreshing. The women were drawn in by the hats, then lingered, intrigued and often disapproving, to study adaptations of fisherman's jackets and sweaters, soft skirts with adjustable waistbands, blouses without a trace of embroidery or tucking. There were even odd-looking shoes, with flat rope soles and canvas uppers, offering a silent invitation to the wearer to stroll in them on sand or rocks. The women who looked, tried and bought them so enthusiastically never suspected that fishing communities all over Europe had used such footwear for centuries. For them, Alouette Doré had invented them and she was a genius.

Geneviève could have sold ice to eskimos. Tall and willowy, her figure had always been good for displaying conventionally smart clothes. Now, freed from a corset, she was the epitome of the modern woman in smooth soft garments which clung seductively to smooth soft flesh but were saved from vulgarity by their sportiness. Every morning she collected her posse of little dogs and set out, clad in a different Doré outfit. One day it would be brilliant white lightweight cotton, fashioned into a sailor shirt and ankle-length pleated skirt and with a sailor's beret topping it all off. A rather chilly morning saw her in an unlined three-quarter length coat of camel-coloured linen, with a chocolate brown jacket and skirt beneath it. The general line, though more formal than many Doré ensembles, was reminiscent of an aristocratic Englishwoman's country tweeds translated into a summer context. Eliane had never seen an aristocratic Englishwoman, in town or country. This suit was another Bonnie Charles inspiration. He had shown her an old photograph of a country house party and suggested that lightweight versions of the women's tweeds would eliminate the need for the ruinously expensive tailoring which was a pre-requisite in the originals.

It soon dawned on all three of the Doré girls that some of the more gamine designs looked better on boyish, petite Elise than on Geneviève, and Elise began joining her in her strolls down the Esplanade. They would return at noon, giggling and making bets about who would arrive first, the trail of eager male admirers or the females who had seen the effect of this new kind of glamour. Eliane was convinced she had succeeded when the men started buying clothes for their women. If the cock likes the feathers enough to bring them home, the hen will soon go looking for them herself, she thought smugly.

By the end of August there was virtually nothing left in stock. Eliane looked at what was there and learned still more about what would sell and what would not. Bathing suits definitely did not. She herself had worn a tricot bathing suit comprising a short-sleeved vest and pants which clung to the upper thigh and stopped short at the knee. Every man on the beach had watched her, mesmerised, and she had optimistically put a dozen suits into the shop. She sold only two of the first batch.

Bonnie laughed at her disappointment. 'Idiot! Lots of your designs suit everyone, but that bathing suit looks good only on girls built like you three. Any of the cocottes would look like German sausages in them, and they know it. Give it a couple of seasons until they've changed their shapes to match yours, then you'll sell the things in hundreds!'

The thought gave Eliane considerable satisfaction. She had nursed a growing dislike for the monumental, over-decorated females ever since Ottilie Deslys had ensnared her at Gaillard. Now, who knew? She might succeed in wiping out the fashionable taste for big buxom women altogether.

Back in Paris, Eliane counted the profits of her first summer success and started experimenting with the possibilities of translating the sporty resort look to townwear.

It proved so difficult that she took even less than her normal minimal interest in events outside her own small world. Only Bonnie's involvement brought her back to earth.

He was not entirely a self-made man: he had been given an expensive education and somehow, mysteriously, had entry to the best London society. But no one ever mentioned his father except to make it clear that he was not the husband of Charles's mother. Rumour identified Charles *père* as anyone from the Prince of Wales to a hugely rich Franco-Jewish financier. Bonnie never discussed it with Eliane but she had heard the tales and could see no resemblance between him and either the Prince or the financier.

Bonnie was a collection of paradoxes. He was an Englishman who spoke better colloquial French than many upper class Frenchmen; he had been raised as a Protestant at a Catholic public school in England; had spent three years at Oxford making influential friends and obtaining a gentleman's third; had held a commission in the Household Cavalry for a while and then had decided he was insufficiently rich to enjoy a military career. He set about making himself a fortune in what later, more respectable, generations would call commodities. Now in his early thirties, he was wealthy and getting more so all the time. He wanted to own half the world. Looking ahead, he saw huge storm clouds which spelled out two things: war and money.

In the late spring of 1914, Eliane was taking a break before the headlong rush to prepare for another Deauville summer. 'Double everything you were considering stocking up with,' he told her when he found her going over a provisional stock list. 'You'll sell it and more again.'

She laughed. 'Really, Bonnie, I know I had a damned good season last summer, but it wasn't *that* good! Deauville would have to become a summer capital like San Sebastian or Baden Baden for me to sell at that level.' Then she caught his expression. 'What do you know that I don't?'

'Oh, lots and lots, little bird. You're so busy feathering your nest these days that you never look up at the sky to see what the weather's like.'

'Stop talking riddles. What's that supposed to mean?'

'Simply, my love, that while you've been divesting France's finest of their underpinnings, Europe has been getting ready for the biggest military confrontation since Joshua showed the inhabitants of Jericho a thing or two.'

'Oh, war, war – everyone goes on about it, but how on earth could that change Deauville this summer? Even if they did start fighting, it's the women who hang around in my clothes, not the men. It won't affect their shopping.'

'This one just might. It's unavoidable, and when it comes it will be like nothing you ever encountered before. Paris isn't London; it's vulnerable to attack from the east. The north coast may look attractive to a lot more than the usual resort crowd by the time this summer comes around.'

Eliane was still dismissive. Had it not been Bonnie, whose interests in coal and steel kept him at the heart of inside international political gossip, she would have discounted the whole thing completely. But he seemed so very sure. . . . A couple of hours later she took out her lists and started adding on a few bolts of cloth here and there. It would always keep if nothing came of his gossip.

Events proved him spectacularly right. When the guns of August began to thunder, he appeared abruptly at the boutique, dressed in British military uniform. Eliane looked up from her work and let out a little cry of protest at the sight. 'What on earth possessed you to join up, you fool? I thought you were in Paris on business.'

He smiled the old cynical grin. 'I was. This is part of it. Don't worry about me. They'll have us all in uniform before long, and first in means best pickings. Now, come on through to the back and let's make some plans.'

'No, I must shut the shop. It's unthinkable to go on now.'

He frowned. 'If you've half the sense I credit you with, you'll do nothing of the sort. Listen to me, Alouette. If you've ever valued my advice, value it now. Stay put. Ignore what the other shopkeepers are doing. Remember what I told you in the spring and by the end of the year you'll be rich.'

Eliane never learned whether Bonnie's family or his business connections moved mountains for him, but someone did. Within a couple of weeks of his first appearance in uniform, he had been transferred from his old regiment to the Allied Coal Commission. He still wore a uniform and bore the title of Captain, but he spent his time at conferences with top industrial and military brass or touring the most unlikely places to procure the vast coal supplies needed to sustain the war effort. In the process he became richer than even he had dared hope.

Before Charles set out on his profitable Odyssey, he returned to Eliane in Deauville to make long-term plans.

'The season here has prolonged itself beyond a bad joke,' he said. 'It has to end eventually, but now even the Government is convinced Paris is unsafe, so this lot are hardly likely to migrate back there when the autumn weather really begins to bite.'

Eliane was watching the first September gale whipping white caps on to the waves and spattering sand from beach to Esplanade. Privately she had wondered how long even the Germans could keep spoiled French socialites cooped up on the Côte du Nord in such weather. Now his remark grabbed her attention away from the storm.

'The Government scared? Does that mean Paris will be attacked?'

'Well, it's certainly possible if the Boches keep pushing the way they have lately. Anyway, the important thing now is the effect it's likely to have. Within the next few days the Government will announce its evacuation to Bordeaux. Then the mass exodus will really start, irrespective of the level of danger. We've got to get in where everything's happening, not stay in this backwater.'

She was beginning to panic. The flight of the rich meant ruin for her if it persisted long. 'Where d'you suggest?'

'Did Christi ever take you to Biarritz?'

'Of course not! When we went south he stayed holed up around Pau until it was time to come back. I told you, darling, I'd not seen a beach since my childhood until you brought me here.'

'All right, here's your chance. Pack a bag and be ready to leave with me tomorrow. Get hold of Elise, give her power of attorney and send her to close down the Compiègne shop permanently. It'll be overrun within weeks but you might as well terminate that bit of business properly as there's still time. Geneviève can do the same here – I shouldn't think there's much left to sell now, anyway, is there?' She shook her head. 'Then we'll all meet up in Biarritz at the end of next week and I'll show you what I've arranged. In the meantime you and I will have a belated honeymoon there, my love.'

He kept his word, taking her south on the train for an interlude of love and luxury in preparation for her entry to the ranks of the rich. But, momentarily, she had misunderstood him. When he mentioned a belated honeymoon, her heart lurched as she assumed he meant to marry her. It took her some time to realise that such an idea had never crossed his mind. When she saw her mistake, she cursed herself for a fool. She had never expected marriage – why wreck her happiness now by pointless hankering after an impossible dream?

Eliane loved Biarritz. It was still warm and balmy there. The stiff autumn gales of the Channel resorts were soft southern breezes here. The people behaved as if they were waiting for a carnival to begin. They were gay, excited and extravagant. War was an unheeded rumour trapped in the chilly north, and nothing was too rare or expensive for those who took refuge in this grand town which seemed still to be locked in the *belle époque*. Bonnie spoiled her, made love to her, bought her presents and introduced her to influential people. After five days, he was ready to unveil his ultimate surprise. He took her to a sumptuous dinner, where a different vintage champagne accompanied every course. Afterwards he gently propelled her towards the casino. She was a little lightheaded on champagne and happiness and had no desire to end the evening at the tables.

'Do we have to, Bonnie? I'd rather go back to the hotel for more champagne – just walk back in this wonderful moonlight. I don't want to be cooped up inside that stuffy casino tonight.'

'Who said anything about the casino? We're just heading in that direction for the moment. That's where we're going – see?' He gestured towards an elegant nineteenth-century villa directly opposite the casino. It was ablaze with light and seemed to be awaiting their arrival.

'A party, Bonnie? Oh, that's different. Maybe just a little while . . . it's such a lovely house I'd like to see it.' As they drew closer, she said, 'Whose is it?'

He reached out and tugged an ornate brass bell pull. The great glass-panelled front door swung open, manned by an immaculate butler. Charles turned to her, beaming. 'Yours, my dear Alouette. Welcome to Doré Modes, Biarritz!' He made a sweeping bow and with a whoop of delight she swept over the threshold into her first full-scale *maison de couture*.

For once the boy inside Bonnie emerged. He led her from room to room, acting the part of estate agent's representative, throwing open doors, describing the daytime view from the upstairs windows with an accompanying flourish of the hand. By the time he brought Eliane back to the ground floor, where the butler waited with yet more champagne, they were giggling together like excited children.

Eliane flung herself on to a *bergère* chair in the ground-floor salon. 'You're so clever! How did you find precisely the right place?'

'You may not care for the answer, but I'll tell you. In my – er – unregenerate days as a man-about-Paris, I often took lady friends to Maison Worth for a spot of shopping. In fact, one could say I spent more time in the damned building than any other Englishman. . . . Anyway, I got to know the place and when I started looking for somewhere for you, I thought you could do a lot worse than start on a similar level to the master. He had an apartment "above the shop", so to speak, so he could keep his eyes open in case important clients were heading for the front door. You've seen the top-floor living accommodation here. Then he set the rest of the house up to look virtually like a society mansion but with displays of fabrics and with rather more mirrors than you'd find in a private house. Otherwise the ladies might have been in their own homes. Of course, you don't have to stick to his formula. You probably have a few ideas of your own.'

She did, and they bore little resemblance to those of Charles Frederick Worth. Over the next couple of weeks, the entire ambience of the house changed. 'I shan't be offering his vast range of materials for a start, so I don't need all those rooms for each different type. In fact, I don't intend to display fabrics at all. I'm giving my customers something like theatre, and I'm going to convert that big salon on the first floor into just that. The little ground floor salon can be a boutique – after all, plenty of the customers will still only want hats or bags or sweaters – and the morning room and dining parlour across the hall will be an office and a fitting room.'

'You make it sound as though they'll be coming here as a place of entertainment.'

'Exactly – and I intend to give them value for money.'

The big salon lost its flattering pink walls and was painted brilliant white. A dais was raised at one end, and the entire wall lined with mirrors. Small elegant chairs of gilded wood, with tobacco brown velvet seats, were ranged at right angles to the dais in two blocks, facing each other across a narrow walkway raised to a height halfway between the dais and floor level.

Bonnie looked at the set-up with perplexity. 'What are you going to do, stage music hall entertainment while they're here? Don't you think the clothes will be enough to keep them occupied?'

Eliane was immune to his teasing tone. 'The Paris couturiers waste too much time treating each customer as if she's the only woman with any interest in the goods. They all do two collections each year, to tie in with the two main social seasons. Instead of showing piecemeal with models drifting in and out of the salons while the women browse, I'm going to do it as a stage show. The full collection will be paraded to a seated audience twice a year, August for autumn, February for spring. In between, individual customers can see whatever designs particularly interest them in one of the smaller salons on the ground or the second floor. With all those mirrors around, and with only three rows of chairs, running the length of the room on each side of the walkway, none of the people at the main shows will need to walk around to look closely at the clothes – the clothes will come to them.'

'Bravo, Alouette! That's a nice touch. And I suspect you've already worked out that they'll be more interested in your goods when they think there's only a limited opportunity to see the full range.'

'Quite. Give me two seasons and Society women will be fighting each other for invitations.'

'You're going to issue invitations?'

'Of course. If I declare open house, I may get little nobodies like Alouette Doré sticking their noses in!'

The style she established in the main salon was to last her for the rest of her career. When she expanded, her new premises also featured a big, mirror-lined salon decorated in neutral colours and with indirect lighting. No decorative clutter distracted the eye. The clothes were all.

The days of Eliane's material insecurity had passed forever. While Europe tore itself apart and buried the old order, she became rich and famous. Ancient nobility and modern war profiteers alike flocked to Biarritz. Enough of the vast profits created by the war found their way to the luxury industries of the Atlantic resort to compensate a thousandfold for the old money lost in the fighting. Eliane turned her face towards France for customers but resolutely away for workers. Just over the Pyrenees were the young girls of Spain, unused to the sort of wages that skilled Frenchwomen could now command. Eliane sent Elise off to set up workrooms in San Sebastian and Irun. Together they exploited the talented embroidresses and seamstresses of the Basque region to produce quality and profit beyond their dreams. The Biarritz mansion housed a small atelier and provided residential accommodation for a limited number of workers to complete urgent tasks, repairs and alterations.

As hostilities dragged on and it became clear that Paris was no longer under threat, Eliane decided the time had come to take the plunge and re-open there, but this time as a couturière, not a mere milliner. In September 1916, a new black marble business nameplate appeared on an elegant eighteenth-century building in Rue Cambon. It said simply: Doré.

Eliane's method of presentation, and above all her own appearance, guaranteed her continuing success. Now into her thirties, she appeared to be barely twenty. She wore her sporty-looking creations with a swagger. Soon fashionable women not only wore her designs: they watched her and copied her walk, her hairstyle, her jewellery. Some of the bolder souls even started to smoke cigarettes in public after she was seen doing so in a restaurant.

For the back-up to her Paris operation, she stuck to the proven formula of Basque employees, this time despatching both Elise and Geneviève to persuade mothers to let their daughters travel to Paris to work for higher wages than they had ever imagined, with the added security of living in well-chaperoned hostel accommodation provided by the House of Doré. It worked like a dream. The cost was minuscule compared with that of Parisian labour, even had the work force been available to meet her demands.

The money rolled in even faster than it had at Biarritz. Elise remained there to run the salon and the Spanish production units. Eliane based herself in Paris. Geneviève had gone through a tearful reconciliation with her baron and spent much of her time commuting between Biarritz, Paris and the Breton château which he had bought for her.

Unfortunately, Eliane showed less skill in running her personal life than her business. At first she was enchanted by the freedom Bonnie Charles gave her. It never occurred to her that he did not regard himself as having any control over her liberty. In her own mind, she was still no more than Bonnie Charles's *irrégulière.* With de Selincourt, the lack of restriction had been a sign of his indifference more than anything else. It was only with Bonnie that she learned what it was like for a man to love her and to admire her intelligence and ability without needing to possess her. But she learned the lesson incompletely. With every day that passed she rose in his estimation as he watched her grasp a new idea and find the most profitable way of using it.

De Selincourt had been grudging with any money beyond her modest monthly allowance. Charles was always willing to listen to an approach for fresh funding to expand the fashion house. Usually, he agreed. When he did not, instead of refusing her as though rejecting a request for a new hat he discussed the project, and as often as not Eliane realised it was a less intelligent move than she had thought. But she failed to grasp that these business conferences were part of his tribute to her as a clever, able woman and not a rich man's indulgence of his mistress. Just as she had reacted to his first investment in her Paris shop, so she continued to behave like a kept woman receiving gifts from her protector. And like all kept women, she nursed a desire to be independent, to owe nothing to any man, even the love of her life, Bonnie Charles.

They spent an idyllic Christmas in the hunting lodge Charles owned in Normandy, a delightful black and white timbered manor some miles from Bayeux. Charles had thought long and hard about Eliane Doré over recent months. Even after six years, each day with her was a fresh start. He often had trouble believing he had known her so long. He was a man with big social ambitions and had set his sights on an aristocratic bride. But Eliane had changed his mind for him. Her personality matched his like a mirror reflection. He wanted her with him for the rest of his life and had decided that whatever she lacked in breeding, she made up for in brains and talent. Together they would be an unbeatable team.

He bought the engagement ring at Boucheron early in December, a perfect Singhalese sapphire the size of a pigeon's egg. He planned to give it to her on Christmas Eve, after they had dined.

Watching her at the dinner table, Charles wondered if Eliane had got wind of his intentions. She was charged with excitement and seemed to sparkle at him. The dress she wore, of midnight blue georgette with a deep Puritan collar in white, accentuated her youthful appearance and made her look like an excited young girl. Then, as they sipped their Armagnac after the meal, she turned to a small side table and picked up a chunky parcel. 'Bonnie, can we do the presents now? I'm so excited about yours that I must give it to you!'

He was taken by surprise. What could she be giving him that made her this excited? His fingers curled around the small jeweller's box in his pocket which held the Boucheron sapphire. Well, his gift would certainly match it.

'Here, quick, I can't wait to see your face!'

Puzzled, he untied the golden ribbon and pulled off the expensive wrapping paper. Inside was one of the glossy black boxes she was using to package her new line of shoes. But instead of reading *Chaussures Doré,* the lid of this had been embossed simply with her name. He lifted the lid, and Eliane's future was irrevocably changed.

Inside the box were stacks of English banknotes, brand new, crisp and impressive. Still bewildered, looking for some joke punchline, he lifted them from their container. At the bottom was a gift card. It said: '*To Bonnie, my heart and all the cash you've invested in me. I said I'd repay with interest. Merry Christmas, darling!*'

Something died inside him. So much for soul mates. For these five years, despite all their sharing and intimacy, she had seen him as a sugar daddy, a useful source of finance until she could stand alone. So be it! Just as well he'd let her give her gift first. At least she would never know what a fool he had intended to make of himself.

Charles was a proud, arrogant man. Eliane was the only human being who had ever got so close to him and she had failed to understand the enormity of his trust in her. His childhood had been as loveless as Eliane's, his solitude as complete, his detestation of people with power over him as great. But he was also at least as tough as she was and instantly disguised the deep hurt she had caused him. Just as well he'd got her a second gifr. Now she need never suspect about the sapphire. . . .

'Afraid you'll have a chilly walk to see what I have for you, old girl. It's in the stables. Come on, we'll go and investigate.'

He used the flurry of preparation over coats and lanterns to cover his unenthusiastic reaction to her gift of money. In fact, if he could have been detached about it, Eliane's was a staggering achievement. The box contained every penny he had invested since 1911, but repaid at 1916 values and with compound interest into the bargain. She was repaying him far more than she would have been asked by a merchant bank – but then a merchant bank would never have lent a sou to a provincial cocotte with no record as a businesswoman. And therein lay the deadly insult. She had taken his money as a mistress takes from her protector; she was repaying as a whore repays her pimp. She had become the archetypal participant in the system she abhorred so deeply. He shuddered with fury beneath the concealment of his greatcoat. Right now if he took her in his arms he would probably strangle her.

All the way to the stables, he fought to keep his tone light and bantering, praising her business acumen, asking her how she had managed without depleting the capital for the rest of the business. She was dismissive of her achievement though obviously delighted to be able to be so. 'As long as this war goes on, I'll double my income every year. And that leaves out 1914 and 1915. It increased tenfold both of those years, thanks to Biarritz!'

They arrived at the stables. A groom came to greet them, alerted by their lantern. 'Ah, M'sieur, I thought you'd be unable to resist a trip out to see him! Come in.'

Inside was a magnificent stallion, jet black and shining like a jewel. Charles bowed ironically. 'Alouette, meet Prince Edward. The Prince made Biarritz back at the turn of the century and Biarritz made you, so I thought the name quite appropriate. And you can hardly think *he* owns you!'

Something in his tone made her hesitate momentarily, but then she was carried away by the grace, beauty and power of the horse. 'Oh, Bonnie, he's wonderful! Quite the best gift I could have had. He must have cost you so much.'

Not half as much as the lesson you just taught me, my dear, he thought, still fingering the jewel box in his pocket.

Back in Paris, Eliane's business went from strength to strength, thanks to her almost psychic understanding of new trends. She had been among the first to raise skirts above the ankles, depriving men of the frisson of covert delight they had previously experienced when women raised their skirts to step up or down. Now she began realising that her wonderful cargo of black hair was wrong for the simple, light clothes she was wearing.

She saw less of Bonnie after Christmas 1916, but was used to his work taking him all over the place and too busy with her own to miss him. Charles kept a permanent suite at the Ritz and Eliane lived there, but he came and went between London, the Western Front, the Riviera and Biarritz, according to the state of his business. London had always been his official home.

He had never stopped seeing other women while he was with Eliane; she had not asked him for sexual fidelity, their bond went far deeper than that. In her turn she liked a variety of escorts, although remaining faithful to him as a lover. At present her favourite companion was an American industrialist whom she shocked rigid when she appeared for their opera date with hair cropped to jaw-bone length. Only when they reached the theatre and everyone started casting her admiring glances did his shock turn to pride at being seen with an innovator the night she launched yet another fashion. He had contacts in the New York magazine world and within the next six months Doré clothes, as well as the Doré look in general, began to feature in the women's press in America.

The first of her designs to be illustrated in the USA was revolutionary even by Parisian standards. It was made of finest wool crêpe in the dark red beloved of Renaissance painters. Having dispensed with corsets, Eliane had now decided the fixed waistline, too, was excessively restricting. So the frock skimmed over the waistline, to a loose sash tied around the hips. The skirt fell in softly-gathered folds, to end a good six inches above the ankles. The neckline – slashed low and edged with ivory coloured insertion – featured self-coloured cutwork embroidery, which was repeated around the hemline.

Most of the French magazines had ceased publication for the duration of the war, so the shorter skirts and hair, lack of corsets and general informality of dress which had evolved over three years in Paris came as a huge shock to a wider female public. The shock lasted all of five minutes, then every girl was bobbing her hair and her skirts and throwing away her corsets. Doré had gone international with a snip of her scissors.

Charles returned to Paris late in the spring, his hurt now successfully concealed, apparently as devoted to Eliane as ever. About that time, Adèle St-Meurice, the daughter of Madame Chaillot who had adopted Eliane's baby, re-entered her life. The emergence of Doré as a transatlantic fashion name had caused one of the Paris newspapers to run a major feature about her and the changes she was making to the female silhouette. A couple of weeks after the piece appeared, she received a letter from Madame St-Meurice.

*Rennes, May 1917*

*Dear Mademoiselle Doré*

*You might have wondered from time to time how your son Edouard was growing up. His father and I often thought of you, but as we all agreed that there would be no contact, we thought it better not to let you know about the boy. Nevertheless, he is your natural child and I felt you would be deeply concerned if you thought he were in trouble. My poor husband was killed in Flanders last November and I have been struggling alone to keep our business going in spite of the wartime shortages. Alas, I was unsuccessful and the shop was closed one month ago. Little Edouard and I are very poor and I fear the child will enjoy none of the advantages you envisaged when you arranged to have him adopted.*

*When I read the article about you in the paper, I realised that you would probably be in a position to help him and would wish to do so if you knew the circumstances. Please do not think I feel you are under any obligation; Edouard is my son now as surely as if I had borne him. But I should hate to see him suffer for my stupid pride. Could you find some way of helping him?*

*Your humble servant*

*Adèle St-Meurice*

Snivelling little bourgeoise, thought Eliane, crumpling the pathetic note and hurling it at the fireplace. These girls look so prosperous and important in their cashmere pelerines but put them in a knitted shawl and a pair of sabots and they fall to pieces! Oh yes, little mother, I'll help you with my son, but you'll know what it's like to be unloved and deserted, too. It never occurred to her that widowhood and bankruptcy might have taught Madame St-Meurice many of life's harsher lessons without her intervention.

Eliane wrote to Adèle St-Meurice, suggesting she send the boy to spend a month or two with his 'Aunt Doré'. In the meantime, she would finance the re-opening of a small dress shop for Madame, and provide stock from remaindered materials in her own workrooms to get round the wartime shortages. Furthermore, if the boy got on well, she would look into the possibility of paying for his education.

She told Bonnie she had sent for her nephew, the youngest son of her elder sister Ninette. Her tuberculosis had degenerated fatally the previous winter and she had left five children. Eliane explained his name and background by saying Ninette had sent him to the St-Meurices to give him a better future than she could manage.

Bonnie had been having second thoughts about his abandoned plans for Eliane. She was so much a part of him now that he was even losing interest in his other women. That had never happened to Charles before, in spite of a number of great passions. When he saw Edouard, he had no doubts about whose child the boy was. It did not alienate him; the sight of the handsome boy with his even handsomer mother moved him to greater tenderness than he had experienced even before her Christmas blunder.

In the months that followed, Charles watched in growing perplexity as Eliane swung between proud possessiveness of Edouard and exasperation at the boy's simplicity. Eliane and Bonnie normally shared a suite at the Ritz, but when she received Adèle St-Meurice's confirmation that Edouard was coming to stay, Eliane hastily opened up the five-room apartment over the Rue Cambon salon. It had come with the lease on the whole building but until now she had not got round to using it.

When Edouard joined them, Eliane took to giving elaborate luncheon parties in the apartment, where she paraded the boy like an exotic pet. He was a straightforward child, intelligent without being precocious, conservative and shy after his simple bourgeois upbringing. Since his father's death his education had been supervised by the parish priest, in whose house he had boarded during the week while his mother worked all day managing a more successful businesswoman's shop, earning a little money to supplement the meagre Army widow's pension.

Bonnie quickly grew fond of the boy and his affection made him give Eliane a second chance at the prize she had never known was lost to her. 'He's a good little chap. I think he needs a proper father and mother, not to be treated as a cross between a gypsy and a dependent cousin,' he told her. 'With my connections, I'm sure you and I could find some legal way of adopting him.'

Eliane stared at him. Eleven years ago she had gone to infinite pains to ensure that this child was never attributed to her and now here was her lover, encouraging her to pretend the kid was hers. Unbelievable! It never occurred to her that this was a tacit proposal of marriage.

'Stop over-reacting, Bonnie, just because he's a poor orphan. So were we all, once. He'll be all right. I'll gladly pay for his education. I owe it to my sister's memory –' here she did have the grace to avoid his eyes – 'but that's all. No adoption, and that's final. I think the sooner we start sorting out a good school for him the better. Since you're so interested, how about England? A touch of the *Milord* may make him a little less dull!'

Charles's face had been growing colder by the moment. When he spoke, it was in icy tones. 'Alouette, do you ever give a thought to anyone or anything apart from yourself and that goddamned business of yours?'

His tone stung her like a whiplash. 'Of course I do. You're on my mind for most of the time, for a start.'

'If you can make yourself believe that, you'll believe anything! I look like your idea of a storybook gentleman; my escapades with other women mean I don't make too many sexual demands on you; I understand your need for freedom – but you don't think about me at all in the way I mean! You think about me as I affect *you*, otherwise I'm of no account. You don't think about making me happy, about understanding me, about avoiding giving me pain –' he held up a hand to silence her as she indignantly tried to interrupt – 'but that's not what I'm talking about now. I'm quite grown up, I'm tough and you can't hurt me – not too much, anyway. But I'm desperately concerned about young Edouard. He's a human being, Alouette, and he's very vulnerable. He needs stability and love, not to be sent to a completely foreign environment just because you have big ideas about turning him into an imitation of an English country squire.'

'Oh, so it's too good for him, is it? I bet when you have a son he'll go to a public school in England!'

'Of course he will. He'll be part of my world, and so are those schools, that way of life. But this little boy is French, bourgeois, and likely to grow up as a small town businessman. His entire background is alien to what you now want for him, but you don't care, do you? He's your little wind-up toy and you intend to make him dance to your tune – exactly what you're determined no one will ever do to you.'

'You bastard! Who the hell d'you think you are? I'll do just as I like, when I like! You're only right about one thing – that no one's ever going to own me. But apart from that, you know nothing about me!'

He did not bother to argue further, simply giving her a long, sad smile. 'All right, Alouette, have it your own way. If you're quite determined to do this, you might let me suggest the school. Perhaps I can help the boy that way.'

She tossed her head and turned away from him. Bonnie walked out, left the apartment and went back to the Ritz.

Next time she heard from him it was by letter, saying he had been called back to London unexpectedly and did not know when he would return.

Eliane cried a little, wondering how other women could quarrel with their lovers and then wind them around their little fingers, while she only succeeded in alienating the one man she wanted. But then a vendeuse came up from the salon and asked to see Mademoiselle about a modification to a design and the incident was pushed to the back of her mind.

Edouard became more and more of a nuisance as she got busier. She put off contacting Bonnie about the choice of school because, deep down, she was a little embarrassed about her behaviour and their quarrel. In the end, she left it so long that the new school term was almost on her and she decided on the spur of the moment to consult an English friend of Charles's whom she ran into at the theatre. He was a rich, dilettante nitwit who found Eliane's aim of gentrifying her 'nephew' thoroughly laudable, and enthusiastically agreed to help.

'Nothing but the best, Alouette! Accept nothing but the best. It's really Eton, Harrow, Charterhouse and the rest, you know. Start at the top – I assume you can afford to. Tell you what: I was at Harrow. I'll pull a few strings, see if we can arrange something for next year. In the meantime I'll give you the names of a couple of tip-top prep schools where you can send him this year, and a good crammer for the holidays to see he's up to Common Entrance when it comes.'

As a result, Edouard's immediate future was decided without further reference to Bonnie Charles. In September Edouard was shipped off to a well-known preparatory school in Sussex, after minimal explanations from Eliane to his adoptive mother and with vague promises to the boy himself that she would see him some time in the holidays. As far as she was concerned, he then effectively ceased to exist while she concentrated on expanding the business to meet mushrooming orders from Elise down in Biarritz. He was forced back into her mind in mid-January by a furious Bonnie Charles, who arrived at the apartment looking as if he were about to thrash her.

'Bonnie – what a surprise. I didn't expect . . . Why, whatever is wrong?'

He pushed past her into the hallway. 'I think it's about time that for once in your life you came out of your bloody Decourcelle romance and started living in the real world. You're destroying your son for some stupid whim, and quite honestly I don't think you're even interested!'

The colour drained from her face. 'Wh-what are you talking about? I have no son.'

'Balls! Stop thinking everyone in the world except you is stupid! I know the kid is nothing to do with your dead sister. You're so self-centred you wouldn't have bothered to see him when she died, you'd just have sent money to finance Adèle St-Meurice. Instead of that, you drag him up to Paris and then send him abroad, far from all he knows. Of course he's your son! He even looks just the way you used to when I first knew you at Compiègne and you wore stable lads' clothes. So isn't it time you showed him a little real care and gave him a decent life? If you don't, so help me, I'll have him taken away from you!'

'What are you talking about? I've got him in a perfectly marvellous school in England, and next year he's going to Harrow.'

'Not if I have any say in the matter! What do you know – really know – about Edouard?'

'What's there to know about an eleven-year-old boy?'

'You're not stupid – though God knows I'm beginning to have my doubts – and you should know better than that. Think about his upbringing! While his mother was working, the priest looked after him. Doesn't that tell you something?'

'Why should it? Someone had to keep an eye on him.'

'It would have been more usual to use a local child-minder. If he was being educated by the priest, and looked after by the priest's housekeeper during the week, didn't it occur to you that it was because he was from a religious family?'

She shrugged. 'Well, I suppose it stands to reason.'

'Yes, it does. And they were very religious. You might also have asked yourself how many eleven-year-old Breton boys have set foot outside France, let alone been sent off to live among strangers in another country. After you've reached some conclusions about that, consider the English character as satirised by foreigners. Xenophobic, jingoist patriots who particularly hate the French. That's a little over-stated perhaps but it will serve as a summary of your typical eleven-year-old English prep schoolboy. And you abandoned your French son to that, then said he couldn't come home for Christmas because he had to attend a crammer!'

'How – how do you know all this?'

'He couldn't stand any more. They tormented him about the way he spoke; the way he held his knife and fork; but most of all they baited him about his religion. It's a Church of England foundation – he was the only Roman Catholic pupil. When it got really unbearable he had one person he could turn to – me!'

'But he didn't even know you were in England!'

'Maybe not, but he knew I was English and that I cared about him. So he ran away, caught a train to London, and did an intelligent thing for a youngster. He went to the French Embassy and said Captain Charles would know what to do if they were able to contact him. They had no trouble in tracking me down, of course, and I took him off to spend Christmas with me.

'Unless you sort out something for him, Eliane, I'm taking him away from you – don't think I can't do it, either. Adèle St-Meurice is his legal mother. If I give her the money to bring him up comfortably and tell her how unhappy Edouard is, she'll simply take him home and there's nothing you can do about it. Now, are you prepared for me to do that to you, or would you rather sort it out yourself.'

She was trembling. She had never seen him so angry and did not doubt his intention of carrying out his threat. 'What do you want me to do?'

'I've engaged a tutor for him and he'll prepare for Common Entrance at my London house. I've sorted it out with the school and they agreed to wait until I'd seen you before taking further action. I want you to approve what I've done and then I want you to withdraw him from Harrow. I've enough pull to get him into Beaumont, my old school. At least that's Catholic. Now, will you agree?'

She affected an indifference she was far from feeling. 'Oh, don't fuss so, Bonnie. Have it your own way if you feel that strongly – I'm sure I don't care. I was told Harrow was the best, but if you think you know better. . . .'

His jaw tightened as he tried to control his temper. 'In this case, a good school in Rennes would have been the best, but given that the damage is done, we'll compromise on Beaumont. And after he's in, no messing around making him stay in England for the holidays. He goes back to his mother in Brittany, understood?'

'Yes, yes – stop fussing, for God's sake! Now that you've deigned to come back, let's forget all about the wretched boy and have a glass of champagne.'

'If you gave me one now, Alouette, I'd throw it in your face. I'm off.'

He turned and left, without a backward glance. Eliane stood in the doorway wondering forlornly if she would ever see him again, and asking herself what on earth she could have done wrong.

By the following morning she had decided that time would make all the difference. He would come round eventually; he always did. They had spent months apart before now and there had been nothing wrong at all. They were both busy, successful, independent people. Why, look at their latest separation! It must have been almost six months and he'd shown up eventually. . . .

But even with her ostrich mentality, Eliane was forced to admit that his return this time had hardly been planned as a reconciliation. He had come for a showdown and when it was over he had gone again, with no indication that he would ever return.

Soon her mixture of nervousness and guilt matured to anger. Let him try and make her come round! She'd show him she didn't need anyone, not even him. Some day he'd realise that unless he made the first move, they'd broken for ever. Then he'd come running back soon enough!

Satisfied with this re-orchestration of the situtation, she turned her attention to the business again. It was almost a relief to be left to herself. There was so much to be done.

And so winter became spring and spring summer – the last summer of the Great War. Everyone knew it was only a matter of time now. All the talk was of exhaustion, of the great popular longing for peace. Eliane began thinking in terms of light, fluttery cottons and smooth adaptable jersey as the bases of her first peacetime collection. The real shortages of wartime had been biting for a long time now, and even a couturière as successful as she had trouble in finding the materials she needed. That was how she re-discovered jersey. At Rodier, the top fabric supplier to the couture industry, she had been begging the senior managers to find her something she could use in quantity. They only shrugged dismissively.

'Everything useable has been used,' said the domestic sales director. 'In fact, Mademoiselle Doré, I'm beginning to think you'll have to go into men's underwear manufacture, because jersey is about all we have left.' He gave her an apologetic smile but she stared at him as if he had shown her the Holy Grail.

'You mean you still have plenty of jersey in stock? Show me!'

'Very well, Mademoiselle, but I think you're wasting your time. After all, who would wear it?'

'My customers, if I know anything! What d'you think I used for the first informal jackets and skirts I made? I moved on because there were other materials I wanted to try out, but if your jersey is the right weight, I'd make it my first choice, not a substitute when nothing else can be had.'

He took her to one of the larger stock rooms. It was crammed from floor to ceiling with bales of undyed cotton and wool jersey. A bale of each was broken out and Eliane tested its weight and drape. She was jubilant.

'I must have been crazy not to have thought of this before! Of course, your jersey is of a better quality than I've ever used before – I might have known that Rodier would supply superior cloth, even for old men's underwear. I'll take every scrap you have.'

The weeks which followed were a flurry of activity as Eliane experimented with different dye shades and remade her whole collection to show off the fall and cling of the new material. She knew before anyone outside the atelier had seen the clothes that this collection would be her most sensational yet. The midinettes were begging for offcuts to make their own versions of the new line – always the best sign that a designer had got it right.

She had stopped expecting any quick reappearance by Bonnie now. She still saw the other men in his circle, but was too proud to mention him. Forewarned by gossip that there was a coolness between them, his friends did not refer to their split.

Charles had never wavered from his lifelong friendship with Christian de Selincourt and once the animus of their own parting had worn off, Christi and Eliane became better friends than they had ever been lovers. They dined together occasionally and saw each other often at parties. Any race meeting or polo game was likely to throw them together. But de Selincourt seldom sought her out at the salon. It was too immediate a reminder of his lack of business acumen when she had asked for his backing. Eliane was surprised, therefore, one September afternoon when her head vendeuse came to tell her that Monsieur de

Selincourt was downstairs and wished to see her.

'Of course, Marie. Send him up at once. He must be here to announce the end of the War at the very least!'

De Selincourt was obviously ill at ease. He kissed her with unusual tenderness then held her at arm's length and contemplated her face, as though trying to read her mood. Eventually, embarrassed, she broke his scrutiny with a laugh and a dismissive gesture.

'Come on, Christi, don't be intense. What is it, a smut on my nose?'

'It was just that . . . that is . . . dammit, Alouette, have you heard from Bonnie lately?'

She flushed and looked away, biting her lip. 'Since you mention it, no, not for months. He's sulking about something that's not rightly his concern at all and he just won't come round. Well, if he thinks he can send you to placate me he's mistaken!'

'No, dear girl, I came on my own account. He hasn't been in touch.'

'Then why mention him?'

'Clearly none of your customers reads the English papers – or not within a few days of publication, anyhow.'

Panic began to rise in her. 'What is it, Christi, an accident? God damn it, he always did take too many risks! Is he badly hurt?'

'Don't make this harder, Alouette, please. It's not that. He – he was married last Saturday, to Lady Venetia Lamington.'

Her world darkened momentarily. 'He was what? Tell me this is some kind of joke like we used to play at Gaillard.'

'No joke, Alouette. He hasn't been in France to my knowledge since last winter. He never mentioned anything like this then. It must have happened since.'

'Or the bastard has been leading all of us up the garden path.' She strove for self-control but although her expression did not change, she felt two huge tears escape her eyes and roll down her cheeks. So that's what happens to spent tears, she thought. They hang unromantically on your jawbone and drip off to wreck your white collar. The novels never tell you that.

She fought not to faint. The whole room seemed to be slipping away. Oh, Bonnie, Bonnie, why? You were the only one I thought would never leave me, the only one I cared for. Why did you do it? We had everything together.

Did you? said a little discordant voice. Did you really, or was he exactly what *you* wanted, without your needing to think of him at all? Eliane pushed the thought aside. Her one love had forsaken her for a well-born Englishwoman. What would a Decourcelle heroine have done?

She managed a laugh. It was high-pitched and a little shaky, but it was a laugh, just. She fluttered her hand dismissively. 'Oh, my, I do over-react at times. I had Lady Angela Mainwaring picked out for him and he went for the wrong bride! I'm sorry, Christi, I really should learn to stop crying when I'm thwarted, shouldn't I? Tell you what, take me out to dinner this evening and we'll tear the bride's reputation to pieces! Bring some amusing people along. I haven't seen most of your crowd for ages!'

She was the last to leave Maxim's that night, and by then every one of the party except Christian de Selincourt was convinced she had thrown over Bonnie Charles and driven him on the rebound into the arms of his English bride. But when de Selincourt left her at the Ritz, Eliane waited until he had gone then turned back into the Place Vendôme. It was well after 2 a.m. but she knew she would not sleep, and felt that if she entered the suite she had shared with Bonnie, the walls would close in to crush her. She turned away from the grand hotel, heading aimlessly south towards the Seine. The Place and the adjoining Rue Castiglione seldom failed to impress her with their perfect balance and beauty. Now they seemed cold and remote. Where the Rue St-Honoré crossed Rue Castiglione, she turned and made for the Palais-Royal. Eliane told herself it would be amusing to look in the Rue St-Honoré shop windows. Really, though, she wanted to keep away from the Seine. In her present mood her sense of self-preservation might fail her.

The small, exquisite shops which always entertained her so now seemed to be something culled from a nightmare. That stuffed Persian cat there, who could possibly want that? Those hideous over-decorated chocolates . . . didn't they know there was still a war on and that such ostentation was out of place? A top class hat shop . . . oh, Christ, hadn't hat shops got her where she was today? Eliane walked on, her throat dry from too many cigarettes and too much champagne, her feet leaden with the weight of her despair. She felt the pull of the Seine once more and veered south momentarily into the Rue St-Roch. Tall windowless buildings were precipitous cliffs at this dark hour. A wedge of light and raucous sound spilled from the door of a rough bar and she thought better of the diversion. Her death wish wasn't so strong after all. The customers in there were no respecters of wealth and dignity. She was safer back where she'd come from.

She found herself in the Palais-Royal. Why had she wanted to come here? It was four o'clock in the morning. The colonnades were blank and empty, her footsteps' rattling echoes sounding like a ghost's passing. The little old-fashioned shops were secret and dark, some of them shuttered. The atmosphere of centuries pressed down on her and for a moment she was frightened. She hurried out into streets scarcely less silent than the square and headed back into the Rue St-Honoré, but this time on the side east of the Place du Palais-Royal. Now there was more activity. Eliane collected her wits. Of course – Les Halles. She was heading directly into the stomach of Paris and the workers were up preparing the feast.

Her haunted journey started to take on the character of a medieval moralist's painting – the panel that showed hell. Something prevented her from turning back. She moved onward, her pace quickening, and around her the traffic grew. Hand-carts, horse-drawn vehicles, burly men with sacks or bloody carcases slung on their shoulders, all hurried towards the great central markets. There were virtually no motor vehicles, the war had seen to that, but there was enough food to stock a giant's larder.

Flickering street lamps cast a garish light on the bloodied corpses of sheep and pigs. Through the soaring cast iron archways she saw gigantic beef carcases, hanging from steel hooks like washing from an obscene clothes line. It seemed inconceivable that anyone would ever wish to eat them – or that she herself would ever eat again.

Eliane skirted the central halls and found herself in front of the church of St Eustache. If ever she had been ready to swallow the comfort of religion it was now, but St Eustache hardly seemed the proper setting. A vast edifice, modelled on Notre Dame, it shouted self-importance and civic rectitude. She stood in the dim nave and surveyed the cold expanse of stone that stretched before her, garnished with sculpture, painting and stained glass, and her head finally began to clear. Whatever she was seeking, it was not here. She turned away. Wishing to avoid the meat market, she veered down the Rue St Denis and rested for a while beside the Fountain of the Innocents. The peaceful splash of the water, doubly serene against the background racket from the adjoining market, calmed her.

I'm light-headed, she thought. This isn't heart-break – it's exhaustion. I'd better get home. . . . But she was too tired to have a clear idea how to get there. This was hardly the area to find a cab and she had lost her bearings. The Rue de Rivoli was somewhere along that way, but where?

Then the smell hit her – warm, reassuring, enticing. Suddenly it was irresistible, all she wanted. She forgot the nausea induced by the meat market. Eliane turned into the St Merry quarter and everything was different. She was in a street full of restaurants. Market porters, wiping filthy hands on bloodstained aprons, were shouldering into the little bistros to eat breakfast. Onion soup, that would drive away everything. Eliane was no longer thinking about love, rejection, death, or even the revulsion the meat market had caused in her. She was thinking about food. She followed two burly porters into a bistro from which yellow light spilled enticingly. Inside the smell of food, wine, steam and tobacco smoke was choking and tantalising. She sat down at a marble-topped table. A decrepit waiter shuffled over and slapped a litre of *vin rouge* on the table, along with a thick tumbler. She poured a large glass of wine and ordered onion soup, followed by an *assiette de charcuterie*.

Afterwards she was convinced the soup had saved her sanity. The beef broth was rich, with globules of clear fat floating in it, along with delicious soft onion slices and a big chunk of toasted bread, a raft for skeins of bubbling golden-brown cheese. The *charcuterie* comprised about ten different kinds of cured meats, along with little pickled cucumbers, that morning's freshly-baked bread and a pot of creamy-white butter from Normandy. Eliane ate steadily for forty minutes and drank half the wine. When she had finished, she felt reborn. She was no longer thinking of Bonnie. She was alive and refreshed and another day was starting. She had enough money to buy and sell everyone in this little place. She had enough money never to be frightened or cold again. She was not going to die because she had lost a man.

She left the bistro and wondered why she had been confused about the way to the Rue de Rivoli. It was just through that side street, two minutes away. The first light of day was streaking the sky peach and pale green now. The air felt country-fresh after the fug of the restaurant. She took it in great gulps, filling her lungs with oxygen and new hope. Eventually a cab came along, as inevitably as the new day. She climbed in, returned to the Ritz, and slept as if she had no troubles.

He was unable to stay away from her indefinitely. She knew he was in Paris shortly after the Armistice, on winding-down work for the Coal Commission. She pushed aside any thought that he might seek her out, but was excessively conscious every day that he was walking the same streets, breathing the same city air as she. And she wanted him as she had never been conscious of wanting him since that first night on the platform at Pau station.

When he came to her at last it was almost an anti-climax, except that seeing Bonnie Charles could never be disappointing. Eliane was working on a jacket, as usual re-shaping it on the model. She was utterly preoccupied by her work and as she discovered she had run out of pins, simply held out her hand to where her assistant had been standing, snapping her fingers impatiently. Her hand was clasped hard and she knew by the texture of his grip that it was Bonnie. All chagrin, all desire for revenge melted as though they had never been. She let the shears she had been using drop and they swung like a silver pendulum from the velvet ribbon around her neck. 'Welcome home,' she said huskily, her throat suddenly constricted by unshed tears. She turned away from model and staff without a word, and led him off to the apartment on the upper floor.

Outside the front door, she drew away from him and opened her arms. Bonnie smiled, instantly remembering his gesture on *le Sleeping* from Pau all those years ago. He swept her up, carried her inside and strode into the bedroom with her. She began to speak as he laid her on the big bed, but he pressed his finger softly against her lips. 'Not now, my love. Later, not now.'

He undressed her reverently, as if she were a valuable piece of sculpture, occasionally pausing to stroke her hair or touch her cheek. Finally, when she was quite naked, he sat beside her on the edge of the bed. The words he spoke brought the tears coursing down her cheeks in a seemingly endless stream.

Bonnie brushed them away, his own eyes suspiciously moist. 'See what you made me do,' he said. 'All that tough little French girl pretence pushed me away from you. It took marriage to make me realise what I'd lost. I'm not going to talk any more about it unless you want me to, and even then not until much, much later. I only want you to know that it's you, only you, now and always. Is that enough to be going on with?'

The tears went on flowing but she nodded mutely, her hand locked vice-like around his.

Hours later, they were sitting drinking pink champagne from the ice box in the tiny service kitchen, which was the nearest thing Eliane allowed to domesticity in her apartment. Charles was absent-mindedly caressing her bare shoulder with his finger.

'All right, Bonnie, you don't appear to want to bring it up, so I will. Please tell me why you did it.' Eliane knew she probably would not like what he had to say but she needed to hear it, and she sensed he would not broach the subject without her invitation.

He turned her face towards his so that he could see her expression. 'Are you sure you really want to know?'

'I don't want to, I'm sure I *have* to. Otherwise I'll never know a moment's peace of mind again. I'll always be wondering whether you betrayed me or I destroyed us without realising it. I must know which, or I'll go crazy. So tell me, which was it?'

He considered the matter silently for a moment, then said: 'Both – but before you judge me too harshly, let me say that I betrayed you only because you had destroyed us first. Nothing else could have made me do it. You behaved abominably – not towards me, just all-round dreadful – and I was stupid enough to decide that meant the end for us, so I went off and, to use that appalling English expression, made an excellent marriage. As soon as I'd done it, I realised that even hating you as I did then, I loved you at the same time. I loved you more than anyone or anything I've ever known, and I didn't acknowledge it until too late.'

Eliane still had no inkling of what she had done to alienate him so completely, but that could wait. First she had to know about his marriage. 'What's she like? Was it she who drove you back to me?'

'Yes, yes, yes, my darling! It took about a month of

married life to make me understand that whatever didn't work for us, we were made for one another in so many other ways that no one else would do. I'd always avoided being tied to one woman before and when I woke up to what I'd done in marrying this one, I realised that my motives for staying unattached had been intelligent and true. You are the only one I ever could have been tied to. And now I'm hers for life, dammit.'

That stopped Eliane in her tracks. 'But Bonnie, why? Even English Society is gradually beginning to accept the idea of divorce. Surely, in time. . . .'

'She's expecting our child.'

He had not intended it to come out so suddenly, so starkly. She looked as if he had hit her, but recovered herself with remarkable speed.

'Does that make so much difference?'

'I'm afraid it does. I suffered enough from not having a proper, traditional family background. No child of mine will endure the same thing. This baby is going to grow up with a mother and a father, and they will behave as conventional parents should, at least on the surface. I shall quite understand if that means you don't want us to continue together.'

'Now you're back, I don't think I could survive another parting,' she said. 'I've been pretending to myself all these months that I'm all right without you, but really I've been only half alive. Oh, my Bonnie, I've missed you so dreadfully!'

As they kissed, she held him like someone clinging to wreckage in a stormy sea, but gradually her grip eased and he felt the tension mounting as she braced herself for the inevitable inquisition. He was determined to be honest with her. Finally she slid away from him and spoke.

'Okay, what did I do that was so terrible?'

'I'm almost afraid to start this, my love, but I suppose it has to be said. It might help you to remember that it makes no difference to the depth of my feelings for you. I could wrap it up in a dozen different ways but what it amounts to is simply this: you are so totally engrossed in yourself that you have time for others only when their interests directly affect yours.'

'In other words, I'm a self-centred little bitch.'

'If you want to put it that bluntly, yes, but there's a lot more to you than that – otherwise I shouldn't be here.'

'All because I wasn't prepared to be a nursemaid for Edouard!'

He winced. 'Oh, God, I was afraid it would come down to that. No, Alouette. You have to pin it to one disagreement, don't you? It's more a matter of your whole way of looking at life. Edouard was just a part of it, though I admit your treatment of him brought it all to a head for me. I'd been uneasy for a long time before that. You have a vision of what you think you want – security, a masterful lover, popularity, fame – then there's what you *really* want. And the reality is security, independence and fame. The trouble is that you muddle together the two. You'd be just as happy alone with your business as you could ever be with a man – happier, probably – but because that's too unconventional a life even for the unconventional Mademoiselle Doré, you tell yourself you really want the lover and the friends. As a result you cause havoc among those who are closest to you, or in this case me, because you want them there but you really have no room for them. You take them for granted, impose your personal preferences on them, have no thought for what they want or need – and the result is that you lose them, as you lost me.'

'But I was always thinking of you!'

'Very likely, my dear, but admit it that you were thinking primarily about presents you could buy me to make me think how discerning you were; men you might impress; witticisms you might utter; all the things you thought might enhance you in my eyes. That's not quite the same as thinking of me all the time in the sense of wanting to make me happy. You were trying to make yourself happy by giving me pleasure – rather a different thing, I fear.'

'I think you're trying to justify going off and marrying

that English bitch and if this is the best you can come up with. . . .' She flushed and tailed off into silence, because he was shaking his head and smiling sadly as though to dismiss a child's tantrum.

'We both know I'm telling the truth, Alouette. Now shall we leave it? It won't help either of us to keep going over it. I want you now as much as I did the first time I saw you at Gaillard. I love you, too, faults and all. If that's enough for you, here I am. If you also require me to change my assessment of your character as the price of reconciliation, I'm afraid we're finished forever.'

She looked away. 'I can't go on without you, Bonnie.' The voice was small, childish, lost. It almost swept him away in a storm of compassion and love. But a doubtful voice still asked him if she was answering from the heart or as the central character in another popular newspaper serial. He would never know.

Charles's choice of wife held a strange irony. Having concluded that his passion for Eliane was leading nowhere, he had decided to finalise his break with her by making a useful marriage. He did not need to marry money, thanks to the war he would always have more than he knew what to do with, but he did need a little more social prestige. Until now his unofficial connections had secured him entry to the best houses, but such an arrangement was always precarious. He wanted to become part of the Establishment by right, and marriage constituted a reliable passport.

Lady Venetia Lamington was the daughter of the Earl of Northwich. She was twenty years old and widely admired as one of the beauties of her generation. In seeking out his wife, Charles had deliberately looked for a type as unlike Eliane as possible. It was not until after their marriage that he realised the irony. His bride looked like a slimmed down version of Ottilie Deslys.

She also proved to have some attitudes in common with Ottilie. She thought men should be flirted with, deferred to and generally treated as though they came of another species. Such a view was totally at odds with Bonnie's idea of successful male-female relations and the rupture started early. Venetia did not hold conversations, she gossiped. She did not think but followed the conventions laid down for her by her class and sex. Within a month Bonnie thought he would die of boredom. Whatever the failings of his wayward little Frenchwoman, she had never bored him for a second. He began wondering just how much good his Society passport would do him if it confined him permanently to a world full of Venetia and her cronies.

She was pregnant within four months of their marriage. By then their life had settled into the rigid lines which she assumed would comprise their permanent existence: formality, triviality and a mutual determination to be seen doing all the right things at all the right times and places. Their first family Christmas at her father's country seat was too much; Bonnie fled back to Paris and Eliane.

There matters might have achieved the classic three-way balance of wife, husband and mistress so common for their time and social position, but Venetia overstepped the mark. By now Eliane was well known in England also as the smartest name among young dress designers. Had she been a music hall star or a cocotte, Venetia might have tolerated and ignored her, but the fact that Doré was a successful businesswoman rankled. She had been aware of Charles's relationship with Eliane before they met but it fell within the accepted conventions for a man of his type. When he resumed the liaison within months of his marriage, and furthermore appeared to be making it semi-public, the Earl's daughter decided it was necessary to assert her superiority.

Venetia bided her time. She would be better armed for the fight as a radiant young mother than as a heavily pregnant wife. So she waited until the summer. Early in June she had the satisfaction of producing a healthy son – all the better to hold Bonnie with, she thought. Now she started her campaign. She had looked after herself during her pregnancy, exercising regularly, eating sparingly and giving up alcohol. Within a month of the birth, her wedding dress fitted her once more. Now was the time to strike.

Bonnie had returned to London for the final month of Venetia's pregnancy but within a fortnight of his son's arrival he was off again, pleading further winding-up business abroad for the Allied Coal Commission. 'Strange that it always takes you to Paris, darling,' said Venetia with exaggerated innocence.

He did not bother to hide his irritation. 'Hardly, since meetings are held alternately in Paris and Brussels. I can get to Brussels and back from Paris much faster than from London, so there's hardly anything strange in basing myself there. Any complaints?'

'Oh, none. In fact it's most convenient because as soon as I'm up and about I shall join you to buy new clothes. I'm sick of going around looking like a whale as I've had to for the past few months. I'm going to buy lots and lots of lovely clinging clothes in that new jersey fabric.'

If she had expected a strong reaction to her proposal to join him in Paris, she was disappointed. He merely said, 'Let me know when you're coming so that I can arrange to meet you.' That, apart from a clipped farewell, was that. He left for Paris the next morning before Venetia was awake.

A number of Venetia's English friends were already in the French capital when she arrived there. The fighting had placed it out of bounds for so long that this post-war summer was the first chance Society women had had since 1914 to do any shopping in the world's most fashion conscious city. Now they travelled to Paris in droves to stock up with luxury clothing before going off to the summer resorts.

Venetia joined Bonnie at the Ritz, where he had reserved a suite for them both. Until a week earlier he had been living there in another suite with Eliane. Once established in Paris, his wife set about crucifying his mistress.

From the beginning Venetia took every opportunity to belittle Eliane's skill as a designer and to sneer at what she produced. For a less talented couturière, such treatment could have spelled ruin, for Venetia's title and reputation as a fashion arbiter were formidable weapons. But the Doré look was irresistible and Venetia's attack met only limited success even among her closer associates.

It was different when she attacked on a social level.

Suddenly, Eliane began to notice slight sneers on formerly friendly faces when she arrived at parties and receptions. It took her a while to discover that small eddies of gossip were making the rounds about her having been a tart and a draper's assistant who failed as an actress and took to dressmaking when her charms proved inadequate for holding on to rich men. She sought out Bonnie.

'I've been doing well with Society since before the war, wouldn't you agree?' she asked.

'Of course – why should I question it? They know a good thing when they see it.'

'And socially – no problems about getting invited to smart affairs and so on. Not haut monde, I'm no social lioness yet, but certainly the smart types are always happy to have me around.'

'Yes, darling, but what's all this about? You sound almost unsure of yourself, and that's unlike you.'

Suddenly she was crying. 'It is unlike me, Bonnie, but only that I show it. I've always felt like an outsider but I've managed to cover it up because people treated me so well I convinced myself it was all in my head. Now it's different. Last time I walked into a party at Maxim's, a bunch of people I know, and whose wives come to the salon, all sneered. I heard one say something that ended with "amusing little midinette for five minutes upstairs after the shop shuts".'

'They said *what*?'

Charles's tone was ominously calm. His expression told a different story.

'There's lots more like that. You know yourself that

Paris is full of so many people with shaky backgrounds like mine that nobody throws stones too fast. But all of a sudden, since this English Society crowd have been here, things are different. I can't understand why they're so awful and patronising. The clothes almost sell themselves yet sometimes I hear these dreadful remarks from women who are wearing my designs. It's almost as if someone has declared a personal war on me and started spreading malicious gossip. I don't know how much more of it I can stand, Bonnie. What shall I do?'

Her tears had stopped but she was on the verge of crying again. A black suspicion started edging into his mind. 'When did all this start?'

'Shortly after I moved back to the Rue Cambon apartment. I was in two minds about going back to the Ritz as a sort of defiant gesture, but I didn't want to embarrass you while your wife. . . . Oh, no!'

He nodded. 'The same thought had occurred to me. It's something of a coincidence, don't you think, that all this mud-slinging started when she established herself here?'

'But, Bonnie, that can't be true. Good God, this sort of thing has been going on for centuries. Men have wives and mistresses who usually ignore one another's existence. From the little you've said about the way she treats you when you're alone together, she's hardly in the grip of a grand passion for you. Why on earth should she feel so hostile to me?'

'I think maybe because you'll never simply be my mistress. She must feel threatened. I do hope I'm wrong, but if I'm not, I promise the problem will stop.'

They parted and he returned to the Ritz. He was seldom there at this time in the afternoon, so Venetia was not expecting him. As he entered the small vestibule outside the suite's drawing room, he could hear her talking beyond the half-closed door. Obviously she was telephoning someone. He stood and listened.

'. . . But my dear, don't let the fresh-faced boyish appearance deceive you! I happen to know she's as old as sin and she had various careers before she started calling herself a couturière. I had a most amusing conversation over cocktails the other evening with that actress woman, Deslys, and if you heard what she had to say about her. . . . No, I couldn't, I promised not to breathe a word! Oh, well, all right, if you really swear you'll keep it strictly *entre nous*. . . .'

Before she could say any more the telephone was taken from her hand and the receiver was firmly replaced. She gasped and jumped up from the chair where she had been sitting. Charles struck her an open-handed blow which flung her halfway across the big room. She stumbled and almost fell before she managed to save herself by clutching a chairback.

'Bonnie – I didn't – what are you doing? If you touch me. . . .'

'I have no intention of touching you again for the moment.' His voice was low and even and terrifying. 'But if you ever so much as hint anything like that again, I'll beat you within an inch of your life, and I'll dare you to try taking me to court for it.'

'You wouldn't. . . .'

'Oh, but I would, and at the moment I can't think of many things I'd enjoy more. But I shall save that as a last resort. The alternative is that you and I get together to discuss arrangements for our son's christening. Like who the godparents shall be. Of course, your very good friend Eliane Doré will be at the top of the list.'

'You wouldn't. . . .'

'You're boring enough normally, but when you repeat yourself every other sentence, it's positively insufferable. Once again, yes I would; I shall; you will. As a little postscript to your campaign of vilification, you are going to establish Alouette as the couturière beloved by English Society women. She will be godmother to our son and you will let the gossip columnists know that she's a close personal friend. You will start buying Doré clothes and being seen in them whenever possible.

'You will also start making little lighthearted remarks about this practical joke you and Alouette had going between you to see how quickly malicious gossip got back to her. But that is to be used only to people with whom you have planted such gossip. As far as the rest of the world is concerned, nothing like that was ever said. She's your favourite designer and you wouldn't dream of going away without a couple of trunks full of her summer clothes. Oh, and one last thing: I'm moving out of this suite and into one on the next floor. Eliane will have her old suite back. I shall be appearing in public with you but otherwise I expect to see as little of you as possible. Understood?'

Venetia Charles rubbed the side of her face where clear imprints of her husband's fingers were beginning to show red against her creamy complexion. She nodded mutely. He turned and left.

It never crossed Venetia's mind to disobey Bonnie. She carried out his instructions to the letter, convinced that if she failed he would kill her. There was no one to whom she cared to admit what she had tried to do to Eliane Doré so there was no one she could turn to for advice. Her apparent sponsorship set Eliane on yet another run of success. The few new arrivals from England who had been hanging back from patronising the new couturière were suitably impressed by her apparent familiarity with Society and her friendship with Lady Venetia Charles. Eliane made her first trip to England for the christening of Alexander George Edward Charles and was photographed for all the best papers. Her visit was wildly successful and she returned to France after making all sorts of valuable new social and business contacts.

But the interlude of malicious gossip had shaken her. Popularity as a designer and her financial success during the war years had given her a sense of invulnerability. It had been a long time since she had felt like the little nobody from Josselin. Nevertheless, for a couple of weeks in the summer of 1919, her world tottered. Thanks to Bonnie's reprisals, a couple of months later she was stronger than she had ever been, but she made herself a promise that her next goal was acceptance by the highest echelons of high society. Nothing else would guarantee her safety.

On first returning to Paris, however, thoughts of self-preservation and advancement were pushed to the back of her mind. She embarked on an idyllic interlude with Bonnie Charles which she always cherished as the peak of her romantic life. Having told her why she had driven him away, he did not refer to the matter again, but concentrated on making her happy and trying to wipe out the fears she experienced as a result of Venetia's abortive revenge.

After her triumphant appearance in London during July for the christening, Eliane spent August in the Pyrenees with Geneviève before resuming her life with Bonnie in Paris. Geneviève was happier now with her baron, but in spite of her château and the handsome permanent financial settlement he had made for her, she felt insecure. Eliane mentally blessed her own business success. She had at last reached the point where she would never need to depend on a man for the material necessities of life and although the emotional insecurities remained, at least she was free in practical terms.

One morning they were sitting together over breakfast on the sunny balcony outside Eliane's hotel room. Geneviève was scrutinising her niece's face. 'I hope I conceal my thirty-six years as well as you do your thirty-four, darling,' she said. 'This morning you look about twenty.'

Eliane looked round her with exaggerated secretiveness. 'Sshh . . . this morning I *am* about twenty – and shall continue to be for a very long time. As long as I look younger than I really am, I plan to *be* younger than I really am. If there was some way of getting at the births register in Rennes, I'd destroy all the records!'

'I think you would, too!' Geneviève abruptly became serious. 'Please be candid with me. Am I wearing as well as you?'

Eliane's answer was a loud laugh. 'You have only to study your effect on the men down in the lobby for the answer to that one, my love! If you continue to bloom so disgracefully I shall have to start dropping loaded remarks about older women to maintain my flagging spirits! Why is it bothering you so much all of a sudden? I always thought you of all people had a pretty accurate idea of your own attractiveness.'

'Oh, it's just – well, things are changing, or about to change, I think. Henri's wife has taken a turn for the worse and I don't think she's too likely to see the new decade in.'

Eliane was riveted. 'So when's the wedding?'

'That's the trouble. He always said that was all he was waiting for and since I left to join you when you set up the business, he's never been less than completely attentive. But I start getting panicky about my age from time to time, and I wake up at night wondering if when he's free he'll find someone younger.'

'But, darling, he's been keeping you for more than ten years, and even when you were estranged, you never thought he so much as looked at another woman. Why worry now?'

'Because I'm conscious of time passing. Because although you and I look young, we both know that mistresses should have youth or motherhood on their side. In my case, both appear to be receding possibilities. I know Henri is ten years older than me, but I don't have to tell you that it doesn't matter for men, particularly when they're rich. What if one of those exquisite little twenty-year-olds gets her talons into him?'

'You'll just have to see none of them gets the opportunity to trap him. That shouldn't be too hard for a woman of your resources.'

'My resources!' Geneviève's pleasing contralto voice held an unusual note of bitterness. 'My resources comprise a degree of skill as an embroideress, experience as a casual couture model and intimate knowledge of the skills of a kept woman. Hardly a great achievement for someone of thirty-six.'

'Nonsense! When you think of what we came from, it's miraculous. I'll be calling you Madame la Baronne by this time next year, you wait and see.'

'Look at what you've done, Eliane. You've managed to build a life for yourself that doesn't depend on the whim of any man. You're safe.'

'But I couldn't get started without the bastards, could I? Even when you're independent, girl, you have to start on your back, saying yes to men. Roll on the day when it will be different, but I don't think either of us will see it.'

In September she returned to Paris and Bonnie. When he met her from the train, she realised afresh the strength of his physical magnetism. He had bought himself a huge powerful motor car which was currently his favourite toy. He came striding down the platform wearing a voluminous motoring coat and a pair of leather driving gauntlets. There was a boyish happiness mixed with his buccaneering air that made her laugh in delight. Any lingering thought of living without him vanished.

As they finished dinner that evening in their suite at the Ritz, he took her on his lap and kissed her gently. She smiled back at him. 'My God, we're getting to be quite the middle-aged married couple, aren't we?'

'Alouette Doré, only you would make such an outrageous statement! You are wearing a negligée of antique ivory lace for which I paid the equivalent of a skilled artisan's life savings. We have just consumed oysters, foie gras and out of season strawberries, and you think we're like an old married couple? No wonder I'm so crazy about you!'

She began to relish everything they did for itself, instead of for its novelty or smartness. And she began, very slowly, to understand what it meant to take an interest in Bonnie instead of thinking about him only as he affected her. It paid unexpected bonuses. She asked a question about a painting, and found herself being shown around some of the masterpieces in the Louvre. He was astonished that she had never set foot inside that repository of art treasures before.

'I told you very early in our acquaintance that you were a little philistine, but I was joking. It seems I should have taken myself seriously,' he said.

'I suppose it never occurred to you that they weren't exactly falling over themselves at the orphanage to tell us about the Old Masters and the great men of French literature. They were far too busy putting us to work in the laundry and the sewing room. So now society has a debt to me and you're going to repay it. I want to know all about French art and literature and – and everything.'

'This afternoon, or am I allowed to extend the cultural enlightenment over a few days?'

It turned out to be a thoroughly enjoyable experience for them both. Eliane revelled in her introduction to the most beautiful artefacts produced by her civilisation; Bonnie was able to instruct a pupil who combined the naïvety of a child with the aptitude of a highly intelligent adult. His only problem lay in containing her greed for it all.

Eventually he called a halt. 'Eliane, you'll have me bankrupt if this goes on! You work all night on your confounded dresses, snatch a couple of hours' sleep and then pop up as fresh as paint, expecting a full day around the galleries and museums. I have to do business when my associates are in their offices, and that's seldom at three in the morning.'

'Hah! So you're bored with me already, are you? All right, cast me aside as a cultural untouchable!'

'Come here and kiss me, you wretch. No, I'm not abandoning you, but I am asking for a stay of execution so that I can get some work done. We're now in late October. I need to complete a lot of business between now and early December, but while I'm at it I'll draw up a sort of Parisian Grand Tour for you and in the New Year we'll really get going. How does that suit you?'

'Oh, that will be wonderful, darling. It will give me something to look forward to over Christmas. I was dreading it a little, you know. I'm getting too used to having you around.'

They were silent for a while, then he said: 'I've been thinking about Christmas. To the Devil with 'em all; I'm not having another farce like last year. They all hate each other while leading this incredibly stuffy, formal life down at their ghastly old Victorian mansion. I'm damned if I'll stand another year of it. I'm staying with you.'

Hope leapt in her momentarily, then died. 'But what about Alexander? I can't see you walking out on him like that.'

'Alexander will be all of six months old by then. Somehow I don't think he'll be too bereft if I'm not in attendance. It's one reason why this should be our Christmas, yours and mine together. Next year I probably shall feel that I want to be with him for at least part of the time. This year I can be all yours, with ribbons on. Only please, my love, no cash Christmas presents this time!'

'Oh, I love you I love you I love you!' She sprang at him and embraced him, not even noticing his reference to her *faux pas* of a couple of years ago. He sighed. There were some things she would never learn.

Eliane bustled through the next month or so, her excitement mounting in anticipation of the fun she would have at Christmas and after. At the end of the first week in December, Charles returned to England briefly. Venetia greeted him frigidly.

'If this goes on much longer, I might consider divorcing you,' she said.

'Try it, my dearest. You'll have to go for restoration of conjugal rights first if you want to sue for desertion, and the minute you do I'll be back here for as long as it takes. Then I shall go off as soon as possible and resume my life where it was rudely interrupted.'

'But what if I sued you for adultery and name Mademoiselle Doré?'

He laughed in her face.

'You'd never take the blow to your pride! You, stand up in public and admit that your husband had deserted you for his cast-off mistress as soon as the ink was dry on the marriage register? You'd never live it down!'

She digested that in silence. He was right. She started again, attempting to dismiss what had just passed between them. 'Presumably now at least you're back until after the holidays?'

'Actually, no. I'll take a look at Alexander, see a few people and go back to France by the twentieth. I hardly think they'll call off the festivities at Lamington just because I'm not one of the happy band.'

'But I shall be a laughing stock! You can't do this to me!'

'No? Just watch me!'

He turned and left the drawing-room, spent the next hour up in the nursery with his son and the nanny, then left for his club. It was the pattern for the remainder of his stay.

Charles found Eliane waiting impatiently on the platform at the Gare St-Lazare when he got back to Paris. She looked sensational, with a cheeky little helmet-shaped hat pulled tightly down over her eyes and a big, soft, masculine-styled coat belted casually at her uncorseted waist. She slipped her arm through his and sauntered with him to the ticket barrier.

He looked down at her, enjoying everything about her. 'You get better every time I see you,' he said. 'Some day I might make you a really interesting proposition.'

'Oh really? Surprise me!'

Suddenly he was serious. 'All right. If there was ever a chance of my getting free, would you consider marrying me?'

She stopped in her tracks, much to the irritation of the hurrying passengers whose exit she was blocking. 'You don't mean it.'

'I've never meant anything more sincerely in my life. I only wish I could promise to deliver – that is, if you'll have me, of course.'

'But what about Alexander? You said. . . .'

'I know what I said. I also know what I want, what I need. And I shan't be any less visible as his father because I'm no longer married to his mother. The more we're together, the harder I find it to contemplate a future without you at its centre. Now, what's your answer?'

'Yes – a thousand, million times yes, however long it takes!'

The people behind them were delayed even further as he swung her off her feet and kissed her.

They spent Christmas in solitary intimacy at the Ritz, totally absorbed in one another. Immediately afterwards they were planning a trip to the Riviera in Bonnie's new car. Then business intervened. Eliane's head vendeuse contacted her to say that an American magazine wanted a major interview about that year's styles and about Paris's continuing role as world fashion capital after the war. Worth and Poiret were the other two couturiers being interviewed and that meant it would have been lunacy for Eliane to refuse. Unfortunately the only possible date for the interview was December 30th, the day they planned to be halfway to Nice.

'You'd be a fool to call it off just because of our trip and I'll be the first one to tell you so,' said Bonnie. 'Anyway, there's a perfectly workable solution that only means you giving up the motor trip down. I'll leave as planned and you catch the train immediately after you've done the interview. We'll both arrive on New Year's Eve and see 1920 in together in Nice. Can't get more romantic than that, can we?'

'Oh, Bonnie, you think of everything! That's wonderful.'

After lunch on December 29th, she waved him off from outside the Ritz. He looked like a glamorous illustration from a popular magazine. Just before kissing her goodbye, he reached inside his motoring coat and took out a bulky envelope. 'Here's some homework to keep you busy on the train, just in case you had ideas about running around loose and picking up new admirers!'

'What is it?'

'Your cultural timetable for when we come back to Paris. I've been amusing myself by drawing up book lists and places for us to see together. Seriously, you might find it interesting to look through on the train and we can talk about any extra things you might want to put in. Now, see you in a couple of days and don't speak to strange men. Most of them will have intentions almost as dishonourable as mine!'

He kissed her again, then turned his attention to the car and roared off out of the Place Vendôme.

Two days later, on the morning of New Year's Eve, as Eliane's train carried her south, Bonnie Charles was killed instantly when his car blew a tyre and overturned. His widow had the remains shipped back to England for a private funeral and burial in her family vault.

# Chapter Eleven
## Doré and Andrea

*Well, now we're really moving! I didn't think I could ever talk about Bonnie's marriage, but I managed it somehow. I did once go on at that novelist girl in an oblique sort of way about dressing his wife and added a few lies about liking her, but I contrived to get on my high horse and look icy when she asked questions about how it really hit me when I got the news of the marriage. This time, at least I was able to tell Andy how much it hurt; how very, very much. . . .*

*Still, no use dwelling on that now. God knows, he paid. He'd not have been driving south on New Year's Eve if we hadn't separated and then come back together. But then, Bonnie was never intended to make old bones. He went out at the best time.*

*Come on, Eliane, face up to it! All this self-congratulation is a pathetic attempt to forgive yourself for dodging telling her the truth about Edouard. She knows something. I'm sure of it . . . that's why I keep getting edgy. But what? How much? Bet Eugène has been blabbing out of school. The little fairy never did learn to keep a still tongue in his head! Whoops – even I know that's unreasonable. The boy has carried more than his fair share of secrets, and he's done it when secrecy would bring him no personal advantage. He's done it for me. I'm glad he's coming to the races tomorrow. On balance I'd like to see him and* la vedette *really making friends.*

*For once I'm feeling comfortably drowsy without the awful little pills. Must be the prospect of a lovely day with lovely horses tomorrow, and Andy looking like a goddess in her first Doré suit. Then a good solid week of work on the collection to follow. What could be better?*

Andy knew the Bois de Boulogne as well as anyone who had lived in Paris, but she had never before attended a meeting at either of the great racetracks there. When she was a child her mother had shown no interest and as a student it had never crossed her mind. Now, thrilling to the spectacle of brilliant silks, top class thoroughbreds and Paris's most expensive fashions on display, she was entranced and wondered why she had stayed away so long.

She looked wonderful herself and she knew it. The previous Monday, before a gruelling session of reminiscences, Doré had taken her into the big first-floor salon, instructed her to stand before the multiple mirrors, and had dressed her head to foot in that season's most stunning outfit.

Peering up at her, a pout of concentration on her fierce old face, Doré had reached sideways to where a vendeuse stood in attendance with a rail full of dresses and suits and accessories. 'Hmm, as you insist on keeping that outlandish hair colour, there's only one real possibility – black and white. Like . . . this. . . .'

She shook a dress and jacket free of its linen dust cover. 'Go on, put it on. The floor covering will protect the hem, don't be timid.'

Andy let her casual pants drop and shrugged out of her cotton shirt. Doré looked at her approvingly. 'Christ, if I had that figure now, what I'd do with it!'

'I still find plenty for it to do, thanks very much!' But there was no hostility in Andy's response.

The vendeuse helped her into the dress. It was of heavy silk jersey, glossy jet black, accompanied by a dazzling white jacket braided with black and with the classic Doré brass buttons. An ornate, slim belt completed the ensemble, sinuous as a snake, comprising thongs of black and white leather interwoven with the entwined Ds which were another Doré trademark. A pair of medium-heel black and white sling back shoes were offered, along with a black leather chain-handled shoulder bag with linked-D clasp. Doré started selecting costume jewellery from the tray which had been brought by another assistant: a bevy of neck chains of black baroque pearls and gold links; a pair of giant baroque pearl ear studs with gold surrounds, like miniature war shields.

'And now, the coup de grâce!' said Mademoiselle. The vendeuse handed her a big Breton sailor hat in gleaming black Bangkok straw, its brim swooping back from the face with almost impossible, effortless elegance. Doré pressed it firmly on to Andy's head, awarding it like a military decoration as she had to thousands of models over the years to indicate her seal of approval on an outfit ready for showing.

'Right now, turn around and find out if you like what you see.'

Andy did so – and gasped. 'Hell, Doré, now I know what the man meant when he said the rich are different. No wonder, with you to dress them!'

She knew she had never looked so impeccably smart and never would again. There was nothing sexual about her allure, but a great deal that was sensual. Clothes like these were the ultimate outward expression of self-esteem.

Doré was grinning like a happy child. 'You were made for my designs, you great big Anglo-Saxon! When you leave here, you're taking a whole wardrobe full. I couldn't ask for a better advertisement!' She reached up impulsively and kissed Andy on both cheeks. Andy embraced her frail, bird-like little body and felt oddly moved.

The rest of the week had been hard on the couturière. She had obviously tried to be honest, reporting her relationship with Bonnie Charles as she had seen it; laughing bitterly about the way the Press had swallowed the lines on how she and Lady Venetia were bosom friends. Andy did not have the heart to press the matter of her son. Clearly Doré had not wanted to tell her – not yet anyway – and she had been so eager to set the record straight on other things that Andy left it for the moment. They had last seen each other on Friday evening. Now it was Sunday and Doré's party met for an early lunch at the Ritz before going on to Longchamp.

For Doré it was like coming home. From their arrival through to the late afternoon, she was the centre of an ever-changing group of old friends, young admirers and acquaintances of all ages.

The big race came and went in mid-afternoon and Andy's attention began to flag. Her ultra-glamorous appearance attracted a stream of smooth-talking admirers, few of whom she found interesting. She began to wish Steb was with her and welcomed the chance of rescue when it was offered.

'How about taking a walk outside?' said Eugène. 'I enjoy being a spectator at these things but once it reaches this stage I've seen most of what I want to see and I hanker after something fresh. I haven't strolled in the Bois for longer than I care to remember.'

Andy agreed readily, Doré was dismissive. 'Go, go – it's all the same with you tourists! Don't know one end of a good horse from another. Tell me where you're heading and I'll have the mechanic pick you up in the car when we leave.'

They debated. 'I know,' said Andy, 'something I haven't seen since I was a little girl – the Shakespeare Garden! D'you know it, Eugène, over at the Pré Catelan?'

'Well, I know of it, of course, but I don't recall ever visiting it. Yes, why not?'

'Okay. Doré, we'll go along the Cascade Walk and end up at the Shakespeare Garden. See you later, and don't tire yourself!'

The couturière patted the arm of the Comte D'Agde, who had just joined her. 'Don't fuss. Henri will look after me as he invariably does when I'm all alone. Go and see your garden!'

They wandered off together, Eugène immaculate as

always in a morning suit; Andy still glorying in her new outfit.

The Shakespeare Garden is a charming French conceit set in the heart of a small park which in turn nestles within the Bois, the overall effect resembling that of a nest of Russian dolls opening from within each other. It contains all the plants and flowers which are mentioned in Shakespeare's plays and poetry.

The Bois in summer always made Andy feel she was strolling inside a Monet or a Renoir. The crystal clear sunlight streamed through the foliage of the big trees, brightly splashing the grass and paths. The fresh green all around lent youth to the faces of the middle-aged and enchantment to the faces of the young. The Pré Catelan was a particularly favoured spot, with its children's play area and attractive restaurant.

Andy felt relaxed now in St-Meurice's company and he was certainly more at ease with her than previously. At first they walked in companionable silence, then St-Meurice started talking about the progress she was making with Mademoiselle.

'Oh, she seems to be letting her hair down now. I think she trusts me a little more each day.'

'Is she sticking more or less to reality?'

'She's given herself a hard time facing up to what happened between her and Bonnie Charles at the end.'

'Ah yes, Charles. Life might have been very different for many people if that had turned out otherwise.'

His reaction intrigued her. 'You know a bit about him, then?'

'Mm - very little, but enough to think Mademoiselle might have been less of a Medusa and happier in her later years if she had used her head and let him make an honest woman of her.'

'You really think he would have?' Andy had been asking herself the same question.

'I *wish* he had. It would have made a great deal of difference to the boy.'

'Ah, yes, Edouard. She's still sticking to the line that he was her nephew. She says he belonged to the elder sister Ninette who died during the First World War, but that couldn't be right, irrespective of what you told me, because later she told other people that the boy was Elise's.'

'Yes, I've heard the Ninette version, too. I wonder how she plans to treat her other little brush with maternity?'

'Eugène, I hate to be such a doubting Thomas, but are you . . . that is, how sure are you that the boy was hers? Don't think I suspect you of deceiving me,' she added hastily, 'it's just that as she's so tight-lipped about it I wondered how on earth you came by the information.'

He gave her a long, grim look and did not answer for a while. Then he merely said, 'I'm too sure for there to be any room for doubt.' He gestured ahead. 'Look, we've arrived. Let's see what your famous garden has to offer.'

Embarrassed by the deterioration in their earlier rapport, Andy turned to the plants around them. She bent to pick a small frond of aromatic greenery and rubbed the leaves to release its sunny, spicy smell.

'There's rosemary, that's for remembrance,' she said, and tailed off, having finished what she knew of Ophelia's mad reverie in *Hamlet*.

To her astonishment, St-Meurice continued the quotation, in English: '. . . Pray you, love, remember. And there is pansies; that's for thoughts . . . there's fennel for you, and columbines, there's rue for you, and here's some for me: we may call it herb o' grace o' Sundays – oh, you must wear your rue with a difference! There's a daisy. I would give you some violets, but they withered all when my father died – they say he made a good end. . . .'

His words froze her. He had simply recited the introductory catalogue of plants, but when he reached the reference to violets, he declaimed the words, enunciating each syllable and gazing coldly at her as he did so.

'Oh, Christ, Eugène, I must be blind and deaf! I never asked you what Edouard's surname was – I thought of him as Doré. It was St-Meurice, wasn't it? If you weren't his son, you couldn't possibly know so much about what happened to him!'

He smiled tiredly. 'Well done. Better late than never. As it happens, he did make a good end.'

'How?'

'He was an officer-instructor in the cavalry school at Saumur when the *Wehrmacht* moved in on the city in June 1940. He was one of those who died gallantly, defending France against impossible odds. It was the week his mother moved in with the Nazis' head of propaganda at the Ritz.'

The warmth went out of the sunshine. Andy clutched at a straw. 'Did she know?'

'Eventually, yes. There's no telling when she found out; not immediately, perhaps. But when she did, it didn't stop her for a moment. She went right on enjoying the privileges of collaboration.'

'Oh, no!'

'You'll get used to the idea. I'm still with her, after all. She must have some redeeming features, must she not?'

'It's hard to think so, I imagine, seen from your point of view.'

His bitterness spilled over. 'Well, you'd better learn, and fast, because you're in a similar position.'

'I don't understand. . . . What on earth are you driving at? My father was English!'

'And your mother?'

'Now I'm beginning to think you're crazy! You know as well as I do that my mother's surname is Chabrol.'

'Perhaps, Mademoiselle Vincent, you would care to hazard a guess at Geneviève Doré's married name when her baron finally made an honest woman of her. It shouldn't be too hard. . . .'

Eliane Doré's voice cut into the conversation like a whiplash. 'Eugène, I sometimes think you must have been the sort of small boy who pulled the legs off flies. Cut it short, since you've seen fit to spill your guts and ruin everyone's day! Andy – my Aunt Geneviève became Baroness Chabrol in 1923. She brought up my daughter Loulou under her own name. Loulou's father was the Duke of Conway.

'And now, if everyone has had enough melodrama, perhaps we can go back to the Ritz. I want a glass of champagne and a short sleep before dinner.'

She turned and walked briskly back to her Rolls-Royce, which had slid up silently beside the gates of the Pré Catelan while Andy's attention was riveted on Eugène St-Meurice.

The drive back was silent, but the looks exchanged by Doré and St-Meurice said more than twenty conversations. In other circumstances Andy would have found it amusing, but today she was going through too much personal turmoil for the humour to strike her. St-Meurice looked truculent; Doré outraged. Occasionally their eyes met – perhaps 'collided' was a better description – and shied away. Once, twice, a dozen times, Andy wound herself up to speak and then thought better of it. How did one begin a conversation after what had just happened? 'Hi, Granny, fancy meeting you at the races' hardly struck the right note. Perhaps 'Oh, Grandmama, what big teeth you have. . . .' She felt hysteria bubbling close to the surface and hurriedly glanced out of the car, trying to concentrate on the sunny street instead.

Finally they stopped at the Rue Cambon premises. Doré leaned forward and jabbed Eugène's thigh with her forefinger. 'You – troublemaker – I want to talk to you back at the Ritz.' She turned to Andy. 'Clearly you and I have a great deal to discuss which I'd hoped to talk over calmly, later on. It can't be helped; now's as good time as any, I suppose. Lunch tomorrow. Will that suit you?'

Andy could only nod dumbly.

'Right. My usual table at the Ritz, 12.45.' Suddenly the brusqueness dissolved and for a moment she was a pathetic old woman. 'Don't be too hard on me in the meantime.'

Andy melted, stepped half into the big car and embraced her. 'Don't worry, Doré, I'll be there.' She was about to add a few reassuring words when she caught Eugène's cold stare over the old woman's shoulder. They say he made a good end. . . . With a small shiver she disengaged herself and turned away.

At the Ritz on Monday Doré was all brittle friendliness, anxious to please, flirtatious, defensive. The waiter poured white wine and left them with the menu. Doré's river of social chit-chat petered out and she looked straight at Andy for the first time that day, a nervous child trapped inside a worn-out body.

Andy sighed. 'Look, let's shelve the preliminaries and concentrate on the explanation. Why all the secrecy? Why on earth was I never told? I simply cannot imagine my mother being too ashamed of her background to admit to it.'

'There's more than one kind of shame, Andy.'

'What's that supposed to mean?'

'I take it you are referring to the stigma of illegitimacy. Even in my medieval day, when the father was a duke it did away with a lot of moral indignation. No, it wasn't that sort of shame. Of course your mother wouldn't have cared about that.'

'Then what?'

'We had a quarrel – a very serious quarrel. We had never got on well, even when Loulou was a child. Come to that, she was little more than a child when we had the big row, the one that was never patched up.'

'What caused it?'

'I think you must get your mother's version first. It's not that I don't want to give you my side – I lay awake all last night trying to find the words. In the end I decided I had to take a back seat. Your mother must have her say first. I owe that to her.'

'It was the war, wasn't it?'

'Yes.'

'Eugène says you were living here with a high-ranking Nazi right up until the Germans left.'

Instantly Doré was all ice-cold dignity. 'I lived with a half-English German nobleman who did his duty for the government of the day.'

Andy was exasperated by the evasiveness of the answer. 'You seem to have a life-long determination to ignore war, whoever else it hurts. For you, it's just an excuse to get rich or an opportunity to exploit an influential lover. Haven't you *any* principles?'

'Don't preach to me about principles! You made money out of war too, my girl. Vietnam made your name!'

'Yeah, but I got half my arse shot off while I was making it. I paid my dues, Doré. What currency did you pay with, your children's blood?'

Fury mottled Mademoiselle's face. The hand that clutched the Baccarat wine glass trembled violently. 'If this place were less public, I'd slap you.'

'Be my guest – at least it would show you had some real human feelings!' Andy stopped, realising she had better control her tongue. Doré was gasping for breath and anger had visibly affected her. The younger woman made a huge effort to put things on a less acrimonious footing.

'Look, let's calm down a bit. It *is* generous of you to tell me to get Mama's story first. I'll go and see her. She should be at home in Brittany now. I can go over the material you recorded for me from Bonnie's death to the mid-twenties while I'm at it, and do a preliminary summary of what we've covered to date. Then I shall come back and we'll discuss our family relationship more calmly. I'm sorry I sounded so judgemental just now. I've no right to take such a biased view as your supposedly unbiased biographer, but remember I had no idea when I took on the assignment that we were connected in any way. Come on, let's be friends – over lunch, at least.'

Doré glared at her for a few moments, then managed a half-hearted smile. 'All right. You may see it differently when we've talked properly. Let's go on working for now, and perhaps you could go and see your mother next week.'

But the rapport they had enjoyed before seemed to have gone for good. For the first time, Andy began to see the Doré who made enemies. The couturière talked about the literary and show business names she had known in the 1930s, and it seemed in her eyes all of them were third-rate. This playwright had stolen the ideas of an unknown English dramatist. That painter was a talentless charlatan. Paul Colombes, still regarded as the genius of French cinema and theatre, came in for the biggest helping of venom. Until now Andy had found it impossible to believe Doré was so old. Today it was impossible to believe she had ever been young. They battled on through course after course, Doré picking at her food, Andy eating like a navvy from nervousness. Nothing can save today, she told herself. The sooner we part company, the better. She concentrated on being as pleasant as possible.

As they were finishing their coffee, a fat woman passed their table, wearing an expensive but mass-produced copy of a Doré suit. Doré glanced at her and said, in a tone the woman could not fail to hear, 'Insignificance in twenty volumes!'

Something snapped inside Andy. She stood up, pushing back her chair so violently it almost overturned. 'Sorry, Doré. You'll have to find someone else as your straight man. I've had enough. I'll give you a call when you've had time to spit out the sour grapes.'

Before the couturière had time to respond, Andy had hurried from the restaurant. She telephoned her mother in Brittany as soon as she got back to the Rue Cambon and arranged to arrive at Rennes by train the next day. She made another brief call, then left Doré's magnificent apartment to spend the night with Esteban Ortiz.

'Do you want to talk, or is silence and alcohol of more use to you?'

Andy looked at him sharply, but there was only concern in Steb's voice and face.

'Do I look that bad?'

'In a word, yes. You're as beautiful as ever but you seem to have had the stuffing knocked out of you. What the hell happened?'

She gave him a weary smile. 'Now would be the ideal time to be the sort of girl you wish I was. I could collapse in tears and you'd kiss away all my cares. At the moment it sounds like bliss.'

'You can cry all you want, lean on me all you want, ask me to sort out all you want – and I promise that I won't hold it against you when you want to go back to being a macho woman again!'

'Steb, thanks. I really do appreciate it.'

'Hell, I've got so used to your bloody-mindedness the past couple of weeks, I think I'd hate it if you came over all soft and pliable now. I was proposing a temporary amnesty for my sake as much as yours.'

She managed a half-hearted playful punch at his arm, then slipped exhausted into his embrace. 'Honestly, love, it's been a really shitty day. You have no idea how much I want to talk about it, but right now I don't think it would do any good at all. Before we get too settled, I'd better confess one thing, though. Tomorrow I'm going away, for at least a couple of weeks. There's someone I have to see. When I come back, I hope I'll have sorted my head out and then I probably will want to talk. Can you forgive me for being so secretive?'

'It's not easy. When our women talk of going off to meet mysterious someones, we Latin lovers start thinking in terms of other men with flashing eyes and waxed moustaches, waiting to tie you to the railroad tracks if you don't submit to their evil demands. But okay – just this once. All the same, isn't there anything you want to get off your chest now?'

'It's not really that sort of misery. Actually it's a family thing that can only be sorted out with the family itself. Telling someone else won't help at all – and that's no insult to your kindness, it simply wouldn't. The best way to help me now will be to spend an evening ignoring all of it.'

Steb nodded, held her for a moment longer, then drew away. 'Come on. When in anguish, reach for food.' He started towards the kitchen.

'I don't think even that will help, the way I feel tonight.'

'Can this be half-a-duck Vincent? Pull yourself together, woman. In the kitchen there's a gigantic platter of *vitello tonnato*, and I do believe I picked up two of the biggest *choux pralinées au chocolat* you ever saw at the patisserie today. Go on, force yourself!'

'Are you sure you haven't any Italian blood? Your preoccupation with food seems decidedly odd in a native of a country where they all seem to wear nettles in their underpants to mortify the flesh.'

'I've been working in Milan for a year, remember? And if all food freaks are closet Italians, you should be slamming out Puccini in a throaty Neopolitan tenor!'

'Well, at least you can make me laugh, and anyone who's able to do that tonight can't be all bad. Lead me to the veal.'

They ate and drank, and afterwards he mixed her favourite apéritif, champagne and *crème de myrtilles* liqueur. 'No cognac for you, far too depressing in your present state. Float away on some bubbles instead.'

They had dined at the open french windows, looking down from the apartment's balcony towards the gardens in the Place des Vosges. Now they moved their chairs outside in the soft evening air. The surroundings and the champagne had a soothing effect on Andy, and Ortiz's presence gave her an added measure of security. He was a very undemanding companion and managed to keep the conversation lighthearted without apparent effort.

'I finished my Lady and Unicorn sweaters,' he said, 'but the colour range really got to me and I've been playing around a little to see what they'd look like integrated into a full collection. Would you like to see what I came up with?'

Oh Christ, Andy told herself, he's trying to take my mind off my family problems and unknowingly he frog-marches me straight back to it all! Aloud, she only said, 'Yes, I'd love to.'

Moments later she was glad she had kept her reservations to herself. The drawings he showed her were sensational. For the time being she forgot the Doré debacle in her excitement at his prodigious talent. 'Steb, these are marvellous! I don't know how you've done it, but you've designed clothes like nothing I've ever seen before. I'd kill for some of these outfits!'

'So much for fashion being a minor pastime!'

'Well, I still believe that, so if *I* think this stuff is the tops, a real fashion buff will drool over them. Who have you shown them to?'

'No one, that's the embarrassing part. I'm a fashion designer and I don't know where to take my designs.'

'Oh, come on, they'd queue in the rain for these, surely?'

'I don't know so much. I'm doing it the wrong way round, and frankly I don't think any of these will ever see the light of day. Normally someone like me spends years working his way up specialised branches of the business and eventually is acknowledged as a master capable of doing a full couture collection. But by then, unless you're a designer who's come up through one house, you're a freelance consultant producing "guest" collections or regular projects for the top names. Eventually, when a couture house needs a revolution at the top, they pick one of these big boys. I have an awfully long way to go yet.

'No one would take me in at the top on the strength of just this – it could be a flash in the pan – but even if it were not, to accommodate me and my style they'd have to shove aside their established hierarchy. No, unless you know of a top fashion house where they're short of a chief designer and wide open for a fresh start, I can forget this lot and get back to my knitting.'

She thought of the House of Doré, of the opportunities

for a fresh talent there, and almost told him the real reason for her presence in Paris, of her own close link to the business. But caution triumphed and in the end they moved on to discuss something else.

As the last of the evening light faded from the sky, Ortiz stood up and held out his hand to her. 'Come on, time for bed. If I can't comfort you any other way, I can love you back into good spirits.'

'Now that sounds like the best idea you've had all evening.'

She was awake soon after first light, running again and again through the crazy, extraordinary story which she still had to unravel fully. A couple of weeks before, she would have been flattered to learn she was a descendant of Alouette Doré, but the old woman's more recent behaviour had saddened and angered her. Andy had grown to like and respect Eugène St-Meurice during her time in Paris, and she had glimpsed the savage hurt he had suffered at Doré's hands. Then there was her own mother. Why had Marie-Louise never referred to her illustrious parents? The hurt there must be just as bad. What a lot of cruelty for one frail little woman to have inflicted. Had it not been for Doré's boorish behaviour on Monday at the Ritz, Andy might have been prepared to believe there was some explanation for what she had done. But the scene in the restaurant had revealed a self-seeking, blinkered harridan who cared for no one but herself. What a heritage!

Now she had to go and confront Marie-Louise, and much as she loved her mother, she knew they might fall out for the first time in ten years merely on account of the discord sown by so much secrecy. She tried to promise herself she would not give Marie-Louise a rough time, but feared even now that she might not be strong enough to resist doing so. She started to get up.

Ortiz stirred and turned over, instantly alert as he realised she was already on the move. 'Don't tell me – you were going to slip into the kitchen, put on an apron and rustle up croissants and *café au lait* for two!'

'Actually I was thinking more along the lines of a shower and a cab. I think I have a choice between your hunger and thirst and the early train. But stick around. When I get back I'll get you enough croissants and coffee to start a brasserie.'

'Promises, promises. You're going off with the guy in the waxed moustache and I'll never see you again.'

'Don't worry, now that I've learned you're not all bad, I'll be hard to shake off.' She dropped the bantering tone. 'Thanks for being so kind to me, Steb. And thanks for not making a big thing about where I'm going or anything. I really couldn't have taken it at present. Let's hope when I get back it's all sorted out.'

'I'd appreciate it if you felt like telling me all about it then – I'm practically giving myself a hernia with the strain of being so reasonable. If you weren't so god-damned sensitive about your privacy and independence, I'd have another try at prising a phone number out of you.'

But she was shaking her head before he had even finished. 'I can't, Steb. Believe me, I'm not being nutty – I have good reasons for being so secretive. Give me a little time and I hope I'll be able to talk to you properly. I just can't do it now.'

She showered, dressed and was gone in less than twenty minutes. By 8 a.m. only a faint trace of her scent gave any indication that she had been in the apartment. Ortiz lay in the big rumpled bed, wondering if he would ever see her again.

# Chapter Twelve

## Doré

## 1920–1924: Unsentimental Education

Losing Bonnie permanently felt much the same as when she first heard he had married Venetia Lamington. Eliane had thought then, too, that she would never see him again. She had survived. She would survive again.

But then there had been the challenge of heights yet to be scaled. Now she had the security she had always wanted and was at a loss to fill her empty days. She talked it over with Geneviève, the only person apart from Bonnie who had seen her vulnerability. 'I thought I was all right alone, that he was just my lover, but I was so wrong,' she said. 'Knowing he's gone has shaken me. I've no confidence any more. I'm the little tart from Saumur again, skulking around the paddocks at Compiègne, hoping no one will point me out as a fallen woman. What'll I do?'

Geneviève was brisk. 'Be a bit more realistic for a start. I know his death was devastating, but that's not the problem now. You need to move on and you haven't worked out how to do it yet, so you think it's because he's not there any more. Face it, Eliane, you'd used up the world you and he shared. If Bonnie had lived, he'd probably have been the first to look for something new. Now you'll have to do it on your own. It could be just as exciting.'

'Thanks for defining my problem. I was asking for a solution.'

'Coming up. When you had Bonnie, you could tag along with him around all the important people. Now you have to do it on your own merit and you're scared. But there's no reason why you should be. Just complete that Grand Tour he started you on. I've seen you looking at it, treasuring it like a magic talisman just because it was the last thing he gave you. He'd despise that. It's only important if you put it to the use he intended. Read the books, look at the pictures, listen to the music and see the plays. By the time you've done it all, with your other talents you'll be unstoppable.'

'But how?' It was a desperate wail.

'Use what you already have. You want to impress the social lions. Be realistic. Plenty of them want to impress you. You're a very fashionable young woman, Mademoiselle Alouette.'

'Young? I'm thirty-five in a couple of weeks.'

'I know that. You know that. They don't. You look twenty, damn you!'

Geneviève was right. When Eliane started studying the invitations which came her way, she saw immediately that many were from the sort of people who could give her the cultural polish she lacked. And so began her friendship with Magda Robles. They had met at a reception a year before and ran into each other again at a dinner party in the spring of 1920. Magda was fascinated by the look Eliane had created and dropped broad hints about getting to know her better. At first Eliane was reserved.

'Who is she, anyway?' she asked Geneviève. 'Everyone seems to know her, but she doesn't *do* anything except be seen.'

'Darling, when you're Magda, that's all you need to do! She's France's artistic soul, according to nine-tenths of our best-known modern painters. She's a Pole, born in Russia, brought up in Belgium in her arty grandmother's house. She does have talent – she's a marvellous pianist – it's just that she hasn't had time to give many concerts in the past ten years or so because she's been married to one millionaire and one magazine publisher, not to mention affairs with half the big names in the art world. She's been painted by everyone worthwhile, starting with Bonnard, and though she claims to be a philistine who never reads a book, she always manages to know exactly who's doing what in the world of the arts. In short, she's exactly what you need right now.'

'Yes, but am I what she needs? What's in it for her?'

'Oh, you'll pay, but it's a price you can afford. She ran away from her publisher a couple of years ago to live with Antonio Robles, the painter. The publisher divorced her and she married the painter, but they're both madly extravagant and his painting doesn't earn enough to keep them in the style they like. Play the generous hostess and they'll be as helpful as you could wish.'

And so, without either woman acknowledging that it was at least partly a commercial arrangement, Magda began teaching Eliane about the arts and introduced her to a world at which Bonnie Charles had only hinted. In the ensuing months, Eliane visited countless exhibitions of paintings and sculpture by strange young men whom no one mentioned again. She sat through concerts where long silences were punctuated by jagged spates of atonal sound which confused or bored her. She also met Picasso, Dali, Bakst, Stravinsky and Cocteau. And she was completely bowled over by the St Petersburg Ballet.

The Russian dance company had revolutionised French taste in ballet, bringing brilliant colour, wild modern music and astonishingly athletic choreography to a previously sedate, formal area of the arts. The artistes who performed the new entertainments were perpetually in debt, always exhausting their resources before the next windfall arrived. Magda was their heroine. From her chaotic, none-too-clean but highly original drawing-room, she nagged aristocrats, impressed rich social climbers, procured influential lovers for cast members – all in the interests of keeping the company afloat. Eliane watched her in admiration tinged with distaste for the chaos of her gypsy existence.

Magda was aware of her attitude and it merely amused her. 'You're too keen on order, Alouette. Our world isn't like that. Neatness and solvency are bourgeois virtues. Who wants to be bourgeois?' And she was gone, on to the next piece of artistic wheeler dealing. Was she aware of the chaos she had just sown in her new friend's mind? Eliane was never sure. She went away and brooded on what Magda had said and came to a couple of startling conclusions about herself.

She had always believed her life to be the ultimate example of the French adventurer's rejection of the middle classes – *épater la bourgeoisie*. Now she realised that she wanted to astound them, certainly, but she wanted to impress them, too, to make them envy her, and therein she failed to live up to the 'don't care' aspect of the adventurer's catchphrase. In an awful way she was too much like them entirely to reject their standards. So she would always be a rebel in clean petticoats. Funny, Magda had seen that where she had not. Now Magda really spat in their faces and enjoyed it. If she were run down in the street, she'd be wearing torn stockings and soiled underwear. Eliane would meet such a fate in new silk hose and spotless Swiss cotton knickers. But they'd both be just as dead. Eliane silently conceded that she would never really fully absorb what Magda Robles had to teach her.

Still, one thing was clear: Eliane certainly had no wish to be labelled a bourgeoise and one way around that was to observe Magda's act and copy it for herself. She watched Magda play Lady Bountiful, unobtrusively learning from her about bohemian society as she had once learned about the sporting world from the horsy set round Christi de Selincourt.

The day she took her first independent step as a patron of the arts was intoxicating. Felix Kusnikov, the ballet impresario who ran the St Petersburg troupe, had visited Magda in her Montparnasse apartment while Eliane was there. Ruin was staring them in the face yet again, he said. The account for the costumes on the forthcoming production of *The Balinese Warlord* was unpaid. They were due to open next week and the costumier had impounded the goods, refusing to release them unless settlement was made in full.

'Don't tell me,' said Magda, 'you were counting on the opening night takings to give him even a little on account!'

Kusnikov nodded in morose silence.

'So what now?'

'No costumes; no gala opening; no more St Petersburg Ballet. As simple as that!' Kusnikov's voice dripped melodrama.

'How much is necessary to save you?'

'At least two hundred thousand francs.'

Magda burst out laughing while Kusnikov assumed an expression of outrage. 'Oh really, Felix, stop looking so tragic! I know I work the odd miracle but even if I hadn't already pawned my diamonds for you this month, I couldn't help you with a sum like that. I don't know enough rich social climbers who owe me a favour.' He looked resigned. 'Still, I'll do my best. Sit and talk to Alouette while I make a few calls next door.' And she swept out in a rush of overpowering scent.

They eyed each other warily for a couple of minutes. Then Kusnikov rose and started pacing nervously about the room, worrying at a lamp fringe or a curtain trim occasionally. Into the lengthening silence, Eliane said quietly, 'I'll give you the two hundred thousand, but only if you promise not to tell Magda.'

He stopped in his tracks. 'You, Mademoiselle? But why? We could not possibly repay your investment!'

She was gaining confidence with every breath. Now she stood up, smiled broadly and said, 'Look on it as sponsorship of a great cause rather than investment, my friend. Anyway, it's not much more than small change to me!' Which was not quite true, but impressed her almost as much as it did Kusnikov.

She was on her way out but turned at the door. 'Come over to the Ritz for a drink this evening and I'll have the money for you. Oh, and one other thing. It's Alouette or Eliane now - never Mademoiselle. Understood?'

'Perfectly - Alouette. I look forward to seeing you later.'

Why did she feel a thrill of guilt, like a successful thief, because she had succeeded in subsidising the ballet without using Magda as her intermediary? Perhaps it was something to do with the sense of power it gave her. Pay and you control. Interesting. Until now she had seen wealth purely as a means of liberation from the dominion of others. Now she was beginning to see it could make her the one who dominated and the feeling was decidedly pleasant.

That evening, Eliane exercised her newly discovered power on Magda and Antonio Robles. 'I've been thinking about these Italian museums and churches and so on that you two keep talking about,' she said. 'If neither of you is too busy, perhaps you'd care to be my guests and guide me around this summer. I've had enough of the Pyrenees to last quite some time.'

Antonio was as enthusiastic as Magda. 'That's a wonderful idea, Alouette. Of course, there's only one way to do it - first class all the way. If one can afford it, the only place to stay in Venice is the Danieli. Every city in Italy has somewhere of that calibre and if you are to establish yourself in the position you deserve, you must be seen in such hotels from the start.'

Alouette smiled secretly as she agreed. And you must be seen there with me, of course, at my expense. So be it. I should have realised a long time ago that most of the things one wants are for sale if one can raise the money to buy them.

Strangely, her understanding of the commercial aspects of their relationship did not lessen her liking for the Robles couple. They knew what they wanted, so did she. Both sides were getting value for money.

Magda went to work to ensure that Eliane acquired the cultural background she had lacked until now. She taught her friend the odd and already slightly outdated vocabulary which had marked out the pre-war member of the upper class. Raincoats were rubbers; chauffeurs were mechanics; cars were parked in motor houses. The terms shared an old-world air, as though they were survivals of a more leisurely era. By implication, those who used such language had established their social roots before the arrival of the new, fly-by-night generation. Daily, Eliane learned new tricks and daily it became harder for a stranger to recognise her as anything other than a cultured woman entitled by birth to her lofty position in society.

Meanwhile, a real friendship was growing between Eliane and Magda which had little to do with their original arrangement. Eliane no longer wanted to imitate Magda's outrageous personality; it was enough to enjoy it by spending time with her. Magda, in turn, was given increasingly frequent glimpses of an intensely private Eliane who would remain unknown to practically everyone else. She liked and admired what she saw.

Magda was a prodigally generous character and recognised that few other people shared her tendency to fling money, gifts and invitations at friends in need. When she discovered a similar, though less obvious, quality in Eliane, she warmed to the self-contained little woman. Eliane's generosity was screened by an elaborate show of indifference, as when she arrived one day bearing a Doré dress box. She handed it to Magda as if it contained scraps.

'I don't know if you'll find a use for that. See what you think.' She was so nonchalant Magda thought that at most it was a try-out version of a sweater or blouse, and began opening the package with no more than mild anticipation. The outfit inside almost stopped her breath.

'Don't gush – go and try it on. It might be useless. I just thought it could solve your party frock problems, that's all.'

A couple of weeks before, she had told Eliane she had

nothing to wear to a Jungle Ball which she was attending as the partner of one of Kusnikov's dancers. The invitation was of some importance to Magda, because it came from a Society hostess and she received few such accolades. The one social area where Eliane had a head start on her was that of the haut monde; the best people regarded Magda with suspicion as an adventuress and a companion of artists, so this event was a breakthrough for her. But she was without funds and had no amusing costume which could guarantee her the desired stunning entrance. Eliane had been dismissive at the time, merely murmuring that she was sure something would turn up. It had, courtesy of hours of work at Doré Couture which Magda could not have financed in a hundred years.

Still babbling with gratitude, Magda took the box to her bedroom. She emerged minutes later, delighted with what Eliane had created for her. The colours were barbaric and tropical – a poisonous but seductive green, paired with bronze and ivory – all calculated to point up Magda's lush red-blonde and cream colouring. The costume was a sheath of skin-tight silk jersey, so closely embroidered with sequins and flat beads that the base fabric was invisible. The back, which extended up into a head-dress, was in jungle green. It slid seductively round Magda's curves before fading into bronze scales and then into ivory, covering the wearer to floor level, and with the green back ending as a yard-long pointed train. It transformed Magda from a seductive woman into a sinister female serpent and looked more expensive than anything she had ever owned.

'Mmm – I seem to have gauged your size quite well. I stole one of your old camisoles and worked from that. Yes . . . it should ensure you get noticed, if nothing else.'

That was all. Eliane dismissed her friend's incoherent thanks. It was the first of many equally generous presents, which Eliane managed to deliver in a manner that distinguished them from the bill-paying she had always done as the apprentice patron of intellectual society.

They both still treated that as a commercial activity.

Magda could not give the couturière material gifts in return; her money was always gone before she had it, and anyway Eliane was so much richer that it would have been pointless. But she understood instinctively how to respond. Although capable of slashing malice on a level with Eliane's own, she usually treated Doré with gentleness, particularly when she sensed insecurity or loneliness in the other. She learned rapidly that Eliane had lost the ability to deliver kindnesses kindly - she proffered them almost as insults, her acerbic delivery often convincing the recipients that she thought them worthless. Magda learned to look behind the often extreme opinions, recognising that they came from the lost child in Eliane whose responses had been frozen and twisted by tougher formative years than most women had known. Slowly, too, she learned to distinguish between a genuine plea for solitude - Eliane needed to be alone quite often - and the dismissive line which disguised aching need and was a cry for help wrapped in barbed wire.

Eliane never understood why she allowed Magda inside the emotional fortress which she had built over the years. No one else entered, not lover, not friend, not family. Geneviève was already inside it with her - she never tried to hide anything from Geneviève - but her aunt lacked Magda's eccentric sensitivity and although she loved Eliane better than Magda ever would, she never understood her half so well.

During the first year of their friendship, the two women forged links which would be broken only by death. Occasionally they fought like wildcats - Magda was unrepentantly childish and Eliane was experiencing for the first time the sort of friendship which most little girls enjoy before adolescence. Her deprived youth had been an emotional desert and now, with Magda, she got a chance to catch up. Sometimes she wondered whether it would be good to unwind like this with others, too, but she always drew back. That was a sure way of getting her head chopped off. Magda was different, possibly unique – although she must never be told that. No, if she started letting her hair down, the whole world would soon think they could take advantage of her. Let them see her as a tough little piece if they chose: after all, she was, wasn't she? But somewhere, always out of reach, hovered the notion that perhaps life would be less lonely, more comfortable, if she softened a little. Her memories and her sense of self-preservation always kept it at bay.

Soon it dawned on Eliane that she was enjoying herself – really enjoying herself – for the first time since Bonnie's death. She wanted to look at pictures, to talk with the men who painted them, to listen to music and ask the composers to explain the stark modern sounds. Gradually she began to live again. It became easier and more enjoyable every day. Some time early in the spring of 1921, Eliane realised she was secure at last and that all that remained was the acquisition of suitable trimmings. She must choose an appropriate frame for the freshly-completed masterpiece that was Alouette Doré.

She had achieved her personal fashion look with scarcely any conscious effort. Her instinct told her what was right and what was not. But she was acutely aware that this certainty wavered when applied to furnishing and decorating a home. It was her main reason for living at the Ritz. Who would expect her to stamp any personality on an hotel suite? The Rue Cambon apartment was another matter and it made her nervous. Bonnie had left her with no guidance – after all, he was the one who had introduced her to living amid the anonymous luxury of the Ritz – so she reverted to memories of Christian de Selincourt's Gaillard and Pau establishments for inspiration. The result was a pleasant but bland collection of painted eighteenth-century chairs and ormolu-trimmed cabinets. She was beginning to amass a haphazard collection of small precious objects and these were displayed on the tables and inside the ornate cabinets. But they were the only objects which said anything about the personality of their owner. The furniture was merely a pale reflection of the world she abandoned with Christi.

Eliane was in Magda's apartment one day, looking at the dusty but distinctive souvenirs of her friend's misspent youth. Fingering a length of embroidered cloth, she sighed. 'I wish my apartment reflected my personality the way this place reflects yours,' she said.

Magda was amused that anyone with plenty of money should regard this as a problem. 'Darling, it's absurd for a woman of your resources and creativity to live in such a boring setting. Expand a little – think out your home as you think out the way you like your body to look. You can't just exist as a gypsy with a scattering of indifferent Louis XVI pieces and some good bibelots stuffed inside your caravan!'

Eliane was irritated enough to forget she had asked for advice. 'I never saw you as an arbiter of domestic chic. This place is always inches deep in dust and completely chaotic.'

Magda struck back with a degree of malice, 'Yes, darling, but at least the clutter is original and not bought by the metre from some gallery in the Faubourg St-Honoré. It says something about Magda Robles, even if it's just that she's a messy bitch. That interests people, intrigues them. Your personality intrigues, but unless you're careful the fascinated admirers will find there's nothing beneath the surface to merit their continued interest.'

Eliane's memory stirred with a remote echo of Bonnie telling her about Oscar Wilde's story *The Sphinx Without a Secret*. Magda seemed to be touching on the same thing, but from a different direction. That settled it. She'd better pay attention.

'What do I do about it? There's hardly any point in getting you to direct a re-furnishing and decorating plan. It'll just reflect Magda Robles, not Alouette Doré. But I'll take as much advice as you want to give me.'

'All right, what do we have? You are grown up, very artistic, discriminating and with a strong line on what you don't like. What *do* you like, Alouette?'

'That's the trouble! I think of likes and dislikes only in terms of clothes and jewellery, and my tastes in those change with the seasons, otherwise I'd never manage my collections.' She hesitated, then went on, 'Perhaps that's what puts me off furnishing anywhere. It's so – so rooted, somehow. I like things to change all the time but if I had the decorators in that often, it would drive me crazy!'

'My dear girl, that's no problem. You've always told me how much you like rich colours and patterns. You must have seen those wonderful screens they import from the Far East.'

'I'm not sure. What d'you have in mind?'

'A solution, Alouette. You simply have the whole place painted in creamy golds and whites and peaches – shades that flatter people – then you spend a fortune on Coromandel screens and scatter them around or fold them up as the fancy takes you. You'll never get tired of them because you can put them away for a while when they become a bore. And another thing – stop being so orthodox. You, of all people, who got going by mixing old and new, plain and fancy – mix things up a bit now. Just because classical Greece and Quattrocento Italy and Manchu China had nothing in common historically, it doesn't mean they can't be a wildly successful mix decoratively. We'll start going to art and furniture auctions and seeing what you fancy.'

So Magda freed Eliane's mind in the decorative sphere and she created a grand luxe interior style that was to be imitated almost unmodified for fifty years. Within six months of their original conversation, the Rue Cambon apartment was an enchantress's cave. Subdued lamps on lacquered Japanese side tables threw their diffused beams on soft golden walls and produced a honeyed light that made everyone beautiful. A perfect torso sculpted centuries before the birth of Christ adorned the carved eighteenth-century French marble mantelpiece. Japanese fans were spread on the lofty walls to display their full beauty. And six priceless Coromandel screens, decorated with birds, flowers and pagodas, completed the unique look of the huge drawing-room. A couple of the original staid antique armchairs remained, but were made more interesting by their contrast with the vast, plain club sofas which Eliane had ordered covered with tobacco-coloured suède.

The fitted bookcases were filled with exquisitely bound first editions of the French classics to which Bonnie had introduced her in 1919. And after Magda had left, lavishing praise on the baroque opulence of her protegée's home, Eliane added her own secret touch of self-indulgence. She unpacked a case of books, bound in leather and with gilded page edges like the collectors' items already on display. These were rather different. Their spines announced them as *Les Miserables, La Dame aux Camélias* and *Madame Bovary*, but inside it was another matter. There lay her own special weakness, disguised as culture - *Les Deux Gosses, Ambrose, La Rose* - the shopgirl romances of Decourcelle to which she was still secretly addicted. With a sigh of private pleasure, Eliane opened a volume masquerading as Zola's *L'Assommoir* and began to read *Les Deux Gosses* for the fifth time.

Time sped past so quickly that Eliane was frightened her life would be finished before she had wrung from it every drop of fulfilment. She certainly did not feel fulfilled yet, although she finally felt safe.

Her interest in ballet introduced her to a scattering of Russian friends. Unlike the members of the ballet company, they were mainly aristocrats who had fled their homeland when the Revolution destroyed the old life. Some still had money but most had little more than grand names and vague hopes of capitalising on them. Eliane was introduced to Grand Duke Alexis Romanov, nephew of the murdered Tsar Nicholas, at one of Magda's parties. Almost before she realised it, she had embarked on a shallow affair with him. Alexis was still in his mid-twenties and Magda teased Eliane about his youth and exalted pedigree, but never about his lack of money. Somehow that was too close to home.

'So he's young and from one of the world's great aristocratic dynasties,' said Eliane. 'So what? Neither of those things was on my mind when I got mixed up with him.'

'Funny, but I believe you,' said Magda. 'I wonder why. God knows it would be the most natural thing in the world for a girl like you to fall for someone so nobly born. It would be the ultimate passport to Society.'

'Rubbish!' Eliane's interruption was unequivocal. 'I don't call a dispossessed refugee the crème de la crème, however high his standing might once have been. It just doesn't count any more, Magda. To be impressive it has to be real. Ideally, that means an English title. French and Spanish are next best, although even they're just a little bogus, and then perhaps the small genuine kingdoms like Scandinavia or Holland. But never an ex-country like Holy Russia. No – I'll tell you why it suits me, though I'll kill you if you ever pass it on. With Alexis, I'm in control. Bonnie Charles was the last man in my life to whom I'd ever play second fiddle, and he never wanted me to. I realised the other day that I'm rich and famous and getting surer of myself every day. I can behave now as if I were the man and they the helpless little *irrégulières*. It just happens that my Russian Grand Duke is perfect material for that.'

Disappointed, Magda shook her head. 'Oh dear, Alouette, there's something inside you that's locked deep in a block of ice, isn't there? I wonder if anyone will ever really melt you?'

'I sincerely hope not. When you melt it's dangerous. You go all soft and then you get hurt. It's best to stay frozen so long as most people don't notice your chilly state.'

'But do you make love to Alexis? I should have thought that was inevitable. He's hardly the sort you could hold at arm's length for long.'

'Of course I do! What a waste it would be not to. He's far too good-looking and physically fit just to be my escort.'

Magda awaited further confidences, but they were not forthcoming. Eliane had found a pliable sexual partner in the Grand Duke, one who complied unquestioningly with her strange whims. She had discovered that certain circumstances enabled her to enjoy making love more than her earlier affairs had led her to expect. If she could retain a position of dominance, she became aroused and often achieved fulfilment. The first time it happened almost by accident. She came back to the Rue Cambon apartment from riding in the Bois de Boulogne, wearing breeches, boots and an English-cut tweed jacket over shirt and tie. Armand, her manservant, had already let the Grand Duke in before going off duty. Alexis stood in the drawing-room as she entered and stared at her in admiration.

'You look marvellous, Alouette, almost like a swaggering little stable boy.' Fleetingly, she remembered Ottilie's depraved riding costume. Although she dismissed that memory, his words and the old incident combined to excite her. She strode across the room and stood in front of him, her eyes challenging him to look away.

'Does it excite you to see me like this, Alexis?'

He smiled, always ready to participate in sexual exploits. 'You always excite me, but especially when you're so – so assertive.'

He moved forward but she anticipated him. 'No, Alex, allow me!' She pressed her body against his, her hands moving to his trousers, opening them and exploring him with an audacity which aroused and shocked him. She pressed on, the sheer strength of her will and her awakening libido forcing him back against the wall. He was very tall and powerfully built but there was no question of who was in command of their embrace. When they kissed, it was she who thrust her tongue between his lips; she who began unbuttoning his shirt; she who suggested they moved to the bedroom. Once there, she insisted on undressing him, but only removed part of her own clothing. In the big bed she pushed him back against the pillows, relentlessly caressing, exploring and inflaming him in the manner that an expert male seducer would excite a new mistress.

Alexis enjoyed her domineering behaviour. Almost instinctively he reacted with a coyness which was far from masculine. Eliane was becoming wildly excited and when she was ready for him to enter her she straddled him, saying, 'Come on – let me have it now!'

He reached an orgasm quickly but Eliane was still restless and aroused. She continued to touch and caress his temporarily quiescent body and was eager for more love-making. He spoke hesitantly: 'That was wonderful. My – my first mistress used to come to me like that.'

'And?' Eliane was avid for the details.

'Well, she liked me to put on girl's clothes when we did it. You know, satin nightgowns and drawers. . . .' An image wound seductively through Eliane's mind of the excitement of slipping her hands inside silken lingerie on to his big athletic body. Immediately she began caressing him again.

'Did you enjoy it, Alexis, when you did that?'

'Very much, my love. Perhaps you'd like it too?'

When he next visited Rue Cambon, she wasted no time on preliminaries, moving across to pour him champagne and trailing a hand provocatively along his thigh as she did so. 'Why not go into my room and see what I've bought for you?' she said.

He knew what would be there. When Eliane joined him twenty minutes later, he had dressed himself from head to toe in the satin garments which awaited him. But he had taken it further than she had expected, raiding her bathroom for lipstick, eye shadow, mascara and scent.

To Eliane he had become an irresistible travesty of a woman. When she embraced him, it was even better, for he was already fully erect and the sensation of his rock-hard penis beneath the delicate fabric made her crazy with desire. She pressed her hands to him through the satin, exciting both of them almost unbearably.

'Quick, on the bed! I want you this instant!' It was an order, not an invitation.

Alexis lay across the bed and she drew up the heavy satin, slipping down on her knees between his legs as she did so. Her lips engulfed him and she felt the luxurious fabric brushing her cheeks as she bent over his body, savouring him as the tide of her desire rose. When she could no longer endure the delay, she rose and slipped out of the simple robe she was wearing. The sight of this big, masculine man perversely appearing as a woman excited her more than any preliminary she had ever experienced. Once again, she straddled him. This time it was even better than before. Now that she was on him and his manhood had disappeared inside her own body, she really felt she was the man and he the woman. Each thrust of her body on his felt as though she were burying herself in him, and when her climax carried her away, in her mind she was a man fulfilling his sexual function.

She had no intention of ever telling anyone about that experience. She sensed it was an aberration which Alexis had indulged only once before and that he was unlikely to boast about what he did when he was alone with Eliane. The image of a Grand Duke in a negligée was hardly flattering to him.

Long afterwards, she reflected how strange it was that Alexis, never a figure of major importance in her life, had nevertheless made waves which influenced her whole world that year. Both her collections were intensely Russian and proved her most successful to date. High boots in soft leather, peasant tunics with huge tight-cuffed sleeves and side-fastened high necks were the major innovations. Beautiful beaded embroidery on evening gowns of rich dark silk were very popular with her more dramatic clients. Eliane's hats were cossack shapes and in the autumn she paired karakul fur versions with an artfully feminine adaptation of a Russian military greatcoat, double-breasted, with a big collar, padded shoulders and military-style belt. The customers were entranced.

Whatever she said to Magda on the subject at first, Eliane was later forced to admit that the affair with Alexis gave her a social acceptability she had never achieved before. The Russian aristocracy might theoretically be nothing but a memory, but the fact remained that a Grand Duke's prestige was exceeded only by that of an English duke. Paris Society was now ready and anxious to meet Alouette Doré and she used her celebrity to the hilt. It added to her other advantages that she was all but unaware of the transformation which her new self-confidence had wrought in her.

Although Eliane's first major successes had come years before, she had achieved them on the strength of her own lifestyle – which conventional women found fascinating – and because the look she devised struck women as being sensible and comfortable as well as smart. She had not made herself sufficiently socially visible actually to be the model on which these women re-designed their images. She had delegated that task to Geneviève and Elise. But with prosperity and recognition, her own beauty and flair had developed until she was now the most striking woman at many of the events she attended. Everywhere women watched her, listened to her and copied everything, from the length of her skirts to her speech idioms and the way she held her cigarette. This year it was severe wool jersey and velvet by day, silk jersey and satin by night. With total disregard for anatomy, Eliane had moved the waist to where the backside used to be and had abolished the backside completely. The breasts had not so much ceased to exist as flowed into the general smooth shape.

When she was taxed with creating an unnatural silhouette, she laughed scornfully. 'Why have you suddenly woken up to the fact that women aren't the same shape as their clothes?' she asked one observer who took her to task about it. 'Until I came along, everyone was staggering around in whalebone armour, with breasts that were half belly flesh pulled up, and bums that were half breast flesh shoved down. All I did was throw away the whalebone and pour a little jersey over the top. I'm not telling women where their waists and bosoms should be – I'm making them look good and permitting them to breathe while they find out for themselves!'

In the meantime, Eliane enjoyed herself inside the poured jersey. Her shape was perfect for it – small, high breasts which hinted at their presence without destroying the line of the knitted cloth; a neutral waist, concealed beneath the waistless shape; a small backside shaped like an apple, pert beneath the dropped waist; and long, curvy but slender legs, apparently bare, in short skirts and flesh-colour stockings of finest knitted silk. Her hair was cropped and combed into a cheeky half-curl at the back of her neck. When not exposed like the coiffure of a small, naughty schoolboy, it was covered by a tight little hat pulled down over eyes and ears. In her short skirts, short hair, dark woollens and crisp white cotton collars and cuffs, she looked absurdly young and perversely sexy. It was sometimes hard to tell whether she was a boy or a girl. To the people she attracted, it scarcely seemed to matter.

Alexis's use of her scent in the privacy of the bedroom turned her thoughts to a new line of business – perfumery. For the first time she realised what a powerful erotic stimulus scent could be. She resolved to find a fragrance which would leave all her competitors standing.

'I'd better start trying to find out a bit more about the whole thing,' she told Magda. 'I'm sure the world is full of people whose life's work has been perfume, and who'll think I'm being brash and arrogant, but that's the way I got into fashion, so why not? I've got some very definite ideas about scent and nothing on the market approaches what I have in mind.'

Magda was a practical woman despite her pose as a good-natured muddler. 'Darling, what you need is a nose. I'll arrange it.'

'Are you sane, Magda? Because if I hadn't heard it I wouldn't have believed you'd made that remark.'

Her friend smiled. 'A nose is a man with a very acute sense of smell and – if he's good – a magical talent for blending essential oils. A good nose can make a top perfume house forever, because once he's established the scents, the formulae belong to the house. Noses are usually trained chemists and they make a lot of money.'

'How come you know so much about it? You're not normally interested in the wheels of commerce.'

'No, but it just so happens that one of my little White Russians is exactly what you've been looking for. . . .'

'Oh, no, Magda, not another one! Just because I occasionally share my bed with a goddamned Romanov it doesn't mean I've a soft spot for every hotel doorman who claims to have commanded a troop of cavalry before the Revolution!'

'It's not like that, darling. This one is quite genuine and he's certainly no candidate for charity. When Guerlain or Wertheimer hear he's on the loose, he'll be snapped up on a very tasty contract. But he could be yours if you treat him right!'

The man was a chemist who had worked for the court perfumier at St Petersburg before the Revolution. In recent years he had lived on the family jewellery which he had brought with him from Russia in the hope of starting his own perfume house on the proceeds. But Souvaroff lacked the clout and experience to break into French perfumery and now he had run out of money. Eliane talked to him, instinctively grasped that here was a man who knew his trade inside out, and retained him for a sum which made her peasant soul flinch. In return he was to bring her riches which made a lifetime's couture earnings look like chickenfeed.

She sent him off to Grasse on the Riviera, where all the finest ingredients were prepared for the use of the big manufacturers. His only guidance was a list of the odours which Eliane considered to have the right ambience for the scent that she would launch. On the basis of these, he was told to bring back something distinctive, which would make its wearer think of riches and romance at the same time.

'I know I can lead them by the nose,' Eliane told him. 'It's the most important and neglected sense we have. The scent that's tickling my imagination is a mixture of jasmine, Russian leather, Bulgarian roses, Tonkin musk, magnolia . . . nothing from a European country garden! Everything remote and intense and –'

Souvaroff stopped her with a smile. 'Say no more, Mademoiselle. I now know precisely what you require.'

He was gone for six weeks. When he returned he brought half a dozen small phials containing samples of his preliminary work. 'They all share an underlying theme,' he said. 'Flowers are the top note – the romance you wanted – and spices, woods or leathers provide the underlying richness, depending on which blend you choose. Come to that, you need not choose just one. You could launch three or four.'

'No, M'sieur.' Eliane was sure of her ground. 'I never want to sell more than, maybe, three, and I'll launch them at long intervals over the next ten years, to give each rarity value. And there is to be no similarity between them. Each will be a unique type.'

Souvaroff nodded. 'I see you understand the business side better than I do.'

As soon as she sniffed the fourth sample, Eliane knew it was her scent – almost. She explored the possibilities of the rest, just to be sure, but none was in the class of this one.

Souvaroff was delighted. 'Yes, Mademoiselle, this is

my favourite too. Luxury and riches coupled with an almost childlike appeal to the senses. It is very beautiful, is it not?'

'Slow down! It's almost there, but not quite. It needs something extra . . . a touch of vulgarity among all that class and wealth.' He tried to break in but she silenced him. 'Shut up, man! I'll remember in a minute what it is, but you're deafening my nose!' She sat silently for some time, occasionally sniffing again at the little bottle. Then she laughed, impatient at her own slowness. 'Of course, I know! Grass and mushrooms. . . .Can you do it for me? I want the smell of new-mown grass and that rich earth you get from mushrooms when you pick them early in the morning. Is it possible? Can such smells be fixed?'

He was looking at her with new admiration. 'Indeed they can, and quickly. I compliment you, Mademoiselle Doré. I would never have thought of them, but in minute quantities they will bring out this scent to perfection.'

Within a couple of days he had produced a new version which was exactly what she had envisaged. He was as pleased as Eliane. 'Now you have the dreadful task of choosing a name and a perfect container,' he said.

How wrong you are, Eliane thought. This is such a complicated product that only utter simplicity in its presentation will do. To Souvaroff, she merely said, 'What did you call that one to distinguish it from the others when you were blending?'

'Oh, I just use alphabetic code letters. That was the fourth so it was D.'

'Then that's what I shall call it. After all, D is my initial, too. That must be a good sign.'

She dismissed his horrified protests and went off to look at bottles with Magda and Geneviève. After a couple of hours at Lalique's trade showrooms, she was close to despair.

'This is insane. The price that company asks, just for a package! And there's nothing I'd put a drop of pond water in, let alone the perfect perfume.'

'But Eliane, Lalique's the best there is. Women all over the world collect his scent bottles,' protested Geneviève. 'I have a dressing table full of them.'

'More fool you! He should stick to his gorgeous jewellery and stay out of bottles. Everything I've seen this afternoon looks like frozen phlegm!'

'But you've seen every standard pattern they produce,' said Magda. 'I suppose they could design a special range for you. There must be something, surely. . . .'

'Frozen phlegm, I say! There has to be something better.'

On the way back to the Ritz, Eliane ordered her chauffeur to stop the car. 'Let's take a look at what's in the shops,' she said. She had chosen to stop outside an expensive pharmacy on the Rue de Rivoli, which sold expensive scents as well as general toiletries and dispensed medical prescriptions from a specialist counter. They were confronted by ranks of the same bottles she had seen in Lalique's showrooms, but now filled and ornately labelled.

With an exaggerated shudder, Doré turned away. 'No, I'll not consider it. Far too elaborate. Now look at the purity of those little bottles up there.' She pointed at the chunky glass flasks in which the pharmaceutical materials were kept, their bevelled glass stoppers reflecting the light of the sun broken into its prismatic colours. She stopped. 'That's it, of course! Why didn't I think of it till now? We'll simply get Lalique to make perfect scaled down copies of the dispensary flasks and use those. They'll be irresistible.'

She was right. The new scent was on sale in the salon in time for Christmas. The distinctive little square bottles carried austere white labels, overprinted with the typeface she used for her nameplate and stationery. It simply bore a large letter D, supported by the name Doré in the bottom left-hand corner and her Rue Cambon address bottom right.

They sold out three times in the first month of production, and Eliane knew she had a world beater.

Romance ceased to be a driving force in her life. Alexis posed no problems; he was simply there and that suited Eliane. She knew now that she liked a man in her life but did not want him to become a preoccupation. Business filled that slot and now she threw herself into marketing her scent, perfecting her couture collections and developing her social role as a leading patron of avant garde ballet, painting and literature.

Paul Colombes was the rising star of literary Paris, an astute, multi-talented man of about Eliane's own age. She met him, as usual, through Magda Robles, and sensed immediately that they might have much in common. She saw him from time to time at parties, but always fleetingly. She did not begin to know him well until they were both invited to work on a new St Petersburg Ballet production, *Jeunesse Dorée*. It was a modern piece, a slight story about well-heeled young people heading south by train for a Riviera holiday. To her well-concealed delight, Eliane was invited to design the costumes. Paul Colombes, already well-known as a writer, was also a talented illustrator. He was designing the sets. To set the seal of success on the project, Stravinsky had written the score and Picasso painted the stage curtains.

Eliane and Paul got on well from the beginning. His flagrant homosexuality removed any question of erotic challenge which might have scared off Eliane, while her obvious devotion to her business reassured Colombes that she was not likely to pursue him under any romantic delusion. There was an undercurrent of unease between them, though, which both sensed – Eliane more than Colombes. She had trouble in identifying it and finally discussed it with Magda.

'Why should I feel so uncomfortable with him? He's very interesting, wants to understand everything and try to design or make most of the new things he comes across. Neither of us is interested in getting romantically involved with the other, so why do I get so scratchy?'

'If you'd grown up with a bunch of brothers and sisters as talented as yourself, you'd understand completely,' said Magda. 'As you didn't, you'd better read what Freud says about brothers and sisters and apply it to yourself and Paul. God knows you're as alike as peas in a pod! It's a bad case of sibling rivalry, at least that's what Freud would call it.'

'What nonsense, we're not at all alike.'

'Oh, but you are! Admittedly for different reasons, you both grew up isolated, more talented than those around you and without knowing you were especially gifted. Each of you got recognition later than you might have done, but, once it arrived, easily and in a big way. You both got rich by what you did, and you both work in fields that sort of waver between art and craft and business. It's amusing to watch you competing. At times you could be twins!'

Eliane was irritated at the whole idea and rejected it out of hand. Magda merely shrugged and smiled. 'Okay, I couldn't care less - but you did ask. Now you have my view, I'll make a little suggestion, too, though you won't want it. Don't expect too much of him.'

'What an idiotic remark! That's even worse than the sibling rivalry thing. I don't expect anything of him.'

'Please yourself, I happen to disagree. And I'll persevere because I love you and you're going to get hurt if you ignore what I have to say. You and Paul *are* very alike, but you're not identical. I think in some things he's much more sensitive than you, and I'm sure that you've a hundred times more courage than he has. Some day, his sensitivity will make him cowardly in front of you - it might even make him let you down badly. When it does, try not to blame him too much. He's no more or less perfect than the rest of us, but you might start thinking he is. And when you're disillusioned about things like that, I suspect you're completely unforgiving.'

By now, Eliane was wishing she had not raised the subject at all. 'Oh, this is all getting very boring,' she said. 'Come on, let's discuss something else. I think I shall start avoiding Paul Colombes altogether if my acquaintance with him has this sort of effect on you.'

So it was dropped. Eliane half-heartedly attempted to confine her relationship with Colombes to their work on the ballet, but the chemistry between them went on working and they found one another far too interesting to keep at arm's length. Soon they were dining together a couple of times a week and sharing their new discoveries in books, paintings and music. Gradually, through Paul, Eliane got to know many of Paris's homosexual intellectuals. Their current idol was the ultimate gilded youth, a blond boy from the Haute Savoie with the features of a corrupt cherub and a temperament to match. Just nineteen years old, he had recently finished his first novel and was tipped to become the literary giant of his generation.

Virtually every homosexual man and many of the heterosexual women in Paris Society were actively trying to seduce Alain Raymond. Colombes was among them and he was successful. This led inevitably to a stream of mournful confessions to Eliane about how callous and promiscuous his new lover was.

Eliane's response was brisk and tough. Magda was more gentle with him. Between them the two women offered a complementary confidante service. Countering Magda's softness, Eliane followed the 'get up off your knees and fight back' school of advice.

After a few weeks of Paul's outrageous complaints, Eliane was unable to resist meeting Raymond. This time she had no need of Magda's illuminating opinions. She recognised immediately, beneath the arrogant exterior, a character very like her own at that age. The vital difference was that there was no sense of potential conflict with Raymond. They shared similar emotional scars rather than being on a collision course towards social stardom. Here was another young spirit terrified of being possessed by lovers, panic-stricken at the thought of owing his future to the patronage of others. Convinced that his churlish promiscuity was no more than a defence against such possession, she tried to warn Paul that he would achieve more with Raymond if he pestered him less. She might as well have saved her breath.

'Alouette, you just don't understand. I'm so crazy about the boy I want to be with him all the time and I get frantic at the thought of anyone else laying hands on him. But he seems to lead them on deliberately just to make me jealous.'

'Very well, but you're going to lose him altogether if you aren't careful. Ease up on the kid.'

Next time she saw Alain Raymond at one of Magda's parties, she talked to him about it. 'Alain, couldn't you be just a little kinder to poor Paul? He adores you and he can't help being so overpowering. Don't give him such a hard time.'

'But he stifles me! He seems to think because I'm poor and live in that hovel near the Place du Tertre that if he throws money and cocaine and clothes at me, I belong to him. I don't want to belong to anyone - ever!'

Eliane impulsively put an arm around him. 'Good kid. Keep it that way! Look, if you're ever in a real hole and you don't want to go to Paul or any of his little friends for help, come to me. I'll give it, and there'll be no strings. I understand you better than anyone else you'll ever know, Alain.'

He smiled wanly. 'Thanks, that means a lot. I only hope I never have to take you up on it.'

'So do I, but for your sake not mine. I want you to be free and successful on your own terms.'

All too soon, he was forced to ask for her aid. It was a sticky summer night, the city simmering unhealthily in the thick swelter of late June. Thunder had rumbled distantly since noon, but by eleven that night the relief of rain had still not arrived. Eliane's manservant came discreetly to her side as she entertained dinner guests. 'Yes, Armand?'

'Mademoiselle, Monsieur Colombes is downstairs, very distressed. He asks if you will go down to him.'

'But why didn't you bring him right up? You know he's always welcome.'

'Of course, Mademoiselle. He refused to come up when he learned you had company. He says he needs to see you privately.'

Colombes was in the dimly lit entrance foyer of the Rue Cambon building. She hurried across from the lift and took his hand. 'Paul, what on earth is wrong?'

He made two false starts before he was able to tell her. Finally it came out on a burst of tears. 'It's Alain! He's dying – dying in that foul hovel up in Montmartre, and he won't let me help. The only one he'll allow to save him is you.' He spat the last word while Eliane stood frozen.

'How long have you delayed coming to me?'

He was unable to speak, breaking into fresh sobs and hanging his head. Losing patience, she gave him an impatient little shake.

'Tell me, you stupid bastard! If he's dying, this is no time for you to play the tragedy queen!'

Her savage tone jerked him back to reality, at least momentarily. 'He – I – that is, I tried to help him when he got sick; begged him to come to me in Montparnasse, but he'd have none of it. Then he got weaker and weaker, and finally he said he'd accept your help if you had time to see him. Otherwise, he preferred to manage alone.'

'Yes, go on. How long ago was this?'

'That's the trouble, Alouette. It was nearly two days ago! When he said it, I just flared up. I felt so jealous of you, started getting ideas about what you had going with him, so I just stormed out. I thought if he'd only take your help, he could damned well wait till you visited and tell you himself.'

'But I don't even know where he lives, you fool! I simply told him once that I'd help if he needed it with no strings attached. He asked you to tell me because he was too ill to come himself, didn't he, and you let him down? How was he when you left?'

'He was practically delirious. It's some sort of frightful fever and it really scares me. . . . Where are you going, Alouette? Christ, whatever it is might be infectious. You can't intend to go there yourself?'

'You cockroach-shit! Of course I'm going to him, and you're coming with me. Armand – tell the mechanic to bring the car round, and you'd better bring a couple of sets of clean sheets down from the apartment.'

Raymond had been alone for more than thirty-six hours. The stench in the room was indescribable. He had been too weak to get out of bed and had fouled the sheets repeatedly. Eliane gagged as the smell hit her, but pity overcame her disgust.

The noise of their arrival briefly revived Alain and he reacted as if the Virgin Mary had come in. 'Alouette – thank God you're here. I . . . can't . . . breathe properly and I'm so very thirsty . . . but you'll help, won't you?' He drifted into unconsciousness again.

Eliane turned on Paul Colombes. 'You should be crucified, you bastard! You've killed him.'

With her usual supreme indifference to other people's plans, Eliane had stopped off en route to the rooming house to collect a physician. He had been about to go to bed and was furious at the intrusion, but Elianc thrust sufficient money at him to guarantee his attendance. He examined Raymond quickly but thoroughly, then turned to Eliane with a sombre expression on his face.

'I'll arrange an ambulance immediately, Mademoiselle Doré, but he's unlikely to survive the night. It's typhus. He'll have picked up the infection from these filthy surroundings, insufficient food, contaminated water supply. . . . These days it needn't be fatal if we get them in the early stages, but this boy must have been sick for at least a week. He has no chance of survival now – he has no strength left.'

Paul was sobbing again. 'Shut up, you pathetic thing,'

Eliane hissed at him. 'At least let him see you looking normal if he regains consciousness.'

As they waited for the ambulance, she questioned Colombes about Alain Raymond's private life. 'How could he exist like this? He was always immaculate at parties and opening nights. He couldn't have kept it up from here.'

Colombes' voice was flat and mechanical. 'No – he kept a business suit and a *smoking* at my place. He also sent his shirts and underwear to my laundry, but he wouldn't accept anything more. He used to come back to this rat trap because he said at least it was his own.'

'But his novel! He was supposed to be ready to storm the heights.'

'Oh, six months from now he would have, but it was his first book. The publisher's advance was pitiful and it would have been well into the autumn before he saw any of his royalties.'

'And you cut him off from a lifeline just because of your stupid possessive jealousy! You disgust me, Paul. Once we've got him to the hospital, please make your own way home. I don't want you anywhere near me for a while.'

'Oh, I couldn't face coming to that dreadful place! I'm taking something of the poor boy's – his watch, perhaps, that wouldn't be infected, would it? – and I'm going home to cry myself to sleep!'

Eliane fought down the impulse to strike him. 'Don't say any more – just go. Your presence won't make any difference to Alain now, he's beyond that.'

She had always recoiled from disease, horrified at the destruction it wrought and the danger it entailed. But she sat beside Alain Raymond in the ambulance, clutching his sweaty hand and soothing him in his delirious ravings. At the hospital she saw him briefly after he had been washed and changed and put into a clean bed. He had another lucid moment when she went to his bedside. He grasped her hand with surprising strength, raised it to his lips and kissed it before slumping back against the pillows.

'Thank you, thank you,' he murmured. 'You made me clean again before the end, Alouette. Thank you for that. I feel easy now. . . .' He lost consciousness, his grip slackened and his eyelids flickered closed. The hospital doctor ushered her out.

'Is there any chance?' she asked.

He shook his head. 'We can make his last few hours comfortable, Mademoiselle, but nothing more. He is beyond medical help now. Who is his next-of-kin?'

'For all practical purposes, it seems I am. Send me all the bills and tell me what arrangements must be made. I'll see to it all.'

He died soon after sunrise. Eliane was as good as her word. She contacted his parents, a bourgeois couple in Chambéry who had been proud of their son's rise to fame, and broke the news. She arranged a funeral service and drafted newspaper announcements and Magda helped her with the stream of telephone calls.

After they had done what was necessary, Eliane went back to the foul tenement near the Place du Tertre. The place had been closed and locked since they took Raymond to the hospital. It stank like a charnel house. Almost automatically, she began stripping the bed, clearing away the used crockery and overflowing ashtrays. At least his parents would find a clean place when they came for his few shabby possessions –

Then, suddenly, the whole thing was too much for her. What was she doing here, in this filth and decay? She never did this sort of clearing up for herself, and here she was working away for the benefit of a couple of bereaved strangers. Suddenly she felt she would vomit if she did not escape the smell and the squalor. Eliane abandoned her task and hurried down the steep narrow staircase. Her chauffeur was standing outside by the car. She took three or four deep breaths of the fresh warm summer air, then got into the Rolls-Royce.

'Serge, please see that room is cleaned and the boy's possessions are packed up to return to his family. But first, take me home – the Ritz, not Rue Cambon.'

The Rue Cambon apartment contained a closet full of the exotic, oversized women's clothes in which it pleased her to dress Alexis. Suddenly that perversity seemed just another facet of the corruption that she shared with the rest of Paris Society – the world that had killed Alain Raymond. Perhaps the Ritz wasn't far enough from those closets of silk and satin and ostrich plumes. Perhaps she should get out of the country for a while. Magda and Antonio were all right; she'd go with them. Then, when she was a safe distance away, she could write to Alexis and make the break tactfully. When she came back, she could start afresh, clean and uncorrupted. She'd continue to socialise with these people, but never let them stain her again.

Hesitant about what she really wanted, Eliane drew into herself for a while, seeing none of her usual friends, even forsaking the Ritz restaurant at lunch-time and seeking out obscure places where she would recognise no one. In the hours of solitude, she started reading more, and for once required something stronger than an unrelieved diet of Decourcelle.

Her literary tastes had started catching up with the sophisticated titles on her shelves, although she still remained more low-brow than she chose to admit. But in this time of uncertainty and confusion, she sought material which was more challenging than her usual fare. At that point Eliane turned up a scribbled note that Colombes had sent her before the tragedy of Alain had severed their friendship. She had asked him if he knew someone who would be willing to act as a sort of literary tutor in her general reading and this was Colombes' response. Remembering vaguely that it had come with a booklet of verse, Eliane read it properly and looked for the little poetry collection.

*'Alouette – these might interest you if you're on the look-out for a poetic schoolmaster,'* Paul had written. *'The poet is an odd type, lives for God and his verse and just scrapes by as a publisher's proof reader in between writing. But he has a fine mind and is the best-read man I know, so if you want someone on whom to sharpen your intellect, this could be the one. He could certainly do with a bit of tactful financial patronage!'*

Perhaps it's time I gave God a try – everything else seems to have failed, she thought. She realised she would have to contact Paul Colombes if she wanted to find the poet, Pascal Davide, and arrange to meet him. At first that was almost enough to put her off, but she thought better of it. Paul wasn't that much of a villain. She knew something of the torment of jealousy, and when she had cooled down after Raymond's death, accepted this as the reason for Paul's delay in coming to her. After all, the doctor had said the boy's illness had started the previous week. Even if Paul had come as soon as he was asked, it would probably have been too late.

She sat down to read Davide's poems which were enough to convince her that a religious phase wouldn't help at all. Nevertheless the project had achieved something: she went ahead and called Paul.

Colombes was wary when he answered the telephone. 'Alouette, this is a surprise. Have you called to abuse me again? I wish you wouldn't – I feel bad enough already.'

'As a matter of fact I rang to see how you were. Do you feel like coming over for supper?'

He brightened immediately. 'That's the best suggestion I've heard since – well, you know. Thank you, Alouette. I'd love to.'

Eliane discovered a new sensation which gave her a degree of consolation. Forgiveness and a conscious effort not to condemn could help the person who forgave just as much as the forgiven. Until now her world had been too harsh for her to learn the virtues of reconciliation. She tried to explain it to Paul, but found it impossible to put her emotion into words. Instead she was particularly gentle with him. He blossomed, and after a while even began reminiscing about Raymond.

When they parted at the end of the evening, he embraced her and kissed her cheek. 'I'll blub if I try to say too much now,' he said, 'but I'm more grateful to you than you'll ever know. I can get back to normal now.'

Alone again, Eliane sighed. It had helped her a little to make up with Paul, but hardly enough to shake off this terrible sense of futility. She was beginning to feel she might be happy again in Paris some day but her earlier inclination to get away had been sound. Italy would do her good.

Magda and Antonio were full of enthusiasm. 'Oh, yes, darling, the Venice Lido will be at its best. Let's go at once,' said Magda. And she waved her social entrepreneur's wand to produce a round of parties and treats for Eliane among Venice's cultural lions.

At first it worked well and the memory of squalor and of the unforgettable smell of that room began to fade, eclipsed by the beauties of St Mark's Square and the Lagoon at sunset. Magda finally managed to convince Eliane that the fancy dress parties to which she was addicted really were fun. Eliane took to them with the fanaticism of a convert, and developed an enthusiasm for costume balls, parties and charades that was to last her throughout the 1920s and '30s. But it was a temporary respite. The images of disease and corruption kept returning, unbidden, waking her at night or spoiling her normally avid enjoyment of parties. Too soon she found herself anticipating them only as an opportunity to meet a string of new aristocratic friends who would boost her business.

On one such occasion, they were at a full dress reception in an ancient *palazzo*. Eliane was wearing a flowing white georgette gown and a magnificent diamond necklace, but her initial pleasure in the evening and in her own beauty swiftly faded. She slipped away with the vague plan of walking back to the Danieli, where they were staying.

It proved to be a longer walk than she had anticipated and, when she came to a little deserted square, she sat down to rest for a moment on one of the ornamental benches. A figure started up in surprise. It was a young man, handsome in faultless evening dress, who had been stretched out asleep. He jumped up and handed her to a seat with a mocking little bow. There was something about the whole incident that reminded her of her beloved cheap novels, and she talked to him for a long time, eventually strolling back with him in the general direction of the Danieli.

When they arrived, she was amused to discover that he, too, was a guest at the hotel. The night porter greeted him as an old and valued client. Eliane stood beside him, amused, intrigued, waiting to be invited on some glamorous escapade the next day. Holding his room key, the young man turned to her with a cherubic smile and bent over her to whisper his invitation.

'Your room or mine?' he murmured. Horrified, she turned away without speaking and hurried to the safety of her suite. It was useless to try and escape by fleeing Paris. The corruption was everywhere. The whole world was sordid and stinking and she was powerless to order it any more. She locked herself in her room, barely controlling her tears, and next day told Magda she was returning to Paris.

Magda and Antonio were bewildered when she left them so abruptly after instigating the whole trip, but she told them she was still paying so they were not excessively concerned. But Paris proved little better than Venice. Now she was home she was as isolated as she had thought she wanted to be, because her usual social set had migrated en masse from the capital for the summer. In the end she was grateful to be able to work on her next collection. When even this failed to keep her fully occupied, Eliane could no longer ignore the overpowering feeling that she was about to fall into a void.

Geneviève had been less and less in Paris that spring. Her baron's wife had died in 1922 and the eighteen months which had elapsed since had made it perfectly respectable for him to plan a second marriage. Geneviève's terror of being passed over for a young girl proved groundless. In mid-August Eliane received an invitation to their September wedding. The knowledge that there was to be a church as well as a civil marriage ceremony made her crow with delight. Say what you would about the Doré girls, they had a knack of getting their own way eventually! There could not be that many *irrégulières* who had held on to a lover for almost twenty years and finally married him - and his title - at the age of forty.

But when her initial pleasure on Geneviève's account had subsided, Eliane felt even worse than before. No matter that at the wedding reception she attracted as much attention as the bride. No matter that male and female guests alike treated her as one step short of royalty. She was an outsider. This was not her world and never could be. Geneviève fitted into it in law now, as well as in fact. A wedding ring and a title signified her status. Eliane was abandoned, alone and friendless. From now on, even her beloved Geneviève would have someone else who came before Eliane in her affections.

Her sister Elise was unable to make up for the loss of Geneviève. She had fallen victim to the family curse of tuberculosis the previous year and although Eliane was financing the best medical care in a Swiss sanatorium, her little sister was not even strong enough to travel to Brittany for the wedding. It was unlikely that Elise would ever recover sufficiently to return to Paris. Ninette had died years ago, and Eliane preferred to have as little as possible to do with her two brothers.

Even in the depths of despair, though, she knew that she would survive. She was less sure of ever finding a cure for the malaise that had afflicted her about the time of Alain Raymond's death. Her little family circle had fragmented and the social side of her new life held a sleaziness which depressed her inordinately.

The Christmas party season seemed to arrive almost before she was aware of the passage of autumn. Good God, she thought, I'm on the edge of my thirty-eighth year. Where's my life gone?

She heard about Georgiana Cranley through one of the few acquaintances she still knew from her days with Bonnie Charles. 'You'll be fascinated, given your appetite for inside gossip,' said the man. 'Georgie's entered in the register of births as a blacksmith's daughter, but how many English blacksmiths' daughters have you heard of who are received in the best drawing-rooms in Mayfair? It's never discussed openly, but it's common knowledge among the best people that she had a right royal father – wrong side of the blanket, of course, but she's not suffered by it.'

Intrigued, Eliane took a good look at the woman crossing the room to meet her. She was big and fair, her almost masculine walk toned down by a voluptuous figure. At a time when the preferred feminine shape aped that of an adolescent boy, Georgiana's height and grace eliminated any sense of excess that might have been created by her big, firm breasts and wide hips. She wore a Doré frock from that season's collection and looked ravishing in it. Eliane was torn between professional interest in the compliment Georgiana's beauty paid her design, and a surge of personal attraction towards the woman.

'Mademoiselle Doré, I'm so delighted to meet you! I've been preaching the gospel of your clothes to my countrywomen for so long I feel we've been friends for years.' Her big well-manicured hand enveloped Eliane's in a firm handshake. The Frenchwoman felt as if she had been scorched, such was the magnetism Georgiana exuded. 'Let's find another drink and talk about the look you have in mind for us all next summer.'

Georgiana monopolised her throughout the evening and during the following week she seemed to pop up everywhere Eliane was invited. She was married to a moderately wealthy American whom she had met when he served in Europe during the war, but they seemed to have agreed to live amicably separate lives unless one or the other wanted the right escort for a formal occasion. During their various conversations, Eliane gathered that Georgiana had far less money than she would have liked. She seemed an ideal employee for the select unofficial payroll of socialites and aristocrats Eliane had recruited to model, promote and sometimes even design items for the house of Doré. During the second week of their friendship she decided to sound out the Englishwoman on her scheme. Georgiana was among her dinner guests at Rue Cambon and Eliane suggested she should stay on when the other members of the party left. Once they were alone, she mentioned a possible working arrangement and Georgiana was delighted.

'How marvellous! Are you sure you mean it? Being paid for wearing your designs, and throwing parties where my English friends can see me showing them off, is almost too good to be true.'

'Of course I mean it, Georgie. You'll be a great asset. I always know when you've been to an important do in Paris these days, because the next day there's invariably a knot of Society women at the salon, demanding to be made to resemble *La belle Cranley*. The trouble is, they're very seldom six feet tall with skin like a peach and legs like a racehorse!'

'Good God, you made me sound like the first successful cross between flora and fauna! Am I that bad?'

Eliane clasped her hand impulsively. 'Oh no, quite the reverse. You're gorgeous. That's why I want you wearing my clothes.'

There was a momentary pause, then Georgiana put her hand over Eliane's. 'Do you ever get a feeling that you might want me *not* wearing them, Alouette darling?'

Confused, Eliane looked away, but did not withdraw her hand from the other woman's grasp. 'I don't understand you. What d'you mean?'

'Oh, I think you have a fairly good idea. Come here and I'll show you.' She drew Eliane into her arms and kissed her, not the socialite's polite peck but a deep passionate caress, pressing open Eliane's lips with her tongue and stroking her bare arms and shoulders as she did so. She prolonged the moment for some time without any protest from Eliane, who felt herself drowning pleasurably in the embrace.

When they eventually drew apart, Eliane said: 'But you're a married woman!'

Georgiana laughed heartily. 'My God, Alouette, you can't have moved in the circles you frequent and retained any illusions about marriage. Charlie goes his way and I go mine. He has some pretty odd tastes, too. Married or not, I enjoyed that as much as you did, and you don't seem to be complaining.'

Eliane flushed. 'No . . . but you did take me by surprise.'

Georgiana laughed again. 'Nonsense! I've been watching you all evening and you've been positively flirting with me. Come on, don't go all modest and aloof. Have a little more champagne. I'm told it does wonders for one's inhibitions.'

They drank together, then Georgiana stood up and drew Eliane to her feet, immediately sweeping her into a more urgent embrace. Eliane was overwhelmed by a new excitement. She thrilled to the combination of passion and softness which she had never experienced before. Georgiana's big, firm breasts were crushed against her and she felt the other woman's nipples hardening through the flimsy layers of silk that were their evening dresses. Georgiana's hands slid down her back, caressing her spine, then squeezed her small round buttocks. Releasing Eliane, she stepped away from her for a moment and murmured, 'Turn around, darling.' She undid the tiny buttons at the high neck of the couturière's gown, turned her again and slipped the garment down over her shoulders. It fell around Eliane's ankles with a sensuous rustle. Now Eliane was wearing only soft satin knickers, stockings and garters. Georgiana eased the panties down over her boyish hips and let them fall, too.

Eliane stepped out of the clothes towards her and Georgiana turned silently to have her own gown unfastened. Eliane undid the buttons, then ran an exploratory finger gently down Georgiana's spine. The Englishwoman gave a sharp gasp of excitement and turned back to her.

Eliane gazed in delight at the big, heavy breasts. It had never occurred to her before, but she found women's breasts very exciting. As Georgiana embraced her again, she buried her face in them, sucking the nipples and revelling in the sensation of their becoming more and more swollen between her lips. After a few minutes, Georgiana sank to her knees and buried her face in the springy black hair which curled between Eliane's thighs. Her tongue pressed inside Eliane and began to stimulate her in a way no man's hands or mouth ever had. She was racked by spasms of excitement and slid to the floor. 'Please don't stop, Georgie, I've never done anything like this before. . . .'

'I've no intention of stopping, darling. I've only just started.' Her fingers trailed provocatively along the silky flesh of Eliane's inner thigh, stimulating her so sharply that the touch was like ice or flame. Georgiana stretched out full-length beside her, caressing her small, round breasts, covering her face and shoulders with kisses and finally moving downwards again, returning to the centre of all Eliane's feverish excitement.

The affair with Georgiana had an odd effect on Eliane. In her initial euphoria she believed it had cured her of the conflict between her hitherto constant need to have a man in her life and her nervousness of male domination. But in fact it seemd to work in reverse. She stopped fearing sexuality because now she knew she could achieve fulfilment without surrender. But she still felt all the social unease of lacking an admired male lover whom she could display publicly like a trophy.

Georgiana settled into her life as though she had always been there, but was no more successful at sealing the gulf at Eliane's feet than any of the men in her past. Georgiana joined the élite unofficial staff and Eliane returned to her business and social interests, with interludes in Georgiana's arms to add spice to her life.

Shortly after Christmas, Georgie planned to return to London for a month or so. By now she was staying in the Rue Cambon apartment and when Armand answered the door on the morning before New Year's Eve, the caller was for her not Eliane.

Having spent a while talking to the visitor, she came back to the drawing room. 'Alouette, are you too busy to be sociable? There's someone here you'd love to meet, I think.' Moments later, she introduced the caller. 'Alouette, may I present St John Montagu Granchester, the Duke of Conway?'

Over Georgiana's shoulder, a smiling face that could have been the Englishwoman's twin greeted Eliane. 'Hello there. All my friends call me Jack. I hope you will.'

# Chapter Thirteen

## Andy and Marie-Louise

There was one very good reason why Andrea Vincent and Joel Handford had never been lovers: her mother got there first.

Their long and well-publicised affair had fed the gossip columns for years, for they were both uncommon types – literary stars who also possessed physical glamour. They had even managed to part friends and now Joel maintained sporadic contact with both Marie-Louise Chabrol and her daughter.

Andy had been on Joel's mind a lot since their talk earlier that summer. He liked and admired her but was conscious that all her knockabout experience had failed to quell a reckless streak which just might lead her into disaster. He had been less interested in her questions about Doré than in the Umberto Report. After her call from London he made discreet enquiries among American underworld contacts which convinced him that unless she was careful the Umberto exposé might be her last. When Marie-Louise Chabrol wrote to him in mid-June he was half expecting it. Within a couple of days he had set his own affairs in order and flown to Europe to join her.

He met her in Josselin, in a hotel-restaurant which did not serve the best food in France but which enjoyed his favourite romantic view. The huge windows of the dining-room opened on to the River Oust and the château on the far bank, with its splendid towers adorned by conical tiled roofs which gave them the look of giant pepperpots. Joel and Marie-Louise ate and drank together like young lovers, then got into her battered Deux Chevaux to drive back to her home in Broceliande, France's last medieval forest.

P'tit Barenton was a perfect little manor house, surrounded by ancient broad-leaved woodland, an appropriate home for his enchantress. Marie-Louise pressed the great nail-studded front door closed behind them both and came to his embrace like a tired child.

'Oh, you look so good – so solid and untouched by everything!' She was obviously badly in need of masculine comfort.

He kissed her, long and slow, memories flooding back with every touch. 'You look pretty damned good yourself, old lady. Now, how can this battered knight rescue you from the dragon?'

'The hell with the dragon – I parked him outside with the Deux Chevaux. Let me get used to you again before we start on that one.' They moved towards the staircase, for the moment seeing nothing but each other.

The renewal of their affair was a bonus for Marie-Louise but her overwhelming feeling at his return was one of relief.

'So now you've used me as your helpless sexual plaything, how do you expect me to help handle the Great Andy Crisis?' Joel was beside her in her bed at P'tit Barenton. Since his arrival three hours before, all he had seen of the house was the hall, the staircase and this room.

'As a matter of fact your timing is so incredible that I was wondering if my good angel had sent you. Andy's coming in the next few days. She knows about Doré – Eugène spilled the beans, and there was a bust-up apparently. I gather she and Doré have called a temporary armistice but once they've talked things over, Andy wants to come up here and get my side of it. I'll find it difficult to blame her if she gives me a hard time.'

'Darn. I thought perhaps the whole thing had blown over and I was going to get a couple of blissful weeks of unrestrained passion with no strings attached.'

'No, you hedonistic animal. You have to be my refuge

and strength, and work for your wild oats for once!'

'Did I ever tell you you've got the best ass I've ever seen on a fifty- four-year-old widow?'

'Stop distracting me. We have a few days at most, then I need some answers for Andy.'

'Well, the truth has a lot going for it – the truth, the whole truth and nothing but the truth.'

The situation came to a head faster than Marie-Louise had anticipated. That evening she received Andy's call announcing her arrival the next day. After putting down the phone, Marie-Louise turned to Joel. 'Right – get your trousers on and start looking like a responsible father substitute. We're about to be up to our necks in family recriminations.'

Andy came into Rennes on the noon train. Marie-Louise was waiting on the platform. 'How can I feel so affectionate towards any woman who looks so much like Jeanne Moreau?' Andy asked in mock dismay. 'You get younger and sexier each time I see you. If it goes on much longer everyone will be saying I'm *your* mother!'

Marie-Louise relaxed with a sigh of relief. Thank God for Andy's generous spirit. She might be impulsive and almost criminally naïve for a thirty-four-year-old, but she was wonderfully tolerant and adaptable. All Marie-Louise's carefully rehearsed introductory remarks deserted her. She embraced her daughter, kissed her, and said: 'I have to start by saying that a lot of what Doré has told you is probably true. Let's get out of here before we go into it any further, though.'

Still wondering what on earth she would say, Marie-Louise drove them back towards Paimpoint in the car. She began awkwardly: 'I should have talked to you about this years ago, but I thought it was all too ugly for a child. Then suddenly you were grown up and I managed to push it aside by telling myself it no longer had any significance. It did, of course, and given your grandmother's identity, I suppose it was inevitable that one day you'd learn the truth. I can't say how sorry I am that you learned like this. It's such an old, shabby story that it shouldn't matter so much.'

'I have no doubts about you, Maman. I never have. Nothing Doré could say would shake my faith in you. But as for the "old-and-shabby-story" line, for Christ's sake, you're a novelist - you know that just isn't true! It's dynamite, even to someone who has no connection with it. When you're as directly involved as I am, it pushes every news story in existence off the front page. One of the world's most famous women manages to produce a child by one of the world's richest aristos, and to conceal it for more than fifty years, so thoroughly that not even her own grand-daughter is aware of it - and you dismiss it as an old and shabby story! Come on, be your usual honest self and admit you find it hard to live with.'

'Okay, I had that coming. It's disconcerting but I'm more or less echoing the way I found out about Doré myself. Before you get too self-righteous about it, I might point out that you made your awful discovery at the ripe old age of thirty-four. I was barely twelve, I adored the woman I thought was my mother and I didn't care for Alouette at all. Perhaps one of the reasons I was so secretive is that even now I get a lump in my throat just thinking about that day.'

Andy was instantly contrite. 'I'm sorry, Ma. You must know more than anybody how overbearing she is. For the past three days I've been carrying around the news all bottled up inside, while she took turns at being indignant, injured and downright offensive. It must have been a hell of a lot worse for you than it is for me, but we must have it out now. Maybe it will help if you tell me your side first, rather than waste time on explaining why you've never told me about it.'

'I'll try, but I haven't really thought it through myself, strangely enough. I dealt with the end of it - we'll come to that later - and I'm terribly grown-up about that, at least. But if I own up, it's the early stuff that did me more damage, although it was fractionally less dramatic.

'When I tell you what it was like being a little girl with La Grande Mademoiselle at my elbow, you'll see how inevitable it was that I'd rebel some day. Sometimes I look back on the 1930s and it seems I spent the whole decade struggling with her – struggling for a proper education when all she wanted was to get me interested in *Vogue*, dancing classes and the *Almanac de Gotha*.'

'But she's the most vehemently un-clinging woman I've ever met, and she despised that sort of snobbery. How could she have been so keen on it for you?'

'Surely you've realised by now that your grandmother is a classic French peasant underneath? Anything she can't have she derides and despises, tries to turn it into a thing of no value. She decided very early on that she hadn't a chance of being accepted as top drawer, so she's spent her lifetime expressing contempt for class attitudes. But suddenly, in me, she had the opportunity of presenting a sort of born-again Doré, a mixture as before but with an undeniably aristocratic pedigree. What a chance! It's like an ugly little girl growing into a beauty. She changes from a prig to the biggest flirt in the room before you have time to blink!

'Anyway, there I was, trying to read all these wonderful books and get the best out of the splendid education Geneviève was setting up for me with private tutors, and along would come Alouette and demand to know why I wasn't off somewhere learning how to curtsey. What made it a hundred times worse was that I didn't even know she was my mother. It made even less sense when such interference came from a rather remote aunt, who drifted in on a cloud of expensive scent now and then, countermanded the orders my mother had given, of which I thoroughly approved, then went away again. The fact that my adored Geneviève usually went along with her wishes, however reluctantly, put the tin hat on it.

'The crunch came when I finally betrayed far too much political sophistication for my age – and of the wrong colour, too – and she hit me with the announcement that she was my mother. Strange, but one of the things that made it hurt most was my own prudishness. Poor old Geneviève was so conscious of her own demi-mondaine background that when she went respectable as Baroness Chabrol she became twenty-four carat genteel, and brought me up that way. My Aunt Alouette always seemed terribly wicked to me in those smart clothes and talking such fast Parisian slang. I didn't know what a tart was, but if I had, I'd have seen her as Alouette. Imagine the shock of learning you're Mary Magdalene's daughter when you thought all along you were the Virgin Mary's little girl!

'Not that I got much time to brood about it. She packed me off to a Swiss boarding school almost immediately, and of course I thought she'd done it to spite me for not wanting to be her daughter. That made me even more determined not to care about Society or clothes or a top-drawer marriage. I hated it at the school, but at least they had a sound academic reputation as well as teaching the usual débutante things. By the time I got back to Paris after the surrender to Germany, I was a real little Commie and that finished things between us.

'Odd to think of it now, but if she'd played her cards right then she might have won me over. By my mid-teens I was interested in fashion and scent and make-up in spite of myself, and all the other girls at the school were always on about how glamorous Doré was and taking sides in that ridiculous gossip column feud she had with Schiffini. I was impressed in spite of myself. But instead of playing on the things she shoved at me when I was a child, she tossed me straight into a dinner party with a bunch of elderly Nazis. That did for my closeness between us, and when we met up during the Liberation. . . . Well – let's talk about that later.

'Luckily, Papa had come into my life while I was in Switzerland. I got to know him quite well in 1938 and '39, when he was shuttling around Europe on his crazy self-imposed mission to make peace with Hitler. He used to stop off in Geneva and take me out. When Geneviève died I was heart-broken, and he was terrific then. He'd had a step-father whom he worshipped, and who died young. He understood how I felt and in his inarticulate way he was very kind. One thing I'll say for him – he understood a lot more of Doré's character than she gave him credit for. He set up a trust fund for me in Switzerland and from the age of fifteen I had my own money. It enabled me to live separately from her and to enrol at the Sorbonne. If you had to be young in occupied Paris, that was certainly the best place to be.'

'But wait a bit, Marie-Louise. What happened to Doré from when she and Conway broke up in 1930 until the shit hit the fan in the Second World War? She can't just have gone into limbo, descending to chivvy you in Brittany and then trailing off to re-run the 1920s in a different colour range for the '30s! For a start, there must have been all sorts of funny business with Eugène. There must be reasons for his continued loyalty to her even now, if she was so heartless over his father's death.'

'Ah, yes – Eugène. We had to get to him some time. Before we go any further, I must tell you that whatever I may have suffered from Doré, Eugène has had tenfold. You see, I escaped. He didn't. She's feasted like a vampire on him and I have no idea how he endured it. Has he said –'

Andy cut her off: 'Ma, I've seen an awful lot of Eugène lately and I'll probably see an awful lot more of him. I want to know about us – Doré, you, Conway and me. He can wait. Right now what puzzles me is how you can bear to think about Doré without spitting poison.'

'Because for all her trying, she never once got what she thought she wanted. The truth is, of course, that she has what she really needs – the fashion house, fame, public acclaim. But she's always thought she wanted the love of a good man, publicly acknowledging her. That's just the half of it, though. When I eventually grew up, I started doing research on her.

'I learned very young that Alouette wasn't going to give me any straight answers. When I was on my own, first in occupied Paris, then with you after Teddy died, I had a lot of time on my hands. So I found out about her. It was good practice for a writing career.'

'But you never wrote the book.'

'Too close to home, my girl, and I'll hazard a guess it will be for you, too. No, I did something far more important than that. As I uncovered the rotten start she had, the awful things she had to do to stay alive, the way people treated her when she was a nobody, I began to understand and feel sorry for her. And once I understood her, I even began to love her. Why did you take a liking to her when you first met?'

'Hmm, let's see . . . she turned out to be far more realistic than I'd expected, she had fewer illusions than anyone I can think of except you, but most of all she radiates toughness and courage.'

'More or less the qualities I found in her. I don't know why, but they are the things I've always admired. I like survivors who've come through against all odds, and my God, she was a survivor! Once I understood and respected her, it was a shortish step to love.

'There was one extra element that took me up that step – learning how generous she was. Not many people make it to the top from origins like Alouette's. When they do, it's a safe bet that they're tight-fisted and selfish, however rich they get. Not Doré. All her life, she's been giving. The tragedy is that she's so emotionally crippled she can't give from the inside, so she gives her possessions. Time and time again I'd come up with someone she'd helped. At times I used to think there wasn't an undertaker in Paris she didn't subsidise, there were so many funerals for impoverished artists paid for by her. Nobody's ever heard about these things, so she wasn't doing it for glory. She paid for people's holidays, made their clothes, bought their groceries, rented their apartments. And all the time she made bad-tempered noises to sugggest she did it all for sound selfish business reasons. It puzzled me for years. In the end I decided it was because she understood about human dignity and thought everyone was entitled to their share. If she could give it to them with a little money at the right time, she did. It was her way of compensating for being unable to give them herself. So here I am, half trying to protect the old bat against my demon daughter. If she wasn't in such a lather, she'd be the first one to appreciate the joke!'

Andy was smiling at her mother. 'You know, when I got here I was really bothered about you, for about the first time ever. I just couldn't square your keeping quiet about Doré with everything else I knew about you. I can't say I'm any closer to grasping it, but you're certainly doing a terrific snow job on Doré.'

'Just don't push me about the big finish. I'm finding my feet now, but it's always hard for me to talk about and I can't manage it yet. How much do you know about the Duke?'

'Very little. I've picked up the odd snippet in general reading over the years - you know, Lord of London, the man with the best yacht, the Henry the Eighth of the twentieth century - that sort of thing. But nothing much about him and Doré. The split came before she'd covered it in her reminiscences.'

'Well, on the assumption that you'll go back to her eventually for the rest of the story, I'll pass on as much as I know. It was funny getting to know him in Geneva - as if I was looking at someone through the wrong end of a telescope. I developed quite an affection for him, but I so despised all he stood for, especially his politics, that it never amounted to more than that. You can't be proud of a father like Jack Granchester. You just stand back and exclaim over him like Mount Rushmore or the Eiffel Tower - or a dinosaur's skeleton.'

At that point Joel arrived with a bottle of wine and glasses, staying to provide moral support for Marie-Louise by chipping in with bits of the information he had picked up while researching his own Doré book.

Marie-Louise was well-informed about her parents. For years she had done direct and indirect research on Doré and Granchester. Gradually she filled in the story of the Duke and the couturière – their meetings; their extensive travels; Doré's visits to his English estates. After a while, though, Andy became perplexed.

'There's something wrong about this. All I've ever heard about Doré in the last month goes right against her risking her standing and everything at the age of thirty-eight just to produce a second illegitimate kid – particularly when she apparently didn't give a damn about the first one.'

Marie-Louise stopped in her tracks, staring at her daughter. 'You mean – you mean she didn't tell you?'

'Tell me what?' Andy's confusion was obvious.

'She'd never have given birth to another bastard. God, no! It never occurred to me that when she confessed about me she'd miss the vital bit. My dear girl, if I'd been a son, you would never have existed and today Doré would have been the Dowager Duchess of Conway. She married the Duke secretly three months before I was born and because I turned out to be the wrong sex, they got an equally silent divorce in 1930. Whatever they say about top people not being able to hide their skeletons, those were the days when unlimited wealth could buy you an awful lot of privacy. You and I are both the legitimate issue of the last Duke of Conway, and inheritors of a fair chunk of his money!'

# Chapter Fourteen

## Doré
## 1924–1930: Being There

*I didn't realise until now how much difference that head-strong stubborn girl had made to me. Funny, after just a month she seemed to have been here always, and now she's gone. I'm feeling lonelier than I remembered I could be. Oh, Conway, I might have known that any fruit of our love would combine some odd traits. At least she's missed your stupidity and my secret yearning for respectability – but otherwise she's inherited a lot from both of us.*

*She must come back! I can't give her up now that I've found her at last. I never could get close to Loulou; there was something too controlled and remote about her even as a little girl. But this one is all fire and passion and talent, and I adore her. She's what I would have given anything to be, what I was looking for without ever knowing it – she's free. If I can't have that for myself at least I can get some joy from watching her live it. . . .*

*But what if she doesn't come back? I have to admit it would be my own fault. I really blundered by not telling her about our connection at the very beginning and that snake Eugène could be guaranteed to put the worst possible face on it when he blabbed to her. I did try to mend a few fences at our lunch, I really did, but I still felt so shocked about how she'd found out that I was on edge and all my nastiest faults were on display. The only one who could ever handle me when I got like that was Magda, by laughing at me for being childish. No one else ever understood that was the only way to treat me when I was difficult.*

*If I ever see Andy again, should I go over my side of the*

*time with Conway, or should I accept that whatever Loulou's faults might be, she always tries to be coldly honest? I've no doubt that she'll tell Andy the truth as she knows it – but is that the whole truth, my truth? I don't know. Even after all these years I don't know if I made the right decision in parting from you, my crazy English duke. . . .*

The Duke of Conway stayed only a short time on that first visit, but he made his admiration for Eliane quite clear. After his departure, she waited for a show of jealousy from Georgiana and was almost disappointed when none came. She simply expressed interest in Eliane's impression of Jack Granchester and appeared happy to gossip about him.

'My dear, he's getting a positively Henry the Eighth reputation! He's just seen off wife number two, and given his much-publicised quest for a son I should think number three will be along in a minute like a London omnibus.'

'Hasn't he got any children, then? He must be well into his forties. Most men have had at least some by then, unless there's something wrong.'

Georgiana became more serious. 'It's rather sad, really. He's got a daughter from his first marriage and there were two sons. But one died of influenza as a baby and the other was drowned at the age of six in a frightful accident on his estate near Cambridge. He blamed his first wife for that – God knows why, because neither of them spent much time with the children. As in all well-ordered households they were looked after by armies of nannies and governesses and their parents were practically strangers. But Marguerite showed signs of recovering after a normal period of mourning and Jack couldn't forgive her. He was never one for the merely normal. He was still at the stage of threatening to raze the estate and sow its fields with salt or something equally melodramatic and she was beginning to say that there would be other sons in time. Not with her, there weren't.

'And then, of course, they divorced and he was raging about London looking for a suitable mother for the heir. He did everything but measure the width of their hips before commencing his courtship! Eventually he teamed up with the daughter of a family known for its immense over-production of children, notably male. Either she was the one barren member of the clan or something had happened to Jack's virility by then, because no child arrived at all – not that he gave her much time. They divorced last year, after less than four years of marriage. Two divorces in ten years would normally be too much for English Society, but of course this was Jack Granchester, impeccably aristocratic and one of the world's richest men to boot. He's still welcome at Court and in all the best drawing-rooms and half the Mamas in London are panting to let him try fathering the next duke on their virginal little girls.'

'And d'you think he will?' Eliane was intrigued.

'Mmm, I suspect not. The Granchesters have never been too good at rearing sons. Jack isn't the son of the previous Duke; he's the grand-nephew of the one before that. The First Duke was one of only two sons and Jack himself the only boy. There were two sisters and only one of them has sons. But of course, if Jack dies without a son the title will be extinct because there'll be no descent in the male line.'

'But what about his sister's sons?'

'The dukedom descends in the male line, which means that only the son of a son can inherit. The son of a daughter doesn't count.'

Eliane considered this in silence. The man made her nervous. He might have problems in producing children but apparently he was a keen and successful lover. Scarcely a day passed without the newspapers carrying gossip items about his latest flirtation. If only half of them were true he must seldom have an empty bed. But what a challenge! If he was really prowling around looking for a third duchess, perhaps. . . .

She pulled herself together abruptly. This was absurd! If there was one European society in which it was as impossible as in France for a woman in trade to penetrate the aristocracy, it was England. The only exceptions to this rule were the occasional actresses who seemed to drive a certain type of nobleman crazy enough to marry them. But it had taken Eliane too long to erase the atmosphere of fringe show business and the demi-monde from her background for her still to consider herself part of that class of charmer. The Duke, if he found her attractive, wanted to get into bed with her, not to make her his next duchess. Really, Eliane, she thought, at thirty-eight you should have outgrown these absurd notions!

Georgiana was watching her with a degree of amusement. 'Speculating on your chances, darling?'

'Momentarily – and deeming them non-existent. I'm surprised you're not more concerned, given your interest in me.'

The Englishwoman roared with unladylike laughter. 'Christ, Alouette – you must be without rivals in your capacity to make the most bizarre circumstances fit a conventional slot!'

'And what's that supposed to mean? I'd be fairly put out if I thought you were getting tied up with some man.'

'Don't be ridiculous. You can hardly see us going off hand in hand to a rosy old age as inseparable lovers. Look at yourself – look at me. We're fashionable, attractive women, typical of our time and social position. We don't belong among that poor crowd of neurotic females who live together as imitation man and wife with the "male" one wearing a monocle and dinner jacket, any more than we'd fit in as wives and mothers in small provincial towns. We give each other pleasure and we're friends, but let's not pretend we're the great loves of each other's lives. I should be delighted if you teamed up with Jack, although you'd give his ideas about women quite a jolt. Why not encourage him a little and see what happens?'

Next day Eliane got the chance to do so – and not

entirely by accident. She encountered him again at the Ritz and joined his party for lunch. 'What a coincidence! You spend so much time in Paris and yet I've been here since the war and we've never run into each other before. Now it happens twice in twenty-four hours.' Her tone was light and teasing but he blushed like a schoolboy.

'I – er – couldn't resist asking a few questions about your favourite haunts . . . usually I go to Maxim's or smaller restaurants, and I never stay at hotels. But someone told me you're often here, and so. . . .'

He fell silent and indicated the group of people he had brought along as protective colouring. Eliane laughed, pleased at the compliment. 'I'd hate to disappoint you after so much trouble, *Milord*, so of course I'll join you.'

'Why are you making fun of me?'

'I'm not – I wouldn't dream of it. What makes you think that?'

'Well, "*Milord*" – it makes me sound a trifle improper, what the older generation in my youth used to call a Stage Door Johnnie.'

'Good God, aren't you sensitive? It was just a little joke, not at your expense – at my own if anything. As we were talking I realised you were the first Englishman I'd met who really *was* a *Milord*, that's all. Don't Englishwomen make jokes?'

'Not very often, with me anyway. They tend to be too busy trying to impress me.'

'What an awful bore for you. You should escape to Paris more often. I'm sure no self-respecting Frenchwoman would give you such a hard time.'

'Don't be too sure of that, either. Frenchwomen try to impress me with a totally different aspect of their characters. Unfortunately it can be equally wearing after a time.'

'Hmm, I'm beginning to see what you're driving at. Before we join your friends, I can put you straight: there isn't the remotest chance that I shall try to impress you with either my marriageability or my bed-ability. There – that should make you more comfortable with me!

Come on, you're keeping your guests waiting.' With a radiant smile she moved in front of him to the circular table where his party were just ordering drinks.

Jack Granchester spent a lot of time in Paris but had always moved in a different social circle from Eliane's. The few friends they shared, like Georgiana, were outsiders in English Society, tolerated there as exotics because their family or business connections were good. The English friends who accompanied him now enjoyed impeccable social standing, so Doré was as unknown and intriguing to them as any other gossip column star of the day. They showered her with attention and she played mercilessly to the gallery. Conway made a minimal contribution to the gaiety, preferring to watch Eliane sparkle. She won his seal of approval when one of her new acquaintances asked what she was planning to do that evening and she said she was attending the Comte de Gratien's costume ball. The Duke had been invited too, as had two of his luncheon guests, but it was clear that among the English colony in general invitations were rarer than hen's teeth, and highly prized. Here was an enchanting, talented woman who seemed able to break all the rules, move in and out of café society and still command the friendship of the French haut monde.

Conway escorted her to the foyer when she departed for Rue Cambon at three o'clock. 'Would you consider permitting me to escort you this evening? It would be a privilege.'

'Only if you're wearing something interesting. Don't say you plan to go as an English maritime hero or something!'

He wondered if he were blushing again. It was a costume ball, the theme was Neptune's kingdom and he had intended to go as Sir Francis Drake. Oh well, he still had time to find something unusual. For once he managed to be devious. 'You'll just have to come with me if you want to find out – but I can assure you it's nothing so dull!' That was enough to win her consent.

They parted, arranging that he should collect her from

Rue Cambon after dinner. Granchester spent the rest of the afternoon and evening in mounting panic, wondering what on earth he could wear to replace the apparently contemptible Sir Francis Drake. By cocktail time he was convinced he might have to show up in ordinary evening dress and pretend he had no truck with dressing up. But that would be frightful! The last thing he wanted this scintillating creature to do was to dismiss him as a poor sport. Exasperated, he went out for a walk to clear his mind.

He was about to turn back towards his house in the Faubourg St Germain when he saw the answer in front of him on a street corner. The ancient and shabby oyster seller was standing beneath a street lamp, balancing a wide, shallow basket containing his wares and holding a chunky oyster knife in one hand. The other was shielded by a chain-mail half glove, designed to minimise the number of cuts he suffered from splinters of shell. Moments later the old man was heading for home to spend his most prosperous New Year's Eve ever, having sold the duke his entire stock, basket and implements. He had made a profit on the deal of almost six months' income.

At ten o'clock, the doorman at Rue Cambon telephoned from the lobby. Eliane took the call personally. 'Mademoiselle, the Duke of Conway's chauffeur has come to collect you. He says, His Grace's compliments and he'll join you at the ball. He's been delayed by urgent business.'

Hmm, so much for all that ardent admiration, thought Eliane. When it comes to the crunch a business meeting is more important than escorting me. Well, if someone else carries me off before he gets there, it's his hard luck!

She was not too irritated because she was so delighted with the ingenuity of her own costume and wanted no distractions from her own grand entrance. Her costume was exquisite. A sliver of aqua silk jersey covered her from throat to toes, embroidered with thousands of turquoise, green and white paillettes and crystals. Her black hair was covered by an intricate silver diadem shaped like a conch shell and about her floated – literally, thanks to the support of a clutch of helium-filled amber balloons – a cloud of aqua and white chiffon. She was the physical incarnation of a sea mist.

She had made a suitably gratifying entrance when an indescribably down-at-heel figure shambled in, his shabbiness accentuated by the glamour of everyone else in the ballroom. All around, scandalised guests were asking how a street vendor had gatecrashed an event closed to half of the very best society. Couture gowns were twitched out of his path; angry mermen and exquisite pretend matelots started forward for the pleasure of ejecting the interloper. Eliane remained firmly in his path, mildly curious about the man's ingenuity in gaining entrance. He reached her side, snuffled some obsequious compliment about her costume, and said, 'P'raps I could open an oyster or two for Mademoiselle. Like that, would you, lady?'

Then everyone started exclaiming about the Comte de Gratien's wit and originality in laying on appropriate street vendors to represent the humbler side of Neptune's kingdom. As they were drawing around, chattering animatedly, the pedlar finished opening the first oyster and handed the half shell to Eliane. A single, perfect pearl nestled in the polished interior.

'Well, never know our luck, do we, lady. Hang on – I'll do you another.' And he returned to his knife and shells.

After her first gasp of amazement, Eliane examined the man with greater care. He opened the second oyster and handed it to her. A second pearl, the twin of the first, appeared. She clapped her hands and gave a delighted laugh. 'Conway, you charlatan! Since when have oysters obligingly cleared out their own bodies before producing the pearls?'

Instantly they were the centre of an admiring crowd, all giggling at his originality. Conway took it all in his stride and went on nonchalantly opening oysters, which he handed to Eliane. Each contained a pearl and her expert eye quickly discerned that they were perfectly graduated to form the central section of a necklace. After tinkering with about twelve shells, he delved into the bottom of the basket.

'Ha! See here – there's been a special delivery to save us all a little time. For you, Mademoiselle, direct from the seabed!' This time he handed over a closed scallop shell. Knowing it must have been doctored like the oysters, Eliane took it carefully and parted the upper and lower sections. Inside were at least a hundred more pearls. 'If they meet your exacting standards, perhaps we can find a handy mermaid to string them together for you.' He delivered the line with theatrical relish, for the ears of all the guests, then lowered his voice. 'But I think Boucheron might do a better job if you took them in after the holiday.'

Eliane was all but speechless. It wasn't the financial value of the gift, although this was immense – she was already a connoisseur of pearls and possessed a fabulous triple strand – so much as the wonderful romanticism of the gesture, its originality, and the cachet which his public affirmation had given her. It was practically the only topic of conversation for the rest of the evening.

For Eliane and Granchester, though, there were other things to discuss. He handed her glass after glass of champagne, gazing at her, talking fast and inconsequentially. All his life, Jack Granchester had been cursed by the combination of a quick mind and a superficial intellect. His curiosity raced and probed and ranged over everything his eyes lit on, but he always dropped one subject to hare off in pursuit of another before his listeners had time to grasp what he was talking about. All too often, his audience was an immature débutante whose mother had propelled her to his side with the sound of wedding bells deafening her sensibilities. She would hover before the Duke in mounting confusion, understanding nothing he said and twittering with rising anxiety as she felt his impatience mounting. It never occurred to such young girls that the irritation was with himself, not with them. Eliane was immune to such insecurity. Over the past twenty years she had heard all the fluent conversation she wanted and more. She had learned that the body and the nervous system often made far more sense and spoke more honestly than the tongue.

Now Conway stood beside her, trapped inside his peculiar semi-articulate view of the world, bewitched by her unconventional beauty and instinctively grasping the vital fact that she wanted nothing from him beyond his company. She was also rich enough in her own right to accept his wildly excessive gift without batting an eyelid. No one could accuse Alouette Doré of gold-digging. Why bother, when she could earn all the money she wanted by franchising another boutique or launching another scent? Granchester was used to women who either rejected his extravagant presents with expressions of outraged propriety, or who grabbed them avidly but with utmost secrecy. None of them had ever reacted simply as if he had given them an orchid or a cocktail. Eliane captivated him merely by existing.

The ball ended with an English-style breakfast at five in the morning. 'We're close to my apartment,' said Eliane. 'I don't want to climb into a closed car; let's walk. You can ride on from Rue Cambon if you like.' So they strolled together along the Rue du Faubourg St-Honoré, with Granchester's Rolls-Royce gliding silently at walking pace a hundred yards behind them. He had put his oyster-seller's gear into the limousine before they set off and now they made an even odder couple, Eliane with her glorious mist of chiffon and balloons drifting around her, the Duke in his workman's clothes at her side.

She stopped abruptly at the corner of the Rue Royale and looked up to her left. A short distance away, the neo-classical façade of the church of Sainte Marie-Madeleine stood in floodlit splendour. 'When I go, I want my send-off from the Madeleine,' said Eliane. 'Look at it – as phony as my costume jewellery, but so elegant.'

He became gloomy. 'I wish I could find some way of not getting a send-off at all,' he said.

'Whyever not? It'd be frightful to have to hang around when your day had passed. Better to die at your best, not when you're an old wreck!'

'I wasn't thinking of that. I was thinking about – about my sons who died; about the other sons I've never had. . . . Unless I do, there'll be no Third Duke.'

He had caught her full interest. 'Why is that so important? I can't grasp the vital nature of that sort of continuity.'

'You ask hard questions – I've never really tried to talk about it. But it – well, it feels like a sort of recognition that we have deep roots, that we're part of the bones and blood of England. For no very good reason, I've always felt it would be a tragedy if that had to come to an end.'

The simplicity of his reply touched Eliane. Gently, she put her hand against his cheek. 'Why are you so isolated? There should be people and things that matter more to you than the few words which separate you from the rest of us.'

'Maybe I'm scared at heart that there's very little else to me. Wouldn't it be terrible if my title were all there was?'

'Yes, of course – but it isn't. Perhaps the title has held you back, have you ever thought of that? You're a fascinating man. If you'd been able to see that fascination as one of your own qualities, not just part of the glamour of the aristocracy, you'd be much happier, wouldn't you?'

'I shall never know, Alouette, because as long as I can remember, I either have been or have been about to become the Duke of Conway.'

She squeezed his hand. 'Well, I know. You would be remarkable whoever you were.'

He returned the handclasp gratefully. 'Even if it isn't true, thank you.'

He had an engagement in London on January 2nd, and had business there for too many days over the next couple of months to make Paris a suitable base. Otherwise, he would have been at her side constantly. As it was, he left the French capital at noon on New Year's Day. To Eliane's surprise, she was really sad to see him go.

The following evening, Georgiana bounced back into the Rue Cambon apartment. 'Well, where's Jack? Don't say he's forsaken you to return to the Great Wen? I thought you'd be at the "come with me to the casbah" stage by now!'

Eliane stifled her irritation and said, 'I'm not sure whether I want him to take me to the casbah or anywhere. He draws me, certainly, but he scares me quite a bit, too. He's so intense; he seems to feel everything twice as strongly as anyone else.' She tried to dismiss the matter. 'I shall concentrate on the business and leave all that nonsense to sort itself out.'

The Duke was less fatalistic. His personal messenger arrived daily with huge baskets of flowers. When Conway returned to England, he began writing to her on a daily basis, showering her with compliments and accounts of his doings. Eventually, surprised at the frequency of the deliveries, she discovered he was keeping two messengers shuttling back and forth between Paris and London so that one of them was always available to rush his latest thoughts to her. He had a sure intuition in wooing women and had sensed it would be unwise to deluge Eliane with more jewellery and expensive baubles. Given the cost of the messengers, bouquets and letters were sufficient. He knew that the trivial nature of what they carried would impress this woman more than if they bore exotic gifts.

Eliane got on with her work, but less single-mindedly than with any collection since Bonnie's death. The Duke intrigued her, interested her, scared her; and she felt a profound empathy with the lonely boy who had looked out of his blue-eyed, adult face early on New Year's Day. But above all the almost mythic quality of the title of duchess twinkled at her from behind his daunting figure. She responded to his somewhat ponderous letters with sharply observed, funny notes. Eliane lacked formal education but her naturally acute powers of observation and an unselfconscious ability to transfer spoken idioms on to paper made her a lively correspondent. Conway's French was perfect, so there was no language barrier. Her funny, scrappy letters, her apparent ability to forget he existed for days at a stretch, her huge self-made wealth, mature beauty and total independence proved an intoxicating mixture for the Duke. His letters grew longer and more yearning; the invitations to cruise or hunt or spend time in an English country house came thick and fast. Eliane turned them all aside, responded with descriptions of her life and Paris and got on with her life.

It was not a conscious strategy – she had not the faintest notion of the kind of behaviour that would ensnare a billionaire nobleman – but it worked like a magical incantation. Four weeks before Easter, Armand answered the door at the Rue Cambon apartment. He was confronted by the usual Conway messenger, all features save his long legs obscured by the biggest bouquet the manservant had ever seen. Armand held the door wide. 'Better bring them straight into the salon, my friend. I'll never manage them,' he said.

The messenger shuffled into the drawing-room with his fragrant burden. Eliane was sitting on her suède sofa, playing with imitation precious stones which she planned to use for that season's range of costume jewellery. 'My God – Conway will soon be sending me the whole of the county of Kent if this goes on,' she said.

'He would if he thought it would advance his case, Mademoiselle,' replied the messenger, and put down the flowers, revealing his identity. It was Jack Granchester himself. 'I thought if I came in person you might pay more attention to my invitations.'

She was disarmed by the romantic gesture. He stood in front of her, grinning his irresistible grin, and waited for her response.

Eliane laughed and raised her hands in an attitude of surrender. 'All right, I'll come quietly!'

Instantly he was beside her. 'I thought we could start

with a brief cruise on one of my yachts – Marseille to Venice, maybe – and then back to the Riviera. Or if you're tired of the Mediterranean, maybe you'd care to come to my Welsh estates for the Easter holiday. . . .'

'Wait, wait! What I had in mind was a dinner engagement or a night at the opera, right here in Paris. You may have been bombarding me with letters and flowers for three months but you seem to have forgotten we've actually met only three times! I'm certainly not planning to sail off into the sunset with you on the strength of that, even with Venice to tempt me.'

In the end, though, she did just that, and her big golden-haired companion banished the disagreeable memories of her last visit to the city on the lagoon. Conway had made up a party of half a dozen friends for the cruise, to convey that his invitation was no mere seduction ploy. Eliane would have died rather than tell him how much the yacht he called his pirate ship impressed her, but it had a greater effect than all the conspicuous consumption by the rich and famous she had seen in France since the beginning of the Great War. *Gay Buccaneer* was a four-masted schooner of around a thousand tons, two hundred feet long and powered by auxiliary twin screws, although Conway preferred to keep her under sail whenever possible. She carried a crew of forty. The black hull and snowy white deck gave her a rakish air, but below it was a different matter. Had it not been for the vessel's motion, Eliane might have imagined herself to be in one of his English houses, an understandable mistake as Granchester had turned his estate architect loose on the yacht's interior decoration.

An ornamental doorway surmounted by a shell-shaped architrave led to oak- and pine-panelled cabins, furnished with scaled down copies of Queen Anne furniture. The master suite even boasted a four-poster bed complete with silk Florentine embroidered curtains. The complement of just eight passengers left plenty of space, as the yacht was fitted to accommodate sixteen. No lover of the sea, Eliane fell in love with the vessel simply because it was so opulent.

Granchester behaved with complete propriety aboard *Gay Buccaneer*. Eliane might have been a débutante chaperoned by old family friends. Released from anxiety on that score, she had a wonderful time. Staying in Venice as a guest at the Danieli, she had been of the privileged class. Moored there aboard the Duke of Conway's yacht, she attained real social distinction. Alone in her stateroom, she admitted she was impressed.

The return voyage surpassed the outward trip. They sailed at leisurely pace around the toe of Italy, then out into the Mediterranean, pausing for a few days off the rocky, deserted coast of Sardinia. Eliane basked on the white sand of a small cove and watched her companions swimming in the emerald sea. But even then, with the holiday at its most idyllic, she had no wish to give up Paris for such remote beauty. She had abandoned any attempt to keep her skin fashionably pale. In the salty sunlight of Europe's best beaches, her naturally olive skintone had deepened to glorious coffee colour. She looked younger, healthier and wilder than since her girlhood gallops through Compiègne Forest.

At Monte Carlo they caused a sensation.

Eliane was astonished to learn that Jack Granchester had occasional gambling crazes. When he said he fancied stopping off at Monte Carlo for a few evenings at the tables, she was incredulous. 'You, gamble? What on earth for? What would you possible hope to gain when you practically own the world?'

'Come, you exaggerate, although I grant you I own too much for the money to matter.'

'So why do you do it?'

'Simply because it's thrilling to try and predict where the dice will fall or which card will turn. I like pitting myself against chance, that's all.'

He was being honest. She watched, fascinated, as he bobbed from table to table. Sometimes worried croupiers would follow him into another room in the casino with piles of chips he had won merely by letting one plaque ride on the black and forgetting about it as his attention wandered to another game of chance. At one stage he was playing four tables at once. Thus he won thousands of francs and she was amused to see less lucky – and poorer – gamblers gritting their teeth at the injustice of it all. 'To them that hath, it shall be given,' she murmured to herself.

But spectacular as his gambling was, one evening was hers alone. Eliane had put on a white silk jersey evening frock with a handkerchief hem that varied from knee to ankle length. The colour contrasted so vividly with her suntan that she would have passed for an Indian had she been wearing a sari. Admiring eyes followed her wherever she went. Half an hour after their arrival, she stood talking to Daisy Nugent, one of her fellow passengers who had joined the casino party.

'Darling, by tomorrow half the women in Monte will be staining themselves with permanganate of potash to imitate your colouring,' Daisy said. 'No one is talking of anything else – except Jack's usual crazy gambling, of course. It'll be a long time before they forget *this* ducal visit!'

Outwardly dismissive of the observation, Eliane was secretly delighted at the impact she was making – and shrewd enough to attribute at least part of it to the flamboyance of her companion. When they eventually left the casino, Conway looked outrageous, a Bolshevik's caricature of a capitalist. He had absentmindedly stuffed a mixture of thousand-franc notes and uncashed chips into the pockets of his dinner jacket. Occasionally a banknote would drift free and float away on the evening breeze, doubtless to brighten some Monegasque street cleaner's dawn shift.

The next night they were back and attendance had increased noticeably as the news spread that the mad English Duke and Mademoiselle Doré were going to be at the casino again. They did not disappoint their audience. This time Eliane wore acid yellow crêpe-de-chine, with a high neckline and no back. Her short black hair was held in place by a glowing band of topazes and her lovely bare back was enhanced by a long rope of topazes and pearls. There were gasps of admiration as Conway handed her out of his Rolls-Royce.

But that was only the beginning. The Duke set out on an orgy of table-hopping and in less than an hour had won more than a quarter of a million francs. Eliane was watching an American oil magnate losing considerable sums when she caught the excited murmur spreading through the room. 'The English Duke . . . a record run . . . he's won eighteen times straight on the black. . . .' The gamblers were moving in the direction of the next room, drawn irresistibly by the lure of someone else's exceptional luck.

Eliane arrived to hear someone close by say: 'He's up to twenty-one now and still his luck's holding. He passed the house record at nineteen.'

At twenty-three consecutive wins, Conway glanced up, saw Eliane, raised a hand in greeting and left his place. 'It would be a shame to spoil everyone's illusions by leaving on a losing try, wouldn't it?' he said, grinning like a schoolboy as the excited onlookers applauded behind him. He was half a million francs up on his night's play. 'You have their hearts and I have their envy, so let's leave on a high note and go back to the pirate ship for some supper.'

She strolled beside him to the car, feeling as if she were flying. He was silent all the way back to the harbour. As they walked to *Gay Buccaneer*, she said: 'What's wrong, Jack? I thought you'd be bubbling after such a success. Have I offended you?'

He smiled. 'Quite the reverse. I've been wondering at your superb independence. You are the only woman I know who would have gone about her own business in that casino while I was off somewhere, winning or losing a king's ransom. My women friends normally cluster at my elbow while I dispense the Granchester millions at the tables.'

'You should have told me, I'd happily have stayed there. But it's years since I was at Monte Carlo and I was enjoying watching everyone making their deals with fortune. Anyway, you could lose a couple of kings' ransoms without noticing, so you didn't really need me, did you?'

'Don't change. Clinging women make me panic. I'm endlessly fascinated by your – your completeness. You don't really need anyone, do you, Alouette? I'd gladly spend a lifetime trying to make you need me.'

'Never try, Jack darling. Take risks, keep faith with me and let me run free and perhaps we'll still be together when we're very old.'

His face was full of wonder. 'If I ended it now, you'd let me go without a fight, wouldn't you?'

'Of course. I'd never try to hold a man against his will. I spent most of my girlhood fighting to be capable of surviving alone. Now I've learned how to do it, I'm not going to run after some man who no longer wants me.'

'If only I'd met you fifteen or twenty years ago – how different life would have been. . . .'

'You can say that again. For one thing, you wouldn't have been gazing deep into my eyes on the most expensive waterfront in the world tonight. You'd probably have forgotten my existence. At eighteen I was very dull fare!'

'You've come a long way then, my Alouette. Please don't fly away and leave me.' He tilted her chin and kissed her fleetingly on the lips. Then he turned and led the way aboard *Gay Buccaneer*. That night, as naturally as dining or walking together, they became lovers.

There had been another she loved more than Jack Granchester, but there was no one who could hope to match him for sheer larger-than-life style. He did not know what it was to be thwarted in a material desire. There was only one thing in the world he wanted which he had not so far managed to attain – a male heir. The longer she spent with him, the more determined Eliane became to present him with one.

He was a keen but unimaginative lover, but she

experienced no feeling that she was under threat from him. Given the stakes she was playing for, she therefore encouraged him to make love to her whenever there was an opportunity. Conway, still besotted by this unique Frenchwoman, responded enthusiastically. Eliane brooded to herself about the chances of conceiving now. She knew she could bear a healthy son: Edouard was testimony to that. But that was nearly twenty years ago. How sure was she that she could still bear a normal child? This time the thought of motherhood held considerable attractions. Conway's status held unlimited glamour for her, but only if she were his legitimate consort. Anything less would make her just another hanger-on and her pride would not let her be that. She must either be Doré, alone and unrivalled, or she must occupy a position at the very top of the heap. At the Duke of Conway's side, this became a real possibility.

There was a further reason for her interest, one she was reluctant to admit even to her secret self. Although his origins were at the opposite end of the social scale from her own, she felt a kinship with him in his sense of solitude. She had learned to handle her own; poverty was a tough taskmaster. The riches which had protected him had made him defenceless against isolation, and every time she glimpsed this in him she wanted to cherish and care for him. Eliane suddenly felt very maternal.

Jack Granchester grew more bewitched by her each day. At the end of their cruise she agreed to accompany him to London, where Georgiana was investigating the possibility of opening a Doré boutique in Bond Street. The Duke would then go on to his estate in North Wales where he planned to host a big houseparty over the Easter holiday, and Doré would join him with Georgiana when his other guests started to arrive. In London, Eliane moved into a suite at the Ritz and Conway went to his Brook Street mansion. He owned a vast town house in Park Lane, but it was too big even for such a lavish host as he and rumours regularly appeared in the newspapers that it was being sold to property developers. In the meantime it stood empty, acting as a repository for his fabulous art collection. He went there only when he wanted to show off the paintings to new friends.

He took Eliane to see them the evening before he departed for the Anglesey estates. Normally a lover of modern art, she nevertheless gasped in wonder at the supreme quality of the classic English portraits and Dutch Old Masters which adorned his walls. She was spellbound by a Reynolds portrait of one of his ancestresses, wearing a golden satin gown of such perfection that it seemed almost possible to feel the texture of the fabric by reaching up and stroking the canvas. 'Ah, I could live with her forever,' Eliane murmured.

He became gloomy. 'Might as well take a good look at it now. Never know when it will have to go with these damned Bolsheviks getting into the saddle.' He always referred to England's Labour Party in such terms.

Eliane was aghast. 'But surely your wealth is beyond anything they can do in the way of taxation? You own the most desirable parts of London and half the English countryside. You can't seriously mean to sell something as irreplaceable as the Golden Countess!'

He refused to be shaken from his depression. 'Take the shirts off our backs if we let 'em! Well, I've no intention of allowing them to beggar me. I'll sell up and invest in the Colonies first!'

She sensed it was time to be silent. Already she had learned that Jack Granchester was capable of backing himself into impossible positions as a result of silly arguments, then having to do something he preferred not to, simply because he had threatened to do it. She had no intention of being instrumental in causing the departure of the Golden Countess to the mansion of some New York magnate. They filed past other works, the value of which would have bought and sold small European countries.

'I really should think about moving some of them down to Earls Hill,' said Conway. 'The Brook Street house isn't big enough to do them justice and I've nowhere else in town. Once I get round to doing that, I can sell off this great barn. That'll be one in the eye for those damned Socialists, even if I keep the pictures. The money I'd raise on this place would buy half Australia.'

Eliane concentrated on the paintings and kept her comments as neutral as possible. The next day, Conway went ahead to the Welsh estate while Eliane toured possible boutique premises with Georgie. Her friend was vague about the Duke's Welsh mansion. 'You have to experience if for yourself,' she said. 'It would be a shame if I spoiled it by trying to describe it in advance.'

In the event Earls Hill was every bit as surprising to Eliane as Georgiana had hoped. Although both women were to spend a couple of weeks there, Georgiana was staying in London a little longer than Eliane in order to say goodbye to friends who were leaving for the Far East. 'Off you go and have a romantic interlude with Jack,' she said. 'Not that it's likely to be too intimate, knowing his propensity for having half the neighbourhood in residence at any given time.'

'Just how big is this place, anyway? At least you can tell me that,' said Eliane.

'Big enough for no one to get under anyone else's feet. In fact the odd stranger has been known to get lost on the way to the bathroom in the middle of the night!'

Eliane had intended to arrive early in the evening, to enjoy the legendary approach to the mansion. But a last-minute appointment to sign the lease of the Bond Street shop she had eventually chosen meant she caught an afternoon train from Euston which did not arrive in North Wales until after dark.

Bangor Station was a bad start. Even on a warm spring night it was a grim, desolate little spot. From a mean forecourt beyond the wooden footbridge, the main road to the Isle of Anglesey sloped unpromisingly uphill past shabby terraced houses and cavernous chapels. The only attractive feature of the dark journey was crossing

Telford's lovely suspension bridge, strung like a steel necklace across the tongue of sea which separated the island from the Welsh mainland. Dim lamps illuminated its stone pillars and the beginnings of its intricate metalwork. Beyond the bridge lay the village of Porth Aethwy, more attractive than Bangor thanks to its rocky perch overlooking the Straits. Within moments the limousine was through the narrow main street and heading off in darkness along the margin of the sea.

Eliane had rejected the brown Windsor soup and dry roast mutton offered in the restaurant car aboard the train. She was looking forward to a late supper with Granchester as the big car swung off the winding road through high ornate iron gates. The drive sloped upward for a couple of miles, climbing through woodland and twice crossing above public roads on its own bridges. Finally they arrived in a small courtyard outside a relatively modest door. The chauffeur ushered her from the car and rang the bell. Eliane was shown into a hall, again of modest proportions.

'Mademoiselle, His Grace is expecting you, of course. Please follow me.'

The butler flung open a door and Eliane felt like Alice in Wonderland. Instead of the traditional inner hall she had expected, before her stretched a gallery so long that the two figures approaching from its far end were little more than specks. She shook her head, expecting her usually infallible sense of proportion to return. It did not. The gallery really was as long as it seemed and the two tiny figures advancing towards her were her host and a companion. Eliane would never admit it, but she was even more impressed than when she had first boarded the Conway yacht.

Eventually the Duke was within speaking distance, his sister Alice by his side. 'Sorry you had to wait,' he said. 'The gallery takes a bit of getting used to. My great-uncle had it built to give him the opportunity to take walks when the weather was too bad to go outside. One grows accustomed to it; the whole place is built along the same lines.'

If anything, this was an understatement. The next two weeks introduced Eliane to a level of extravagance she had not dreamed existed; few people in England knew of it, either. The Granchesters had amassed a vast fortune from property since a series of marriages of convenience in the eighteenth century. They came from modest merchant stock but by Victoria's reign they had been rich enough to make the usual claims to illustrious ancestry reaching back to the Norman Conquest. Genealogists claimed that Granchester was a corruption of the French *Grand Chasseur* and that an ancestor had been William of Normandy's head huntsman. Not that true antiquity mattered. The Victorians regarded landed wealth as the ultimate qualification for noble rank and therefore it seemed only natural that England's greatest landowner should receive the last ducal title to be granted outside the blood royal.

The First Duke did not attain the satisfaction of seeing a son taking the succession. His heir died young, leaving a couple of daughters. The title passed to his dead brother's only grandson. The boy - Jack Granchester - grew up accustomed to having his every whim satisfied almost before he made it known. He was just thirteen years old when he succeeded to the dukedom. Since then, no one had ever refused him anything, except a surviving male heir. He did only moderately well at Eton, was a good if unimaginative officer in the Household Cavalry, and obediently joined in the upper class English ritual of early marriage to produce an heir and assure the succession.

Tonight he had the air of a boy out to impress a new friend with his model railway and pony. In some ways he was still an overgrown spoiled child, but he did everything with panache. Although more impoverished aristocrats sneered at the vulgarity of Earls Hill, all who were invited flocked to his legendary houseparties.

As they approached the great house's dining-room, he

said: 'Everyone's just about to come out from dinner, but I'm sure you weren't rash enough to eat the railway company's mutton. Would you like something on a tray while you're changing?'

Eliane accepted, disappointed in her hopes of a romantic supper with him. But when she arrived in her room she changed her mind. Finally, she had found a setting to match those described in her novelettes. Who would have thought that an English duke would share the same ideas of comfortable living as a pot-boiling French fiction writer?

Her big room was furnished with the most expensive antiques. The silken Persian carpets on the floor were of a quality normally reserved for wall hangings. A marvellous fire crackled in the marble fireplace. The sheets and pillowcases on her vast four-poster bed were of the finest white Irish linen, the pillowcases monogrammed with the Conway arms. The fragrant woodsmoke in the fireplace mingled with the more delicate aroma from the masses of hothouse blooms in tall vases and fat Chinese porcelain bowls. Eliane was relieved no one else was there to see her girlish wonder as she looked at it all.

Why was this room so special? She was rich enough to decorate in such style herself though she had never considered doing so. She recognised that part of the magic lay in the realisation that such ostentatious comfort was duplicated in the seventy or eighty guest rooms throughout the great house. 'Now that really *is* impressive!' she murmured to herself.

So was her dinner. When she emerged from her bath, a maid arrived with a succession of trays bearing consommé, slices of cold roast veal in a tuna fish mayonnaise, hot cutlets of Welsh spring lamb with tiny new potatoes, and a bowl of hothouse fruit from the Duke's greenhouses. A bottle of Dom Perignon accompanied the food. The maid opened it, apologising for taking over the butler's function but adding that His Grace had thought Mademoiselle would find this arrangement more private.

Eliane stifled her impulse to giggle at his jealousy disguised as consideration, and turned to her supper.

In due course she entered a drawing-room whose size would have amazed her had she not seen the long gallery first. When she was introduced to her fellow guests, though, the sense of wonder returned. It was not a literary or cultural gathering, but it seemed that no one of significance in European High Society or Conservative politics had been left out. She often reflected later that the scope of the house party was defined by the Prince of Wales on one hand and Winston Churchill on the other. Churchill had been a friend of Granchester since the Duke's days of military service in the Boer War, when Churchill was a foreign correspondent in South Africa. In many respects he represented a more educated, developed version of the Duke's political views. He took to Eliane as if he had chosen her personally to be his best friend's mistress.

'I've heard a great deal about you, Mademoiselle Doré. My wife tells me no woman of taste wears any other designer's frocks these days.'

'I wish that were true, but yes, enough of them come to me to keep me out of the soup kitchens.'

'Something tells me that a woman of your calibre would always find some way of staying out of the soup kitchen. You have "survivor" written all over you, Mademoiselle.'

'Hardly the most flattering characteristic, surely? And please call me Alouette or Eliane. "Mademoiselle" sounds like a governess.'

'I can think of a lot of men who would have given their fortunes to be educated by a governess like you, and of course it's flattering to be told you're a survivor. Beauty and grace – even talent to a great extent – all of those are accidental. You have no say in how much of them you get. But the drive to survive, that's different. We all have a little of it but only those with great moral and spiritual courage have the strength to develop it properly. I think you've done that in most unpromising circumstances. I hope those days are far behind you now.'

She nodded, warming to the man and impressed that he had sniffed out the aspect of her character which responded best to flattery. The Duke was playing the perfect host among the various groups of guests and Eliane found herself spending most of that evening in increasingly intimate conversation with Churchill. As the party was breaking up, he took her aside and said quietly: 'Jack needs a woman like you – independent, realistic, no nonsense about crowds of interfering kinfolk. Don't run away from him, even if he becomes overpowering. With a woman like you at his side, he could be great. You have the sort of fighting spirit he lacks, although he has plenty of courage.'

They parted at the drawing-room and Eliane stared after him, impressed that he had described her as being beside Conway, not behind him. It implied an equality of status which flattered her still further.

The weeks which followed unfolded like the 'happy ever after' of a fairy story. On her first morning, the Duke took her on a tour of the hothouses, where she exclaimed over the azaleas and orchids and unashamedly fell on the strawberries, nectarines and peaches which were ripening there in out of season profusion. The gardener who accompanied them watched in horror. As they left, Eliane whispered: 'What did I do wrong? Isn't one meant to eat the fruit? I thought it belonged to you?'

He laughed. 'Tomlin has been with me all his working life and I don't think he's ever seen what he would call a "toff" eating the fruit straight off the tree. He expects us to take it from cut glass bowls when it's been decently washed and dried.'

Everything at Earls Hill was enormous – not merely twice as big as the same thing anywhere else, but a hundred times bigger. The island was subject to fierce gales blowing in off the Atlantic and after a particularly ferocious storm on her fourth day, Conway told Eliane that more than three thousand trees had been blown down.

'But all I noticed was that one old chestnut down by the lodge,' she said.

He smiled. 'One can lose a lot of fallen trees in fifty thousand acres.'

'You really own that much land?'

'Oh, yes, and that's just the North Wales estates. If I count in the Scottish and Shropshire land there's more than double that.'

The wonders of such extreme wealth were never-ending and when he begged her to stay at the end of her two weeks and cruise on his yacht to Scotland, she found the invitation irresistible. By now the French dress designer was an enthusiastic convert to English country pursuits. The activities themselves did not hold any special magic, but Eliane's competitive instinct surfaced with a vengeance. In Scotland, Granchester introduced her to salmon fishing. At first she participated almost from self-defence, after a couple of days of complete boredom as a spectator. But as she learned to cast and was taught about the wily nature of the quarry, she became genuinely interested in the sport. Within a week she was fishing from daybreak to dusk.

When she was not fishing, she rode, hunted, or played golf or tennis. Always fit and strong, she was now in peak physical condition and looked more like a twenty-year-old than a woman approaching her forties. She imagined she had left any notion of fashionable dressing behind when she travelled north from London. In fact she was as chic in the Highlands and in north-west Wales as she was in Paris, and the influences she picked up while participating in English country house life were to be reflected throughout the rest of her 1920s collections.

The Scottish trip was extended from a fortnight to a month. Georgiana was in Paris, acting as her deputy, but although she had a natural business sense and was in tune with what Eliane wanted, she was not a couturière. Nor was Doré a country gentlewoman. At the month's end, she told Granchester with real regret she had to return to the business, but was nevertheless aware of missing her own world also. For the third time that week, he proposed marriage.

They were standing in the wild garden of his Highland hunting lodge, watching a blazing sunset. 'Eliane, what possible reason can you have for refusing me? I have enough money to keep us going from now until the end of time. Your refusal makes no sense.'

She gave him a sad smile. 'The fact that you think I need a reason to stay unmarried is enough, Jack. I think anyone needs a positive reason to marry, not to stay single. At present I have all I could want. Why change things?'

He looked downcast. 'All right, let's put it another way. Is there anything that would induce you to marry me?'

'Yes. If I were expecting your child. But at my age and with no sign after the past few months, that doesn't seem too strong a possibility, does it?'

'What if you were? Would you marry me then?'

'Without second thoughts – but don't start chasing rainbows.'

He sent her south in his Rolls-Royce the following day. Eliane checked in to the London Ritz for a couple of days to do a little shopping in London before returning to Paris. Next day she went to her new Bond Street boutique to review its progress. It was unusually hot and she had been dashing around all afternoon. She fainted while preparing to leave the shop and the manageress insisted on calling a doctor. Within twenty-four hours, Eliane telephoned the Duke of Conway with the news he had been longing to hear. She was pregnant.

Jack Granchester was jubilant. Eliane insisted on continuing her planned journey back to Paris, but he had joined her there within a day of her arrival.

'What's the French equivalent of a special marriage licence?' he asked. 'The sooner we're married, the better. You can't back out now, can you?'

Eliane looked at his big, boyish figure and was reminded of the clumsy but good-natured Newfoundland puppy which Geneviève was raising in Brittany. A wave of real love for the man swept over her.

'No, I can't. I promised you. But there are conditions.'

He began blustering. 'Nonsense – out of the question. We were meant for each other, everyone says so. What conditions?'

'Jack, I've heard you talking about your dream of a son. What if we marry and I have a daughter? You're no young boy, but you're certainly young enough to father a son if you marry someone else. I don't want to tie you to me if we have a daughter.'

'Don't be ridiculous! If you're suggesting that I wait and see what you produce before deciding on marriage, you'll defeat the entire purpose of the delay because if it is a boy he'll be illegitimate and unable to inherit the title.'

'I wasn't thinking along those lines at all. You are one of the richest men in the world. I refuse to believe that you are unable to buy total privacy with that money if you want it desperately enough.'

'So?'

'So, contrive some way that we can marry legally but with complete secrecy. Then I spend a very quiet few months away from the spotlight. Once I've had the baby, if it's a boy we announce our marriage. If it's a girl, we get an equally quiet divorce –' she raised her hand to still his protest – 'and go on as we were before, giving you the opportunity to marry again and produce an heir. You'd better get to work on it quickly, Jack, because those are the only terms on which I'll have you.'

He stared at her in mounting perplexity for a while, then roared with laughter. 'Whoever called you "*Gentille Alouette*" was crazy – you're the toughest street fighter I've ever encountered. My dear, dear Eliane. There can never be any other woman for me after you, and you're quite right to suggest this lunatic arrangement. It ensures that I shall be your willing slave for the rest of my days.'

Eliane gave a sceptical sniff. 'Hmm, let's reserve judgement on that until we see what the stork brings, shall we?'

She was right about his money buying total secrecy. They took a summer cruise aboard *Gay Buccaneer* and the press performed their usual story-seeking manoeuvres at Marseille, Cannes and Monte Carlo. There Granchester gave them plenty to keep them occupied. Two of his guests were a much married prima ballerina and her latest lover, both of them itching to create a big enough scandal to precipitate even her complacent Swiss banker husband into taking divorce proceedings. A pre-arranged public row of theatrical proportions erupted aboard the yacht as the lovers were confronted by one of the ballerina's old flames. Old and new lover went over the side together and were widely photographed fighting in the water, where they were joined by the ballerina, intent on saving new love from the fury of old.

It was the best story the gossip columnists had obtained since Conway's second divorce, and far more photogenic. The lovers left the yacht under an apparent cloud of ducal disapproval, the press followed en masse and *Gay Buccaneer* sailed off to an unspecified destination. The only mention of Doré's name in the subsequent coverage was as 'among the other passengers was. . . .' In Corsica, some seventy-two hours later, a middle-aged couple went through a civil marriage ceremony in the town hall at Bonifacio. Eliane's father had not married her mother until she was expecting her last child. Her birth certificate therefore recorded her as Eliane Bonheur, her mother's maiden name. Granchester held several minor titles over which the dukedom took precedence. With complete legality, he was registered as Montagu, Baron Ruthin. Their obscure aliases were swallowed by an uncaring bureaucratic machine on the island and did not re-emerge until their equally obscure divorce in 1930.

Eliane Ruthin gave birth to a baby girl in London in March 1925, just two months after being present at her spring show. Only Geneviève and Jack Granchester knew anything about her pregnancy.

During her pregnancy, Eliane had often speculated as to her reaction if she bore a daughter instead of the much desired son. She had assumed that, whatever the child's sex, she would feel no stronger emotional tie to it than she had towards Edouard. Only the disappointment of not producing a boy would move her one way or another. Her daughter, Marie-Louise, therefore came as a surprise.

The baby was born in the Mayfair house which had been Jack Granchester's wedding present. Eliane had retired there at the beginning of the eighth month of her pregnancy and the story had been circulated that her physician had ordered three months' complete rest and seclusion after a year of overwork. The Duke's personal physician attended her, backed up by the best obstetrician in Harley Street. A team of nurses had been imported from the Continent, supplied by a Swiss agency renowned for its discretion in such circumstances. All in all, thought Eliane, if the press got through that security net, they deserved the story.

But no one penetrated her cover. Geneviève joined her for the last three weeks, bringing news, books and gossip from Paris, and Eliane enjoyed the peace. She had a fairly easy labour and her baby was small though robust. As Eliane held her for the first time, she was swept by an impulse of tenderness towards the child so intense that it shocked her. Her mind was filled by the realisation that this scrap of new life was a part of her, a part which would perpetuate her blood and possibly her talent, if not her name, long after her own death. At last she had something to fill the empty space resulting from her lack of religious conviction. This extension of her flesh would carry her to a sort of immortality, and some day might produce yet another generation to continue the line. It was a wonderful thought, so appealing it swept away any regret that she had failed to produce a son. Without any recourse to logic, she was sure that a girl would be a more likely repository of her own talent. Here was a future for the House of Doré!

During her pregnancy Eliane had thought over her possible role in Conway's life and was already less sure that she was willing to pay the required price to be a duchess and mother of the future duke. In recent days it had been growing increasingly obvious that Granchester would not tolerate any continuation of the couture house once she was officially his wife. Now, quite suddenly, as she held her daughter in her arms, she knew beyond doubt that the couture house was more dear to her than any human being. This child already had a purpose. She would succeed Doré as the Empress of haute couture. Of what value was a dukedom compared with that?

Jack Granchester showed no sign of seeing it her way. Instead of growing increasingly concerned about the child's sex as the pregnancy advanced, he fell more deeply under Eliane's spell. Once or twice, when she touched on the chance that it might be a daughter, he had been almost dismissive. 'I want a son, of course. But I no longer want anything more than you. If it's a girl, I shall resign myself to being the last duke. I shall still leave a dynasty when I die and any child of yours will be very special. The only reason I'm not pressing you now to announce that we're married is that someone might learn too much about your condition. But as soon as the baby is born I want to tell everyone that I have a third – and last – Duchess.'

Eliane dodged the larger issue by treating it flippantly. 'Hmm, isn't there a poem called "My Last Duchess" about a duke who'd bumped off his wife?'

'Don't make fun of me. I've never been more serious, Alouette.'

Part of Eliane was delighted by such devotion, but it made her nervous, too. She began to suspect that once they shared parenthood, he would become determined to make public their marriage. When that happened, closure of the fashion house would inevitably follow, and nothing would induce Eliane to approve that.

She was still deeply involved with the Duke, her love a combination of reverence for his larger than life qualities and relish for his undeniable charm and physical attractiveness. But she had learned she had no need to be seen as his wife to reap the social benefits of association with him.

Since their affair had become public knowledge in France and England – particularly since Conway had made it clear that Doré acted as his hostess at Earls Hill and Granchester House – doors had opened to Eliane that even her previous exalted position had not merited. It seemed that she did not need to be his wife to be treated as his official consort. Once the beau monde observed her welcoming Winston Churchill or the Prince of Wales to the Duke's French hunting lodge, or leading the ladies out after dinner at Earls Hill, no drawing-room in Europe was closed to her.

Even the staid Queen Mary was heard to say that, 'Alouette is too fine a character to tolerate those Mayfair lorgnettes being flourished at her by mamas who want Granchester for their daughter.' Truly the nobody from Josselin had arrived. She did not need to become a duchess to occupy a place at the top.

The baby had Eliane's golden skin and strange granite-and-water eyes, but from her father she inherited a mop of red-gold curls. From the beginning she was beautiful. There was nothing of the wrinkled, red new-born look about Marie-Louise. Granchester was spellbound. On his visits to Eliane, he spent long interludes gazing at his daughter while she lay in her carved olivewood crib, apparently contemplating a serene, secure future. Eliane quickly recovered her strength and within a couple of weeks was visiting her Bond Street boutique as a dry run for her return to the salon in Paris, where Georgiana was once more running things in her absence.

'You can't be planning to go back?' The idea was incomprehensible to Granchester.

'Of course. Has fatherhood made it unnecessary for you to visit the Scottish and Welsh estates, or to go to your regular business meetings at the Park Lane management office?'

'That's quite different. . . . No, I see. It's only different if you're my Duchess, isn't it?'

Eliane nodded without speaking, her eyes carrying a silent challenge.

'It's time to talk, my darling, I know.'

He behaved so well that Eliane almost weakened. Over a dinner comprising all her favourite dishes, he flattered her, flirted with her and made it clear that she was the only woman with whom he wished to associate. With perceptible effort, he refrained from blustering and emotional blackmail. He simply pleaded, and in doing so almost won her.

He also had a gut instinct for using money with flair and Eliane was still enough the little girl from Josselin to be impressed by this. After the soft sell of the dinner, in which he agreed there could be no question of her giving up the couture house, she resumed her preparations to return to Paris. But he had meant something rather different. Two days later, she was crossing the hall at Earls Hill, on her way to the stables, when he emerged from the library and called her over.

'I have a little something for you. Come and see.'

A few yards along the corridor was a large study, seldom used because the Duke had no intellectual pursuits. At least, it had been a large study until two days previously. Now it was a first-rate imitation of her main Paris atelier. Cutting tables, equipment and fabrics were all arranged as though awaiting her touch. She turned to him. 'How did you do this?'

'Simple. I just got my London manager to telephone your *directrice* in Rue Cambon and asked her to place an order for all the materials and equipment with a London supplier who would be able to deliver here. Then I told her you wanted her to get on the Golden Arrow yesterday and come here as fast as she could manage. She arrives tomorrow. Now you can do a lot of your preliminary work here if I need you when you feel you should be creating!'

After the first satisfaction of being married to a man capable of financing and realising such a project, Eliane had a few doubts. Wasn't there just a hint that the 'working here in case I need you' line meant 'working here because it wouldn't suit me if you worked elsewhere'? She felt slightly less free – and less impressed.

But in the end a mere man, even such a rare one, could not compete with Rue Cambon. And he certainly could not compete with Eliane's sense of independence. She did most of the advance work on the next collection from the Earls Hill atelier. Then, a month before the show was due, she joined him for breakfast one morning, wearing a travel outfit.

'I didn't know you were going to town.'

She smiled at him, assuming her most friendly tone. 'I'm not, darling. I'm off to Paris.'

'But – but you can't! I told you, I need you here. You can do everything in your workroom. . . .'

'You know that's not true. If you want to keep me, you're going to have to live with my spending a good part of the year in Paris. If you find that unacceptable, we shall have to talk about that divorce.'

She had taken care to preserve her friendly tone of voice, but he was aware she would not be thwarted this time. When she said they could divorce if he didn't like her proposal, she was quite prepared for him to call her bluff. Nevertheless, he was too used to getting his own way to give in without a struggle. This time he let her go. Next time it might not be so easy.

The next attempt was not long in coming. After a couple of weeks he joined her in Paris and was soon pressing her to announce that they were married. She refused, not even wishing to discuss it.

Granchester was bewildered. 'Alouette, I thought you insisted on secrecy only because you wanted me to be free if we didn't have a son. If I'm happy this way, what other reason do you have to keep our marriage secret?'

'Because in the end, we must divorce. Right now you think marriage to me, with Marie-Louise thrown in, is a perfect life. But I'm sure that as time passes, that yearning for a son will come back and I'm hardly likely to have another child now. The gynaecologist was quite surprised I'd conceived this one. Even if you manage to handle that without becoming bitter, you're an obsessive type.' She broke off, laughing to reassure him. 'I love you that way, so don't pretend it's not true! But because you hang on to your objectives doggedly, you'll never learn to live with me carrying on as a couturière. You've already proved that without the outflanking operation you tried at Earls Hill. If I don't keep on as a designer, I shall stop being the independent creature you adore and become just another pointless social butterfly. You'll be bored with me in six months and starting divorce proceedings in twelve. It just won't work.'

'But what do you suggest? I can't give you up, I just can't!'

'There's no reason why you should. I love you just as much and my life would seem empty without you. But I think we'll be better just going on as we are. Believe me, one day, in a few years perhaps, you'll find some girl who would make the perfect mother for your heir. By then you may be tired of me . . . but even if you're not, we'll give each other up then and get a quiet divorce. Until that happens, we'll go on as we have for the past year, with the added fun of Loulou.'

He grumbled but had enough good sense to see that her viewpoint was more realistic than his own. 'And after all, you really are my duchess, aren't you? It's just that only you, me and Geneviève know about it. Oh, all right then, but I'll never want a divorce, you'll see!'

She was privately convinced that he would, but as time passed she began to hope he would remain constant. The life which opened up to her over the next three years was one of pure pleasure.

They agreed that it would be far less complicated if Marie-Louise were based at Geneviève's estate in Brittany. Geneviève was, if anything, more devoted to the baby than its parents. She had no children of her own and this was the daughter she would have loved. Neither Eliane nor the Duke had any reservations about sending off their much-loved only child to a remote estate. It was what usually happened to babies in the Duke's circle anyway. Geneviève and her baron were frequent guests at Conway house parties in France and England, so Doré's and Granchester's return trips to their home in Brittany were regarded as unremarkable.

In the meantime, Eliane continued to dictate the fashion taste of Europe's richest women, and of a growing number of American socialites. After the first flush of new love wore off, Eliane privately recognised a more tangible new influence than romance – the effect of English country house life on her designs. It came at an appropriate time, after the Russian look had started to pall and before her clientèle began thinking she was running short of new ideas.

Conway was a social dinosaur even among the richest and most conservative families in England. His tastes were archaic and his wealth limitless. He still ran the estates like a medieval *grand seigneur* and the staff wore livery. Eliane had seen nothing like it and thought it far too chic to be confined to servants on a remote Welsh estate. She was particularly impressed by the butlers' and footmen's indoor uniforms, which comprised waistcoats in chevron stripes of black and royal blue, worn with the usual trousers of the servants' morning uniform, and shirtsleeves. Earls Hill had acres of corridors, freezing in winter, and there was an alternative winter jacket coloured like the waistcoat but with long sleeves in plain black to keep out the chill. She designed a whole series of separates and suits around this theme, the sleeveless waistcoats worn with royal blue silk blouses, the jacket versions as suits, combined with plain black skirts which echoed the men's uniform trousers.

A chance compliment about the quality of the tweed in the Duke's country clothes led to his introducing Eliane to the rural mill owner on one of his Highland estates who produced all the wool for Conway's suits. Eliane was fascinated by the whole process and the mill-owner was equally captivated by her appreciation of the best cloth. She returned to see him several times and eventually they collaborated to create a range of lightweight tweeds, suitable for women's town styles which Eliane would use to maximum effect for the next fifty years.

Liveries cropped up again when the Duke took her shooting in the Welsh mountains. Here the beaters wore Melton overcoats in a rich blue, darker than the indoor servants' waistcoats, braided in bright yellow. Their hats were oddly antique-looking hard-crowned billycocks with little cockades of more bright yellow braid. Eliane fell in love with them. Her next hat collection featured the billycock again and again, and the braiding became a more permanent influence. First she used it to trim her versions of the beaters' coats, semi-fitted shapes with braid patterns down the back shaping seams, the Melton cloth of the originals now replaced by midnight blue cashmere. But after that season she returned repeatedly to the braid and used it to trim suits and coats. It became so much her fashion signature that it was the first touch the cheap copyists imitated.

The Duke found the separations caused by her business interests less galling than he had expected. He himself had a wide range of commercial and political interests and Eliane made determined efforts to bring her working diary into line with his. Nevertheless, the effect on them both was inevitably one of estrangement. A similar lifestyle had worked well with Bonnie Charles, because of his enthusiasm, his constant new projects, his insatiable desire to do and see new things. Whenever he and Doré had been reunited after separation, they scarcely stopped talking for days. But Jack Granchester was of a different mettle. Although seldom in one place for more than a few days, he rarely did anything unexpected. He might be in North Wales one day, the Scottish Highlands the next, Norway a few days later and then the French Riviera, but his activities at each destination were eternally predictable. He shot and rode in Wales; shot and fished in Scotland; fished and fished in Norway; shot and hunted wild boar in Languedoc; and visited the casino in Monte Carlo.

Meanwhile, Eliane continued to enjoy the better aspects of their relationship. She took great pleasure in living up to her new status as grande dame when she was in Paris. While retaining her domestic set-up at the salon and her suite at the Paris Ritz, she also signed a lease on one of the most magnificent apartments in the capital, in a two hundred-year-old mansion on the Rue du Faubourg St-Honoré. The term 'apartment' was misleading: it occupied the mansion's entire ground floor and included a large garden. The reception rooms were worthy of a medium-sized palace, and that was how Eliane used them. The lavish entertainments she gave there ranged from masked balls and fancy dress parties to diplomatic banquets and concerts by leading musicians. For the more important functions, Granchester was invariably at her side, demonstrating his delight at the talent and independence of this woman with whom he had chosen to share his life.

Eliane reached the pinnacle of social and cultural prestige when she threw open the main salon for the premier of a new production by the St Petersburg Ballet. Her modest start as a secret backer for Felix Kusnikov had become an informal sponsorship arrangement and now she was always one of the handful of top patrons of any new St Petersburg production. The latest work, *Gigolo*, was a vehicle for Mikhail Pushkin, the sensational new male dancer whom Kusnikov had managed to smuggle out of the USSR with the help of a large subsidy from Eliane. Now she provided further support by launching *Gigolo* from her own salon.

The memory of that evening would always remain with her as the essence of all she had striven for. Coincidentally, Conway was unable to be present, and she basked in the glory alone. After the performance, she turned away from a group of France's most famous Society names and her eyes met Magda's. Her former mentor raised her glass towards the younger woman and said, very quietly, 'Salute the Empress!'

'That didn't sound altogether friendly, Magda, my love.'

'Really? Perhaps you're being a little over-sensitive. No insult was intended, Alouette. I'm thrilled to see you succeeding so brilliantly. And as *Vogue* said the other day, you did it all on your own. Do you truly believe that?'

'Of course not! Without friends like you to give me a leg up, I'd still be reading novelettes and going to see revivals of *Chu Chin Chow*! You taught me practically all I know about dance and painting. And you dragged my reading into the twentieth century, too, come to think of it.'

'But you never tell the world that - just murmur it to me over the umpteenth glass of champagne.'

'It's a hard world, Magda. I thought you'd learned that when you were a kid, the same as me. I invite you here, don't I? I dress you free of charge; I take trips with you; I am grateful. But I don't intend showing that gratitude by telling the whole world what an ignorant little nobody I was before you dragged me up by your apron strings. It's unrealistic to think I would.'

'I don't ask that. It just bothers me that when you have people who are genuinely fond of you, you treat them well but no better than the ones who'd sell you down the river if you stopped paying them. Georgiana, for instance. How long would she stay around if you didn't give her a salary and an apartment as well as superb clothes? There are a lot of her sort in your life. Sometimes I worry that you can't tell the difference between them and the ones who really love you.'

'Maybe I can't. Maybe I have to go on being Lady Bountiful to all of you because I have a sort of blindness that stops me from knowing who my real friends are.'

'Poor Alouette! Forty-two years old and you can't tell the difference! Let's hope you never have to find out the hard way.'

But it was something which caused Eliane little disquiet. By 1928 she employed more than fifteen hundred workers. She was a millionairess if the reckoning was in sterling or

US dollars, a billionairess in francs. If there ever came a day when she needed help, there would be so much money that even then she would not need to find out who loved her for herself and who for her fortune. No one was more aware of this than Eliane herself. It did not make her trusting, but it gave her boundless self-confidence.

There was no question that the St Petersburg Ballet cost her a great deal of money. Magda, who genuinely admired Eliane and who also loved Kusnikov and his company like an exasperated mother does her wayward children, watched the relationship with mixed feelings. She wanted the ballet to survive, and if it was to do so, Eliane's continued support was essential. But she knew that once the brake of Kusnikov's respect for Eliane was removed, any successor of his would attempt to milk her. Magda was not altogether sure that Eliane could handle such a challenge.

Her doubts were resolved in the summer of 1928. She had spent some time in Venice on the Lido with Doré and a number of other fashionable Frenchwomen. It was the year that women took to shorts. Eliane had reacted with disgust. 'I'm not a footballer, I'm a woman!' she said. 'No one sees my bare knees under a pair of sawn-off trousers.'

Doré's answer to the new style made her and Magda – whom she dressed free as usual – the fashion toast of Venice. Eliane had a vivid memory of the one time she had looked through her son's new clothes, when they had shopped together in London just after the Great War, before he entered his English boarding school. It was not maternal instinct that had made her examine the boy's kit but the couturière's insatiable curiosity about fabric, cut and style. The cotton pyjamas had intrigued her – what a perfect get-up to wear out of doors on a hot day! At the time, what she had in mind was protection of female arms and legs from tanning unfashionably.

She had actually got one of the midinettes at Rue Cambon to make up half a dozen sets and had worn them privately when she stayed at friends'' villas on the Côte d'Azur. But she had never gone public with them, at first because even she lacked the audacity to be seen outside a friend's villa in trousers, later on largely because she had stopped caring about the sun darkening her skin. Now the suitability of such clothes for beach wear came back to her. She designed beach pyjamas in soft white cotton – with a more formally-cut silk version for evening wear. Eliane wore this revolutionary outfit to the beach with a vast, beaten-up straw hat and a pair of canvas shoes. It made every fashion page in Europe. After she had queened it around the Lido for a few days, the Duke of Conway arrived aboard *Gay Buccaneer* and Eliane went off with him to cruise the Adriatic.

'Do join us, Magda. You know how the charm of yachts wears off for me after a couple of days. At least we can get off and explore some of those funny little Dalmatian islands together. Jack always wants to fish or swim or talk very naïve politics and I don't care for any of that.'

Magda declined regretfully. 'I have to stay. You know how frail Felix looked when we saw him? Well, he's worse – far worse.'

They had run into Kusnikov with Mikhail Pushkin in a seedy little bar a couple of nights before. He had looked ghastly and Eliane had been horrified at the degeneration of the man since his appearance at the *Gigolo* première in April. Instantly, Eliane was all concern. 'Is there anything I can do? Should I stay too?'

'Oh, God, darling, not with with Jack in tow! You know how he gets when he's on about *les pédérastes*! I don't know whether poor Felix could handle it but I'm damned sure I couldn't.'

Eliane nodded grimly. Granchester's obsessive dislike of homosexuals was one of his less endearing features and lately it had been much in evidence when he had attended the ballet in Paris. She fully understood Magda's reservations.

'Okay, but make sure you radio the yacht if he gets any

worse. The rate that tub wallows under sail, we'll be within range for a couple of days.'

It did not take that long. The *Gay Buccaneer* had been at sea for only four hours when a radio message came from Magda. It appeared that Kusnikov was dying. The Duke might have loathed Felix and his friends, but he loved Eliane and was only too willing to return to port when being with a friend mattered so much to her. By the time she got to the squalid rooming house where Kusnikov and Pushkin were staying, it was all over. The place was a ghastly reminder of the squalid tenement where Alain Raymond had met his end. This time, though, the victim had not been abandoned. Magda was there, and so were Pushkin and Boris Vasili, another young dancer with the company.

Eliane turned on Magda. 'Why is he living in such a hovel? I saw he had enough for a good hotel – the Danieli – even if he hadn't spent so much on cocaine and little boys!'

Magda shrugged. 'By the end he was buying cocaine for the little boys and *their* little boys – a lot of money can go straight down the drain when you're on that path. He'd have died in the gutter whatever you gave him, Alouette. The man just had a natural allergy to money. Anyway, the poor devil's beyond it all now. He got pneumonia. Incidentally, he didn't collapse in a restaurant. He's wearing his dinner jacket because it was the only warm thing he hadn't pawned.'

Eliane was standing at his bedside, crying silently from a mixture of sorrow and rage. Eventually she looked up. 'To think a man of his talent had to end like this. Magda, I promise you that whatever happens later in our lives, I'll see you don't end up this way – but you have to promise the same for me.'

Instead of laughing, Magda merely embraced her. 'It could never happen to you, darling. You have too much self-respect. But thanks for thinking of me like that. I don't feel so sure about myself!'

Mikhail and Boris were doing a creditable impression of a Greek tragic chorus, wailing, sobbing and declaring their lives were over. Funded by Eliane, they went off on a two-day drinking spree while she and Magda arranged the funeral.

'He had nothing left, Alouette. Looks like a pauper's end.'

'Nonsense. He was a great man. He goes out as he lived, in style. I'll pay all the bills.'

So the greatest ballet impresario of the century was buried at Venice's island cemetery, San Michele, mourned only by Eliane Doré, Magda Robles, Mikhail Pushkin and Boris Vasili. Just before they joined the cortège, Magda came to her in agitation. 'Alouette, I don't think the boys are too keen on a dignified farewell. They're next door being a little – well, extreme.'

Eliane went to talk with them. 'We're both prostrated by this, Alouette – prostrated!' said Pushkin. 'We can't go in some bourgeois procession to the island. Boris and I will go every step of the way on our knees. It's what *he* would have wanted!'

Eliane looked at them in contempt. 'Since when has either of you two considered what Felix wanted? You danced like angels, so he endured you, but if either of you think you gave him a moment's joy beyond that, let alone knew what he wanted, you're mistaken. Now pull yourselves together and let's go.'

They glared at her mutinously but then fell into line and followed her down the steep stairs. Outside, however, as promised, they flung themselves to the ground, again moaning like tragedy queens, and started shuffling forward on their knees. Eliane smiled down at them. 'Up, boys! Let's show a little respect for the Master!'

Pushkin tossed his head defiantly. 'We know how to give an artist's farewell. Leave us be!'

She squatted beside them and said in a low, sweet voice: 'If you two aren't up off your knees and walking in two seconds, I'll see you never take another sou out of the

St Petersburg or any other dance company I'm connected with.' She stood up and smiled again. 'Come along, dear boys, master your grief – after all, even you two must have doubts about your ability to crawl on water!'

They were on their feet instantaneously, she chivvied them aboard the launch and the rest of the funeral passed off without incident.

Eliane rejoined *Gay Buccaneer* the next day. Kusnikov's death had shaken her – not merely the fact that he had died, but the circumstances of it. She had no wish to perish in lonely obscurity, attended only by a couple of paid hangers-on, and for the first time began to feel her world was peopled by too many such creatures.

After cruising the Adriatic, the yacht headed south to Corfu, then turned north-west towards France. Conway was eager to proceed from there to Scotland to put in some shooting at the start of the grouse season. Eliane simply yearned for dry land and emotional security.

Throughout the cruise she had tried to reason herself out of this craving for safety. She was secretly married to a duke, possibly to the richest non-royal nobleman in the world; the union was not made public only at her behest. She was a very rich woman in her own right. Where then was the seat of her insecurity? During long lonely nights of self-scrutiny, she had decided it lay in her belief that people always let you down eventually. As a result, she felt safe only when she could control her own surroundings, deriving her comfort from things – buildings, clothes and furniture – rather than people. It seemed to her that the answer was La Madeleine.

Eliane had seen La Madeleine for the first time a couple of years earlier. It was a small estate on a private promontory high above the Mediterranean between Monte Carlo and Menton. The area was being developed piecemeal for the millionaire market, with beautiful luxury villas in extensive secluded grounds. This would never be a mass holiday playground. The estate she wanted derived its name from a legend that Mary Magdalene had stopped here briefly to rest when she journeyed to southern France after the Crucifixion. It was said to be the first place she had found peace. Originally, Eliane had dismissed her desire to buy the property as a passing whim. She was mostly based in Paris then, and as her liaison with Jack Granchester was at its most intense, it seemed stupid to acquire yet another house so soon after moving into the Faubourg St-Honoré apartment.

But the property was still for sale and Eliane found herself longing for it like a child for a new toy. Now, as she said goodbye to the Duke at Monte Carlo, she came to a decision. La Madeleine would be her security. She went to see the estate again and promptly agreed to buy it. The house which came with the land was little more than a glorified farm and she had never considered living in it. She knew exactly what she wanted of her new home. She had already discussed her ideas with Magda during her first period of interest in the place, and Magda had recommended a young architect, Jules André, as the best man to design the house she had in mind. Eliane moved into an hotel in Roquebrune and contacted him. Within two days he had travelled down from Paris. After they had thoroughly inspected the site together, Eliane sent him on another journey.

'I can tell you precisely what I want inside the place,' she said, 'and for the outside, I'll send you to look at a building whose mood I want you to capture for me in the new house. You're going to Brittany to take a good look at the convent-orphanage of Josselin.'

And so the convent became the model for Doré's paradise in the southern sun – but a convent transformed and built in the way Eliane Doré outlined. The textures and moods of the exterior of the ancient religious foundation translated readily to a luxurious southern house.

There on the rocky cape, amid hedges of lavender, André created a dwelling of clay-tiled roofs and terracotta terraces, big arched north-facing windows and quiet courtyards. It was a house for browsing through, for relaxing and restoring the spirit.

As she had warned the architect, inside the house Eliane's own ideas reigned supreme. She wanted to create a place which would be a haven for others as well as herself, a place to which guests would flock because they found it irresistible. With such an incentive, how could she ever run short of company?

First came the matter of personal privacy. That was provided for by the very nature of the guest accommodation. It comprised a series of double suites with their own bathrooms, to which they connected by a private foyer. The foyer, in turn, connected with the landing. This allowed guests to cut themselves off but permitted the maids to enter the bathrooms for cleaning purposes and to go into the foyers to leave breakfast trays. The trays were supplied with extra Thermos jugs of hot milk and coffee, so that any guest who wished to go back to sleep could do so and still look forward to fresh coffee without the bother of summoning another servant. Eliane's own accommodation occupied a separate wing and consisted of two suites of bedroom, dressing room and bathroom, with an interconnecting door between the bedrooms. One suite was for her, the other for Conway.

All the big airy reception rooms opened on to terraces among olive trees and more lavender. Eliane wanted no dramatic decorative effects – after all, this was a place of rest and restoration, not an art gallery. Everything was painted a soft pale taupe or beige, even the modern Bechstein grand piano. Most of the easy chairs and sofas were covered in coffee-coloured suède. Everything was soft, quiet and welcoming.

The house was ready in just a year and when she started filling it with people, Eliane established a way of life which blended perfectly with the surroundings. There was a rule of absolute quiet around the main building during the mornings. 'My friends are all mature men and women, not youngsters,' she told each new party of house guests.

'They need their morning to recover from their social lives. That's why the pool is some way from the house. If any of you is energetic enough to go swimming or walking in the morning, there's a pool house where you can drink and chat, also tennis courts and miles of paths down to the Cape.'

The house came to life from mid-day on. Even then the keynote was total informality. Large meals were prepared and set out as a cold buffet in the big dining room, along with a couple of hot dishes for those who preferred them. As guests arrived for their meal, they helped themselves from the table then went out to eat on the terrace under the wistaria and vines, surrounded by the scent of lavender and Mediterranean herbs. There was no pressure to extend or curtail one's stay; it was a big place, capable of accommodating twenty guests in the main house, even given the lavish size of the accommodation. Once one received an invitation, it was for an unlimited stay.

La Madeleine was seldom empty. A constant stream of off-duty business associates spent time there. Old friends loved it and new ones kept up a barrage of hints for invitations. Eliane smiled secretly. At last she had found a way of surrounding herself with the warmth of humanity, held captive by the lure she understood best: perfect, understated comfort combined with style. And when she felt tired of them, she could cut herself off and leave them to their own devices. Her private wing looked out on its own small walled garden with a fountain and spectacular views. Everyone who stayed at La Madeleine was aware that Mademoiselle was never to be visited there. She always emerged to see her subjects. She had no desire for them to come to her.

She came closer to achieving perfect contentment there and then than at any other time. Marie-Louise came down for the summer with Geneviève. Her son Edouard had stubbornly gone his own way and entered the Army, where he was now carving himself a career of some distinction. He had married young. 'Snatched the opportunity while my back was turned,' Doré had said with a sniff when she heard he had married at the time that her own affair with the Duke was in its early, euphoric stage. Now the young couple had a baby son and Eliane encouraged them to visit La Madeleine at every opportunity. She felt no warmer towards Edouard now than in the past but had decided it would be good for Marie-Louise to grow up with the companionship of another child, particularly such a close relative as little Eugène St-Meurice. With a prudent bourgeois eye to Eugène's future prospects, Pauline St-Meurice persuaded her husband to accept the summer invitations.

To perpetuate the myth that Marie-Louise belonged to the baron and baroness, Eliane suggested that the child's surname be changed to Chabrol. Only Granchester, Geneviève and her husband called the child Marie-Louise. Ever since her Gaillard days, Eliane had indulged in the upper class English habit of giving nicknames, which had also been a popular practice among Christian de Selincourt's Anglophile set in the 1900s. Now the habit was as much a part of her as her use of the term 'mechanic' instead of 'chauffeur'. Marie-Louise was Loulou. It gave just the right air of lightness and grace and of not taking life too seriously, though in fact Eliane had very firm plans for the child's education as a young woman of breeding and fashion. Conway hated it, but had the sense not to say so.

Conway also hated La Madeleine, and was less restrained about showing his feelings there. The design pleased him well enough, but he felt the interiors were 'too modern by half'. On his third visit he announced loudly that he felt one could carry poverty chic too far. For the first time, Eliane suspected him of being unfaithful to her. Jack Granchester lacked the vocabulary to come up with such a glib, fashionable judgement himself. Those words had been uttered by a woman – and an envious one, by the sound of things.

But it was the guests rather than the surroundings that most irritated Conway at La Madeleine. To the Duke, an ideal day began early with a large, convivial breakfast.

One then went outside, preferably in a large group, and did things - tennis, riding, swimming. Then there should be a copious luncheon, formally served by an army of attendants, followed by a snooze, more violent activity and tea. Nothing could have been further from the pattern of days at La Madeleine. When the guests began to emerge shortly before lunch, swimming was the most energetic thing they ever contemplated. The self-service buffet was anathema to Granchester, and as if that were not enough, one had to try and converse with a bunch of scented pansies about ballet and books. Not even books about field sports or sailing, either. They read incomprehensible philosophical novels which didn't seem to have a story. They referred to artistic movements he had never even heard of. At La Madeleine, Granchester felt he needed to wear his philistinism as a badge of masculinity.

They both accepted they would not be at peace together on the little estate, and their romantic interludes were spent now in Paris or in England. The relationship still had its moments: he was on hand at Rue Cambon when she launched her triumphant collection featuring sailors' berets, white bell-bottomed pants and navy reefer jackets, all directly inspired by the workwear of his crew aboard *Gay Buccaneer*. She was the centre of attention in London when she gave a dinner party for Conway's daughter on the night of her Coming Out ball, and designed the girl's ball gown into the bargain.

But, imperceptibly at first, he and Eliane drifted apart. Conway loved her as much as ever; she was unique among all his female acquaintances and he would never tire of her. The truth was that she was beginning to tire of him.

Granchester's wish to satisfy every desire the moment it was experienced, a trait which had beguiled Eliane at first, came to annoy and then depress her. The Earls Hill atelier was merely its first manifestation. Next time, it was her health. She had suffered occasional migraines since girlhood and when they struck she knew that a darkened room and strong sleeping draught were the only remedies.

During their second summer together, they were staying in Scotland when she suffered a series of particularly severe attacks caused, she was sure, by the pace at which she had lived and worked that year. The Duke would not listen to such explanations. Within twenty-four hours of the second attack, Eliane was mortified to be confronted by Britain's top neuro-surgeon. Conway had ordered the man driven up from his Harley Street practice to devise the ultimate miracle cure. Eliane was furious, but helpless to stop him.

It was the same with almost everything. A casual remark about not knowing which shade of mink she preferred resulted in the delivery of a coat in every available shade within three days. When she reminisced about a horse she had loved in Christian de Selincourt's stables, he managed to conjure up a stallion of identical size and matching markings to those she had described to him. Eliane discovered the curse of unlimited wealth – the ennui which could result from being able to satisfy every whim without any anticipation or effort.

In an attempt to stop Conway from sapping her normal appetities and pleasures, she began to spend more time away from him. Inevitably, as she failed to keep up with his sporting and political interests, he drifted towards other companions. That was the one thing that Doré would not countenance. Christian de Selincourt had given her no choice about sharing his favours. Bonnie Charles had ruefully admitted having a wandering eye however much he loved her. In each case she had loathed having to endure such promiscuity, but was given no choice. With Jack Granchester she had made it a condition of their relationship: if he wanted Doré, there were to be no other women, even casually.

The fact that he was beginning to bore her did not mean that Eliane wished to give him up. When she was told that he had been seen in the company of a succession of glamorous young actresses, as well as a recently-divorced countess, Eliane attacked. It was autumn and she was with him at Arcadie, the estate in south-western France where he went boar hunting. Eliane had just arrived and was dressing for dinner when he came to her room.

She watched him in her dressing table mirror as he moved across the large room towards her. As he bent to kiss the nape of her neck, she said: 'I'm amazed you have the energy left for that.'

He froze. 'What do you mean?'

'I imagine I made myself quite clear. Most of Paris and London appears to know what's going on. It was inevitable that I should hear eventually, surely?'

He avoided her eyes for a moment but then decided to hold his ground. 'Look here, Alouette, I'm sick of all this chasing around from fashion house to perfumery to boutique. All right, I know it's supposed to maintain my interest in you, but how can I go on being interested when I never even see you? I'm not denying I've seen some other women lately. I don't like an empty bed and I don't like placing my sister at the end of my dinner table as hostess. I want you there, where you belong. I don't know whether you realise it, but this is the first time we've been able to look forward to more than a week together for over a year. I want to tell everyone you're my wife and that Marie-Louise is our daughter, but you're making it bloody impossible. Frankly, the entire arrangement is beginning to lose its charm.'

Hmm, she thought, he must be upset. He's using Loulou's full name in front of me. But she only said, 'There, you see? I told you you'd get tired of me! You can't be so deeply in love with me if you're unwilling to accept terms that make me happy.'

'Don't be ridiculous. You always tie me up in knots. I'm not quick with words like your funny little effeminate intellectual Parisian boyfriends, but I can say that you're twisting things to make them what they're not. I love you and I want you – but I want you with me, always, as my Duchess, not as some visiting celebrity passing through on the way from one set of bright lights to another. If you insist on calling that unwillingness to accept terms that make you happy, you're right.'

He stood glaring at her, like a small boy caught slightly in the wrong but by no means ready to submit to authority. Eliane normally laughed at such a performance, but this time she felt a surge of irritation. She jumped up and strode across to the Duke, glaring up at him. 'All right, forget about all the clever words. I'll tell you the truth of it. I'm your wife, behaving just as I said I would when we married, and just as you agreed I might. In spite of all that, in spite of my having been absolutely faithful to you, you're jumping into bed with every woman who crosses your path with the right sort of look in her eye. I'm not putting up with other women's cast-offs and I'm not going to be pitied by people who whisper that I'm not enough to satisfy you. Now make your choice, Jack. You can have as many women as you like, but not if you plan to come back to me afterwards. I have no intention of hanging around here while you make up your mind, so I'm off to La Madeleine tomorrow. Come for me on the yacht if you decide you prefer me to them.'

Before he could say anything in reply, she had stalked past him and started down the staircase. There was a group of guests already sipping drinks in the drawing-room and Conway's social sense prevented him from storming after Eliane and making a public scene. Throughout dinner and the talk and card games which followed, she behaved as if nothing were wrong. When he tried her bedroom door that night, it was locked. She did not answer his knock.

Next morning, the Duke was up and out at dawn, inspecting his boar hunting territory and talking to a couple of farmers who claimed the beasts had damaged their crops. When he returned at breakfast time, Eliane was gone. A note awaited him, which merely said: '*If I see you on the Riviera, I shall assume we might still have a future together.*' It was unsigned.

Conway collected her from La Madeleine three days

later and whisked her down to Cannes where *Gay Buccaneer* was waiting. She was very happy to see him, as always after even a short separation, and left it to him to mention their quarrel. He had planned their reconciliation on his usual grand scale. They were alone apart from the crew, who remained discreetly invisible. A perfect dinner table for two had been set up on the after deck and they dined together against a backdrop of the jewel bright lights of the Riviera shore. Throughout the meal they talked of inconsequential matters. Only when they had finished did he stand and extend his hand towards her. 'Come on, let's walk. The time has come for us to settle things.'

They strolled together along the deck, eventually stopping to lean against the rail and look out at the bay. 'You're right, Alouette,' he told her. 'Whatever the reasons for my cheating you, you had a right to expect better behaviour. You never pretended things would be any different. Well, I've done a lot of thinking and I've decided that if I have to put up with you running the fashion house to have you with me, I'll do it. The other women are nothing. I can give them up without another thought. I think I was just using them to work out my resentment of your independence.'

He reached into the pocket of his dinner jacket as he spoke, and took out a small shagreen case. 'I hope you'll accept this as a symbol of my contrition. Do what you want with it – I know your ideas of appropriate settings are different from mine so I've left it in its naked state.'

She opened the case. Inside was the biggest flawless emerald she had ever seen. She gazed at it in silence for a moment, then took it out, fascinated by the iced fire deep in its green heart. Then she drew back her arm and flung the gem as far as she could out to sea. It made a small plop and disappeared forever in a flash of phosphorescent water about fifty feet away.

Jack Granchester was stunned by her action. Speechless, he stared at her for some time. Eliane broke the silence. 'You said it was mine, to do with as I wished.

What I just did wasn't just a silly whim, Jack. That stone would buy and sell several of the people I know. Certainly I don't think any of my friends could even contemplate buying a lover's gift of that value. But to you it had the significance of a bunch of violets. I think that's why I'll have to be the one who puts a stop to what we have.'

He finally managed to speak. 'But for God's sake, why? I've accepted all you said. I've come abjectly back to you with a present worth several kings' ransoms. Forget the emerald. I don't give a damn if you prefer to feed it to the fish rather than wear it. But what else could I possibly do that would make any difference?'

'Nothing. Nothing at all – that's the trouble. You could never stop being you and you could never stop thinking secretly of me as an emerald or a racehorse or a new piece of property. Sooner or later we'd have this same conversation again and I'd end up throwing another fortune over the side of a yacht. You can't help being a proprietor and I can't help needing to be free and self-sufficient. We've had nearly six good years. I think it's time for that secret divorce we once talked about, before things start turning sour between us.'

'No, I won't – can't – accept that! I love you. I'd give up practically anything for you, Alouette. You don't mean what you're saying. You're trying to punish me for those other women.'

'That might have been true a few days ago, but not now. There's nothing I'd ask you to give up, darling. It's more that as long as you are you, it won't be possible for you to accept my freedom. And the older we both get, the harder you'll find it. I'll always love you, but I can't go on living with you, even informally as at present. There would be other women eventually, whatever you say now, and no one gets away with humiliating me. My little show of temperament the other evening wasn't even a sulk compared with the sort of rage I can muster when I'm really stirred up. Come now, we'll always be dear friends, nothing can change that. I shall always need to talk to you, and to know you're there. But I won't stay married to you. Remember our bargain. If either of us wanted to end the marriage, we could, as quietly as it began. Anyway, whether you believe it now or not, if we divorce you'll start thinking about another duchess and the possibility of a son, and eventually that will make things easier for you.'

He pleaded, reasoned and eventually ranted for half the night. Eliane listened, never matching his anger, forcing herself to remain calm. She truly loved this man, but after her own fashion. And finally, in her forties, she had come to recognise that continuing the relationship with him would become an unbearable bondage. With the realisation had come an uncomfortable splinter of doubt which told her that it would inevitably be the same for her with any man. It seemed she was destined to travel alone.

At last Conway accepted her decision as final. She shared his bed that night and lay awake until dawn, simply holding him in her arms and making soothing noises. It made no difference to her resolution, though. The following morning she left *Gay Buccaneer* without looking back. The Duke sailed within hours. After that they communicated with the utmost discretion through their lawyers, and in due course managed to arrange a divorce which was as quiet as their marriage had been. The duchess who never was returned to her empire in Paris. The Duke turned his thoughts to a male heir. Within the year he was married to a twenty-five-year-old blonde from the English shires.

# Chapter Fifteen
## Andy and Marie-Louise

Joel had been taking as much weight off Marie-Louise as possible over the past two emotion-laden days. The trouble had not arisen from Andy's reaction but from Marie-Louise's own problems with her distant past. During her first session of reminiscence, she had repeatedly deferred discussion of what had happened between her and Doré during the war. Eventually, after midnight, she said she was too tired to continue, and promised to cover the rest of the story the following day. Andy realised the strain her mother was feeling and agreed to the postponement.

But that night Marie-Louise was unable to sleep. The one time she dozed off, she woke, sweating and shivering by turns, and clung to Joel until the sharp edges had worn off her nightmare.

'That does it,' he said. 'I'm giving you a hefty sleeping tablet and you're staying up here in the morning. I'll manage young Andy until you get your head together. There's no reason for you to suffer like this just because your daughter's doing her own version of *Roots*.'

Marie-Louise protested half-heartedly but soon agreed. As a result, the next day Joel told Andy the family history would have to wait and took her off for an introduction to the forest which had been the birthplace of the myths of King Arthur, Merlin and Morgan-le-Fay.

'But surely that was England, or anyway, Wales? I never heard the tradition started here,' said Andy.

'Just shows you how much damage a bad translation can cause. The Cornwall of the English story was really Cornoaille, here in Brittany. If you don't believe me I'll show you all the magic places here in the forest. We'll start with Merlin's miraculous spring. After all, it gave your mother's house its name, and she's been putting me through a PhD course in local folk history for the past few days, so you might as well share the knowledge.'

The spring of Barenton was not exactly accessible. They drove round and round the quiet forest roads, getting lost three times although Andy insisted she had read the map properly. Finally they turned down an overgrown lane past an ancient row of workmen's cottages. An old one-armed man was working in one of the gardens and they asked him for directions.

'The spring? Hah – just up the lane. You'll find it when it wants you to. Sometimes it doesn't like to be disturbed by strangers. Come inside and I'll show you some pictures of the way it used to be.'

They entered his tiny living-room, cool and still after the strong sunlight and teeming insect life of the garden. He reached up for two faded photographs hanging beside the fireplace.

'There, you see? That's Barenton before the First War. I still had my left arm – there I am playing the accordion. We used to go up to the fountain wearing our proper traditional holiday dress on July 14th – Lord knows why we used a French holiday as the excuse, but we did – and we'd eat a picnic, and sing and dance to the old tunes, and the bird in the pine of Barenton would sing and the water would bubble like champagne. Doesn't happen any more, of course. It had all died out by the time the Second War came. But those of us who know still go up there now and then to listen to the bird singing in the pine tree or to drink from the spring. Make a wish for me if you get there.'

They said goodbye and went back out into the sunshine, moving on foot up an overgrown path, across a meadow and steeply down to the bank of a hidden stream which moved fast and deep beyond a screen of young trees. Dark blue dragon flies hovered and danced a couple of feet above the water, their midnight iridescent colouring adding to the atmosphere of mystery. They slogged along, scratched by brambles, slipping on the steep slope, always pushing up the tiny valley towards the spring.

Suddenly they were in a clearing which was bare except for one ancient tree, the Barenton pine. Below it was a rough square trough, modestly bordered by paving setts and, at the side opposite the outfall, by a fallen menhir obviously taken from one of the region's myriad collections of standing stones. 'Somehow I feel I have to whisper,' murmured Andy, 'and what's more, I'm sure something is watching me from the trees. Trouble is, I'm less sure that it's friendly!'

'I've a feeling there's nothing to harm you if you respect the place,' said Joel. She realised he meant what he said, and somehow the words seemed appropriate, not cranky.

The spring, though inconspicuous, was breath-taking. The water in the trough was about five feet deep but so clear that it appeared to amount to a few inches only. It obviously had an exceptionally high nitrogen content which produced an effect like champagne bubbles. Andy squatted beside it and dipped her hands into the sparkling depths. She drank, and as she did, Joel said, 'Don't spill any on Merlin's stone. If you do it's supposed to rain for forty days and at this time of year that could wreak havoc with the tourist trade!'

He sat down beside her and Andy rested her head against his shoulder. At that moment, the bird in the pine tree, whose melody was reputed to be sweeter than that of his brothers outside the sacred grove, burst into a flood of song.

Andy raised her head and grinned. 'Okay, father figure. You've set up the perfect surroundings for a bit of the old straight-from-the-shoulder advice. I know you well enough to suspect you of sticking a tape recorder up that tree to create a sympathetic atmosphere of birdsong!'

'It's a shame to see such cynicism in one so young, but part of modern life, I suppose.' He became serious. 'Look, I'm not trying to stop Marie-Louise telling you her big secret. In fact it's not that big; more sad than anything else. But I think if you get it from her without any other explanation, you might miss out on a few things. When she tells you, I know you'll fail to understand how she can bear to have anything to do with Doré, and knowing your current bug-eyed worship of her you'll start kidding yourself it's all because of her mega-magnetism and nothing to do with Marie-Louise. In fact it's quite the reverse.'

'As I still don't know what it's all about, I can hardly agree or disagree with you, can I?'

'Put it this way: for a teenage girl in love it was possibly the worst betrayal of all. Marie-Louise deserves some credit, not just for managing to survive and turn into a fine woman, but for even getting round to forgiving Doré eventually. I don't want your old bag of a grandmother to claim the credit for that. Marie-Louise gets her courage and generosity from her own inner strength - and from the example of Geneviève Chabrol. If you want a heroine from Alouette's generation, forget your grandmother and pick on your great-aunt.

'It's ironical that from what I heard, Geneviève always thought Alouette was better than her at everything worth doing. But in the end Alouette became an emotional monster and Geneviève brought up a child to be one of the best, most understanding women who ever lived. Everyone who knew her seems to agree there was a sort of shining quality about Geneviève. She only thought she was a nobody because Alouette was so talented in worldly ways. But think of it - an orphan kid, dragged up with no education worth talking about, and the first rich, important man who has an affair with her falls so deeply in love he stays around for nearly twenty years, then risks being ostracised to marry her and introduce her to his world. She must have been quite something, don't you think? She never designed a couture collection, but by God she did a pretty fine line in human beings! She was the solid gold Doré. Don't muddle her up with the battered piece of costume jewellery you admire so much. She deserves better.'

Andy gave him a gentle smile. 'Haven't you forgotten something? The one person in the world who loved Alouette to distraction was Geneviève. The old girl must have some redeeming features, so don't be too hard on her. Come on, let's get back to Marie-Louise. She'll always be my real heroine, just as she's yours, so the big finish is unlikely to change my views.'

They returned to P'tit Barenton to find Marie-Louise refreshed and in better spirits. She and Andy went off together for another session while Joel went to make some calls. He rejoined them to go and dine in a local restaurant. As they prepared to leave, the telephone rang and Marie-Louise went to answer it. Moments later her voice cut across their small talk, unusually high and agitated. 'Andy, this concerns both of us!'

Her daughter turned back into the hall, puzzled. 'But no one knows I'm here except Doré . . .'

Marie-Louise was doing little talking and a lot of listening. Eventually she said 'Yes, yes . . . I see. Well, if you're sure . . . Otherwise one of us can drive her down through the night. You're positive? Okay, Eugène. If there's any change, please call me, whatever time it is. There's a phone extension right beside my bed. Good night, and – and thanks.'

She hung up and turned, pale-faced, to Andy. 'Doré had a stroke an hour ago. She's not in any immediate danger and she's under sedation now. They won't know until tomorrow or the next day how extensive the damage is. Eugène thinks she'll want you if she's aware of anything when she comes round. No point in going tonight but can you catch the early train tomorrow? I'll come with you, of course.'

The two women clung together mutely for a moment, then Joel came and parted them. 'Come on kids, our date's still on. There's certainly nothing we can do here tonight except worry, and Marie-Louise has just said that

Eugène was adamant that there's no point in any of us going to Paris immediately. Get going. It might be your last chance to switch off for some time.'

Andy started to protest, then nodded. 'You're right. I can't bear to sit around imagining the worst.'

Marie-Louise was less certain. She sagged against Joel, who had moved to stand protectively behind her. 'I know she's an old bitch, Joel, but I don't want her to go out as a drooling prisoner in a useless body. It feels wrong going out to enjoy ourselves now. For the first time in my life I find myself wanting to pray.'

He took her by the shoulders, turned her around to face him and touched her lips with a gentle, reassuring hand. 'Get drunk instead, baby. It's more effective.'

# Chapter Sixteen

## Doré

## 1930–1944: Götterdämmerung

*Why don't you ever recognise the best times while they're happening to you? I read a story once about a man who sold his soul to the Devil on condition that he could stop his life at the moment he wanted and spend Eternity at that point. Every time something wonderful happened, he thought there'd be something better tomorrow and postponed calling it quits. In the end he was left as a drunken old tramp under a bridge in the rain, but as that was the last day of his life anyway, he had to take it as his Eternal Moment. Sometimes I know just why he made such a hash of things – I often thought the best things were just the dress rehearsal for something better.*

*Those endless days of success in the thirties . . . how could I ever hope to convey to Andy the feeling of power, the sheer pleasure of being on top of the heap? In a way, I suppose I never behaved more sensibly than ending things with Conway, although plenty of people thought I was a fool. After all, look at what happened to that poor next Duchess of his. Sure, she had all the money and prestige, but she couldn't enjoy it because he treated her as if she were a cross between the secretary of a family business and the star inmate of a harem. He couldn't do that to me because we never made our marriage public. He always had to court me. If I'd had a son instead of Loulou and come out publicly as his Duchess, I could have kissed my independence goodbye forever.*

*Yes, I missed Jack a lot from time to time. I was lonely. But I've always been lonely, except for a little while with*

*Nico. If I'm honest, the compensations of being back in Paris at the very top would have made up for leaving Jack ten times over. The parties alone were enough to keep me going . . .*

The parties were certainly impressive. The smart press gushed about them; more radical papers called down fire and brimstone on the useless drones at the top of Society who spent more on one evening's entertainment than would be needed to re-finance a dying business in a depressed region of France. Eliane often questioned her own unending capacity to enjoy them, but she never tired of the excitement of being at the centre of such extravagance. Suddenly everyone wanted to know her. The years of association with the Duke of Conway had bestowed on her the social cachet to open any door. She was asked to design costumes for a steady stream of prestigious theatrical and dance productions, her couture collections achieved almost legendary status, and her income rose to levels she would have believed impossible even ten years before.

The reason for her greater material prosperity was not the clothes but her growing perfume sales. About the time she was supervising the renovation of La Madeleine, she had received an approach from the Reynaud brothers. Simon and Jacques Reynaud had built a colossally successful multinational fragrance empire, largely on the strength of cheap mass-produced scents which sold in chain stores throughout the Western world. Having cornered the lower end of the market, they had increased profitability by using their contacts abroad to launch more expensive products through exclusive outlets. Already they had manufacturing plants strung across North America in addition to the French factories which supplied Europe and the Middle East. They were satisfied with their progress in the cheaper and middle markets but now they wanted a top class product.

Paris was the only place for rich women to buy rare,

exotic scents. They visited the specialist perfumiers like Guerlain, or stocked up with the scents their own couturiers produced while they were in Paris on their annual clothes-buying trips. It was virtually unheard of for couturiers to sell their branded perfumes outside their own salons or boutiques. Now the Reynaud brothers came to Eliane with a franchise proposal which would give them the right to manufacture D and distribute it worldwide. She would receive a large down payment on signature of their agreement, and a royalty on every bottle sold. They finalised their partnership in June 1930. By 1932 she was making so much money from the US royalties alone that the couture side of the business was modest in comparison. How those American women must love their scent, she thought, and how I love the American women!

She needed her hefty income, for her spending was also on a grand scale. She did not hang on to the palatial Faubourg St-Honoré apartment for long after the break with Conway; it had been a conceit of hers to keep pace with him and she preferred the Ritz and Rue Cambon anyway. After the unforgettable moment when the St Petersburg Ballet actually staged a premier in her Faubourg St-Honoré drawing room, she felt she had derived the maximum satisfaction from the place. As soon as the break with Jack Granchester became permanent, she quietly divested herself of her urban palace.

But La Madeleine cost a fortune to maintain in the manner she had always intended. Eliane had learned that for her, business and pleasure would always mix inextricably. Many of the people who called themselves her personal friends were also on a sort of unofficial payroll, one which had originated with the employment of people like Georgiana back in the 1920s. She had learned that when aristocrats turned to trade to boost shrinking fortunes, their great names assured them of success. If she backed them and bought up much of what they did, she not only shared that success for her fashion house but also attracted personal kudos as a woman of impeccable taste.

So La Madeleine housed a constant flow of exalted guests, who lived free and high at Doré's expense. Her business reaped the benefits but the overheads were breath-taking.

Then there were the international Society women whom she dressed free of charge in return for the favourable publicity their custom brought to her house. It was a variation on the La Madeleine theme, and was theoretically cheaper, given that the merchandise cost her far less to produce in her workrooms than the retail value of the clothes. But some of the women favoured with this arrangement were audacious when it came to the quantities of clothing they took. One or two had to be restrained from acquiring the entire collection free of charge, and gradually Eliane evolved a set of rules for the number of garments permitted, strictly related to the recipient's social prominence.

There were family obligations, too. Edouard was determined not to accept a centime from his mother, but his wife Pauline, intent on establishing their young son's security, had pressed him to agree to have a trust fund set up for the boy. In return for her generosity, Eliane was able to brow-beat Edouard and Pauline into sending the child to spend much of his summer holidays in Roquebrune, or with Geneviève in Brittany, where she herself was a regular visitor. Not that she was that interested in the child herself but his presence was good for Loulou, almost as good as her having a brother of her own. Then there were the expenses of raising her daughter – nothing but the best for her, and the prospect of very expensive schools in the future. Conway had set aside large funds for her but Eliane made it a matter of principle to provide for the girl herself.

Family expenses did not end there. She now supported her two brothers, though grudgingly. Really, she reflected, it was more blackmail money than a gesture of family solidarity. They had got in touch when she was at the height of her relationship with Jack Granchester. Although Eliane interminably told everyone how 'systematically non-snob' the Duke was, her instincts shrieked a warning to her not to test his egalitarian spirit by introducing her threadbare brothers. And when they began seeing her featured in the newspapers as his constant companion, they showed growing interest in such an introduction.

Paul had some sort of job running a little bar and tobacco shop. He lived in the adjoining hovel with the woman who had shared his life for ten years without benefit of marriage, and their four children. Now it seemed the owner of the little business wanted to capitalise on it and retire to the south. Unless Paul could buy the place, he and his family would be homeless. It was a modest investment, he wrote to Eliane on grubby ruled paper, and he would come to Paris to discuss it with her the following week if she didn't have time to reply now . . . She hastily sent him funds for a deposit on the business and forwarded the balance before her scruffy kinsman could appear on her doorstep. Gaston was even worse. He had followed their father along the fairground trail and was a penniless tinker. The minute he heard she had financed Paul in his bar, he demanded similar treatment, using his brother's tactics. Almost before she knew it, Eliane was the backer of a small hardware shop in Rennes. The demands did not end there. Having established contact, the brothers kept up an irregular stream of whining requests for subsidies.

It had been a bad year for tobacco sales. . . . One of the children had been sick and needed special food. . . . A new ironmongery line had to be bought in if Gaston was to remain competitive with his rival, but profits did not run to such an investment. . . .

Each time she stumped up with less than good grace, Eliane asked herself why she so resented the requests. The money involved was less than she spent on her meals at the Ritz. It amounted to no more than petty cash to a woman of her wealth. But she knew the answer. They had never done anything for her, had never shown any interest when she was an abandoned waif, and now they wished to exploit her because they sensed she had a weakness. She went on paying up and hated them for their rapacity.

But her brothers were of no more importance than buzzing midges in the summer of her life. She allowed herself a small self-indulgence in the spring 1931 collection, to mark the passing of any matrimonial ambition. For the first time, her show ended with a wedding gown. This had long been traditional with all the couturiers except her. She had always scorned the practice and knew that the inclusion of such a design this year would draw immense attention to her as a glamorous, star-crossed lover. It was her lust for publicity rather than sentimentality which prompted the inclusion of the gown.

It was a beautiful design, made up in white slipper satin. The long skirt was unusually slender for a wedding dress, falling in close-cut panels over the hips before flaring slightly towards the hem. It featured a long train, overlaid by another formed by the fine veil which cascaded from a tight-fitting little head-dress. The bodice had long sleeves, unpadded shoulders and a high waistline, from which rose a large stand-up collar which gave the whole silhouette an antique look. A row of forty tiny spherical buttons, covered in satin, ran down the back from collar to hips. Drawings of the lovely wedding fantasy appeared in magazine after magazine, many accompanied by speculative copy asking whether this was Mademoiselle Doré's farewell to a lost love. It was very good for business.

Other changes made her early thirties collections markedly different from previous years, particularly her swing from black to white. As the virtual inventor of the little black dress, Doré had done more than any other designer to make black the smartest colour of the 1920s. Now she abandoned it, along with short skirts, flat chests and dropped waists. Her thirties frocks were longer, often in white, with more emphasis on the breasts and a very definite, though still uncorseted waistline.

'Doré re-invents the feminine woman' cried the headlines, following through with drooling descriptions of the beauty of her white satin, tulle and sequins, and praising her talent for turning the hard-edged flapper into a softer *femme fatale* for the new decade.

She herself appeared to go from strength to strength in beauty and elegance. Nearer fifty than forty, she looked more like a youthful twenty-five-year-old. Privately Eliane attributed her ageless looks to the assurance with which she could now approach fashion. The immediate effects of her relationship with Conway had passed into fashion history by now, but her years at the top of English Society had given her real insouciance to back a natural ability to feign it. The cupboard full of mink coats could only have been afforded by the man who bought them for her; only the inspiration of his cultivated shabbiness could have told her how to wear them without ostentation. She kept them, unworn, for a long time before the answer came to her. Of course! Fur was warmest when worn inside, wasn't it? She'd give them a look to combine English sang-froid with the opulence of pre-Revolutionary Russia. . . .

Out of her musings came a quartet of English-cut trenchcoats apparently made of standard heavy cotton gaberdine. Inside, though, they were wonderfully different. Each raincoat had a full mink lining. The left-over skins from the conversion of each of the Conway coats went to make fur berets to wear with the raincoats. Eliane kept only one of the original minks intact. It was a marvellous raven-dark model, doubly impressive in an age before black mink had been developed. This one she wore as a coat, but even here her informal approach was in evidence. Half the time she wore it the way students were beginning to wear their extra sweaters – thrown over her shoulders with the sleeves knotted together in front to stop the coat slipping off. A gossip columnist even alleged that Mademoiselle's casual habit with her mink had brought at least one dowager to the edge of apoplexy on seeing her in it for the first time.

No one could ever call her a copyist, because she drew

inspiration from so many sources and combined them so uniquely that the result never looked as if it derived from the work of others. The change of style from twenties to thirties came as a result of what she had seen in furniture design and interior decoration. Suddenly she was aware that people whose drawing rooms in the mid-twenties had been dark, rich and sharply defined in the high Art Deco manner, had gone over to white or beige drawing-rooms with glass-topped tables. Closed windows, drawn blinds and low lights were giving place to tall glazed doors, muslin curtains and brilliant sunlit interiors. The black dresses and cropped hair that had reflected tough chic were out of place against such back-drops. She who had invented the Little Black Dress abandoned it, creating bias cut skirts to be worn with flowing chiffon blouses and picture hats to frame soft, jaw-length, wavy hair styles.

To those who had followed Doré's development as a couturière, it was a surprising departure. Magda was openly mystified. 'I'd never have recognised these designs as yours, Alouette. I must have missed something, because to me they look like the sort of thing you'd say trapped women. What happened to your girl who ran and swam and played tennis?'

Eliane grinned: 'She decided to change for the evening, and she grew up a bit, that's all. Come and see the day clothes – you've only seen my evening frocks today. They'll change your mind.'

Slowly, Magda began to see what she meant and decided she liked the result. Eliane's twenties clothes had freed women and made them audacious. In a sense they had overstated their message, teaching girls to behave, dress and look like cheeky boys. Now they had learned feminine self-confidence, she was giving them easier, prettier garments, which allowed a less than perfect body to be alluring. They could also be realists by day and fantasists by night. Doré day clothes were evolving as crisp suits, easy resort clothes and simple dresses which could be played up or down with the use of different accessories. But at night they were shed like chrysalids, to reveal frilled crinolines, flowing trains of mousseline de soie and lavish beading on chiffon or silk jersey bases. The look was universally admired and copied.

'That's another thing,' she told Magda, 'I regard copies as inevitable, but these fancier lines show who spends money on originals and who goes for the cheap stuff. There's no way to fake top quality beaded hand embroidery.'

Eliane would have considered herself the unassailable queen of couture had it not been for an interloper who seemed set on challenging her in every field. Anita Schiffini was an Italian of impeccable background who had been forced to earn her own living in Paris since the death of her husband in the late 1920s. Her crazy trompe l'oeil hand-knitted sweater had first drawn the attention of the fashion editors. She had applied the wild artistic ideas of the Surrealists to fashion and had achieved instant celebrity.

Everything she did was anathema to Eliane, because the woman was challenging her supremacy in the world of art and letters as well as the couture. Until now she alone, of all the designers, had been associated with the intellectual avant garde as well as the fashion world. Schiffini quickly built up a cultural salon as famous as Doré's and the literary and artistic lions frequently flitted from one to the other. Eliane fought her new rival like a wildcat, even adopting the technique which had been used against her years before. When she first started making her mark, one of the top couturières who had gone through the long, arduous apprenticeship system to reach the top had sneeringly referred to Eliane as the Milliner. Now Eliane copied the slight and called Schiffini the Italian. She never referred to the rival designer as anything else.

The effect of Schiffini's arrival on the scene was minimised by Eliane's sensational success with her perfume, and by yet another new departure in her career: she was discovered by Hollywood. Her ex-lover the Grand Duke

Alexis had found that California was a natural haven for exiled aristocrats with little to offer but a title and an exotic European background. He moved there in the mid-1920s and by 1930 had a successful public relations company. When a movie mogul client wanted introductions in Europe to enliven a planned holiday, Alexis wrote to Eliane and arranged a meeting. It was a great success and within months Doré paid a visit to Hollywood with Magda Robles as her companion. She returned with a commission to produce the stars' costumes for three major films. It was yet another stride forward in her progress towards international acclaim.

But everything did not go according to her wishes. Loulou was not turning out to be the daughter Eliane had hoped for. She had seen the child as a future leader of Society, a talented couturière with an aristocratic background - in short, a carbon copy of her mother without the disadvantage of humble birth. From the moment she first picked up a book, the little girl appeared to have other ideas. She was a voracious reader, an early writer, eternally curious about the world about her. She showed minimal interest in pretty clothes and amusing children's parties. Her idea of fun was an afternoon alone with a book or an expedition to the woods to look at rare plants and listen to birdsong. As she grew older she resolutely refused to be impressed by the fluffy daughters of the French nobility with whom Eliane encouraged her to play. She adored the gamekeeper and the groom's son at Geneviève's estate because the one told her about animals and the other taught her to ride like a gypsy. She also enjoyed the visits of Edouard's son, Eugène. He was proving to be a talented artist and Loulou would sit with him for hours, watching as he produced sketches of the plants, birds and wild animals she loved so much.

Eliane was more captivated by her daughter every time she saw the child, but this stirred ferocious protective instincts which inevitably led to conflict. She contemplated Marie-Louise's development grimly. Hmm, lot of good that will do her, she thought. If I wanted to bring up a convent schoolteacher she couldn't be better, but a would-be *locomotive?* Never. I'll have to send her away to school.

She was forced to put off detailed consideration of such a plan, as for the moment Loulou was not even aware that Eliane was her mother but thought herself to be Geneviève's daughter. Marie-Louise was only dimly aware of the intense scrutiny directed at her. She enjoyed the visits of the charismatic woman who surged into the château on a cloud of scent and energy; she enjoyed the exotic presents, too, although she would have preferred still more books.

Occasionally Geneviève made a cautious approach to Eliane about telling the child who her mother and father really were. 'I can't help feeling that the longer you leave it, the worse it will be for her. I know your reasons, darling – she may be indiscreet if she's told too young – but defer it too long and you'll risk losing your daughter. Anyway, I love her as if she were mine and I have feelings in this, too. I don't want her to think I ever wished to keep things from her.'

'Don't worry, Fairy Godmother, no one's going to tarnish your precious crown!'

'Eliane, don't be so cruel! You know I'd do anything for you. I'm just concerned for Marie-Louise, that's all, and if you won't see the damage you're doing, I have to try to tell you, no matter how I hate doing so.'

'Okay, Geneviève, I'm sorry. It's just that I'm a little disappointed in the kid, and worried about how and when to tell her the truth.'

'But why are you disappointed? She shows signs of having a brilliant mind. Most parents would be thrilled to have such a talented child.'

'Most parents would be happy if their brats went on to be civil servants or teachers! Loulou is going to be special, but turning her into a bluestocking won't give her the sort of start she needs.'

'I hate to say this, Alouette, but you're already too late. I know she's still very young, but she's never going to care a rap about impressing the right people or wearing the right clothes. She simply isn't made that way.'

'We'll see about that. Another year or so and we start looking at the right sort of school.'

'Not England, please! Remember what it did to Edouard.'

'I wouldn't dream of England! The last thing I want is for her to turn into one of those great hulks who dash about waving lacrosse sticks and gushing at big dogs. No, Switzerland's what I have in mind.'

And there the matter rested in an uneasy truce between the two women until the child grew older. Eliane was secretly ashamed. She adored Geneviève and knew her own explosive bad temper over Marie-Louise was caused by a mixture of guilt and jealousy. As the circumstances were entirely of her own making, she knew that she had no grounds for blaming Geneviève, which in turn made her feel and behave even worse.

Marie-Louise's own intellectual precocity revived the dispute in 1936. That spring, Paris was a very different city from the wild, alluring honeypot it had been in the 1920s. The country's right-wing political parties were trounced in the April 26th general election and during the month that followed, employers were rocked by a series of lightning strikes organised by underpaid workers throughout French industry and commerce.

Outraged, Eliane raised her voice along with all the other employers to criticise the ungrateful workers who dared to campaign for better pay and conditions in such tough times. Didn't they know that the rich had problems too? One June morning, her maid wakened her earlier than usual – an event justified in Eliane's world by nothing short of death or national disaster.

'Mademoiselle, Mademoiselle, you must wake up! The doorman from Rue Cambon is out in the drawing-room. The staff have locked you out of the salon!'

Eliane was thunderstruck. For a moment she simply sat in bed, staring stupidly at Marthe. Eventually she found her voice. 'Give me my wrap, then send him in. I have to hear this straight from the horse's mouth.'

Marcel Granville stood before her moments later, shifting his gaze around the room in embarrassment to avoid confronting his employer without her frock or make-up. 'So what happened, Marcel? How did they get in and turn you out, for a start?'

He was indignant enough to look her in the eye. 'Turn me out? The little bitches never let me in! It was the apprentices who live in the staff hostel who started it. When I got there at 7.30, two of the young madames were already down at the door. "Not you, Marcel," they said, "you're a boss's man. Only workers who believe in solidarity get in today!" And there I stood outside, with them inside, until the first midinettes arrived. They'd obviously planned it all yesterday, because when they came the girls opened up, and the women marched in. I tried to follow and they all turned on me and hustled me out. "Go on back and tell Mademoiselle no one except occupying workers gets in until she meets a delegation to discuss our demands," they said. I hung around to see what happened at normal opening time. One of the apprentices came out and pasted up a placard on the door to say the place was occupied, and – and I don't know how to tell you this bit – she hung up a Doré shoe box, all tied up with pretty ribbons but slit on top like a moneybox, with "Fighting Fund Contributions Welcome" written on the side! I didn't wait to see how the customers took it. I came straight to tell you, Mademoiselle.'

He stood in gloomy silence, awaiting her reaction. What he got was blank-faced incomprehension. 'But they can't do this. Don't they know the state the country's in? I could replace them twenty times over within five minutes – and probably at lower wages!'

'Just try it, Mademoiselle. I think you'll find the National Guard couldn't winkle them out, let alone get a new work force in. Anyway, they say that nothing can be done until you agree to see a workers' delegation.'

'Well, that's a non-starter. I have no idea what a workers' delegation is and I'm too old to start finding out now. You'd better go back to the salon, take up your normal station outside and tell any customers who arrive that we hope to be back to normal very soon. I shall come down when I'm ready - and *not* to meet a delegation, or whatever, but to ask my workers what they think they're doing! Off you go, Marcel, and thanks for coming to tell me.'

Eliane deliberately moved at her normal leisurely morning pace, taking a long bath, debating which outfit to wear, getting her favourite hairdresser round to her Ritz suite to make sure she would look her best for the confrontation. Having applied perfect make-up she completed her image by twining her triple-length rope of pearls round her neck, and then had her limousine brought round to the Place Vendôme entrance. She could easily have walked to Rue Cambon through the Ritz Corridor, but a motorised arrival would be infinitely more effective.

But she was wasting her time. When she mounted the steps, the staff refused her admission. One of their organisers, a young apprentice seamstress called Annette Lebrun, stepped out with a sheaf of hand-written papers.

'Mademoiselle,' she said, 'the workers' organising committee told you they wished to send a delegation. We will not admit you until you agree to meet our elected representatives. In the meantime, these are our demands. Come back when you've considered them.'

Before Eliane had time to react, the girl thrust the papers into her hand and retreated inside the building. The door was barred again and Doré remained alone on the steps, locked out of her own *maison de couture.* She turned, swept back down the steps and into her car. 'Back to the Ritz, Serge,' she said, then sat in silence, furiously crumpling the written demands.

The workers were making only reasonable requests for better conditions - a decent limit on working hours, written contracts of employment, weekly instead of monthly payment and paid summer holidays. Many other businesses already offered such conditions, but the French couture industry was notorious for its bad conditions and Doré's ateliers were no exception. She could easily have afforded to provide what the staff requested, but now she was simmering at her public humiliation and was in no mood for appeasement. She called Marthe.

'Tell Reception to get me a secretary as quickly as possible. I need to make an announcement to these brigands.'

When the secretary arrived, Eliane dictated a notice of dismissal. 'I want a master copy of that typed up in triplicate as a Notice to Employees,' she said. 'I also want it done in letter form – three hundred copies. That's the number of employees involved in this charade. When they're done, my mechanic can take them round to the salon.'

She sent for Serge. 'When you take the letters of dismissal, paste up the three notices first, then post the three hundred copies through the main letterbox. The letters make it clear that if they don't leave quietly, I shall have them physically evicted.'

Having delivered her edict, she ordered Marthe to pack a bag for her and arranged to go off to stay with Geneviève for a week.

Eliane forced herself to leave without checking the employees' reaction to her dismissal notice. Let them stew! Let them wonder when the gendarmes would be sent in to turn them out on to the pavements. Give them a week to cool off and they might change their tune about delegations and workers' rights. They'd see what happened to upstarts who tried to lock her out of her own premises!

After the long motor trip to Brittany, Eliane was close to boiling point. Over pre-dinner drinks, she delivered a tirade to Geneviève that would have made the views of Louis XIV look advanced. Her aunt smiled gently, trying not to appear amused by the workers' rebellion. 'And do you think they'll come to heel because you've stormed off?'

'I sincerely hope so, for their sakes. If they do, I may

consider re-engaging the most skilled workers – as long as they weren't ringleaders, of course.'

'Don't you think they have a right to live decently?'

The voice floated out from behind a high-backed chair. Eliane and Geneviève stared at each other in astonishment. 'Marie-Louise, is that you? Come over here at once – I had no idea you were in the room. Why didn't you come out before and say hello to Aunt Eliane?'

'You were talking when you came in and I didn't get a chance. Then I got so interested in what Aunt Eliane was saying that I listened for a while. But you didn't answer what I asked, Aunt Eliane. Don't you think they have rights too?'

'You're far too young to understand, Loulou. One day you'll realise we can't all get just what we want.'

'Please don't call me Loulou. My name's Marie-Louise.'

'I prefer Loulou. What's wrong with it?'

'Nothing, except that it's not my name.' The eleven-year-old girl's stare was unswerving. 'Anyway, aren't you going to give me a proper answer? I know we can't all have what we want all the time, but you and Maman and I and Papa and lots of our friends seem to get a lot more of what we want than these people. I've been reading Papa's newspapers. Some of them can't pay their rent, and they only have meat for dinner on Sundays. We get meat twice every day except when one meal is fish. And we go away on holiday. And now Papa is getting older, he doesn't need to work to keep us. We have enough money for him to stay at home and for us to be comfortable. Some of these poor people have to go on working until they drop, and you just said you wouldn't agree to give them pensions when they were too old to work any more. It's not fair, Aunt Eliane. You can't expect Maman to agree with you, surely? She's far too kind to go along with horrid things like that.'

Geneviève had flushed and was searching for words to deal with Marie-Louise. 'I really think you're much too young to discuss such matters, my dear. Please go to your room now and leave us alone. We don't want a nasty argument.'

'Why not, Maman? You're too shy to tell Aunt Eliane the truth and she won't listen to the poor people who work for her. She bullies them and then comes rushing up here to hide from them. What good is that when she could be talking to them, trying to sort it all out?'

Eliane lost her temper. 'Get out of here now, you insufferable child! I will not be spoken to like this by my own daughter!'

The awful reality of what she had said stopped her dead. Loulou had started determinedly towards her as she spoke. Now the child halted and stared at Eliane, a stricken expression on her face.

'Your own what?' But before either woman could answer, she whirled around and rushed from the room.

Eliane started forward. 'Loulou, wait! You don't understand, child. Come back!' But there was no response, only the receding echo of the girl's shoes against the flagged floor of the hall.

She turned sheepishly back towards Geneviève. 'Oh, Christ, I'd give anything not to have said that. Any child who was less quick on the uptake than Loulou wouldn't even have noticed, but that one? What a way to find out.'

'Yes. What a way to find out.' Geneviève's face was ashen. Her voice shook. 'I'm trying not to blame you for this, Eliane, but it's hard. I think, if you'll forgive me, I must excuse myself. Apart from anything else, Marie-Louise needs me now rather more than you do.' She put down her drink with exaggerated care and left the library.

Eliane dined alone. A parlourmaid brought her a note from Geneviève saying that she felt unwell and would be staying in her room. The baron was away on a hunting trip and was not planning to return for a couple of weeks. Next morning was no better. Eliane went out for a ride mid-morning. When she returned the house was silent. She sat in the library and read the newspapers for an hour, then Geneviève came in.

'I'm sorry to have left you to your own devices for so long, but Marie-Louise is inconsolable. I've sent her off to stay with Pauline and Edouard for a few days. She's fond of Eugène and I think it's safer for her to confide in him if she must talk to anyone.'

'Confide? You mean you admitted that what I said last night was more than a slip of the tongue?'

'Really, Eliane, sometimes that child is more adult than you! Of course I did. She'd never have believed anything else. I had no alternative but to tell her that it was a secret marriage and that you would fill in the details for her as soon as you were able. In the meantime I said all the usual things about loving her even more than a natural mother would because I'd chosen her, and so on. But she's bitterly hurt. There was no excuse for you to let go like that.'

'Nonsense – I'm having a very rough time! No one thinks of what I'm going through, only of Loulou. If she hadn't been eavesdropping on us, then cheeking me with the most monstrous views, none of this would have happened. I know it's rough on her but she brought it on herself.'

'Heaven help you on the day we all get exactly what we deserve! Now look, we have to be pleasant to each other if you're staying for a while. I'm very fond of you; you've been my best friend all my life. But if I have to put one of you first, it will always be Marie-Louise. You can take care of yourself; she can't. I suggest you spend the next few days thinking out a way of discussing this entire matter with her and making it clear that you love and want her. You won't make up for your behaviour, but at least you might make her feel a little better. I'd prefer it if you go back to Paris at the week-end, because Pauline is sending her back on Sunday and I don't think it's wise for you to be here when she comes home.'

Eliane nodded silently, her cheeks burning with humiliation. In the event she held out only until Friday morning, then left early, without seeing Geneviève, explaining in a note that she would work out some way of discussing the whole matter with Loulou as soon as she had sorted out the dispute at the fashion house. Back in Paris she spent a frightful week-end. None of her friends was in town and she paced her Ritz apartment like a caged tigress. On Sunday afternoon she took a taxi past the Rue Cambon premises, preferring its anonymity to her instantly recognisable limousine. The occupation was clearly still going on, with two placards now adorning the front of the building and a couple of pretty vendeuses accosting passers-by to put their case. Furious, she returned to the Ritz.

On Monday she sent for her lawyer and her business manager. They spent the day going over the costs involved both in staying closed and in giving the work force what they demanded. Her advisers favoured settlement, but Eliane was now doubly keen to hold out.

'It's not just the financial cost, it's my personal standing,' she said. 'How much respect will they have for an employer who comes crawling the minute they try ordering her around? I didn't build up a successful business by giving in at the first sign of trouble.'

'Mademoiselle, if you don't bend a little this time, there may not be a successful business for much longer. The delegation contacted me this morning and said that if we don't achieve some sort of compromise, they'll ensure you won't get an autumn collection out. You know what that would do to sales on the couture side.'

She dismissed them and spent the rest of the day fuming in solitude. There must be a way out – there must! Now it wasn't merely a matter of backing down in front of the workers, it was having Loulou know she was defeated too. It never occurred to her that her daughter might respect her more for showing humanity to her employees.

The week dragged on with no sign of settlement and Eliane received reports that the strikers were getting substantial donations from passers-by and from sympathetic trades unions. On Thursday her lawyer returned.

'Mademoiselle Doré, unless you settle, I think you are facing ruin in the couture business. After this is all over, you'll be a perfumier and no more. You need your workers. You're half-way through a collection and even if you called off this one, the next one would be a disaster too because you'd still be breaking in a new staff. No one has ever launched a couture collection with a completely untried work force following a season in which they missed one show altogether. You'd be a laughing stock.'

Still she could not bring herself to give in. She retreated into solitude once more to seek a way out. Her excuse for capitulation came from a new and unexpected source – Hollywood. Only hours after the meeting with her advisers, Eliane received a call from a man who introduced himself as Nicol Alvarez. He had been sent to see her by the head of the film studio for whom she had designed costumes in the past.

'Mark Schulberg has a new project in mind, Mademoiselle Doré,' Alvarez told her. 'I'm the art director for this movie and he asked me to contact you while I'm here in Paris and have a few preliminary discussions about tying in costumes and set designs.'

Her first impulse was to dismiss him out of hand. How could she get down to new work with her present staff relations problems? But she knew Alvarez's work and had admired his gorgeous Art Deco-style drawings for more years than she cared to remember. Even when she had troubles, the chance of getting to know him better was irresistible. Eventually she agreed to dine with him that evening.

Nico Alvarez was a Spaniard from the Basque region, but he had attended an art school in Paris and had worked in the French capital from the early 1900s until 1930. He was one of the handful of decorative artists who had created the extravagant paintings, furniture, jewellery and room settings which combined to form the Art Deco movement. In California he had specialised in the more ostentatious epics, dressing dancing girls in cascades of beads and painting exotic designs on their legs. He gloried in the aura of decadence which his work conjured up and enjoyed a legendary reputation with women.

His looks surprised Eliane. She had expected a big, dashing, arrogant figure along the lines of Magda Robles's husband. Instead she was confronted by a slender man of average height, bespectacled and conventionally dressed. In spite of his nondescript appearance, he possessed a personal magnetism which made conventional good looks irrelevant. She was instantly captivated.

The movie project was the tale of a rich young woman who tired of her smart friends and the unending round of Society entertainments which made up her life, and left everything behind to find her true self in the world's remotest places. It almost went without saying that these places were the most exotic locations imaginable, all written in to give full licence to Alvarez's rococo imagination. Eliane would be required to create virtually a full collection to clothe the Society girls in the earlier sequences, and another wardrobe to ensure that her heroine looked impeccable as she fought her way through rain forest, a Far Eastern seaport and mountain wilderness. Eliane found the new commission as irresistible as Alvarez himself.

He was unaware of the salon occupation, as he had arrived in France only that morning. Eliane refrained from telling him about it until after she had established the deadline for the film costumes. When he told her this would be mid-September, she silently resigned herself to giving in to her staff. They had her over a barrel. To mount the winter collection and to get this commission completed on time, they'd be on virtually twenty-four-hour shifts from now until the autumn. Any thought of starving them out, or even locking them out and taking on a new work force, was out of the question. She accepted the commission, parted from Alvarez with a firm arrangement to dine with him again the next evening, then returned to her suite, contacted her lawyer and told him to arrange a meeting with the delegation.

She met them in a ground-floor salon at the Ritz. The younger members of the delegation looked around wide-eyed and impressed. They had never been anywhere so luxurious. In fact Eliane had chosen it in preference to her suite because the suite was even more expensively appointed. Somehow her earlier refusal to consider the women's demands would have appeared doubly churlish against such a background.

If Eliane had expected a twentieth-century version of a French Revolutionary mob, she was mistaken. The women were quiet, dignified and sensible. Once the two spokeswomen had conquered their initial shyness, they put their case well. Eliane kicked a little, extracted a few reciprocal concessions, like a workers' guarantee to stay for whatever overtime was required as long as they were paid, and reduced the holiday pay in return for providing free holiday accommodation in a seaside hostel to be opened by the company. But these were mere details. The workers had won a resounding victory and they knew it. After an hour they were ushered out, chattering like sparrows in their surprise at Doré's abrupt surrender. They still did not know about her Hollywood assignment.

Emerging from the negotiations, Eliane was almost too angry to speak. Privately she promised herself that the eight women who had conducted the negotiations would not work in the garment trade for much longer. After that, she turned her thoughts to Loulou.

When she had calmed herself sufficiently, she telephoned Geneviève. 'I don't think I can achieve anything by going over this whole mess with the child; it's best that you reassure her and then let it drop. I'll see her at the château this summer – oh, and I've arranged for both of us to receive details of three excellent girls' schools around Geneva. It's high time she was off to one of them. She can go in September.'

Geneviève was horrified. 'But, Eliane, Marie-Louise

has been moping around the place for days, waiting to talk it all over with you. You can't just abandon her now – what will she think?'

'As I'm no expert in the thought processes of eleven-year-old girls, I haven't the faintest idea. Before you start getting too sentimental about her, though, think of what I had to put up with at her age. No one was even prepared to keep a roof over my head, least of all my family. No, Geneviève, you're being too soft with her. A few tears now will toughen her up for later on. Try not to worry. It will sort itself out. I'll be up to see you all in about six weeks.' Before Geneviève could raise further arguments, Eliane hung up.

She felt thoroughly ashamed of herself for once. What she really wanted was to travel to Brittany immediately, take Loulou in her arms and tell her how proud and happy she was to have such a daughter. But between them loomed the spectre of the fashion house lock-out. The sense of humiliation she felt prevented her from seeing that the little girl would probably be delighted she had finally behaved justly. To Eliane, there was never any grace in defeat.

In her anger and frustrations she turned increasingly to Nico Alvarez. He fascinated her, combining as he did talent, sex appeal and intellectual capacity. Others were less charmed by the man. Magda, always ready to blunder in good-naturedly with unwanted insights, was the first to warn her.

'Darling, you were never part of his circle before he went to America. If you had been, you wouldn't go within a mile of him now. He had about a dozen different sorts of nasty reputation – fortune hunting and a taste for kinky sex to name the two most obvious.'

'Rubbish! Why should someone as talented and successful as Nico need to be a fortune hunter?'

'You haven't seen how fast he can run through all that

money he earns. When he left Hollywood he didn't go willingly – they threw him out on his butt.

'He'd got above himself, went crazily over budget on his first directing project, screwed up the film he was put on as art director when they cancelled the one he was directing, and finally insulted the head of production so outrageously that they told him to forget any future in Hollywood movies. I imagine that for old times' sake, the studio boss let him act as messenger boy to you on his way back here to leave him a few rags of pride. Of course, he'd already taken the precaution of marrying an American oil heiress who's set him up in one of the most expensive interior decorating businesses I've ever seen. That one won't starve, but why should you give him a leg up? If you want a boy friend or an intellectual sparring partner, you can have half the rich and clever men in Paris. That one is poison.'

'What if I don't want half the rich and clever men in Paris? Oh, Magda, can't you sense the electricity around him? He gives off sparks. He excites me.'

'Mmm . . . yes, I remember back in the twenties he excited a couple of the best-looking kids in town quite a bit, too, until he showed them what he enjoyed in the way of bedroom romps. I heard that neither of them was ever likely to lose the marks.'

'I don't believe it! He's far too civilised for such nonsense. That sounds to me like the malicious gossip there was after his fashion drawings were published. All the prigs decided he must be depraved because he drew women who looked sensual instead of twee.' She allowed herself a dreamy little smile, 'I should imagine he'd make a very considerate lover.'

'Look, Alouette, he's a bad lot. And when I say that, you know me well enough to realise I know what I'm talking about. Don't touch him.'

That was enough to set Eliane headlong on a path of flirtation with Alvarez. She got up to leave Magda's apartment, saying as she went: 'Never tell me to keep off the grass, Magda. *You* should know *me* well enough by now to understand that will only make me roll around on the lawns stark naked!'

Alvarez was a delightful companion. He had a fund of salacious stories about Hollywood; he was refreshingly open about his stormy relationship with the studio and his abrupt departure; and best of all, his divorce from his heiress came through within a week of his arrival in Paris. He neglected to tell Eliane, or anyone else, that the lavishly appointed shop which was his wife's farewell gift had been more in the nature of a bribe to get rid of him.

Now he courted the couturière with the skill of a hunter after the most elusive quarry. Sensing her sexual nervousness, he tiptoed around that aspect of their relationship. Their physical contact was flirtatious, teasing, in the manner of a sophisticated young playboy encouraging a nubile schoolgirl who was not quite ready for her first lover. The approach captivated Doré, as he had known it would.

Magda had not gone into detail about Alvarez's unsavoury political reputation along with everything else. He preached a peculiar form of intense nationalism that had much in common with fascism but was above all his own creation. It involved championing the traditional role of France as the acme of civilisation, and carried with it a galloping paranoia about the intentions of all other foreign powers – especially Russia, Germany, Britain and the USA. In the 1920s he had spread such views in a periodical called *Marianne*, after the idealised girl who was the traditional French equivalent of Uncle Sam or John Bull. Now he began to persuade Doré to join forces with him to revive the title, which had folded for lack of financial support before he left for America.

Suddenly she developed an interest in politics, though of such a variety that none of her older friends was prepared to discuss her new enthusiasm. In her set, the strange views she picked up from Alvarez appealed only to such survivors of the old nobility as still espoused the most eccentric right-wing views, and even they tended to look away in embarrassment when the subject of the re-launch of *Marianne* arose.

Alvarez would never have succeeded in swaying her from her normal cynical non-involvement, except for one thing. Every cartoon he produced for the dummies of the re-launched periodical featured a pilloried, downtrodden Marianne, representing the spirit of France persecuted by the other European powers and by France's own left-wing politicians. Nico's cartoon Marianne always bore a remarkable resemblance to the young Eliane.

The summer was well advanced by the time Eliane tore herself away from Paris and went to visit Marie-Louise before the girl was sent off to her Swiss boarding school. Geneviève had managed to persuade Doré to send Marie-Louise to the school which offered the best academic education. Once that was settled, Eliane attempted to make amends for her appalling blunder during the seam-stresses' sit-in. But the child had become quiet and with-drawn and it was impossible to know whether any of her conciliatory gestures found their mark.

She was quite relieved when September came. Marie-Louise went to school and she could return to Paris, to Nico Alvarez and her new role as publisher of a political journal.

Magda was beginning to panic about the relationship. She had known Eliane for more than sixteen years now, and believed she had never seen her closer to marriage. Magda possessed the intuitive common sense Eliane had always lacked. God knows, she thought, that one makes enough of her own mistakes in trying to deal with ordinary people. Guided by a maniac like Alvarez, she'd ruin her-self within a year, particularly if he could get his hands on her money.

But Eliane was not listening to Magda or anyone else. The first issue of the re-launched *Marianne* appeared, with the Marianne-Eliane caricature figure nobly defending her innocence in a prisoner's dock, facing an obviously crooked jury which comprised Hitler, Stalin, Mussolini, Roosevelt and Chamberlain. The new magazine attracted plenty of public comment and Eliane cared little that most of it was adverse. At least they were talking about her as some kind of intellectual heavyweight, not just as a couturière who ran a cultural salon on the side. That would be one in the eye for both the Italian and the garment workers' union!

She decided that if Nico proposed, she would marry him. They could be an unbeatable team. This was what she had always needed, a man who appealed to her intellect as well as her emotions. She arranged for him to travel with her to La Madeleine the week after the first issue of *Marianne* was published.

Before they left, Nico threw a post-launch party. He had just made a lot of money out of a big interior decoration job and wanted to show Doré that he, too, knew how to spend. He hired a suite at the Ritz for the occasion. For the first time, Eliane felt slightly uncomfortable with him, largely because some of his guests were so outlandish. Predictably, there was a lavish sprinkling of French, German and Italian fascists. There were also members of the ultra-conservative monarchist group in France, largely made up of aristocrats whose titles pre-dated the 1789 Revolution. Then there were various obscure writers, political theorists and others who supposedly gave Alvarez's views intellectual respectablity. Eliane had met many of them before and individually they had seemed perfectly acceptable. It did not cross her mind that she had never been interested in politics before and therefore had not tuned in to the more extreme aspects of their characters. She was aware, though, that together they all seemed to share a certain chilling intensity. After an hour or two of their company she wished to be gone, but was unsure whether because of boredom or unease. As Nico's hostess, however, she could hardly depart before any of the guests had left. Instead she moved unobtrusively away from the hub of the celebration and eventually sat down in a corner.

'Really, Mademoiselle - don't tell me you find Pierre Laval's view of the future less than captivating?' At that moment, Laval was holding forth about France's glorious non-violent future in the centre of the biggest group of guests.

'Hmm - he gives the Auvergne a bad name. The sooner he's gone, the better!' Then she remembered where she was and the sort of person she was likely to be talking to. For the first time she paid proper attention to the man who had addressed her.

He stood out from the rest of the party as if he had strayed there by mistake. Against him they all began to look a little seedy. The man was around forty years old, unusually tall, with a lean but muscular frame which appeared to have been designed to show off the expensive English worsted suit he wore. He had a smooth, fair-skinned face, bright blue eyes and light blond hair cut in a smooth, unoiled style. Intrigued, Eliane tilted her head and smiled enquiringly.

'Ah, no, we've not been introduced, have we? I am Otto von Schirach, one of the commercial attachés at the German Embassy. And you, of course, are the immortal Mademoiselle Doré - or should I say Marianne?'

Her smile broadened. 'I should have known from those looks you were a member of the Master Race. You must be at the top of the Führer's list for use as propaganda material!'

'I hardly think so, Mademoiselle. I find my country's present methods of self-promotion somewhat, shall we say, strident? I prefer a quieter, more dignified approach to the world.'

He was a marked improvement on anyone else she had met that evening and she stayed with him. Von Schirach seemed determined to avoid the topic of politics and she began to enjoy the sort of lighthearted evening she had been accustomed to before Alvarez had pushed her head first into the political arena. Eventually the random chatter of guests separated them, but von Schirach returned to her side a couple of times during the evening.

Next morning, he telephoned while she was dressing. 'It was wonderful to meet a living legend and find her so much livelier and lovelier than one could hope,' he said. 'I thought perhaps you might let me go on enjoying your company over lunch.'

She was truly sorry she could not accept the invitation. 'I leave for the Riviera this afternoon, Baron. Otherwise I'd be delighted to come.'

'No matter. Perhaps when you return?'

'Perhaps. Although . . . if you're not too busy, you might like to join the party in my house at Roquebrune some time next week?'

'I should love to, but I have to return to Berlin for some meetings in a few days. I hope you'll let me accept the invitation when I return, though.'

'Of course. I look forward to it. And please call me Eliane - Mademoiselle Doré makes me feel like an elderly companion.'

'Very well. I hope you'll call me Otto. Have a good trip. Goodbye for the moment.'

When he had gone, Eliane wondered why she felt a twinge of regret. She shook herself, dismissing the feeling as a childish whim. It was simply that he had represented a return to more frivolous realms than those she was exploring with Nico. 'About time you concentrated on serious matters, my girl,' she muttered.

At La Madeleine she settled down for a holiday spiced by her growing closeness to Nico. So far, he had done nothing more than kiss her, unless one counted the steady flow of seductive talk which he directed at her whenever they were alone together. But she was in no hurry for things to proceed in that direction and was happy merely to flirt with him. Apart from anything else, it enabled her to dismiss Magda's awful warnings about his sexual reputation.

A number of her Parisian friends and business associates

were staying at La Madeleine. As the days passed, luxury and calm worked their magic. The company was entertaining, Nico continued to be charming, and Eliane looked forward to teasing Magda, when she arrived, for crying wolf.

She was surprised one day after lunch when Nico challenged Mikhail Pushkin to a game of tennis. Nico was very fond of his food and wine, smoked heavily and was fifty-three years old. A couple of sets with someone as fit as the twenty-five-year-old dancer might not be a good idea, particularly following the large meal they had just consumed. But Alouette could hardly play the mother hen. Instead she strolled down to the tennis court with one of her female guests to watch the two men. Alvarez was more athletic than he looked and he put up a good show, especially given that his opponent was a professional dancer, almost thirty years younger than he.

As the two players changed ends, Nico walked towards her, grinning broadly. 'See? There's plenty of life in this poor old body!' Then, instead of taking up his position for the third set, he continued to approach the women, smiling in preparation to say something else. Mikhail called out impatiently to him to get back on court, but he merely raised his racket without turning, in a gesture that suggested he had more important matters to deal with.

As he lowered his arm, he suddenly crouched, then doubled over, letting out a harsh groan as he did so. He fell and Mikhail started running towards him, while Eliane and Catherine Duplessis started forward from their own seats. Alvarez's face was blotched and he was sweating profusely.

'Pain . . . terrible pain . . . chest and jaw . . . and my arm . . . aaah!' His disjointed murmuring rose to a pitch of anguish and he jerked forward as another spasm of pain hit him, began vomiting and then lay still.

'Mikhail, Mikhail, what's wrong with him? What the hell is wrong?' Eliane was almost hysterical as Pushkin drew level with them.

He bent over the older man and rested a hand lightly over his chest. Then he knelt hastily beside Alvarez and cleared the vomit from the man's mouth with his fingers. 'Catherine – take Alouette away. Not something you need watch. . . . I think it's his heart, Alouette. I'll try to revive him, but I'm afraid he's had it.'

Catherine Duplessis did not need to struggle with Eliane to draw her away. The sight of the preliminaries of Mikhail's resuscitation attempt were enough. She gagged and turned away and the other woman supported her back to the house. All she could see was that congested, vomiting face translated to her shadowed bedroom. What if they had become lovers, as Magda had feared? He might have been making love to her when that happened. He'd have died on her . . . in her . . . By the time they got to the house, Catherine practically had to carry her.

Catherine sent two servants down to the tennis court, then telephoned Monte Carlo for an ambulance. Nico Alvarez was dead, killed by a massive coronary occlusion, long before the vehicle climbed the steep drive to the house.

Eliane was devastated, not so much by Nico's death but by the manner of his dying. There was too much of the earthy countrywoman in her make-up for her to be overly squeamish about unpleasant sights, but something in the entire episode brought her face to face with the sneering rictus of death – her own inevitable death, not Nico's. The nightmares she suffered in the months that followed were always the same. He was making violent love to her in her darkened bedroom at La Madeleine when he was seized by the fatal attack she had really witnessed on the tennis court. In the dream he died in her embrace and it was as though he were dragging her still living flesh with him to the tomb. Soon she fled the house, unable to bear the memories. She never went back, and the great estate which she had created as her paradise on earth went on the market the following spring.

Back in Paris she was at a loss. She withdrew her backing

from *Marianne*, which promptly folded, and set about severing all connections with the odd people she had met during its brief revival. Then, tentatively at first, she re-emerged into her old circle.

After the first ache of loss had eased, Eliane thought about the handsome German baron who had been her only worthwhile new acquaintance during the interlude with Nico. She made a few desultory enquiries about him but gave up when she was told he had not returned after his trip back to Berlin. Not that it mattered much. Eliane decided that she was better at business than at love. Now she was in her fifties, it was about time she started regarding men as nothing more than friends. It was safer that way. She flung herself into the affairs of her fashion house with greater vigour than ever.

To the public, there seemed to be no change in her way of life. She was still seen at all the most fashionable parties and first nights; still threw her own spectacular entertainments. The difference was that nowadays she was one of a large mixed party or was escorted by a male acquaintance instead of a lover. Her friends noticed and whispered to each other that she was nursing a secret sorrow for Alvarez, pointing out that she had even sold La Madeleine because it was the scene of his death. But she had recovered quickly from everything except the torment inflicted by her own imagination. Soon he was little more than a phantom in her memory, less real than men from whom she had parted much longer ago. A year after the tragedy, Eliane already had difficulty in recalling the details of his face, although she had total recall of Bonnie Charles down to the veins on his hands and the set of his shoulders. From Nico, only the horror of her brush with mortality remained. His face had faded, but the nature of his death still hung sharply defined in her memory.

When Marie-Louise had been at school for a while, Eliane made further attempts to reinstate their relationship, travelling to see her in Switzerland from time to time. The child was easy prey for Eliane's brand of personal magnetism, but their very different ideas for Marie-Louise's future formed a barrier between them.

War had once meant overnight success for Doré, but there was no Bonnie Charles behind her in 1939 to pinpoint the commercial possibilities. Two hours after the declaration of hostilities between France and Germany, the House of Doré was empty. Instead of dismissing it as the inevitable but temporary result of such momentous news, Eliane panicked. Without waiting to discuss the matter with anyone – who would have been able to give her the answers, anyway? – she closed.

She would never admit it, but the closure came almost as a relief. For the past year she had felt less and less equal to competing with Schiffini's apparently effortless expansion into her own fashion territory. The war gave her an opportunity to opt out of the contest. Eliane was never certain how the Italian couturière had gained such an ascendancy. She knew that her own attitude to fashion as something which developed rather than changing each season carried an in-built weakness. Eventually the clients got tired of seeing endless re-workings of the same look. They might pay lip service to her supremacy, but inevitably they wanted something which made them feel young and new and original. Schiffini had absorbed many of the eternal lessons Doré had taught the fashion trade. She took up the simplicity and comfort of unstructured clothes, but she teamed these traits with the use of wild, singing colours, crazy embroidery, and hats that would stop the traffic on the Champs Elysées.

Eliane had spent years trumpeting that such things were mere gimmicks and unworthy of her. Now she could hardly climb down, but she watched with mounting alarm as Schiffini drew a storm of publicity with her gimmicks and went on to use the interest generated by them to sell understated, classical clothing that out-Doréed Doré. By the end of 1938, Eliane was secretly running scared. For once she had put aside the principle of no dramatic changes and launched a collection for summer 1938 which brought to Paris the flamboyance of the flamenco dancer and the bullfighter. Her evening gowns with their cascades of black and white frills exploding at hip level from a slim-fitted maillot-shaped bodice, created an urban version of the gypsy dancer; her jaunty little suits of thigh hugging knee-length pants worn with heavily-embroidered jackets cropped at the waist conjured up pictures of the matador's suit of lights. The look was universally publicised and brought a flood of orders, but it was not mainstream Doré and both Eliane and her long-term clients knew it. She had no idea of where to go from there.

With the outbreak of war, she found her answer – temporary retirement under the cloak of patriotism. A brief announcement was sent to the newspapers but with all the other sensational events of that week, it made no more than a paragraph or two. The Doré boutique remained open to sell perfumes and accessories, but otherwise the fashion house effectively ceased to exist. Eliane withdrew into her suite at the Ritz and devoted herself to gloomy contemplation of the future. For the past two years she had been surrounded by determinedly superficial social butterflies and pessimistic right-wing French nationalists. One group represented the ultimate defeatism; the other refused to think of anything beyond tomorrow afternoon. Now, in her self-imposed solitude, Eliane discovered the superstitious peasant in her was still perilously close to the surface and ready to propel her into flight at a moment's notice.

Edouard was no help, of course. He had salted away that wife and kid of his somewhere impossibly remote and was now preparing to be a hero. Eliane knew the mettle of the French army and had nothing but contempt for it. Instead of feeling pride in her son's patriotic fervour, she despised him for failing to share the mass defeatism which had swept the officer class since war had first come to seem inevitable. Edouard had refused to heed her offer to 'arrange' his departure from the military, and had returned to his post as an officer-instructor in the cavalry school at Saumur. Eliane would have died rather than admit that at least part of her contempt for his stand came from her own memories of the place. She had not admitted the connection for years and Geneviève's death had cut off any direct reminder she might have received of those tough times. Now her son was training a new generation of the very cadets who had introduced her to the demi-monde.

Like a rat in a maze, her mind sought a solution, eliminating dead end after dead end. Those who remained dear to her were scattered beyond reach: Magda visiting New York and unlikely to return while such storm clouds threatened France; the Duke of Conway tucked away on his Scottish estates after Winston Churchill had warned him his pro-Nazi views had no place in London; Georgiana back in England, loyalties to her Italian second husband conveniently shelved. God, had it really come down to this, so few friends that when the stalwarts were scattered, no one remained to her? She realised with dismay that it was true. She had plenty of friends, all right, but they were people like Colombes or Grand Duke Alexis – reeds who would look to her for support, not offer it themselves.

Eventually, having reached the point of despair, she came up with a long-neglected name – Christian de Selincourt. Christi had remained a friend over the years, but he had married eventually and since then they had seen very little of each other. It was not that he thought his wife would resent Eliane, rather that Eliane kept asking herself why he should finally have chosen to marry such an ordinary woman when he could have had her. It was not the sort of attitude which makes for an easy friendship so by 1939 it was more than two years since Eliane had seen de Selincourt. Convincing herself this had been more by oversight than design, she promptly decided to contact him.

'Alouette, darling! God, it's years since we talked. How are you? What are you going to do with yourself while this idiotic business is going on? I see from the papers that you've shut up the business at last!'

'It hardly seemed appropriate to be selling expensive frocks when people's husbands and sons would be dying in next to no time.' It was the first explanation that sprang to mind, but having offered it, Eliane decided she liked the sound of it. Yes, it had the right degree of gallantry and dignity. She'd use it again . . .

'What was that, Christi? Leaving Paris? Well, really I hadn't given it much thought. We have to set some sort of example, don't we? Can't go running off and leaving all the little people trapped here at the first hint of trouble, after all.'

'Come off it, Alouette – I know you, even after all this time. You never gave a shit about the man in the street. Besides, it's not the little people who'll get bashed on the head when the Boches arrive. They'll be out looking for people like us, leaders of Society. Who knows what they'll have lined up for us? It may just be a case of keep your nose clean and we'll ignore you, but they could do anything from confiscating all our property to deporting some of us as a lesson to the rest. They did a lot of that sort of thing in Austria, and Austria joined up with them voluntarily, remember.'

'You don't think we're going to beat them, then?'

'Don't be crazy! Our army was in a hundred times better shape in 1914 and we weren't up to a decisive victory then. This time round they'll force us back beyond Paris within a few months. And what will our skylark do then, poor thing?'

Suddenly she was shy. There was no easy way of telling this man that in spite of all her money and prestige she was as solitary as she had been when he plucked her from behind a Saumur shop counter more than thirty years ago. 'Well . . . my friends are nagging at me to join them in America.' Another lie. Magda was the only friend she had there and such an invitation had never crossed her mind. Eliane swept on: 'But I'm nervous about leaving the business at such an unsettled time. I really must stay in France. I – that is – I wondered what you and your – er – wife were planning to do.'

'Funny you should bring it up now, we were just discussing it.' Only Christian could be naïve enough not to realise that almost every couple in Paris was discussing the immediate future at that moment. 'We've just taken a house close to that place I used to lease at Pau when you and I were together. I bought it in the end, you know, but Caroline doesn't like it so we've moved a couple of miles from there and I'm still looking for a buyer for Les Eyzies. Hey – I don't suppose you . . .?'

Ten days later, Eliane Doré became mistress of Les Eyzies, the house from which she had eloped with Bonnie Charles in 1911. Good connections and black market gasoline had got her to Pau and back in the comfort of her chauffeur-driven limousine. Now that she was not daily confronted with her closed couture house, she was able to convince herself for hours at a time that her life was not totally dislocated by the war. At the back of her mind she nurtured an idea of converting a wing of Les Eyzies to comfortable self-contained family accommodation to which she could lure Edouard's little family, and eventually Edouard himself. All right, so he was dull, but he was her only son and with Loulou at school in Switzerland, her only real family right now. In the meantime, she had a little nest for herself and a friend close at hand, even if he was some other woman's husband.

By the end of October, Eliane was installed in Les Eyzies, along with her inevitable screens and little precious objects. To a woman of her wealth, removal did not entail upheaval; she paid others to smooth away any disruption. To her the major move involved nothing more onerous than going to bed in Paris one evening and in Pau the next. But the disruption in her way of life was another matter. She had chosen to forget the ennui which had made her scheme to opt out of the annual winter exile in Pau during her years with de Selincourt. Within days she was recalling vividly that only the prospect of Bonnie Charles's presence had lured her down there during that final year. It had been suffocatingly provincial even with Christi's local cronies from the horsy world to liven up the duller locals. Now even they were absent.

Eliane rode, went fishing, walked a lot. And in the evening she sat alone with her books, staring into her crackling log fire and wondering why it was so much easier to enjoy solitude in Paris than here.

Gradually she was forced to admit that the sort of solitude she talked about so much in Paris tended to amount to one evening a week alone, or an afternoon spent away from the excitement of the galleries and shops. Here, where true solitude was the norm and an event of any sort a remarkable exception, she learned she was more gregarious than she had chosen to believe. She had assumed she would see a lot of de Selincourt and his wife. Had it been left to them, she would have, but a couple of dinners with them were more than enough for Eliane. Christi huffed and puffed about the political situation, most of his remarks falling into the 'it would never have done in my day' category.

Eliane watched him, aghast. Why, Christi, she thought, you've become an old man in the couple of years since we last met!

Indeed he had. He was in his early sixties but his outlook was that of a man in his mid-seventies. It was as though the eternally irresponsible youth of her own young days had become ancient with no proper middle age to separate the two periods. She was sad but determined not to keep going back to be bored. Caroline de Selincourt was likeable enough, with a cultivated mind and a love of literature and music. But she preferred to pursue these interests for her own amusement, rather than to sit around putting them on public display with the endless discussion indulged in by Eliane and her literary friends in Paris. As far as Eliane was concerned, there was no point in reading a book unless you could be publicly patronising or incisive about it afterwards. No, she concluded as her chauffeur drove her back from the de Selincourt house after their second dinner together, their company most certainly won't keep me happy. I'll have to find someone else.

She made a start next day, taking out her address book and beginning to work through those of her social acquaintances who had still been in Paris when she left. By now there must be plenty of amusing people who'd value a luxurious bolt-hole in the country, with fine food and wine and the only price to provide entertainment for the châtelaine. After all, she couldn't be the only Parisian who didn't want to be trapped there after the inevitable débâcle.

After half a dozen calls, it was dawning on her that no one else appeared to be thinking that way. It was obvious that Paris was changing, but it seemed to be as lively as ever. They were all talking about a brilliant new girl singer called la Môme Piaf who was packing the Elysées Bar every evening; about the odd things the couturiers were doing – Creed turning out perfect miniature fashion collections for evacuee children made from off-cuts of his high fashion fabrics; Molyneux keeping his workers on at slack times to knit for the troops. Eliane was the only one who had closed down and her abrupt departure had amounted to no more than a nine days' wonder.

The streets were full of glamorous young Polish and English servicemen in uniform who added a dash of adventure to daily life, but the non-aggression pact between Hitler and Stalin had secretly convinced many French power-brokers that they too could reach an accommodation with the Führer which would make outright war avoidable. One way and another, Paris at war sounded like more fun than Paris at peace. By the time she talked to Paul Colombes, Eliane was almost weeping with frustration. How insanely stupid she had been to cut and run! Bonnie had always told her she should disregard her impulsive first reaction and act on her second thoughts.

This time she seemed to have ignored his advice with dismal consequences.

'Alouette, dearest! How wonderful to hear from you. When are you coming back, my love? You're missing so much.' Colombes was at his most gushing.

She gritted her teeth and made an effort to sound light-hearted. 'As a matter of fact I was calling to find out if you'd care to come for a nice long stay now I've settled in down here. It's the most perfect hideaway, you know.'

He cut her off with a dismissive laugh. 'Me, leave Paris now? Don't be absurd, it'd cost me my career. The arts have never been more active – the place is bubbling. My advice to you, darling, is to get back here fast and to start having parties again before they forget that Alouette Doré was ever anything more than a scent manufacturer!'

That did it! Colombes was right. She had remained the centre of France's most fashionable social coterie by being everywhere that was anywhere. Memories were short in that section of Society and she was becoming more passé each day. The sooner she got back the better. Eliane wrote a letter to Edouard, telling him she had bought him a lovely house at Pau; that she knew his feelings on the matter but had gone ahead anyway, in case he needed it. Whenever he, Pauline and young Eugène wished to move in it was waiting for them. She had stayed there for a few weeks to make sure everything was as it should be and now, having done all she could for his welfare, she was returning to Paris to see if she could be of some use. . . .

She sat back in satisfaction and re-read the finished letter. It was so good she had already convinced herself that Edouard's future security and comfort had been the real reasons for her exile in Pau. Now, having set things up for him, she was free to return to her natural habitat.

Paris was more exhilarating than she remembered it at any time since the 1920s. Immediately after her return, Eliane attended Noël Coward's special benefit production of *Spring Fever*. She wore gorgeous white silk jersey evening pyjamas under a cashmere evening jacket lined and trimmed with honey-coloured mink. Next morning all the papers featured the autumn look Doré would have launched for Society if the war had not inspired her to close her fashion house. La Grande Mademoiselle had returned.

The strange hot-house life continued throughout the winter and spring. As France's reluctant war effort progressed, the shortages were reflected in the disappearance of coffee and of much of the material the fashion industry had turned into men's and women's clothing. Across the Channel in England, such conditions resulted in drabness and an air of make do and mend. Paris, as always, rose to the occasion, at least when it came to superficialities. The girls in the streets looked as smart as ever, although their fashionable frocks were made of increasingly unlikely materials. Hats became more fantastic each day, partly because the bits and pieces which made them up were not so hard to get; partly because they had escaped the dictates of rationing. Shoes looked like creations from a surrealist's workshop, with manufacturers surmounting the lack of leather by using felt for the uppers and great chunks of sculpted cork of increasingly exaggerated height and shape for the soles. Lack of petrol made non-official cars a rarity and by the spring of 1940 bicycles were the chic form of transport for young and old alike. Dinners in private homes became more fashionable than restaurant parties because the state of war meant that one ate and drank better if one were rich enough to pay black market prices and employ a private cook.

Like many other rich Parisians, Eliane ensured that her chauffeur bought petrol on the black market and that her new cook received sufficient cash to pay the vast prices for unofficial real coffee, good meat and all the other essentials of high living. She had never employed a cook in Paris before, arranging to have food sent in from the Ritz if she was entertaining at the Rue Cambon apartment, but the new arrangement made her table one of the best in the capital. She still wore clothes fashioned from the most expensive fabrics and topped by the rarest furs. When questioned about them she smiled sweetly and said she was having her pre-war wardrobe remodelled to avoid the shortage of materials.

By Easter she and her friends were convinced that the war would fade away into the biggest non-event of the twentieth century. Edouard had paid one visit to the Pau house and had installed his wife and son, but flatly refused to stay himself. He preferred to remain at Saumur, drilling his young officer cadets and secretly helping to train them in dirty fighting techniques passed on by veterans of the civil war in Spain. Whatever his mother and her circle might choose to believe about the prospects of hand-to-hand fighting, he had other ideas.

In mid-April they were shocked at the speed and immediate success of the Germans' invasion of Norway and Denmark, but hastily dismissed it as something too remote to affect France. Perhaps they would have dismissed the invasion of the Low Countries on May 10th, too, but there was no time. On the evening of May 13th, French troops on the Meuse, confronted by a small advance party of General Guderian's panzers, panicked, threw down their guns and ran. Behind their terrified artillery, the French infantrymen fled too. By the next night, Guderian had crossed the river with two of his tank divisions, had swung round and was racing westward towards the sea – or Paris. Neither Eliane nor her friends were reassured by the general's choice of the Channel. They watched in mounting fear as the Germans cornered the British Army and much of the French force, and when the miraculous evacuation of Dunkirk rescued thousands of them beyond all expectation, the Parisians knew they would be the next victims.

At first Eliane was determined she would not panic again. I'm not ending up in that dull little town with egg on my face for a second time in one year, she told herself late one night as she sweated in the dark, wondering what would become of her. But her resistance did not last long. The refugees were straggling through Paris on their way south and west, grim-faced, homeless. Eliane saw her first groups of them in the street one morning and recoiled as if touched by a leper. She rushed home and poured herself a large cognac. She seldom drank spirits but today she could hear her own teeth chattering.

Shakily, she sat down on her big sofa with a second drink and tried to analyse her fear. It was so simple she almost laughed at herself. After so many years of wealth and privilege, the sight of those dispossessed people had taken her back to her orphanage days! Looking at the bleeding feet poking through shoes worn out by days of walking; seeing the pathetic bundles of cloth that contained all the bearer now owned; looking into those eyes which had no home on which to fix, she had tasted convent soup, had smelled the laundry room and felt the despair of the destitute. It was not going to happen to her. Better a fool in Pau than a penniless refugee in the ruins of Paris!

Eliane sent for her chauffeur. 'You've learned how to wring gasoline out of stones in the past few months, Serge. Now's your chance to exercise all your magic powers. We're going to Pau and I don't know how many chances we'll have to refill en route. See what you can do. I shall want to leave at dawn tomorrow.'

He regarded her expressionlessly. 'You think we have a chance of finding any unblocked roads, Mademoiselle?'

She laughed. 'Why do you think you've gone on working for me all these years when the Depression could have bought me any number of servants for less than I paid you? Because you're the best mechanic in the business, and you know side roads that not even the map-makers have discovered yet. Get some rest tonight but make sure you set aside time to plan us a good escape route. Now go – I have plans to make.'

Eliane had intended to dine at the Ritz with Angela Fenwick, an American who had lived in Paris since 1930 and who wrote for a number of US magazines. She telephoned to explain that she was leaving.

'Hey, how would you like some company?' said Angela. 'I'd love to do a feature on what it's like heading south, and if you can put up with me on the road we can travel together.'

Eliane's maid, Marthe, loathed the provinces even more than her employer. Eliane sent for her after making her arrangements with Angela Fenwick. 'I'm leaving town tomorrow, I don't know for how long. Is there any point in asking you to come?'

Marthe glowered. 'Where was Mademoiselle thinking of going?'

'Well, I'm aiming at the house in Pau I bought for my nephew. You know, you quite liked it when you travelled down with me the week I bought it. Of course, I don't know whether we'll manage to get that far with all the problems.'

'Hmm - even if we did, I wouldn't fancy it. Those turnip-bashers couldn't hold an interesting conversation to save their lives. I'd rather stay here and make trouble for the Germans!'

'None of that, Marthe - not when I can hear it, anyway! I'm not interested in wars. You won't come, then?'

'Don't know. I shouldn't think there'll be too many grand ladies looking for maids in the next couple of weeks. I'll have to think of some other way of earning a living if I do stay.'

'Oh, that's no problem. I'll go on paying your wages. After all, I shall be back eventually and I want someone I trust to keep an eye on things. Let's put it this way: if you're not going to lose money by it, do you prefer to come along with me or stay here and guard my personal things?'

'Well, there's no contest, is there, Mademoiselle? I can't manage out of Paris, whoever's in charge here. I stay.'

'Right. I assume that the Germans will take over places

like this when they arrive, so your first job will be to pack up all the personal things I leave here, label my trunks with a suitably impressive warning to leave well alone, and put them into storage in the baggage rooms in the hope that our new masters will have more to do with their time than look through ladies' luggage. After that, I suggest you move in at Rue Cambon. The more I think about it, the happier I am that you want to stay here. We could hardly clear my rooms there, and I'd give a lot more for my chances of hanging on to my screens and things if you're there to stand guard.'

She spent an hour or so allocating various items to different trunks and crates, chose a small collection of clothes and accessories for her exile, then went to bed, leaving Marthe to pack what she planned to take with her.

Angela was staying at the Ritz too, and they had breakfast together in Eliane's suite at 5.30 a.m. 'The Nazis should be proud of themselves,' said Eliane with a sniff. 'They've succeeded where all else has failed, and managed to wake me before dawn for once in my life.'

An hour later, Serge was steering the big car out of Paris. Already, many of the refugees heading south were on the move, walking or riding bicycles. There was even the occasional horse-drawn vehicle. Angela was saddened and felt guilty at their luxurious mode of transport as they passed groups of people laden like donkeys with the few belongings they had saved, or with rags wrapped around their feet because their shoes had given out. 'If only we could let one or two of them in . . .'

Eliane was unmoved. 'Stop the car and open the door and we'd be killed in the rush,' she said. 'Take it from one who once had nothing – the other penniless ones will have the last crust out of your mouth. You stay alive by holding on to what you have.' They did not discuss the matter again.

As the morning wore on the road became increasingly crowded. Serge had warned Eliane that there would be problems whichever route they chose and she had planned their daily mileage accordingly, but it began to look as though she would have to halve the distance she had hoped to cover each day. The people they passed had been walking for anything up to a week. They had no idea where they were bound – except that it must be south, away from the conqueror. They walked the road, slept in the fields, dived for the ditches when planes machine-gunned them. They filled the beautiful French highways that early summer in a huge, sullen, tragic flood, flowing forward slowly but inexorably. And among them, shielded by a huge luxurious car, was a woman whose indifference to their plight was almost as monumental as the struggle itself. To Eliane, the refugees existed only as an obstacle to her speedy passage away from the same threat that drove them.

Eliane had thought she could avoid the worst crowds by travelling down Route N7 and staying at Vichy and Toulouse on the way. Serge agreed that the more direct routes through Bordeaux or Limoges would be completely choked because they ran closer to the west coast and appeared to offer a quicker escape from France. If their thinking had been correct, Eliane reflected, the westerly routes must be completely choked. They finally got to Vichy at almost 10 p.m. Eliane, unaccustomed to being thwarted, was almost spitting with fury. Her temper worsened at the Reception desk in the Hotel du Parc when she realised there was not a room to be had in the whole town.

'We can at least provide dinner in the restaurant, Mademoiselle,' said the manager, impressed by her famous name and silently cursing himself for having parted with the last room to a Dutch diamond merchant an hour before. 'While you eat, I will have the night porter ring every establishment in Vichy and see if we can locate something suitable.'

Realising his good will was all that stood between them and a night in the car, Eliane became suitably charming and swept in to dinner. After a cigarette and a glass of champagne, she became better tempered. Then she started sharpening her claws.

All around them were seated those who had departed Paris early and well-prepared. Before the débâcle of the May invasion, huge picture hats had been the fashion accessory of the season. When the Germans began their drive westward, these were replaced by headscarves as their owners put aside frivolity and prepared for flight. But not these women. The females in the restaurant at the Hotel du Parc looked as though they did not know what war was. They wore their huge hats, gestured grandly with immaculately-manicured nails, laughed a lot and drank a great deal of champagne. At any other time, in any other circumstances, Eliane would have regarded their behaviour as normal. Tonight she felt tired, grubby and an outsider, and she hated them all.

Raising her voice sufficiently for everyone at their end of the room to hear, she said to Angela: 'Well, it's the height of the season, it seems. How lucky we are to have happened by. How fortunate that there is still somewhere to enjoy oneself.'

'What's that supposed to mean?' The question came from a beefy man at a nearby table.

Eliane's smile was pure poison. 'Only that everyone's very gay here and it's quite pleasant. So different from the roads out there with everyone shuffling along on soleless shoes.'

'D'you expect me to go and join them? Just because we managed to get out before the roof fell in, you think we betrayed France!'

'Well, didn't you?'

If his wife had not managed to pacify him, the man would have lunged over to their table for a real row. Angela Fenwick sighed with relief as the woman nervously persuaded him back to his chair and poured more wine for him. 'Alouette, for God's sake – why provoke them? After all, they're hardly doing anything different from us.'

'That's not the point. Who are they to make me an outsider, sitting there with those fat-cat smiles on their stupid bourgeois faces while we don't even have a bed or a bath for the night?'

Angela was beginning to wish she had not made the trip. Alouette Doré in a corner was obviously a lot different from the social *locomotive* who had all Paris at her feet.

The evening was saved by the night porter, who slipped quietly into the room and spoke to Eliane. 'Mademoiselle – I fear there is not an hotel room available in the whole of Vichy, but I have a suggestion which might help if you are really desperate. My brother is in the militia and he is on duty tonight. I have checked with him and he would be honoured if you would care to have his bed. If you do not mind sharing with your friend, it would accommodate you both, perhaps.'

The idea pleased Eliane more than the reality. It was at least thirty years since she had slept anywhere so humble and she was prepared to hate it. But there was a certain flattery implicit in the man's eagerness to help her. She gave him one of her best smiles and he puffed up with pride. At the last minute though she managed to avoid closer acquaintance with the militiaman's quarters thanks to the intervention of one of the restaurant's clients.

'I gather you are experiencing accommodation problems. Permit me to assist – I am the manager of the Hotel Royale across the square.' The man had been sitting at a table beyond the irate guest who had yelled at Eliane and clearly sympathised with her views. Now he had come to join them and gestured kindly but dismissively at the night porter.

'Unfortunately I cannot offer you a proper room – no one in Vichy could do that tonight – but there is an attic where I could have a bed put up. There is room for only one person, but maybe your travelling companion would be able to manage with a reclining chair in the linen room? Neither space has access to good washing accommodation, I'm afraid, you'd have to use the hotel's restaurant washrooms for that.' Accommodation for the chauffeur was not mentioned. It was assumed he would sleep in the car.

Eliane agreed enthusiastically. Better an attic in a proper hotel than a bed in some tinpot cottage. Angela, consigned to the linen room, had other ideas which she kept to herself. But Eliane was content. She purred and flirted with the man, invited him to join them and generally behaved like a débutante on her first date. Angela made an excuse about taking a walk and went out for a while. When she returned, Eliane was alone again, but glowing with satisfaction. She was ready to leave.

'Alouette, surely the offer of an attic for the night can't have improved your temper so greatly?'

'No, but his behaviour did. How old would you say he is? Thirty-five? Forty?'

'Hmm, something like that, I suppose. Why?'

'Well, my dear, he thinks I'm the most beautiful woman he's ever seen and, if I'll share it with him, I can have the best suite in the hotel indefinitely. Not bad for a woman of my advanced years, eh? I turned him down, naturally, so it's the attic after all, but it gave me a splendid boost.'

Christ, the world is falling apart and she can put it out of her mind because some third-rate gigolo in a provincial hotel would like to boast that he's laid Alouette Doré, thought Angela. She's in a class of her own!

That night was hell. After only an hour in her attic, Eliane realised she should have accepted the militiaman's offer. It was very hot. The attic's one window was a tiny glazed skylight and the tiled roof over her sleeping space had absorbed the full heat of the day. Now it combined with the warmth which rose from the hotel beneath to produce a well-nigh unbearable temperature. It was not even possible for Eliane to go and sprawl in a cool bath. Instead she rose about six times during the night and trekked down to the ground floor, where at least the restaurant washroom was cool and spacious. She tried one of the public bathrooms on the way back to her attic, only to find it inhabited by another guest who had been unsuccessful in obtaining a more orthodox bedroom.

By the morning she was ready for a fight. It was

fortunate for the manager who had offered her the little attic that he was not on duty until later, otherwise he would have been quickly disillusioned about the sweet nature of the mature beauty he admired so much. Angela was stiff in every limb, but the prospect of spending the day with Eliane in such a viperish mood was infinitely worse than her aching joints. Fortunately providence intervened in the shape of a call from Eliane's maid in Paris.

Eliane had told her to try the Hotel du Parc on the assumption that they would be staying there. Marthe reached her there because Eliane refused to take breakfast at the Royale after such an uncomfortable night, and went back to the Parc for her croissants and coffee. By now the hotel was buzzing with the gossip that Alouette Doré had been there the previous evening. She was recognised instantly and when the call came a page was sent to summon her from the restaurant.

'Mademoiselle Doré? Marthe here. I thought I'd better let you know. The Boches have moved in –' Eliane winced at the indelicacy of the term at such a time – 'and they've shown no signs of wanting to take over the apartment wing. At present it seems they're content with commandeering the ordinary guest rooms. I don't suppose you'll be interested in coming back, but if you are it looks as though your suite will be okay after all. . . . At least all your nice things should be safe now.'

'Not interested in coming back, Marthe? It's the most interesting suggestion I've heard since I left! Expect me by the end of the week.'

'But, Mademoiselle, you'll hardly have got as far as Pau by then. Are you feeling quite all right? Has the heat affected you?'

'No, but the crowds have. Suddenly I don't feel the need of country air after all. Thanks for calling, Marthe. See you in Paris. Oh, and Marthe – make a couple of tactful enquiries about where we can put Mademoiselle Fenwick if the Germans have taken over her room. She can hardly stay with us, can she?'

Eliane sent a page to find Serge, who was having breakfast at a café, having cleaned himself up at the local barber's shop. He took the news of their proposed turnaround impassively, merely saying: 'Mademoiselle realises, of course, that it will take perhaps twice as long again to get back, given that we're travelling against the traffic this time and that there'll be even more people on the move than yesterday?'

'We'll manage somehow, Serge. Anything's better than sleeping in a hot attic without a bathroom.'

Really? he thought. Perhaps you'd change your mind if you spent a hot summer night in the back of a limousine.

Somehow, Eliane managed to charm a local garage proprietor, introduced by her hotel manager admirer of the previous evening, who was honoured to fill Mademoiselle's car with gasoline and provide an extra ten gallons in cans for only fifteen times the peacetime price. 'Right now I'd pay a hundred times that to get back to Paris, but don't tell him!' Eliane murmured to Angela.

At first their progress through the suburbs of Vichy was not too bad. The people who had stumbled in overnight were just stirring themselves, although it was now late morning. News of the capitulation of Paris two days before had finally seeped through to them. It would galvanise many into a last-minute dash for the coast, but even they were still digesting the news. Doré's party made good use of the lull to clear the streets of Vichy and start north. But once they re-joined the N7 it was bedlam. The traffic heading south had swollen enormously since their journey started and was now augmented by other travellers who, like Eliane, had decided to return home. After an hour they had travelled only a few kilometres and her ill-humour was returning swiftly. Then she had an idea.

'Angela – if you'd booked up to go off for a summer spa cure before wrecking all the good work on the Riviera, would you bother to take it if an invader marched into your country the day before you started?'

'Diets and mud-baths as normal in spite of adversity,

you mean? God, no. If there was one time I'd forget figure control it would be during an invasion.'

'Just what I thought. Well, about twenty kilometres north-west of the main road is a rather pleasant spa town called Bourbon l'Archambault. I spent one of the most comfortable and boring weeks of my life there back in 1930 or '31. This would be the beginning of its high season in normal times and there wouldn't be an unreserved bed in the place. I have a suspicion that some of their customers won't turn up this year. Perhaps we could do worse than try it.' She raised her voice: 'Serge – fork left as soon as you can get off this sewer of a road. I feel in the mood for exploring the countryside.'

The big chauffeur shrugged and did as he was told. Mademoiselle was a capricious old bat at times, but she usually knew what she was doing.

They arrived at Bourbon l'Archambault about four o'clock. Eliane was right. Compared with the places they had been in the past few days, it was a ghost town. The arrival of the limousine acted like a magnet on the locals. 'I feel like the new sheriff in those cowboy movies, who comes to save the place from the bad guys,' said Eliane with a giggle that was almost girlish.

And I feel monumentally relieved that I'm not going to have to cope with another of your temperamental outbursts, thought Angela, for it was clear that the place was as deserted as Eliane had predicted.

They stopped at the first hotel of any size. 'Whatever the accommodation is, we'll take it,' said Eliane, 'as long as it's not an attic and a linen room!' As it happened, the Hotel Archduchesse had rooms with baths for all three of them. This time even Serge was to be rested and refreshed. Angela and Eliane had a glass of wine in the bar before going up for their baths. The hotelier, delighted to have guests at last, recommended the town's best restaurant. He had closed full meal service in his own establishment because the demand was so small.

Eliane had not enjoyed a bath so much since the first

one in old Longchamps' tub when she was a child. 'And it's even better when you don't have to mess around with an old goat afterwards to pay the bill,' she told herself aloud. The bath water was filthy when she got out. She wondered where all the grime and dust could have come from. Her stockings were full of runs and holes and there was a mark on the back of the skirt she had worn ever since leaving Paris. 'Who cares? I'll leave it all behind. Some lucky chamber maid can get it cleaned and boast she owns a Doré original.' The conceit amused her and she dressed in a fresh suit of raw silk, feeling as though she were already back in Paris with all Society at her feet.

At the restaurant, the patron was apologetic. 'I cannot offer you ladies à la carte tonight,' he said. 'What with the war and shortages and this new crisis. . . . there's just the one prix fixe menu, but I assure you it's all fresh and there's plenty of it.'

Eliane was still feeling expansive. 'I'm sure whatever you have will be admirable, M'sieur. Serve away!'

He was staring at her, suddenly fascinated. 'Are you – that is – forgive my impertinence, Mademoiselle, but aren't you Alouette Doré?'

Instantly she was all graciousness, royalty stepping from her throne to receive a loyal subject. She inclined her head. 'I am, M'sieur. I hope that won't prevent you from serving me my dinner!'

'On the contrary. I'm most honoured to meet you. I will ensure you have the best we can offer.' And he bustled away, muttering: 'Such an honour . . . such an honour!'

They started their meal with a hot salad topped with soft-boiled eggs. 'This food is wonderful!' said Angela. 'Who said there was a war on?'

She had not spent much time out of Paris and had virtually no experience of good provincial cooking. The dinner was a revelation. The salad was followed by mountain trout, then by a leg of lamb, studded with garlic cloves and braised in white wine. A feather-light open tart of fresh cherries on top of *crème patissier* completed the meal. They made huge inroads into all of it. Finally Eliane sat back, groaning, over a cognac. 'I've eaten like a ravening wolf and enjoyed every crumb. I suppose I can always tell myself it makes up for what we didn't eat in the past seventy-two hours!'

Angela laughed, somewhat ruefully. 'Best make the most of it now, Alouette. I can't see much more food like this being available now you're an occupied country.' Eliane said nothing, merely looking sidelong at her friend with a cynical smile that suggested she knew better.

They stayed in Bourbon l'Archambault for three days, sending Serge on a reconnaissance trip on the second to check the traffic on the main road. He returned to report that the tide had turned; the flood from the north had almost ceased and the heavier flow was now coming back from the south as people who had panicked at the thought of prolonged fighting acknowledged the Armistice and set off to see if their homes had been looted. Serge felt the movement would have thinned enough by the fourth morning for them to return to Paris in a day's easy drive.

It was late afternoon when they walked into the foyer of the Ritz. The swastika flag of the Nazi régime flew outside. Inside the hotel, though, things seemed much the same. As Doré approached the wrought iron door gates of the Place Vendôme entrance, one of the Ritz's assistant managers saw her, gave a start and shook his head frantically at her, as though signalling her to come no further. She gestured back, with a look that said, All right. If I can't come to you, come to me.

The man hurried out through the arched doorway, very flustered, and said: 'Mademoiselle Doré, are you sure you wish to come in? You – you know that the Occupation Force has taken over the entire hotel?'

'What's that to me? I understand from my maid that they've said they won't need the apartments around my suite.'

'I – er – I don't know about that, but d'you really want to live here with them?'

'As long as they don't want to share my suite, I have no feelings one way or the other about it. Now, shall we go in?'

'You'll have to report to the *Kommandantur,* Mademoiselle Doré. Standing orders. Everyone here who's not part of the Occupation Force must do so immediately upon arrival.'

Eliane gestured at her hair and clothes. 'I've been on the road for nearly a week. I'm filthy. If you think I'm seeing anyone before I've bathed and changed my clothes – and had my hair washed, if I can get my maid round here fast enough – you can think again. What sort of impression will your precious *Kommandant* have of Frenchwomen if I see him like this?'

She swept past the protesting assistant manager and into the lobby, where she realised immediately why he had been so cagey about her entry. Previously invisible within the deep portal were two *Wehrmacht* sentries. On the far side of the lobby was a lone civilian who, in spite of the warmth of the day, wore the soft hat and leather coat now associated throughout Europe with the Gestapo. So the fussy little man had been trying to protect her, to give her a chance of walking away if she had failed to realise before that the Germans were in residence. Very kind of him, but quite unnecessary. She could look after herself. It never entered Eliane's head that the assistant manager had hoped no self-respecting Frenchwoman would want to live at the hotel while it was occupied by an enemy power.

In her suite, nothing appeared changed. Eliane suspected no one had even made a search, which was a promising beginning. The Germans were snobs the same as anyone else, and a lustrous name like her own was worth cultivating, she assumed.

She telephoned her maid, expecting that someone would listen in and not caring. 'Marthe? I'm back at last, round at the Ritz. Yes, please come as soon as possible. I want my hair washed. I shall take a bath while I'm waiting. Please bring that black dinner gown. I see from my wardrobe here that you moved it back to Rue Cambon. Any problems?'

'None, Mademoiselle. Welcome home. I'll be there as soon as I can. I hope you didn't have any . . . trouble.'

'Trouble? Of course not. Why on earth should I have? Come on now, hurry and get that dress ready.'

She hung up and went to run her bath.

At 7 p.m. she arrived at the *Kommandantur*. The outer office was being run by a German woman who was the epitome of what the French would come to know as *Souris Gris*. They were dowdy, forbidding valkyries, with hairy legs, heavy jaws and severe hairstyles. If that's an example of German womanhood abroad, thought Eliane, the French girls will have a ball entertaining the German troops.

The sour-faced secretary said, Yes, the *Kommandant* was still in his office. On announcing Eliane, she discovered he wished to see Mademoiselle Doré at once. Knowing she looked wonderful in her slinky, spangled black dress and her legendary pearls, Eliane made her grand entrance. The *Kommandant* was not alone. A handsome, elegant figure leaned against the fireplace in the big room. It was Otto von Schirach.

He stepped forward. '*Herr Kommandant*, permit me to introduce your charming visitor. This is Mademoiselle Eliane Doré, the couturière. Eliane, may I present General Bernhard Heinlein?'

After the formal introduction, she turned to Otto. 'What a lovely surprise – it's so long since I've seen you! It must be four years since you left Paris.'

'I could hardly have returned to France sooner, given the state of diplomatic relations between our two governments in the last couple of years, could I? But now I hope I'm back for a long, long time.'

Heinlein was standing patiently waiting to claim Eliane's attention. 'Mademoiselle, I had naturally heard you had returned to Paris. I'm delighted you felt sufficiently secure to come back to the Ritz. May I assume you will continue to honour us with your presence?'

She smiled. 'As long as I'm not in the way, Herr General. I'm not planning to give any wild parties or disturb the peace in other ways.'

He managed a small, polite laugh. 'I regret I am unable to enjoy your company for long this evening, although I hope to do so when I am less preoccupied on state business. However, I believe that Baron von Schirach wishes to entertain you, unless you have another engagement?'

She turned to Otto. 'Another engagement, after my travels this past week? All I had in mind was dinner and an early night.'

Otto gave her a teasing smile. 'Well, may I at least share your dinner?'

'With pleasure.' She turned back to the general. 'By the way, what about my travelling companion? She's an American journalist, Angela Fenwick. She was staying here before we left, in one of the rooms which your people have taken over. I've put her up at my apartment in Rue Cambon for the moment, but perhaps she could return here?'

General Heinlein intervened. 'We shall have to see, Mademoiselle. Frankly, I think it unlikely. But I am sure we can offer excellent substitute arrangements for Miss Fenwick if it is not convenient to you for her to stay in your apartment.'

Eliane nodded her thanks. The sooner Angela was out of the apartment the better. She might not live there herself, but she liked to have it available. She had only offered it on this occasion because she had wanted to make her entrance to the Ritz unencumbered by a companion.

They talked of small matters for a few minutes, then the General made his excuses. He had an appointment elsewhere at eight o'clock. Otto escorted her down to the restaurant.

Seated at her old table, Eliane felt as though she had never left – except that the temporary departure and return had brought the bonus of this handsome man to keep her company. She smiled her most beguiling smile.

'So, Otto. Tell me why a humble minor commercial attaché from the old days is suddenly persona grata with the top people and given automatic entry to the best places. Before the war you had to rely on your personal connections for that. Now it seems you have the political clout, too.'

Again he treated her to that private smile. 'You, of all women, know that things are seldom what they seem, Eliane. Commercial attachés have many non-commercial uses.'

'Tell me something else, something more personal. I always meant to ask you before but somehow I didn't get round to it. You are the only person I know who calls me Eliane, not Alouette. Why?'

'What name do you call yourself, privately, inside your head?'

'Eliane.'

'That's your answer. You *are* Eliane, not Alouette. I'm only guessing, but I would think that Alouette was a cheeky nickname given unthinkingly by an irresponsible young man a long time ago. You permitted it to bc uscd because in those days Eliane was someone to be ashamed of. Perhaps she was poor; perhaps she was lonely; probably she was dispossessed, without friends. And Alouette? Oh, she had friends. After all, they named her Alouette, didn't they? Fast friends, useful friends, friends who could give her a good start. So Eliane was locked away and Alouette took the stage. But when Alouette had established the Doré name and reputation, you found her a vulgar memento of a past best forgotten. The trouble was that the fashionable world identified you with that scheming little skylark and you couldn't get rid of her. You tolerated her but she only ever shared your nest. To yourself you were always Eliane. To me you are always

Eliane. You have no need to be anyone else.'

Eliane felt a huge load slipping away, one she had scarcely known she was carrying. He really knew her, well enough to make that observation and to get it right. No one else ever had: not Bonnie, not Jack, not Nico. The next question slipped out almost involuntarily.

'Are you in love with me, Otto?'

'Do you still need to ask?'

'I suppose not, after what you just said. I realised you found me attractive when we met before, but it was so fleeting I'd never considered your feelings might run so deep.' She laughed, suddenly struck by the obvious reason for this oversight. 'Apart from anything else, there's the small matter of age. I must be at least ten years older than you.'

Now it was his turn to laugh. 'And you know without my needing to tell you that you look about twenty years younger than you really are. There is no reason why that should make the smallest difference. You are everything I want, everything I could ever want. It might seem a trifle sudden to you, but I've been carrying it around with me for almost five years, like a primed grenade. Now, Mademoiselle Eliane, it's about to explode.'

She reached for his hand. 'Thank you, Otto. Now I even feel twenty years younger than I am.'

Von Schirach had a suite on the same floor as her own. She wondered whether he would have relinquished it if her reaction to his declaration had been unfavourable. Then she smiled to herself. Hardly! He was an important man in the machine that was running France now. It was far more likely that she would have received her marching orders. So what? Conquerors always got their own way and she found this one extremely diverting.

He spent that night in her suite, but left before Marthe brought her breakfast tray. Eliane awoke alone. There was a note on the pillow beside her. *'I don't think we need make an announcement to the world yet, do you? I'll see you later, I hope. My love, always.'* She tucked the missive inside the drawer of her night table. Quite right. Marthe would guess soon enough, but there was no need to beat her over the head with it. . . .

Over the next few days they laid the foundations of an intense but very private love affair. Eliane was adamant that she would not be seen publicly with von Schirach. It had nothing to do with his nationality and everything to do with his age. 'I've no wish to give my enemies cause to gossip about my being seen out with a man young enough to be my – well, my nephew, if not my son! I may not look my age, but some of them have been around long enough to know how old I am to the month! We're companions within these walls, acquaintances outside. Okay?'

He smiled. 'Whatever you say, my darling. I must say I find it ironic that you're probably the one woman in Paris who won't be seen publicly with a German because of his age. At least it's original!'

Eventually, Eliane decided she could no longer put off getting up to date on the whereabouts of her children. Edouard must be back at Les Eyzies by now with Pauline and Eugène. He'd be wondering why she'd never arrived. Then there was Loulou. She'd been clamouring to come home to Paris since the war started. Now the Armistice had been signed, Eliane thought she might consider it, but not until a few months had passed and enabled her to see how the Occupation worked. She would write to her daughter, but she could telephone Edouard.

It was a long time before Eliane made contact with the Pau estate. The Parisian telephone system was working well but elsewhere the connections were very patchy. Eventually, though, she got through. Fifine, the housekeeper she had engaged before Pauline's arrival, answered the telephone.

'Hello, Fifine, it's Mademoiselle Doré. I'm back in Paris. If M'sieur Edouard has arrived home yet, please put him on.'

'Oh, Mademoiselle, he hasn't! Thank heaven you

called, I'm so worried – I –' She broke off as someone took the telephone from her.

'Hello, Tante Eliane. This is Pauline.' Eliane's heart sank. The voice was dulled with worry – or sorrow.

'What's wrong, Pauline? Where's Edouard?'

'I wish I knew! If only there were some way of finding out, but I just can't get through – I don't know what's going on . . .' The dullness in her voice dissolved and the younger woman was sobbing. 'Oh, God, I'm so afraid, Eliane, so afraid! He said he'd never give in, whatever the politicians did. Said they were betraying France and that we should fight to the last drop of blood, that living under the Nazis was worse than dying bravely, and now I can't contact him – can't even contact Saumur. It's as if someone's put a big black curtain down on them all . . .'

Forcing herself to stay calm, Eliane interrupted her. 'Don't be hysterical! What could be wrong? France surrendered a week ago. There was no fighting along the Loire Valley, was there? The Germans drove the British into the sea around Dunkirk, cut off the remains of the French Army and then advanced to Paris. He was safe from the action down at Saumur. He's probably caught up on the road somewhere between the nearest main railway and you. Stop worrying.'

'Don't be so damned complacent – don't you have any idea what's happened?' This wildness in her normally meek daughter-in-law stopped Eliane in her tracks.

'What are you saying? What do you think is going on?'

'I don't know what they're telling you in Paris, but it's common knowledge down here that plenty of our fighting men refused to recognise the surrender. They fought on – some of them are still fighting.'

'But there was no one for him to fight in Saumur, you silly girl!'

'Don't you dare call me a silly girl! I'm sick of your patronising tone all the time – particularly when you don't know what you're talking about. They held the damned garrison against the Germans, don't you understand?

When the Germans came to take Saumur after the surrender, the cavalry officer cadets held the garrison against them. Edouard is one of the most senior officer-instructors at the cavalry school. Now where do you suppose he'd be if something like that happened?'

Eliane felt faint. 'Oh, no! No! When did you hear about this? How certain are you?'

'I'm certain of nothing! Even this is speculation. I heard a rumour, passed down the line by some good people who want to tell us what's really happening in this poor betrayed country of ours. They say that's what happened in Saumur, but I can't get through and no one will issue papers for me to travel there. The German authorities deny that anything has happened and say it's a temporarily restricted area. But if the people who brought the rumour are right, he's probably dead. They took the garrison a couple of days ago, with no prisoners. Apparently they wanted to show the locals how tough they could be. No survivors is what I heard. Don't try to console me. If you want to do something for me, just use whatever influence you may still have to find out if they got him, then tell me.' Pauline was sobbing wildly now and her impassioned voice tailed off. 'Please, please, just find out and tell me he's all right. I can't live without him. . . .'

Fifine was back on the line. 'Mademoiselle? I think I should hang up now. Madame is very upset. What she told you . . . the men who brought the news seemed very sure. I cannot say more, you understand, I'd better go to her now, but please see if you can find out any more.'

'Yes, Fifine, of course. You go to Madame. I'll ring when I know something. Give Eugène my love.' She hung up.

She brooded about the conversation for more than an hour, then asked the hotel switchboard to obtain Edouard's usual Saumur number. The silence that ensued confirmed her assumption that someone had listened to her conversation with Pauline. Eventually a courteous German voice came on the line.

'Good day, Mademoiselle Doré. Our apologies for the delay, but there is some problem with connections outside Paris. I'm told this is a military number. Could it be that it has been discontinued following the cessation of hostilities?'

Eliane fought to keep her voice calm and as polite as his. 'Possibly, that's what I'm trying to find out. My nephew's wife has just been telling me some confused story of a skirmish down at Saumur and I was concerned for my nephew's safety. I had expected him to be demobilised and back at home in Pau by now.' After all, she thought, if they were eavesdropping, I'm not telling them anything they didn't learn five minutes ago.

There was another long pause, then the silky-voiced German operator was back. 'Mademoiselle, I regret there seems to be a considerable delay. We shall continue to make every effort to trace your nephew – through the German administration at Saumur if we cannot make contact in any other way. If I am unable to reach you in your suite, I shall see that a message is left for you at the *Kommandantur*. Is that satisfactory?'

'Completely, thank you. Please hurry though. My nephew's wife is in a dreadful state.'

'Of course, Mademoiselle. Goodbye.'

Otto brought the answer towards the end of the afternoon.

When she opened her door to him, Eliane knew her worst fears were confirmed. She stood aside mutely and he walked past her into the drawing-room. Without turning to look at her, he said, 'He was your son, not your nephew, I take it?'

'Yes – and you've just told me what I was trying to find out. He's dead.'

Otto turned to face her at last. 'I wish I did not have to tell you this – wish it were not so. But at least you will know the truth this way. I also have permission for you to tell your daughter-in-law. News of the Armistice was circulated to all French military units. They were ordered to lay down their arms – by their own Supreme Command, you understand, not by us. We expected a certain amount of opposition in the circumstances, and we should have known Saumur would be an obvious place. The cream of the Army, cooped up hundreds of miles from the nearest action, unable to express their patriotism in the one way they understood, and all of them young and hot-blooded. Of course there was likely to be trouble.

'The instructors from the cavalry school took charge. The town was a natural strongpoint – that was why it was sited there in the first place, no doubt. They held out for three days and the *Wehrmacht* had to smash the centre of Saumur to pieces to get them out. Too many of them died, including your son. The few survivors are being put into a military prisoner-of-war camp in Germany, but don't hold out any hope to your daughter-in-law. Her husband was one of the dead. In other circumstances he would have been posthumously decorated. I'm sorry, Eliane. I wish more than I can say that I was able to tell you he was safe in a prisoner-of-war camp.'

She turned away from him and walked to the tall windows that overlooked the Place Vendôme. Poor Edouard, the most significant thing about him had been his death. And that wasn't his fault, it was hers. He had never been anything to her but an occasionally amusing pastime. She had been incapable of seeing him as an extension of herself, the way the books said mothers felt about their only sons. She'd done her best for him, but always in a practical, material sense. Now here she was, trying to imagine how Pauline would feel, and failing. She knew that Otto was watching her anxiously, afraid that the news would turn her against him because he was one of the invaders. But he was part of her life, and Edouard never had been.

Deep inside, Eliane hoped no one would ever call her to account for her indifference. Although she felt no guilt at continuing to fraternise with the Germans, she did feel an obscure shame at the absence of guilt. For a moment she was honest with herself and faced the knowledge that if anyone ever confronted her with this monstrous coldness, she would deny it.

But in this one moment she simply did not care, and she knew why. When she was poor and friendless, she had coupled with youths she hardly knew as a way of staying alive. Out of those loveless unions had come a baby – a baby she had not wanted and whom she was ill-equipped to care for. She had handed him over to more prosperous guardians with a sigh of relief, for her own sake as much as for his. That was the truth of her relationship with Edouard, not the later nonsense of treating him like a performing animal or sending him off to school in England. She had been incapable of any emotional link with him because her own emotions had been malformed and stunted before he was ever conceived. Her one regret was that Edouard's adoptive mother had ever contacted her. It would have been better for her son if he had never known his biological mother. Perhaps now he would have been a stolid middle-aged shopkeeper, not a dead hero in an unmarked grave.

Otto was watching her carefully. Now he spoke. 'Do you want me to go, Eliane? I know there's nothing I can do to make this better. Please believe me when I say that no one wishes more than I that this had not happened.'

She turned to face him. If there was anyone she could confide in, at any time, it was this man and now. She began to marshal her thoughts, then stopped. Why? Why tell anyone, ever? The futility of confession overwhelmed her. It achieved nothing. To purge guilt, one had first to feel guilty, and she did not. Since her father abandoned her to Providence and Mother Church, no one had felt any obligation to give up everything for her above all others. Why should she pretend a responsibility she did not feel for life's waifs and strays? She was fifty-five and had always fended for herself with minimal help from the world. Let them do the same.

She looked at Otto with her brightest smile. 'Don't concern yourself. It's not your affair.'

# Chapter Seventeen

## Andy and Marie-Louise

### Extract From Andrea Vincent's Working Diary

*Tuesday August 3rd, 1978*
I never thought that my own mother would feature as a primary source for the Doré biography, but it looks as though she's done a lot of research on the middle years, as well as the parts where she was a central character. She told me about her split with Doré while we were travelling back from Rennes to Paris today. There's nothing I can do here yet, because Doré is still in a light coma. There are signs of her coming out of it and the physician is optimistic about her chances. But how many chances do you have left at ninety-three? We all know she's practically at the end of the road but will she have to endure her last days in a horrible half world, lacking the power of speech or movement, or will she recover sufficiently and last long enough to finish helping prepare her biography, and see it ready for the publisher?

It's rather peculiar: the woman's vitality is so intense that even now we are all sitting here willing her to live, hoping against all reason that she'll recover sufficiently for another few months of relatively comfortable life. One would think we were worrying about a forty-five-year-old rather than a nonogenarian.

Rather than sit here brooding, I'm trying to draft what Marie-Louise has told me as a written narrative. The more I learn about my grandmother, the more inclined I am to try a sort of non-fictional novel as the appropriate form of biography. . . .

* * *

Marie-Louise felt sick with excitement as the train headed back towards Paris. It was hard to imagine the French capital as an occupied city with an enemy army in command. Since 1939, Eliane had refused to allow her to return to France, even in the school holidays, so she had no idea as yet what it was like under wartime conditions.

Serge met her at the Gare de l'Est. 'Mademoiselle is waiting for you, Mademoiselle Loulou. There are guests for dinner this evening, so she was unable to meet you in person.'

Marie-Louise shrugged. 'I don't mind. I suppose it would get you into trouble with Mademoiselle if I asked you to call me Marie-Louise instead of Loulou?'

He smiled at her and nodded almost imperceptibly.

'Okay, Serge. It's not important, anyway. I hope we aren't going to the Ritz.'

He was stony-faced again. 'No, Mademoiselle, Rue Cambon.'

She nodded. From the newspapers she had learned that the Germans had taken over the Ritz. She had been keeping her fingers crossed that her mother was no longer living there but with no high hopes. In fact Doré had moved back to Rue Cambon the previous day to prepare for Marie-Louise's arrival.

The girl was dismayed at the prospect of a dinner party on her first night in Paris. She had planned to discuss her future with Eliane but clearly that was out of the question now.

At Rue Cambon she was shown to one of the guest bedrooms. Marie-Louise was impressed in spite of herself. When Geneviève had brought her to Paris as a child, they had always stayed at the Ritz. She was a stranger to everywhere but the drawing-room in this apartment.

As if the luxurious bedroom were not enough, a dress rail had been brought in, with half a dozen Doré evening dresses hanging on it. Her mother's maid gestured at them. 'Mademoiselle says will you choose something suitable for yourself, Mademoiselle Loulou, as she knows your size but not your taste.'

Given a chance, I'd wear them all at once, thought Marie-

Louise. I wonder how many other sixteen-year-old girls have a choice of six couture gowns for their first grown-up dinner party?

Each dress came complete with matching bag and shoes. A cascade of Doré's celebrated costume jewellery had been left on a lacquered tray on the dressing table.

In the end she did not choose a dress at all. At the end of the rail was the loveliest ensemble of them all – a suit of evening pyjamas in midnight blue silk jersey, with a flower-printed crêpe-de-chine blouse in gold and three different toning shades of blue. Marie-Louise felt as if it had been created for her. It had, although Eliane would never have admitted it.

When Marie-Louise finally walked into the drawing-room, Eliane was standing beside the fireplace, waiting for her with unconcealed curiosity. 'Bravo, Loulou – you chose the right one!' she said. It was the closest she came to a formal greeting.

Oh, God, thought Marie-Louise, she's going to make me compete and perform from the very beginning. Well, at least I cleared the first fence.

Doré was speaking again: 'Come and have some champagne, I think you're old enough now. The others will be here in a few minutes. I thought it would help if I introduced you immediately to some people who might be useful to you.'

'Useful, Aunt Eliane? In what way? You know I want to register at the Sorbonne if they'll have me at my age.'

'Don't be absurd! If you persist in that, you can do it in a couple of years when you're eighteen. Meanwhile you can get to know some really cultivated people. Education doesn't begin and end at university, you know.'

Here we go, thought Marie-Louise. 'Stick with me, kid, and I'll put you in pictures.' More to slow Eliane's galloping monologue than for any other reason, she said: 'I take it you still want me to call you Aunt Eliane. I thought "Maman" might take their breath away rather.'

Eliane flushed and glanced at her sharply. 'If that's

your notion of adult dialogue, I'd stop right there. Irony does nothing for you.'

Marie-Louise returned her look without wavering. 'It was just a straightforward question. We've hardly had sufficient time together for me to find out what you want.'

Eliane was almost intimidated by her daughter. When she thought of herself at sixteen, it was impossible to reconcile that memory with the self-assured young woman Marie-Louise had become. She had been prepared for her daughter's intellectual precocity. She knew from her school reports that the girl was academically exceptional. But she was not ready for such social sophistication. Marie-Louise wore her evening clothes without a trace of self-consciousness, although she had chosen the most extrovert outfit on the rail. She had applied make-up expertly and now she was sparring with Doré without any sign of nervousness. She was also exceptionally beautiful. Eliane was unable to decide whether she loved or hated the girl.

Further confrontation was avoided by the arrival of the first of her guests. Paul Colombes and Mikhail Pushkin arrived at the same time as the Vicomte and Vicomtesse de Terrasson. Jaime Haro, the newspaper columnist, brought a female nightclub singer called Martine. Magda Robles arrived last, with Otto von Schirach.

Marie-Louise went through the ritual of introduction to all these people with a degree of shock. She knew from the anti-collaborationist imported newspaper she read in Geneva that Pushkin, Haro, the Vicomte and his wife were all actively pro-German, and that Paul Colombes regularly appeared at places where prominent Nazis met socially. Magda was apparently non-political – but she had returned to France from a safe haven in America soon after the Armistice so presumably was not anti-German. Marie-Louise had never heard of the nightclub singer but as the girl was with Haro there were no prizes for guessing her views. That left Otto von Schirach – and his allegiances were obvious.

It was a strange evening. The guests were very friendly and Marie-Louise found it easy to keep lightweight conversation going. Eliane made sure that the small talk was steered away from the girl's family background, apart from the initial references to her as Geneviève's adopted daughter.

'Ah yes, your poor mother died two years ago, did she not?' said the Vicomte. 'Such a charming lady. I think the loss of your father was simply too much for her, as she was in delicate health herself. They always seemed so perfectly happy together, she seemed to lose the will to go on without him.'

Marie-Louise murmured a suitably anodyne reply. In her wretchedness when Geneviève had died so soon after Baron Chabrol, she had sought some way of blaming Doré. Had the couturière's cavalier treatment of Marie-Louise hurried Geneviève to her grave? For some months, Marie-Louise had added such a possibility to her list of grievances against Eliane, but when her grief had retreated somewhat, she faced the fact that Geneviève was probably the one person alive for whom Eliane had an unselfish affection. The baronness's death had probably hit Doré as hard as it had her daughter.

The guests passed on to other topics, among them to the round of plays and exhibitions scheduled for the coming season in Paris. Marie-Louise's nimble intelligence allowed her to cope effortlessly with surface conversation, while a deeper layer of attention was devoted to her mother and observing the way she reacted to the others. It was not long before she decided that Doré and von Schirach were involved with each other. She remained outwardly impassive but inside she was going through turmoil.

Since she first began reading adult books, Marie-Louise had reacted instinctively against the ultra-conservatism of her background. Her political thinking had continued to develop along the lines she had first expressed to Eliane in Geneviève's library during the 1936 midinettes' dispute. The grand issues of the Spanish civil war and of the general struggle against fascism and national socialism had carried her away. Now she was in the full flush of youthful left-wing political idealism. Association with people like those seated around Doré's dinner table was anathema to her, and only her innate courtesy prevented her from making a scene.

But there was enough trouble in the offing between her and Doré over what she wanted to do with her life without the complication of a political row. Time enough to argue about the Nazis when she had set up independently of her mother – if she ever wanted to see Doré again after she managed to free herself.

Eliane had no idea of the bombshell her daughter was about to break. Her emotional antennae warned her there was likely to be a row, but she assumed it would stem from Marie-Louise's pent-up resentment at the clumsy way she had been told about her birth, aggravated by a clash of opinion over what she should do with her future. Eliane concentrated on trying to show the girl how entertaining life in Paris could be, and on keeping her exchanges with Otto as few as possible to avoid arousing Marie-Louise's suspicions.

But Eliane was too self-centred for such a delicate task. It had not occurred to her that the last thing a lively, highly educated sixteen-year-old would find entertaining was a table full of middle-aged political extremists and non-participants. She also thought it was enough to keep the width of the table between herself and Otto, and to see that someone else lit her cigarettes.

When the last guests had departed, Otto stayed for a few minutes, talking to her quietly in the vestibule of the apartment. Eliane embraced him and kissed him good night at the moment when Marie-Louise emerged from the drawing-room.

She flushed and retreated. 'Oh – forgive me. I – I thought you'd gone. . . .' It was quite true. They had left the drawing-room at least five minutes before and Otto had already said his good nights.

Eliane sighed in exasperation. 'Oh hell, children! You'd better go and I'll deal with her.'

'Be careful, Eliane. She is not a child any more. She doesn't like you very much and she hates me for reasons I can do nothing about.'

'Nonsense! I'll talk some sense into her. It's about time Loulou learned a little about the realities of this world.'

When she went back into the drawing-room, Marie-Louise was trembling like a nervous woodland animal ready for flight. Doré gestured impatiently at one of the sofas and moved towards the drinks table.

'For heaven's sake, stop flapping about and sit down. You're grown up enough to accept that I get involved with men like any other woman. It's no big deal. Let's have a drink and talk things over.'

Marie-Louise's voice held the flat calm of approaching hysteria. 'I don't want to sit down. I don't want to discuss your sordid collaboration. We have nothing to discuss. I'll sleep here tonight. In the morning I'm leaving.' She made for the door.

'Don't be a damned fool – I'm your legal guardian, remember. If you won't listen to reason, you'll have to do what I tell you! In any case, you'd soon change your tune if I cut off your allowance! I'm your parents' executor. You can't touch any of that inheritance until you're twenty-one.'

Her daughter's laugh was almost a sob. 'Before you become the Great Dictator, think about it! Just try making me stay and see what I tell your fancy friends. They'll know within five minutes that I'm your real daughter – and who my father is. That should take their minds off the latest Paris chit-chat!'

'You wouldn't dare!'

'No? Try me. And forget about the money, Mother dear. You must know I've been seeing my father occasionally in Switzerland. He said you and he talked on the telephone from time to time.'

'Yes, but what has that to do with your financial circumstances?'

'He may not be the world's greatest thinker, but he knows you quite well and he seemed to anticipate you'd try making me do what you want. So just in case, he's given me a trust income: more than I need, actually. Papa can't seem to think in small numbers. Anyway, what he's allowing me would buy me a decent little apartment if I wanted to saddle myself with property, and pay my fees and keep me as a student. And it started six months ago, not on a promise of good behaviour when I'm twenty-one!'

Damn Conway! Damn him, damn him! I might have known he'd blunder into the way somehow. . . . Eliane needed to blame someone and while her mind cast about for an alternative means of holding on to Marie-Louise, she silently cursed the girl's father.

Thwarted, she adopted a conciliatory tone. 'Look, Loulou, I might have over-reacted a little. I was nervous about how you'd take the idea of Otto and me. I wanted us to get on well, not to fight, so I tried to be tactful about it. But I'm not ashamed of our friendship. He's no Nazi but an old-fashioned aristocrat - why, he's half-English, like you, and he was educated in England. You can't believe he's associated with Hitler's mob of thugs.'

'And you can't believe he isn't! Really, I know you're no master of political theory, but you can't seriously imagine that somebody who's here in an official capacity for the Third Reich is just a non-participant, along for the ride! They vet the people they send abroad for everything from Jewishness to the slightest hint of disloyalty to the Führer.'

'I tell you it's not true! He was a friend of mine years ago, when he was just a Paris businessman.' Not quite true, she thought, but it sounds good and he could have been. . . .

Marie-Louise shook her head, an expression of disgust on her face. 'I don't know why you're bothering. You've never caused me anything but misery. Why do you even want to tie me to you? I suppose it's because you'd like someone to control. Well, you picked the wrong one, Mademoiselle Doré. I hate everything about you, and I want nothing from you. Now, if you want to, you can order me out. I'll find somewhere to stay, no doubt. At worst I can go back to Switzerland. Otherwise, I'll stay here overnight and tomorrow I'll leave. I intend to register at the University if they'll have me so young. If they won't, I shall spend the time until I am old enough reading and studying on my own. I might even try to do something for France, to make up for the treachery of you and your kind.'

With that she left the drawing-room. Eliane started after her, in fury and misery. 'You're still a child – you don't know the half of it. If you'll just come and listen to sense. . . .' She drew level with Marie-Louise and plucked at the girl's sleeve as she did so. Marie-Louise broke her grip with such ferocity that the shoulder seam of her jacket split.

'Leave me alone – I understand everything, you old whore! I've found out enough about you since you blabbed about being my mother to know just what you are. All that pretence about making it on your own! You started on your back, and you set yourself up with money you earned like that. Just because you invested it in a business, you think that makes you better than the girls who do it in alley-ways. Well, it doesn't! It makes you just like those old madames who put their savings into respectable restaurants in the provinces – you just put yours into a couture house instead. All you know about is grasping men and money, and trampling anyone who gets in the way. I know you don't care two hoots about politics – all you care about is Alouette Doré! Well, I don't – and now I want to get as far away from you as possible!'

With that, she pulled herself free. The jacket sleeve came away completely. Sobbing, she rushed into her room and slammed the door, locking it behind her.

After a sleepless night, Eliane heard her depart next morning. She made no attempt to stop her.

# Chapter Eighteen

## Doré
## 1944: Eclipse

Otto was finishing his packing when she awoke. Nothing – not even the Nazis' evacuation of Paris – made Eliane lose sleep in the morning. Now she watched impassively from the doorway as he snapped shut the locks on a document case. Seeing her, he smiled with some embarrassment and gestured at the collection of luggage.

'Not a great deal to show for four years of my life, is it?'

She ignored the comment and said, 'What are you going to do? They won't stop chasing you at the French border, and even Germany won't be safe for much longer.'

That amused him. 'Dr Goebbels may be prepared to die at his Führer's side. I have other ideas. I shall return to Berlin now, naturally – I am a loyal German. But once hostilities end I'll consider my duty done. I made arrangements a long time ago in case something like this should happen. The Allies are not going to take their revenge on me.'

He came to join her at the door, took her hand and raised it briefly to his lips. 'The trouble is, my enchantress, that I have no desire to go anywhere without you. My plans include both of us. Are you coming with me today?'

Momentarily she was troubled, appearing scarcely to understand what he meant. When she finally spoke, it was with an air of bewilderment. 'Coming, Otto? But where? The Allies will have all France within weeks. There *is* nowhere to go.'

'There are other countries than your lovely France, my dear. For the moment, there is Germany. Then, eventually, it will be somewhere in South America, or possibly Portugal or Spain. Does it matter, so long as we are together?'

'Yes, Otto, it matters. And it would matter more every day, once we had run away. I've loved you for years, but for years I've designed nothing. My fingers itch for the feel of pins and scissors. Without my work I should die of futility. I closed the salon because I would not work with the shortages the war was bound to cause. Now it's coming to an end and you're suggesting I move away from the one place in the world where my work is fully valued. Do you seriously think a couturière of my standing could re-launch from Lisbon or Rio? Paris would laugh me out of existence!'

Von Schirach was gazing at her with mounting incredulity. 'My dear Alouette, do you think you'll ever be allowed to run a fashion house in Paris again? You were on the losing side, remember? You'll be lucky to save your neck, let alone your business!'

'I'm not afraid of that Communist rabble –' she gestured contemptuously towards the street below – 'they wouldn't dare lay hands on me.'

'I think you'll find you're wrong on that score. If you stay here, at the very least you'll be used as a scapegoat for a lot of others who welcomed us. At worst, the mob might reach you before the military. If they do, I don't think you'll get through alive. Please, my love, cut your losses and come with me now. I have to leave with the General Staff in an hour.'

She turned from him wordlessly and went back into the bedroom. There she sat before the triple mirrors on the dressing table, searching her own triplicate reflection for an answer to the dilemma. In all honesty, there *was* no dilemma. Otto was handsome, cultivated and charming. She loved him enough to spend many more years with him. But when he was weighed against her need to re-start the couture house, he came a hopeless second. As she sat there brooding, von Schirach quietly came into the room.

Eliane pushed back her chair, rose and folded the hinged side mirrors across the central glass, as though shutting up an icon. Then she turned to face him.

'I'm sorry, Otto. You go alone.'

There were tears in his eyes, but he shrugged with painful nonchalance. 'Then you're dead, my darling. If you change your mind I shall be downstairs for at least three-quarters of an hour. Someone will fetch my luggage soon. Try to keep yourself safe.'

He left. Somehow a kiss would have been inappropriate to their parting.

After two soldiers had come and gone with von Schirach's luggage, Eliane went to the tall window which overlooked the Place Vendôme from the suite's sitting room. Below her, all was bustle. Officers hurried to and fro, briefing dispatch riders, allocating car space and generally preparing to make the débâcle of their retreat as dignified as possible. Eventually, the big armoured Mercedes saloons began to leave in twos and threes. Otto von Schirach came to stand outside the hotel's main entrance. Twice he gestured to his driver to delay a few minutes more. Then a senior SS officer approached, they spoke, and von Schirach finally moved towards his car. As it swept out of the Place, he raised his hand in a final salute to the woman who stood concealed by the fine white mesh of the Ritz's curtains. After the last of the cars had gone, it was as quiet as a country village on a summer afternoon. Eliane opened a book and sat down to her pretence of reading. She had no idea what was going on all over Paris. She knew it was self-imposed ignorance because the radio would be broadcasting some sort of account of events, but whatever they broadcast would be of little interest to her now. Eliane was attempting belatedly to follow Bonnie Charles's advice: reject your first panic-stricken reaction, give yourself time to analyse the real situation, then act in such a way that your own interests will be best served. The volume about Richelieu was for form's sake, she had not taken in a word of the text. She was seeking salvation and it was elusive.

Even after she had conquered her panic, Eliane recognised she was in trouble. She had been visibly involved with a senior Nazi for four years. In her favour, she could prove she had retained her financial independence, and it was a fact that she had been the first couturière to close down when war was declared. Had she gone on trading during the Occupation, many of her customers would have been German. A faint glimmer of hope began to warm her. Perhaps she had a chance after all . . .

But Eliane was a past master of the value of propaganda. She knew the greatest threat came from intangibles – she was a glamorous, immensely conspicuous target with enemies even within her own circle, and the people who were being liberated today in Paris would want some famous heads to stick on spikes. She would make an illustrious corpse and there would be plenty of people willing to hand her over. On the other hand, there were an awful lot of celebrities to choose from if one wanted well-known Parisian traitors. Throughout the Occupation, couturiers had sewn for the Germans; film and theatre actors had staged their most celebrated performances; ballerinas had cavorted and orchestras had made music. Most of fashionable Paris had gone on singing and dancing without pause. Would all of them now be prosecuted?

Eliane's mind went round and round the subject for most of that night. Somewhere along the way she checked on practicalities with the Ritz's manager, inviting him to join her for dinner. He was clearly ill at ease, but he had made a profession of courteous service to the rich for so long that refusal would have been unthinkable to him.

He told her that although the administrative top brass and most of the senior military had now left Paris, there were pockets of *Wehrmacht* all over the city, many prepared to fight to the death for the Führer, many more with little choice in the matter. There was likely to be skirmishing for some days. The Allies were close to Paris but there was talk of the German military commander having made some sort of secret deal to pull out quietly rather than let Paris be destroyed by heavy fighting or blown to pieces as Hitler had ordered. Whatever the truth of the matter, it seemed the capital was temporarily an open city.

Pouring champagne for Eliane, he said: 'I have no wish to interfere with your plans, Mademoiselle, but might it not be prudent for you to leave quietly while things are so chaotic? It's true you will run a risk if the Resistance stops you, but frankly I think they'll be too busy picking off Germans to prevent you going anywhere if your papers are in order. For a few days, at least, I think they'll put off arresting French civilians and concentrate on taking control of the city first.'

Eliane laughed. 'If I'd been planning to leave, I'd have gone with Baron von Schirach and travelled first class all the way to Berlin. No, M'sieur, I'm a Parisian. If I left now, it would be for good. I plan to re-open the business again once all this nonsense is over. To do that I have to be here in Paris.' The confident sound of her own words surprised her. 'Anyway, you're not preparing to escape and you've been waiting on the Germans hand and foot for the past four years. I'd have thought you'd be one of the first the Resistance would come looking for.'

His smile was unreadable. 'No, Mademoiselle, they look after their own. I have remained at my post for the last four years for one reason only – it was where I could be of most use to my country. And now I think perhaps I had better get back to work. There is much to be done.'

He rose and went to the door, turning back to her briefly as he reached it. 'You are safe from betrayal by me, Mademoiselle Doré, but I cannot guarantee my staff. Many of them work for the Underground and many more who do not are seeking ways to ingratiate themselves now the Nazis have gone. Take care. If the authorities get you, it will be merely unpleasant, but if the mob find you first it could be fatal. Good night.' The door closed silently behind him.

Eliane finished the bottle of champagne, then prepared for bed. In the night she heard the distant rattle of gunfire as the battle for the streets began.

Throughout the days of late August, Doré stayed in her suite. She watched from behind her drawing-room curtains as the Americans arrived in the Place Vendôme, a group of war correspondents among them. Perhaps now she was safe. The manager called to see her again and she broached the subject.

'I'm not afraid of official justice; I've done nothing wrong. What bothers me is the chance that I'll be cornered by the rabble. Surely now that the Americans are here – especially those reporters – I'll be safe from personal attack?'

'It's impossible to say, Mademoiselle. Collaborators are still being rounded up in the streets and some of them are beaten up before they're handed over to the authorities. I confess that it sickens me. We should be preparing to live together in peace, now, not starting new enmities. Unfortunately not everyone thinks as I do and for the time being I think you are safer in your suite. You still run the risk of being arrested, but if you are in your rooms they will simply take you away to the Conciergerie without any sort of impropriety.'

'Hmm – what a prospect. If I'm a good girl I get a safe conduct to the dungeons!'

The manager shrugged. 'I'm afraid that's the best advice I can offer, Mademoiselle. I'm sure the presence of a few American journalists at the Ritz will not guarantee your safety if you appear in public.'

But Eliane was beginning to find the solitude unendurable. She had tried to reach Paul Colombes, Jaime Haro and a couple of other friends who had remained in Paris and worked under the Nazis. None of them answered their telephones and she assumed they had been arrested. They were as unlikely as she to flee Paris. To her own surprise, she was also anxious about Loulou. Eliane kept telling herself that she and her daughter had ceased to exist for each other when Loulou became aware of her relationship with von Schirach. She would never forget or forgive the things Loulou had said that day. But still, the girl was barely twenty even now. How was she managing? Was she even alive? Given the views she had expressed when they parted company, she was probably up to her eyes in the Resistance. Doré was determined to try and locate her. But for that she needed help and she was unlikely to find it within this room. She would have to venture out soon.

That afternoon she received a note. It seemed the manager was sincere in his desire to ensure she emerged unscathed. He had located Angela Fenwick, the American journalist who had joined Eliane on her abortive journey south after the fall of France. Angela had left the country when America entered the war. Now she was back as one of the US correspondents and the manager, recognising her as Eliane's one-time travelling companion, had told her the couturière was in hiding at the Ritz. Angela's note said: *'Darling – I smell a story. Can I do anything to help? Love from the Press.'*

'Well, my dear,' Eliane said aloud, 'for a start you can contact the Duke of Conway in England.'

She ventured out to meet Angela, rejecting the manager's suggestion that they lunch in her suite. They ate at Eliane's old table in the restaurant. Eliane compromised on her initial adamant refusal to discuss the Occupation by offering a non-attributable account of what it had been like to resume normal life in Paris after the coming of the Germans. After all, she had to offer something in return for Angela's contacting Jack Granchester.

In the end the price was higher than she had anticipated. As Eliane left the restaurant, she narrowly avoided bumping into a woman dressed in the uniform of a junior housekeeper. The incident occurred only because the woman had stopped to stare at her. Eliane stepped aside, glared back and hurried towards the lift. Now she had finally emerged from her suite, she was going to get out and start living again. And first she would locate Loulou. Back in her bedroom, she changed her clothes, then returned to the foyer, all the time vaguely disturbed by a feeling that she had met the housekeeper before. But that was absurd – she simply never had anything to do with the Ritz's junior domestic staff.

As she re-crossed the foyer and emerged into the afternoon sunlight, she remembered. Of course! The woman hadn't always been a hotel housekeeper. In 1936 she had been a junior seamstress at the Rue Cambon, and a garment workers' union organiser into the bargain. She had been one of the strike committee with whom Doré had eventually been forced to settle. Still, they had lost in the end. By 1939, Eliane had ensured that not a single one of the ringleaders remained on her staff. . . . As the significance of the woman's identity dawned on her, a man and a girl fell into step on either side of Eliane.

'Not so fast, Mademoiselle. You're not going anywhere yet,' said the man, gripping her elbow and turning her back towards the hotel entrance.

'Get your hands off me! I go where I please.'

'Not any more, you don't,' said the girl. 'You have a business appointment with us, and then there are a few people down at the Conciergerie who'd appreciate a little chat. Come on, girls – we've got her!' She raised her voice on the last words and four other women moved to join her. One of them was the ex-seamstress. They formed a tight group around Eliane and forced her back inside the hotel. Was it coincidence or self-protection which ensured that for the first time Eliane would recall, there was no one at the Ritz's Reception desk?

'I know her suite number,' said Annette, the housekeeper, and got the keys from the board. They thrust Eliane into the lift and took her back to her suite. Inside the drawing-room, Eliane made a dash for the telephone, but the young woman snatched the receiver from her with one hand and struck her sharply across the face with the other. 'None of that, you treacherous bitch. Sit on that chair - now - or I'll really slap you around!'

Eliane thrust past her angrily and sat down. She faced her captors, fury displacing all fear. 'When you've finished playing your childish game of cops and robbers, perhaps we can go down to the Conciergerie and get this farce over and done with.'

'Not so fast, Your Ladyship!' It was ex-seamstress again. 'You two - tie her arms. We're going to give you a little token of our appreciation first, Mademoiselle.'

As her accomplices tied Eliane roughly to the chair, the woman produced an outsize pair of dressmaking shears and a set of barber's clippers. 'We're going to give you the style all Paris is talking about - *La Collaboratrice!*'

Eliane's courage collapsed. She was back in a Breton fairground tent, aged thirteen, the prisoner of a country barber. The one thing that could reduce her to gibbering incoherence, and they'd happened on it! She let out a shriek of protest and attempted to overturn the chair, but the man steadied it.

'You damned whore, we'll show you who's in charge now!' The former seamstress bent close to Eliane, her breath sour in the couturière's nostrils. She was panting with excitement and a sheen of sweat coated her thin face. 'Just keep still, or you'll lose an ear as well as your hair.'

The clippers churned against Eliane's scalp and the hair fell in hanks on the pale, sun-dappled carpet. She fought hysteria, nausea and faintness. She must not lose control in front of this trash! Her pride was all she had left. But mentally she was wearing sabots and a sacking apron, and feeling herself count for nothing. Her dignity was disappearing along with her hair.

At that point the door burst open and a female voice yelled: 'Stop that this minute - you're as bad as the damned Gestapo!'

Eliane was positioned with her back to the door so was unable to see the intruders. Whoever they were, they seemed to have authority. Maybe Reverend Mother . . .?

She shook her head, desperately trying to clear it. No, no . . . that was the other time, and then no one had helped. Now help was at hand, but too late, too late. . . . Her pride and freedom were lying in little curls on the carpet. They couldn't stick it back . . .

She was drifting in a shadowy half world, but she became aware that her persecutors' first shouts of protest had been silenced by the newcomer's air of authority. They stopped, work of destruction half completed, and stood sullenly around Eliane's sagging figure.

'We have a proper warrant for Mademoiselle Doré to attend the Conciergerie for questioning and we'll escort her there. Now, get out!' This time it was a man's voice.

Protesting again, the group began to leave. As the last of them passed from the room, her rescuers came into her field of vision. The woman was Loulou. She knelt beside her mother, tears running down her cheeks. 'Oh, Doré, what have they done to you?'

Eliane made a superhuman effort to snap back from the dark places into which she had been slipping. 'Nothing that can't be mended, thanks to your timely arrival. Untie me and let's see how much damage they managed to do.'

Loulou freed her with shaking hands, then paused. 'Mama – are you sure you want . . .?'

'If the world is about to see me like this, I'd better find out what a treat they're in for. If you daren't show me, I'll look for myself.'

Stumbling slightly, she rose and moved into the bedroom where she looked at herself in the triple mirror. What she saw nearly unhinged her completely. Only one hank of hair remained, hanging drunkenly askew from her left temple. A trickle of blood was coursing down her cheek where the seamstress had nicked her, startled by Loulou's arrival. The rest of her head was nothing but uneven grey-black stubble. Her skull appeared to have shrunk to the size of a pin, with two great burning eyes staring crazily from an ancient, lined face. It seemed that Eliane had graduated from maturity to senility in a few moments of physical abuse. Lunging forward on her stool, she crashed the side mirrors shut over the central glass, leaned over until her face touched the surface of the dressing table and howled in anguish. 'Why, oh why, didn't they just kill me and have done with it?'

Loulou, who had followed her into the bedroom, cradled her like a child. 'Come on, Mama, it'll grow again. We'll find something to cover your head decently and then go to the Conciergerie.'

That only provoked a fresh storm of weeping. 'Go out like this? I couldn't! You can cover my head, but what can cover my face? Nothing will get rid of that look; it's as if I've had a stroke. . . .'

'Mama, you have no choice. We really do have a warrant. I've known for days that you were here, the manager told me. He asked me to watch over you until something was sorted out. You'd never have seen me if these rats hadn't sniffed you out. I was hoping you'd decide to go off to Switzerland for a long rest before they wised up to your being here. But now the news is out, the Conciergerie really is the safest place for you. That bunch will be back, if I know their sort, with more helpers than Pierre and I could control. And believe me, they wouldn't let you go quietly with a scarf to hide your shame!'

Loulou glanced over at her companion, as if for corroboration. 'She's right, Mademoiselle. Even the normal arrests can be a problem if people find out we're bringing in a celebrity. If you let us take you now, we have a closed car round at the back. I think the manager can arrange an unobtrusive coat or something, and with that and a quiet arrival, we should get you in there with a minimum of fuss.'

The man was talking sense. Even in her numb state, Eliane could see he was smothering his personal feelings about her in deference to Loulou. He seemed okay. The kid was in good hands.

'All right, I'll come along in disguise – not that anyone would recognise this old hag as Alouette Doré, anyway.'

Ten minutes later, wearing a maid's cheap lightweight topcoat, her shaven head wrapped in two heavy silk scarves bulked as high as possible to conceal the lack of hair underneath, Eliane slipped through the staff entrance and into an anonymous saloon car outside. The absence of weapons and the concern shown her by her two escorts misled the crowd waiting at the Conciergerie and they assumed she was a witness attending an identity parade. Eliane realised her good fortune when a van full of male detainees trundled to a halt seconds behind them. The men, who were cooped inside the van in locked cages too cramped for proper sitting or standing, were chivvied down into the forecourt with blows from rifle butts to their legs and backs. Members of the crowd managed to discharge the odd kick or punch against those who stumbled near them. One woman spat full in the face of a well-known stage actor whom Eliane had seen perform many times. She shrank against Loulou, afraid he would recognise her. But the man stared at her blankly and she realised that right now she bore no resemblance to the Alouette he knew from theatrical parties.

Inside the Conciergerie, Eliane's papers were processed and a formal holding charge of outraging public morality recorded. She turned back to Loulou, helpless in the face of such organised hostility.

'What now?'

'I'm afraid they'll lock you up, Mama, for a day or two at least. It's not as bad as it seems. The cells are clean and you can receive parcels of food from outside. I'll arrange that through your friends, if you like.'

Eliane nodded silently. A woman came to lead her away. Loulou, clearly a favoured operator, stayed with her as they moved along a dank corridor. 'May I spend a few minutes with my mother?' she asked the wardress.

'Yes, but no more, Mademoiselle. You know how strict they are.' She withdrew and Loulou turned to her mother urgently.

'Now listen carefully, Doré, so you won't be scared or

worried at what happens to you. When they have the next big group of prisoners together, they'll either take you off to the *Vélodrome d'Hiver* for a few days, or direct to the transit prison.' Here she hesitated.

'Where's that?'

'I – it – it's at Drancy.'

'Drancy? But that's where they used to put the Jews en route to Auschwitz and Buchenwald! My God, what are they going to do?'

Loulou stiffened. 'So you knew about Auschwitz and Buchenwald! I was hoping your lack of interest in anything outside yourself meant that at least only ignorance tied you to those pigs. It looks as if you knew pretty well what they were doing!'

'I hadn't the least idea what they were doing but I did know they shipped out people they didn't like – Jews and Communists and so on. And I knew they went to camps somewhere in the East, and the names of some of them. It wasn't my world, Loulou. I didn't make it and I couldn't have altered it. I just wanted to live my life as quietly as possible. It wasn't my affair, that's all.'

Her daughter was rising to go. 'I have to help you. I love you in spite of what you are. But that doesn't mean I have to like or understand you. I don't. Just don't be frightened at Drancy. They won't be using your precious skin to make soap!'

She turned and left. The door was closed and locked behind her.

The next couple of days passed in a cloud of misery for Eliane. On the second morning, Marguerite Ivry, a well-known cabaret singer, was pushed into the cell with her. She was back at the Conciergerie after a spell in the *Vélodrome d'Hiver,* Paris's big indoor bicycle stadium.

'I think they're using it deliberately to frighten us,' she whispered. 'The police used it as a transit camp when they rounded up all the Jews in '42. There are thousands of supposed collaborators crammed in there now. I actually saw Sacha Guitry in the men's side, wearing a Panama hat and pyjamas, of all things! The poor man had obviously been knocked about.'

'How come you're back here so soon then? I thought it was next stop, Drancy after the *Vélodrome*.'

Marguerite shuddered. 'They have their doubts about me, that's all. I was denounced by a bitch who used to top the bill at *Les Trois Chats* before I got the star spot. She's saying it was because I had a Nazi boyfriend who ordered the manager to take me on. It was a lie – though I did have a German boyfriend – and now they might just let me go and forget the whole thing.'

'Lucky you. I think they'll throw away the key over me.'

'Why, darling, who are you?'

There it was again. A week ago there wouldn't have been a woman in Paris – or many men – who failed to recognise Alouette Doré immediately. So far it had occurred to no one to connect this shrivelled old woman with the couturière. Let's keep it that way, she thought. 'Oh, just a dressmaker who chose the wrong way to stay alive during the Occupation.'

The singer was content with the story and chattered away inconsequentially for the next couple of hours. At noon the cell was unlocked again. Eliane held her breath momentarily in case the wardress gave away her name. But the woman might have been working for her. She merely jerked her head in Eliane's direction and said, 'You – come on. Time to move on.'

Eliane followed her out through a gloomy hallway beyond the cell corridor and through into a rear yard. 'Just as well for you that your daughter's such a good girl,' said the woman. 'If you think you've had it tough, you should see what's happened to some of your lot when they came in publicly through the crowd out front.'

In the yard another unmarked car waited, driven by the man who had helped Loulou bring her in. The wardress hustled her into the front passenger seat, slammed the door and locked it from the outside. Eliane noticed the inside door handle had been removed. The car slid away under a high archway and into an alley, turning away from the front of the building where they could hear the usual crowd baying at some new arrivals.

They drove in silence for some time, then Pierre said, 'You're going to Drancy, in case you were wondering. The *Vélodrome* is full to the brim right now.'

'H-how long am I likely to be there?'

'Don't worry, it's not equipped with gas chambers!' His voice oozed the contempt he had suppressed in front of Loulou. 'We only use it for short-term transit, although some people won't be out this side of Christmas. Normally you get a hearing within a fortnight and then go on trial. Unless you get off, you serve your sentence in Fresnes Prison.'

'Prison? But that's absurd! I've done nothing wrong. . . .'

'Nothing beyond betraying your country! Such a trivial matter, eh?'

'I don't involve myself in schoolboy heroics.'

'Ah, that explains why you didn't let your son's heroic death stop you screwing a representative of the prople who killed him, practically while he was dying for his country.'

She was trembling violently. 'I'd have stopped Edouard if I'd had any idea what he planned. But he wouldn't even listen to his wife when she tried. He insisted on going on with it. I took care of his family - still do - and I couldn't stop living my life just because he had, could I?'

'Other mothers have been known to do so. Other mothers have also been known to help their countrymen to throw out the invaders by working secretly against them. Even if they're too scared for that, other mothers have withdrawn to the country out of the enemy's way, so they won't need to have any contact with them. You seem to have rushed into Hitler's arms crying "My hero"!'

'Don't be so damned pious. I never went anywhere near Hitler.'

'No, only his head of French propaganda. And by

Christ, you helped his cause by being seen all over the place with high-ranking Nazis and French traitors like Laval. You couldn't have done more damage if you *had* met Hitler.'

She was fighting back the tears, conscious that a few shreds of self-control were all she had left. 'Okay, knight in white armour – if I'm such an ogre, why has my daughter attempted to make things easier for me?'

'God knows! I wish she'd let the mob shave you from head to toe and tattoo your face with swastikas. Because she's one hell of a girl, I suppose.'

Anger swamped Doré's misery and she turned on him. 'That's enough, you bastard! Thousands of people did worse than me and they're walking around loose because they were less well-known than I am. Why should my daughter reject her mother on the strength of that?'

'I'll tell you why, you old bitch! Because she's in love with an English airman she met when he was passed down the line through us. He stuck around as part of the Resistance after a foul-up left us too short of trained men to go on. The Germans got him and because he'd chucked away his RAF uniform when he teamed up with us, they practically took him apart before they shipped him off to Germany. If he's still alive he'll never be much use for anything after the war – and your naughty little girl is having his baby!'

Eliane gripped the dashboard until her knuckles whitened. What would she have done if it had been her and Bonnie? Simple – she would have killed any member of her family who went anywhere near the enemy. Her daughter had swallowed all the hate and despair she must have been feeling and had rescued her from the tightest corner she had ever been in. For the first time ever, Eliane wished herself dead. This was a shame she must always carry. There would never be anyone she could tell.

Pierre drove on in silence, ignoring her abject misery. Realisation penetrated her self-preoccupation. 'You love her yourself, don't you?'

'Of course. I'd do anything for her, go anywhere. But I'm not the one she wants. It's Teddy Vincent or nobody for Marie-Louise, and if she can't have him she prefers to be alone. Ah, at last. Here we are at your country mansion, Mademoiselle.' He swung the wheel savagely and brought the vehicle to a halt outside the gates of Drancy.

The Drancy complex had started life as low-rent accommodation for working-class families in a dowdy northern suburb of Paris. Later it was turned over for use as police barracks and later still achieved notoriety as the collection point for Jews en route for the extermination camps in Germany and Poland. Now the fourteen-storey blocks were the temporary home of Parisians accused of collaboration. Its sinister reputation had prepared Eliane for something far worse. It was dowdy and run-down, but there were common rooms as well as cells, and outside there were scrappy areas of green where the internees could walk. The interior walls were whitewashed and bay windows gave an open view across the compound.

It was still only a matter of days since the last groups of Jewish prisoners had been freed. Eliane was put into a room where much of the furniture had been overturned, as though abandoned in haste. In the corner were broken pieces of bric-a-brac. Still sick at heart from what Pierre Fouquet had told her about Loulou, she straightened one of the rickety chairs and sat down wearily, trying to blank it all out. Her glance moved over the shabby interior, seeing nothing to command her attention until she noticed splashes of yellow like autumn leaves over by the window. Intrigued in spite of herself, she rose and went to investigate. The 'leaves' were yellow fabric stars, torn off and discarded by the Jews as they received news of their liberation from Drancy. Holding one of the tragic little objects, Eliane stood alone in this relic of German oppression and sobbed until she could cry no more.

No one at the transit camp paid her much attention. She was still reticent about her identity and none of the people in authority seemed inclined to reveal it; possibly not many of them had been told who she was. Twice a day the prisoners received food of sorts, but it was unpalatable stuff, largely potato soup, and most of the internees appeared to have resources to pay for food parcels to be sent in. Eliane had suffered such trauma in the past week that she was indifferent to what she ate or drank. She made no effort to send for food or to contact any of her friends outside. Her chance confession that she knew something of the nature of German extermination camps had apparently destroyed any rekindled affection in Loulou because she did not hear from her daughter again. As the days passed, she sank further into black depression, convinced that nothing would save her now and that she would end her days in jail.

She had been in Drancy for nearly two weeks when she was ordered to the camp administration building. The officer in charge was talking to a middle-aged man in British military uniform. Eliane expected to be taken to wait in another room. Clearly this caller was nothing to do with her. But she was wrong. As she was ushered in, he came to meet her, shaking hands as though he were meeting her at a smart social event. 'Mademoiselle Doré, I presume. I'm James Michaels. I've been asked to come with Angela Fenwick and escort you back to the Ritz.'

Eliane never remembered much of the drive back to the First Arrondissement. She had thought she would never see it again. All she ever recalled clearly was wondering whether her legs would carry her when she got out of the car. It was her own limousine and Serge was driving. By now it was late September and the few civilian cars in the streets were no longer subject to arbitrary interception by partisans.

It was assumed that those who could get hold of enough petrol to drive about were on official business.

Angela had suppressed all reactions beyond her first horrified gasp when she saw Eliane. She took her through to the shower block at the rear of the administration building and bathed and dressed her. The couturière seemed incapable of performing these tasks for herself and merely huddled in the bath, trembling and whimpering. Angela had been warned about her friend's shaven head. She had brought scarves and an all-enveloping hat, as well as an outfit of very plain clothes – nothing to excite attention. In the car travelling back, she put her arms round Doré and held her gently in an attempt to still the woman's incessant trembling. The farther they travelled from Drancy, the more Eliane relaxed, but it was clear her recovery would take a long time.

Once she was installed at the Ritz, Angela got hold of a doctor, who prescribed hefty doses of tranquillisers. Colonel Michaels left them outside Eliane's suite, with instructions for Angela about where he could be contacted. Then the journalist got to work to bring Eliane back to normality.

It was much less difficult than she had expected. When she had first seen Doré again at Drancy, she was half-convinced the woman had permanently lost her sanity. Nothing in her behaviour on the way back to the Ritz reassured Angela.

She had bargained without Eliane's vagabond resilience. The tranquillisers put her to sleep for a full twenty-four hours. When Angela looked in on her shortly before noon next day, she was sitting up in bed, attacking a bowl of coffee and a plate of croissants. She still looked deathly pale and her head was swathed in a silk scarf. Otherwise she seemed quite her old self.

'I don't believe this! When I left you yesterday, you were at death's door.'

'So would you have been if you'd been barbered and locked up by that bunch of Communist bandits. What was there to live for if I was going to spend the rest of my days in surroundings like that?' She turned her attention to her second croissant.

'You mean you can bounce back, just like that?'

'Don't be childish, Angela. You're too intelligent for such nonsense. Of course not. But I'm a realist, and I believe in taking advantage of any opportunity I get. It appears that, thanks to you, I have one hell of an opportunity and I plan to use it. I have an awful feeling that I shan't like the price I have to pay, but given the alternative, I'll live with that.'

She's made of iron, thought Angela. Love her or hate her, you have to admire her toughness.

The designer was regarding her closely. 'So when are you going to spill the beans about my dramatic rescue?'

'I thought you'd never ask – I'm not sure whether I'm allowed to tell you. I'm not even sure whether I should know anything myself. That stiff upper lip type came to see me after I'd told the most senior American Intelligence man I know that you wanted to contact the Duke of Conway. I said how did I go about it, and he said leave it to him. The next thing I knew, Colonel Michaels was at my table down in the restaurant, asking leading questions about His Grace and how I knew him. I explained it was for a friend and that you were the friend; also that you'd been taken away by some tough-looking types soon after you asked for the favour. And that, my dear, was that.'

'Come on, there has to be more. Michaels didn't just come back to you out of the blue and say: "Off we go to bust little Alouette from jail." What did he say when he came back?'

'Ah, that's where it gets really exciting. He was gone forever and a day. When I first made contact, I thought they'd be back after a couple of quick phone calls. No chance. In the end I thought this guy Conway must have dropped dead without anyone noticing. Then, two days ago, I walked into the restaurant again and there was Michaels at my table as if he'd just popped out to the men's room for a minute. He told me that if I'd care to collect some suitable clothing for Mademoiselle Doré and be ready to go with him the next morning, it had been arranged to release her from custody into his and my joint care.

'Naturally the girl reporter in me was all agog to know who'd fixed it. I made some incredibly gauche remark about not realising His Grace still had so much pull. Michaels got quite snippy and said of course he didn't, but that the Duke of Conway had not been Mademoiselle Doré's only English admirer, or her most influential one. Alouette, does he mean who I think he means?'

Eliane merely smiled. She was feeling much, much better.

Finally, she said: 'Now the painful bit. Let's have the conditions, Angela.'

The American woman became solemn. 'I think you've guessed already. Only the obvious. There's no question of your remaining in France, let alone Paris. It's not just the fact that you collaborated; they'd have to exile half Parisian Society if that were the criterion. It's the identity of the man. Von Schirach was apparently a much bigger fish than was officially recognised – a top Intelligence type – and your exalted admirer seems more than a little concerned that people might start suspecting you'd acted as some sort of high level go-between, given your pre-war connections with England. They have therefore issued safe conduct for you as long as you undertake to leave for Switzerland within the next week, to become a permanent Swiss resident and not to return to France for at least three years. If you agree to all that, no charges will be brought against you.'

Eliane burst into scornful laughter. 'They must be out of their minds! Me, a go-between for the English and Germans? I may be an unfeeling old bitch about the sufferings of others, but it's because I'm self-centred. That same self-centredness is a guarantee that I wouldn't be interested enough in their stupid politics to act as a go-between for anything. Still, if it gets me out of hot water, who am I to complain? Some day, Angela, I'll be able to find a way of expressing my gratitude to you for your part in this.'

'You've already agreed a price, remember – a non-attributable account of life in occupied Paris. If you like, I'll travel with you to Switzerland and do the piece while you're settling in.'

They both knew that however lightly she treated the matter, departure would be bitter for Eliane. The presence of a friend, even one comparatively recently acquired, would soften it somewhat.

Just before their departure, Eliane was drinking champagne in Angela's room. She had been preoccupied for most of the afternoon and now seemed to be winding herself up to ask a difficult question.

'I – I don't suppose you've heard anything from a kid called Marie-Louise Chabrol or a young man called Fouquet – Pierre Fouquet?'

'No. Should I have done? I'll try to look them up if you want me to. There isn't much time, though.'

'No, no. If she'd wanted to contact me, she would have done by now. It's not important, not important at all.'

They left for Switzerland at dawn on September 30th. Eliane did not see Paris again for almost four years.

# Chapter Nineteen

## Doré
## 1948–1978: Born Again

The rain fell in a steady curtain. It seemed to have been coming down like that forever. In Paris, thought Eliane – in Paris when it rained you looked in the windows of the boutiques; you hurried along the Ritz Corridor from Rue Cambon, as dry as on a sunny day, diverted by the stupendous jewels and amusing trinkets in the showcases. You emerged at the other end to the effusive greetings of the hotel staff, and the maître d'hotel came to escort you to your usual table. You ate lunch with someone amusing, your friends stopping to chat as they passed by. And afterwards, after a leisurely cognac and a last cigarette, you went back to the salon and did an evening's work on the next collection . . . as a way of life there was nothing to beat it. Certainly nothing here. What was that wonderful line of Orson Welles's in his new movie *The Third Man*? 'A thousand years of peace and all the Swiss have invented is the cuckoo clock!' He must have been forced to hang round Geneva in the autumn.

It was four years since Angela Fenwick had come to get her out of Drancy. It felt like four hundred. At the time, exile had seemed an attractive alternative to imprisonment and public humiliation. After all, she had been close to sixty years old, a sensible age for any woman to retire. What a pity she had not hung on to the resolve that had been so strong when Otto left. She'd told him nothing would make her budge from Paris, but within a month, a short spell in detention and a little roughing up by a gang of women had changed her mind. Well, she'd been right first time when she sent Otto off alone. Another apt quotation flitted into her memory: 'Better to die on your feet than live on your knees.' How true! Right now she wasn't so much living on her knees as flat on her face. And what had happened to those who'd stayed? Nothing! Chevalier, Guitry, Lifar, Colombes, Pushkin – all the people they'd said would never work again – they were all back at the top, a little embarrassment now and then about all they had to cope with while she, who had led a blameless life throughout the war, was abandoned here, a forgotten pariah. And now, to cap it all, this mountebank Dior was enjoying a crazy success by cramming women back into abominable fancy dress the like of which they'd given up before 1930. If she'd been in her rightful place, she'd have stopped all that. . . .

Eliane raged to herself for some time, partly aloud, partly inside her head. There was no one to hear. She only needed two servants in this weather-house of a villa, and they were both out. She had been growing increasingly bored and frustrated by Geneva for most of the time she had lived there, but today's tantrum was something special. *Vogue* was carrying a feature on the latest styles from Dior. His New Look had exploded into the world of haute couture the previous season, shattering everything that went before and provoking legendary reactions. Everyone still spoke of the way the journalists and clients were tugging at their skirts as they left the first showing, in a subconscious attempt to mimic the sensational longer clothes of the models they had just seen on the catwalk.

Coming after a period of stark austerity, the New Look had inevitably carried all before it, if only because it yelled luxury and conspicuous consumption. It made women look soft, frail and vulnerable. On the surface it was all rounded shoulders, swaying skirts, bosoms and softness. Underneath it was a suit of over-tight armour, its boned and stiffened linings built over the murderous little waist corset called a *guêpière*. When Eliane saw the first pictures of the innovative style she was thunderstruck. My God, he's put women right back inside the prison I let them out of in the twenties, she thought. It'll never catch on – it can't!

But by the next season, virtually every couturier in Paris had followed Dior's lead. For the moment, at least, the comfortable fashionable woman was dead. This season's magazines made it clear there was no move away from the New Look. It had even been copied by the cheap ready-to-wear trade, never an impulsive market even in times of plenty. If the mass market was prepared to commit itself to such extravagant designs at a time of post-war fabric shortages, it must be here for good.

Still bemoaning the iniquity of it all, Eliane went to her library and booked a phone call to her lawyer in Paris. Her Swiss attorney could not answer this one for her.

Maurice Chaumet was unable to conceal the surprise in his voice. He could not remember when Mademoiselle Doré had last telephoned. These days there could be little to concern her in Paris.

'Maurice, hello! How are things in the City of Light?'

God, he thought, she even sounds like an exile. 'Much as usual, Mademoiselle. Nothing out of the ordinary but we still have the occasional shortages. Much better than England, though, from what I hear. It sounds as though they're rationing themselves out of existence.' She bit back an impulse to tell him to shut up about England and tell her more about Paris, as he said: 'Anyway, to business. What can I do for you? Nothing wrong, I hope.'

'No, nothing, but . . . I was wondering . . . how'd you think people would react if I came back?' She heard his sharp intake of breath and tried to safeguard herself against the indignity of rejection. 'For a short visit only, of course.'

He was silent for long moments, then replied: 'It's hard to say. Occasionally there's still the odd eruption of ill-feeling against someone prominent who was, er, involved with the Occupation, but it happens less and less.'

'From what I can gather, most of the big literary and

entertainment names who were given a hard time are back in favour now.'

'Mmm, I suppose it does look like that from the outside. From here it's a little different. I was seated two rows from Colombes at the theatre the other evening and the couple next to him got up and left when they realised who he was. I think they all have to put up with that sort of thing from time to time.'

She gave a contemptuous, dismissive little sniff. 'Who cares about people like that? I think you've answered my question. I might take a little trip back there soon. I'll be in touch if I do. Thanks for the information.'

He held the receiver long after she had disconnected. How did you tell a living legend that so far as Paris went, she was dead? She would have little to fear from popular hostile reaction because in the past four years people had forgotten her as thoroughly as if she had shut up shop in 1919, not 1939. He slammed down the telephone. What the hell! Let her learn the hard way. She'd probably had it easy enough since 1944, sitting on a pile of money in Switzerland.

The return to Paris was a devastating experience. Eliane's old friends were glad enough to see her, but then, Colombes and Magda regularly stayed with her in Geneva, and even Mikhail Pushkin had been there two or three times. Most of the other people she knew nowadays were not based in Paris, and the Ritz restaurant and some of her other old haunts seemed to have filled with newer, younger faces since her departure. They were faces which showed no glimmer of recognition for Alouette Doré.

For a few days, Eliane was almost content to stroll the old familiar streets, smell the air and re-charge her spiritual batteries with the electrical current that was the atmosphere of Paris. She was staying at the Rue Cambon apartment because she did not yet feel equal to returning to the Ritz as a guest. Even the apartment was no ideal haven, for the last time she had lived there for any length of time was when she was suffering her appalling nightmares after Nico Alvarez's death. Eliane was rapidly coming to the conclusion that her life was all past and no present. This was not at all what she had intended. She had not exactly visualised a triumphant return, but she had been considering the possibility of re-opening to show this upstart Dior how women were meant to look. Now it was clear that no one wanted to know. She had more or less decided to cut short her stay and return to Geneva, when a short reference to her appeared in the gossip column of a Paris daily paper. It was not the sort of entry she was accustomed to.

The cross-head said WHERE ARE THEY NOW? DEPARTMENT and the item went on: *'There was a sad lack of dukes, ballet dancers and poets around the Place Vendôme this week to greet one of the big names of yesterday, who used to be regarded as The dressmaker. . . . When Alouette Doré swept back into the Ritz, only the doorman was there to say hello. Her last performance there was better attended, if only by Wehrmacht sentries and Nazi officials. Ho, hum, where are the snows of yesteryear?'*

As Eliane finished the paragraph, she tore the paper in two and threw it to the ground. She called the concierge of the Rue Cambon building. 'When my maid returns, please tell her I wish to speak to her immediately. I shall be leaving before the end of the week.' Then she rang the small company office which was the only working unit on the former salon floor. 'Natalie, please get hold of my mechanic and tell him to see the car is ready to go at a couple of hours' notice. I may be leaving earlier than I planned.' After that she locked herself into the bathroom and cried for half an hour.

The ringing telephone disturbed her orgy of self-pity. She tried to ignore it, but a small voice deep inside her still suggested it might be the welcome she had hoped for so she rushed from her refuge and answered it. Natalie, who screened all incoming calls, said, 'I'm so sorry to bother you, Mademoiselle, but I don't quite know what to do with this call. The young man says he's your great-nephew. Do you want to speak to him?'

Her grander hopes dashed, Eliane was nevertheless grateful that someone wanted to contact her. Then a terrible thought crossed her mind. It could be some grasping member of Gaston's or Paul's brood. Both her brothers must be grandfathers by now. . . . 'What's his name?' she asked with mounting suspicion.

'St-Meurice, Mademoiselle – Eugène St-Meurice.'

She sighed with relief. Maybe the time had come to tell the boy he had a grandmother. . . . 'Put him on, Natalie. Of course I'll speak to him.'

She invited Eugène to dine with her at the Ritz. The young man seemed bemused, both by the luxurious surroundings and by Eliane's flattering attentiveness. He was just twenty and rather shy, and she had never shown any interest in him before.

When they had ordered, she gave him a dazzling smile and said, 'Right, young man, down to business. Tell me what you do with yourself here in Paris – you are living here, I take it?'

'Yes – well, that is, for the moment . . . that's one of the reasons I wished to see you. I – I wanted to ask your advice, and possibly your help.'

Suspicion tugged at her. Was he going to touch her for money? It certainly sounded that way. But what about his trust fund? 'Why, Eugène? I'd have thought a young man like you would have everything sorted out in Paris.'

'Well, that's the trouble, I have, but Maman has other ideas. I don't want to hurt her, but it looks as if I'll have to unless I want to end up living a life I know I shall hate. I've just done the basic course at the Beaux Arts. I knew a long time ago that I'd never be another Picasso or Van Gogh, but fine art wasn't my main interest anyhow, so it didn't matter.'

'What was?'

'Fashion. Ever since I was a little boy, I've loved working

out how people put clothes together, what makes one woman's dress look wonderful and another's look like nothing on earth. I'm not a bad graphic artist – certainly decent enough to make a career in advertising or magazine illustration – but what I really want to do is get a job in a fashion house. If only yours were still open . . .' She was about to remark that he couldn't have much going for him if a niche in the family firm were the height of his ambition, when he went on, 'You're just about the greatest designer ever and I'd have given anything to learn something of your techniques. But as you've closed down, that's out of the question now.

'I've been pestering the fashion houses with designs, doing little fill-in holiday jobs with one or two of them – anything to try and break in at the right place. But apart from a couple of tiny assignments, they all say I'll have to work with dressmakers for a few years and then come back and try again.'

'And?'

'And so I wondered if you could advise me whether it is worth going that route, whether I'd learn enough to make all the time worthwhile. After all, you got to the top from nothing. You must know the best form of training.'

A tiny imp of devilment was beginning to stir inside Eliane. To think she'd chosen the wrong child, because she'd assumed only a woman would take over from her. Perhaps Loulou wasn't cut out to follow her into the business, but Edouard's son might be. . . . The thought brought with it all sorts of instantly formed notions of starting again, of re-opening purely to mould this boy to carry on in her tradition. It was a beguiling idea, but what if he had no talent?

'I can't possibly advise you without knowing whether you're any good, Eugène. It's not just a matter of being able to draw well – or even a matter of being able to draw at all, come to that. I could never manage more than a stick-man. All my garments were designed on the model. But if I saw some of your work, I might be able to give you an opinion.'

'Would you be interested in looking?' His face was radiant with hope.

'Why not? Who knows, we may have another Dior in you.'

He scowled. 'No, whatever I may be, not that. He trusses up women like chickens ready for the oven. I've tried following his style because no one will look at anything else in Paris at present, but the shapes I like are nothing like that.'

She smiled even more broadly. 'I think we may have a lot in common, young man.'

After dinner they drove to the small flat he rented close to the Boulevard St Michel. It was painfully clean and tidy. I certainly don't have a carefree bohemian for a grandson, thought Eliane. His portfolios were like the apartment, orderly and properly classified, the work he preferred to do in one folder and the New Look adaptations in another. As Eliane looked at his original work it was difficult not to show excessive enthusiam. The designs were brilliant – smooth, graceful and fresh, but without a trace of the pads and bones which gave the New Look its structure. The New Look file was another matter. Probably because he disliked the style, his drawings were stilted and derivative. Hardly surprising no one was interested in the kid if he'd been showing them that stuff.

When he had finished showing her the material, he glanced at her shyly. 'Well, what do you think? Is there any point in my going on?'

She took a deep breath and for once was generous and straightforward in her praise. 'You have a great deal of talent, Eugène, but there's a lot against you. Forget the New Look! You weren't meant to handle such nonsense – no bad thing, I'm the same. But it does mean trouble if you start trying to get started now. Your designs need a more casual, popular attitude to fashion. It will return, but God knows when. You'll have to bide your time and wait for the right moment – I don't know whether you're prepared to do that. You also need to improve your practical experience of the fashion business, and while you're showing such unusual drawings, I don't quite know who'll take you on . . . but we can come back to that later. Right now I'd like to know why you came to me for advice if you weren't hoping I'd stake you.'

He shrugged. 'That had nothing to do with it. I thought if I were very, very lucky you might be able to introduce me to a couturier who'd be prepared to give me a beginner's job, but I had no great hopes of that. It's more on the family level. You see, I know this is what I want but my mother is behaving as if I'm insane even to consider it. I think I just wanted to be able to say that the family's one expert thought I had talent.'

'Ah, the formidable Pauline! And what does she want you to do?'

'She wants me to leave Paris for a start. She likes the idea of my going down to Toulouse so I'll be nearer home and taking a teaching diploma in the local art school. Then, she says, I'll be secure for life if I don't make a success as what she calls a proper painter.'

'But you told me yourself that you'll never be any good as a "proper" painter!'

'I know, but she won't accept it. She says I'm being too modest and that my stuff is wonderful. She frames everything she can nag me into parting with and sticks it on her drawing-room walls. Really, Aunt Eliane, it's dreadful stuff, sort of immature Degas on a bad night at the ballet, but she's convinced I'm his spiritual heir! That's really why I needed to consult you. It's a family matter. The trust you set up for me will keep me alive. I need a job to make it up to a good income, but I can survive on it, and I'm prepared to if it means I can learn to be a couturier. It's not about money, it's about hurting Maman. She had such a terrible time over Papa, I hate to think of having a row and making her unhappy. But I can't sacrifice my whole life for that, can I?'

Too damned right, thought Eliane, as her instinct to control came into full play. Here was her grandson being held back from a successful career by a silly little nobody without the guts to stand alone on her own two feet. . . . She decided it was time for a little bit of enlightenment from her to encourage him.

'Eugène – how much d'you know about my relationship with your father?'

'Well, I know you more or less financed his upbringing, paid for his education and so on, after his mother died.'

'That isn't quite the way it was.' And you're not going to get quite the straight story either, she thought privately. 'Edouard was really my son. But I – I couldn't earn enough as a shop assistant to keep him and look after him, so I had to give him up to my sister to raise. When I'd built a successful business, I got him back. So you see, you're my grandson. That's really why you have the trust fund. I'll be settling more on you later, but that'll do for the present.'

Eugène expressed surprise but did not appear exactly amazed. I expect he had his suspicions before, she told herself. He must have guessed his talent came from somewhere and those lumpish parents of his could hardly be the source. In her supreme egotism she never paused to ask herself whether this ingenuous youth might already have known more than he admitted about his antecedents. She neither mentioned his father's death nor asked questions about how his mother had adjusted to her sudden widowhood. Why rock the boat? Eugène St-Meurice might eventually provide a solution to the frustrations which plagued her. All she needed was a little time to think up an appropriate plan of campaign.

Eliane decide she had been silent too long. She shut the final portfolio of sketches and stood up. 'If I were you I'd forget teaching brats to paint catkins or whatever – because mark my words, that's what happens to everyone who gives up the risky road to success in favour of a little security. Your mother made her own life and she has to live it. . . .' She passed on hurriedly from that, uncomfortably aware that Pauline had no say in the skirmish which killed her husband at Saumur. 'You have to make your own way. I need time to think. If you're free tomorrow, come round and see me at Rue Cambon around noon. I may have come up with something by then. Now, I must be going. At my age I need all the beauty sleep I can get!'

All the way back to Rue Cambon she fought an impulse to whistle. She was feeling better every minute. This meeting could turn everything around. Really, that idiot Pauline had no idea of how to win. What was it Winston Churchill had told her – that she had the instincts of a street fighter? At the moment she felt more like a clever fox descending on a pen of stupid chickens. She almost danced into the apartment. 'Marthe, forget about packing. You'll be delighted to know you don't have to ship me off to Geneva yet. We're staying at least another ten days.'

In Montparnasse, Eugène St-Meurice was sipping a large drink and thinking over the events of the day. He had mixed feelings about it. In one sense it had been even easier than he had expected. In another, it had created unforeseen complications. He was under no illusions about the blood tie between himself and Alouette Doré. Pauline had told him the couturière was his grandmother shortly after Eliane's influence had persuaded the Germans to confirm that Edouard was dead. In fact, she had returned to the matter again and again, drumming it in to her son that the woman must have been collaborating with Edouard's killers to have been in a position to find out the truth about the Saumur action.

Pauline had involved herself with the local Resistance in an attempt to avenge her husband's death, and had shipped Eugène off to continue his education in Paris so that he would be out of harm's way if she were caught. The trust fund Eliane had set up for his education became directly available to him as soon as he was living away from home. Early in 1942 he was placed in lodgings with a girlhood friend of his mother. He took private art lessons while attendng a lycée in Paris. On his sixteenth birthday he moved into a small apartment. By then he was already enrolled for a number of courses at the Beaux Arts and it made him feel grown-up and independent to hang round the student cafés in the Boul' Mich' area. That was where he encountered Marie-Louise for the first time since her last pre-war summer holiday from Switzerland. They clung together like orphans for a while, and over the next couple of weeks she filled him in on her rupture with Doré when she had returned to Paris after the French surrender.

Eugène had been scandalised by what Marie-Louise revealed about their family history. His obsession with Alouette Doré dated from then. A little anarchic part of Eugène wanted to be Eliane. Another part hated her for her apparent indifference to his father's fate.

He was full of sympathy and admiration for Marie-Louise, who was at the height of her passionate involvement with Teddy Vincent. It was indiscreet of the girl to tell him what she was doing in the Resistance but Eugène was now all the family she had. She trusted him instinctively and he honoured that trust. When Teddy was captured and Marie-Louise was cut off from the other members of her Resistance group, she turned to Eugène for consolation and no brother could have been more supportive. They stayed in touch throughout the terrible days of July when many of her group were picked up, and Marie-Louise first became certain both that Teddy had been deported after torture and that she was several months pregnant. Later, Marie-Louise told him she had intervened to stop Annette Lebrun and her friends from venting their spite on Eliane. Later still, when she discovered her mother had known at least something about the Nazi death camps and had turned a blind eye to it, they discussed the whole matter together before Marie-Louise decided to sever all connection with Eliane. Eugène had remained her constant companion until her baby was born and she heard that Teddy Vincent was still alive. Finally, he had escorted her to a Channel port when she left France with her baby to marry the crippled airman.

Since then he had been prey to seesawing emotions about his grandmother, a situation which seemed doomed to last. He simultaneously idolised and was repelled by her. She was his ideal woman and the reason he hated the thought of any physical relationships with women. Tangled inextricably in this emotional undergrowth were his own ambitions to reach the top of the couture business, and a genuine love for his mother which nevertheless he knew he would sacrifice to get what he wanted in the fashion business. For one thing was certain: Pauline St-Meurice would not tolerate co-existence with Alouette Doré, and if her son chose to be reunited with the couturière then Pauline, regretfully, would disown him.

Eugène had no intention that Eliane should ever know any of this. Instinctively he understood her better than anyone else – they were very much alike – and he knew she would have no more to do with him if she suspected the extent of his information about the skeletons in the family cupboard. To Doré, anyone who knew so much about her weakest points was a threat, and one did not welcome such a person into one's private world.

Next day, when Eliane met him at Rue Cambon, she was almost girlish. At present the business operation consisted only of the ground-floor boutique and the first-floor administrative office. The great mirrored salon was shrouded in dust sheets. The ateliers were bare and dusty. All the merchandise for the boutique was produced elsewhere to Doré's specification.

They made their tour then adjourned to the Ritz for lunch. 'Well, what do you think of it?' said Eliane.

'It would be presumptuous to say. I'm far too inexperienced.'

'Good boy – a little humility never hurt anyone at your age – but keep it for me, don't let outsiders see it or they'll mistake it for weakness. Now, I've been thinking, trying to weigh up what you need and see how it compares with my own plans. Maybe we can help each other.

'I have plans to come back to Paris and take up where I left off. I thought I'd said all I had to say in fashion, but when I see today's styles I realise I'm still needed. The trouble is, as for you with your lovely designs, there's no place for me at the moment. So while these fools are playing about with their padding and their nasty little corsets, I thought we could make some preparations for the future. I made a couple of calls this morning to old colleagues. There are two couturiers who'll be prepared to give you a training place for the next year – just a very humble fashion assistant, but it's the best start if your training has been on the fine art side before.

'Now you don't need to make up your mind yet. You can take one of these jobs and see how you like it. After the year is up, if you feel you've learned enough, you can join me and start doing some basic design work on the boutique merchandise. Nothing very exciting at first, I promise you, but later on you could get to the very top. I'm going to start planning for a major re-launch. It'll take at least two years, possibly more. Then we'll see what we shall see. Are you with me?'

Eugène struggled to keep a gleam of triumph from his face. He'd done it! She had accepted him, given him his first and second steps on the ladder, and, unless he made a real mess of things, guaranteed him a brilliant career. Who could ask for more? And he had a year in Paris, working at a couture house ostensibly unconnected with Doré, in which to prepare his mother for the inevitable rupture. It couldn't be better.

'I – I don't know how to begin to thank you. . . . I no longer even know what to call you. Should it be Aunt Eliane or – or Grandmother?'

'Call me Grandmother just once in public and your future ends at that moment – possibly your life, too! From now on, I'm Mademoiselle, or Mademoiselle Doré. You're about to become one of my staff and that's what all of them have always called me. Don't imagine you're being victimised. At various times I've numbered some of my best friends on my payroll, and in their working capacity they always called me Mademoiselle, too. It's simply a mark of professionalism. Another thing – don't waste time on over-effusive thanks. Just do well in your work. I only like tangible forms of gratitude.

'Now, I shall go back to Switzerland and start planning. You will go to work. I want you to stay with me as often as possible when you can get away for a weekend or when you get a vacation. We're going to have a great deal to talk about in the next couple of years.'

At first it was all a wonderful dream to Eugène. He loved his work at the fashion house, although it was very humble and involved long hours. He was getting invaluable training for the only career he wanted, and he knew it. Things didn't work out too well with his mother; she began complaining that he never spent any of his time off with her and inevitably it came out that he was visiting Eliane. The row which followed estranged mother and son permanently and Eugène felt a deep sense of guilt about the entire business. His mother was not very old but she was isolated and lonely. He had given her pride and purpose and now she was bereft. Still, he thought, it's a tough world, as Mademoiselle keeps telling me. You have to protect yourself, because no one else will.

But after he left the couture house and joined Doré full-time, he found his own life a lot less than perfect. He had expected her to be a bit of a slave driver and a perfectionist; what he had not bargained for was her viperish jealousy. The compliments she had paid his work in Paris were untypical. She had been lonely and on her best behaviour then. Now she sensed a younger, more talented rival racing to overtake her. She wanted him there as her successor but she had no intention of permitting him to steal her glory while she was still in charge.

It made for some bruising encounters, and time and time again Eugène withdrew at the end of a meeting, feeling he could not take another day of her. Still, he thought, he was learning from one of the best teachers there was. He had a sure inheritance lined up. He would simply have to learn to take it.

The hardest bit was when they came to detailed discussion of the Paris re-opening. Eliane had hit on the idea of linking it with an exclusive franchising operation with a top New York department store. It was a brilliant concept, combining her legendary reputation with the cachet of a Parisian re-launch to boost the birth of the New York venture. This in turn would pump much needed funds into the couture side, which would eat cash in the early days. Eugène was full of admiration for her imaginative business sense. He felt less reverent when he discovered how minimal his own participation would be.

He submitted a portfolio of new designs to Doré while she was finalising the business plan. The clothes were carefully judged to suit the general design philosophy of the House of Doré and Eugène knew instinctively he had got it right. They were the best designs he had ever produced, retaining the Doré mood but incorporating something extra that was bang up to date. Eliane looked at them in silence, her face looking increasingly grim as she turned each page. Finally she snapped the portfolio shut and looked up at him, forcing a smile.

'Well done, Eugène. Pity no one'll see them.'

'What? But I don't understand. . . . I thought you told me to prepare a whole range of designs so you could choose a dozen or more for inclusion in the re-launch collection.'

'Mmm, but I don't think they share the same overall, shall we say, tone, of my work. No, we might put some through the boutiques, but not haute couture yet. Don't worry, my boy, there'll be other collections.'

'But Mademoiselle, you know this sort of design isn't suitable for boutique production. It's couture style. It cries out for the grand finish!'

'Boutiques or nothing, Eugène, and be thankful. I'm not promising that, either. We'll see how they make up for mass production. Now, the main thing is to set up the American deal before we get everything else going.'

Eugène disguised his chagrin until later, when he was alone. It had been inevitable really, and he should have prepared himself. God knows he'd seen enough people fall victim to Doré's malice in the past year. It seemed that the resentment which had started when she saw the New Look had taken root and was colouring her attitude to anyone who showed signs of a talent that threatened to eclipse her own. Probably a mixture of age, bitterness over her rejection by the French after the war, and a mounting desperation about having no new ideas of her own. He snorted with exasperation and flung down the magazine he had been idly flicking through. It was all very well to understand why she behaved this way, much less easy to handle when her malice was directed at you.

He concentrated on Eliane's negotiations with her American contacts. She had no intention of committing herself to a Paris re-opening until she had a deal set up with New York. It was nothing to do with the money – she was worth enough for the couture house to run at a loss for the rest of her days. It was a matter of not losing face. If she had a US deal all sewn up and reported in the trade press, no one could say she had come back to couture because she was lost without it. She could look them in the eye and say she had to re-open her Rue Cambon salon to give her ready-to-wear empire the upmarket backing it needed. So everything depended on the American deal. Without it, there could be no reborn couture house.

Doré decided to make a first approach through Angela Fenwick who, as editor in chief of *Mode International*, was now one of the most influential voices in modern American fashion. In September 1952, Eliane wrote to her friend:

*My dear Angela*
*You, of all people, know that my work is everything to me. This summer I decided I had been away from it too long. I've often told you that some day I'd create a new*

*style to suit this new world, but that I was awaiting my moment. I think that moment has finally come.*

*Now I'm writing to ask your advice. I need hardly tell you how Paris has changed. It's no longer enough to have a maison de couture here and talk down from the commanding heights to the world below. One needs a wider public. I'm therefore planning to achieve mass sales by appointing a top concessionaire in the United States – either one of the most important wholesalers or one department store if you think such an outlet would achieve the desired volume. In any case, I'm in your hands on this. You know it must be someone with the best possible fashion reputation and I shall trust your judgement completely in selecting that concessionaire.*

*The clothes would be manufactured in the United States on the basis of toiles sent from Rue Cambon and my profit would come from royalties on each garment sold. Once the wholesale deal is tied up, I can re-open the couture house as a shop window and image builder for the ready-to-wear.*

*My first collection will be ready in January. I think it would be best if the nominated concessionaire came to Paris to make his selection: the atmosphere is right here. I'd love you to be here too, of course, as my guest. Please let me know soon what you think, as my decision to re-open the maison de couture depends on whether a successful concession agreement can be set up.*

*As ever*
*Eliane Doré*

Angela Fenwick telephoned the moment she received the letter. 'It's a wonderful idea, Alouette,' she said. 'I'm convinced the future lies in that sort of deal, and most of the American rag trade shares my feelings. But Paris is so conservative it's in danger of losing out. The big New York wholesalers are getting sick of waiting for the French couturiers to come round to the idea and they're already looking towards Italy – or even Madrid, God help us – as an alternative. Pitch the collection right and the sky's the limit.'

Eliane made much of the American woman, complimenting her on her insight, even suggesting the possibility of an advance visit to see the collection being made up. In the end, though, they agreed that Angela should accompany the nominated wholesaler, with an additional incentive of exclusive editorial coverage of the production and shipment of the first toiles, to run in *Mode* the month the ready-to-wear range was launched in the shops.

Once the negotiations had started, Eliane began commuting between Paris and Geneva, still testing the atmosphere in France for hostility, always ready to flee if it showed itself. But all she encountered was indifference. The years of exile had turned her into a physical shadow of her former self and that, coupled with a sudden collective move away from memories of the Occupation, seemed to have pushed her out of everyone's thoughts. The attitude aroused mixed feelings in her. She was relieved that the path had apparently cleared itself for her permanent return to the city of her triumphs, and at the same time resentful that they had forgotten her so utterly. We'll see how long that lasts, she told herself. Nevertheless, it meant that by early November she could safely ensconce herself, along with a full staff of expert workers, in the Rue Cambon building. At that point rumours appeared in the papers about the couture house re-opening. She made sure that her spokesman issued nothing but bland statements to the effect that she was doing experimental work for the overseas market and that no firm plans of any kind had yet been made.

And so Eugène, stifling his bitterness, was drawn into watching Doré in the full flush of active creation. She had already spent considerable time choosing fabrics which appealed to her, thinking out what she termed the logic of modern clothes, and putting together in her head her initial thoughts on what shape and style should be made up in what material. From the beginning he found it unnerving not to be able to refer to drawings. He knew that other top couturiers had been known to work in this manner, but there was something so hit and miss about the assembly of Mademoiselle's garments that after the first week or so he began wondering just who was really responsible for them, she or her tailors and cutters.

After a couple of weeks he could not resist the temptation to find out what her workers thought about it. He singled out a senior tailor, a man who had been with her in the great pre-war days and had come back from his own modestly successful business to work for her again. Eugène had the human touch his grandmother lacked and was already on good terms with all the members of staff who knew him. He went to work on this man in earnest and within a couple of days they went off together for lunch, at Eugène's invitation and on the pretext that he wanted to benefit by the older man's experience. That was precisely what he planned, but in a way Emile Ponthieu never suspected.

Throughout the meal he kept up a stream of chit-chat about the nuts and bolts of the couture business. Even this was no waste of time – Emile was highly skilled and a mine of useful information. But it was the answers to his casual questions when they were relaxing over the second bottle of Beaune which proved most riveting.

'It's so bewildering for a new boy like me with no workshop training before now.' Eugène was at his most ingenuous. 'I don't understand how Mademoiselle manages to make that jump from a length of material draped around a girl's shoulders to a tailored suit without hours of pattern cutting and dry runs on muslin, let alone drawings. I suppose that's just because I'm so green!'

Ponthieu leaned over and slapped his shoulder sympathetically. 'Nonsense, my lad – it's what we've all been asking ourselves since the twenties.' He lowered his voice, looked round exaggeratedly as though to check that no salon eavesdropper was in the restaurant, and said: 'Of course, the answer some of us came up with was that she sort of doodled with shears and we designed the clothes – but I shouldn't be saying that to the boss's nephew, should I?'

'Oh, come on, Emile. You and all the other staff know she's harder on me than on any of you – and that's saying a lot.'

'True, kid. Sorry, I know you're no stool pigeon. Look, as you're such a decent type, I'll tell you. Your aunt had a great eye for what was right in fashion, and she had it like a clairvoyant, about ten minutes before most other people. She also had a lot of influential boyfriends and a great deal of luck when she was first getting started. Now don't get me wrong: you have to be talented to do what she's done. But she's not what she thinks she is. I've seen samples of her cutting and sewing. It's professional all right. She knows enough to tell whether we know our jobs inside out, and I'm sure that when she had to she could turn out clothes herself. The trouble is, she's convinced herself over the years that she really does make up the clothes on the models when in fact she doesn't do anything of the sort.'

'But that reputation! All the publicity when she was at the top of the heap. . . . They all said she personally designed and finished the collection.'

'Of course! It was great publicity. Who'd have cared if the press had been told that Emile Ponthieu was the best thing that ever hit the house of Doré, or that Henri Maurois the cutter was the natural successor to Madame Vionnet? We went along with it because it kept us well paid. At first there was nothing wrong with it, it was a good gimmick. And we didn't under-estimate the importance of that vital flair her creative suggestions and instructions gave our work. Trouble is that now she really believes she does it all herself, and it's beginning to interfere with the amount of work we get through because she's not so sure of herself any more.'

'I don't understand.'

'Well, plenty of top couturiers only put across the feel of what they want in their collections. These days a lot of them admit it and even publicise the names of the designers they employ. Mademoiselle never did that, of course. She employed tailors and seamstresses of such skill that they were her real designers – and kept them anonymous. Oh, we'd never have been anything without her, but she'd never have been anything without us, either. The best way to think of her is like a rich patron building a house, with us as her master masons, her architect and so on. She'd express an idea and we'd adapt it. But then it was as though the patron decided to make a few marks with a stick in a patch of sand to indicate the outline of his idea and, when the craftsmen had made it, went round telling all his friends that he'd not only designed the place himself but also completed the wood carvings and slapped on the odd wall painting. Couture just doesn't work like that, my friend. The puzzlement you're feeling is that of a true professional, even an inexperienced one, confronted by an eternal amateur.'

'Well, it seems to have worked well enough before.'

'Yeah, but don't imagine it'll work now. I told you, she's no longer sure of herself. Nor should she be. For Christ's sake, she's approaching seventy and soft from living a life of the greatest luxury. Only she would have the nerve to imagine she's still in touch with what the majority of women – even prosperous women – want to wear. The one area where La Grande Mademoiselle was truly inspired was choosing the right materials at the right time, chucking away corsets, setting women free. That's why she was able to go on year after year, pumping her ideas through us and having them turned into something terrific. Trouble is that everybody's heard that old story once too often, and she's never come up with another idea that big. I can tell you now that if she doesn't, she may as well give up on the frocks and retire again to live on her perfume profits, because the business has no room for big-headed has-beens.'

All the man said had a devastating ring of truth. Eugène knew instinctively that Doré no longer had that spark which had propelled her to the top. She had exhausted her ideas, as Emile feared, and the skids would be under her unless something could be done to make her take a different line. With great effort, he asked a casual question.

'Any thoughts about which way she could go?'

'Oh sure, but who'd listen to me? Funny thing is that my thoughts are a sort of development of what she taught me in the thirties. Strange that she seems to have forgotten and I remember. . . . She always made a big deal of looking at where people were now and where they were going. And she took a lot of trouble considering exactly who she was aiming at. Now it occurs to me that a lot of the problem with what she's trying to do today comes from confused thinking about her customers. If she wants the expensive ready-to-wear market, she's hardly going to do well with outfits for the polo grounds or garden parties. She doesn't seem to know how women live today, and she's thinking in the wrong income bracket.'

'Emile, you're a marvel. It's so straightforward I could shoot myself for not having worked it out before. We could still make it if we went along those lines.'

The older man shrugged and became morose again. 'Kid, I know that, you know that, but does Mademoiselle know that? And if not, are you going to be the first to tell her?'

They stared at each other glumly. Then Emile said, 'What the hell, I can always go back into business with my son-in-law! Let me treat you to a cognac before we return to the lion's den.'

After that, Eugène watched Doré's every move. With his new knowledge, it was painfully obvious that everything Emile had said was true. The empress of couture had been a bright little girl on the make who had used her opportunities to the hilt, made a couple of lucky swipes at an edifice that was crumbling anyway, and been given all the credit when the entire building collapsed. Ever since then she had been living on her reputation and the quality of her staff.

He did a lot of thinking, too, about Emile's views on the way a new Alouette Doré should have approached production of a mass market collection. It made too much sense to ignore. He took out his own rejected drawings and, even allowing for considerable personal egotism, saw designs which fulfilled the criteria Emile had suggested. His clothes were perfect for a woman with plenty of money but with a lot more to do with her life than attend parties and watch polo games. His suits would let a woman go shopping or to lunch looking chic, but they would be equally suitable for a boardroom meeting. Doré's cocktail and evening gowns were beautiful, but required a full-time personal maid to maintain them properly. His own designs could be entrusted to a good commercial dry cleaner. He remembered one of his grandmother's favourite aphorisms: 'Fashion must go down into the street.' The trouble was that his did and hers no longer worked below the first-floor drawing-room.

'Mademoiselle,' he murmured to himself, 'sooner or later you'll have to accept that either we go over to my designs or you bomb.' Somehow the thought cheered him, even if he had no idea how to convey it to her.

She bombed with a vengeance at the private show for Nathan Rose.

The workers in the atelier sensed her failure before the New York wholesaler even arrived. They had seen the garments as Mademoiselle went through the ritual of her final personal viewing, when she assembled her choice of accessories along with the outfit on the model. Doré herself made quick, bright, brittle remarks. Whatever else had deserted her, her intuition was wellnigh infallible, and now it was telling her something was badly wrong.

All the ensembles were up to her pre-war standard, there was no doubt of that. But nothing had moved on. Everything seemed fixed in the late 1930s. Sleepless and desperate, Eliane had even asked herself in the depths of the night whether her desire to wipe out the events of Occupation and its aftermath had frozen her forever in the 1930s. Whatever the reason, she knew she had it more wrong than she had previously thought possible. In the final days of alteration, checking and re-cutting, she practically butchered some outfits in her frantic determination to work miracles. They refused to be re-worked and when the tailors had re-made the slashed garments, Doré was left with the same unsatisfactory, dated shapes which had ignited her fury in the first place.

Angela watched in mounting anxiety as model after model strode down the salon in the traditional no-frills Doré manner. Where was the lightness, the freshness, the evolution of classic themes into something new? All she could see was a succession of neutral-coloured suits with tops that looked positively shapeless compared with the decisive structure of a post-New Look peplum jacket, and soft floating silk evening dresses which would bestow instant invisibility upon any woman who wore one in a room peopled by the current crop of gloriously-beaded strapless crinolines. As the staid, understated styles repeated themselves endlessly on the catwalk, she hardly dared meet the eyes of the man who had been so delighted when she offered him first option on Doré's ready-to-wear début.

Eliane's arrival at the end of the showing made matters even worse. In an attempt to create a dramatic effect, she had made excuses not to meet Nathan Rose until the end of her private show for him. There was no suggestion of rudeness – she had arranged a reception and dinner for him that evening, and all sorts of diversions should he be at a loose end in Paris after his business was completed. But Rose had naturally expected to see the apparently ageless beauty who had been so widely photographed right up until the eve of the war. Instead he was confronted by an old woman, clad in a cropped black jacket and a plain grey skirt. Her face was a route map of lines and wrinkles.

Her hair was an impossible shade of black beneath an odd-looking hat which seemed crazily dated when worn indoors. Eliane saw what she wished to see in her looking glass. The black jacket and grey skirt would have looked like a witty feminine parody of a man's formal morning suit if it had been worn by a young woman. Given her age, it merely looked like a dowdy provincial pensioner's idea of what smart townswomen wore to see their lawyers.

Fortunately, Nathan Rose was a courteous and civilised man. Angela thought of some others she might have approached and winced at what they would have done to Doré. It was still pretty bad. Having seen his reaction to the clothes, she wondered if he would even stay to dinner with the couturière.

He stayed, and was polite. But he was determined not to mislead Eliane with false suggestions that he was impressed. Rose had been raised in a tough school and believed that when bad cuts were necessary, they should be inflicted quickly and cleanly.

Eliane fluttered around him, flirting like a teenager. Somewhere along the way she said: 'I insist we leave business until later. I want to hear all about New York. It seems everything happens there these days, not here.'

'I think you could say that,' Rose replied heavily, with a significant look at Angela.

She was so embarrassed she found herself fluttering too. It was no use. Nothing could put off the evil news forever. As soon as they had finished their dinner, Nathan Rose turned to Eliane, a look of sadness on his face. But his words were no less wounding for all that.

'Mademoiselle, before you start going into detail, I have to tell you something which is extremely painful to me. Unless there's a whole alternative collection I haven't seen, I regret I cannot do business with you.'

'I don't understand, M'sieur. I didn't expect to sell you the entire collection, of course. It was deliberately comprehensive so that you could make a selection appropriate to American tastes. I thought perhaps thirty or forty of the hundred designs. . . .'

'Mademoiselle Doré, there wasn't one outfit on that catwalk that I'd be confident of selling to fashionable women in New York. I realise all the styles were in keeping with your look, but I expected that look to have changed with the times. From what I could see, those were remakes of clothes you were showing in 1938 and '39 – and they weren't revolutionary then.'

Eliane belatedly stood on her dignity. 'Forgive me, M'sieur. I should have realised such a new country would be interested in futurism, not in design classics. Forgive me for having involved you in such a waste of time.'

'Oh, don't worry about that. I've arranged visits to Dior and Lanvin while I'm here. They may come up with something more appropriate to the US market. Perhaps some of the English buyers would be interested in your collection. I hear they have more . . . er . . . classic tastes there.'

Eliane rose unsteadily. 'My apologies, M'sieur, but I feel a little tired. I have been very busy, you know, preparing for the foreign buyers. If you will excuse me, I will ask Angela to act as hostess for the rest of the evening. Good night.'

'Hold it a minute, Nathan, I must just have a word with her,' said Angela. She caught Eliane in the lobby. 'I'm so terribly sorry, Alouette –' she struggled to think of something more positively encouraging to say – 'maybe the timing was a little wrong.' It sounded lame even to her.

Doré managed a travesty of a smile. 'That's it absolutely. Wrong by about fifteen years! I should have dropped dead in 1939. Good night, Angela. Don't feel you have to see me again before you go home. We both need time to recover from this one.' Then she turned away towards the lift, stepped in and vanished from Angela's sight.

The Rue Cambon staff had never been told they were working on a collection aimed solely at American mass production. Eliane had fed them the story that she was running a trial line in order to decide for her own satisfaction whether a comeback was feasible, as much as for new markets. She had added that a few overseas companies might look at the result with a view to franchising abroad. As a result, she was not required to explain herself to them when the Americans did not buy. Eugène was another matter. He had been at the salon the evening of the disastrous presentation, although he had been ordered to stay backstage. Now Eliane found he was the only person she could turn to. Magda Robles and Paul Colombes were both out of the question. Magda would commiserate and Paul would crow. Eliane was not sure which would hurt most.

So she put the weight of her bitterness and despair on the frail shoulders of her grandson. He was surprised by his own reaction.

Eugène had suspected that the collection would be turned down. It looked flat and insipid, and nobody was going to pay to copy such qualities. He had expected to feel triumphant when she was rejected, almost avenged for her treachery against him. He felt all this, but on its heels protective and resentful on his grandmother's behalf.

'The man's a philistine! Didn't he realise he was being given a chance to handle an immortal? You don't judge such work by ordinary standards!'

A large tear trickled down Eliane's cheek. She squeezed his hand and smiled tremulously. 'Some day I'll thank you adequately for that, my boy. At least I have your support. That counts more than anything.'

They both knew it did not, but she was surprised to realise it mattered more than she would have suspected. He was equally astonished at how important her gratitude was to him on a purely emotional level. Almost immediately, however, self-interest started to insinuate itself.

'Mademoiselle, you've had a terrible shock. Don't let's go over dead ground immediately. Take a break, unwind a little. Perhaps a short trip back to Switzerland or to the Côte D'Azur would be sensible. When you feel a little better, may I ask your permission to discuss things with you again? I think I may have the answer.'

He had the answer all right, although it took him virtually the whole of Doré's period of spiritual recuperation to work out a sufficiently tactful way of saying it. Emile Ponthieu had prophesied that Doré would fail because she lacked any contact with contemporary attitudes, needs and ideas. Eugène had all those. Now he had to convince Eliane that future collections would be by Eugène St-Meurice for Alouette Doré. The arrangement would differ from that at several other couture houses in one basic aspect: only the two of them would know the designs were his. His price would be inheritance of the couture business on her retirement or death.

It proved easier than Eugène had anticipated, partly because Eliane had taken a worse beating than at any time since Bonnie Charles had married Lady Venetia Lamington, and partly because he phrased the suggestion in such a way that she could pretend he was merely acting as a 'young ideas' consultant. Eugène discovered he had a talent for dressing up unpalatable suggestions.

'What I had in mind,' he said, 'was to bring you the sort of sketch notes that I make from observing people's changing tastes and so on. You could consider them and come up with your own designs, using my sketches more or less as research notes. Then, when you had decided what was right and what wasn't, I could brief the cutters. We'd tell them you'd got me to sketch your designs so you could be free to do other things while I worked with them to produce the basic garments. Then you could step in and bring them up to finished standard.'

She accepted it completely. They both knew, without any open acknowledgement, that he was putting before her not merely the offer of credit for his original designs, but a method of palming them off on her staff in such a way that it need never be admitted she no longer devised the clothes. She would still get to do what the cutters secretly called her 'slash and burn' routine on the part-finished garments. They had always had to re-make many outfits because of this, so there was no reason why she should act differently now. It was a perfect solution.

No one ever needed to tell Eliane Doré that there was no such thing as a free lunch. She knew Eugène's price to the last centime. Graciously accepting his proposal, she said: 'Of course, Eugène, as time goes on we shall have to start incorporating more of your original designs into the collections, so that when I finally decide to retire and hand over to you, the transition will be smooth.' They both knew she was really saying: 'I accept your price, and you'll get it eventually.'

It did not matter that he could tell no one of his triumph. The Rue Cambon staff, engaged on short contracts for the Nathan Rose collection, were signed on permanently and told they would be producing another experimental range which Eugène had sketched for Mademoiselle. Then he went to work, at last free to run things until she arrived with her silver scissors to hack at a few token ensembles. It went like a dream. Eugène was pretty certain that Emile Ponthieu had guessed the truth, but no one else ever gave any indication that they saw how things had changed. Eugène's confidence grew every day as he anticipated a presentation to another New York wholesaler who would say yes where Rose had said no.

Doré had other ideas. She never forgot a failure nor forgave an insult, and she never permitted repetition of circumstances which had caused her pain. There was to be no second private show.

When Eugène was satisfied that the collection was almost ready for presentation, he went to see Eliane about making arrangements to nominate a wholesaler. Halfway through his progress report, she silenced him.

'I have a better way, Eugène. Have you ever considered that it might be more profitable and less painful to us to let someone else negotiate with New York? They can pay for the couture house re-opening into the bargain. How's that for a neat little suggestion?'

'I don't know about neat, Mademoiselle. I don't even understand how it would work. If anyone takes the misery from us, they'll want to take the profit too.'

'Not necessarily. What if they stand to profit quite separately on other business if they back us on the franchising and the couture come-back?'

'I think you'd better explain in terms a simple country boy can understand.'

'Of course – the Reynaud Brothers! They got into one hell of a flap because a little bird told them I'd been talking to big bad Americans about mass production. They hated to see a new profit source going out of the window.'

'No doubt. That merely means they'd like to hive off our profit.'

'Not all of it – and they'd pay through their well-trained noses for what they did get. It's really quite simple. For ages they've wanted to expand their sales of D in the States but I've restricted them because they couldn't satisfy me that they could assure quality control if they manufactured in North America. If there were a department store concession operating, it would boost perfume sales, and if I lifted that manufacturing restriction in return for them doing the fashion franchise leg-work . . . and that's just the beginning. They've put forward a sensational range of very expensive beauty products – skin care and make-up – which they want to launch under the Doré name. I'd get the usual royalties on the scent, similar royalties on the cosmetics, ditto on the clothing concession. They'd sell the concessions and take on *all* the Paris couture re-opening expenses in return. How's that for a deal?'

'In just two words, Mademoiselle, too good. There must be a snag.'

'Well, of course, they'd require a shareholding in the main company . . . but have you the faintest idea of what it costs to run a couture house these days? And on top of that, they'll effectively give you and me unlimited salaries from their side of the perfume business, by writing off our living expenses as business expense accounts!'

Red lights and alarm bells were flashing and ringing inside Eugène's head. 'Don't touch it, Mademoiselle! Keep the company and finance the couture re-opening yourself. We'll slay New York with the new designs and you'll cover the couture costs again and again. Make this deal and one day they'll control us.'

Eliane was naturally indomitable and she was recovering her confidence faster with every day that passed. Now she was ready for Eugène.

'Don't be so suspicious. I've been dealing with the Reynauds for more than twenty years and they've treated me fairly. Since you're so concerned, perhaps you'd like to sit in on the negotiations.'

'I'm certainly not letting them take place without me, if you're planning to go on using my . . . that is, if you and I are going to continue collaborating on your collections.'

'Don't attempt to dissuade me, Eugène, I'm not listening. I tried doing a concession deal by direct negotiation and look what happened. Okay, so now we've got the designs right. You don't think I'd push my luck with Angela Fenwick by asking her to put up a second buyer, do you? She was very gracious about the last fiasco, but I'd never approach her again from a position of such weakness. No, my ideal would be to have Nathan Rose come crawling back at the end of my first new couture collection and tell me he was wrong in 1952.'

And that was precisely what she got.

It was just as well, for as it happened they still needed Rose's commercial muscle. Early in 1953, Eliane showed her first couture collection since 1939. Everyone from Doré herself down to the humblest apprentice midinette was convinced it was a winner. The clothes were delicious – quite different in mood from anything else in Paris, strongly reminiscent of classic Grande Mademoiselle but with an indefinable freshness which made them special and new.

The last model paraded to warm applause. Immediately

afterwards, Nathan Rose reached Doré moments before the rest of her admirers. He beamed at her. 'Mademoiselle, I've never been so happy to be proved wrong. May I congratulate you on a brilliant collection and ask if you're interested in renewing our initial negotiations?'

'My door is always open, Monsieur Rose. It's good to see someone prepared to be so gallantly wrong.' Neither of them chose to admit they were referring to different errors – Doré to the wholesaler's poor judgement of her genius, Rose to his premature assumption that Eliane was finished. As it was, everyone was able to get a little of what they wanted.

Eliane referred him to Jacques Reynaud and within forty-eight hours the perfume magnate had concluded an exclusive tie-up with Rose for ready-to-wear, as well as a guarantee that stores offering the clothes would carry the cosmetics and scent too. By then, Eliane and Eugène were discovering the full extent of their need for a Nathan Rose.

The European press had decided to go for Eliane's jugular. As she said months later, she could have shown the greatest collection of all time and still they would have carved her up in print. They seemed to have formed an unconscious conspiracy to ensure that her comeback would fail. Something about this fabulous figure from the past screamed to be torn down. Perhaps they simply perceived a better story in her destruction than in her resurrection. Whatever the reason, they were out to finish her. Nor was it confined to the fashion press. There were even a couple of men of letters scattered among the specialists who duly produced razor-sharp words and proceeded to slash her with them on the pages of the quality glossies.

The Parisian papers were the first to unleash their scorn. The British and German press followed on the heels of the French. By the time the dust settled, everyone had written off Alouette Doré as a permanent has-been who had re-opened simply to boost her scent sales. It was confidently predicted in the European trade press that there was unlikely to be another couture collection. Drab colours, tired lines, lack of structure in a structured age – all these charges were flung at her as proof of failure. She was even criticised for using flat-chested, narrow-hipped models. This last accusation infuriated her more than any other.

'The stupid, brainless bastards!' she said, putting aside the third paper. 'They know as well as I do that every model in Paris is shaped that way, otherwise she couldn't get a job. They've been padding out the models with horsehair for the past six years, and they try to rub out anyone who refuses to go along with it now. Perhaps someone will tell them eventually that padding might work on a skinny beanpole model but it looks like hell on a naturally curvy woman.'

It was the naturally curvy women of America who saved her, in their thousands, courtesy of Nathan Rose's wholesale operation.

It showed in the first sales statistics to arrive from New York. When the Doré lines appeared in two Fifth Avenue stores, every suit had sold out by the second day. The dresses were not long in following. American women who wanted to be both fashionable and mobile were rediscovering what rich Frenchwomen had learned and forgotten in the 1920s – one could run across the road or climb a steep flight of steps in a Doré without feeling crippled afterwards. The skirts allowed long strides; the sleeves permitted the arms to be stretched fully. The shape was in the cut and quality of the material, not in the bulk of the padding or the rigidity of the bones. Middle America was getting to know Alouette Doré at last and had no intention of letting her retire again.

In Paris the papers maintained a morose silence. In London a couple of fashion editors had the courage to admit they had been wrong. Very slowly, Europe began accepting that La Grande Mademoiselle really did appear to be immortal.

Eugène knew that Eliane had finally accepted the reality of their new success when she retired to Switzerland for a month to have a face lift. No one was going to mistake her for an eccentric grandmother again.

The years that followed had a disturbing duality for Eugène. The fashion house went from strength to strength and he, at least, knew it was largely down to him. After a while the Reynaud brothers were obviously aware of it, too, although they never let Doré suspect their complicity. But Eliane herself became increasingly convinced that the two annual collections were all her own designs. This gave Eugène no more than the odd stab of irritation. After all, it was only what he had expected from the start. What bothered him far more was that his grandmother used her power increasingly to veto the very originality which had saved the house. As the Yé-yé age dawned, bringing skirts that looked more like broad belts, along with panty-hose and kinky boots, Eliane flung out a growing proportion of Eugène's more innovative designs.

She seemed bent on stopping him from developing along the very lines which had brought their original success. Easy fabrics, freedom of movement, lack of clutter, clean lines - all were features of the young look which revolutionised fashion in the sixties. She rejected it all, instead of allowing Eugène to work it into the Doré collections.

His initial designs took the new trends and applied to them the famous Doré staples. As early as 1963, he brought her the briefest of mini-skirted suits, saved from vulgarity by matching ribbed tights and sweaters which gave the tiny skirts and brief jackets the look of elegant trimmings above a splendidly simple body suit. Eliane laughed the idea to scorn. Two seasons later, Courrèges brought Paris to a standstill with such a look and set the style for one branch of couture throughout the sixties. Eugène brought her tailored coats whose ultra-short skirts were once more balanced by the matching colour of the thick tights which went with them. She rejected them out of hand. ('Who wants to look like an overgrown schoolgirl on a winter outing?') Valentino drew everyone's eyes to Rome with such a look in 1967. Close to despair, Eugène changed tack and experimented with the superb heavy matte jersey developed by Swiss fabric manufacturers. He gave it even more impact by using pin-tucks and smocking techniques more usually associated with crêpe-de-chine on traditional children's dresses, and added the final touch with fine kid and snakeskin trims. She hated it. ('Baby-clothes for leather fetishists!') In 1969 Jean Muir was acclaimed from Tokyo to New York when she showed snakeskin over pin-tucked fluid jersey in London.

Eugène was trapped. Eliane let through only what he considered his bread-and-butter designs. As the years passed, the house became a fashion institution. Other couturiers changed with the seasons; Doré went on re-working the same look for customers who had no desire for a new image. Sales were good but static. There were no troughs but no peaks either. The most Eugène could hope to get past her was something like his classic re-working in silk of the English tweed-and-cashmere look. It produced a lovely, flattering collection, but was far too understated for his taste.

His tragedy was that he knew he could have achieved what he wanted if he had been prepared to gamble. Now he was established as the right-hand man of one of fashion's all time greats, plenty of houses would have taken him seriously. Had he shown his own designs to any one of six leading couturiers, they would have taken him on, as a freelance designer at the very least, and within a couple of seasons he would have made his name independently of Doré. But he was a prisoner of his own lust to own the House of Doré, and of his inexplicable desire to protect Eliane from a changing, hostile world. So he stayed and was prosperous and unhappy.

The Reynaud brothers were unhappy, too. They were not in business to stand still, but to progress. In 1970 Jacques Reynaud came to him and suggested that he put pressure on Mademoiselle to retire and leave the designing to him. Eugène shook his head wearily. 'She'll die in harness. I can only suggest you pray she goes soon, because there's no other way she'll relinquish control, to me or anyone else.'

Jacques looked at him oddly. 'Eugène, don't you ever get tired of jumping every time she cracks the whip? You're a talented man. Why waste your life under her thumb?'

'Don't worry about me. I'm fine the way I am.'

'It may not be possible for you to continue that way forever. We've had enough. Neither of us is young anymore, and really, since the 1950s, we've only stayed in business for fun. It's stopped being fun now because we're not expanding anywhere. If you can't get Mademoiselle to move over, we're selling out.'

'You can't do that! She only went into partnership with you because she'd worked with you for so long. She'd never tolerate strangers.'

'She has no choice in the matter. I never understood why her lawyers didn't insist on a buy-back clause in the company articles, so that we had to offer our shares to her, but they didn't. As a result we can go to whoever we choose, and we've received such a generous offer that no one else would dream of matching it.'

'Try me. Rather than let part of the business go elsewhere, I might attempt to raise the funds.'

Jacques Reynaud laughed. 'Oh, Eugène, you haven't got this sort of money, or any chance of access to it. Not even Mademoiselle could raise the capital. We're getting out of the whole business, not just couture. Remember, we rolled the whole thing together. Reynaud Perfumes owns forty per cent of Doré Couture. To get hold of the garment business you have to be able to afford to buy the whole operation. We sell products in a hundred countries and our worldwide sales last year alone were nearly $800,000,000! No individual could bid for us.'

Eugène was shaken. He had never been at all interested

in the perfumery and cosmetics side of the business, and the immensity of the figures involved came as a shock. His only consolation was that Mademoiselle had insisted on Reynaud Perfumes becoming a shareholder in Doré, rather than agreeing her business should become part of their company and take a shareholding in it. If she had done that, they could have swept her away without even consulting her. But after the shock came curiosity.

'Just who *is* big enough to bid for you? You're clearly not just selling off your business in shares.'

'No harm in telling you now, I suppose. The deal is all finalised. It's Cavalieri.'

'Surely you don't mean the Italian ready-to-wear firm?'

'None other.'

'But they're not big enough for that sort of capital outlay! They'd never manage it.'

'I confess I was a little surprised, but they own far more than you'd think. Their designer separates are only the cherry on the cake. They supply a number of the big international chain stores with own-label knitwear through one subsidiary that's never publicly linked to them; they have their own stores throughout Italy and South America; they have a middle-sized cosmetics operation, a chain of expensive hairdressing salons and, would you believe, five luxury hotels specialising in slimming and beauty treatments!'

'God, they're everywhere. It sounds like a front organisation for the Mafia.'

A long silence fell on the room. Then Jacques said: 'I don't recommend you make jokes like that to anybody else.' A moment later he forced a laugh. 'Come on, this is getting melodramatic. We're selling out to a very up-and-coming company which will take a lively interest in the development of Doré enterprises. I hope you'll feel you want to co-operate with them, that's all. By the way, I can't take you up on your lunch invitation. I have to arrange a few things out of town this afternoon. Look after Mademoiselle, Eugène. Try to persuade her we've all had our day sooner or later.'

Eugène sat alone at the big table for a long time after Jacques' departure. If his own blunder just now had revealed the true identity of the new owners of Reynaud Perfumes, they wouldn't need a controlling interest in Doré Couture to have things their own way. He had read enough over the years to know that the Honoured Society knew how to make things happen to their advantage.

# Chapter Twenty

## Pavane for a Dead Infanta

The coma changed to natural sleep during the second day. Towards evening on Wednesday, Doré awoke and asked in a croaking voice for a cup of China tea. The nurse at her bedside hurriedly sent for her doctor. By the time he came, Eliane was becoming strident in her demands.

'What is all this nonsense? Did I pass out or something? What am I doing with all these vultures flapping around me? Where's my tea? Doesn't anyone listen to me any more?'

Entering her room, the doctor said, 'I take it you feel better.'

'Hmm! I might if someone would give me a drink. I'm as dry as the Sahara.'

'All in good time. Only a few sips of water until I've examined you properly.'

He went over her thoroughly. The fingertips of her left hand were numb and there appeared to be some loss of sensation in her left leg. Otherwise there was no visible deterioration. Dr Antonin sent the nurse to order Doré's tea, then turned back to his patient.

'Now, before you start playing the tyrant, let's get a couple of things clear. You've managed to reach a great age, against all the odds given your smoking and your determination to go on working until you drop. Now you've had a stroke – a slight one, but it's a warning that you could have another at any time. You're to take far more rest. Above all, no business at all. Monsieur St-Meurice can handle all that for you. You should have given him his head years ago anyway.'

'My work is my life.'

'You say that like a little parrot, Mademoiselle. I'm not going to argue, merely to tell you it'll be just that if you try to do any more, because it will cost you your life. Now, whether you wish to die immediately or go on living in relatively good health is up to you. I'm sure you won't last long if you carry on taking an active part in the business.'

'But what am I to do with myself?' It was the plaintive wail of a child.

'What all other retired women of means and intelligence do – pursue your interests. For a start, you could go on working with the young lady out there – who is it, Mademoiselle Vincent? – I'm sure it wouldn't harm you to continue work on your biography.'

'Andy's out there? Why didn't you say so? Send her in at once. Oh, doctor, that's quite a different matter. If she's back, of course I'll retire!'

Antonin was taken aback at the transformation in his patient. He had no idea that she had assumed Andy had left permanently.

The nurse looked at Antonin questioningly. 'Any restrictions on family visiting, doctor?'

'Mm, yes, for a day or two, just as a precaution. Let them all pop in and out for a few minutes at a time. Not too much excitement. She can start getting up tomorrow morning and in a couple of days she can go out for short walks. From tomorrow I want her moving about in the apartment as much as possible. Plenty of rest, of course, but certainly after a week or so she should be going out for drives and short strolls without trouble. I'll leave full diet and general care instructions with the prescriptions.' He turned back to Doré. 'Welcome back to the world, Mademoiselle. Remember, it's more or less up to you now whether you'll have a chance to enjoy it.'

Outside he talked to Andy, Marie-Louise and Eugène. 'She's made a remarkable recovery, but it's really more like a remission at her age. Given her strength, she could last for years, but I'm inclined to think she'll just fade away some time in the next few months – in her sleep if she's lucky. Treat her gently and try not to excite her too much, although I fully understand that with her temperament that's asking a lot of you all!'

The next couple of days were paradise for Eliane. She staged a positively theatrical reunion with Marie-Louise, and acknowledged Eugène for once as the support he was. There was an element of melodrama in both meetings. But with Andy she seemed to behave with utter sincerity.

When they were alone, she said: 'Did you come because you forgive me, or because you just reacted automatically to a call to duty?'

Andy embraced the frail old woman. 'I came because I love you. There's nothing for me to forgive.'

'I think there is. I thought of it again and again after you'd dashed off. Your mother left like that nearly forty years ago. It was my fault then, too. You can't blame a sixteen-year-old girl for starting the sort of row we had.'

'Doré, you're going to have to stop this! The doctor said no excitement and I can see you getting het up already. Listen to me for a moment and then we'll let the whole thing drop. You haven't told me the whole truth, but you've probably got closer than you ever did before. I just want to say I understand why you are what you are. You're pretty marvellous anyway. There are things about you that I hate, but at least I understand. There's no need to keep apologising just to stop me going away again. I love you and I'm not going anywhere. Before I drop this conversation, though, I'd like to know one thing. What was your real reason for getting me to write your biography?'

The ancient eyes opened wide. 'Reason? You already know it – I don't want to be forgotten, and I want the record set straight.'

'You'll have to do better than that! I happen to think you don't give two hoots about being forgotten. I do believe you care about the way you're remembered, though, and that's a different thing.'

Eliane glanced around to make sure they were still alone

before she answered. 'I read a very interesting article in a literary magazine a few months ago. It talked about the fashion for writing biographies and it quoted Billingham, the English novelist. You must have heard what a private man he is; won't normally tell anyone what colour his sweater is, let alone any details about his past. Well, he'd actually commissioned someone to write his biography – chosen a well-known writer and thrown open every bit of private correspondence, all his notebooks and a list of his living friends and kinsmen into the bargain. Guess what he said when they asked him to comment? He said he wanted his biography written like he wanted his head blown off, but he knew that sooner or later every literary hack in the business would be working on a different version. He'd worked it out that if one talented writer produced a biography with full access to the existing sources and the subject's support – with personal approval of the manuscript, of course – that it would kill the market for all future attempts. Think of it – by going through it all once himself, he had a good chance of stopping any future snoopers thinking it worthwhile to take another look!'

Andy was forced to admire Doré's reasoning. 'And you thought you'd try the same thing – give me ten times more information than you had given anyone else, tell me a few awful secrets and then turn me loose. I presume that means there are things I still haven't found out.'

'If you want to speculate about that, my dear, feel free to do so. I don't think you'll get very far. But I'm content for you to produce a book covering all the information we've discussed and what Loulou has added. I suppose I have to include Eugène in that too.'

'But you make it obvious there's more – more than any of us three knows.'

Again the innocent look. 'Conjecture, dear girl, pure conjecture. You go off and write the biography. I'm satisfied that you'll present a portrait which I find acceptable.'

She would not discuss it further. When Andy, stung by

curiosity, tried a little pressure, she smiled smugly and reminded her grand-daughter of the doctor's warning about excessive excitement. 'You're an infuriating old woman, Doré,' said Andy, 'but I don't want to lose you yet, so settle down and get some sleep. I'll see you in the morning.'

Marie-Louise stayed for a week, but by then Eliane had improved so much she felt able to return to Brittany. 'Joel will be furious to be alone, after coming all that way at my invitation,' she said. 'Anyway, I miss him. Andy, I've been meaning to ask you . . . how would you feel about acquiring a step-father?'

She burst out laughing. 'Really, Ma, I don't think it counts when you're in your mid-thirties! He's hardly going to bring me up wrong or send me to bed without any supper, is he? Does that mean he's asked? I was rather hoping he would.'

'Yes, he asked me just after we got the news about Alouette. I love him, and I'm damned lucky to get a second chance with him.'

'I never understood why you let him go before, but I was abroad and you'd split up when I got back.'

'Strangely enough it was all wrapped up with the Doré business, indirectly at least. A lot of it was that we were both still a bit too egotistical but I toppled the whole thing by getting caught up with the old witch again. You see, I'd always vowed I had no time for her; that I'd loved Geneviève Chabrol as a mother, not Alouette Doré, and so on. But I'd remained fascinated by the woman all those years, and I'd quietly researched her all the while I was writing about other subjects. Every time I ran into someone who'd been around when Doré was at the height of her fame, or when she was on the way up, I'd interview them. I pieced together a huge quantity of material, and as I did, I began to move from hatred to grudging respect. That turned to admiration and I ended up with an odd sort of love for her. God knows her faults are huge, but she has some impressive qualities, too, particularly her courage and her sheer determination to survive.

'Of course, I'd never told anyone about any of it, and suddenly there I was, faced with the boyfriend of the moment doing the big biography of Mademoiselle. Furthermore, when Joel was approached to do the book, we were going through a rocky patch together. Doré did one of her classic prima donna routines after a couple of weeks of reasonably close collaboration. Joel isn't too good with ladies from the fashion business – he's more used to bull fighters and cowboys – and he flared up and stormed out. I confessed all to him, intending to offer him my research material. He launched into a tirade about what she'd done to me and I blew up in his face. After that there was no going back and we ended up walking away from each other.'

Andy was aghast. She was starting to have difficulty in believing that one small fierce woman, who had set her world on end so recently, had also turned her mother's life upside down. The more she heard about Doré, the more she realised the woman's pervasive personality coloured all their lives. 'And you still manage to care about her?'

'Oh, fanatically! Once I got over the early resentment, it was almost a love affair. She's firmly a part of my life and I can't imagine trying to dislodge her. It's very hard to capture her charm because she's a mistress of understatement, but I can think of one example straight away which says a whole lot. Remember I told you about the time she got me back from Switzerland and introduced me to her dreadful collaborator friends? Well, she wanted me to dress up in the latest fashions to impress them, but her sense of personal freedom was such that she put out a whole rail full of clothes for me to choose my own outfit. However much she wanted me to succeed, she wouldn't dream of presuming to dictate my choice of clothing. That was pure Doré.'

Andy took her to the station, promising that she would be back in P'tit Barenton as soon as Doré was sufficiently recovered. They made time to stop at a restaurant for lunch on the way.

'We've sorted me out,' said Marie-Louise. 'Now what do we do about you? I heard you on the telephone to someone the other morning.'

'Eavesdropper! You did, and it's about time I admitted that it's getting serious.'

'So who is the mysterious caller?'

'A dreamy-looking type I picked up just after I got here. It turned out he knew Eugène and the rag trade crowd. I've had a bit of a thing going with him – purely physical at first, but believe me, you wouldn't blame me! He's a dead ringer for about four Italian film stars. The trouble was, he had all the Latin macho trimmings and I didn't like that at all. He didn't know how to get hold of me, thanks to my rather patchy attempts at personal security. But while I was with you in Brittany, Eugène took pity on him and told him where I was. Hence the call. When you have time, I think I'll introduce you to him and. . . . Why, Marie-Louise, what's wrong?'

Her mother responded with a shaky laugh. 'I – I'm probably being silly and mother hen-ish, but ever since the Umberto trouble I get extremely nervous at any mention of Italianate men and macho Latin behaviour. Are you sure he's all he seems?'

'Oh, you're too easily worried. One, he's Spanish, not Italian; and two, the macho bit applies to Spaniards as much as Italians.'

'You can't have been that sure if you didn't tell him where to find you. Why did Eugène let the cat out of the bag? He knows you're more or less in hiding.'

Now it was Andy's turn to look troubled. 'I asked myself about that at the time. There was no reason for him to let Steb in on the secret. I told Eugène I wasn't head over heels about the guy because he was too intense. And come to think of it, he should have known the fact that Steb works for an Italian firm would be bound to make me uneasy, however unconnected it might be.'

'Just who does he work for?'

'Oh, er, I did know . . . something like an opera title . . . you know what I'm like with rag trade names. . . . Cavalieri.'

'Look, darling, I know it's none of my business, but let me make a note of it and ask Joel to make a few enquiries when I get home. I'd be much happier.'

'All right, if it makes you feel better. But stop worrying! I want to introduce you soon, then you'll *see* he's exactly what he seems and no more.'

She saw Marie-Louise off at the Gare Montparnasse and went back to Rue Cambon. For the next couple of weeks she went over the tapes and notes for the biography, checked out some of Marie- Louise's research with Doré, and followed Eugène around as he finished off the collection. They had postponed it until the end of August and he was handling it faultlessly. When Andy exclaimed over his ability he was on the point of telling her he had been designing the collections for more than twenty years, but stopped himself at the last moment. Why let Doré down now when he had shielded her for so long? He would be running the fashion house soon enough.

Doré had made a few contributions which kept her quiet about the overall collection as it moved towards its completion. With her customary attention to detail, she regarded one item in particular as the key to next season's look. One evening she called Andy to her bedside. 'I have something for you, my dear, a little preview of the collection. I hope you'll like it. Take a look in that box on the night table.'

Intrigued, Andy picked up the long, narrow container. 'Open it,' Doré urged. 'It's something of a prototype, I hope.'

Inside the flat box was a metal belt, the interwined links mimicking the small D-shaped designs which in gilt had become a house trade mark. But this was not a gilt. It was surprisingly heavy and it glowed darkly, like gunmetal.

'Why, Doré, it's lovely! But I thought the gilt Ds were a lifelong favourite.'

'Yes, yes, but this season we're concentrating on a range of fabrics in crimsons and slate greys. I can't think of any two colours less suited to gold. Steel or silver is made for those tones, and there's something businesslike and assertive about steel so I chose that. It seemed to cry out for much bigger links than the gilt Ds, too. Please wear it for me with the right outfit.'

'I'd be honoured. I hope you hand over something terribly pricey in crimson and grey to go with it.'

Doré's attention span these days was noticeably shorter. She gestured vaguely. 'Ask Eugène, he's in charge of all that.'

Pleased with the gift, but slightly saddened at the old woman's increasing weariness, Andy said good night.

Later, lying in the darkness in Doré's bed at the Rue Cambon apartment, she was unable to sleep. For the first time, she was oppressed by sadness for her grandmother, where before she had felt the old woman had exactly what she needed, as well as what she deserved. Now Andy saw a different picture. After a lifetime of going for what she wanted, of throwing aside the humble ambitions of her sex, this symbol of female independence and achievement was left alone. There were no memories of a long marriage, of children growing and leaving and returning with grandchildren in tow; no one man Doré could look back on and truly believe she was everything to him; no special place for Mademoiselle. However fine they were, dress fabrics lacked life. They fell in crumpled heaps when they weren't filled with people. And the people she knew . . . hadn't they made up for the lost family life? Had they hell! Now, at the end, it was horribly clear that Doré had got what she paid for. The people who clustered around to warm themselves at the fire of her success – they'd been there for the fine surroundings, the fame-by-association, the glittering parties. As the living legend grew old, it was finally obvious that whatever the secret of her allure, it had not been her lovable character.

Will I be like that? Andy wondered in the dark. Doré's not indulging in wishful thinking when she says we are alike. I have all her drive and independence and rage, but I've been saved from her coldness by a childhood full of Marie-Louise. Which is all very well while I'm young and sexy and have lovers and friends and my mother's still around. What happens when my career has excluded everything else and I'm a very old celebrity whom everyone remembers and nobody wants to know any more? She shivered at the bleak prospect. And into the void created by her depressed spirit there came a comforting image – Steb Ortiz.

'Oh, come on, that's straight cheap romance!' Andy was so exasperated with herself that she said it aloud, adding, rather more quietly, 'But what's so wrong with cheap romance? When you see the alternatives . . .'

Suddenly she was aware of the real difference between Alouette Doré and herself. Doré had never really been the central figure in any man's life. She had come closest with Bonnie Charles. He had realised her value, but too late. The others? The Duke had wanted to put her at the centre of his world, but more as a specimen butterfly, collected, chloroformed and transfixed by a pin. Andy had been offered more several times, with different men, but none had seemed quite worth giving up other elements of her life. Her reaction had become so routine that she had assumed Esteban was no more than a passing dalliance. But this was different. When had she ever missed a man before? Now a little nagging loneliness told her she wished it were not so long since she had seen him, made her hope she would be with him again soon.

'Well, my girl, you can do something about that, at least,' she said. 'Call him tomorrow and see if he still stirs you up; and then, who knows? Now, for God's sake stop talking to yourself and go to sleep!'

Eugène was more comfortable now about his and Andy's relative positions in Doré's scale of priorities. He had talked to Eliane soon after Andy's flight to Brittany. The old woman had been hit harder by her grand-daughter's rejection than by anything in her long life. It devastated Eugène because he wanted to mean that much to Doré and knew he did not. Nevertheless he made himself available, as usual, while she shouted and sobbed and protested against fate. In the middle of it all, she said something which made him go cold.

Bemoaning Andy's departure, she said: 'And to think I was going to divide Doré Couture between the two of you!'

Keeping an impassive expression was the hardest thing he could ever remember doing. 'But you've changed your mind now,' he said, apparently without emotion.

'Oh, yes. If she goes tearing off like this over one disagreement, God knows what she'd do if she was under pressure in the business. I've altered things a little. I hope you're happy with it, but I thought it was for the best.'

'What have you done?'

'I've left Doré Couture to you and the holding in Reynaud Perfumes to Andy. The perfume company shares have a higher paper value than the couture business, of course, and Reynaud Perfumes' holding company owns forty per cent of the couture house, but I thought. . . .'

He sighed with relief. He didn't give a damn about Reynaud Perfumes. He didn't want the money . . . he wanted the couture business. He'd cope with the Cavalieri involvement afterwards, and he could do it better without a family partner.

Eugène was feeling more and more like an inexpert juggler with too many balls in the air at once. Cavalieri had started pushing him some time ago. Get the old woman out. We won't displace you, we know you can run the company, but if you don't get her to go peacefully, we may remove her without the option. . . .

Andy had been heaven-sent at first. When she let slip that she was hiding from interests not a million miles from Cavalieri's, he thought a quick tip-off might be a good bargaining counter. It was. They took the heat off him over displacing Doré and encouraged him to get Andy within surveillance range. He had told them he had no wish to be involved in violence. There was no question of that, they had assured him. If she was in Paris working with Mademoiselle, she wouldn't be yapping at their friends' heels in London. That was all that interested them.

So he'd co-operated. His new associates regularly assured Eugène that their foot soldier was only in Paris to protect his interests; that once Eugène was in the saddle all such irritations would disappear. But as time passed Eugène wondered how long it would be before they decided he was not running things as they wanted. There might, after all, be worse forms of servitude than that imposed by La Grande Mademoiselle.

It was late afternoon and Eugène was standing in the mirror-lined salon, making the final adjustments to a suit of vivid silk evening pyjamas, which reflected classic 1930s Doré but also managed to capture the whole fashion spirit of 1978. Andy was watching him, totally absorbed. He checked the last buttonhole, looked at his watch and said, 'Okay, everyone, we can stop on time today – it's all under control. Thank you for all your work.' There was a ripple of approval as the staff dispersed. Such punctuality so close to collection time was unknown with Doré.

Andy left the salon with him. 'This collection is different. Why? I thought she'd finalised the designs before she got sick.'

He gave her a secret smile. 'Oh, it's surprising how many nuances slip in when someone else finishes things off.'

They headed upstairs to the apartment.

As they walked in through the door, Eliane came out of the drawing-room. 'Ah, Eugène, at last! It's no use, I can't hold back any longer. I want to go down and see my collection, make sure it's going to look right!'

He looked slightly troubled, then shrugged. 'Tomorrow, Mademoiselle. They're packing up now. We've all but finished the final preparations. You can see everything tomorrow.'

She started to move away, grumbling a little at his laziness in stopping so early in the evening. 'No stamina, that's the trouble with everybody these days. No . . . no. . . .'

They both raced towards her as she fell. Eugène rolled her over to face them and supported her gently in his arms. She gazed up at him, her face suddenly drenched with tears. 'No time now,' she murmured. 'No time at all.' Then she died.

Eugène carried Doré into the master bedroom and laid the tiny, shrunken body on the bed. He was dry-eyed but his face wore the expression Andy had seen on the faces of men whose closest comrades had just been killed in battle. After long minutes of silence, she touched his arm gently.

'She'd have wanted to go like this, Eugène.'

There was savagery in his look. 'She wouldn't have wanted to go at all!'

He walked out and left Andy to shed private tears for her grandmother.

Eventually she became aware she was no longer alone. Doré's maid had come in.

'Mam'selle Vincent – a word, please . . . I don't think M'sieur Eugène . . . that is . . .' the words tailed off and she started crying quietly.

'What's wrong, Nadine?'

The maid struggled for self-control. 'Mam'selle – he's calling the funeral directors. He's arranging for them to take Mam'selle away . . . strangers will get her ready. She couldn't bear that, really she couldn't, but I can't be the one to stop him. I'm just a servant.'

The problem had not occurred to Andy. Now she was at a loss to offer a solution. 'But Nadine, someone has to do it. What had you in mind?'

Confused, the maid flushed and looked away. 'I – that is, I thought perhaps, Mam'selle, you and I could . . .'

'Me? Christ, I wouldn't know where to start! And I'm not sure I could handle it,' she added lamely.

Nadine was almost pleading now. 'I know what is necessary. I'd do it all, gladly, but I know Mademoiselle Doré would be against that. It would have to be someone close. Please, Mademoiselle Vincent – it would have meant so much to her . . .'

Suddenly, Andy understood. She had to, however distasteful she found it. The love she still felt for Doré demanded it.

'Okay, Nadine, you win. Hang on – I'll deal with M'sieur Eugène, then we'll attend to it.'

Eugène tried to resist at first. 'Don't be absurd, Andy. The idea is barbaric. Nadine is nothing but a peasant. You really shouldn't encourage such nonsense!'

'Doré was a peasant, too, at heart. I think Nadine's right.'

'In that case it's just as well that I'm the one who's arranging the funeral. Mademoiselle was a major figure. We can't have her laid out by a couple of amateurs. It would show!'

'You can't mean you intend to have an open coffin?'

'Of course. People will want to pay their last respects. We'll have the body embalmed and then it will be in the right condition to lie in state.'

'No chance. Have you any idea what they'll do to her? They'll make a slash down her torso, draw out her guts and fill her up with sawdust to make sure she keeps good and fresh for the gawping multitudes. Presumably you think she'd approve of *that!*'

He paled. 'I – I didn't think of it that way.'

'Well you can start now. What's it to be, loving amateurism and a closed coffin from Nadine and me, or a professionally-stuffed dummy from the embalmer? Make up your mind. I don't have all night!'

'Very well. I'll ask the undertakers to come tomorrow. If you insist on this charade I believe it's traditional to sit with the corpse after it's been prepared.' He closed his eyes with a show of exaggerated distaste, but Andy was left with the impression that he was secretly relieved at her intervention.

Back in the bedroom, Nadine briefly embraced Andy. 'Thank you, Mam'selle - you'll never know how much this would have meant to her.'

'I think I'm beginning to get some idea. Right - you'll have to show me.'

Eliane had been reluctant to face death but she had been determined to choose her own outfit for her last appearance. Nadine opened the big walk-in closet in the dressing room and took a sealed dress bag from a hanger at the back. It contained a cream suit of fine Irish linen, braided with dark blue and with a dark blue silk blouse. From a drawer she took an outsize handkerchief of finest cream lawn.

'A handkerchief, Nadine, now?'

'Her jaw, Mam'selle. You see? It sags when we die . . .' She began to cry quietly.

Gradually, Andy did as the maid instructed her, learning that what had seemed to be a grisly task was really an effective way of letting out her grief. Together they washed her grandmother's body, dressed it in the chosen clothes and scented it with her own extra-concentrated blend of D. Then Nadine fetched Doré's cosmetics box and Andy made up her face. They both understood instinctively that although the coffin would be closed, this was the way Doré would want to encounter the Maker whose existence she had so often denied. As she finished, Nadine handed her a jar of light-coloured foundation cream and a box of matching loose powder.

'But I've done her face, and that's so light . . .'

'Her hands, Mam'selle. Didn't you ever notice? Every day she did her hands with this pale cream and powder, then set it with a damp sponge. She had naturally brown hands and when she was young they used to laugh at her and call her a peasant because her hands were sunburned. I think I was the only one she ever told, and that was just because it slipped out one day when she felt old and tired . . .'

That made Andy cry in earnest. How many other childhood sneers had Doré swallowed without showing the hurt? No wonder she turned into such a monster . . .

When she had finished her grandmother's last toilette, she folded the old woman's hands on her breast and straightened the immaculate clothes. Then she remembered one of Eliane's early stories.

'Jewellery, Nadine. Did Mademoiselle have a box for special bits and pieces?'

She found what she had been looking for in the bottom of a carved sandalwood box. It was a little topaz ring, its gold setting worn thin with time and heavy use. It was pretty enough but obviously at odds with the expensive costume pieces around it. Inside the shank, almost worn away, was engraved 'G to E, 10.12.04.' It was Geneviève's Christmas present.

It was appropriate that Doré should go on her last journey wearing the gift of the one person who had loved her unstintingly, without asking any return.

Andy was wearing the steel belt which her grandmother had so recently given her. Now she took it off and slipped it about the old woman's waist. It would be her own tribute. She stood back to study the effect and for a moment it was as if Doré spoke to her. Gunmetal with cream linen? What a faux pas! I could never be seen dead in it!

The impression was so vivid that Andy laughed in spite of herself. No, it was more appropriate that Doré should be buried wearing just Geneviève's simple jewel. She would wear the belt on her grandmother's behalf.

When they had finished, Nadine went to fetch two massive candelabra from the drawing room, filled them with tall white wax candles and placed them at Doré's head and feet before lighting them. When she had finished, she gestured towards a chair beside the bed.

'Mam'selle Vincent – may I have the honour of sharing your watch with Mademoiselle Doré?'

Andy nodded, tearful again. Whatever Doré had lacked, here was one woman who had obviously loved her. As they took their places, Eugène came into the room. He carried a spray of the silk camellias which had been part of Doré's fashion signature. Without speaking, he leaned over the bed and placed the flowers between his grandmother's cold fingers. Then he kissed her forehead, turned and left.

She had been lonely, almost solitary, in those last years. No one attending her funeral would have guessed it. The Madeleine is a big church. On that day it was packed with the famous and infamous from all over France and the fashionable world. All the women seemed to be wearing Doré originals and everyone claimed to have been her friend.

'I wish I believed she could see this,' Marie-Lousie whispered. 'She'd thoroughly approve. It's the one time she'd regard vulgar display as excusable.'

Only the service was to be held in Paris. Long ago, Doré had bought a plot in a Swiss cemetery and had arranged for her remains to be transported there. Appropriately for a woman who had not relished sharing her bed in life, she had chosen a double burial plot and her grave was separated from all the others by a closely-fenced expanse of turf.

Back in Paris, after the interment, Marie-Louise, Eugène and Andy attended a meeting with Eliane's lawyer at the Rue Cambon apartment. As a little sentimental gesture to her grandmother's memory, Andy wore a crimson and grey tunic, fastened at the waist with the chunky steel D-link belt. Minutes later, when she learned what the couturière had done to Eugène in the way of sentimental gestures, she regretted the impulse.

Doré's will was straightforward. Marie-Louise was to inherit her mother's jewellery, books, screens and antique furniture. With the exception of some small pensions and bequests to long-serving members of staff, the couture company and the holding in Reynaud Perfumes was split between Eugène and Andy. Doré had also taken the opportunity to make a post-mortem announcement of her marriage to the Duke of Conway and to direct that the Press should be informed that Marie-Louise was their child.

*'At the last, I feel that my grand-daughter's status as my legitimate descendant must be reflected in the scale of her inheritance,'* she had provided in the will. *'Therefore, Andrea Vincent will inherit 55 per cent of my holding in Doré Couture and 55 per cent of my shares in Reynaud Perfumes. Eugène St-Meurice will receive the remaining 45 per cent of each.'*

Apart from this bombshell, there was nothing unexpected about the document. When the lawyer had left, Andy turned apologetically to Eugène. 'I swear I knew nothing about this! It never occurred to me she'd leave me anything. She knows I've got a comfortable income coming to me in trust through Marie-Louise from the Conway Estate. I never dreamed this would happen. It would be more balanced if she'd at least divided it evenly.'

After the first shock, St-Meurice had managed to get himself under control. He smiled dismissively.

'We should have known that in the end Mademoiselle's subconscious desire to be a good bourgeoise would conquer the gypsy in her. At the last she had to show she valued legal status above all else. Never mind, I'm used to being a subordinate by now. Please excuse me. I know we're dining together before you leave tonight, but I'd like to go back to my apartment for a while.'

He walked out. Andy shut the door behind him and leaned against it, sighing heavily. Back in the drawing-room, she scanned her mother's face, seeking her reaction.

Marie-Louise was as uneasy as Andy. 'I really thought the old bitch had relented and turned into one of the good guys at the end,' she said. 'Oh well, she always was good at fooling people. She was still a harpy under the skin, it seems. Legitimate descent, my eye! She didn't care about that. It just appealed to her manipulative nature, knowing she'd sow the seeds of dissent by doing something like that. I really can't forgive her for double-crossing Eugène.'

Now Andy was puzzled. 'I can see she was ungenerous, but aren't you over-reacting in calling it a double-cross?'

'You don't know the half of it. Doré never made a come-back in 1953! She'd have sunk without trace if it hadn't been for Eugène. She hasn't designed a commercially successful garment since 1939. Her come-back was really Eugène's début. He's been ghosting designs for her ever since then, from a mixture of loyalty and the hope of inheriting the business. I imagine some people inside the house guessed the truth, but I'm the only person he ever told about it.'

'Oh, God, and now she's cheated him!'

'It looks horribly like that, doesn't it?'

'What are we going to do about it?'

'It's rather up to you, but I suspect we're both thinking along the same lines. Come on, let's have a stiff drink and talk it over. We'll work something out.'

By the time Eugène was due to return for dinner, they had settled things. Andy's inheritance from the Conway estate was enormous – far more than she was ever likely to be able to use. She had been unaware of its size until now because it was administered by Marie-Louise and did not become Andy's absolutely until her fortieth birthday.

'Not that you need worry about that,' said Marie-Louise. 'You can have as much as you want whenever you like. You just never needed it before, apart from the small allowance you've received since your teens, and I saw no reason to complicate your life unnecessarily with it when you were so clearly capable of earning a good living for yourself. In fact it's not only enough to free you from ever working again – you could keep a small town with it!'

'Which brings us to a far more humane use for my legacy from Doré.'

'I think so, Andy. After all, it would almost amount to

stealing to take the poor man's inheritance now, wouldn't it?'

She nodded. 'I wish I'd told him before he went off. He was looking so down, and trying so hard to hide it.'

'Never mind. You'll cheer him up fast enough now. Look, I'd rather not stand around like Lady Bountiful's handmaiden. I'm going to make myself scarce. Give him my love and tell him I've gone off to meet some friends of Joel's. I hope he's pleased.' Marie-Louise got her coat and left.

Eugène arrived about ten minutes later. He looked a little pale but otherwise was his usual self. Andy greeted him with a light kiss on the cheek, explained Marie-Louise's absence and led him into the drawing-room. As she poured drinks, he excused himself. 'I left something downstairs in the ground-floor lobby. I'll just go down and pick it up.' In fact he merely went down a floor to the couture salon and unlocked the door which connected it with the staircase up to the apartment.

He re-joined Andy and raised his glass to her. 'A toast to the new Empress,' he said, unable to keep a thread of bitterness from his voice.

'Sorry, Eugène, you've got the wrong heir apparent. I'm abdicating on accession. D'you think they'll charge me capital gains tax?'

He stared at her, momentary bewilderment rapidly displaced by alarm. 'What are you saying? Tell me, quick!'

'Okay, okay, there's no hurry – no one's going anywhere! Marie-Louise told me what you've been doing for Doré since she re-opened. I can't let her get away with diverting the lion's share of inheritance to me. My grandfather left me far more than I'll ever be able to spend. I'm making over everything Doré left me to you. I'll stay in Paris tomorrow instead of going back to Brittany and draw up the papers with the lawyer. Does that make you happier? Hey, you look as if you've lost a tenner and found a penny. What's wrong?'

As she spoke, the doorbell rang. Andy frowned. 'Odd –

must be the security man coming to check on something. The internal phone must have gone on the blink.'

As she started to get up, Eugène thrust her aside. 'Stay where you are! Don't come after me, do you understand?' He rushed into the hall, slamming the door behind him, and opened the front door to one of the two Cavalieri foot soldiers who had tried to run Andy down in the Rue de Rivoli.

The youth looked at him quizzically. 'Thought it was supposed to be her,' he said in a low voice.

'It's off. I'll explain tomorrow. Don't hang around now! Quick, or she'll overhear. . .' He might as well not have spoken. The Italian put a hand inside his leather bomber jacket and drew out a gun with a silencer fitted. 'Put it away, you fool – what d'you think you're doing?' cried Eugène.

The assassin smiled. 'We don't just want her. We decided to make a clean sweep while we're at it. It makes no odds to me whether you or she gets it first. *Ciao,* Eugène.' He fired twice at point blank range.

Andy, completely mystified at Eugène's behaviour, had reached the drawing-room door. She opened it as the *mafioso* started across the hall. Andy saw St-Meurice's body and gasped. Then she turned and ran from her pursuer, zig-zagging in the hope of presenting a poor target. At that range it was pointless. Something punched her in the back with vast force and her legs gave way beneath her. No pain, just complete absence of feeling from the small of her back down. There was a time, centuries ago, when she'd felt something like this before, but not here. Where, when . . .? The floor swam up to meet her and she reached out for it as for an old friend. Doré, she thought, I just know this is all your fault. . . .

In an American-style hamburger restaurant some ten minutes from the salon, Marie-Louise reached into her bag for cigarettes and lighter, only to realise she had left them at the apartment. She could easily have replaced them here –

they stocked her brand – but she was superstitious about the lighter. It had been Teddy Vincent's last gift before the Gestapo got him and for more than thirty years she had kept her promise to carry it always. She told herself that this time it was unimportant; that her desire to regain the talisman was just an excuse to barge in on Andy's *tête à tête* with Eugène. But at heart Marie-Louise was as superstitious as her mother. She was already half convinced that there was a purpose behind her forgetfulness, that somehow it was pre-ordained she should return now to the apartment above the couture salon.

Marie-Louise gave herself an impatient little shake. 'Come on, you fool,' she said aloud, 'go with the feeling and get back there. They're not going to eat you, for Christ's sake!' The odd look she got from the couple at the next table settled it. She'd rather be cold-shouldered by Andy and Eugène for gate-crashing their confidential talk than be mistaken for a nut who talked to herself. As her steak and salad arrived, she stood up, left enough money to pay for it beside her untouched plate, and walked out. Now they'd be convinced she was cuckoo! Perhaps they were right.

Minutes later, she decided she had been summoned by Andy's guardian angel. Arriving back at Rue Cambon, she was admitted by a puzzled security man. 'Ah, Mademoiselle Chabrol, good evening. Perhaps you can solve a little problem without my having to disturb your daughter and Monsieur Eugène. Do you recall whether any of you have been in the main salon since this afternoon – showing it to one of your visitors, perhaps? No? In that case, I'll have to come up and ask Monsieur Eugène's advice.'

'What's wrong, Louis? I thought this place was like the Château d'If once locking-up time comes.'

'That's just it, Madame. As a fail safe, all the doors and windows on the alarm circuit have to be shut on the inside when the system is switched on. If they're not, the circuit's not complete. A bleeper sounds in the control room and the sources of the break show as flashing lights on a floorplan.'

'My God, it sounds like an alert for World War Three!'

'You're telling me. It's all tinkling and twinkling like New Year's Eve right now but I checked myself that everything was closed when I did the 5.30 rounds. Half an hour after the place is cleared, the duty man always does that, then he goes back to the office and switches on the security system everywhere except the apartment. That's integrated to the main system by whoever's up there when they settle down for the night, just by pressing a button. The main switch does two things. It automatically locks all the doors and windows and activates the alarms. What bothers me is that two doors which I know I closed are open now – the main one from the salon to the apartment and the fire escape door from the salon to the emergency stairs at the rear.'

Marie-Louise suddenly felt cold. Just the combination to allow a break-in to the apartment with a way out after the burglary. But that was absurd! Who would burgle an apartment before dark and when three people were expected to be present? No one, if robbery were the real motive. But what if the intruder had something else in mind?

The implication slammed home. 'Come on, Louis, forget the alarms – get up to the apartment, fast!'

Doré's opulent apartment looked like an abattoir. The first bullet had caught Eugène in the carotid artery and severed it. Walls, floor and furniture were splashed with crimson. Even had there been no second bullet, he would have bled to death before help reached him.

The security man cried out, turned away and started retching. Marie-Louise yelled: 'Andy – Andy, where are you?' and stepped over Eugène's body as though it were a log, oblivious to his fate in her fear for her daughter.

Andy was lying in the drawing-room, sprawled face down where the bullet had stopped her zig-zag flight from the gunman. Marie-Louise experienced a fleeting memory of another time when her daughter's life had hung in the balance. Then, too, she had lain twisted, face down, with an ominous bloodstain on her back. Only then she had been in expert hands, en route to a Vietnam base hospital. Now she was alone and, for all her mother knew, already dead. Marie-Louise pressed her fingertips to the pulse point behind Andy's jaw. There was still a faint flutter, barely discernible.

A silent voice inside her head said, Let her go. With a major wound there on her back, she'll probably never walk again. Even if you save her life, she won't thank you if she passes a lifetime confined to a wheelchair. . . . Marie-Louise dismissed the thought. That was something to handle later. Right now she must do her best to save Andy.

Louis came into the drawing-room, grey-faced but calmer now. 'I'm sorry, Madame, but I've never seen anything like that before. It was – oh, God, not Mademoiselle Vincent too!'

Impatiently, Marie-Louise cut him off. 'Not yet, but she's bad. Call an ambulance, fast. I'll get through to the police on the other line. I want a motorcycle escort to take her through to the hospital.'

In less than half an hour, Andy was in a private intensive care unit at the best hospital in Paris. The apartment and salon were crawling with police. Eugène's body was photographed then removed. The evening stretched interminably ahead of Marie-Louise. The police were sympathetic but determined not to let her go to the hospital until they had questioned her thoroughly. As she was almost as mystified as them about what had happened, she was irritated by their persistence. Finally, just as an inspector finished his initial questioning, the hospital called.

'Mademoiselle Chabrol? We've taken a good look at your daughter and we'll have to operate if there's to be any chance of her walking again. The bullet is lodged against the spinal column but at such an angle that we can't see how much pressure it's causing without operating. It could even kill her if it's left there.'

'And she'll recover completely if you operate?'

'I wish I could be that confident. Put it this way: it's the best chance she has.'

Marie-Louise had understood for a long time what it was to be alone, but she had not passed such a night since she waited in a Paris attic in 1944 for confirmation of her nightmare belief that Teddy Vincent had been taken by the Gestapo. Teddy had been her first hostage to Fortune; Andy was her second. Was this one to be sacrificed too?

This time Fate was kinder. A pearly dawn had already broken when the surgeon's registrar came to find her. 'Mademoiselle Chabrol? We have taken your daughter up from the theatre now. You cannot see her yet, but Professor Dulac says she will make a full recovery.'

Marie-Louise fought down a dizzying surge of relief. 'How can he be so sure, so early? Does he mean just her life, or her life and her legs?'

'Her legs, too, Madame. Although the bullet was lodged close to the spine, and at an awkward angle, it had penetrated with far less force than we anticipated. She was incredibly lucky. Perhaps you didn't notice the heavy belt she was wearing. It appears to have been made of steel plates. The bullet went right through one of them. It penetrated her back but had virtually spent itself first. Another centimetre would have paralysed or even killed her. As it was, she appeared to be in a weaker state than she actually was because she'd lost a lot of blood by the time you found her. She'll have a sore back for a couple of weeks, but after that a scar is the worst she'll have to worry about.'

Doré – you saved her! Marie-Louise said a silent prayer of thanks to her dead mother for designing that last belt and insisting on giving it to Andy. The tension drained out of her and she felt sweat bead on her forehead. She smiled wearily at the young surgeon.

'Thank you for the news. May I stay here somewhere until my daughter is able to see me?'

'Of course, Madame. We can give you a room next to hers. You could probably do with a few hours' sleep. By this afternoon she should be strong enough to see you for a few minutes. I'll find a nurse to take you up there.'

Marie-Louise followed him, at peace with the world.

'Come on, Marie-Louise - you know me too well to imagine I'd let the bastards get away with this, and with Doré's life work into the bargain. No chance. I'm fighting!'

Two weeks after the shooting, Andy was still in the hospital, but irritation was a sure indicator of her progress. Marie-Louise sighed and tried to remain calm. 'I don't like it, either, darling, but only you could have the nerve to fancy your chances against the Mafia. They've made three attempts to your certain knowledge and they've come closer every time. Next time you won't be wearing armour-plated costume jewellery.'

'Mother dear, you have an outdated attitude to the Mob. The old Moustache Petes might have gone for revenge at all costs, but the new generation likes low-profile, high-profit operations with minimal bloodshed.'

'Then why have they been so keen to spill yours all over the pavement?'

'Easy - they thought my big mouth threatened their profitability when I was a probing journalist. Now I'm a potential fellow business boss it's another matter. To tell the truth, I think that by the time they got round to this little exercise, poor old Eugène was their real target and I was just an added bonus. They wanted him out of the way so they could asset-strip the couture business without awkward objections from someone whose primary involvement with the couture house was emotional. If I can put up a deal that makes financial sense to them, I'm in with a chance. And if I do it in a manner that makes me look as tough as them, I'm home and dry. It's not just the Jews who admire a bit of chutzpah!'

'Oh, great, so you're going to get yourself as dirty as

they are by involving yourself in business with them, just to prove you can't be beaten.'

'Uh-huh. I intend to buy them out.'

'Now that really *is* chutzpah!'

'Not at all. You, proud parent, are going to stake me. You and the Conway millions, that is.'

'I don't believe this. Are you sure that bullet didn't ricochet into your brain?'

'Look, Ma, the only way I've managed to forget the pain in my butt the past few days has been to do some intensive reading. Joel obligingly ferried in the source material. I now have a pretty good idea of how much Grandpapa left. I also have a good idea of how much Cavalieri would want for their share in Doré Couture. The two sums are remarkably similar.'

'Idiot girl! One, they'll never sell out to you; two, even if they did, what on earth would you do with a couture house? Eugène was the brains there for twenty-odd years. Do you imagine for one moment that you can simply swan in and re-create the House of Doré?'

'Not on my own, but with a little help from my friends. . . .'

'Name any two dozen.'

'Okay: you, for money and moral support. Joel and my own TV contacts for promotional talent. He can take my material and write the all time definitive Mademoiselle biography which will propel Doré Couture right back centre stage. I'll come out of the closet as the glamorous descendant who's picking up the torch and is leading fashion towards the twenty-first century. Seraphine Junot will run the administrative side. After Eugène she knew more than anybody else about the business. And – the big finish – Steb Ortiz will design the clothes.'

'Well, at least you have the good sense to name a talented fashion entrepreneur and an original designer. But how much good will the rest do if Cavalieri refuse to co-operate?'

'I plan to sell them on the idea that they'll do much

better with me than without. And by "with me" I mean by letting me buy out of direct partnership and leaving them with the reflected glory of our couture success to boost Doré Perfumes and Cosmetics. I simply can't see my way to wresting that bit back. But I'll come up with something some day. Doré once told me her only tactical rule was never to forget a favour or forgive an insult. I couldn't agree more, and I think shooting my arse half off is enough of an insult to qualify! I also owe them for Eugène. He might have let the killer in, but that was thanks to Doré's final betrayal. I'll get them one day. In the meantime, I plan to move them sideways a little.'

Joel Handford had arrived half-way through this policy statement and now stood grinning at Marie-Louise as she struggled to come up with further objections. She turned on him. 'You've been encouraging her, I can see it! She'd never have got going on this by herself.'

'Nonsense. All I did was provide her with books and newspaper clippings. Then I listened to the basic plot and threw in a few suggestions, but that's all. She's at least as much of an idiot as me, and probably a good deal braver. I think we could be in for a fun winter. She's convinced me it could work, and the alternative – the pair of you selling out to Cavalieri – sure sticks in my throat. I'm prepared to play my humble little part, so you'd better start thinking about cashing in your old man's life savings.'

Marie-Louise began taking the whole matter more seriously. She had been worrying about the Cavalieri situation ever since the shooting. They had both jumped to the conclusion that Eugène had turned Judas in his misery at losing his just inheritance, but had united instinctively in the face of police enquiries and had insisted it must have been an ordinary burglary. With the collection about to be shown, this was not as preposterous as it might have sounded in another city. The French knew how much money there was in high fashion and that pirates were willing to take big risks to get at the best designs. The Rue Cambon shootings could just have been a fashion hi-jack that went wrong.

Throughout the investigation, Marie-Louise assumed they were protecting Andy by their silence – and possibly Eugène's good reputation, if that mattered any longer. She had told herself that Andy would quietly sell out the business to Cavalieri and that would be that. But all the while she had been afraid her daughter's combative nature would rebel against such passive acceptance, or alternatively that Cavalieri would not rest until they had succeeded in eliminating her altogether.

But now it seemed there was an alternative solution – that of beating the opposition at their own game. She might have expected Andy to react like a cock-eyed optimist, but Joel was usually cool-headed in circumstances like this. If he was going along with Andy, there must be a chance of success. Marie-Louise turned to another aspect of the proposal.

'What about Esteban Ortiz? I know his commitment to you is likely to override the professional one to Cavalieri – but are you really sure he has no idea of their real business?'

'As sure as I can ever be. I've asked him how he'd feel about joining a re-vamped Doré with a free hand as chief designer. He thinks it's a wonderful idea but he still has his macho thing about me being the boss. He's gone off to think about that one. He's promised to give me an answer before I approach Cavalieri with a firm proposition. Obviously, if I don't have a designer, it stops being such a good idea. Strangely enough, it's the fact that he's still worrying about the threat to his manhood that convinces me he's genuine. If he were with them, he'd either turn me down flat to encourage me to sell, or he'd say yes to keep me happy and then stand back to wait for them to blast me into the next world.'

'Mmm – you have very shaky criteria for judging someone's sincerity, my girl. Still, you're on unsafe ground altogether, so I suppose this idea is no wilder than the alternatives. Okay, I'll go along with putting up the Conway money to buy Doré back into the family. You get well and finish off your nasty little plan for cutting out Cavalieri.'

Andy beamed triumphantly. 'There you are, Joel, what did I tell you? She's always been a sucker for hare-brained schemes. We'll beat the bastards yet!'

Marie-Louise covered her face with her hands. 'What did I ever do to deserve you as a daughter?'

It was another month before Andy was well enough to tackle Cavalieri. During that time the posthumous collection had been hailed throughout Europe and America as the best Doré in twenty years. Now, the papers were asking, who could hope to fill the shoes of La Grande Mademoiselle? After a while the odd story began to appear with the suggestion that the Italian fashion company which controlled the Doré perfume subsidiary might buy out the family interest in Doré Couture and put in a top modern designer. Two magazines even named the likely couturier - Pierre de Castellane.

Steb Ortiz came to see Andy a week after she was discharged from hospital. He had spent a lot of time in her room during the first days after the shooting, but once she made her proposal that they should work together, he disappeared.

'Well, hi there - I thought we'd lost you! Surely the prospect of a woman boss wasn't all that daunting?' She had missed him and was spiky as a result. Ortiz smiled, undeceived.

'We've been through that phase, haven't we? I came back because you asked me to consider something crucial, Andy. You know very well it's something that matters a lot to me and I wanted to think carefully before I made my decision.'

'And?'

'And let's be clear about one thing: if I become the new Doré chief designer, I won't be working *for* you, we shall be working together.' He raised a hand to silence her heated interruption. 'Before you go on, I assure you that's not my hot Latin temperament speaking. Any name designer in Paris will tell you the same. If you accept that, my answer is yes – when do we start?'

She let out a whoop of excitement. 'You certainly know how to surprise a girl! To tell you the truth, I was half expecting you to come back and turn down the job, then ask me to marry you.'

'Marry you? It'll be bad enough working with you! My only chance of keeping you in line is to treat you rough. I'll be your lover but not your husband.'

She giggled. 'You say the nicest things. That solves a lot of problems. You don't want to do anything silly like moving in with me, I suppose?'

'Perish the thought! Give up Miguel's splendid apartment in the Marais to move in over the shop? No chance, lady.'

She put her arms round him and managed to plant a kiss on his jaw before he held her away from him.

'Aren't you going to ask me what prompted my decision?'

'Actually I had some far more burning questions in mind . . . like finding out whether my back is all better yet. But okay, if you insist. What prompted your decision?'

'Castellane. I've seen the newspaper stories. If Cavalieri wished him on you, you'd end up with a garbled pastiche of my knitwear ideas. He's been following me around like a bloodhound recently and I'm just waiting to see my ideas popping up in his next ready-to-wear range. I'll never get another chance like the one you're offering me and if I can't kick my stupid male ego into line to grab it, I deserve to be upstaged by that second-class copyist. Madame, I await your orders.'

'That'll be the day. If we manage to stay together for more than the next five minutes, we'll still be fighting when we're old and grey!'

Abruptly she became serious. 'Thanks, Steb. I promise not to lean on you. I love your work and I know you'll be a sensation. Now all I have to do is persuade Cavalieri to give me back Grandma's company.'

'Why bother? They're a good firm – their ready-to-wear is very attractive and they've always had a reputation for willingness to try new ideas. Surely they wouldn't object to your engaging me and trying me out on your haute couture? And even if they did, you own the controlling interest.'

She tried to detect a hint of insincerity in what he said but it seemed genuine enough. Only someone who knew Cavalieri's antecedents would suspect that she might be unable merely to outvote them. As far as he was concerned, all she needed to resort to was a boardroom manoeuvre. Momentarily, Andy considered telling him the full story then decided against it.

No – however pure his intentions, knowledge was power, and she intented to stay in control. 'Let's just say I prefer not to share the driving seat. I'll arrange to see Cavalieri himself next week, make him an offer and after that, let's hope we have a business.'

Lorenzo Cavalieri was not nicknamed Lorenzo the Magnificent for nothing. He looked more like a suntanned New York banker than the classic picture of a *mafioso*. Regular training had given him a perfect physique. His glossy black hair had distinguished wings of silver at the temples.

Everything he wore was hand made. He had been educated in the best schools, and at the appropriate time had married the beautiful daughter of an aristocratic Roman family. The days of the Sicilian thug made good were long gone.

Andy travelled to his Milan knitwear company headquarters to meet him. Marie-Louise was almost frantic when she heard the plan.

'But you can't walk into the lion's den like that! It's suicide. For God's sake meet him here in Paris. He's bound to say yes to a meeting in the salon. After all, he owns a piece of it too.'

'I'm not in hiding, I'm as much of a hunter as he is. He

has to understand that, or he'll think he can tread on me any time he likes. I want to come across as being as powerful as him.'

'You're turning into a megalomaniac, and a suicidal one at that! At least take Joel with you.'

Andy laughed. 'Oh, really, Mama, what d'you think poor old Joel is – the US Cavalry? I can just imagine Lorenzo the Magnificent quivering in his shoes as Pussy Cat Joel ambles into the room and ripples his middle-aged muscles! No, I go alone. There'd be some excuse for taking Steb, because he's to be the designer, but he's not in on the details and I've no intention of telling him for a long, long time yet. That means a solo trip. In any case, if they want to bump me off, a minder's not going to stop them killing me. To survive I have to be as impressive as them, and I intend to be.'

Her mother shrugged helplessly. 'Okay, but don't expect me to say you know what you're doing, I'm not at all sure that you do. Be lucky.'

In spite of his good looks, cultivated tastes and fabulous wealth, the most impressive thing about Lorenzo Cavalieri was the air of stillness that surrounded him. Meeting him was like stepping into the eye of a hurricane.

Stop doing his job for him, Andy told herself irritably, trying to dismiss his aura of power. He's just a successful gangster who wants to launder his crooked profits through my company and I'm not going to let him. He also kills people, her less courageous self murmured.

'You've come a long way for such a short meeting, Ms Vincent,' said Cavalieri. 'Surely nothing required such urgent discussion that it could not wait until after you had recovered fully from the recent – er – unfortunate business of the burglary? We were not thinking of asking for any immediate policy changes.'

She registered the slight increase of emphasis when he reached the word 'immediate'. 'No trouble, Signor Cavalieri. I'm in excellent health now and we have to discuss the appointment of a new designer, if nothing else.'

There was a silence. Cavalieri's eyes had not moved from hers since she started speaking. Finally he said: 'Perhaps, as you have decided we should talk so soon, we should move on to something more basic. Given your tragic mishap and the loss of Eugène St-Meurice, perhaps you would prefer not to take over the business at all. I realise you have a strong sense of family tradition, but it's not as though your own career to date has prepared you for such a business. I gather that the underworld has interested you more than the world of fashion.'

So we're being fairly frank, are we? she thought. And aloud: 'You wouldn't be about to formalise those little teasers I've read in the papers about buying me out?'

'Why not, Ms Vincent? I think we at Cavalieri would be far more at home running Doré Couture than you would be. I have fairly definite views on the direction couture should take in the immediate future, particularly when it can be harnessed to related lines like ready-to-wear and perfumery. That is the way we would want to see things moving.'

'Yes, I rather thought so . . . on a par with so many others that there'd be nothing unique about Doré any more.'

'Perhaps not, but those other companies are taking a particular route because it is logical and profitable. If you merely wish to preserve a museum-piece fashion house, perhaps you are out of touch with modern marketing realities anyway.'

'Perhaps, but if I am and I own the entire Doré fashion business, it won't matter a damn.'

'But you don't. Cavalieri owns a sizeable chunk of the company, Ms Vincent. We would have strong views about such a development.'

'What if I offered to buy you out?'

His laugh was silky. 'You have a sense of humour, I see.' He tapped a slender file which lay in front of him on the leather desktop. 'This contains an up-to-date summary of the company's assets. Our holding is worth almost a billion pounds sterling.'

'And I, Signor Cavalieri, am worth more than two billion sterling. Give me back the company and you can have half of it – and in a very useful form: high value real estate in England, Austria and Canada; a nice little gas field and a slice of oil stock. There are a clutch of good hotels, too, which would ice the cake of your own hotel holdings just beautifully.'

If the man had been still before, he became positively frozen now. 'You would exchange half the Conway fortune for a fashion house?'

'Yes – if it really did buy you out. But I'd want the scent and cosmetics interests back from your main company, too.'

'I don't think we would like that. Anyway – why? These assets you offer are of far more potential value than couture. Why plunge into the fashion and beauty business when you can live like an aristocrat on the interest from your interest?'

'Basically I'm just an old-fashioned busybody, I suppose. Oh, and one other thing . . . I like the idea of staying alive.'

'Why should you not stay alive?'

Andy had always suspected that the softly softly approach was not her strong suit. Now she abandoned it without regret. 'Because some little friends of yours – perhaps even employees – seem to think it would be a good idea if I didn't.'

His expression of surprise was just a little too slow in appearing. It seemed he wasn't too concerned whether she suspected him of villainy. He merely said, 'That sounds as though you've been reading too many crime stories late at night.'

'I never read fiction, Signor Cavalieri. Real life is always quite vivid enough. Look, let's stop behaving like inscrutable Japanese tycoons. I'm prepared to say quite openly what I want, and to tell you what I'm offering and why. I have family reasons for wanting to carry on with the fashion company. You know enough about my past to appreciate that I'm unlikely to feel able to collaborate with you and your associates. That means boardroom squabbles and an unavoidable loss of profitability, hardly desirable in an organisation as efficient as your own. But you're not wedded to the idea of a couture house, are you? Anything will do, from property to oil, so long as it gives you a flourishing front behind which to carry on your own family interests. So, I'm offering to buy you out by exchanging your couture holding for equally useful business. I don't think you can afford to say no.'

'That's rather a sweeping statement. Have you considered what might happen if you refused to sell out to us as I asked earlier, then started running Doré Couture in a manner we did not approve?'

'Oh, yes, I've thought of little else lately. I know precisely what would happen. You'd repeat your offer, possibly upping the stakes a couple of times. If I went on refusing to sell, I expect I should soon have an accident. And this time, I don't think my luck would hold out. Frankly, Signor Cavalieri, I don't advise that course of action.'

He had the grace to smile. 'You must be feeling confident if you think you can afford to patronise me, Ms Vincent.'

'Oh, I am. Until the last couple of months, I was a well-known TV journalist and no more. Your kind have been bumping off people like that since the last century and no one has taken a lot of notice.

'As of August, it was a different matter. Now the whole world knows I'm the legitimate descendant of the last Duke of Conway and the most famous dress designer who ever lived. You and your associates like a certain amount of privacy in order to run your affairs efficiently. The last thing you want is to have every popular scandal sheet in the world sending out reporters to investigate the sensational assassination of this year's biggest celebrity. You could try it, of course, but I can't imagine you'll be that foolish. You pull out of some business ventures every day, realise your assets and go off to invest them elsewhere. I think you'll decide it makes more sense to do that with Doré Couture than to stay around, wipe me out and then have to clear up the mess.'

'I still haven't acknowledged any connection with these shadowy criminal forces to which you refer. It could all be a figment of your imagination.'

'Well, if it is you still have no good reason to refuse my offer, because I do own the majority interest in Doré Couture and I do intend to develop it according to my wishes, not yours. If you're a law-abiding businessman there's nothing you can do to stop me and you may as well sell out now.'

For the first time he smiled with some warmth. 'Whatever your other qualities, you are not without courage. Perhaps we can do business. But tell me one thing. You just said you'd want the Doré scents and cosmetics back from the main Reynaud Perfumes company. I see no reason why we should go along with that, too. Your proposition is all very well for Doré Couture but we don't have to give you the perfumes as a bonus.'

'It would be much, much wiser. You see, I have plans to launch at least two more fragrances through Doré Couture – Mademoiselle and Alouette. I've already registered the names. And if you don't include D and Doré Cosmetics in the sell-out, I'll simply base my entire marketing campaign on the line that the two new scents are for young women of fashion who would have used D half a century ago but now want something up to date. Within a year you'd only have faded movie stars and retired madams bothering to buy their bottles of D any more.'

For a long time Cavalieri said nothing, but sat staring blankly at the file on his desk. Finally he met her eyes again, this time with a flat, hostile glare. 'It seems we have nothing further to discuss, Ms Vincent. Please instruct your financial advisers to draw up an exact list of the assets you are offering in return for our share of Doré Couture plus re-purchase of the perfume franchise. I think the rest of the deal can be conducted by our accountants.'

He rose to see her out. At the door of his office he shook her hand. Andy was unable to resist a parting shot. 'Cheer up, Lorenzo. With me tucked away learning the fashion business, at least you won't have to worry about what's on television any more!'

She left without waiting for a reply.

Andy had no real fears that she was in danger in Milan. Even if Cavalieri changed his mind, he was hardly likely to mess his own doorstep by getting rid of her here. She simply found it oppressive. Back at her hotel she called the airport and discovered there were two flights out to Paris that evening. She made a reservation with Air France, told Reception she was checking out immediately, then started to call Marie-Louise to tell her of the change of plan. But she changed her mind. Her mother would only get anxious if she rang now to say she was coming back soon, and she had no intention of breaking the news of her victory over the telephone. No, she'd fly back to Paris and call from the airport . . .

It was nearly midnight when they landed at Roissy. Andy was still too high on success to feel sleepy. Throughout the flight she had been planning her business future. The more she thought about it, the more she understood Doré's preoccupation with style. Pictures of Steb's lovely Lady and Unicorn knitwear flitted across her mind. They'd make wonderful accessories to up-dated classic Doré suits . . . Still absorbed in her plans, she disembarked. She had only hand luggage with her so once through Passport Control she headed for the exit. She froze as she glanced towards the terminal door. Esteban Ortiz was coming towards her.

Oh, Christ, no – not him too! Did I really get things that wrong? She turned aside, panic-stricken, as he saw her and raised a hand to attract her attention. Cavalieri must have had someone watching her movements at the hotel and they'd tipped off Steb to catch her before she got back to central Paris. . . . even as the thoughts raced through her mind she was frantically looking around for some means of escape. Nothing more brilliant than standing still and screaming occurred to her. He must be going to bundle her off somewhere in a car and in due course there'd be a story that she'd been kidnapped for ransom. Yes, it had to be something like that. Oh Steb, why did it have to be you? The only hollow reassurance was that he could hardly bump her off here in the busy concourse. At that moment he caught up with her, reaching out and grabbing her arm.

'Hey, what's got into you? I half kill myself getting out here to meet you off the plane, and instead of rushing to my arms you take one look and run as though the devil were after you. What are you playing at?'

Almost hysterical now, she pulled away from him. Passers-by were beginning to take an interest. 'Stay away from me, you murdering sod! If you think I'm going off somewhere quiet with you, you've another thing coming! What did they promise you for this little job?'

'Have you lost your mind? I suggest you go to that phone booth and call your mother. Perhaps she'll be able to talk some sense into you. I obviously can't.'

That slowed her down a bit. If he wanted to get rid of her, where did Marie-Louise fit in? Maybe he was going to force her to say something to deceive her mother. . . . Nevertheless, it was the only chance she had. They arrived at the bank of phones and she dialled the Rue Cambon apartment. Marie-Louise answered almost at once.

'Andy? Why on earth are you ringing? Didn't you see Steb? He's out at Roissy to meet you.'

The tension receded a little but now Andy was totally bewildered. 'What – how did any of you know I was coming back tonight? I only decided on the spur of the moment.'

'So I gathered from the hotel when I called. Really,

Andy, you're one of the most inconsiderate people I know! To fly home without letting me hear about that delicate meeting with Cavalieri, and to leave no message! Joel practically had to blackmail the desk clerk into telling him you'd booked a ticket on the evening Air France flight. We were still pretty nervous and as Steb was having a drink with us, he volunteered to come and meet you, just in case anyone was waiting for you. . . .'

'But how did he know there was a chance of danger? I've told him nothing.'

Marie-Louise was beginning to sound exasperated now. 'Because I thought this business had gone far enough, and that you had to take a chance and come clean with the man. You can't conduct a relationship with a lover when every day you wake up wondering if he works for the Mafia!'

'You told him everything?'

The telephone was removed from her hand, gently but firmly. Steb broke into the conversation. 'It's okay, Marie-Louise. I'm on my way back with her. You'll never get any sense into her head on the telephone. See you soon.' He hung up and turned Andy in the direction of the concourse.

'Now, lady, to the car – come on, march! For once I'm going to be as macho as I want, even if you go back to playing boss lady tomorrow. Your mother was absolutely right! We wouldn't have lasted five minutes with all that Mafia nonsense hovering around us. For a great big grown-up girl you are stupid beyond belief at times.'

Andy sagged against him, tears of relief starting to trickle down her cheeks. 'So you – you had no secret connections with the Cavalieri family? They never made any little suggestions about the sort of work you did for them – I mean apart from the knitwear?'

'Do you have any idea how long it takes to train as a fashion designer? It took me the best part of ten years, and you seem to think it's something I could just absorb on my days off from shooting up Sicilian policemen! I take your word about the nature of the Cavalieri operation, I admit I've heard a few rumours over the couple of months I've been with them. But surely you must have realised they wouldn't use the specialist fashion staff as hired thugs?'

'Well, they do it in the movies. . . .' Even in her own ears it sounded unforgivably lame.

He turned to her again in exasperation, took one look at her doleful face and then burst out laughing. 'Oh, hell, at this rate I really just might have to marry you. I don't think you'll ever learn how to look after yourself!'

Arm in arm, they left the terminal and went out to his car. Esteban gestured at the glove compartment. 'Before we set off, take a look in there. Marie-Louise asked me to bring something out for you, said something about having had it repaired for you and you wearing it as a good luck charm. All I can say is that it's a damned heavy good luck charm.'

As he spoke, Andy had taken a chamois leather pouch out of the glove compartment. She opened the drawstring fastening and a familiar, sinuous chain of steel D-links flowed out on to her lap. It was the prototype Doré belt which had intercepted the foot soldier's bullet. Marie-Louise had ordered a repair job instead of a replacement and for once Andy understood the superstition attached to such a talisman.

'It's a bit conspicuous to wear everywhere, but I'm tempted,' she said. 'What with this and you riding shotgun on me, I should be proof against all attackers from now on.'

Steb eyed her with mock amazement. 'Me, ride shotgun on you? I thought you were going to take care of me – boss lady.'

*More Compulsive Fiction from Headline:*

## JANICE YOUNG BROOKS

# CROWN SABLE

**A dazzling saga in the bestselling tradition of A WOMAN OF SUBSTANCE**

**Irina Kossok arrived on Ellis Island possessing only the clothes on her back and a fierce determination to make her American dream a reality. But the crowded violence of the New York tenements was as harsh as anything she had endured in her native Poland. And the loving, hard-working Peter Garrick offered her irresistible security as his wife.**

**Irina's passion to escape the immigrant ghettoes brought her to the attention of society furrier Jacques Neptune. As his protegée, she entered a world of luxury – the fashion houses and salons patronised by the wealthy and the glamorous; the ballrooms and nightclubs of Manhattan's social elite. But Irina's increasing success left her torn between the two worlds she now inhabited. And the memories of her old life had power to cast a threatening shadow over the glittering promise of the new . . .**

FICTION/SAGA 0 7472 3067 6 £3.99

*More compulsive fiction from Headline:*

# MALCOLM ROSS

**A rich West Country saga**
**in the bestselling tradition of POLDARK**

# *On a Far Wild Shore*

Young, beautiful and newly widowed, Elizabeth Troy travels to her late husband's Cornish home hoping to find comfort in its fertile hills and valleys. But she is shocked to discover the vast, decaying acreage of Pallas is now solely her responsibility – a legacy as unexpected as it is unwelcome.

Elizabeth's plans for her inheritance provoke the bitter hostility of her sister-in-law, Morwenna, whose word has been law at Pallas for thirty years. To bring the troubled estate back to prosperity Elizabeth must look for help elsewhere. And there are many very willing to be more than a friend to the widow – David Troy, a poor relation whose sober exterior hides some disturbing secrets; Courtenay Rodda, the sensual newspaper proprietor; and James Troy, the rich and worldly wise American cousin who begins a thrilling but dangerous liaison with Elizabeth . . .

'The book is beautifully written, the characters depicted with a passionate realism that held me entranced. I simply loved it!' Patricia Wendorf, bestselling author of *Larksleve*.

**FICTION 0-7472-3001-3 £2.95**

Headline books are available at your bookshop or newsagent, or can be ordered from the following address:

Headline Book Publishing PLC
Cash Sales Department
PO Box 11
Falmouth
Cornwall
TR10 9EN
England

UK customers please send cheque or postal order (no currency), allowing 60p for postage and packing for the first book, plus 25p for the second book and 15p for each additional book ordered up to a maximum charge of £1.90 in UK.

BFPO customers please allow 60p for postage and packing for the first book, plus 25p for the second book and 15p per copy for the next seven books, thereafter 9p per book.

Overseas and Eire customers please allow £1.25 for postage and packing for the first book, plus 75p for the second book and 28p for each subsequent book.